GARDEN OF THE GODS

VOL. 2

A. A. DARK

Mad Girl
PUBLISHING
PITCH BLACK™

Mistress B-0042
Garden of the Gods
International Bestselling Author
A.A. Dark
Copyright © 2023 by A.A.Dark

All Rights Reserved

AUTHOR'S NOTE

Garden of the Gods is a collection of standalone novellas
shadowing the lives of the Mistresses and Masters who occupy
it. Although each main character will only have ONE book, they
may appear in others throughout the series. Some stories will
also have BDSM elements, but these stories are NOT BDSM.
Mistress and Master is a title, showing nothing more than
ownership. The scale of darkness in the stories will range from
Pitch Black, Static White, to the extreme, Oblivion. Please be
aware of this before you dive in. The rating will be in the blurb
of each book. Trigger warnings are all over the board. If you are
not comfortable with dark reads, please DO NOT read this
series.

RULES

Rules are subject to change. If you neglect to follow these rules, you will undergo an investigation/trial where punishment is evaluated by the Board and Main Master, Elec Wexler. Punishment can range from fines to lockup in Hell Row to Death.

1) Keep your hands to yourself.
    2) The only property you may destroy is your own. (slaves included.)
    3) You are a number. Your peers are a number. Use them.
    4) Respect your neighbor's privacy.
    5) GOTG is NOT to be discussed outside of this facility.

GLOSSARY

W

    Virgin slave. Wears a white robe during the auction.

B

    Nonvirgin slave. Wears a blue robe during the auction.

D

    Docile, drugged slave. Can be w or b. Heavily trained. Good for elderly or those with disabilities.

M

    Male slave.

Crow

    (fc: female crow, mc: male crow) Ruined, disfigured slave. Convicts fall into this category. Black robe during the auction. Usually the cheapest slave.

Blank slate

    Mostly male slaves who have undergone forced indoctrination through various scientific methods. (Brainwashing, programming, training, etc.) Most remember their identity but have key parts of their past erased if it could pose a threat or alter their role as a slave. They're programmed to be focused solely on their Mistress or Master. They are made to be obedient, loyal, and protective.

*Master numbers written out throughout the stories are capitalized. (Ex. Twelve-twelve.) Also, the word Master throughout is capitalized. (Ex. Master Twelve-twelve.)

*Slave numbers written out will not be capitalized. The word slave throughout will not be capitalized outside from the beginning of a sentence.

"THE MORE HURT SHE GETS, THE MORE VENOMOUS SHE GROWS."
-EMILY BRONTE, WUTHERING HEIGHTS

PROLOGUE

Garden of the Gods
Colorado Springs underground facility

What started out as forty-four Mistresses had now turned into more than I could count. One hundred? Two? The Main Master's voice echoed through the speakers from the large auditorium, but I stayed just outside one of the entrances with my only remaining slave. We were near the room we'd been assigned to for the males and others like him. I could have gone inside, but I was too captivated by our handsome Main Master who walked the stage. He had such charisma, and he knew just how to capture an audience.

"Welcome to the second auction for the Garden of the Gods. For those who didn't make it to the first, I'm going to recap this as quickly as possible. You've taken the classes. You've learned the rules. Even though our slaves have been trained, you are going to have to earn your titles. The B's in front of your number are for a reason. This is the Beta stage. Some of you will make our foundation, some of you won't. Your outside status got you here, but that means nothing inside the Gardens. You are a

1

number. That's it. Your identity means absolutely zero. Here, there is no power or favoritism. This world is mine, and you better hope like hell you can follow the rules, or you won't survive in it." His eyes scanned the large room and his tone lightened. "On the plus side, a lot of you have made it this far and that speaks volumes. I have high hopes for most of you."

A smirk tugged at my lips, and I blindly reached back, taking my drink from my blank slate I'd gotten from the first auction. I was already buzzing pretty good, but that didn't stop me from finishing off the Vodka and Sprite.

"Another."

One word was all it took for the tall, deeply tanned male to turn and head back to the bar. My gaze lingered, taking in the width of three-eleven's shoulders in the fitted suit. I'd never dressed him up outside of jeans and a t-shirt, and he'd only just started going outside with me the last few weeks. But I didn't want to think about what led up to that, or why I needed him to begin with. The thought ignited the aching hole in my chest. It was a reminder of the laughter. The whispers. Three-eleven was my armor in more ways than protection. I'd grown close to him since it'd become only the two of us, but I didn't want to think about that either.

"For those new to us tonight, I don't think I need to go much into how this place is not Whitlock1. The rules are different. The location is different." I turned back to the stage. "I am *not* the old Main Master, Bram Whitlock. A few Masters from the first auction had to learn that the hard way. You can not buy yourself out of trouble. You cannot *buy me.* I will never let the Garden of the Gods fall."

A small bump against the back of my shoulder had me glaring at a Master who put his hand up apologetically as he headed through the door, returning into the main auditorium.

"Let's recap bidding for those who don't know. First, we have the white, or w's. These are the virgins. We also have the b's: or blue." He paused. "Not virgins. We also have the d's, who now have their own room at the back right, behind all of you. They're docile, trained, and good for those who are looking for a long-term slave. Lastly, come the black, or as we call them, the crows. These could be fun for anyone looking for a bloodbath or just a fun time. They're the convicts. The disfigured. The old. *Repulsive*." He stopped at the end of the stage. "You get it. Also in that category, you'll find the breeders. I want to make a note of some changes in this category." His hand rose through the pause. "Listen to me closely. I won't repeat it. You are not allowed to bid on them unless you've already gone through the steps and signed a contract with me. We had a few try last auction even though this was already stated in bold caps in the pamphlet. If you bid on a breeder, and you haven't met with me, your bid will be revoked and I will fine you ten thousand dollars for wasting my time. Breeders are special. Breeders are for only those I approve of."

"For those looking for our programmable, 'blank slate' males and *now* females, your auction is just through that door off to the right. The information was in the packet, but just in case you missed it last auction, these are those who have had a portion of their memories erased. They're aware. They know who they are, but they only remember what we want them to."

Female blank slates? Interest was there but faded just as fast.

"The last few weeks have been exciting, to say the least. I've watched some of you grow in your role. The majority have done great with following rules. For those who are new, pay attention."

"What you buy is yours. You can do whatever you want with it. Fuck it. Kill it. Share it. Marry it. Love it. Eat it. Destroy it." Hesitation. "I don't care so long as you follow the rules. Your business is your own. I can't stress that enough."

"If you look down the arm of the chair, you will see a button. Do not." He stopped for what felt like ever. "All of you listen and listen good. Let me say it again since others from the first auction learned the hard way. *Do not...* press that button unless you are sure you want to bid. We do not have a lay-a-way plan. You cannot get your slave on loan. If you don't have the money, don't bid. At the Gardens, there's no such thing as accidents. If you bid, you buy. If you can't pay, I will take my payment however I want. Don't believe my threat, *test me*. I'll take everything you own on the outside world and you can remain here with the slave you couldn't resist. This life can be simple if you just do as you're told. The rules are easy. Complete acceptance into the Garden of the Gods is not. You all signed a contract to get this far. Abide by it, and Alpha status will be yours."

Lights flashed, racing around the edge of the large auditorium. I didn't bother sticking around to see anymore. I glanced at my slave, taking my new drink as I headed for our room. It was time, and I was more than ready.

MISTRESS B-0042

Expectation was the root of all disappointment—Murder was the antidote. In my twenty-four years, I knew nothing. *I'd experienced everything.*

Growing up with a famous athlete for a father, I became buffet for the industry. He'd been so determined to have me become someone that the predators ate me alive. Sure, I succeeded, but not because of them. Everything I had, I worked my ass off for. Did I get credit for it? No. Rumors had weight with the elite, and if you didn't play by the rules, the allegations became your identity.

They became mine.

I wasn't naturally talented. Beautiful, yes, but a huge rock star...no. Despite that I had a unique voice, I'd never be one of the best in the world. I wouldn't go down in history for selling out crowds or from making millions on tour. I knew that. Pistol, Master A-0077, had known that too when we dated. He didn't care anymore than I did. It wasn't until I declined a deal with the Devil of Hollywood that any dream I had of getting by on passion alone was lost. I lost it all. I lost him.

Rumors. Expectations. Death would have been better than

having everyone including him, turn their backs on me. What was my life if it wasn't mine to control?

Whispers, I was used to. Dirty looks, I tried not to let get to me. The only reason I was here was because of my father's name and money. That, and I was nearly impossible to control. Everyone knew I was a mess. *They all knew.*

Failure.

Used.

Washed up.

The Whore of Hollywood.

Didn't that make me the perfect pair for the Devil? How many times had I cursed myself for not giving in and taking the stupid deal? A million. Instead, what did I do? I broke. I was still self-destructing, and I wasn't sure when or how it would end.

Reaching over, I grabbed my drink from three-eleven. He was sitting at my feet, staring ahead like the perfect blank slate he was. No conversation. No judgements. No fucking expectations.

"Do you like him?"

I turned, looking up and over my shoulder to a woman with shoulder length red hair, cut not that differently than my old style. Now I was a wavy blonde, and the extensions reached to the middle of my back. I had always had dark hair or some random fun color, but I'd never gone blonde. It was nice. It was new, and so far from the real me.

"I'm sorry?"

"Your slave. I'm guessing by how well-behaved he is that he's a blank slate?"

"Yes. I bought him at the first auction." I tried forcing a smile. It wasn't often people came up to talk to me. "I like him. He's convenient."

The woman's face lit up. She looked close to forty and was wearing a gold sequin dress that hugged tightly to her curves. It glistened in the dim light, sparkling as she glanced around the room, lowering not only her upper body but her voice.

"I'm thinking of getting one, but I'm on the fence. Is he good for...all things?"

I glanced at three-eleven. I wouldn't know if he were good for sex or pleasure but given he followed orders, I couldn't see why not.

"He'll do whatever I tell him. *Anything*. And he'll do it to the best of his abilities. If you're not looking for...drama, I say go for the blank slate."

"Are you getting another?"

My smile matched the eagerness from the one she'd given me before.

"I want the drama."

"Goals." We both laughed, and her hand came out. "I'm Mistress B-One-thirteen."

"B-Forty-two."

Her hands were soft as we shook but cold to the touch.

"It's nice meeting you. I should go start the hunt. I hope I see you around, Forty-two."

"I hope so too. It was nice meeting you."

She pulled back, waving as another woman at the far end of the room seemed to notice her. I let out a sigh, taking a big drink before handing it back to my slave. I went back to the book, flipping through the pictures at record speed. I didn't need details. I needed a certain look. A cockiness. One that told me this man wasn't broken by this place. He'd have a chip on his shoulder, and it wouldn't take him long to show his true colors.

People swarmed the area, going this way and that. Couples laughed. Women either continued to look or bid and leave with their slaves. I paid attention to the screen, but no one anyone had chosen drew me in.

"Just take a seat and grab a binder. Did you read the pamphlet?"

My head whipped around at the Main Master's voice. He was everything I wanted, and someone I'd never come close to having. He'd give me a good fight. Maybe kill me. It was too bad he'd sworn off women. He hadn't said as much, but if he dated or showed interest, I hadn't caught it. He sure didn't show interest towards *me*. Who would? I was pretty much blacklisted from being fucked as well, not that I probably would go that far with anyone.

Standing, I took quick strides in his direction. He was talking at an increased volume to a woman who had to be in her seventies. Maybe eighties. At my approach, he leaned in, pointing her towards one of the empty sofas a few feet over.

"Main Master."

"Mistress, how can I help you?"

"I can't find a slave." At the sarcasm in his look, I rolled my eyes. "What I mean is I can't find what I'm looking for *in* a slave. Do you happen to know which ones give your guards the most trouble? The fighters."

Interest flickered on his face. "You won't find those in your book. They're not for sale until I deem them ready."

"But that's what I'm looking for."

"You want to get killed?"

Was I silent a little too long?

"Not killed."

"Really? That's not what I hear."

"Anything you hear from these entitled idiots can't be trusted. I'm fine, and I'd be more than okay if you got me the type of slave I wanted. Besides, I have a special code to shut them down for a reason.

"If you're looking for someone to control you, then you want a Master."

"Are you offering?"

Another look that told me I didn't stand a chance in hell.

"Well, can I beat one of those? Break them? Kill them?"

"We both know the answer to that." He seemed to think but shook his head. "I'm not giving you an unsafe slave. You could die. I'm not going to be responsible for that. Find you a slave from our selection. If you're good enough, you can make them however you want. If you want them to rebel against you, manipulate them into it. Twist their mind, Mistress. Make them think they have power. Then…take it away." His lips jerked back on one side, and his tone turned to velvet as he stepped in even closer. "You may find the challenge quite to your liking. Can you do it? How good are you, Forty-two?" He paused, moving his gaze to my mouth, only to come back up to my eyes. "Do you like to play games?"

My lips parted through the spell of his sex appeal. For seconds I couldn't even remember how to speak. Did he really remember my number? Wait…*was he manipulating me?* I was so confused as I tried to find my voice.

"I…do. I think that sounds like something I might like to try."

His face and voice went back to normal, bewildering me even more. "I believe you'd enjoy it. Besides, I'm curious if you can do it. Go take another look. Keep me updated on how it goes." At a call from across the room, Elec nodded, hesitating as he seemed to question saying more. "Maybe you're not ready for a talk. Maybe you are. Just know, I've been monitoring your situation, and I have some ideas. Those will come when I think you're ready. You're stronger than you think. Braver too." Another pause. "Don't disappoint me and let them win. Grab some coffee and have the time of your life. That's what we're here for. Enjoyment. This place doesn't have to be a prison. Put that strong mind of yours to work. They only win if you allow them."

The Main Master left me standing there more perplexed than ever. His advice was just that…advice, but it was the nicest thing anyone had said to me in longer than I could remember. It had

11

me turning around in a daze and walking right into three-eleven. My drink dislodged from his grasp, saturating my black gown. Ice shot out in all directions. Vodka and Sprite sprayed across the floor as the glass shattered. I closed my eyes, breathing through the embarrassment that came from the gasps and laughter sounding throughout the room.

"Mistress."

My lids cracked opened, and I made sure to keep my voice low. "Why are you still here? Get me something so I can clean myself up."

"Of course."

"Do you think she'll take her clothes off here too? Maybe the men should just line up in a train and get it over with."

"If they haven't already."

Laughter.

I wasn't going to cry. I wasn't going to rage. The female voices continued snickering behind me. Any other night I would have turned and gave them the look of death. After Elec's advice, I found myself puzzled on how to react. I was depleted. *I wanted to win.* I couldn't stand being the root of everyone's jokes.

Swallowing hard, I took in a deep breath, forcing myself to smile just the smallest amount. *Shit happens. Shit happens.* This could have happened to anyone. The names...to anyone. People were mean. Ruthless. I was mean. They were just words. I knew the truth.

I glanced over. Elec was talking to a couple, but he was looking right at me. No sympathy. No expression at all. Just watching. Was he waiting for me to snap? To make a big scene? Ten minutes ago, I might have.

"Mistress."

Three-eleven's eyes were on mine. For some reason, I found myself looking into them for the first time. Brown. Dark brown but...*something.* I couldn't place my finger on what I felt when I tried to gaze into their depths. I'd originally bought him for safety. I knew my other slaves would die, and I'd be alone. Having him assured I never would be. But to see him as a person. To acknowledge the secrets I had told him. To think there was someone looking back at me and feeling something over my...life. I couldn't face that.

I took the napkins, patting against my dress. A worker slave was already diving to my feet to clean up the mess. I didn't hurry back to my seat. I took my time, continuing to press into my dress to soak up the alcohol. The moment I sat down, my slave remained standing.

"Would the Mistress like another drink?"

"Yes. *No*." Dammit. I was supposed to be sober for this game. Or was that supposed to be for myself and my sanity? Did I even want that? "Sit, slave. Let's get this over with."

I grabbed the binder, starting over on the regular male slaves that weren't blank slates.

Mind games.

That's what Elec suggested I do. Turn them into what I wanted. Hadn't I pretty much done that with my last couple, or had that been dumb luck? I stayed so drunk, I wasn't even sure. Anger ruled me, and I lived there. Maybe stopping the alcohol might help. This could even be fun. There was appeal to look at this as a game, I just wasn't confident. That disappeared when I lost everything. Was it possible I could get it back? At least some part of a real outside existence? That wouldn't happen with a slave, but maybe if I fought or...who was I kidding? The women talking about me summed up all of the elite. I was fucked.

Flipping the page, I paused as I took in the slave at the bottom right. Then the one on the left. They both weren't bad looking. Most women would have probably found them dreamy, but I had never been attracted to pretty boys. Especially ones that could, *and probably did,* point out any girl in the room to fuck over. They were exactly what I needed, and they couldn't have been more opposite. The one with light hair reminded me of a preppy quarterback while the other screamed bad boy. The one with dark hair and eyes seemed like a mystery. It was intriguing, but I knew what I'd get with him and that had me rolling my own eyes. Maybe I was over men in general. Or was everyone right and I was just over life?

Coffee, that's what I needed.

"Slave."

"Yes, Mistress." No questions. He was ready for an order.

I turned the binder around pointing to the slaves.

"Go put in the information for these two. I want to see them."

His eyes jumped up to mine lowering just as fast.

"Yes, Mistress."

I handed him the binder, not even watching as he headed to the kiosk to go enter the information. At the voice behind me, I jumped.

"I'm already impressed." A hint of a grin. "You like your pairs. That's what you got last auction. Will you use these against each other?"

The Main Master was crouched behind my sofa, his face level with my shoulder. I could have turned completely to face him, but the feel of his breath on my skin was too delicious to part from. Besides, I didn't want to appear desperate or like I was throwing myself at him. He probably got that from every other woman in this place. He wouldn't get it from me.

"I was thinking about it."

"You should." He paused. "Why a fighter? What are you really looking for? Is it the pain from the abuse, the fear, or something more?"

"There's always more." I did turn, then, but I scooted back to the edge of my seat to put space between us. Immediately, I nearly lost myself in his vibrant blue depths. Usually, they were light or dark sapphire. Tonight was different. Tonight, they practically glowed. There was no lust. No want of me. Just a fun curiosity, and I saw it as clear as day. "I hate men. *Hate them* but…apparently not as much as I think. I just want…" I stopped. "I just want to prove myself right. To feel something, even if I do know how it'll end up. It always goes in the same direction. That's fine with me. The more extreme the better. Anger is not much different than love. Most kill because of both."

"They do, and for other reasons." A couple laughed loudly across the room, drawing our attention, but he came back to me. "Your music is good. You made the right choice. I respect your sacrifice." He glanced up as three-eleven came to sit back at my feet. "As you know, the Gardens is big on holding events. If I held a concert in a few months, would you perform?"

"Me?"

"Amongst others."

"Pistol?" My face drew in from distaste, and I couldn't help it

"He's already agreed. That's irrelevant. Would you do it?"

I sighed. "Let's be honest, Main Master. No one wants to hear me."

"Make them."

"How am I supposed to do that? They're the ones who ran me out."

At my number being called, I eased to my feet.

"You're the one looking for a fight, Forty-two. Don't let it fall just to your slaves. Give them something they can't resist. Make them crawl back to you. Show me your willing to work for it, and I'll see if there's something I can do to help."

15

MO3II

I t didn't matter how hard you fought. How...*long* you tried to resist. I battled against my training for months more than most. I could remember that. I could recall the torture I'd gone through for disobeying. It meant nothing. My brain said I was indifferent to my struggles. It was in the past and unimportant. I was content now and at peace once I'd submitted to what I was meant for. Which was *her*, my Mistress. How could I not want to assist or protect her? Fighting was what I'd been born to do.

Growing up in Brazil, my life hadn't been easy. Mixed martial arts was what I lived for. I had competed from my earliest days. I had the scars to prove it. But where my travels ended, was where I thought my life was beginning. The opportunity seemed too good to be true. The recruiter was just too likeable for my taste. If I would have been smart, I would have listened to my instincts instead of jumping on a plane.

Glory.

Money.

Success.

I sold my soul to those things and ultimately this was the price. Could I really complain? Maybe I didn't have the ability. I sure couldn't think into the future without feeling foggy. Then again, why look into the future when the present provided more than I was worthy of?

I belong to her.

I served her.

I was hers to do with as she pleased…and sometimes when life or nightmares were too much, or when she was too drunk to think straight, she'd come to me. Those nights were my favorite. She'd have me hold her, or she'd cuddle in my lap and fall asleep. Other times she'd talk to me for hours as I stared ahead, hearing but not acknowledging. That was the hardest part, but my training was clear. I was a body, not a consciousness. I supported. Aided. I was a provider, not a companion unless it was ordered of me. It wasn't.

"Mistress, if you'll just wait here."

The guard opened a door, giving view to a room that was full of more guards. The two slaves I had put the information on stood in the middle of the room, restrained. They were looking at each other, clearly confused on what was happening. When the guard moved further into the room revealing my Mistress, both men didn't take their eyes off her. Where the dark-haired one looked relieved, the other, not so much. His head whipped to the guard as the man checked his restraints, but the blond was hesitant as he gazed between me and my Mistress.

"You can come in now."

My Mistress glanced at me at the guard's order, and I followed as we headed in the room. I stayed a good two feet back, giving her space, but remaining close enough to protect her if I needed to.

"Hmm." Her heels clicked as she began to pace. Her eyes trailed up and down their nude bodies, inspecting their defined muscles and height, which was decent over her own small frame. The light-haired man didn't react, but the dark-haired one clearly approved of her interest. I didn't like it, but I stayed in my spot calculating their motives and intentions per my duties.

More clicks as she circled them, coming to a stop in front of the blond.

"How well do you take orders?"

There was a pause as he glanced back at the man at his side.

"I believe myself capable of doing whatever you want."

"Good answer. A little too good. You?"

Her question was directed at the one with dark brown hair.

"Better than him."

My Mistress's head tilted, and her lids narrowed as she stepped closer.

"Is that a fact?"

"It is. Name it, and I'll do it."

"Alright. Suck his dick."

The man's smug look melted, and both men's stares connected. A small smile tugged at my Mistress's lips as she headed back in my direction, circling me like the shark she was. Although something in me wanted to smile as well, I stayed stoic. Her hand ran along the length of my lower back, and what had to have been pride made me stand taller. She came to a stop a few inches in front of me.

"I'm waiting, slave."

"I…"

"You what? Aren't so confident in your abilities anymore?" In slow steps she approached them again. Still the slave didn't obey or answer. She went back to the blond. "You don't care for me much. You shouldn't. I am a Mistress. I believe you were prepared and truly understand what that means. That's why I'm going to bid on you."

The brunette's eyes lowered, his face losing all hope as my Mistress once again took him in.

"You, on the other hand, doubt my power. That's also why I'm going to bid on you, so don't pout, slave. You'll be sucking

dick in no time. And I mean that. The three of us are going to have so much fun."

Something flashed on his face but disappeared just as fast as he looked over to me.

"Mistress, can I speak freely?"

Seconds passed. "Sure. Why not. What is it?"

"What's up with that guy? Is he your slave too?"

"He is, but you don't have to worry about taking his cock. He's above your rank. Besides, you couldn't fit it in your mouth anyway. Three-eleven is just for me. Unlike the two of you, *he's special.* Maybe in time you can be special too. Or not. We'll have to see if you can earn it."

The brunette seemed to think, shaking his head. "I'm not really into guys. You, yes, but not them."

Laughter filled the room as my Mistress glanced at me.

"I may have found a winner after all. Slave, does it matter to me if he likes men?"

"No, Mistress."

"If I tell him to suck dick, what is he going to do?"

I met the brunette's annoyed stare answering him directly.

"You will suck dick."

"And if I don't?"

Wider my Mistress's smile grew.

"Slave, tell him what will happen if he doesn't follow my orders."

I took a step forward, placing me directly behind her and only a good foot and a half from him. Our eyes locked, and I could see a resistance behind them. I didn't like it. *Or him.*

"If you don't obey my Mistress, I will unhinge your jaw and put his dick in your mouth for her. *Gladly.*"

The blonde went rigid, but the brunette was better at hiding his emotions. Or maybe he had to see for himself.

"There you have it. Now that we're clear on how this dynamic will work, I'm feeling great about the three of us." She glanced at the guards, nodding her head as she turned and headed towards the main door. Once again, the brunette's voice rang out.

"It'll be you too though, right?"

She didn't answer. As we headed out of the room and back down the hall, I saw her shoulders sag. My training on body language told me she was suffering from lack of self-confidence. Defeat? Was she tired? It was hard for me to read her when I couldn't see her face.

"Bidding will take place shortly, Mistress."

"Thank you."

We left the guard, heading back into the large, opened room. When my Mistress took her seat, I didn't sit. My brain was going crazy trying to figure out what to do to be more of service. It hadn't always been this way. Usually I obeyed my commands, but lately I was thinking more on ways to help. I could do that if she allowed me. And she did need something. I could sense it. Feel it.

"What is the matter, slave?"

"You need something."

Her face was just as blank as mine.

"I need a lot of things."

"What can I do?"

She didn't speak. She didn't even tell me to sit.

"Mistress?" Was that tears collecting? Possibly. I detected she was overwhelmed. It followed her when she returned only days ago. How could three days away make her so upset? I wasn't sure, but I knew what came after her sad episodes. Rage. A lot of it.

"I'm more tired than I realized."

"Does the Mistress wish to return to the apartment? I can bid and bring the new slaves home for you."

Silence.

"I think that's the most you've ever said at one time."

More silence. I had no idea how to respond. It was only a question and a suggestion. Was I supposed to suggest?

"I'm still wet from the drink. I do believe I'll return and take a shower. Here." She took a paper from the end table, jotting down a number. "Do not bid over this amount. If someone outbids you for one of the slaves, let them have them. I'm not sold on either one anyway. If you do happen to win them, bring them right home. Don't let them disobey you. You are above their rank like I mentioned before. Understand?"

"Yes, Mistress."

"Good. I'm going to inform the guard at the desk of my departure and give you control over my bid. You come straight home after you collect them. If one of them tries to run or give you an issue, do whatever you must to bring them to me. If you can't, get a guard. If a guard isn't available and they're still giving you an issue...kill them."

MISTRESS B-0042

I never had doubts three-eleven would deliver my slaves. That didn't seem to matter to Elec or the guard when I requested my slave take over for me. Although three-eleven could bid on my behalf, he wasn't allowed to return without the guards assisting in the delivery. I had been fine with it. Maybe I even understood their precaution. That didn't mean I was happy about it.

The animal in me needed to see what these slaves would do when they thought they had the upper hand. Both were wild cards. Where I expected the blond to fight out of deep-seeded beliefs, I was curious if my brunette rebel would run when faced with something he seemed to be against.

What sort of life did they think they were getting thrown into?

A part of me wanted them to squirm. To be terrified of what I was capable of. I hadn't lied when I said I hated men. I did, but not all. Just most. The pressurized explosion simmered in my gut, igniting from lust to looks. Almost everything they did triggered me.

Throughout my entire life, I hadn't come across a single one that hadn't betrayed my trust one way or another. The majority of men weren't loyal. *Ever.* It was my bitterness over what they had done to me that left me itching to destroy them in every way possible. Especially the two that were no doubt already waiting for me. They feared the worst. They should. I couldn't deny that I wasn't half tempted to end this now. A bloody massacre was exactly the sort of release I needed. If it weren't for Elec's challenge, I would have seriously considered it. I wasn't in the mood for games, and this might turn into my biggest game to date.

Could the Main Master really help me get my life back?

Turning off the blow dryer, I stood and flipped my hair back as I straightened and looked in the mirror.

No makeup. Nothing but my robe covering the scars I couldn't face. Nothing fake about me anymore except half my hair. I wouldn't think about that. I was getting rather fond of the blonde locks that didn't at all remind me of Pistol's new slave. *Bitch. Both of them.* He'd see I wasn't what they claimed. He'd discover the truth, and he could have both of my middle fingers for believing the lies they so easily told about me. Not that he probably cared anyway. It was me who was hurt. He had never really been committed, and that's what I got for letting myself fall for someone who never deserved me to begin with.

"What the hell are you doing, you fucking psycho? I said I wouldn't move. I meant it."

My eyes lifted to the reflection of the door. I didn't rush as I turned. I kept my pace leisurely as I headed for the yelling that continued. I knew that voice, and the outspoken brunette was on a rampage. Had I thought he was mysterious? Well, there was my mystery. It was wrapped in dramatic complaints and protests.

"What in the hell is going on here?" I slid the French doors open, glaring towards three-eleven who had one of the dark-haired slave's arms pinned behind his back while he held the other by the cuff attached to the floor.

"Mistress, he doesn't follow orders."

"I said I'd be fine sitting here."

"If he said you needed to be cuffed, you listen. Did I not say he was above your rank," I exploded. "Slave, finish cuffing him and then break the unrestrained arm. We're not starting out as I had hoped."

"Break—what!"

"*Weren't you trained?* Is it so hard to follow rules?"

Movement at the door had my eyes jerking up. A guard appeared at the doorway; his mouth surrounded by what looked like powdered sugar.

"Is this not your job?" My lips parted. "Are you eating my donuts?"

"He said." His mouth was so full, I could barely understand the tall, lean guard as he pointed to three-eleven.

"He said he'd restrain the slave, or he said you could stuff your face with my breakfast?"

Yelling howled out followed by a pop so loud, I nearly jumped. Three-eleven stood, leaving the brunette rolling and crying out from the floor.

"Did you let this guard eat my donuts?"

"He asked."

"They were not yours to give, slave." My head moved off to the side so I could see the guard around him. "Did you eat all of them?"

"No, Mistress. Just two."

"*There was only three.* Do you usually go around asking slaves for food? Maybe I should take it up with the Main Master about how you're not getting fed. Is that it? Are you mistreated here?"

Fear had his eyes widening. "No, Mistress. We eat fine. I just—"

"I don't want to hear it. Get me more, and grab chocolate ones too while you're down there. Unbelievable. *You.*" I turned back to three-eleven. "I said you could have one. That doesn't mean offer them to every dick under the sun. How bad is his arm?"

"Fucking bad! That son of a bitch zombie. God dammit."

Were we to name calling already?

I took in the odd angle of his arm feeling lust spark in the ice cold within. Forcing the anger back, I let my personality transform almost seductively. "What's your slave number?"

The brunette was moving into a sitting position, wincing and crying out with every shift. The blond was against the other wall, restrained and sitting there quietly. He was the thinker. Calculative. But he'd talk, and when he did it would get him in trouble. He had too much power and ego not to try to use it.

"M1038."

"I don't like it. What's your real name?"

For the briefest moment, he stopped the noise, growing quiet. His reaction was exactly what I wanted. He thought I was interested under my cold exterior. That would give him hope where it didn't lie.

"Dane."

I crouched, letting my robe open as my legs became exposed to my upper thighs. Dane's breathing hitched for the smallest moment, but he wasn't looking there. He was trapped in my gaze as I eased him against the wall to straddle him. He was wearing the traditional grey sweatpants all the male's slaves wore after being bought, and they were hiding nothing of his arousal.

"*Dane*," I repeated, softly, fitting myself against the hard length that rested over his thigh. "Yes, that's better…isn't it?"

"Yes, Mistress. Fuck, yes."

More, I moved, glad he couldn't touch me as I had my fun. The slave was starting to breathe hard. His knees came up, sliding me even more into his lap as he searched for some way to keep me on his cock. At the sound of material shifting, the spell vanished. I glanced back to three-eleven as he kept his eyes on Dane.

"Did you break the bone, or did you pop his shoulder out of place like you did with Omar?"

"I popped it out just in case the Mistress changed her mind."

"When I say something, you do it. You should be in trouble for not following orders. It looks like tonight you're both lucky. Pop it back in."

If I didn't know better, three-eleven's mouth tugged back on the side. It was so fast, I may not have seen anything there at all.

"Whoa, no way. Mistress, please. Anyone but him."

"Stop being a baby or I'll make him finish the job."

I stood, turning to the blond who still hadn't made a sound.

"And what is your number, slave?"

"M-zero-five-zero-five."

"Five-oh-five. That one is better. Let's cut it down to five. Dane and five." I sat on the edge of my bed, letting the robe open once again. The blond's light gray eyes didn't leave mine. He didn't even seem phased by any possible nudity on my part. "Are you gay?"

"No."

"Impotent?"

"No."

"You just don't find me attractive?"

He didn't speak.

"I take that as a no."

"I think your exterior is attractive."

"But not the interior, huh."

Silence. He glanced at the other men, lowering his eyes to the wooden floor before meeting my stare.

"I know who you are. You're that model turned rock star. I used to listen to your music. I'm disappointed that you're a product of this place. I wouldn't have thought that. You didn't strike me as...cold."

"Cold usually equates to death, five, and the industry will kill you faster than you can catch your breath from shock. I may be a monster in this underground world, but at least my soul still belongs to me. That's more than I can say for the rest of the devils you find yourself surrounded by. Tell me." I lowered the top half of my body so that my face was level with his. "What brings you to hell? What are your sins?"

A yell and cursing filled the room as a pop echoed through the space. I didn't even bother turning around as I took in the nervous way five watched my blank slate. Yes, I was going to have to keep a close eye on this one and pray I didn't bite off more than I could chew.

"Your attention belongs with me, not them. How did you get here, slave?"

"A woman from a bar. I left with her. We never made it back to my place. I was shot up with something in the cab. Here I am."

My head shook. "I've heard about these new female scouts. Smart."

His lips curled back at me in disgust, and he didn't even try to hide it.

"I like you."

And maybe a small part of me did. He wasn't pretending to be anything he wasn't. He wasn't saying what I wanted to hear to appease me. That still didn't mean he was safe. If anything, it put my guard up even more. Dangerous. Yes. Alarms were ringing in my head, and they called me home like the lost little girl I was.

Lowering from the edge of the mattress, I moved in until I was right beside him. It took a few seconds, but he finally lifted his gaze to mine. It was intense...yet the Mistress in me spotted vulnerability.

Closer, I moved in, making my voice light and quiet.

"You're not like the others, are you? You don't deserve this life. I didn't ask for this either, slave." I didn't turn on my charm.

I mirrored him like the evil bitch I was. Giving, but not. Showing my wounds but keeping them close. This one needed to think he could trust someone. To relate and connect. "What's your name?"

Time. It played out as he scanned my face.

"How did you not choose this? I think you did. I think you love it."

I nodded, looking down. "You think I enjoyed losing my career and being lied about to the world? Or maybe you think I deserved these?"

Untying my robe, I opened it, not looking at the scars randomly marking my nude body.

"The jagged ones on my thighs, almost gone now from multiple surgeries in my youth, are from a barbed wire fence. I received those at ten when I told my father I didn't want to do horseback riding lessons anymore. He was going to shoot my horse. I tried to save it, but he wasn't ready to jump that fence. My dad shot him anyway while I tried to fight myself out of a mangled mess. You see, my father was determined to have me succeed like him. So much so, he pimped me out to whoever he could to make it happen. Maybe he knew what they were doing. Maybe not. Regardless, it started when I was twelve. The other scars are why I had to leave modeling. They were tired of covering up my pain. My stomach, me. My chest...me. Arms." I jerked up the sleeves on the robe. "*Me*. We all die differently, slave. We either find ways to heal or do what we must to forget it all. That's just the way it goes until we're set free. You fear death, but I long more than most to leave this life for good."

I stood, turning my back on him and dropping my robe completely as I headed towards my other two slaves. Where Dane's eyes didn't miss an inch of me, three-eleven kept his stare on my face.

"We won't be going back out tonight. I'm going to bed. You get out there and wait for my donuts. Lock up behind you." I turned to look at the new slaves. "Three-eleven is in charge if you need anything. If you try to pull something, he has my permission to kill you. This doesn't have to be a bad thing. I need you. You need me. *You* decide what you want to make of this."

MO3II

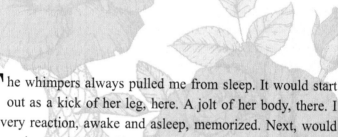

The whimpers always pulled me from sleep. It would start out as a kick of her leg, here. A jolt of her body, there. I had every reaction, awake and asleep, memorized. Next, would be the crying as she tossed back and forth fitfully under the blankets. She'd get so wrapped up in them that by the time she flew awake, she'd be tangled and even more panicked. Without an order, there was nothing I could do but let it play out…*and wait.*

Light snoring stirred from the far side of the room, but with how dim it was, I couldn't quite see whether the dark-haired slave was waking from our Mistress's small sounds. I suspected five was awake from the constant groans and turns on the mat I'd provided before bed. I was closest to the door on one side of our Mistress, the blond on the opposite side, and the dark-haired, Dane, at her feet. None of our presence could stop whatever nightmares haunted her. More, she moved, the first sob escaping.

"Mistress?"

The whisper was barely audible, and it'd come from Dane.

"Don't."

My order was firm. Silence from the slave took over, but our

30

Mistress only got worse. Blankets rustled, and she mumbled something incoherently, sobbing even harder.

"Is she okay?"

"Maybe we should wake her."

My growl had the two men growing quiet again. The rustling increased, and I knew it wouldn't be long now.

"No. No. *Daddy!*"

Gasps filled the room, and I could barely see the outline of my Mistress as she bolted upright, trying to catch her breath. The sobs didn't allow her to. They were loud and not anywhere close to ceasing as she fought the blankets and scrambled from the bed.

"Don't let him get me. Slave, *don't let him get me.*"

She climbed into my lap, just as fast, turning and pulling her comforter down to us. The majority of her body was between my spread legs, and with my bare back against the wall, her head rested on my stomach as she clung tightly around me.

"You're safe, Mistress."

"I'm not. I can't. *Breathe.* You won't let him get me?"

The trembling grew worse as her grip increased.

"I'll protect you. You're safe."

I felt the truth of my words, yet my voice sounded robotic. The slaves didn't make a sound as she continued to cry. Something told me to put my hand on her back, but another part knew I hadn't received an order to do that, so I shouldn't. I stayed still, letting her hold on until she grabbed my wrists, putting them on her shoulders. That didn't happen every time, but I was glad it happened now. It allowed me to cover her nude skin, soaking in the warmth as my hands completely splayed across her back. The softness was jarring to my hard exterior. I added pressure, offering support without moving my touch in a caress. I was here. That was enough.

"I don't want to remember anymore." She sniffled, moving her face down into my hip. The friction had my lids blinking as my heartrate jumped. My own warmth increased, and I could feel my body wanting to react. Wanting, but not giving in entirely. I wouldn't betray my Mistress too. Not if I could help it. I was a vessel, and what I felt was irrelevant.

"Mistress, are you okay?"

Her body stiffened at Dane's question, but she hugged around me tighter. She didn't respond, but it didn't stop him from continuing.

"If you want to talk or something, I'm awake. I'll listen."

"Back off. If she wanted to talk, she would have gone to you."

"Fuck off, *five*. I'm just trying to help."

"Let her deal on her own. You talk too damn much."

The Mistress sniffled but ignored them.

"I wouldn't be talking right now at all if she was okay. All I want to do is check on her and see if there's anything I can do. Mistress, I'm here if you need me."

"She knows, dumbass. Shut up."

"You're lucky we're chained up."

A loud groan vibrated me as she lifted her head.

"Slave, we're sleeping in the living room. Let's go."

"*See, Dane.* You just couldn't stop."

"You're not stopping either. You're still going."

The Mistress stood, and I followed her into the living room. The moment we were out of the room, she slammed the door closed.

"Go get on the sofa."

I headed over, obeying. The cold from the leather penetrated my skin. Even with sweatpants on, I could still feel the chill through the material. It didn't last for long as she threw the cover over me and climbed under, snuggling at my side.

From the moment I became hers, I never laid down to sleep. I'd gotten used to being against the wall. This...this felt too good. It felt even better with her nude body against me. Her leg was even over my hip as she held on. And me, with where she was laying, I could almost imagine I was holding her too. But I wasn't. My arm was underneath, lying next to her on the couch. It wasn't around her like I felt it should be.

"This is better," she breathed out, and then yawned. "So much better."

The last was light. As if she were already drifting off. I wasn't. All my focus went to controlling the hardness between my legs. It was suddenly agonizing. *New.* It had me shifting under her as I tried to get control. Even the action was different. I never moved. I wasn't supposed to, and my behavior was enough to have her reacting.

"Slave?"

Her head rose, and her knee slid down just enough to brush my cock. My teeth ground together.

"I apologize, Mistress. I can't seem to." I stopped, my brow creasing from the confusion and disappointment in myself. "I think maybe—I'm sorry."

Her leg lifted off, and pressure from her hand eased around my length, gripping tight enough to make me grunt. I couldn't stop the sound from coming. Pleasure took me over completely, muddling my mind even more as she trapped my length against my lower stomach.

"What are you sorry for, slave? For this?"

"...Yes. If I could sit up."

"No."

The order had me closing my eyes, trying to breathe through the twitching against her hand. My body was beyond my control. It didn't matter that she wasn't stroking me. The touch was enough for my body to finish what it started, if it wanted to. I couldn't let it. I wouldn't.

"I can't say I'm not curious from what the woman at the auction asked me. You're a blank slate. Were you taught to please a woman in your training?"

My precum increased, pooling against me. It was hot, slick, burning me alive at her words.

"I was, Mistress."

"Such strain in your tone. Such restraint. What did they teach you? To fuck? Eat pussy? To finger your Mistress until she screamed? I'm curious. Can you show passion, or is that beyond you?"

"I can do whatever my Mistress needs of me."

"Anything?"

My entire body convulsed in ecstasy as her hand squeezed, stroking up to the head of my cock.

"No one will know you better than me. They can't. I'm programmed just for you. I can be whatever you need."

A pause.

"But do you want to?"

Did I want to? "I want to please my Mistress, yes."

"Show me."

As if a switch flipped in my brain, I was pulling her underneath me before I could process what I was even doing. My lips crushed into hers, drinking her in as if she were my first kiss. *My last.* Our tongues dueled, and she moaned, crying out into my mouth as my hand firmly gripped the side of her throat.

"*Jesus.* Whoa. No kissing. God." She took heavy breaths against my lips. "You can't kiss me. Anything but that."

But it was too late. I'd already tasted her on my tongue. I'd felt her melt underneath me, and I wanted more. *She wanted more.* The craving was so clear in my mind, but so was her order.

Lowering my lips to the opposite side of her neck, I breathed her in, sucking and kissing along her throat as I still held to the other side of it. My tongue swirled, feeling her hammering heartbeat. I let my teeth graze the softness, nibbling at her, feeling my entire world shift with the new emotions that came with my actions. Shaky, pleasure-filled sounds filled the room, increasing just the smallest amount as I took my time making a path to her breasts. For as many times as I'd seen them, *even felt them against me*, this was different.

Her skin tasted sweet with a hint of saltiness. She even had goosebumps while heat poured off of her. Maybe it was me. Was I the one on fire? I didn't know as I sucked her nipple into my mouth, grazing the hard nub with my teeth. Gently, I pulled against it, sucking even more. A small cry left her, and her legs drew up to my sides.

"They really did teach you. This is so...*real*. Are you real? I mean, still blank?"

My face lifted, and it was dim enough from the light above the kitchen stove that I could see she was baffled.

"I...I am me. Do you wish for me to stop?"

"...no."

She shifted, and her hand pushed past my sweats, wrapping around and sliding down my cock. The grip I still had on her neck secured even more, but I used my other hand to hold to the sofa with almost all my strength.

"You can give pleasure, slave, but you're not the best at taking it. You like this. Don't you."

It wasn't a question, but I felt compelled to answer anyway.

"I do. I don't think I'm supposed to. I..."

Words wouldn't come, but a million scenarios battled against each other in my brain. Did I move back and trap her wrists beneath her as I lost myself in her taste? Lick her? Suck against her until she ordered me for more?

The answer was a mystery, but my response was immediate. On some level, my higher self knew what to do, and he was feasting on the opportunity. It was the taste of her skin that called the most.

I sucked down her stomach, moving even lower as I placed one of her knees over the back of the sofa. I had her spread good and wide as I began tracing my tongue over her slit. Experience merged with training, slowing my own impatience until I knew nothing but the small sighs. The deep inhales. She rocked against me as I held her hips. Time didn't even exist. Only her as the taste of her juices owned me.

"Fuck. God. This." Her head lifted, and she gripped to my short hair, holding tightly as I sucked harder to her clit, tracing her opening but not breaching the entrance. She wanted me to push into her. It was obvious as she moved at a more feverish pace. Her orgasm was right there, and I kept her on the edge, despite I should have given her what she wanted. I should, right? Or was there more pleasure in making her wait?

My lessons blurred with what I felt I should have known. I did know, but I couldn't necessarily recall instances.

"Wait. Wait. Wait."

The three worded cadence came out fast. Nothing. My mind blanked, and I lifted…stopping. Still…aching.

"Too real. Too soon. Take off your sweatpants and lay down on your back."

I obeyed while I tried to process. Had I done something wrong? Too many thoughts. Too many questions. Perhaps that was the reason I wasn't performing as I should.

Laying down, the Mistress's hands immediately began running down my chest. I didn't touch her. I tried not to even react. It was impossible as she lowered, moving her lips inches over my cock. Hot air was almost worse than her touching me. It had my fists clenching as I stared at the ceiling above.

"Don't move. Don't come."

She grabbed my cock, encasing the tip before she slid me in her mouth. A deep sound vibrated my entire being as a rumble tore its way free. My knees were trying to draw up. Even my chest was slightly elevated from the sofa. Nothing I could do muted the sensations that took me over.

"That good, huh?"

Did she want me to feel good?

Her tongue swirled around me, teasing as she brought me

even deeper. The suction was bliss and torture at the same time. To not shoot my cum inside of her mouth was going to kill me. Had this been done to me before? Yes? No? I knew nothing or cared to even try to figure it out as her rhythm turned unforgiving. She stroked, moaning as she went faster.

"Mistress."

"Mm-mmm."

Was that a no?

Fuck it was too good. Too much.

"Mistress. I'm trying. *Please.*"

Her head came up, but she didn't speak. Instead, she crawled on top of me, straddling and easing me inside of her. Slowly, she rocked, inching her way down. Nails bit into my chest, increasing in pressure. Moans started again. Sweet sounds. Hungry sounds. I tried my best to be unresponsive. It's what she wanted. A vessel. Someone to pleasure her without it being a person.

"This shouldn't feel so good. I shouldn't even...be doing this. It's wrong but." She moaned, breaking my skin with her nails. "It's better this way. So much better." She sucked in a breath, finally managing to get me all the way inside of her. Sweat was coating my skin, and I stayed in a pleasure purgatory. Not giving in but taking as much as I could manage. My Mistress was moving now, stretched out tightly around me, going up and down at a slow pace. Her legs were shaking the more she fucked me. Despite laying here like a corpse, I wasn't doing much better. It took all I had to hold to control and not pound into her until I was coming deep in her pussy. I could do that. My mind was screaming to, even if I knew it was bad.

"I see why they want the blank slates. Fuck. So wrong. Too good." She broke off with a cry, her head lowering to the base of my throat.

"Yes. Move. Fuck me, slave. God, I'm right there. Fuck me hard and fast. Come in me. I can't..."

She didn't continue as I wrapped around, holding her against me like a vice. I withdrew, using my strength to pull her down onto me as I began slamming my cock in deep. It didn't take but a few thrusts before she was screaming and writhing against me. Pulsing spasms shook her, the action burning its way into my brain. I pounded faster. Harder. Trying to claim something I couldn't even begin to understand, and with every shot of my own cum, I lost pieces of myself to her even more.

MISTRESS B-0042

"This life doesn't have to be bad. It's quite simple. Be my slaves. Obey. Be loyal. Do everything I say, and you live." The city was packed, but Dane and five were managing just fine as they walked at my side. "Down here, there's everything you can imagine. You may be owned, but that doesn't mean your life has to be miserable. Not if you follow the rules."

"Which are to...cater to you? *Adore* you? All three of us?"

My eyes narrowed at five. "Is there someone else you'd rather be wasting your pathetic time on?"

"Feisty. No."

I slowed, coming to a stop. "Someone doesn't know how to share. That's what this is about, right? Are you jealous over my slave?"

"Which one? The idiot or the zombie?"

My lips tugged back at the edge, but something shifted in me at the name-calling. There was something more than five's attitude I didn't like. It was his demeanor. In the way he kept looking over. I glanced a few feet away where three-eleven was watching but keeping his distance. With a nod of my head, he joined us.

"We both know what this is about." I turned to three-eleven. "Slave, five is jealous of you. What do you think of that?"

Brown eyes met gray but didn't linger as he put his focus on me.

"I think nothing of it. You're my priority."

"Thank you, slave." I turned to five. "That is how you should be."

"I'm not a—"

Blank slate. If you or Dane call him a zombie again, I won't have three-eleven break your jaw, I'll do that myself. That's a promise."

Five's lips twisted, and he kept quiet as I led the way to an outdoor bistro. The tables weren't big, but we managed to find two empty ones next to each other. Dane went to take the table with me, shoved out of the way by five who managed to grab the chair first.

"Why two men and a blank slate? I don't understand. Does he not fulfill you enough? It sure sounded like it last night."

"Both of your training was atrocious. Would you prefer I chose you to fuck last night? Or is it Dane's mouth you're regretting not having? I could solve that this very minute if you'd like."

"His mouth doesn't threaten me. Neither does being with men. If you ordered him to get me off, I'd come down his throat right here just to spite him. Why? Because I think he's a moron."

"Wow." I just shook my head at him. "You are quite the piece of work. I bet the guards didn't get to see this side of you. I'm so glad I did. And so you know, when I tell you you're going to suck his cock, that's not a threat. I'm not saying it as a form of punishment. You *will* suck each other's cocks. You will fuck each other. That's what I want. It's an act, and your preference doesn't mean shit to me. This isn't about you. It's what I like. *I'm the Mistress here.* Now, whether I join someday, I haven't decided. You have to earn that."

A pause. "You're serious?" Five shifted in his chair. "You want us to be together? Sexually?"

"That's right."

He got quiet, glancing at Dane, only to look around the crowded street. *"But why three of us?* Especially if you don't want to be with us like that all the time."

"Because it's what I'm into. It makes me hot and happy. I like variety. Look at the three of you. Your appearances are all different. Your personalities, attitude, clearly different. Sexually, I like to watch men, but I also like choice. I want to feel. The only thing you're making me is annoyed, which isn't a good thing for you."

"You want to feel? Here." He rose, leaning over enough to swoop me in his arms so that I was sitting on his lap. Three-eleven was halfway out of his chair, pure protector drawing in his features as he glared at five. "Let's get to know each other."

"Sit, slave. I'm fine." I turned back to five. "You think I can hear you better by sitting on your lap? Or perhaps you think me weak and incapable of being able to fall for you unless you're treating me like a baby."

"I'm holding you for me, not you. I'm angry. I'm a jealous guy. I don't like that I was stolen from my life regardless it was shitty to begin with. *It was still mine.* I've been in this hellhole for over a year, only to be sold to you, to be..." he looked around, the anger fading into a frown. "Set up with another guy. But I still have you. It's a lot to process. I wasn't sure what to expect. This isn't as bad as I prepared myself for. They told us we could die." His tone dropped. "Truthfully, I'm trying to grasp the entirety of the situation. I don't mind it. I'm not..." He glanced over to Dane. "Really attracted to him like that, but if that's what you want, I guess I could try. But only because of the outcome. If I'm going to belong to you, then I think it's only fair you belong to me too."

"I thought you didn't want me."

"I never said that."

My head tilted. "You pretty much did."

"Maybe I saw you weren't as bad as I thought. I shouldn't have been so quick to judge."

"We all make mistakes."

But he hadn't made a mistake. He was right to be cautious. He had no idea what to expect and that was perfect.

The back of his fingers brushed over my cheek, and I tried not to pull back and cringe. "Was it the horse?"

"What?" I felt myself stiffen on his lap.

"Your nightmare. Was he killing your horse again?"

My lips tightened, and I let out a breath, letting sadness I didn't feel shadow my face. Tears filled my eyes, and I let the seconds span out. His hand settled on my lower back, and I sniffled.

"It wasn't the horse. As crazy as it sounds, the horse was far from the worst of it."

"There was more?"

"So much more."

Dane was leaning forward, closer to us so he could hear. I looked to the side, sweeping over his face with the smallest tinge of interest. A grin just as mischievous as my underlined hint appeared. I returned, putting my attention back on five.

"I was young. Maybe seven. My dad had been out of town for a while, but by some miracle they were letting him come home to visit for two days. A big game was coming up, so I can remember my mom stressing how important it was for us to be on our best behavior." I let the memories come. The numbness followed, the emotions only finding me when I slept. "The moment my dad walked through the door, I knew it was going to be bad. Maybe that's why they let him come home. Maybe they knew he was close to snapping."

"Did he hurt you?"

I glanced over to Dane, and five's growl rumbled through me at the interruption.

"You seriously have no manners. Let her finish."

"I am letting her finish. I'm here for you, Mistress." Dane's hand came to rest on my shoulder, but five swatted it away.

"Go on."

"I'd rather not." I wiggled on five's lap so that I could go back to my chair, surprised when he gripped my hips securely, not letting me stand.

"It'll help if you talk about it."

Fire scorched inside of me. It fed the anger, encouraging me to take the long dagger style stick from my hair and stab it into the side of his neck. I held to the impulsive flames letting them reach deadly heights. As intense as they hit, I pushed them back, letting my body soften once again.

"Maybe you're right."

"I am. What happened?"

Before I could even open my mouth to speak, he leaned in, burying his face against the side of my head. To him, I felt inviting. To anyone on the street viewing us, I had no doubt my face said the opposite. My lids closed, and I reigned in the part that got me into the Gardens to begin with.

"My dad came home on a rampage. They always started out silent. That's how you knew it was going to be bad. We were halfway through dinner when out of nowhere he threw his plate against the wall. He started yelling at my mom about something. I don't remember what it was, but he was so angry. When he ripped her out of the chair and hit her the first time, all I can remember doing is screaming. I must have been screaming a lot because after a while he stopped hitting her and looked right at me. That's when I ran."

"*Monster.*" Dane's head was shaking, and I let the sadness take over again as I lowered my eyes. "Did he…?"

Dane didn't continue, but I knew he wanted to.

"Officially, my mom had been drinking a little too much and fell down the stairs. She had a broken arm, the side of her face was pretty bruised up, and she had a concussion. They didn't take me in. All I suffered was a few bruises and a busted lip. He was about finished by the time he got to me anyway. It's fine though. It wasn't the first time or the last. It's just the episode that somehow makes it into a lot of my dreams."

Arms tightened around me, and five pulled me more into his chest. With my back to three-eleven and Dane, I let my true self shine. It couldn't have been at a worse time. Long blonde hair swayed, and Pistol slowed, dropping his arm from around his slave as he stopped to look over at me. He pulled the sunglasses down, suddenly fuming...and it wasn't at whatever they were talking about. From the way his slave swung her face to look over at me, she'd been caught just as unaware as I had been.

"You're unbelievable, you know that?" For some reason he zeroed in on me, stomping in my direction. It was so unexpected that I didn't even move. I couldn't. I was the instigator in our arguments. Never him. Not until now. "Did you fuck him too just to try to ruin my night?"

"Excuse me?"

Anger hit like a bullet, and I flew forward, fighting through five's arms as I stood. Three-eleven was immediately at my side, waiting.

"The Main Master. He mentioned you may be playing in the Evil Deeds concert in a few months. What did you do to get invited into that? Do I even want to know?"

"Fuck you, Pistol. The Main Master *invited me*. I didn't do shit. You're so brainwashed and gullible, you'd believe anything anyone in your circle told you. For your information, I never fucked anyone. Not while we were together and sure as fuck not in the months following."

"*Right.*"

"I am right. We're over. *We've been over.* Tell me why I'd lie about it if I did? I *wish* I had something to throw in your face. Nothing would give me more pleasure than to watch you fall a peg or two. I did nothing but love you, and what did you do? You turned your back on me like everyone else I've ever cared about and focused more on loving your career and yourself."

His slave pulled at his arm, but he didn't budge. He took in the three men behind me, his eyes narrowing even more.

"You're not playing at that show."

"If the Main Master allows it, yes I am. Are you so threatened by me?"

"Threatened?"

"What else could it be?" My head shook back and forth, disgust taking me over. "You're a rock God. *I'm nothing.* You took the deal with the devil and have golden boy status. You're set for life. I declined, and we all know what happened because of it. *You know what they did to me.* Is that what this is about? Guilt? Is that why you're so angry?"

"Absolutely not. You brought on whatever happened to you."

"Keep deluding yourself. Make me the bad guy if that's what makes you feel better. I don't care anymore. I'm about to rise. When I do, who's name do you think the press will bring up when they beg to interview me? Oh, the stories I could tell them."

Pistol took a step forward, his eyes so narrowed, the color barely showed.

"The only one delusional here is you. Keep my name out of your fucking mouth."

"Or you'll what?"

At three-eleven's step closer, Pistol glanced over, eyeing him up and down.

"You're not playing at that concert."

"The decision isn't yours. It wasn't even mine. What does that tell you?" I smiled, lifting one of my eyebrows at him. "I have the backing of the Main Master, and there's nothing you can do about it. He knows the truth about me. *Ask him.* He saw my sacrifice and what Hollywood did to me. It was all lies. All of it, and now revenge will be mine. Watch for me, *Master Seventy-seven.* I won't need a contract to make it to the top. I'm about to bring the Devil to his fucking knees. You can tell him I'm on my way."

MO3II

Disobedience hadn't even been in my vocabulary until I'd seen Master Seventy-seven in my Mistress's face. I could barely even take in their conversation. I'd been so out of it with the need to spill his blood. Even when he stormed off, ways to kill him blinded me. It'd taken my Mistress's hand on my bicep to break the spell. Even now, back in our apartment, hours later, I still couldn't think straight.

"What is that? Are you writing a song? A plan of action to knock all those fuckers in Hollywood on their asses? I had no idea you dated Pistol Stevens. Holy fuck. That is...bad ass. He's like a...just amazing. And you're a singer? How have I not heard of you? I didn't listen to much music though. I guess I was too busy with work. I really didn't have time to do much of anything."

My Mistress's eyes lifted from the paper.

"Don't say that bastard's name in my apartment. I hate that son of a bitch."

"Sor-ry, Mistress." Dane stumbled over the words. "You do look familiar. I know I've seen you somewhere. But...work. I...I worked a lot."

"Well, *I'm sure trying*."

The sarcasm was thick in her voice. Our Mistress had been focused now for hours. Ever since our swift departure after lunch, she'd been quiet and withdrawn from all of us. Where I was content to watch her, five and Dane were having a harder time. That wasn't good for them. Especially since she reached this stage so soon. It'd taken weeks for her to get here with the last slaves. Now, a day? There was something different with her this time. Before it was fun for her to play her games with the men. Now, she was intense. Withdrawn, but driven to work. What that said for Dane and five, I didn't know. She wasn't happy with either one of them. It didn't even appear she wanted them around.

"What did you do for work, slave?"

Dane's face slightly winced through the title, but she didn't see. She was already looking back down at the paper.

"I...don't think I should say."

Her eyes shot up. "I asked you a question. Now I really want to know. What did you do?"

"It's not something I like to talk about."

"Slave."

The threat in her tone had him letting out a sigh. "I was in some movies."

"Oh." Interest sparked. "So, you're an actor."

"Sort of. Not really."

"What do you mean? You either were in movies and acted or you didn't."

"You did porn?"

Five's question had my Mistress's head whipping back to Dane, repeating slave five like a parrot.

"You did porn? Not that amateur shit, but real porn?"

"It paid the bills. Besides, I was good at it."

"Maybe it'll be five sucking *your* dick."

"*Hey*. What is your obsession with blowjobs?"

"It's fucking hot."

Five threw her a look but her fascination was all focused at Dane.

"Let me see it."

"Seriously?"

"I saw your dick when I bought you. Big...but is it really porn-star-big? I want to see."

"I wouldn't say its overly impressive. Average for the industry. Eight inches, or so. It's my skills that counted."

"Your eight fucking inches?"

Five looked between a mix of surprised and angry. She waved his words away. "Clarify and elaborate, Dane. What are your skills?"

"Are you a squirter, Mistress?"

Her lips parted in surprise only to close. "...Not that I'm aware of."

"That's my gift, and I'm amazing at it. We'll find out soon enough, if you want. And I do this thing with my tongue and fingers when I'm eating pussy. God, I could make you scream so good. What's the most times you've ever come in a day?"

"Six. Once." No hesitation. No pause.

Dane laughed. "That's nothing. We'll break that record in the first half-hour to hour."

"That doesn't sound possible. It was years ago, and I haven't been the same since. Now, show me your dick. I'm serious." The Mistress pointed. "Out with it."

"Now, I'm curious." Five moved to the edge of the chair, across from them. "I can't believe you were in porn. I'm not sure whether I'm intimidated or just shocked."

"You're both."

Dane pulled his sweatpants down, grabbing his soft cock. When he looked at my Mistress, she pointed to five. "Don't look at me. He's who you want."

"Mistress."

Her tone deepened as she stared at five.

"We talked about this. You're the one who said you weren't threatened by men. You'll suck his dick, and you'll do it because I ordered you to."

Repeatedly, his jaw flexed, and he gave me one look before cursing under his breath. He feared me. He should.

"You're coming to stand over here, Dane. I'm not getting on my fucking knees. I'm going to stay sitting right here in this chair."

"This is going to be good." My Mistress stood, putting down the paper and pen as she waved me from the other end of the sofa. "Slave, sit here. You're going to touch me as I watch this."

Touch her?

I stood, taking my place as she unbuttoned the leather pants she wore. The men paused as she took them off. Dane's mouth opened, and he grew harder as she slipped off her panties and climbed on my lap. Her back was against my chest, and her legs were opened to each side of mine. She picked up my hand, placing it over her slit.

"Touch me and make me come. *But not too fast.* You two," she flicked her hand in their direction. "Have at it."

Dane moved in, and five's hesitation was there as he grabbed Dane's hard dick. His eyes closed, and he slid the slave's length in his mouth. He didn't stay that way for long. He turned, continuing to suck, but he joined Dane's intense stare as I massaged my fingers over our Mistress's wet pussy. She liked when the men got to this part. She'd enjoyed Omar and Mitchell's time together, even if they didn't. I hadn't participated then. She hadn't even let me outside the apartment at that point, and she had paid for that mistake.

"I see now why you were in porn. So big." She moaned as she moved against my touch. "That's so hot. Slave, a finger."

Her arms wrapped around my bicep, hugging me closer to her chest. Tightly, she held around me as I used my palm to rub over her clit. My finger pushed deep, and I couldn't stop my own cock from thickening beneath her. She was moving right up against me, and after last night, the memories were all I could think about. I could still feel her tightness around me. Taste her. The need was beginning to interfere with rational thought when it had never been like that before. It wasn't out of hand yet, but the fact that I was aware of it said something.

"Another finger. *More.*"

Five's head moved in a steady rhythm, never taking more than the head of Dane's cock in at a time. Both men were focused on our Mistress. Dane stroked down to five's mouth, his moans growing louder as our Mistress moved against my thrusts.

"She thinks this is hot, but dammit. I want that pussy. Fuck, Mistress. I can make you feel good. Let us come over there. I promise you won't regret it." Dane licked his lips, but I felt my free hand slide over her stomach protectively. She was so wet, enjoying what *I* could give her. I wanted her to keep needing me like this. Not them. Never them. "Mistress."

"Five is yours. I am not. Not yet."

Contentment washed over me. She'd told the other two men the same thing. They never earned her. She may have made out with them, but they'd never come this far. Not like what I was doing now. For some reason she chose me and some deep-rooted instinct had me wanting to keep it like that.

Was that guilt I felt?

I blinked through my duties knowing the emotion didn't belong. It was hard to fret too long on it when she was so into what we were doing. More, five took Dane into his mouth, seeming to get more comfortable as he stared at her private area. I tried not to focus on him and more at what my Mistress would enjoy.

She had said to get her off. To touch her.

I reached under one of her knees, spreading her wider as I eased up her thigh. The way her breath caught encouraged me closer. Higher. Up her stomach, and under her shirt. Higher. Underneath her bra. When I rolled my finger over her hard nipple, she cried out, getting so much more vocal and wetter. My fingers pinched, not too hard. Not too soft. I rocked her against me with my thrusts, teasing my own cock before I realized I was even doing it.

"Yes. Take more of him, five. Just like that. Fuck. Five, more."

The last was spoken through her moan. My Mistress's head went back and forth on my chest as she got closer to her orgasm. I slowed my fingers, rubbing along her channel. My cock was so hard as memories of her riding me took over. I closed my lids letting myself stay there...be there, with her.

Time went by. Teeth bit into my bicep, pulling me from the sensations that seemed so real. Without a shirt on, I was exposed. Free for her to do whatever she wanted. I liked the pain from her teeth as they imprinted into me. *It made me...feel.* It made me hers.

"Switch. Dane, take five's seat. Show me what you got. Make it good, and you may get rewarded." Her breaths were heavy as she wiggled against me. She was trying to prolong from having an orgasm. It was right there. The realization had me easing my fingers from inside of her to rub over the outside of her slit. I took in Dane's defined stomach and the way his long cock slightly glistened from five's mouth. Five didn't seem to hesitate in pulling his sweatpants off. His own cock was already hard, and although it wasn't as big as Dane's, he was still decent in size.

"I'm getting this reward. I'm so going to get it."

"Shut up and suck."

There was almost a playfulness in five's words. Maybe he wanted the reward. Whatever it was, I didn't like it. I didn't even know why, but the thought of the Mistress treating these slaves did things to me. Things that were bad.

"Oh...*fuck*." Five gasped, biting his lip. "Have you done this before, or has it just been too long?"

Dane smiled as he looked up. His tongue came out, flicking over the tip.

"I worked in porn. I've had my cock sucked every which way under the sun. I've never done it, but I know the tricks. I know what feels good."

Something between a moan and groan left the slave as Dane took him in deep, adding suction. Whatever he was doing with his tongue was making five's jaw drop. Thrust after thrust he kept going, deep-throating him on occasion.

"Maybe this isn't so bad. I mean." Five's mouth opened wide. He quickly caught himself, shutting it. The lightest sheen of sweat was collecting on his face, and five let out a low sound, reaching for Dane's shoulder. Where I was curiously watching them, I felt my Mistress's head continually leaning back so she could look up at me. I glanced down, inches from her mouth as she stared. And just like that...it was as if time stopped. Her eyes on mine. Her lips only a kiss away. She blinked rapidly, jerking her face back forward. But she didn't stop moving. She was trembling as she went back to watching them.

"Ooooh my God." The Mistress's head lifted, and her hand fitted over my digits. She added pressure, easing the tips of her fingers in with mine. She was moaning again, moving against me as Dane stroked and sucked. When he licked against the slave's balls, the Mistress cried out, going into spasms against me. I kept my fingers in deep, thrusting. I wasn't sure why, but before I could stop myself, I latched to the side of her neck, sucking against her as my own cum shot from my cock. It caught me so unaware that alarms went off in my head. I didn't have permission to do that. I hadn't been told it was okay. What had I been thinking? Nothing... because I wasn't able to as I came down. I was locked in nothingness. Frozen in place.

Five was moaning out and making sounds. He and Dane

were even going through the motions of…something. All I saw was my Mistress as she turned on my lap, stroking the side of my face. She was studying me. Looking at me differently…until… fear. No, terror. It had her hand stopping on my face, and her eyes growing incredibly wide.

"Three- eleven?"

My name echoed in and out, wavering as if my Mistress was standing far away. I kept her stare, blinking, but I couldn't react.

"Are you okay?"

"Fuck that was unbelievable. I never thought I'd say that about being with a guy, but damn."

Five's voice dropped in tone, and I took in his flushed face as he and Dane began laughing about something.

"Three-eleven? Hey. No, not them. You look back at me. Can you talk. Please, say something." Tears filled her eyes but didn't spill over. "I didn't break you. Please. I didn't. I…please say something."

My hearing came back so loud it was jarring. But it wasn't louder than normal, I just wasn't adjusting very well to it.

"Is he okay?"

Five and Dane approached, both watching me cautiously. Almost…annoyed or angry. Relieved? I couldn't tell. Nothing was making sense.

"What's wrong with him? Did the zombie come too hard?"

Five snickered, and I watched the concern melt from my Mistress's face, turning cold as she slowly turned to look at him.

"What did you say?"

He paused. "Nothing. He was just really into it. Maybe he came too hard and it blew a circuit in his brain or something. He's not right, you know. Whatever they did to him fucked him all up. I mean, look at him. The guy has issues that go beyond… Just…*look*. I'm sorry, Mistress, but he *is* a zombie. A real, living, fucked up z—"

White from her blouse blurred as blonde hair tumbled free,

down her back. My thoughts were starting to return. Rationality faded in. Blood. The spray barely registered as her hand slammed into the side of five's neck.

Everything in me scrambled to react as he grabbed the side of his throat and flew at her, taking her to the ground. The first hit sent her head spinning to the side. Red flashed in my vision and sound completely disappeared for a breath of a moment.

Yells. They still weren't quite making sense but that didn't matter. Instinct was tearing its way through me, from my speeding pulse to the roaring in my brain. I was coming to. Getting a little more responsive as his hand connected with her face again.

"I told you! I fucking told you!"

Her...arm kept swinging. She was fighting. It was only then I saw the gold shimmer of the small dagger-style weapon. Five had blood pouring through his fingers as she kept swinging up at him. She always kept it in her hair. She was always ready. Slices and tiny holes littered five's bare chest as I threw my weight forward out of nowhere, crashing right into him. Sound wavered again, but nothing could have stopped me now that I could move.

No words. No need. I brought my fist down, smashing into five's pale face. Once. Three times. I couldn't stop. Bone caved under my power. I felt it crunch through my fingers and the vibration travel through my arm. Crimson oozed and ran a river from split skin, and all it did was call to me. My Mistress was still yelling, but I didn't even know what it was about. I was stuck again, but in a different way. Before I could think about what I was doing, I pinched onto his trachea, squeezing and crushing it under my hold. A loud popping reverberated through me, and I reared back, punching my way through the delicate area of his throat.

"Die you piece of shit. I told you not to say that. *I fucking said!*"

Death. I hadn't been ordered to do that either, yet there was no coming back for this slave. Not after my abuse. I grew as cold as ice, slowly turning to look at my Mistress. Blood spotted her face and blouse, staining her blonde hair, red. She was staring down as five twitched and made deep, bubbling groan-filled sounds.

"Leave him and let him suffer alone while he dies. Zombie," she growled. "Do you hear yourself, five? Who's the fucking zombie now!"

She twisted her hair back, reinserting the bloody knife-like hair pin.

"Come sit down, right now. Talk to me. What's happening?"

I obeyed, feeling more off than ever. Something was different. I sat down, watching her as her hands cupped my face. Worry. She was shaking as she looked at me.

"I'm not sure, Mistress. I don't know."

"Are you okay? Do I need to call someone?"

My brain hummed. An answer wouldn't present itself. "Maybe. I...

Footsteps had her head spinning and her gaze pinning Dane as he jolted to a stop.

"*What?* Don't look at me like that. I take care of what's mine. You haven't earned your place with me yet, but three-eleven has. No one hurts him and gets away with it. Do you want to call him a zombie too?"

His head shook frantically, and I saw the picture of true fear. Not just for the Mistress, but for me as his eyes landed on mine. The slave wasn't to be trusted. He'd never be the same, and a part of me wanted to get up and kill him for it. By a miracle, I kept in my seat. Barely. I was getting foggy again. Spacing.

"N-No. I. No, Mistress."

"Good. You'll live another day."

MISTRESS B-0042

The body pick-up was the last thing on my mind when I'd called for assistance, yet that's exactly what they kept mentioning. Didn't they know now wasn't the time to question or piss me off?

"Yes, it's just one body. That's not my issue. My blank slate is not well."

"Is he sick? What are his symptoms?"

I glanced over. "He's not sick. That's not what I mean. He locked up or something."

"Perhaps he's not feeling well and should be seen. Concerning the pick-up, do you believe the guards need one body bag or is there multiple pieces?"

I could have screamed. "I stabbed that motherfucker *like I want to stab you*. I didn't cut him up. One body bag will work. *Focus*. My blank slate…he's not sick. Not ill, I mean. It's his mind."

"Can you describe that, Mistress?"

"It's exactly as I said. He locked up. Spaced out. He wasn't normal."

A pause. "How is he now?"

"He's sitting on the sofa looking at me. Three-eleven." I headed over, sitting next to him. "Do you still feel the same? Is anything different from before?"

His brow drew in. "I think I'm okay. I am a little tired, but it is close to our bedtime."

I glanced at the clock. It was not close to our bedtime. In fact, it wasn't even dinner time yet.

"Send guards to pick up this dead body. I'm calling the Main Master."

I hung up the phone, walking over to the paper with all the numbers listed. I dialed in Elec's, beginning to pace all over again.

"Main Master." His deep voice sounded slightly irritated.

"It's Mistress Forty-two. I think I need help."

Silence. "What do you mean? Are you hurt?"

"Not me. I think there's something wrong with my blank slate."

Footsteps suddenly sounded. They weren't fast but they weren't slow. They just were as he cleared his throat.

"I'm actually on your floor. Define wrong. I want to know everything."

The concern in his tone was so different than the annoyance I'd detected before. It had my own growing as I took in three-eleven.

"He appeared fine when all of a sudden he got quiet. He stopped moving and got stiff. I kept calling his name but he wouldn't answer. His eyes were moving but he said he couldn't speak. He couldn't even move his body at first."

"How long did this last?"

I paused. "I'm not sure. Five minutes, give or take? I wasn't myself."

"Were you drinking?"

The disapproval had anger flaring. It wasn't easy avoiding alcohol. I sure as fuck could have used some now.

"I was not. We were…He was helping me." I closed my lids. "He was getting me off."

"So…he got you off, and then what? Did he come, too?"

More footsteps. They were steady, if not on the faster side.

"Five said he did. I'm not sure. I was on his lap but facing away from him."

"Ask five how he knows the slave came? Did the mental episode happen just afterward?"

Glancing at the floor, my lips tightened.

"I can't ask him. I killed him. He called my slave a zombie. I warned him not to do that. I just snapped."

"You don't have to apologize to me for killing your slave, Forty-two. It's your slave. As long as you got what you wanted out of him that's all that matters."

"But I didn't." I pouted. "I don't care. I'm worried about three-eleven. That's never happened to him before."

"Open the door. I'm here."

I hung up, jogging to the barrier and swinging it open. The Main Master's eyes didn't even go to me. They went right to my slave as he and two guards came into the living area. I went to shut the door, stopping as the pick-up guards arrived as well.

Elec walked forward and three-eleven stood to face him. I hurried to their side.

"How do you feel, slave?"

"Tired."

The Main Master's head cocked to the side.

"You're tired? Does this happen often?"

"No, Main Master. I don't recall ever feeling very tired."

He nodded.

"Walk me through what happened. Do not leave out anything you felt, saw, or heard. Start at the beginning."

Brown eyes came to mine, and I nodded my permission for him to comply. Even that had the Main Master's lids narrowing.

"My Mistress wanted me to touch her. To help her reach an orgasm."

The Main Master's hand rose. "And how did you feel about this? Did you want to help her?"

"I did."

"Do you enjoy pleasing your Mistress?"

"I do. Very much."

"Very much," Elec repeated. "As you were helping her, what were you thinking?"

Three-eleven's eyes dropped, moving back and forth as if he were recalling.

"My Mistress liked what was happening. She was watching Dane and five please each other. It was making her very aroused. She liked what I was doing. Then...Dane said." He stopped, looking down and getting quiet.

The Main Master lowered his head, tilting it as he tried to look into the slave's eyes which stared at the floor. "He said what?"

"He wanted to taste her. To... He wanted to come over to us."

"And how did that make you feel?"

Three-eleven's intense gaze rose to meet his, cutting over to Dane with so much rage that I nearly gasped. The Main Master snapped next to his eyes, and three-eleven's stare went back to Elec.

"I felt more than angry. Almost uncontrollable. My hand." His brows came together, the fury I could so clearly see, vanishing. "It held to her. I held to her. I shouldn't have done that. She's not mine. I...shouldn't have."

"Have you done anything else you shouldn't have?"

His lips parted. "I sucked her neck. She didn't ask me to. But I did it, and I didn't even think about it first. It just happened."

"Did you come without her saying you could?"

Three-eleven hesitated, glancing at me but nodding.

The Main Master brought his phone up, texting something as he continued.

"When you came, is that when you got stuck? Is that what it was? Stuck?"

"Yes, Main Master. I couldn't move. I couldn't speak. Five... he made my Mistress angry and attacked her. I think that's the only reason my body started working again. She could have died. I had to protect her. Look at her face. She's bleeding. I failed. I'm sorry." He turned to me. "*I'm sorry.*" He turned back to Elec. "Something is...changing. I've started thinking things. *Angry things.*"

"Three-eleven, do you recall what they're about? Do they revolve around your Mistress?"

"Not at her. At anyone but her. I want the best for her. I want her to be safe. To want to keep me."

"Of course I'm keeping you." I stepped in, grabbing his hand. "You help me. I need you. You've been a good slave. The best one."

The smallest smiled tugged at three-eleven's mouth but it faded as he looked back up at the Main Master. Elec was looking at our joined hands, his mouth slightly pursed as he kept texting things into his phone.

"Given your heartfelt admission, I hate to be the bearer of bad news, but I'm not so sure that's possible. I have to take him. Would you be interested in a new slave? It's on the house."

"*A new one?*" My head shook. "No way in hell I want a new one. I want mine better. What's wrong with him? Will he be okay?"

Elec put his phone back in his pocket, looking between us.

"I can't really say." He turned to three-eleven. "You're having issues following the simplest commands. You pose a risk to your Mistress. Do you know this?"

My gaze went back and forth between them, a bit confused. I didn't understand what he meant. A risk, how? To me?

"I just want to be with her."

"But that's the problem, isn't it."

It wasn't a question. Three-eleven broke my hold on his hand, stepping to the Main Master's side.

"I'm not supposed to love her."

"You're not. Duty and emotions cannot coincide. You know this. That's how people get hurt. You don't want something happening to your Mistress. I know you don't."

"*Love?*"

My question had three-eleven's eyes lowering and the Main Master looking at me as if I were daft.

"He'll have to be reprogrammed and analyzed for a few weeks. I make no promises whether he can return."

"What? That's not fair. I don't want him to leave. He can't leave me."

"It's too much of a risk to let him stay. You heard what he felt when your other slave wanted you. He was angry. He should have not felt that. The emotion shouldn't have even registered. This slave is a killer. All blank slates are programmed to kill. Do you understand? It would have only been a matter of time before he killed your slave. Maybe even you."

"Me? No way. Three-eleven would not kill me." Anxiety was causing me to shift as I looked between the men. I couldn't lose him. Who was I going to go to when the nightmares came? Who was going to protect me without...talking? Dane couldn't do that. He couldn't be quiet for more than two minutes. And I didn't want comfort. Not in the form of pity or self-awareness. I wanted to deal on my own without *being alone*. I wanted three-eleven.

The guards were placing five in a body bag. I glanced over to Dane who was sitting against the wall, now in his sweatpants, his face pale and terrified. Or was he traumatized? He'd never feel safe with me now, and I wouldn't have my slave here to protect me. To watch over me as I slept. I didn't trust this new slave not to take me out when I wasn't looking.

I grabbed three-eleven's hand feeling as if my heart was aching. It shouldn't have been. He was just a blank slate. A slave. He wasn't even a real person. So…why did I feel as if I were losing a part of myself?

"I don't want you to leave."

"Mistress." The Main Master's head shook in warning. "You can't tell him that. I know what you mean by your tone, but he might not." He turned to three-eleven. "That is not an order. She knows you have to go. She doesn't want you to, but she knows its what's best for you."

But was it?

"Can I come see him?"

"No. It might disrupt the reprogramming."

The guards zipped up the body, carrying the bag towards the door. I crossed my arms over my chest more unnerved than ever.

"But weeks? You can't do it any faster?"

"We may not be able to do it at all. We can try. That doesn't mean he'll respond as he should. We won't know until the time comes. In the meantime, you can either take another blank slate, on me, or choose a new male slave to replace the one you just lost. The choice is yours. Think about it."

Elec gestured towards the door, but three-eleven didn't move. I leaned in, again grabbing his hand.

"The only way you get to come back to me is if you get better. You have to focus, slave. Let them fix you. Accept whatever training you undergo." My lip quivered, and I forced myself to stand straighter. "You can do this. I'll be waiting for you."

His hand rose, cupping my cheek. He didn't speak. He didn't even nod. Three-eleven dropped his hand, walking towards the opened door at a determined pace. When he disappeared through the threshold, an emptiness followed.

He wasn't my boyfriend. He wasn't even technically a steady

lover. He was a companion. A protector, yes, but more than that. Three-eleven was my safety blanket. My lethal pet, ready to die for me. It made perfect sense. Everyone loved their pets more than people anyway.

The door closed and all that was left was blood and bruised hearts. Mine. Maybe even Dane's. He and five had bonded over blowjobs, and at the first opportunity, I'd snapped and stabbed him in the neck with the sharp end of my specially made hair stick. It wasn't a good thing. Especially in Elec's eyes. If he was going to help me get my life back, he wanted me stable. It was time I worked harder towards that.

MO3II

ntiseptic. A hint of bleach. Hospital gowns. Itchy blankets and cold cement floors. Had I forgotten this place so quickly? Yes. No. Now that I was back, the familiarity registered almost like home. But it wasn't home. I'd spent months with my new Mistress. I'd bonded with her despite that I shouldn't have. Even if we hadn't talked much, I had been aware of going through the days of helping her. Holding her. Who would hold her now that I was gone? Dane? A new blank slate?

The thought sent my heart jumping on the monitor and lines moving all over the screen as a doctor in a white coat looked at me.

"This keeps happening, Arthur. You guaranteed me when we opened, these blank slates were safe. You said there may be a few hiccups, but that overall, there was nothing to worry about. *They are not safe.*"

The rage in the Main Master's tone came out as a smooth, deadly calm. It left my instincts uncertain on what path the Main Master wanted to take. Half of me expected nothing where the other half was prepared for the worst.

"Main Master, it appears to be a lot of blank slates, but you have to understand, we have thousands. The ones reacting are only a handful of those."

"It's a handful too many. Do we know what has to be done? Can he be fixed? The heiress's slave who massacred her and those Masters couldn't be. We had to put him down. Can we prevent from doing that again?"

"I'm not sure yet. I thought I'd be able to fix the last one but...you can't turn off love or grief. Not all the way. I've tried. The heiress's slave couldn't forgive himself for what he did. He loved her. That's what's turning them. We all know it."

The Master cursed under his breath, reaching for his phone as the ring filled the space.

"Give me a minute."

He left the room, the deep tone of his voice humming through me, even through the closed barrier.

"I want to be fixed. I want to go back."

Dark eyes met me. Kind eyes? There was something sympathetic in the depths, but I couldn't tell as he quickly looked away.

"You love her, don't you?"

"I think so. I mean..." My Mistress's words came back. She hadn't wanted me to leave to begin with. What if they didn't plan on letting me go back? "I feel something, but I mostly want her safe. She needs me to keep her safe. She has bad dreams. I help her through them."

"So, you worry? Would you say your worry overpowers your feelings of love?"

I could say no, but could I truly answer that? The two molded together. They were one. Could you love without worrying, or worry without feeling love?

"My duty is the most important. Keeping her happy and safe is what I'm meant to do."

He looked at the lines, studying them as he came back to me.

"You believe that to an extent, but there's the slightest trace of deception. I can tell when you're lying, slave. Don't do that. It won't get you back to her any sooner. If anything, it'll backfire on you. We can't send a slave back who's capable of lying."

"But I'm not. I do want her happy and safe. I just want her that way with me."

He glanced at the lines, nodding.

"We'll see what we can do. You remember the procedures? You know what you're going to have to undergo? It won't be a simple task."

No. It wouldn't. I'd wish for death. I'd wish for anything outside of the torture of having my brain scrambled like an egg. I was aware of that, but no emotion came through with it. I was still more blank slate than human. I knew that too, and I wasn't sure how to feel about it, or if I even should.

"I want to get back to my Mistress as soon as possible. She needs me. Do whatever you must."

"Alright. We're going to start out with a set of questions. We'll go from there."

The door opened, and the Main Master swept in.

"I have to take care of a few things. The Mistress will want an update. What do you think? Which direction do you want to take?"

Arthur glanced at me, picking up a clipboard. "There may still be hope with this one, but I won't know more until after I go through the questions and scans. I'll give you an update first thing in the morning."

With that, the Main Master left, closing the door behind him. I stared ahead, letting all thoughts fade as I prepared myself for what could be the end. *No lying. No lying.* I wanted to. I wouldn't deny that, but he was right. There was no outsmarting this machine I was hooked to, and the risk was too high.

"What is your name?"

"I am m-zero-three-one-one, referred to as slave three-eleven."

"And what is your human name?"

My mouth opened, and I went blank only for a moment before it came back. "My human name was Ravi Santos. Born in Rio de Janeiro, Brazil, February second, year nineteen-ninety-seven. I am twenty-five years old."

"Very good."

He looked between the monitor and the clipboard before writing something down.

"Were you an only child?"

Again, I blinked, waiting for information to become clear.

"I feel I was."

"And would you say you had a hard life?"

"I…Yes. I can recall a lot of fights. I." I stopped, trying to make sense of what I was seeing. "I'm dirty. Young. I feel as though I may be hungry? Yes. I…I feel I had a hard life."

There was more certainty as the dull emotions became truth and made themselves known.

"Excellent. Do you feel anything about what you recall?"

"…I do not."

More writing.

"Okay." He let out a breath. "Would you say since you've been here that you've grown into the role you have taken?"

"Yes."

"And would you go as far to say that you're even content in this role?"

"Yes. I am."

"What about happy?"

I sat up a little straighter. Was I happy? Did serving my Mistress make me feel that?"

Seconds went by. My head shook as the new overthinking part of my brain kicked on.

"I don't know about happy. I do not think I feel that. I feel… proud. A duty…to be what she needs of me. I have wanted to smile because I believe what she said was funny…but I'm not sure if that's happiness."

"I see."

My eyes lifted from the daze.

"Is that bad?"

"No. Quite good."

A sigh of relief left me.

"Let's talk about your Mistress. You said she depends on you. She has bad dreams, and you help her through them."

"Yes."

"Does *that* make you happy?"

Happy. Happy.

Visions of her crawling down to me, wrapping around me... taking me to the sofa with her all came back. I blinked through them trying my hardest to decipher what it was I felt.

"Maybe a little. I'm not sure. It's a mix of different things. I feel...a purpose. The first few weeks before her slave attacked her, it was all she needed me for. I grew fond of having that role. It was my only one at that time. I...liked providing comfort to her?"

His hand shot up. "Did you feel this comfort too?"

"No. Just purpose where I didn't have any before."

"Okay. So it was pride and satisfaction you felt when providing her your services."

"Yes."

"When you were brought in, the Main Master mentioned a sexual relationship between you and your Mistress."

He paused, looking up at me.

"Yes."

"When did that start?"

"The night of the auction."

"This last one?"

"Yes. She had a bad dream. She...was curious about me that way. She wanted me to make her feel good."

More writing.

"And what about you? Did it feel good for you?"

Just thinking about it made my cock hard.

"It did. A lot."

"At any time during this sexual episode did you find yourself conflicting with your role as her blank slate?"

My eyes closed, the urges and voices returning.

"I did. I found myself wanting to do things she didn't ask for. To touch her. Taste her. I didn't disobey my role until earlier when I was pleasuring her again and I got angry."

"Angry?"

"One of her other slaves wanted to join us. I didn't want him to. I..." My hand lifted. "I put my hand on her stomach protectively as a reaction to that anger. I sucked against her neck when she didn't ask me to."

"I see." The markings against the page sounded like fast scribbles. "Do you recall anything else happening? Any murderous thoughts?"

My back straightened even more as I stared ahead.

"I was angry. I don't believe I was murderous."

"Hmm." Arthur pointed to the monitor. "That's a tinge of deceit, slave."

"I don't think I was murderous when I did that. I don't believe I would have killed anyone. I mean, I didn't kill anyone. If I wanted to, I would have, right?"

He went back and forth looking between the spikes and me.

"It's very light. Almost not there, but it is. That concerns me. You may not recognize the need, but the existence of it lurks below. It's present."

Silence played between us as he began flipping through the pages of the clipboard.

"I would kill for her. I would kill. That's who I am. It is fact. Is it not normal that that part of me rests below?"

His eyes lifted. "Sure. It's normal. You asking me about it *is not*." Arthur pulled the rolling stool forward, taking a seat.

"You are aware more than most. I believe this is new for you.

Maybe even slightly confusing being as it goes against the commands you should be following. I want to give you a chance, three-eleven. I really do. I'm just not sure what will come of it. That gives me pause. We have a no-risk policy. I can't let you go back to your Mistress until I'm certain you are not the same person sitting before me now. When I finish, you may not even care to go back. You do understand this?"

Not want to go back? I couldn't imagine feeling such a thing. Then again, I wasn't going to argue either. I was going back, and reprogramming my mind wasn't going to get in the way of wanting it. I belonged with my Mistress, and that was the end of it. Maybe even the end of me.

MISTRESS B-0042

"I don't want one. I don't see any I like."

The Main Master tried to stay patient, but I knew I was pushing him with how difficult I was being.

"It's not about liking them. *It's about needing them.* You need one. You've made that clear for the last half hour."

"I have, but I want my own. Truthfully, I'm pissed at myself for even telling you. I thought he could be fixed and sent right back to me. Had I known you were going to take him away, I would have stayed quiet."

"Quiet and possibly dead. Mistress…pick…a blank slate. Any. Blank. Slate."

I took in his aggravation, rolling my eyes as I poked at the page a little too hard. It was over the picture of a dark-skinned male with big, round eyes. He was attractive, but not in the ways I was looking for. More…beautiful for a man, like most of the others.

"He looks a little too easy to break. I'm not saying I want this one, but." I made a sound. "Where are your men? Real men? Not boys. Not chiseled abs and model faces. I can't feel safe with someone like that. It's hard to take them seriously. I'm not doubting their skills, but I want to *feel* it. You said they're all deadly. Where's the lethal sniper, secret ops, delta force, CIA agent who has scars on his face from a bomb, and a beard? Or scruff. I'll take that. I want him to have meat on his bones. Muscle, but meat, and he has that look. The one that says he'll break you in half if you get too close. Where's that slave?"

"On the television. For fuck's sake, Forty-two."

"You don't have anything like that?"

"Do I look like a scout? I'm not out there recruiting, and this isn't a buffet." Something transitioned his face from aggravated to intrigued. "Actually, hold on." He picked up his phone, but my hand shot up.

"Not permanently though. I still want my slave. I figure... Two weeks. *Tops.* Then you can bring three-eleven home."

"That's pushing it."

"I take full responsibility for anything that may happen while he's in my care. I know what you said, but he won't hurt me. If he kills my slaves, he beat me to it. I can live with that."

The Main Master looked up from his phone. "That is not okay for his role. It's definitely not acceptable behavior for a blank slate. He needs to serve the purpose he's meant to. He has to follow the rules or he can't be your slave."

"That's ridiculous. You can't sell something to me and then take it away. Why allow us to get attached at all?"

"No one is getting attached."

I felt exposed. The truth had my eyes lowering as he continued.

"You knew the risk. We're in the beta stage. I made that abundantly clear. The only reason I'm giving you a new blank slate to begin with is because I gave your father my word I'd watch out for you and make sure you weren't ever alone. It was a condition I allowed in the contract when you joined. I need you reigned in just as much as the slaves. But I'm warning you now, if you kill this loan, I'll charge the fuck out of you for it. Do not murder this blank slate. Don't mar his skin with any significant marks or it ruins a future sale."

"Scars give character."

"*Don't.*"

"Then don't mention my dad. I hate him. You know that. He may be trying to get me to talk to him again, but he and I are finished. Next time I won't stop. *I'll kill him.*"

"I know you will."

The Main Master's voice was quiet towards the end as he went back to pushing buttons on his phone. Why had I overreacted to three-eleven's lock up? I blanked out when I had too much on my mind too. Wasn't that just the case with him? Safety. Protection. Sex. Maybe I shouldn't have added the last part to our routine. It had been too much. Right? Or maybe I was right to call it in yesterday. I had no idea. All I knew was I didn't feel the same without him, and I wanted him back.

"The guards are getting things ready. I'm on the fence about this, but I'm going to show you three blank slates that fit your...*preference.* They're not available yet because I have something special in mind for them, but I have faith in these three, so I feel okay if you choose one."

"Special?"

"Yep, and that's all you need to know. Do you want to look at them?"

"Are they manly?"

"They're men. Former soldiers as you requested."

My eyebrows lifted in surprise. "Do they have battle wounds? *Beards?* Is there a look in their eyes?"

Had that been excitement in my tone? The Main Master just shook his head, looking at me as if I'd lost my mind.

"Let's go, Mistress. You can see for yourself."

He led me through a pair of doors, weaving us through halls until we were heading into a large area that looked like a lobby. Guards brought in three men in gray sweatpants who's personas were just as three-eleven's had been. Stoic. Standing at attention. No expressions. No emotion. That alone got me excited. If they didn't think, they couldn't judge. Couldn't disobey. They couldn't deny me anything.

I walked forward, fascinated as I took in all three.

"They do have scars. *Proof.*" My mouth was slightly parted as I glanced at Elec, but my intrigue had nothing to do with their rough exterior, and everything to do with their energy. The combination of the two was everything I'd been looking for to begin with. It was perfectly intimidating.

"I like them."

"Good. Finally."

Stopping before each one, I looked past their scars and took in their appearance. All three had dark hair, ranging in depth and shade. Where the first had the lightest, the middle slave had the darkest. Even their skin ranged in color from slightly tan to beautifully dark. None were good-looking in the Garden's sense, but they were ruggedly handsome. It had me walking to the third slave whose light brown eyes stayed fixed ahead like the others. None had beards, but that could easily be fixed.

Again, I headed to the beginning, but I found myself doubling back to the last.

Slightly square jaw.

His lips were on the fuller side.

Killer stare.

Slightly crooked nose, as if it had been broken more than once.

Circular scars resembling bullet wounds were on his shoulder and bicep, and there was a four-inch gash across his pec. A trail of dark hair ran from his chest to the lining of the sweatpants, but I couldn't have cared either way. I kept going back to the scars.

"The third. I want him."

The Main Master nodded. "For a price."

"What? But you said—"

"That I'd get you a blank slate. These are not normal blank slates. You're going to come to see, although they're technically blank, you won't be able to detect it. This is for good reason. It helps them blend in in any situation. In any location."

"I didn't program them that way, you did. I want this look, but I want them blank. I shouldn't have to pay for the extras. You said this was a loan."

"It is. I still want something out of it."

"Something. But...not money."

It wasn't a question.

"No. I want you to try to break him too. Fuck him. Smother him with seduction and make him do everything you desire. Try to get him to fall for you. I want to see how well his training truly is."

"That sounds like I'm doing you a favor. I should be the one getting paid."

He laughed. "I'll tell you what. You do this for me, and I'll do everything in my power to return your blank slate."

"You're supposed to be doing that anyway."

"I'm not going to lie, it's not looking good for three-eleven. Work with me, and I'll work with you."

I glanced at the soldier, turning back to Elec. Could I really lose my slave for good? The thought almost made me sick. It had been years since I had attached to anyone like I had with him, and even there, I'd never opened up to Pistol as much. I let myself crumble to pieces while I cried tears I'd spent a lifetime suppressing. I told three-eleven secrets from my past. I opened my emotions. My world...to a void. A void I'd embraced as my own. A void I'd fallen for, even if I couldn't quite admit it.

"Fine. You have a deal."

He stepped forward, waving away the guards and the other slaves. What sounded like a foreign language left Elec, and he clasped his hands at his front just in time for the slave to bring his stare to the Main Masters.

"State your name."

"M-zero-nine-three-two. Slave nine-thirty-two, Sir."

Elec took out his phone, scrolling through something before more language sounded from him that I didn't understand. When he reached into his pocket and withdrew a small device, I watched curiously. He lifted his hand, and a red light flashed into the slave's eyes.

"This is your new Mistress. You are programmed for her now. You are to serve her to the best of your abilities. You protect her and listen to whatever she commands of you. This is your mission. Do you understand?"

"I do, Sir."

The Main Master turned to me, gesturing to the slave.

"Good luck."

"I don't need luck to break him. Have you seen my life? I don't even have to try. If anyone can screw this soldier up, it's me. I am the bull, and the world is my china cabinet. Let the destruction begin." I paused, moving in closer. "What language were you speaking?"

"A dead one. Is there anything else you need?"

He was already leading me out as my new slave followed behind. My mouth opened, only to close.

"Speak, Mistress. You're not going to start holding back now, are you?"

"No. But it really doesn't have anything to do with slaves. I meant to talk to you, but all this happened." I let out a sigh. "Pistol confronted me in the street yesterday before all that went down with three-eleven. He was angry. *Yelling at me.*" I paused as we headed around a turn and came through the main doors we'd originally entered through. "I started working on new music, but...he said there was no way I was going to perform. I'm not sure I should."

The last of my words were stolen as Elec spun to pin me with ice blue eyes.

"Last I checked, I was the Main Master. I say who performs."
His head shook. "You'd let him dictate your career?"

"Not dictate. I just think maybe—"

"You think what? That you don't deserve to be on the same stage as him?"

My face fell, and I glanced down. How could I not think that? Aside from being a dick, Pistol truly was a rock God. He had the talent. So did I, but I had to give it everything I had to compete. It didn't come naturally.

"I deserve it more than anyone."

"You're right. You do." Some of the anger faded as he let out a breath. "Pistol will get over it. Focus on you. Keep working on your music. I think if you stay determined, you won't even recognize your life in a year. But mark my words." His face grew hard again, and I forced myself to swallow through the threatening energy. "Success is easy to obtain. It is not easy to keep. If you ruin this opportunity, getting it back will be nearly impossible. This is your chance, Forty-two. Already, your name is rocking the boat. Your fight has started, and it's only uphill from here. It won't end until the day you walk away. Are you ready?"

My hands were shaking at his words, but I found myself nodding through the anxieties of what this could mean. I wanted it. I earned it after everything I'd gone through.

"I'm ready."

"I know you are."

Elec swept his hand towards the door housing the main hallway. It was a goodbye. Nothing more; nothing less. We were parting ways until further notice. Hopefully, the next time I saw him was when he was delivering my slave. I really liked what I saw and knew of nine-thirty-two, but I'd have to get to know him.

Giving a nod, I glanced at my new soldier. He was still staring ahead, waiting for a command. I ran my finger along his forearm, towards his wrist. How was he somewhat normal? He appeared more blank than three-eleven had been. "This way, nine-thirty-two. It's time to go home."

"Yes, Mistress."

The heels from my boots clicked against the cement. The slave behind me didn't so much as make a sound. Without shoes, he was lethal. Almost nonexistent like a ghost.

We headed into the main hall, not having to walk far to make it to the elevator. When the door opened, a Master and slave exited, along with two Mistresses who appeared to be without protection or company. Idiots. They'd learn fast enough it wasn't always safe without some form of muscle behind you. I'd learned that too, but it was my own slave who'd attacked me. If it hadn't been for Mitchell, Omar may have killed me. I sure didn't go anywhere without three-eleven after that. Why I had to begin with, I had no idea. Ego? Inexperience? Alcohol? Probably all three.

We stepped on the elevator and before I could reach for the button, the slave was already coming out to stop my hand.

Without me having to tell him, he pushed the number nine for our floor.

"You know where we live?"

"I do, Mistress. Apartment nine-ten. One bedroom, one bath. Eight-hundred-sixty-five square feet."

"Wow." I closed my opened mouth. "What else do you know?"

The door was halfway closed when a hand shot in, aiming to stop it. The slave next to me was such a blur, all I heard were screams before I even realized what was happening. The door opened, but nine-thirty-two was already forcing someone back into the lobby. He had their arm twisted, and his other hand in a solid grip to the back of their neck. Yells and curse words filled the space as I rushed out, trying to make sense of what was happening.

"What the fuck! Let go of me! Hey!"

But my soldier only forced his head lower to the ground until the Master was practically bent over, in half.

"Slave! Slave, stop."

I yelled, running over, but nine-thirty-two wasn't letting go.

"Bitch! *Get your damn slave.* I'll have his life for this!"

"You're the one who tried busting into the elevator. Nine-thirty-two let go of him and come back to me."

Brown eyes glanced my way, letting go immediately as he walked to my side. The Master straightened, his face red as he began stomping my way with his pointed finger.

"Your slave is *dangerous.*"

"He did nothing wrong. What was he supposed to think after your actions to get on the elevator? You couldn't wait or take another one?"

"*No,* it was still opened."

"Barely."

"If you come closer to my Mistress, I will break your arm."

The Master's hand once again came up, shaking and pointing. "See what I mean? He can't do that. Who does he think he is?"

"My protector. That's who. Maybe next time you should slow the hell down and wait your turn."

"I'll be reporting this. I know who you are."

"Is that right?"

"Yeah. It is right. When I tell the Main Master—"

"You leave me for five minutes..." Elec shook his head as he walked up.

"Main Master, this...*slave.* He attacked me for no reason!"

"That's a lie. This Master tried stopping the elevator by shoving his arm through the door when it was almost closed. My slave was merely protecting me from a possible attack. It was heroic if anything. I'm very impressed with his skills."

The Master's head jerked to Elec's.

"Do you hear this insanity?"

"Master Twelve-oh-eight, we keep running into each other like this. I'm headed the long way around to my office. Why don't you follow me, and we'll see what can be done. *Mistress*."

Elec threw me a look. He didn't have to continue. I leaned towards my slave, keeping my voice down.

"Go hit the button for the elevator."

He obeyed, and I followed, watching as the Masters headed off, approaching a turn in the distance. My attention went back to my slave, and I saw him in a new light. One that was proud yet uncertain. This soldier went beyond deadly. What he was trained for was beyond my own blank slate and probably most of the ones available to the buyers. So...if these weren't available to us, who were these special blank slate soldiers going to?

MO3II

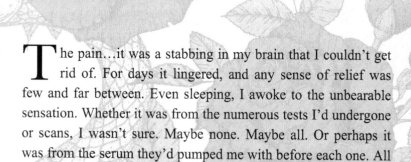

The pain…it was a stabbing in my brain that I couldn't get rid of. For days it lingered, and any sense of relief was few and far between. Even sleeping, I awoke to the unbearable sensation. Whether it was from the numerous tests I'd undergone or scans, I wasn't sure. Maybe none. Maybe all. Or perhaps it was from the serum they'd pumped me with before each one. All I knew was that if it didn't stop soon, I was going to be sick or go crazy.

"You're not going to eat dinner, again?"

It took everything I had to crack my lids open. I took in the guard, waving my hand so that he'd go away. Even that took more strength than I felt I had.

"You know, it should stop soon. Hang in there."

"Wait." My voice was raspy, even hoarse as I cleared my throat to continue. "This is normal? I don't remember this part."

"Yeah. It's a stupid question since you're already aware enough to ask, but you're going through the reprogramming cycle, right?"

"That's right. I want to go home to my Mistress."

"Loyal. Even with your mind reversed back to normal. She's

lucky to have you. Most blank slates would be having a meltdown right now."

Reversed? Would they?

I closed my eyes, holding my palm over to keep out any light that might seep through.

"How many more days of this do I have to go through? When do I get to leave?"

The need to heave was there, but I repetitively swallowed, trying to push the compulsion down.

"The headache usually lasts about two to three days. Then they start the reprogramming."

"I'm on day five."

"Your headache lasted days more than the others. Interesting. I'm surprised you haven't been taken in yet to start the reprogramming anyway. It shouldn't be much longer now. When the pain stops, it happens pretty fast. You sure you don't want to try to eat? I've noticed that helped the others. It might be just what you need. I can come back a little later to get your tray."

"I should try to get something down."

"Good choice. I'll see you after a while."

The sound of the heavy metal door closing made me wince. My fingers spread as I peeked through them, standing to make my way to the tray. What was on my plate had me pausing. It reminded me of...hospital or cafeteria food. The realization had my eyes lifting and my hand dropping. For days I'd been in so much pain, I couldn't even form a rational thought. But now with the guard's words, I had little choice but to face the truth.

Slowly, I glanced around the room. Just the sight had panic edging in.

Meltdown...yes.

Focus.

No, I didn't want to. My brain was trying to fight what was coming. Nothing was right, and everything was blurring together. My Mistress...I wanted her. But...Mistress? *Owner.*

The guard's words repeated, and with it, the knowledge that he was indeed a guard. For what? A prison? No. I hadn't gotten in trouble, and convicts weren't bought and sold, but this sure resembled a prison.

My brain scraped through memories. Emotions came, unstable and thick like clotted blood. My blood? No...five's. My Mistress and I had killed him. Me, a killer? A fighter, yes, but a killer?

For her, definitely.

But who was she aside from a beautiful woman who purchased me?

Her face was as clear as day in my mind. So much clearer than my tough past. Clearer than all my competitions. She was someone more ingrained within me than what I had worked so hard for during my life.

Prison...no. I'd been taken. I knew that. I had been scared and angry. I knew that too. I still felt the emotions towards it, but not comparable to the fear that surrounded my Mistress taking on another blank slate. What if she decided I was a liability, and she didn't want me back? What if she liked him more? What if Dane hurt her? Fucked her? *Tasted her?*

Jealousy was always my biggest sin. It's what kept me single for so long. What was mine was mine, and no one in hell would get close to that. I wouldn't even let them want what I'd chosen for myself. But my life with my Mistress hadn't been like that. I hadn't stopped slaves from wanting or speaking to her like Dane had. I allowed him to live, where I shouldn't have left him with a jaw to speak with at all.

Sweat beaded my skin through the massive memory overload. They weren't new, but the emotions tied to them were.

Rage.

Jealousy.

Envy.

Fear.

Longing.

Love.

Love.

Love.

A groan merged with a guttural grunt. I didn't want to be here. I couldn't be here. Not with her out there. Love, yes. I'd said that, and although I hadn't quite felt it before, my subconscious had known the entire time. But that all was stolen as images flashed in my mind's eye. Me and my mom. Me and my training partners.

My native language came back, and my mom's voice was so clear that where I'd managed to hold in the sickness, I gagged through the shock of overwhelming emotions.

"You're just going to abandon me? For what? So you can try to be some champion? You've done that here. Tell me how it's helped us so far? It hasn't! You have to let go of this dream. You have to go back to Diego. That or get a real damn job. Something, Ravi. Don't you walk away from me! Ravi!"

But I did. I left with her shouting and cursing me for being such a disgraceful son.

"You're going to do it, Ravi. When they sign you, you're going to go to the top. I just know it."

But Luis was wrong. I never made it to my destination. The only television he probably saw me on was the local news as a missing person. If they even knew. Maybe my family and friends thought I just disappeared because I'd failed in my purpose. I had no idea what to think about any of it. About any of *this*.

I squeezed my lids closed, rubbing my thumb and index finger over my closed eyes. Eat. Food. But thinking about the present only had my mind looping back to the Mistress I felt so attached to. I couldn't escape it. Was she eating? If so, with who?

More sounds left me, but I barely recalled as I stood over the small table, picking at my food. The chicken had no flavor. Neither did the vegetables. Maybe they knew I couldn't handle them at this stage. I couldn't recall the food ever being so bland before.

"Harder. No, Ravi. Move faster. Faster!" Luis's voice repeated in my head. *"Duck. Jab. Again. I don't care if you're tired. No one is going to take it easy on you in the ring. Again!"*

I'd been good. So fucking good, and it all disappeared for what? Her?

Just at the thought of her face, I softened. Yeah...her. Maybe I was okay with that. Maybe. If I could only think straight. Even though I could recall my past, I still couldn't grasp thoughts for long. Emotion, yes. But holding to them, no. It was as if I was here, but my knowledge of everything was cycling through a dryer. Around and around. There but not for long. Just tumbling in a never-ending loop as I digested it.

At the door opening, I turned, looking at the barrier. I knew the man that walked in, and mixed emotions followed. I should respect him. Fear him. *Hate him.* That one didn't last long. My brain wouldn't allow it no matter how hard I tried to hold to it. All I could do was study his serious, curious face as he looked at me. Tall. Dark hair. Good looking. Dark suit. Always some shade of dark.

"Main Master."

Still, my throat was hoarse.

"Three-eleven. I see you're thinking clearly."

"A little."

"Do you know why you're here?"

I put down the piece of chicken I'd been holding. No fork. No...utensils at all.

"My Mistress. She called you because something happened to me. I lost control of myself."

"You did. But that's not what I meant. Do you know why you're here? At the Garden of the Gods?"

I blinked through his words realizing my headache was lessening. Not by much, but it was becoming bearable.

"Her?"

"Yes. She bought you as her protector. It was not your choice to be here, but you ended up in my domain anyway. The training you've undergone to become her blank slate has been extensive. Sadly, it didn't last. Do you know why?"

Our conversation in the apartment came back. It had my throat tightening, and me not recognizing the robot I'd been. With as distant as my emotions were for the memory, I couldn't say there wasn't any. It was a sliver of what it was now…but it was all for my Mistress.

"I love her."

He nodded but didn't speak.

"I feel like I'm in trouble."

"Three-eleven, I'm not going to lie to you. You're okay now, but once we reprogram your mind again, you may not come back. Not as the person you are now, and definitely not the one before. We've done this enough to know the track record isn't good. Even if it is, we don't know how long it'll last before something goes wrong again. Maybe it won't. Maybe it will. Some slaves take great to this. Others don't. I am seeing a pattern though. It's one I can't do much about I'm afraid."

It was my turn to be quiet.

"Do you truly love her, or did you succumb to the programming of being hers? See, I'm trying to figure out this pattern I mentioned before. That's why I want to try something."

"Try something?"

"Where the reprogramming may completely destroy you, this may have your own Mistress turning on you. She seems to have feelings for you too, but not with you like this. She wants a body, nothing more. I gave her that, but I'm feeling…a bit…" A smile tugged at the edge of his mouth, "curious."

"She has someone new? A blank slate?"

The Main Master's eyes narrowed as he looked at me.

"Is that a problem for you?"

"No. Yes. I want to be hers."

"If I recall correctly, you want to be her *only* one. Does that still stand?"

My mind was saying to tread carefully. If I screwed up, I may not be going back to her at all. And it wasn't like I was hooked up to the monitors anymore.

"No, Main Master. I know my duty. I just want to be the one my Mistress relies on. Her dreams." The screams and cries came back making me momentarily shut my eyes. "Her nightmares are very bad. I want to be the one to help her through them."

"Maybe you will soon enough. I'm going to have you monitored for a few more days, and I'll decide which path to take. Maybe you'll return to her, or maybe you'll die or are killed during the reprogramming before you get the chance. All I know is your Mistress is doing some testing of her own, and I won't get in the way of that. For now…you stay."

MISTRESS B-0042

B reak him.
    Break him.
  Break him.

It should have been easy. It shouldn't have warranted me doing anything more than what I normally would. After all, I was a professional at fucking shit up without even trying. As I stared at nine-thirty-two, I couldn't get over how there was zero change. None. Not a single thing. I'd carried on as if everything was normal, hoping for some sort of physical reaction out of him, but so far, he appeared just as blank as three-eleven had been. Then again, it would probably help if I showed him some sort of attention. It was hard. I felt…like I was turning my back to my real slave. Even after a week, I couldn't allow myself to lower my walls. Hell, I'd chosen Dane after the nightmares, and he'd been chained to my floor. Nine-thirty-two may have been a shell, but I knew what Elec wanted of me, and I couldn't be vulnerable to another blank slate I might lose.

"Dane, eat."

"Yes, Mistress."

The slave sat directly across from me at the small dining

room table, and the soldier was at my side. Dane hadn't been the same since he witnessed me murdering five. I couldn't blame him, but I was losing patience with his fear and silent nature. I didn't like it. He wasn't like a blank slate. This man had thoughts, and after Oscar, I knew this pattern a little too well. He was watching. Always...*waiting*. It was only a matter of time.

"I'm bored. I think I'll take a break from work tonight." The need for a drink kicked in. The more time that passed, the worse it seemed to get. "I say we all go catch a movie."

My stare went right to Dane. I saw the moment his eyes lit up. He wanted to feel safe. I suspected a small part of him even wanted this to work, given the alternative. But he was smart to know he was on a clock, and I wasn't to be trusted. No one was safe with me. Rage and blood had been all I'd ever known. It was the answer...*and my curse*.

"Mistress, what movie did you want to see?"

Dane's question was forced, but I pretended not to notice.

"There's a few to choose from. I'm trying to debate what I'm in the mood for. I chose one comedy, one romance, and a horror."

"A comedy might be good." He stole a glance up at me. "It might lift the air a little. I know you've been working like crazy, but it's felt somewhat heavy lately."

"I agree. The comedy might be good." I turned to my soldier, knowing it was pointless. "What do you think, nine-thirty-two? Do you like comedy?"

He stopped eating, blinking before lifting his gaze to me.

"I do. I think I'd like to see a movie."

"...you would?"

"I enjoy funny movies. So do you." My stare jerked to Dane, who looked just as surprised as me. I shifted in my chair, realizing I'd never continued prying into this blank slate like I had intended on the elevator. "What movies do I like?"

"Over the Drop. Patty's Landing. Down Raleigh, which was one of my favorites too."

Had I put those on the information packet? How had he known that?

"What was your favorite scene from Down Raleigh?"

My mouth nearly dropped as a smile came to his face. He stabbed his fork into his potatoes, pausing to speak. "Definitely when Edwin tries to outrun the cops but ends up losing his pants to the poodle that jumps the picket fence."

I laughed as my mind recalled exactly the part he was speaking of.

"That might be my favorite too." My head shook in surprise. "So, you have good taste in comedy. What else do you like?"

"Pie. Apple. Cherry. Cheesecake." He took another bite of potatoes, pausing until he swallowed. "Motorcycles. Hunting. *Secret missions.*"

Was the last said with emotion? I was enthralled.

"That sounds better than a movie. I wish we had a secret mission." I glanced at Dane. "Doesn't that sound like so much fun?"

"It does sort of sound badass."

I scooped some of my own potatoes, mischief taking over as we all stared at each other.

"We could go to the city and try to find something to be secret about. Maybe we can choose a Master to follow around. Someone might be up to no good."

"Hmm." I thought over Dane's idea. "Maybe. But how would we know?"

"No idea."

Nine-thirty-two finished eating, sitting up straight in his chair.

"You're the soldier. What could be our secret mission?"

"Nine-thirty-two is forbidden from secrets. His mission now is the Mistress."

91

I frowned. "We just got told to go fuck ourselves by an override. That blows."

"What if the Mistress ordered you on a secret mission with her? Could you do it then?"

He looked between me and Dane. "No."

"What if I called it an adventure?"

"An adventure is acceptable."

I clapped, and Dane's smile was almost back to normal.

"Perfect. We need a special adventure. A daring one. Ooh!" I leaned closer to my soldier. "Do you know where they're holding three-eleven?"

Dane stiffened, but I barely noticed as the soldier's lids squinted the smallest amount. "I believe so. Yes."

"Is it possible for us to sneak in?"

"Whoa." Dane didn't look so excited anymore. "Can we get in trouble for that?"

"I don't see why. I mean, it's somewhere here in the Gardens right?" I turned to nine-thirty-two. "It is here in the Gardens, isn't it?"

His head turned towards the back wall as he pointed. "Underneath the guard's apartments. Below. There's a lab and testing facility."

That did sound risky which was even more appealing. I was never one to follow the rules. I also wasn't stupid. I didn't want to do anything to risk getting kicked out either.

"Dammit. I think that's pushing it. City, it is. Let's go get dressed and find an adventure. Worst case, we find nothing, but we get to smash in faces. That's good for you, Dane. It won't be yours."

I threw him a wink watching as his face paled.

"Lighten up. You're not dying tonight unless you piss me off. I guess that means you better try your hardest to help me have fun. Come on. Let's all go get dressed. I'm not having you both leave here in those damn sweatpants. Our clothes need to be dark. Mysterious but bland, so we blend in."

The men followed me to the room and into the closet. I flipped on the light, scanning the large selection of clothes. This was what I splurged on. A closet as big as my room. After all, I never really planned on leaving here for long. There was only so much that appealed to me in the outside world, and now that I got the majority of it handled, I could stay here as much as I wanted. Unless...the Main Master held true to his word.

I grabbed two pairs of jeans, tossing them towards my slaves.

"They're three-elevens but you both should fit. Well...they may be a little big on you, Dane. And...maybe a little small on you, soldier, but try to make them fit."

My own black jeans were further down. I headed back, snatching those and a long-sleeve, black fitted shirt. Nothing fancy. After all, there was no telling what we were going to be doing. All I knew was before the night was over with, I'd be covered in someone's blood, and I was looking forward to it.

"WHAT ABOUT THAT ONE? HE LOOKS A LITTLE SUSPICIOUS."

"That's the vice-president's son. He's not suspicious, he's paranoid. He married a vegetable. Well, she wasn't always that way. Someone poisoned her down here. I guess he fell in love with her and—" My head shook as reasons why he wanted to marry her to begin with registered. "Anyway, nothing suspicious or exciting there. *At all.*" Flashes of their intimate life or lack thereof had me wanting to roll my eyes...until it dawned on me that there might actually be one. I paused, cocking my head as my eyebrows rose. Them, together, like that? Her, a body. Him, the initiator. Was it so different than what I wanted from three-eleven? He didn't move either...unless I told him to.

My lips twisted, and I pushed Dane's beer back to him, watching as he downed his third one. To say I wasn't upset that I couldn't join in was an understatement. Partying is what I did. Hanging out in bars and clubs was my life. To do it sober? Boring. Absolutely dull. That three-eleven wasn't here on this secret mission was even more depressing. I needed something. Excitement. Fun. I was losing my mind and sinking again, and I couldn't imagine hitting rock bottom without the stability of my real slave. After all, I'd gone this long bottling things up. Especially from therapists. Three-eleven was the first person I didn't have to hide from. Who was I going to talk to now that I'd finally put trust in someone? To vent to? Who was going to listen without judging me?

"Mmm." Dane pushed the empty glass away, gesturing his head towards a Mistress who was heading into the bar. She was alone, and I'd never seen her before. With the way she was dressed, she was either asking for trouble or she had no idea what sort of things happened in the city during the night hours.

"Hold on."

It was all I said to Dane as I took in her short, black dress. It came down to mid-thigh, and the top had a very low-cut V. Her breasts were on the bigger side, and more than one table turned her way as she headed to the bar.

"That's not a mystery; that's trouble. I'm not interested in that." I glanced over. "Soldier, what do you see?"

Nine-thirty-two's eyes were still transfixed on the fucking TV. He'd been watching the outside world's football highlights for the last hour, barely looking away enough to answer me. Maybe I didn't need sex to break him. I could just turn on the damn television.

"Table twelve. The two Masters whispering. Something about a slave and a deal they have. And an upcoming rape. Something about that too."

"Wait, what? I don't see numbers. Where's table twelve? How do you know this?"

Brown eyes lowered to mine.

"Below the screen. The table by the window." He glanced over but went back to the sports. "I read their lips. I'm not sure it's their slave. I can't tell."

The two men were older than me. Maybe at least by ten years, give or take.

"Should we follow them when they leave?"

Nine-thirty-two shook his head. "Nothing will happen tonight."

"Some adventure this turned out to be."

At my sigh, he kept staring ahead, but continued. "I detect a shift in your mood. You need an outlet. We will do that first. Then, we will retire so you can fuck me. Afterward, we sleep."

Dane's eyes widened but lowered to the table.

"I'm sorry, what?"

"You battle depression. You are in the beginning of an episode. You need to inflict pain. Shall I restrain the slave?"

"Whoa!" Dane's hands flew up, and he scooted to the side of his chair as if he were ready to bolt.

"You're safe. Calm down." I rested my forearms against the table, leaning in closer to nine-thirty-two. "We'll go to The Batting Cage. It's my go-to. I'll take out my anger there. As for fucking you." My head shook as I kept eye contact. "Looks won't get you pussy. Not mine. I don't care how good-looking or badass your resume is. I don't even care that you're some-what blank or not. I don't know you, and I don't sleep with strangers."

"We are not strangers. I am yours."

Even though the voice was slightly robotic, I couldn't get over feeling as if this blank slate was more human than blank. Or maybe it was just that he was so much more advanced.

"You're a loan, not mine. I'm done talking about this. Let's go."

I didn't wait for either of them. I headed through the

entrance, not stopping until I was surging through the door to my favorite place in the city.

"Gino!"

"Mistress Forty-two. So good to see you."

"Thanks. Is my room available?"

"It is. It's waiting just for you. I'll have slaves be brought back that fit your criteria."

"Excellent. You're amazing, G."

The male slave beamed a smile from behind the counter. The place was usually packed, but only a handful of Masters were lingering around the doors to the private rooms. Pictures of spilled guts and severed limbs filled the artwork on the walls. Where people left, I knew the ones lingering were either taking breaks or waiting for someone inside. I picked up a spiked bat, throwing the slave a dazzling grin and winking before heading to the very last door. Dane and my slave followed, and I didn't stop them.

"You can't be serious. Are you stalking me?"

The voice had me grinding my teeth as I glanced to the bloody man walking out of the door next to mine. His nearly white hair was stained crimson, and there was splatter over one side of his face. He was in all-black, just as us, and the tattoos covering the exposed part of his body didn't affect me as they once did. I used to find him so dreamy. Now all I suddenly wanted to do was beat his face in.

"Fuck off, Pistol. You wish. Had you not said anything, I wouldn't have even acknowledged your existence. You should really grow up and get over yourself."

"Says the deadbeat alcoholic."

I stopped in my tracks, spinning and pointing the end of the spiked bat in his direction. My soldier took a step forward, but I shook my head at him, making him stand down.

"You're one to talk. At least I'm not a druggy."

"I don't do that shit anymore."

"Well, I don't either. I haven't had a drink in a while."

"You'll cave."

My smile returned as I lowered the weapon and stepped closer.

"*You're counting on it.* I hate to burst your bubble, but I'm not the same person I was when we were together. That Lilian is dead now. You helped kill her with everyone else. Thank God for that." My head shook as I took in his questioning gaze. There was wariness in his expression. Interest, but also caution. "You were always so good at making me feel incomparable to you. You're going to feel so small when I take this world by storm. I haven't even made my move, and yet the universe is already parting a way for me. There's no stopping it, boo. How does it feel?"

"How does what feel?" He let out a sarcastic laugh, but I saw through his walls. He knew something big was happening for me, even if he couldn't physically see it. "You're speaking out of your ass. I feel nothing about it."

"Yeah you do. A part of you has always been threatened by me. Whatever insecurity that revolves around it is about to grow. I hope it eats you alive. Now, if you'll excuse me."

I didn't wait for him to keep up with his stupid charade. Walking through the entrance to my room, I took in the three opened doors that rested almost right next to each other. A restrained crow with dark hair stood in each one. It didn't matter who resembled my father more. They were convicts, the worst of the worst, and they all deserved to die.

I pointed the bat to door number three. *Always number three.*

Dane eased to the far corner of the room, and nine-thirty-two followed. I took the ponytail holder from my wrist, tying back my hair as I breathed in and out. I wouldn't think about how three-eleven wasn't here to pick me up off the floor when I finished. Or how he couldn't hold me until I calmed enough to

A. A. DARK

function. No…I had to try to hold it together until he returned. I could do this. I could face my past. I had to.

Already, my breaths were increasing, and that shake that sent my teeth chattering kicked in. I paced as two larger men forced the older restrained slave to the middle of the room, hooking him to a hoist in the center. From my small height, they never had to lift them high.

"So, we meet again. Someday, Daddy, I'm not going to stop."

"That is not your father."

"Shut up, nine-thirty-two."

I threw the soldier a look and lifted the bat over my shoulder. The slave was wiggling like a fish on a hook. His muffled voice was yelling through the cloth that had been used as a gag, but I didn't hear him. I didn't even really see him. It was the dark hair I was fixed on. It was the memories that haunted me.

"Music?" The laugh had been full of real humor, as if the thought of my singing had been the funniest thing in the world. *"You're telling me after finally finding your place in modeling, you want to piss it all away for fucking music? You don't even know how to play anything!"*

Letting my weight settle on my back leg, I lifted the bat high, swinging at the slave's stomach with everything I had. A whoosh of air left him followed by a mixture of a yell and a cry.

"I do know how to play. I've been taking guitar lessons for six years. And Foster, that producer I was telling you about, he says I'm good. Daddy, music has always been my passion. I told you that before you even put me in horseback riding lessons. I want to sing."

"But you can't. I've heard you, Lilian. Sorry, honey, but you're no singer."

Pain.

"I am. I've actually been told I'm pretty good."

"They're lying. You're not." His face was turning red. *"You're not doing it. You're going to stay in modeling and work*

98

on that contract with La'Ronge and move even further up from there. You have the look. The appeal. You—"

"I have scars! I can't do it anymore. I won't! I'm finished. La'Ronge doesn't want me. I'm too much work. I'm too much of a risk. I'm focusing on music from here on out." I paused. *"I already have a band and everything. We're still learning the ropes with each other, but this is going to pay off. I'm meant to do this."*

Blood sprayed across my face as the spikes tore and dug into the crow's chest, ripping the bare flesh wide open. I swung again, feeling the jolt in my entire body as the spikes lodged in his breastbone.

"I'm not letting you ruin this. You're modeling."

"I'm not."

"Lilian."

"I'm not and you can't make me! Unless you plan to kill me like her."

Whack!

The hit hadn't been unexpected. I knew the consequences for bringing up my mother, and age had never been a factor. My dad swung, and that day, a lifetime of pain came pouring out. My mother's mysterious death. Years of beatings. Enough rage to tease but not to sate. It unleashed the real me. Fed her and turned her into something no one recognized.

"I hate you."

Again, I swung, this time embedding the thick metal into the side of the crow's throat. Gouges brought the blood down like a faucet. That only had me moving to his face. To the bulging, horror-filled eyes that stared at me like the monster I was.

"You killed her. I know you did. *I hate you.* I hate you!"

Bone shattered in his jaw and cheek. The crow's face jerked with my pull as I tried to dislodge the bat, but it was getting too heavy for me to control like I wanted. Visions kept blinding me. From my mom to a collage of my entire life. Moving out had been my new start, but nothing was new. I couldn't escape him. He always came back. He always forced himself in my life and tried to destroy it. The Gardens was the only good thing he'd ever given me, but I couldn't even escape giving him credit for that. I was my father's daughter. I was evil just like him.

"I wish I would have killed you. Someday I will. I'll have a new life. I *am* worthy enough," I yelled out. "I'm good. Maybe I'm not the best, but I deserve something to go right for me. *I belong in music.* Fuck everyone. Fuck Pistol. Fuck *you.* I'm going to be the best version of Lilian Lowe. I'm going to be great, and I'm only leaving you alive to witness it. Everyone will *love* me! I deserved to be loved. I need. I *want.*"

I let out a scream as I swung. Blood, spit, and flesh went splattering over the floor as I caught the side of the slave's head. Yells were deep yet void. Hollowed and more of a humming groan. The slave was doing something between flopping and convulsing. I reared back, needing to just swing until I couldn't lift my arms anymore. To swing again. And again. And again. The bloodier, the more he looked like my father had when I got done beating him with his golf club. Although...my father had lived.

This man wouldn't.

MO3II

There was no smile on my face despite this was where I wanted to be. I couldn't show happiness as I gazed at the two men who were sleepily staring back at me. It was early. Not even sunrise yet, but the Main Master insisted it was time for me to return to my Mistress's apartment. He didn't even wake her. She had no idea I'd been temporarily returned. Not that I'd be back for long. The Main Master didn't think I'd survive the week. I was starting to think he was right. But not so much because of my Mistress. I was at risk there, but it was the blank slate soldier I wasn't sure I liked. The way he was looking at me. It didn't feel right. He felt like a threat. Even the Main Master kept his distance while he spoke quietly to him.

"Did they fix you?"

At Dane's whisper, I removed my gaze from the man sitting in my seat and brought it to Dane's. I was in five's position now, level with the end of the bed, on the opposite side of where I used to sit. I didn't like that.

"I'm fixed."

"You seem different."

"Do I? How so?"

His mouth opened, and his head tilted. "You don't appear angry anymore. Your face is...softer. More relaxed. Are you real now?"

"Well, I'm not dead yet."

The smile was but a quick flash, melting just as fast. "You aren't blank anymore. I can hear it in your voice. Do you still want to kill me?"

"Maybe."

He sat up straighter.

"I'm joking."

"Are you?" There was a nervous laugh, but he didn't seem to believe me. "I'm not sure I like this new humor after what I've seen you do."

"Dane. Shut. *Up.*"

At the Mistress's groggy voice, we all looked her way. She rolled to her side, only to angrily roll to face my way. I swallowed hard, my heart hammering as I waited to see if she'd wake. Minutes passed. Nothing.

"You're not going to kill me, right? I haven't done anything with her. Nothing. *I swear.*"

My gaze narrowed as I moved my attention to the new blank slate. What about him? Had he touched her? Held her? Fucked her?

"Not him either. She calls him a stranger."

Warmth and squeezing tightened my chest. I felt myself loosen at the thought of my Mistress. Stranger...but not me. She'd chosen me. She wanted me. *Or she did when I was blank.* She might not anymore.

"You sure I'm safe? You're not going to—"

"Dane!" The Mistress flew up, rage filling her face as her blonde hair wildly haloed around her. "What the hell—"

She stopped mid-sentence, slowly turning to face me. I saw the moment her expression changed, and what it did to me was almost too much for me to control. I had to remain lifeless.

Remain just as blank as I did when I'd left, if not more so. It was the only way I stood a chance in the long run.

"You're back?"

She threw the covers off, scrambling from the bed. Her weight crashed into me, so different and more consuming than it had been before. The scent of her skin registered, sweet with a tinge of exotic spice. The heat. The softness of her hands as they cupped my cheeks so she could look at me. I was in awe of her beauty. Absolutely consumed by the mere presence of her now that I was somewhat normal. It was heaven and hell at the same time.

"They fixed you? You're better now?"

"I'm better."

I kept it short and sweet. The more emotionless I was, the longer I'd live. She righted the oversized t-shirt she wore, straddling me as she locked her arms around my neck. I would have done anything to hold her. To trap her to me and never let go. Luckily, the soldier's glare kept me distracted enough that I didn't give in to the temptation.

"I was so worried they wouldn't bring you back. We went on a secret mission the other night, and I contemplated breaking in to see you, but it was too risky." Tighter, she held. "I'm so glad you're back. I'm just going to stay like this." She yawned, turning and leaning over to pull her comforter off her bed to wrap around us. "Take your shirt off and hold me so I can sleep. *I need to sleep.*"

I obeyed, tossing the shirt. My arms lifted, easing around her. Not too soft. Not too hard. I was overanalyzing everything to remember how I'd been before.

"Yes. *Finally.*"

My Mistress sighed, yawning again as she melted into my chest and neck. How she could sit up to sleep, I had no idea. It wasn't so comfortable now that I'd been changed back into my old self. Or...what was left of that person. I wasn't him. Not completely. The connection to my past just wasn't there as it had been before. I felt, but what emotions I held over that existence was disappearing by the day.

I closed my lids, falling into the place that made me the happiest. These moments. The ones where she needed nothing but to feel safe in my arms. This was what I had been counting down the hours to. This was my life now.

"Your smell."

She inhaled, sighing deeply.

Opening my eyes, I glanced over to Dane. He was lowered to his mat. It appeared his lids were cracked open, but I couldn't quite tell. His arm was secured to a chain locked to the floor, but he had leeway if he wanted to roll over. When I moved my attention back to the blank slate soldier, he was still looking at me. The Main Master had warned me, mentioning he'd be watching, but I hadn't been sure to take that as a threat. It *was* a threat, or the soldier saw me as one. Unlike Dane, he wasn't chained to the floor, and I didn't like that.

"You're heart." Sleepy eyes met mine as she pulled back to stare into my face. "Why is your heart racing? I can feel it pounding." Her hand pressed into my bare chest and for the first time since she'd awoken, she looked at me. *Really* looked. "Are you okay?"

"I'm okay."

"But you're not." She turned, looking behind us to the soldier. When she turned back to me, I could tell from her expression that she was thinking. "I see. You think he's taken your place." Her voice lowered. "He didn't. I'm doing the Main Master a favor. I'm trying to." She got quiet, mouthing the words. "Break. Him." Her volume increased to a whisper again. "You're still my blank slate. You're not being replaced."

But I wasn't blank anymore, and I was obligated to tell her that whether I liked it or not. Maybe it was the brainwashing or training I'd undergone. Trust came first, and if I didn't disclose the truth at the first opportunity, I'd lose hers. That couldn't happen or I was as good as dead the moment the lie was revealed. I had to take my chance now with the truth but cover my ass good enough to not get killed because of it. It wasn't going to be easy.

"Mistress, I'm not." I scanned her eyes, watching so much emotion flicker through as she kept my stare. "I'm not the same as before."

"I know. They reprogrammed you."

"No."

Her brows drew in, and she shifted on my lap.

"What do you mean, no?"

"They couldn't do it without killing me. You told the Main Master you wanted me back. I'm." My gaze lowered, but I couldn't continue.

"You're what?" Pressure from her hand brought my face up demanding. "Finish. You're what?"

"I'm stuck."

Silence.

"Define stuck."

"I'm somewhere between blank and normal. I can think. I can recall. I can even feel." My head shook. "I just can't do those things all the way. I'm stuck in between. I'm sorry."

For what felt like forever, she scanned my face. Her leg finally lifted, and she eased off my lap. The tightness in my chest squeezed a different way. Not full of love and excitement. This pressure hurt. It ached and made my throat almost feel like it was closing. I wanted to reach forward and refuse to let her get up. To keep her to me. It was a death sentence.

"I see. I…" She didn't go back to the bed. She sat next to me, wrapped in her blanket. Her lips quivered, and a single tear raced down her cheek. "Stuck." She sniffled. "I truly do ruin everything. I broke you, and now they can't fix you, and you're stuck.

Not even normal. Just…in a new place. A place you can feel. One you can hurt."

My eyes dropped from hers. Not because I didn't want to hear the truth, but because it was too painful to see her hurt for me and not be able to do or say anything about it.

"I'm sorry, slave. I am."

"I'll be the same for you. I'll try my best. You won't even know the difference. We can forget this and just…live."

She wiped the tears, wrapping the blanket around her even more.

"To hear you speak so normal its…"

"It won't happen again."

My words were but a whisper. Her chin came to rest on her drawn up knees. Still, she continued to stare at me. Whatever was going through her head, I had no idea, but it was important. And deep. She was thinking hard, and I feared what it entailed. Would she just kill me now? Would she send me back? Maybe she'd want to keep the soldier for good. He wasn't always going to be a stranger.

"Can you be broken again now that the blank slate part of you is gone?"

"I don't think so."

"But you're still blank slate…a little."

It wasn't a question.

"I think so. My memories and past…I felt them stronger when the programming was undone, but each day, the emotions fade. I have no desire to think about it. No sadness or longing. I know it sounds bad, but I don't care about that part of my life at all. Nothing matters but this life here. With you, listening. Helping. Out of the way, but always of service. I still know my duties, and I will not fail them. If anything, I may be able to carry them out even better now. Clarity without feeling."

"But you *do* feel."

God, if she only knew what it was like being near her like

this. I could fill the entirety of space with the love I felt for her, but she'd never know. She wanted a blank slate, and that's who I'd pretend to be.

"To an extent. Not much." And that was the truth concerning anything but her. "Aside from the protectiveness and emotions towards you, nothing and no one else affects me. I feel absolutely nothing."

There it was. The robotic truth I knew she'd hear, and she did. A slight smile came with her nod, and she let out a breath, letting her legs lower as she scooted closer on my mat. Dane's head lifted, but I ignored it as I stayed mesmerized by her beauty.

"Lay down, slave. If I don't have to fear breaking you, then what we do shouldn't matter."

There it was once again. That explosion of my heart. It wasn't just beating. It was running a marathon as if the result would lead me to a place that I'd never been before. A place worth going. *A place worth staying.*

The Mistress glanced around the room as I obeyed, laying on my mat.

"Soldier, close your eyes and go to sleep."

"I'm to watch over the Mistress."

"I am the Mistress, and I'm safe. Sleep or you will leave the room."

I swallowed hard, slowing my breathing as I got still. I kept my stare pointed at the ceiling…waiting…expecting nothing. Wishing for everything.

"I can almost see the old you. The same." She pulled the covers over her shoulders as she moved in, leveling her hands on my chest. "But different." In slow strokes she made a path from my pecs to the band of my sweatpants. I didn't move. My cock thickened, but I tried to act as if my consciousness wasn't even here.

I was a body.

A vessel.

An outlet.

Nothing more.

Fingers pushed past my waistband. "Lift." And I did, allowing her to pull down my pants to mid-thigh, not even removing them. It was obvious what she wanted, and that didn't involve anything other than what it was. Sex, release…from someone she relied on. Me.

The Mistress removed her panties, not bothering to take off her shirt as she straddled me. She didn't touch me as she sat on her knees, hovering just over my cock.

"Get me ready, slave."

My teeth clenched as I brought my hand up between her legs and continued to stare ahead. With how small she was, there wasn't much room in between us. My hand brushed my length, and I tried my best to mute the sensations. This wasn't for me. *It was for her.* She'd see I was no different than before. I wouldn't look at her. I didn't deserve that.

Wetness met my fingertips causing me to bite down harder. She was already so ready, but I did as she said, tracing my finger over her slit. Teasing her clit.

In circles, I took my time moving between her entrance and the sensitive nub. When I made it back to her channel, she sunk down on my fingertip. I inched in deeper, filling her as she moaned and held her weight up over my chest.

"*Yes. Yes.* Another finger."

The gasp as she stretched around my digits made my cock twitch between us uncontrollably. As hard as I tried to ignore the need, this was different than with my blank slate. With him, I had more restraint. That was almost nonexistent as she fucked my fingers, brushing my cock with every downward motion. This was the one place I had to control myself in, or I was as good as gone. If my Mistress couldn't rely on me to fulfill this need, she'd eventually find someone who could.

MISTRESS B-0042

No outpouring of needs. No focusing on his wants. *No expectations.*

I grabbed my slave's cock, fitting it against my entrance as he placed his hand back down at his side. I had been craving to feel him inside of me. Just having him back and knowing I'd probably never have to worry about breaking the blank slate part of him left me in a frenzy. As I rubbed his thick tip against me, he didn't manipulate his movements to try to ease inside or rotate his hips to drive deeper. He was as still as a statue. Like he wasn't real or alive at all. And maybe a part of him would never be again. Stuck. I wasn't sure how to feel about that, but if he still wasn't normal, he was still mine. Still devoted. Still not judging me. Just more coherent when it came to questions. I was okay with that.

I didn't want to know whether I truly broke him or not. I wanted to believe he was the same but better. It had me biting my lip and taking my time as I inched down.

Yes...So big. So...perfect for me.

A smile tugged at the side of my mouth as I focused on the way he stretched me.

This was right. This was what I wanted.

Me, the Mistress.

Him, the broken blank slate.

A plethora of fuckedupness.

Digging my nails into his skin, I focused on nothing but what would bring me more pleasure. I found it in the calm—in his unresponsive body as I used it. There was something in that that made me want to come on the spot.

"Fuck." I looked down, lifting my shirt enough to watch myself slide down his cock. As I rose, I couldn't keep in the moan, seeing myself grip tightly around him. Higher my eyes lifted, appreciating his hard, muscled body, but it wasn't reacting normal. It was... Again, sounds left me as my orgasm tried to take over. "You're holding your breath." The realization made me even wetter as my mind danced in dark places. I glanced up to his emotionless face, clawing my nails down his chest. "You try to fight this so good, but you like this pussy as much as I like this cock. And I have you back. You're mine, three-eleven. I own you..." I stopped, wanting nothing more than to kiss him. To have him kiss me. And he'd like that. Blank or not, I could feel how much he wanted me. *Love. Yes.*

"Did you think about me like this while you were gone? I bet you did. I own more than just your body, don't I?" I paused as he continued to stare ahead. "I do. I have every part of you. I have your soul." I did lower, then, hovering only an inch or so away. "They say you can't find heaven in hell. I think we've found it, slave."

I ran my tongue between his lips, lifting. Three-eleven didn't respond, but the deep vibrations coming from his growl almost did me in. He didn't even look at me. He didn't have to for me to know how he felt about this. My slave was so thick, swelling even more with every roll of my hips. He was perfectly fitting, which made it hard not to take control and play with my own clit. I could get off on him in two seconds flat. His size in me was that good. But I hadn't waited all this time to end it that fast. From the moment he left, this was all I could think about. Me. Him. This twisted new thing I was beginning to crave. Should I send the Mistress from the auction a thank you basket? Maybe I should have a bouquet delivered to the Vice President's son and new bride as well. *I understood the appeal.* I truly, really did.

"I thought I hated sex." I lifted until he was almost out of me, sinking back down until he was buried. My actions were almost rough. Harder. I lifted, increasing the speed. Faster. Harder. Faster. "I was never a fan until you. Something about us together is different. Maybe it's just you. I like how you feel in me. I think about having you inside me all the time now. I *need...*"

What did I need? Did I even know? My mind was conflicted. I wanted to be railed until I couldn't move, yet I wanted it slow. I wanted control more which had me rolling to my knees and lowering my chest down to his. I ground my hips, reaching up to fist his hair as I fell into rhythm. "I need you to look at me. Don't speak. Don't move. *Try not to even breathe.* Just look at me as I come all over your cock."

I got no response, just obedience as his eyes stayed transfixed to mine. I rose higher on his body, only taking in the tip as I lowered, pressing my lips to his. The contact was barely existent. Sensations were torture as I let go of his hair and reached down, rubbing over my clit as I continued to barely fuck him. Again, I kissed him, hovering over his mouth.

"I think I want you to come in me again too. I bet you want to so bad." I moaned, not able to stop the shaking. "I wont ever forget how you wanted to kill for me, slave. I wonder had I not called the Main Master, if you would have done it. Does a part of you want me so badly, you'd destroy anyone who showed interest?"

My orgasm was right there as I tried to breathe and speak through the words. I was trembling, fucking his tip as I could see the blood and murder in my mind's eye.

111

A. A. DARK

"You told him you loved me."

More I massaged my lips into his. Breaking away as I cried out through my need to release. I was trying everything I could to prolong it, but at my slave's escaped groan, I was hanging on by the thinnest thread.

"I'm tempted to have you prove it." I sucked his bottom lip into my mouth, my eyes rolling through the fantasies blinding me. A man...dutiful, loyal. One that was only mine that I controlled. Protecting me. *Killing because of me.* Maybe in secret, so I didn't know. A blank slate who was supposed to be good...but wasn't? Why did that have such appeal?

"Fuck. *Slave.*"

Spasms hit hard. My cries merged with moans as three-eleven's cum shot into me with force. His hands were fisted, and he was biting into his bottom lip as he tried to hold still. He couldn't as I slid down his length taking every inch. Jolts shook his body, followed by the sexiest expression as his lids closed and his face softened. I wanted him again. I wanted to keep staring at him to try to discover who this new person was that I was...*falling for.*

It would be stupid to deny that I had an attachment to him. How far it went, I was terrified to find out. Or maybe I already knew and that was the reason I'd been crying and sick over him getting broken. Anything I grew feelings for somehow was taken from me. It left. It disappeared. It fucking died. And now here I was, pulling my blanket back up and dreamily staring into a face that did weird things to my heart.

Brown color appeared and my slave glanced at me. The softness of his expression disappeared. He was guarded. Gone to be replaced by the blank part of him. That was better, putting me at ease enough to lower to his chest. I kept him inside of me, basking in something I would have never of wanted. But it was him. Somehow that changed things.

For minutes we didn't move. I even began drifting again. It

was the throat clearing that had me lifting my head.

"I see you're happy to have your slave back."

"Main Master."

I lifted feeling my slave's cock ease from me. I didn't have to tell three-eleven to get dressed. My tug to his sweatpants had him obeying me.

"Can I expect these unexpected visits to continue, or have you come to get your soldier?"

Elec leaned against the door's threshold. I wrapped my comforter around me, tighter, standing to face him. I ignored how my slave's cum ran down my thighs, but something about it leaving me in front of the Main Master did wicked things. I was turned on all over again, and I wasn't sure this lust was going to end anytime soon.

"Actually...I'm going to leave him for a while longer."

"But I don't need him anymore."

"I'm not so sure of that." He glanced at my slave. "Let's just make sure. Besides," he shoved his hands in his pockets as he came closer, "your job with him isn't finished. How would you say that's going?"

"I'm torn. I'm not sure." I glanced at Elec, lowering my voice. "I was upset the other night. Sex has never been brought up and yet he felt that was the solution to my...bad mood."

"You haven't had sex with him yet?"

I saw the surprise on the Main Master's face as he closed even more distance.

"I have not. Sometimes that's better."

"And he mentioned sex? He hinted or did he say those words?"

My eyes lowered as I recalled. "He said something like, he saw a disturbance in my mood and that I needed an outlet. As in murder. He wanted me to kill Dane, and afterward... we could retire so I could fuck him. Then, we'd sleep."

Elec's eyes widened, surprising me.

"He said that?"

"In almost those exact words."

He looked between the soldier and my slave. For the first time, I noticed how the soldier was staring at three-eleven. His lids were narrowed, almost closed, and his face was hard. Clearly angry.

"Hey, I told you to sleep. You're awake."

"It is my job to protect the Mistress."

"And I told you I was fine and to go to sleep or I'd send you to the living room."

"I will stay here."

"You better close your eyes."

Elec's expression was one I hadn't seen before. I couldn't even place the emotion as he turned back to me.

"Do the two of you argue like this often?"

"Sometimes. He's not a good blank slate. He doesn't listen for shit. He has a mind of his own. Or maybe it's the orders. He sticks to them. He won't budge if he doesn't want to."

Elec just kept shaking his head.

"Is he not supposed to do that? *Did I break him?*"

I wasn't sure if that was excitement or shock in my tone. Maybe a little sadness? Not for the slave, but because I was right with my fear that I was cursed. Everyone I connected with destructed one way or another.

"It's hard to say. It clearly can't be love this early, but it's something. Attraction, maybe, or just...lust? Whatever it is altered him and it's showing itself right now. Something's happening here. He doesn't like your slave." He paused. "Maybe the earlier instances are unrelated, but time will show a bigger picture."

"*Time?* You want me to keep him here even though he's not listening to me? I thought you wanted me safe?"

"You're safe."

"You think? I'm not so sure. What if he doesn't listen, and

this happens again? What if he tries to hurt my slave."

"He won't unless you ask him to. I don't think this is necessarily aggression. He's adjusting to a new possible threat. Once he realizes three-eleven isn't here to hurt you, he'll be fine. Besides, your slave can take care of himself."

I got quiet, still going back and forth. Three-eleven was sitting up now, almost a mirror of nine-thirty-two as they glared at each other.

"Give it a few more days. Let's see what happens. I want to know he's broken for a fact before I make my decision. The only way I can do that is to keep him here with you."

"And if he is broken?"

The Main Master's brows drew in. "He and the others are soldiers. I'll just keep them the hell away from women."

My head shook. "That won't work for all of them."

"No. It won't." His jaw flexed repeatedly. "I fucking hate lust, love, all of it. There's nothing it doesn't ruin." He seemed to catch himself, going back to look at my slave. "Speaking of Romeo, how is he? Did he tell you he wasn't a blank slate anymore?"

"He did. I still want him."

Elec nodded. "And if he starts killing your other slaves?"

I couldn't stop the smile or heat that flooded my face as I looked down.

Giddiness.

Appeal.

Intrigue.

A new game?

"I'm not so sure he would without me asking." I lifted my eyes to Elec's. "But I think I'd like to see if I could get him to try. He's not programmed as much as he was before. Nothing is off limits if I allow it, and there's something...*really* fucking hot about him being all primal over me behind my back. I like it. I'm going to like driving him to do it even more."

MO3II

C omedy. Had I ever found movies as funny as the others thought? It was taking everything in me to see the humor in the situation. Maybe it was because I didn't watch much television growing up, or perhaps I was still more blank slate than I realized. I wasn't sure, but I kept myself occupied by massaging my Mistress's feet as she laid down and continued to throw popcorn at the screen…or the soldier…or Dane. But not me. She kept sitting up to pop pieces in my mouth, teasingly running her finger over my lips. Then she'd lay back down as if she hadn't just hinted to hours of foreplay or fun again tonight. It was driving me crazy.

"No way!"

The Mistress died laughing, throwing her head down to rest against the arm of the sofa. Dane sat on the floor with the soldier, his face not appearing happy for someone watching such a funny movie. Although the soldier kept turning around and watching suspiciously, he had no problem catching on to the funny scenes. He was just as loud as my Mistress.

"I can't believe I waited this long to watch this movie." She pulled her foot back, sliding her other one over my lap so that I could start massaging that one next. Her heel grazed my cock, and I closed my eyes at the sensations. When I opened my lids, she was smiling. I grabbed her foot, going back to stare at the screen as I let my fingers work their magic. I could barely start before the Mistress pulled back.

"Actually. I have a better idea." She eased to the floor, moving between my legs to put her back to me. "Slave, you massage my neck. Dane and Nine-thirty-two, you have feet duty. One for each of you."

Any hint of a smile disappeared as I watched the men turn back to look at her. They moved in immediately, obeying her command. When she leaned forward and ran her fingers along Dane's cheek, heat flushed my face with the underlining anger. It was the briefest touch before she returned, but it was enough.

"Neck, three-eleven."

I eased her hair over her shoulder. Just seeing the exposed skin, I could taste her all over again. I could feel myself sucking on her throat, feeling her back laying against my chest. Since I'd been returned, all I could think about was having her over and over. Losing myself in her. Being with only her.

"That's nice."

She let out a moan as the men went to work. I reached down, leveling my thumbs to the back of her neck. As I worked in small circles, she looped her arms around my calves, holding on. For something so insignificant, the act seemed to mean more. Trust. As if I were her anchor and she was holding to me for stability. It was enough to calm the jealousy and anger at the other two men touching her. I had to let it go. It wasn't my place to feel so overprotective. If my Mistress chose to act on something, that was one thing. If she didn't and they crossed a line, that was entirely different.

"This is better than Mickey's in Hollywood." Her head

leaned back between my thighs, resting against the sofa as she stared up at me. For seconds she didn't speak. She just gazed up, trapping me with the softness that had suddenly taken her over. I could have done a million things as she kept my gaze. Pulled her into my lap to never stop kissing her. I could have cupped under her chin to keep her in place as I eased my hand through the opening of her baggy, long sleeve, lounging outfit. I could play with her breasts, teasing her until she couldn't take it. "Popcorn, slave."

Or…I could feed her popcorn and lose a part of myself even more as the blank slate I was forcing myself to be.

Reaching over, I grabbed a piece, sliding it in her mouth. Her lips incased the tip of my finger, sucking. I didn't close my eyes like I wanted. Only my cock reacted, but she couldn't feel or see that.

"One more."

Her eyes closed as she let out a slight moan. I knew it was from the men, but it didn't bother me as I picked up another piece of popcorn. I waited for her to open her lids before I hovered it over her opened mouth. For some reason, I didn't lower. I didn't slide it passed her lips. I waited. Watching. Taking in her reaction.

The Mistress closed her mouth, squinting her eyes playfully as her head cocked to the side between my legs.

I lowered it even more, and she lifted her head up, taking it from my fingers. Not before she bit playfully against my digit.

"I'm going to remember your teasing, slave. We'll see how much you like it when I'm teasing you tonight." She lifted her head, and I went back to massaging her neck. When ringing broke through the room, all four of us looked over towards the kitchen counter. The Mistress stood, heading over as Dane paused the movie.

"Hello? Yep, it's me." I stole a glance as Dane slid in closer to the soldier. Whatever he whispered had nine-thirty-two laughing. My bad mood was immediate. I still didn't understand how nine-thirty-two had so much personality being blank. It wasn't right. It wasn't fair. But what exactly was fair in the Gardens? Not much.

The Mistress walked closer to us, jolting to a stop. "Seriously? No, I wasn't aware of that."

My neck craned as I watched her pace, curious who she was talking to. I couldn't tell whether the caller was bringing good news or bad.

"You're joking." She laughed. "Oh. Yeah. I mean." At her pause I turned back to face straight, not wanting her to catch me staring. "Right now? Okay. Well, I'm still working on it, and it's very different than what I usually put out. I haven't even tested it out with my guitar yet. There's a lot left to—Of course. Right. A few verses before...and jump into the chorus? No chorus yet? Two? Alright, alright. I'll sing the first two that lead to the chorus. But no chorus."

She took a deep breath, leading off into a slow hum that transformed into a hypnotic rhythm. All of our heads snap her way as the rich tune merged with slow, drawn-out words.

Higher than the stars, I held all the power.
You're the only one I trusted, but you pulled me down.
My tower doesn't seem as safe now.
Oooh yeah, am I safe now?

Deep, lavish sounds left her as she made a moaning, erotic hum to the beat that I assumed would have been the chorus. Intoxicating energy had me holding my breath as I listened to the song come alive. I'd never heard anything like it before. My Mistress's style wasn't traditional. She was different. Unique, and *good*. So damn good. Shock didn't come close to describing what I felt. Neither did awe. It was more than that, and I wasn't the only one. The soldier was suddenly standing at my side, and

Dane had lifted to his knees at my other side. Me…I was cemented to my seat, and my heart was no longer mine.

Nothing is the same, I think my heart drowned
I look into his eyes, I think my soul's bound
Having him, he makes me feel found
Oooh yeah. I think I'm found now.

She came to an abrupt stop, multiple expressions passing over as she'd been pulled from the tune.

"Really? I." She stopped, her face swinging to all of us in surprise. When her hand motioned for me in a quick wave, I sprung from the sofa, jogging up to her. "Yes, of course. I will. See you soon."

The Mistress hung up, squeezing the phone in both hands as she looked at me with big eyes. Out of nowhere she started screaming and jumping up and down.

"Go get on your suit, slave. We're headed to the Main Master's private lounge. He wants me to test out my new song on his guests! It's nothing formal. He said it's just for fun, but *you're* formal because you're mine. *My guitar.*" She spun, racing for her room. I followed, overwhelmed by excitement for her. Me…*feeling.* For her. Only for her.

"Hey, what about us?"

Dane followed behind, and the soldier didn't have to be ordered to join us. We were all standing at the closet. I was grabbing my suit while our Mistress swallowed hard.

"Dark colors. The ones y'all wore out to the adventure. Put those on. You can come. But best fucking behavior, or I kill you in the most painful way when we get back."

"Yes!" Dane jerked a pair of my jeans free, and the soldier took the black ones next to them. My lids narrowed the smallest amount, but a hand on my far cheek drew my eyes to my Mistress. She stepped in, pulling the back of my biceps so I'd face and move in closer to her.

"Are you going to be okay out there tonight?"

"Best behavior."

Her head shook back and forth. "Give me more than that, slave. Are you going to be okay out there with me tonight? I have no idea how this party will be. It might be loud. It might be a bloody mess. We're talking about the Main Master's private quarters. His lounge. I need you trigger free. Half blank doesn't mean entirely blank."

"I'd kill myself before I ruined this for you, Mistress."

Her lips parted as something washed over her face. "You would."

"Without hesitation."

"I believe you." She nodded. "Get dressed."

DARK GOD STATUS WAS NOT WHAT I HAD BEEN EXPECTING. FOUR sets of guards checked us from the moment we got off the elevator, on the top floor. Even when we finally arrived at the main door, there was no walking in. Another guard in two-tone black camo with a gun at his hip held up his knife…waiting. The need to protect was there, but I knew there was no threat.

"Arm."

My Mistress didn't hesitate, not even wincing as he dug the sharp tip into her skin. Crimson looked black under the red lights, and he waved us in, not offering her a bandage or napkin for her wound. She didn't seem to care as she dropped her hand, letting the blood run free.

More guards parted as we stepped through, heading through a small entrance towards a pair of large, black-trimmed glass doors, two stories tall. They opened for us, and we barely made it through as my Mistress jerked to a stop.

To say the place was dark didn't begin to describe what we'd stepped into. The heaviness wasn't just the feel in the air. The place felt barren. Like a nightly wasteland or oblivion. So black it was a void. Each step felt as if you'd fall through the floor. If there were walls, you couldn't tell. It was infinite and yet swallowing. It provoked fear. The floors, walls, ceiling. It all blended into nothingness. The only lights were a dull red. Even their glow seemed stolen by the surroundings.

Music thumped in the distance, and I kept at my Mistress's side while she stayed looped around my arm. Dane and Nine-thirty-two followed, and with as paranoid as I suddenly felt, I didn't like having them at my back. Especially since they seemed to be connected somehow. I didn't want to think about that. Dane and I hadn't had the best start. I nearly broke his arm. Then... helping kill five. He feared me. He had good reason to, and I couldn't fault him for that. But nine-thirty-two, I'd keep my eye on him.

"Slave...Wow. *Look at this place.*"

The deeper we got in, the more I didn't like it. Glass rooms gave view to three different butchers. Men, who were in stages of dissecting and processing...slaves. Meat grinders. Hatchets. Blood. So much blood was over the floors and stainless-steel counters. For once, I was thankful for the dim red lights. It hid more than they exposed. Death didn't bother me, but there was something about this place that made the most grotesque acts feel a million times worse.

"I see," the Mistress mumbled, pointing to a far stage. "Live torture, there. Processing..." She stopped. "How many people are they torturing at a time?" Another pause. "Oh...shit. There he is. The Main Master."

Against the far end of the club, halfway up the wall, was an elevated booth, almost like a throne. With how dark it was, I could barely make him out, but he seemed to be alone. Slouching...but *watching us.*

"My guitar?"

The Mistress turned to see Dane hold it up. All she did was

nod, leading me towards the ominous booth as her arm trapped mine against her body, tighter.

"Best behaviors. Best fucking behaviors. God, I hope I don't pass out. Or throw up. I can't breathe. I need luck. I need a miracle." She slowed, looking over at me. "You protect me. Keep the bad luck away, at least for tonight. Our future literally depends on this."

MISTRESS B-0042

Something told me not to wear the fancy heels. Stiletto boots, yes, but not the opened-toed monstrosities I'd almost put on. Boots were better with the black mini dress. They were edgier. I needed every ounce of edge I could get. God, what if I didn't pull this off? What if I ruined it like I did with everything else?

Each step promised a fall. Each push from the balls of my feet hinted that I'd twist my ankle and tumble down these stairs to my death. It was three-eleven wrapping his arm around my waist that vowed he'd save me if I did. It instilled power I forgot I had, and that meant more than dependency. It shined a light on the fighter I'd always been underneath the broken shell of my exterior.

"Mistress."

I stopped at the top of the stairs, pausing as the Main Master gestured to the end of the horseshoe-shaped booth. He sat in the center, not any straighter than when I'd spotted him below. Was he drunk? Upset? He sure didn't look normal.

"Main Master." I sat down on black leather, pointing to the

floor for my men. Not a word was spoken from any of them as they took their place.

"What's the name of the song?"

Hesitation had me as heat blossomed. Singing for him had been harder than I could barely stomach. I worried my voice had sounded too shaky, but by a miracle I held it together.

"I haven't decided yet. I only finished this one yesterday. It's the third I've written since the auction."

"Third? That fast? You're determined."

All I could do was nod.

"Good. Very good." He took a bottle, pouring more amber liquor into his glass. "Stop judging me, Forty-two. I allow myself to drink once a month. Tonight is my night, and I plan to get completely wasted. I've earned that."

"I have no doubts you have." I glanced around the dark space, spotting other booths in the distance. Colors were dim, but there were people present. "You mentioned friends you wanted me to play for?"

A smile jerked to the side of his mouth as he brought the glass back to his lips. "The Main Master doesn't have friends, he has…assets and investments." He lifted his glass. "They'll hear you. Your voice is like sex. They won't miss it."

"No, I don't think they will. I'll probably ruin their night and—"

Elec bared his teeth, leaning forward to push his finger against my lips. "*You have got to stop that.* Your lack of self-confidence ends tonight. Three-eleven." My slave sat not a foot away, turning his face to look at the Main Master. "When she talks down to herself, spank her. Put her over your knee and spank her ass until she cries. When she cries, fuck her, sobbing and all. Let her fight you, but don't let her win."

"He takes orders from me, thank you very much."

The Main Master's smile beamed, his lids clearly heavier than normal. They were barely open at all.

"I'm the Main Master. I'm not doing this for me. I'm doing this for you. He'll listen to me, or I'll take him away from you. One of you will learn. Hopefully, both of you."

To argue or fight was pointless.

"Fine. I'll try my best, and hopefully they like it. Like I mentioned before, I haven't played it on guitar yet. It's only the song. I know the tune I'm going for but...I'll try."

"You can't hold a paper with lyrics and play at the same time. I already have a guitarist on the way. You'll sing for him, and he'll figure out the music part of it for you."

My head cocked to the side. "You didn't."

The Main Master laughed, and I cursed under my breath.

"I did. You should know he's pretty pissed."

"It's the story of our entire relationship."

"Seventy-seven is...coming around. Maybe. He's just as much being tested as you are. You're more disciplined, believe it or not."

"I don't want to sing in front of him. He's just going to berate me like he always did."

"Did you ever think to listen to his advice?"

Anger boiled in my stomach, simmering until I pushed my blame at him to the side and thought over the Main Master's words.

"I didn't. I probably should have."

"You'll learn more by listening than by repeating and learning from mistakes. Other people's knowledge might not always be right for what we want, but it doesn't hurt to consider outside options." He finished his drink. "I should write a fucking book."

I laughed, my smile not staying in place as I spotted Pistol heading up the stairs with his guitar. He wasn't with his slave and seeing mine only seemed to make him even angrier.

"Great. Here we go."

I barely finished before he bound up the last two steps, sliding in the opposite side of the booth.

"You're drunk."

Elec reached over, pouring himself another glass.

"And I intend to get even drunker." He gestured the full glass towards me. "She's writing new songs. You'll listen and help her."

"What the hell is going on here, Main Master? First you tell me I can't ask favors of you, and the next thing I know, you're asking them of me."

Elec took a sip, a glare appearing. "Do you want your favor?"

Pistol paused. "I do."

"Then you'll do as I say."

"Play guitar for her, here, so she can…" Pistol looked around. "Entertain your guests?"

Laughter came from the Main Master. He sat up, leaning his forearms on the table.

"You're going to do so much more than that. You're going to take Lilian under your wing. You're going to promote her. You're going to rave how her new songs are the best thing you've heard in years. And you're going to make it believable because despite the war you two have going on, they are. You know she's good."

Pistol's eyes came to me briefly before returning. "I never denied that."

"You never made her believe it, either."

At Elec's words, he looked down at the table as the Main Master continued.

"You are the best in the world right now, Seventy-seven. When Forty-two's music releases, she'll mirror you. And I won't own just one rock god. I'll own two. Both versions: male and female. You can make this hard on yourselves, or you can both be smart and come together. Imagine what you can do if you both stopped fighting with each other, and instead fought for the futures you want." Elec paused. "You're raising your nephew, Pistol. He's pretty much your son. He has no mother or father. Think about what this could do for him."

My eyes went wide as my gaze jerked to the one man I used to think would be the worst father in the world. Could he truly be raising a child? He did appear...sober. Angry, but level-headed, unlike his stumbling past self who was out of control on booze and drugs.

"I don't need to be told what's good for him. I'm very much aware of the future I want him to have. I'm seeing very fast what it's going to take to make it happen." He let out a breath, closing his eyes. "I really don't think it'll work." He opened, looking at me. "No offense Lilian, but I'm trying to stay as far away from drama as I can. When you and I were together—"

My hand shot up. "I don't think either of us are the same people we were in those days. Life was...fucked up. For both of us. And I don't want you to hold my hand through anything. The less time we spend together, the better. But you know what they did to me. *You have to know.* I didn't deserve to be ruined because of my unique creativity. I fucking love the music part of me. It's the only place I feel whole. To turn into some pop princess and change everything about my music?" My head shook. "I'm not a sellout, Pistol. Not even for a dream. I couldn't do it. I've fought for this part of my life, and you know I have the scars to prove it. To give that up, as if none of it mattered? You'd never do that. They wouldn't have even asked you. *You're a guy.* All I am is a pretty face and a sex-sells advertisement. I left modeling to get away from the sexualization. I took out the implants. Jesus...I deserve a real chance at my dream. *Just let me be me.* That's all I ask. If you're not feeling my new music and don't want to back me, I'm fine with that. I truly am because I know I'm proud as hell of what I created. But don't turn your back on me again without it being justified. Just...*listen.* I really think this can be something. It could be a lot better with your help."

"God dammit." He let out a groan, looking between me and the Main Master. "Let me hear it."

I reached into the top of my dress, pulling the paper from my bra.

"Still the same, I see."

My lips twisted as Pistol turned to the edge of the seat, placing the guitar on his knee.

"Words from the heart stay closest to the heart. You know."

"Yes, I do."

Pistol got quiet, staring down at his guitar as I looked over the lyrics. I was shaking again. A glass of water sat a good foot in front of the Main Master, and I grabbed it, taking a drink.

"Okay. Here goes nothing...and everything."

I let out a breath, starting off in a low hum. One word after the next. One face behind my closed lids. I didn't need to see my paper to unlock my soul from the cage it stayed trapped behind. Music set me free. Music was my life. It was also Pistol's. I didn't even make it to the chorus before music enveloped me like a blanket. The chords were slow, like me, twisting and winding in notes that held me captive to their erotic tune. It was everything and more than I could have dreamed for my words. For my song. I may have made it, but Pistol brought it to life with his creative genius, and I couldn't deny him credit. Not even after all the ways he hurt me.

"That is...so fucking good." The Main Master's voice had my eyes opening, but it didn't have me stopping. Pistol was looking between me and the guitar with approval on his face, but my stare turned to find one person. The one who waited for my every order. The one who inspired more than feelings. The one who had me.

My hand settled on three-eleven's shoulder as he stared ahead, and I didn't care that anyone saw. The Main Master didn't seem to give it a thought, and Pistol was all about the music. Nine-thirty-two and Dane were watching, but the way they studied me wasn't my concern either. I was focused. I suddenly had a wealth of hope and belief in what I was capable of. I had the backing of two of the most powerful men in the world, and my future was up to me. I was going to fight to the death for this, *and I was going to win.*

MO3II

The night couldn't have gone more perfect for my Mistress. She was every bit headed for fame. Her future was set, and even the Master I hated the most had left in a surprisingly good mood. But where there seemed to be a light at the end of the tunnel for her, it left all of us lost in the dark waiting for a direction. We got nothing when we got home or when we'd awoken this morning. Not one word. Our Mistress was back to work again, ignoring us as she wrote things down, only to erase and rewrite something new. It was fascinating to watch, but not something the soldier seemed to be able to handle. He'd been in a bad mood for the last hour and growing worse by the minute.

"That's five."

My Mistress looked up from the pad of paper she held, throwing nine-thirty-two a look as she glanced between him and Dane who were sitting next to each other.

"What's five?"

"Sighs. You're aggravated."

"I am now. You're interrupting me."

The soldier paused. "A sigh is an indication of stress and anxiety. My mission is to make the Mistress happy."

"No." Her head tilted as she elongated the word. "Your mission is to protect me and obey whatever I say."

Silence.

"I think the Mistress needs to take a break or the stress will increase. This is protecting you."

Her face hardened, and her eyes flicked to me for the briefest moment. She placed down the pad of paper on the coffee table, moving to sit on the edge of the cushion.

"Alright. You don't want me stressed. What do you suggest I do? How should I relax?"

There was a slight hesitation before the soldier opened his mouth, but he quickly shut it. I saw my Mistress's lids lower, but it was so quick. What was she doing? What was she thinking?

"I will draw you a bath. The Mistress likes baths."

My back straightened against the wall before I could stop it. *Thump-thump. Thump-thump.* For the briefest moment, all I could hear was my heartbeat in my ears.

"Maybe a bath would be nice." She stood, and so did the soldier.

Thump-thump. Thump-thump. Thump-thump.

"You can sit, Nine-thirty-two." The Mistress's eyes came to me, and I could barely breathe.

"Dane."

We all looked towards the slave, who's face was suddenly caught off guard with surprise.

"Mistress."

"Come bathe me."

"...if that's what you want."

There was slight fear in Dane's voice but more apprehension. As she smiled at him, his own lips pulled back at the side. It melted as his gaze suddenly snapped to me.

Whatever he saw on my face, I wasn't sure. It had my Mistress looking in my direction, but she just pulled his arm, leading him into the bedroom door and disappearing from view.

"I am not incapable of my duties."

I glanced at the soldier.

"You're not supposed to be talking."

"I *am* capable."

"I don't understand your kind. Are you not trained to stay quiet unless spoken to?"

The soldier's glare only intensified.

"Do not act like you are above me. You are not a good soldier."

"You're right. I'm not a soldier."

"But that's who she should have. How can she rely on you to protect her when I'm gone? You are not qualified for such duties."

"How do you know what I'm qualified in? You don't know me."

I tried to keep my voice down, but my building anger had no buffer. I was confused. Raging now that my Mistress was now choosing Dane. Had I done something wrong? Was I not good enough? The soldier didn't think I was and that had me doubting myself. If he could sense it, could my Mistress?

"You are slave three-eleven, trained in mixed martial arts, specializing in Brazilian jiu jitsu. You've won four pro fights, winning three by submission and one from a knockout. I know you, Ravi Santos, and I'm better than you."

"Keep thinking that. So did everyone else."

Laughter had me glancing over to the bedroom door. I inched even closer, straining to hear what was being said.

"Exactly, so relax. We got off on the wrong foot. It's just." She paused. *"Three-eleven is very important to me. Slave, when I choose someone, they become mine. I'm very protective over those I care about, and that's not many people. Do you under-stand? Five had no right calling him names. I warned him."*

"You did, Mistress."

"I have a temper. I'm reactive when provoked. It's gotten me

133

in more trouble than anyone knows, and it's a battle I fight constantly. It's why I'm here more than out there. I'm just sorry you had to witness what you did. With five...I couldn't tolerate that sort of behavior. I'd do the same if someone were being mean to you."

I tried to move even closer at the sudden silence, but the soldier started humming. My gaze cut back over to him. "You are not a blank slate. Not a real blank slate."

"I'm special. You are not. Especially now that you've been changed back."

The moment I put my ear by the edge of the opening for the door, more humming. I glared at the soldier, wishing more than anything that I could jump up and choke him out.

"Will you knock that off?"

"Eavesdropping is a sign of insecurity."

"And running your mouth is a way to get hurt."

The soldier stood. "Are you threatening me?"

"Sit down and be quiet. The Mistress will hear you."

"I don't take threats; I eliminate them."

"If you don't sit down, you will force me to call the Mistress back in here and she will be angry that you're misbehaving. Think about it."

The soldier glanced at the door, not looking happy as he sat back down against the wall. More laughter only made us madder. Water finally sounded and just thinking about Dane in there helping her undress, possibly touching her, sent fire through my veins.

Maybe nothing was happening. It didn't matter if it was. The Mistress didn't belong to me. I'd never have claim on her, and I had to accept what that meant. But could I? The slight tremble of my hand said otherwise.

"If you were a good protector, you'd admit you're not qualified to take care of the Mistress."

"I am qualified. Stop talking to me."

"I'm going to state my concerns to her. It's clear to everyone here, she needs to put you in a different position or send you back."

A small growl left me, but I didn't respond. I sat against the wall, moving the foot over, where I'd been sitting before. I let my anger consume me, eating away at me even more. The water eventually turned off, and the Mistress and Dane even returned. I kept my stare down, wallowing in ways to be better.

A mix of lavender and spice filled the room, and I soaked it in. Dane didn't go back to the soldier. He took a seat a few feet away from me as the Mistress reached for her pad of paper. I glanced at the slave, but he wouldn't even look at me. My stomach turned, and my teeth clenched as I battled duty and love.

"I have to admit, nine-thirty-two, the bath was exactly what I needed."

"Because I know what is best. That is my job. It is also my job to inform you when I feel you're making a mistake." The soldier stood from across the room, and I couldn't stop myself from standing as well.

"You think I'm making a mistake?"

Before she could get out another word, he took a step towards me, still staring me down.

"I believe the Mistress has let her emotions get in the way of rationality. The slave, Ravi Santos, must be killed or sent back."

"Killed?" I took a step forward too. "*You can try.*"

"Wait one minute. What did you call him?"

"I called him by his name. He doesn't deserve a number. He's not a protector. He's barely a slave."

"I can protect the Mistress just fine."

But the soldier didn't respond. His stare went to the woman standing in the middle of the room between us.

"Mistress, my mission is—"

"Enough." She closed her eyes, tilting her head back as she

135

breathed in deeply. "I will not hear another word of your concerns. You take orders from me. It's not the other way around."

"No. I have a mission from the Main Master. I will follow it."

Her lids opened, half in shock, half in rage.

"I beg your pardon? Did you just tell me no?"

"The Mistress is not safe."

"Yes I am. You'll stop this talk right now."

"Everyone knows the Mistress is not safe."

"That's it. I've had enough." She headed towards the bar that separated the kitchen and living area. "I'm calling the Main Master."

It was a push from the soldier's leg that had me racing forward. He was going for the Mistress, and she'd barely turned around with her phone in time to see me put myself a foot between them.

"Were you coming after me?"

Her voice was loud as she tried to step around me, but I didn't let her as I kept my focus on the soldier who was now fixated on me. His breaths were starting to grow heavy, and there was a crazed expression as he stepped in even more. Despite the emotions he may have felt, a part of him wasn't quite acting on them. Not yet.

"Call the Main Master, Mistress." My hands lifted. Not only as an expression of caution, but as an opportunity for control. If he decided to act on his need to hurt either one of us, I was going to be ready and have the upper hand. "*Now*, Mistress."

"Calling."

"Soldier, you need to go sit down and wait for the Main Master." His head jerked as I kept my voice calm. "We can let him decide my fate, okay?"

"Main Master. This is Forty-two. You have to come get your soldier."

As if the Mistress's voice was a trigger, he slammed his hands to the side, knocking mine out of the way. The spin of my body only gave me more momentum as I threw my elbow up, catching him right in the nose as he tried to get by me. His head reared back, but where he should have stumbled or fell, he didn't move. It was as if pain didn't affect him at all.

Blood poured from his nose and large hands grabbed my biceps from behind, throwing me across the room as if I weighed nothing. It was her screams that had me trying to react before I even hit the floor. But it wasn't screams of terror. My Mistress was pissed. Murderously so as she pulled her hair free and slashed towards him with the dagger-style hair pin.

"You think you can come after me? Come after me like my father?" Her wide swing was level with his stomach, barely missing as he surged back. "You think you can hurt my slave? *Hurt what's mine too?*"

Again, she swung, not close enough as he lunged to the side. With a quick grab, he held on, taking her back. Her cry was filled with pain as he crushed her wrist making her drop the weapon. His hold as he squeezed around her wasn't any softer.

"Let go of her. She's your Mistress. *Your mission.* You don't want to hurt her."

"Hurting her is okay if it's protecting her. And I am doing that. *From you.*"

My hands lifted. "You want to protect her from me? Why don't you put her outside and lock us in? You and I will handle this between ourselves. How about that?"

For a moment, the soldier seemed to contemplate my idea. The pause had my Mistress's legs dropping out from underneath her, and her using her weight as her arms shot up, breaking his hold. The surprise that she would even know something like that only lasted long enough for the recognition to register. It didn't matter. Instinct had me surging right for him now that she was free.

We hit hard, clipping the side of the sofa as the soldier tried to get his arm around my neck. He spun me into the wall, knocking the mirror off. Had I not been expecting the move, he would have gotten me in a headlock. Luckily, I was able to shuck his hold, spinning us even more as we crashed into the floor. The end table shattered, sending even more broken glass and wood skittering down around us.

"Nine-thirty-two, stop! Nine-thirty-two, stand down! *Charlie one.* Charlie one!" She growled. "It didn't do anything. *Fuck. Yes, they're fighting.* Hurry up!"

The Mistress was staying even with us, close, but not close enough to interfere. I was almost positive she had the phone at her ear, but I couldn't look to see exactly what she was doing. I kept my focus on the soldier who was combating every move I tried to lock in.

"You're not safe. You have to die."

The strained words did nothing but feed the bubbling heat that was scorching my insides. My instability as a slave grew. My uncertainty over what was right or wrong fed my brutality. I swung, smashing into his face, trying to get back to his back. He stayed just out of reach as I focused on crushing bone with even more hits. I punched in quick succession, working him to his side even more. His elbow came back, connecting with my ribs and knocking the air from me.

Not. Safe. Must. Die."

Pain webbed under my eye, branching out into my face as bright lights blinded me. I tried blinking them away, but the next hit came just as fast. A hand wrapped around the front of my throat, slipping free as I used his thigh to push myself out of his reach.

"Must. Die. M—"

I grabbed his shirt, throwing my weight forward enough to catch him unaware. My fist went right for his throat, and all I wanted to do was put my arm right through it. The power behind my hit had a sound gurgling free, and both of his hands flying to his throat. It was all I needed to take his back and cup his chin.

"Slave."

But I barely heard my Mistress. With the other hand, I held to his head, using my weight to twist with everything I had. For as much as time drug out, the snap was fast and loud. I felt it in my entire being, reverberating through me like a million solid 'pops'. It sounded like relief. Like...*I was going to be in so much trouble.*

MISTRESS B-0042

I t wasn't the kill I had been wanting, it was better. More of a challenge than Dane. Also more of a threat. My slave had protected me when it mattered the most. That was more of a turn on than I could have imagined. I wasn't naïve to think it would always be that way, but it counted where it wouldn't have before. It was a start. The ultimate foundation to what I now knew he would do if I asked. Better...*if I didn't*. I warned him when I called out. That should have given him clarity not to act. He still went through with it.

"And that's exactly how it happened?"

Three-eleven sat on the sofa holding the icepack to his eye, staring ahead and nodding.

"That's right, Main Master. Just like that."

"You were on the phone. You heard most of it. I told you he wasn't safe."

Elec shook his head at my words. "He shouldn't have declined so quickly. You said you took a bath at his request. Go back to that part."

I rolled my eyes.

"I was trying to work. He said because I kept sighing that I was too stressed. He suggested he draw me a bath."

"But he didn't, because three-eleven was arguing with him in here."

"That's right."

The Main Master's brow drew in, confused. He glanced to Dane, pointing.

"Where was he?"

"With me, of course."

"With you." A sigh left Elec. "There's the issue. He suggested the bath, but you didn't allow him to accompany or help you."

"Of course not. You said you wanted me to break him."

"Break him," the Main Master snapped. "Not break his damn neck."

"He came after me! Look at my arm. I'm covered in bruises. My slave saved my life. If it wasn't for him, I might be dead right now. Then, what?"

The anger left Elec as he glanced down. "I'm glad you're not dead. And I did ask for this. It just seems implausible. He shouldn't have responded in that manner. He's not a blank slate, per se. He should have been better. What the hell happened?"

"I told you if anyone could do it, it's me. I'm cursed. *You're welcome.*"

The Main Master waved to the guards to take the body bag out.

"Dammit. I can't believe he went downhill so fast. Why would he believe your slave isn't safe? I don't think he'd use that as an excuse. He had to have a reason. You didn't voice any concerns?"

"Of course not. I've always had confidence in three-eleven's abilities. Why do you think I bought him? I saw the list of his skills. He was a professional fighter. I know enough self-defense to know he was more than capable of protecting me."

"Someone told that soldier something."

I glanced at three-eleven, following his gaze to Dane. Although I didn't turn around, I paused as I thought back. Hadn't he been close to the soldier lately? They'd practically been sitting next to each other for days. And they'd only been a foot apart when I told Dane to bathe me. Did my slave realize it too? Given the way he wouldn't take his eyes off Dane, I was pretty sure I knew the answer.

Putting my hand on three-eleven's shoulder, I stood straighter. "I don't know if someone tried to manipulate nine-thirty-two, but if they did, they deserve to die for putting me at risk. I know it wasn't me who doubted my slave. Three-eleven is irreplaceable. Slaves come and go. He's not normal like the others. He may not be entirely a blank slate anymore, but he'll hold that title from me. Where I go, he goes. If he feels strongly about something, I will stand by him. That's just the end of it." I smiled at Elec. "So long as three-eleven keeps me safe, he can do no wrong."

The Main Master's gaze left mine, narrowing as it glanced in Dane's direction. He looked down, licking his lips as a small tug pulled at the side of his mouth. His gaze came back to mine, holding my stare with a knowing only Masters and Mistresses would understand.

"Your slave did good protecting you. I know I'm upset about the soldier, but this was a big lesson for me, and I'm appreciative of it. Between three-eleven and nine-thirty-two, the lab will learn a lot. I feel horrible about your arm. Why don't you let me make it up to you? It's almost dinner time. I'll walk you to one of the restaurants so we can get you a food order to-go. What do you say?"

I looked down at my robe but knew where he was going with this.

"I would love that. If you'll give me a moment, I'll just get dressed." I held out my hand to three-eleven. "Come help me dress, slave."

Without pause he stood, lacing his fingers through mine as we headed for my bedroom. I shut the door behind us, leading him into the closet. I didn't go for the clothes. I grabbed each side of his face, lowering him towards me until he was only inches away.

"We both know why that soldier turned on you. We know who is responsible. You said you loved me."

One of three-eleven's eyes were completely swollen shut. Bruising darkened his face from temple to mid-cheek. Despite the transformation, he couldn't hide what was obvious.

"I do."

"Not good enough. Say the words."

"...I love you."

My lips brushed his. He stayed unresponsive. Detached. It had me pressing harder for seconds before I pulled back, turning my voice just as cold as the mask he wore.

"Everyone loves. It's how they love and what they do that sets them apart from the rest. Show me what loving someone means to *you*. I want proof of how far you're willing to go to protect this love you feel." I reached over, grabbing a floor length, black, long-sleeved dress. As I put it on, I kept my stare right on his. He was intense. Even shaking as he took me in. He was confused on how far he should go. Maybe he was even wondering if I meant what he thought I did. I'd let him figure that out on his own. "When I get back, I better be proud."

I grabbed the black platformed wedges, leaving him behind as I kept at a steady pace. The Main Master was still standing in the spot next to the shattered end table. I took a seat on the sofa, not even looking as I slid on my shoes. My glare was on one person, and he was squirming as I murdered any thought of safety he might have felt he had.

He knew I knew, and with every second that ticked by, he squirmed even more. Panic danced in his eyes, growing as my slave walked from the bedroom door, not moving any closer. I glanced at him, only catching his blank stare for a moment before it transformed to rage. He turned towards the slave, waiting as I stood.

"I'll be back. You two have fun."

Standing, I looped my arm to the Main Master's.

"Mistress, wait. I..." Dane's voice was full of fear as I continued to the door. I didn't look back. I didn't even acknowledge him. It was the scrambling as I got to the doorway that had me turning. My slave had Dane's bicep, holding him still so he couldn't run. "I don't want to stay with him. *Mistress, please.*"

"I'm curious." I paused at the door, projecting every ounce of indifference towards Dane that I held. His life meant nothing. His fear made me happy. His death...not priceless, but worth the cost. "People spend a lifetime trying to express their love. They buy their significant other fancy things. Have mementos made. Some even think a legal union is the answer. Do you know what I think, Dane?"

"What?"

A tear raced down the slave's cheek. He tried jerking again, but he didn't break free from three-eleven's hold.

"I don't think love is the little things. Quite the opposite. I think it's how extreme you're willing to go to prove your love. Anyone can buy flowers or jewelry. Tattoos are just ink and needles. Scars stay, but even that would never be enough for me. *A corpse.* A life. An imprint of a human being...gone...*for you.* What says I love you more than that? Murder is memorable. Death is forever."

MO3II

"My mother was a hard woman to please. She had me working the streets, thieving, selling drugs, doing whatever I could to bring us food or money. Nothing was good enough, and she beat me every chance she got. When I think back, I don't have a single memory of when it all began. Perhaps I was too young. Or maybe I blocked it out because I never wanted to return to begin with. Do you remember your childhood? Your mother? What about all those women you fucked? I bet you couldn't wait to add mine to your never-ending list. You were just so proud of what you did. Did you see her as one of them? Another number? A conquest? Did you really think she was equal to you?"

"No. *Never.* Three-eleven, I swear!"

"You just keep lying. *Be honest with me.*"

Whack!

Whack!

Whack!

Small pieces of wood splintered off from the end of the thick leg of the coffee table. Dane curled even more in a ball, crying out as I beat against him with severe force. Lacerations were bleeding from some of the bruising welts covering his already broken arms and ribs. As I circled around his fetal form, all I kept thinking about was how he manipulated the soldier to try to kill me or have me leave.

"I asked you a question?"

Whack!

Whack!

"Please! I didn't do anything. I didn't mean to dis…re-spect the Mistress." He sobbed, peeking out through one of the arms covering his head and face. "I didn't mean it. I was new to this and being s-stupid. I'm sorry. I promise you; I'm sorry."

"Sorry for disrespecting her?" I swung down, slamming the large chunk of wood into the center of his curved back as he hugged to his legs. "Or you're sorry for trying to get the soldier to kill me?"

A loud cry got tangled with his yell as he rolled and tried to catch his breath. It only had me slamming the end down on his stomach causing him to double over once again.

"You know I love her. You knew that when they took me. I came back here focused on being as blank as I could. As good as I could…*for her.* I didn't threaten you. I was respectful despite all I wanted to do was tear your fucking head off. What did that get me?"

I brought both of my hands over my head to hold the leg.

"Please! Please, no. I only wanted you gone so I'd be safe. You're not okay. I didn't want you to hurt me again. Please!"

"You were worried I'd hurt you?" The thick wood cracked down the middle as I broke it along his side. "I'm not going to hurt you. I'm going to do so much more than that."

Fingers clawed at the floor as Dane tried to breathe and get away. I let him as I broke the leg apart, immediately stabbing the end down on the back of his thigh. Howling filled the space as the top part of the slave's body shot down towards his leg. He was having no issues getting oxygen anymore as he screamed through the pain.

"No more! I'm sorry!"

I ignored him, more needing to speak my mind as I focused. "I think a part of my Mistress may love me too. Maybe not a lot. Not yet, but do you know what I have that you don't? *Time.* I'm going to make her love me too. I'm going to be the best blank slate she'll ever have. The only one she'll ever have."

I pulled the jagged stake free watching as blood dripped to the floor. A trail started to form as Dane tried to make his way to the front door. He had nowhere to go, and he knew it, but he wasn't going to stay still and let me kill him either. If it weren't for the multiple bones already broken from my beating at the beginning, perhaps he would have given me a good chase. Thing was, I didn't have the time or patience for that. It'd already been twenty or so minutes. I was just having too much fun making him suffer. I didn't want it to end. Not after seeing the little touches here and there from my Mistress. Or knowing how much he wanted her. Or what I'd been through the last few years. The beatings. It was all still there. The training. The agony associated with it. I was unraveling into someone I didn't know. Someone just as loyal as they were lethal.

"I'll do any-thing. I'll—"

I flipped him over, stabbing the end into his thigh. The top half of Dane's body jolted forward, and my head whipped over as the door opened. My Mistress took one look at Dane and lifted her eyes to me.

"Good. You're not finished. I didn't get Italian. I settled for steak. Meat and murder. It sounded like the perfect combo." She headed for the table, putting down the plastic, fancy to-go bags. "Continue. Just steer clear from the end of the sofa. I want a front row seat to the end."

Did I smile? God, I had, and I hadn't been able to control it. It didn't matter as the Mistress took out her box, walking in the kitchen to get a knife. I pulled the wood out again, ignoring Dane's pleading as I pulled him further back into the space and grabbed a large, jagged piece of the broken mirror. If my Mistress wanted a view, I'd give her the best one.

"I'll be g-good. I'm. I. I'm sorry. I'll be. Mis-ess"

Dane dropped a shade of color as I pulled him to sit up. I kneeled behind, barring my free arm across his chest until my Mistress took her seat. She was holding a plate, and she placed her wine glass on the coffee table. There was a peppiness mixed with lust as she smiled and started cutting into her meat.

"Continue, slave."

"G-God. Fuck. Fuck, please!" The sobs were so deep, Dane's body shook but barely any sound broke free. "Mistress, p-please!"

"She won't save you." I whispered the words in his ear. "You belong to me now. You betrayed me." I lifted the glass, flattening the edge just under his eye. "My mother used to say, Vingança é um reflexo da dor da sua nãoção. That's Portuguese. It pretty much means, *revenge is a reflection of the pain you can't run away from.* Maybe she was right on this one thing. Maybe she's wrong." I pulled back the glass from the mirror, catching both of our reflections as we stared. "My revenge will be worth both of our pain."

I forced him down, stabbing the end through one of his eyes, pulling out just as fast to embed the glass through the other. The screams became demonic. Dane's body thrashed as he tried pushing against me, despite most of his fingers were broken. Even his forearm was limp skin and protruding bone from the beating I gave him at the beginning of my wrath. Whole, he didn't stand a chance. Broken...I was just playing with my food.

"Shhh." I held my hand to his throat, keeping him from flailing. "Respire um pouco. Take a breath. Breathe."

Please! Three. Th-Th—"

"You're beyond asking for forgiveness."

I smashed the glass on the floor, shoving and forcing small pieces past his lips. I spun his head to my lap, holding my palm over his mouth with a grip he couldn't break.

"Swallow it."

"Mmmhhh. Mmmhhhhh!"

"Swallow it right now or I'll cut out your tongue. You're going to pay for turning that soldier against me. You're also going to take responsibility for how disrespectful you treated my Mistress. For how *unworthy* you are to even look or speak to her."

Muffled sounds hummed and sobbed against my hand as he fought and thrashed. I let a minute go by. Two. More. It wasn't until I saw him swallow and jerk that I let my stare cut up to my Mistress. Her own lips were parted, and her lids were heavy. The plate was sitting on the table, no longer on her lap. Before I could stop myself, the words tumbled free, leaving me.

"She's the most beautiful person I've ever seen." I kept my voice low, and my hand over his mouth, dragging him back up to rest against my chest. I couldn't stop staring at her entranced face as she watched me. My legs latched around Dane's waist, and slowly I eased my arm under his chin, locking onto my other wrist to make the hold secure. I could feel the blood beginning to stream down the bend of my elbow as he silently sobbed. I heard none of it. I just kept squeezing his throat tighter and tighter as his feet tried finding ground to help him break free. He didn't stand a chance. Neither did I as I fell even more under her spell.

"She deserves to be cherished. *Respected.*" Gurgling. A jolt. "She's been fighting for far too long. She doesn't have to do that alone anymore. I'll fight for her." I whispered, swallowing hard as she eased to the ground, slowly crawling her way to me. "I'll fight for you, Mistress. *With you.* I won't say a word. I won't have to."

And I wouldn't. My actions would speak loud enough.

I'd be her protector. A body for her to use as she saw fit. I'd be the one she could rely on when the world became too much. I'd be there for her when she needed someone in her darkest, lust-filled hours. I may have not been a blank slate anymore, but aside from our stolen moments, she wouldn't know the difference. I was hers, and I'd do whatever I needed to keep proving that.

The End

Couple B-0019
Garden of the Gods
International Bestselling Author
A.A. Dark
Copyright © 2023 by A.A.Dark

All Rights Reserved

RULES

Rules are subject to change. If you neglect to follow these rules, you will undergo an investigation/trial where punishment is evaluated by the Board and Main Master, Elec Wexler. Punishment can range from fines to lockup in Hell Row to Death.

1) Keep your hands to yourself.

2) The only property you may destroy is your own. (slaves included.)

3) You are a number. Your peers are a number. Use them.

4) Respect your neighbor's privacy.

5) GOTG is NOT to be discussed outside of this facility.

GLOSSARY

W

Virgin slave. Wears a white robe during the auction.

B

Nonvirgin slave. Wears a blue robe during the auction.

D

Docile, drugged slave. Can be w or b. Heavily trained. Good for elderly or those with disabilities.

M

Male slave.

Crow

(fc: female crow, mc: male crow) Ruined, disfigured slave. Convicts fall into this category. Black robe during the auction. Usually the cheapest slave.

Blank slate

Mostly male slaves who have undergone forced indoctrination through various scientific methods. (Brainwashing, programming, training, etc.) Most remember their identity but have key parts of their past erased if it could pose a threat or alter their role as a slave. They're programmed to be focused solely on their Mistress or Master. They are made to be obedient, loyal, and protective.

*Master numbers written out throughout the stories are capitalized. (Ex. Twelve-twelve.) Also, the word Master throughout is capitalized. (Ex. Master Twelve-twelve.)

*Slave numbers written out will not be capitalized. The word slave throughout will not be capitalized outside from the beginning of a sentence.

"WHEN IT ALL CAME DOWN TO IT, IT WAS ALWAYS YOU AND ME. IT'S ALWAYS BEEN YOU AND ME."- DEAN WINCHESTER

PROLOGUE

MISTRESS B-0019-2 -RORY

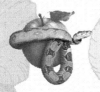

Garden of the Gods
Colorado Springs underground facility

Perhaps I should have been impressed. We were in a private underground city. We were surrounded by top-of-the-line luxury. Guards were stationed throughout for safety, and we had slaves at our beck and call. It wasn't every day that someone got to attend an auction to buy real human beings. I was impressed with that. Thing was, I would have been just as happy in some piece of shit house in the worst neighborhood in LA. I didn't care for materialistic shit like my twin sister did. I didn't even care about the attention we were shown, or the anonymity we were given concerning our true identities. There was only one thing I was here for, and it was for the fun I'd missed after the first auction. I wanted more blood. Sex. As I took in the Main Master walking the stage, all I wanted was for him to get on with the show. I already knew the rules. This time, I wasn't going to jump the gun out of anger and jealousy. I'd be good. I'd do better.

"Welcome to the second auction for the Garden of the Gods,

For those who didn't make it to the first, I'm going to recap this as quickly as possible. You've taken the classes. You've learned the rules. Even though our slaves have been trained, you are going to have to earn your titles. The B's in front of your number are for a reason. This is the Beta stage. Some of you will make our foundation, some of you won't. Your outside status got you here, but that means nothing inside the Gardens. You are a number. That's it. Your identity means absolutely zero. Here, there is no power or favoritism. This world is mine, and you better hope like hell you can follow the rules, or you won't survive in it." His eyes scanned the room. "On the plus side, a lot of you have made it this far and that speaks volumes. I have high hopes for most of you."

Hazel smiled, leaning over to whisper. "That's us. I wonder how long it takes to get Alpha status?"

"No fucking clue. I'm more wondering how long this introduction is going to last. Do we have to listen to this crap? We already know the rules. Let's go head to the room that houses the men. I want to start looking through the book."

"You're so impatient. We talked about the rewards for patience. Instant gratification gets you nothing, Rory. This won't take long."

I almost argued. I wanted to. I was in the mood to fight, and that didn't look promising for whatever slave we ended up choosing. Instead, I buried the anger with the rest, turning back to look at the stage.

"For those new to us tonight, I don't think I need to go much into how this place is not Whitlock. The rules are different. The location is different." I let out a sigh. "I am *not* the old Main Master, Bram Whitlock. A few Masters from the first auction had to learn that the hard way. You cannot buy yourself out of trouble. You cannot *buy me*. I will never let the Garden of the Gods fall."

"Blah, blah, blah. Hazel, I don't have time for this. I'm going to slip out."

"*Don't you dare.* Give it a little longer."

Any longer and I'd scream. The Main Master paced the stage some more, taking in the audience that stared at him like the God he was. While everyone kissed his ass, I was probably the only one who didn't care for him. He made me feel threatened, and that caused me to be defensive and want to lash out. It wasn't a good thing.

"Let's recap bidding for those who don't know. First, we have the white, or w's. These are the virgins. We also have the b's: or blue." He paused. "Not virgins. We also have the d's, who now have their own room, at the back right, behind all of you. They're docile, trained, and good for those who are looking for a long-term slave. Lastly, come the black, or as we call them, the crows. These could be fun for anyone looking for a bloodbath or just a fun time. They're the convicts. The disfigured. The old. *Repulsive.*" He came to a stop at the end of the stage. "You get it. Also in that category, you'll find the breeders. I want to make a note of some changes in this category." His hand lifted through the pause. "Listen to me closely. I won't repeat it. You are not allowed to bid on them unless you've already gone through the steps and signed a contract with me. We had a few try last auction even though this was already stated in bold caps in the pamphlet. If you bid on a breeder, and you haven't met with me, your bid will be revoked, and I will fine you ten thousand dollars for wasting my time. Breeders are special. Breeders are for only those I approve of."

"For those looking for our programmable, 'blank slate' males and *now* females, your auction is just through that door off to the right. The information was in the packet, but just in case you missed it last auction, these are those who have had a portion of their memories erased. They're aware. They know who they are, but they only remember what we want them to."

159

"The last few weeks have been exciting, to say the least. I've watched some of you grow in your role. The majority have done great with following rules. For those who are new, pay attention. What you buy is yours. You can do whatever you want with it. Fuck it. Kill it. Share it. Marry it. Love it. Eat it. Destroy it." Hesitation. "I don't care so long as you follow the rules. Your business is your own. I can't stress that enough."

"Hazel."

She threw me a look that had my teeth clenching. I was too restless to sit still. We'd still have to find a slave. It all took time. The adrenaline pumping through me said I didn't have enough of that. I needed to *go, go, go.* Where, I had no idea. My mind swam with violence and release. Lately, I was never calm. Never still. It was getting uncontrollable. Seeing my sister smiling and staring at the stage only made me worse. Hazel was perfect, poised in her beauty and sophistication. I could stare at her forever and wallow in my toxic envy. If only she could see like me. *Feel what I did.* Not that I'd ever let her. I was in a push and pull, and change wasn't accepted, only yearned for.

"If you look down the arm of the chair, you will see a button. Do not." He stopped for what felt like ever. "All of you listen and listen good. Let me say it again since others from the first auction learned the hard way. *Do not...* press that button unless you are sure you want to bid. We do not have a lay-a-way plan. You cannot get your slave on loan. If you don't have the money, don't bid. At the Gardens, there's no such thing as accidents. If you bid, you buy. If you can't pay, I will take my payment however I want. Don't believe my threat, *test me.* I'll take everything you own on the outside world, and you can remain here with the slave you couldn't resist. This life can be simple if you just do as you're told. The rules are easy. Complete acceptance into the Garden of the Gods is not. You all signed a contract to get this far. Abide by it, and Alpha status will be yours."

Finally. I didn't wait as I stood. Lights ran the edge of the floor, making their way over the top arches of multiple door-ways. Commotion stirred as heads spun from the stage to the nearest entrance as a line of beautiful women dressed in sheer white robes awaited their cue. I was already heading for the exit. This time I'd be good. This time…I'd do so much better.

MISTRESS B-0019

HAZEL

I had always been the reasonable one. The responsible one. I was definitely the dependable one. When it came to anything significant, Rory found some excuse to run off or hide. She'd never admit that, but I knew my sister better than she knew herself. If I had to describe my identical twin, only one word came to mind: selfish. I could drop another ten adjectives including: greedy, sly, cunning, smothering, bitch—that was a noun— evil. Yes, evil amongst tons of others. If it was negative, it was Rory. From her dark clothes to her melancholy and mopey outlook on life, it's just who she was. And me, I was her complete opposite. Not that anyone would agree. For identical twins, people couldn't tell us apart. Rory was great at pretending to be like me. She even blamed me for her fuck ups, and if I wanted to be honest…I *had* pretended to be her, even taking the blame as her on more than one occasion. We swapped identities so many times, no one knew who or what to believe anymore. Rory and I were okay with that, *sometimes…*

"What about this one?"

"You've said that three different times to men who weren't even close to your taste." I flipped to the next page inside the black binder, scanning over the slaves as I tried to ignore Rory picking at her nails. Her leg was bouncing so hard and fast, she was shaking the entire sofa. "I don't even see why you're so excited. The moment we pick, you're going to do the same thing you did last time."

"Disappear? *Yeah...*"

She rolled her eyes as if it were obvious and there was no other way.

"So, we're playing this game again? I bond, and you come in and fuck it all up. Why can't we just meet him together from the beginning? We share him like we talked about, and just do our own thing."

"Hazel, we didn't talk about that. You said that's what we should do, and I said it was boring as fuck, and I'm not here for a shitty time." Dark hair swayed despite she had the curls piled high on her head. Had she put enough pins in like I told her to? No. Her dark, curly hair was about to go tumbling down her back at any moment. "Let's just pick one already. I need a drink, and you're already driving me crazy."

Flipping the page, I let out a deep breath, taken aback as my eyes locked on a gorgeous face at the upper right of the page. I knew the moment Rory spotted him too because she inhaled, moving in closer.

"Bingo. Tell me you're seeing the same hotness I am."

"Do you think he's *too* hot?"

Rory laughed, a smirk appearing. It had my own face sobering. She'd completely ruined everything last time, and I still hadn't forgiven her for it.

"There's no such thing. The hotter, the more fun. They should really have *all* stats on this page. I wonder how big his cock is?"

"You should come with me. I'll know before you."

"You'll see it, but I'll be the one fucking it. *Prude.*"

"Shut up, Rory. Let's pick two more to be sure."

"You pick two more. I want this one."

"I'm not getting two men again. You'll just kill yours and steal mine. It's pointless. It works better this way. Besides, with only one, you'll have more restraint. You need to work on that anyway. Your temper is getting worse."

"If it's worse, it's your fault, Hazel."

Sequins sparkled as she stood from the black leather sofa. She threw me a challenging look, lifting her clutch to her stomach.

"I'm going to get me a drink, fuck a Master in one of these dark hallways, and I'll be back late. Don't wait up for me. I trust your judgement. Besides..." that evil smile I knew so well appeared as she bit against her bottom lip. "Do me a favor and don't mention me to this one. I want to see something."

"See what?"

Her eyes glanced to the door where the guard stood, only to come back to me.

"Do you remember what we did to Jimmy Pierce a few years ago?"

It was my turn to smile, and it was genuine. It hadn't been anything too bad. "That was a pretty good game we played."

"Yeah. That was fun. Let's do something like that." Rory took a step back. "Put him in the cage. Always in the cage, Hazel. Don't get soft and bond like you always do. That was your mistake with your first slave, and I hope you learned your lesson. For the millionth time, we're not here for a relationship. Cock and blood. That's what we're here for."

"You mean that's what *you're* here for? Slut."

"Jealousy only makes you uglier, Sister. I may have killed your slave, but it was only a matter of time before your true colors showed. I did you a favor. You know how stupid you get when you're in love. All you do is obsess and focus on them. Then you're destroyed when you finally flip out and kill them. It's pathetic."

"You just can't stand that I'm not focused on *you*."

"Because you're mine, Hazel, face it. You're my twin and no man is ever going to come between that. *Ever.* We stick together. We're all we have left."

"Are you still here?"

"No. I'm off to hunt down a Master while you settle this slave in. *Have fun.*"

The sarcasm was thick as she spun and headed from the room. As I continued to flip through the binder, I didn't find anyone I liked better than the slave who'd caught both of our attention. I stood, heading for the kiosk. Even as I entered the information, I still took in everything I could about the slave. Only when I got back to my sofa did I finally shut the binder and lay it down. I didn't sit. I knew it wouldn't be long. Besides, Rory had me all riled up. She drove me mad, and there wasn't anything I could do about it.

"BC-Nineteen." The voice paused, and I froze as I took in the good-looking guard, scanning the room for me. "Mistress Nineteen."

Have fun. You're mine, Hazel.

I wanted to growl or scream. Rory was becoming out of control. She could have men, but I couldn't. Men liked me. Some, anyway, not that they got a chance to get close. *But she wasn't here now.* She'd never know.

As I headed towards the giant guard, I made sure to keep eye contact, breaking away for a moment to take in his lips. His mouth started to widen into a grin, and I didn't miss his interest as I slowed in my approach.

"I'm Mistress Nineteen. Do I get your name?"

There was hesitation as the guard began leading us down the hall.

"Jackson Banks."

"Ooh. I like that name, but I think I like a lot more than that."

Brown eyes glanced over towards me, and his surprise transitioned to interest. *A lot of it.* It had me slowing, and the shy part of me wanting to take over. Seduction wasn't my strong suit. In truth, I didn't have a clue what the hell I was doing, but the guard was still stealing glances at me. It made my mind race making my thought process derail completely.

I searched for something to say. A witty comment. A seductive proposition. Nothing came to mind, making me even more aggravated. How could she be so good at this? I wasn't, no matter how hard I tried to portray this side of her. She was better. Prettier. Sexier. Everything from her slightly fuller lips to her more exotically shaped eyes screamed the better twin. Her breasts were bigger. She had a smaller waist and more curves. She was even a quarter of an inch taller than my average height. Her hair was shinier. I saw all of that, but no one else did. To them, we were the same. They were clueless. *They were blind.*

"There's a lot of doors down this hall." I licked my lips, my heart hammering through the anger and thrill. "Are they all occupied?"

Sweet. Shy. Dammit! I could still detect my real self under the invitation, and the guard's own hesitation didn't help my nervousness.

"Are you curious or does the Mistress need something from me?" His lids narrowed as if he were battling his own demons, but he continued anyway. "If you're requesting, I'm allowed… and…I'm pretty sure the next room is unoccupied."

Rory was probably already pinned against a wall getting fucked. I could do that too. Men wanted me…just not normally more than they wanted her. But this guard was interested, and he was attractive with his height and round eyes. His jaw had just the right definition, and he looked fit under that dark uniform. He could have been everything I needed. That could pose a problem. It could be the answer to a lot more.

"I'm requesting."

My soft voice nearly cracked. The guard slowed, almost

appearing speechless. He spoke something into his mic, grabbing a card. He took a glance at me as he tapped the end against a sensor. Darkness opened up like a black hole, and more, my heart thudded in my chest. I could do this. *I wanted to do this.* Rory would be so pissed if she knew. It was okay for her, but no matter how many times she encouraged my behavior, she was twice as fast to mess things up for me the moment I obliged.

Stepping inside, I could barely catch my breath as an arm swept me in against the guard's hard body. My eyes rolled, closing at the spicy scent of the cologne. As the door clicked behind us, it trapped us in the pitch black. I let a moan leave me as his hands grabbed my ass, bringing me impossibly closer. I fisted into the front of his shirt, and I met his tongue with all the vigor Rory would have. I could feel her take me over as scenes from our past rolled through. I'd seen her make out and fuck so many men. Rory took what she wanted, including me. There wasn't anything she didn't get if she went after it. She had a classic beauty with a rebel twist. Men didn't stand a chance if she targeted them.

"Shit, you taste and smell good."

I moaned into Jackson's mouth, breaking away. "I was just thinking the same about you."

Inch by inch, my dress lifted on my thighs. The guard's hand pushed up, cupping my skin firmly as he moved higher. Rory was wearing the same thing. She was probably feeling the exact scratchiness of the sequins as it moved up to her hips.

"I don't have to see to know I'm feeling lace. You're so beautiful and sexy." The tips of his fingers made a circle over my clit. He pushed back even more, massaging my panties over my entrance. "Tell me what you need, Mistress."

I clung to the guard's uniform shirt as if I were dangling from a cliff. I drew him in closer, forcing the words from some vault I kept hidden inside.

"I don't need a slave for sex. I want *you*. Fuck me but make it fast. I don't have much time."

Vertigo hit as I was spun. My hands shot out to the wall, not prepared for the emptiness at not holding onto the shirt anymore. Clinking sounded from a belt, and I'd know the sound of a zipper from anywhere. My panties were pulled down and when pressure rubbed against my entrance, I could see Rory's face. Her mouth parted through the lust. Her eyes were in slits as she was here yet not. The power would put the hint of a smile on her face as she basked in the thrill of winning. I could see her, and yet, I was still mentally seeing myself as his finger slid in me. I was her. She was me. We were both lost and tumbling through the rights and wrongs of a world we should have been doomed to forever. No one was safe with us outside of here. She wasn't to be trusted, and if I wanted to be completely honest with myself, neither was I.

The guard's finger disappeared, and pressure took its place at my entrance. For the smallest moment, I almost jerked away and ran from the room. The pleasure and my racing mind were the only things keeping me rooted into place.

"Oh...*fuck*." Jackson let out a deep moan as he stretched me. I was so wet and yet it was far from easy for him to fit. It wasn't him. *It was me.* It was Rory, and her constant monitoring and overbearing attitude that made it impossible for me to make a real connection so I could get this far. That had been my problem. I wasn't going to be that person anymore. I made that mistake with my first slave, and he ended up dead before I could make a hint of progress.

The guard withdrew, only to push even deeper. I sucked in air, my eyes shooting open to nothingness. My jaw was dropped from the shock, but Jackson couldn't see that. He was starting to thrust and wrap around me as he pushed to unbelievable depths. What felt like a sigh of relief left me as I adjusted. My body softened, and I let the guard use me as I tuned into all the sensations sparking through.

"Jesus, you feel unbelievable." Fingers pushed between my legs as he rubbed his digits over the top of my slit. I jolted at the sensitivity, and I moaned feeding from the burn that intensified. "I was too distracted to look. You're not married, are you? You're part of a couple."

"Married? No way. I'm a twin."

"No Master to deal with. I like that even better. That is…if you wanted to keep something like this going."

My heavy lids opened, and my nails dug into the wall. All thoughts stopped, splitting off and multiplying into what seemed like a million more. Had I thought this would be my secret to bask in during the impossible times with Rory? Had my mind even drifted to these possibilities? It had, even if the repercussions were…lifechanging.

"You'd like to be with me after this?"

"Are you kidding?" Harder he thrust. "Why wouldn't I want to be with you after this?"

"I…don't know. You're the first person I've been with in four years. The second person, ever. I don't usually do this." One of my hands dropped from the wall, digging into his thigh as he made sounds in my ear. Why was I telling him this? I wanted to be Rory. I was ruining my mystery. I was damn near confessing my entire life. But it could work in my favor. With how hesitant this guard was…*I knew it would.*

"Four years?" More moans. "Second person?" The shock was apparent. "I'm glad you chose me. I'd like to please you more than this. Often, and as much as you want."

His cock was getting thicker inside me. With how his fingers kept teasing, I was finding it hard to even process his words. I was moving against him faster. Needing more. Needing release for the first time in weeks. It was right there when lately I'd been nothing but opposed to even trying.

"I like this. I." My hand lifted from his thigh, gripping his wrist as he built me up even higher. "*Jackson.*"

"Fuck. Fuck."

"*Jackson.*"

I pushed my weight down against his fingers. The added pressure had me sucking in breaths. My sounds grew louder, and I felt my orgasm edge. Minutes went by and it didn't fade away like I expected. With the smallest shift of his fingers, every part of me seemed to explode. Spasms shook me, and the hold around me tightened almost unbearably. There was pain, but also pleasure as I closed my eyes and focused on the way his cum pumped into me.

"Son of a bitch. Oh, fuck."

The guard finished but he didn't move. He just held me trapped against him, which I liked even more. As much as I tried to be like Rory, I wasn't her. I didn't get angry at too much affection. I craved it on deeper levels than I wanted to admit, and the only reason I avoided it was because I knew what would follow if I got attached. Rory would destroy it. *Destroy him.* She always did.

"Wow, I." Jackson pulled out, moving in the darkness. Something sounded and the next thing I knew, he was pushing some sort of cloth between my legs. "I'm sorry. I didn't ask if you wanted me to pull out. I was so swept away I didn't even think about it."

Swept away? I smiled.

"It's okay. I didn't think about it either. Truthfully, I didn't even think you'd be interested in me."

My volume dropped as I removed the cloth from between my legs and pulled up my panties. I turned, immediately met with a pair of soft lips. The kiss came out of nowhere. With the darkness, I wasn't sure how he could even see. It didn't matter as he pulled me back into him, ravaging my mouth, and taking the cloth.

"You really have no idea how beautiful you are, do you?"

"My sister is the prettier one."

"I doubt that." Another kiss. "I want to see you again."

"I." All *I* could see was Rory. "Maybe. My sister is…complicated."

"You have to get her permission?"

Wiggling from his arms, I reached back, pulling the handle to the door. Light flooded the space and brown eyes soaked in every expression I must have been going through. I was so conflicted. This was not what I expected to happen. Despite my schemes, I truthfully thought he'd fuck me and be done with it. *Be done with me.* Rory was great at putting me down to the point that I was starting to believe her. This could work. Seeing Jackson behind her back could be good.

"My sister is overbearing at times. Jealous, even. Maybe I can get away without her knowing. I mean…if that's okay with you. I understand if that's too much to deal with." I stopped. "But if it's not, maybe we could meet somewhere?"

A smile appeared, and he joined me, stepping into the hall.

"We have apartments here, too. I have a roommate, but he won't mind. You can come see me any time I'm not pulling guard."

Happiness soared as I mirrored him.

"I would love to come see you."

"I'm off tomorrow."

Tomorrow? So soon? My mouth parted, but I kept quiet as we took a right onto another hall. As we came to a stop outside of a door, Jackson didn't open it. His gaze studied my face, and I wasn't quite sure what he saw there. Could he sense my hesitancy? My fear? His frown told me he might.

"You don't seem like a killer to me. Is she the bad one? Is she the reason you're here?"

My eyes lowered. "Rory wouldn't like this. She's—"

His finger pressed to my lips, and he reached down grabbing

a pen from his belt. When he flipped my hand and wrote on the inside of my palm, my heart was racing.

#04921

"That's my cell number. Call or text when you want to meet. If I'm not working, I want to see you." His digit returned to my lips, making a path and dipping in the center just the smallest amount before he pulled back. "Your slave is waiting, Beauty. I really hope you call."

MISTRESS B-0019-2

RORY

I was drunk. Way past drunk, but who the hell cared? Not the Master whose name and number I'd crumbled and thrown in the trash. Not the other three I'd nearly collided with when I tried getting on the elevator. My sister didn't even seem to care as I walked into the bedroom to see her smiling and staring at the damn wall. It had me wanting to lash out. To ask her what the hell happened that made her so happy. I didn't say a word. Those would come, but not until I dealt with the slave that was no doubt responsible for her good mood.

Had they hit it off? Was she already giving him those sad, love-me eyes she gave to every man who looked her way?

Hazel was so weak. So desperate for someone to love her. Didn't she see the most important person she'd ever need already did?

I pressed my hand to the doorframe, steadying myself. Glancing around the room, I took in our elevated bed. The way my sister sat on top of it was as if it were a throne, and she was the queen of this underground kingdom. She was so high and mighty. So pure and in control of herself. And me, I was obviously the peasant doing her bidding. Hadn't I gotten us down here? Fucking Mistress Nineteen-dash-two. I should have been the original Nineteen, but no. Even she got the better number. Nothing I did made me win in her eyes. Didn't I kill the slaves so she could see how unimportant they were? How they didn't matter, just like everyone else who tried to come between us? She'd never see what I did. Hazel only viewed me as the destroyer. And I was. I didn't deny that. It was the reasons that she neglected to see.

I did everything for her.

For us.

Our DNA made us bad. There was nothing wrong with that, but Hazel refused to face facts. She held to light and dreams as if they'd save her from the inevitable. There was no outrunning what was in us. The sooner she embraced the truth and realized she was just like me, the faster we could focus on what we needed to become. No more arguing. No more competition. We'd be *one* like we were always meant to.

Pushing from the wall, I tore my eyes from my sister to look at the soundproof cage hidden underneath her. With only four feet of head clearance to move around, the slave didn't have much room, but that was the point. He wasn't a guest in our home. He didn't even deserve to see it if we didn't want him to. But I couldn't quite focus on my reasons as I approached. As much as I wanted to head up the steps and grill Hazel, I withdrew my knife, heading to the entrance of the cage instead. The light oak concealed the slave from view. The moment I reached and opened the slat on the door, the man's head lifted. He was illuminated by the soft glow of the interior lights, sitting with his legs drawn up. His brown hair was a rich walnut color almost muting the deep green shade of his eyes. Had they not been so vibrant through his fear, I might have been more focused on his shaky hands as they lowered from hugging around his shins.

"Mistress."

I didn't answer. I opened the door, turning to close it behind me. The slave looked even more nervous as I crawled in his direction. Maybe it was the predator in my gaze, or perhaps he'd glimpsed my knife. I was too drunk to care as I continued to crawl until I was climbing on his lap to straddle his sitting form.

Dark, thick curls blocked my line of sight. I blinked to bring the slave into focus, shaking my head to get my hair out of my face. It was wild, just like me. I was beyond thinking. Instinct drove me and it had me pushing my free palm against the slave's bare chest until he was cautiously lowering.

Seeing him look up at me with his handsome face, so careful, so concerned...he and Hazel didn't get far. They might not have spoken at all. My doubt had me trying to read him even better. Just the thought that she was throwing herself at him left my eyes closing. I could have ended this right here and now. I wanted to. My fist was so tight around the tiny little pocketknife I held. It wouldn't have caused much damage, but enough if I stuck it in the right place. No. I'd be a good girl. Hazel said I needed to learn restraint, and she was right. I'd be good, and then she'd stop being so mad at me.

"Do you think I'm pretty."

I reached back, unzipping the dress to pull it over my head. When I unhooked my strapless bra, the slave swallowed back the fear, nodding.

"Show me how pretty I am, slave. Make me feel it."

The wariness didn't subside as the slave reached up, flattening his hand on my sternum. I could feel his trembling all through my body. I grabbed his wrist, moving his palm over to my breast. The touch was light, not at all like someone who wanted to continue or even go further.

"Are you truly so afraid?"

My voice was loud making the man stiffen beneath me.

"If you'll just tell me what you want, Mistress, I can try to do it."

"I told you what I want. I said make me feel pretty. I'm not sure what you think that means, but this is not it."

"I can try again."

My mouth twisted. "Don't bother. I'm not having you ruin my mood completely." I licked my lips, feeling them pull back to the side through the slight smile. "Moxley stay."

The slave jolted, stiffening under my code word to shut him down. There would be no fighting. No running. The slave laid there paralyzed as I moved in. "Since you failed to obey, you get three cuts. Maybe next time you'll be more inclined to give me what I want. And not just give it to me, slave. You better try your hardest to make me happy, or I'll kill you like I did with the others."

I opened the knife, lowering to press the blade over his defined pec. The slave was in decent shape which I liked. What I didn't care for was how weak and broken he was on the inside. *Just like Hazel.* Did he have no spine? No backbone to fight? No skill to lie to impress? At least Hazel would have succeeded as a slave. She knew how to follow rules. She didn't just excel with orders, she reinvented them. Made them better. Unlike me who couldn't follow the simplest rule. At least I wasn't weak. Just...lost.

"When I release you, you're going to forget the fear. You're going to become strong. Confident. If I say fuck me; you're going to fuck me so good I can't get enough. And that's all I really want from you. Sex. Blood." Crimson broke over the blade as I pushed down. "I do love to watch people bleed. You're going to like it too. Next time, I won't have to say the magic words. *You're going to want this.* We're going to fuck, covered in your blood. Show me your life is mine without me having to take it. Give this to me and you'll live. It's that simple."

The line of blood elongated as I added more pressure and moved down a good inch. It spilled over the split skin, running towards the side of his body. Green eyes stared hollowly ahead, but I knew the slave was very aware of what was happening, even if he couldn't respond to it. I'd learned that with the last slave. He preferred this over being responsive through the wounds. *Weak.*

"Look how pretty you bleed. See..." I rocked my pussy against him. "This isn't so bad, right? You're going to love this. Beg me for it. I'll make you feel so good."

My hand eased over, starting the next cut. Just seeing the red gush over metal had the anger retreating and the lust returning. It was one or the other with me, and lately the lust just couldn't outweigh the rage Hazel stirred up with her lectures and rules.

"Do you think you can behave if I bring you back? Can you please me, slave?"

Another cut. More blood. The slice was deeper sending crimson to the middle of his chest to pool in the dip between the muscles. I flattened my hand, moaning as I smeared the substance from shoulder to shoulder. The outline of my fingertip sent me in a frenzy. I was moving against him even more, still humming with arousal from the last Master. He couldn't get me to come. He hadn't cared to try. This slave...I could make him do whatever I wanted.

"We're going to try this again. I'm going to bring you back and you're going to fuck me like your life depends on it because...*it does, slave.* I had every intention of you living throughout the night, but I'm not impressed with what I've seen so far. Change my mind. Are you ready?"

"Moxley." I paused, lowering to bite against his bottom lip. "*Run.*"

The slave sucked in a deep breath; his eyes wide with terror as he panted."

"I'm waiting. Don't make me shut you down again or you're not going to come back."

Lips crushed into mine, and the slave's hand latched to the back of my neck, keeping me in place. I met his tongue, moaning as he wrapped his arm around my waist, spinning me to my back so he could get on top. He was still breathing hard and shaking as he lifted enough to stare down into my face.

"That's all you got, slave?"

For a moment I wasn't sure if he was going to continue or try to kill me. Maybe he didn't know either. Our eyes held and he seemed to calm the smallest amount. The slave reached down, lifting the hand that held the knife. He brought it to his chest, adding pressure from his body as he leaned in and captured my mouth again.

Was that an invitation for me to cut at will?

The action completely puzzled my fuzzy head. I let him kiss me and steal me further away. Fingers gripped to the lining of my panties, twisting them in his fist enough to have them cut into my skin. It was tight. Almost too tight. Fabric made a ripping sound and my lids cracked open just in time for him to jerk and tear them free. The atmosphere shifted to such a foreign degree, I could have cut the air with my knife. Green eyes were glowing in the light. Blood was smeared up to his neck, and I could feel the stickiness all over my chest and breasts. I was suddenly in awe, and my lust had nothing to do with boredom. This was different. My need was more demanding.

"Better."

Fingers explored over my folds, sliding along my slit as he teased between my entrance and clit. I brought the knife back up expecting him to stop or balk. He didn't. The slave didn't even flinch as I leveled it against the other pec and pressed in. A drop of blood left him, falling onto me with the weight of a thousand fists. My heart slammed into my chest. It pounded and rattled against me. It was one thing to force my fantasy on someone, quite another for that person to comply and give me what I wanted. That hadn't happened yet, and now that it was, it was so much better than I expected. *It was real.* Shared.

"Kiss me more." I cried out as his finger slid in deep. I didn't have to repeat the order. The slave lowered, sweeping his tongue back in my mouth. Another finger stretched me, and he drank in my moan while I rocked even faster.

"Blood and sex." The slave's stare was intense. Almost angry as he pulled back. "You're not going to kill me?"

"Not if you give me what I want."

His lips were back and on mine but only briefly. He lowered, sucking down my blood covered chest, making his way to my breast. Suction drew in my nipple, and I cried out as the thrust became demanding.

"I like this. Fuck. I." A cry left me as he went to my other breast, sucking that nipple into his mouth as well. With his teeth, he tugged against the nub, withdrawing his fingers to rub circles over my clit. "So good."

My eyes opened from their heavy state as his hand grabbed mine with the knife again. As he led it to his neck, all I could do was try not to come all over his fingers. I had no idea what he was doing, but the fantasy and risk was enough to have me nearly screaming through a release.

"Slave."

But he was already pushing the tip of the knife into his skin. Red ran a river down his throat as my mouth parted through the sight.

Pressure. I barely realized he had pushed down the grey sweatpants and his cock was fitting against me. My legs spread even wider, and he knew what I wanted. He lowered, surging his cock into me as he gave me perfect exposure. I buried my fingers in his hair, holding around his back tightly as I rubbed one side of my face against the warm wetness from his wound.

The slave was already pushing so deep. With how my head was lifted into his neck, he pushed into places I could only dream of. Tighter, I held around him, feeling his life force flow down my cheek, and onto my own neck and chest.

"Fuck. Oh, God, yes."

The slapping sounds were loud as the thrusts turned into pounding. The friction against my clit was a delicious undoing. I built and built. I held on tighter, growing louder with my cries. The slave ground forward, sending my legs shooting out with the spasms. My nails clawed in deep, and my world spun as ecstasy stole any sense of rationality. Moans followed mine, and I locked my legs around the slave's hips as he went to pull out. The action only had him collapsing on me even more, finding my lips again as he jolted through his own release.

It was hot.

Different.

It was a promising start.

MISTRESS B-0019

HAZEL

"I s he dead?" Rory looked up from her pancakes, only to turn her eyes back to her plate. "I saw you when you left his cage, last night. You had blood all over you. You were in there for a damn hour. Should I be calling for a pick-up?"

"Stop being so pissy. The slave's not dead." She smiled, keeping her gaze down. I tilted my head, trying to see her better. "He's…quite the slave. He actually obeyed me. He let me cut him." Only then did she look up. "A lot. He looks like my own personal fucking corkboard. It was beautiful, Hazel. I think I like this one."

My brows lifted in surprise. "That's new."

"Right? I didn't see that happening. Good cock too." She let out a small moan. "I'm impressed. You did good choosing him."

"…You saw him too. Well…"

Silence played out between us. I wasn't sure what to do now that Rory wasn't battling some overpowering need to filet the slave alive. I expected to be playing therapist again. Her last slave couldn't handle Rory's needs. Now that this one did, where did that leave me?

"Are we still playing our game?" I picked up a piece of bacon, biting and chewing slowly as her emotions shifted.

"Yeah, of course. It'll be fun. He'll have no idea what to expect once he meets you. You're so proper and good. It'll be different from me. It'll fuck with his head. Ooh!" She shifted in her chair to face me even more. "You should go into your lectures about manners and patience. Be the mom. You were always good at that. He won't know what to think."

I turned back to my food, losing my appetite.

"What's the long face for. I'm not saying anything we don't know, Hazel. Don't tell me it suddenly hurts your feelings."

"When have you ever cared about how I feel?" I stood, picking up my plate and heading for the trashcan. "You tell me not to behave a certain way and then freak out at me when I'm more like you. I'm tiring of these games. It's not even fun anymore."

"Hazel, stop being overdramatic. You haven't been the same since last night. What was up with you anyway when I got home. Why were you smiling?

"I can't smile now?" I rolled my eyes. "Maybe I was thinking about a life without you in it."

Rory stood, glaring. "Take that back. That's not even funny. That's just mean."

"Welcome to how I feel. You think I like being called a prude? How about a mom? Good? Proper? Remember when you called me a fucking square all through high school? Vanilla? It's only mean if it hurts your feelings. Stay with the slave and have fun. I'm going into the city. I have some shopping to do anyway."

Shock disappeared as anger took over. "You're going shopping now without me? We shop together. You know that."

"What I know is you go out all the time by yourself. It's my turn, Rory." I sighed, trying to calm. My voice softened as my hand came up. "Play your games. Have fun. I'll be back later."

"I don't think so."

"Are you serious?"

"You're not going, Hazel. Not alone."

"I can't go to the store, but you can go off and fuck Masters? Maybe I'll find me a Master to fuck too. That might be just the fun I need."

The laughter that filled the space only had me snatching my purse from the counter. I grabbed my phone, glaring as Rory put herself in the middle of my path.

"Those Masters out there would eat you alive. Don't even think about being so stupid."

"But you can be stupid. Just not me."

A groan left her, and she rolled her eyes. "We're not the same. Not even close. If you want something to do, take the slave with you shopping. I'll stay here and hide out until it's my turn with the game." Her lids narrowed. "Stay away from those Masters, Hazel. I mean it. I better not hear that you're messing around with one. They'll kill you, and maybe not even on purpose. They're not normal men. They're not safe."

"I'm not safe," I snapped. "I'm so sick of this. I'm going shopping, and I'm not taking the stupid slave. You don't like to share anyway."

"I'm sharing! Jesus. Take him. You'll need the protection anyway."

"I said I'm going alone."

Rory grabbed her plate, throwing it at my feet. Glass shattered as she stomped her way over to me, getting an inch from my face.

"You're taking the fucking slave, Hazel. I'm not telling you again."

"And if I don't?"

Hands leveled on each side of my face, holding tightly. I grabbed her wrists, squeezing and trying to remove them as she added more pressure. The slap came so hard and fast, I didn't have time to even comprehend the move. She clutched back to my face, moving her hands back to lock in my hair on each side of my head.

"You're taking the Goddamn slave. Do you hear me?"

"Let go of me, Rory."

"Say it. *Say it!*"

At my sob, one of her hands slid free and she connected to my face again, this time so powerfully my head spun at the force. It had been years since Rory physically assaulted me, but I would never forget how crazed she'd become back then. I had been sure she was going to kill me. She'd almost succeeded. Had I forgotten how unstable she truly was? The look in her eyes said everything. She wouldn't just kill me. She'd kill us both.

"I'll t-take him."

Tears poured free, running down my heated flesh. My cheek throbbed, and I sobbed, again, hating that I did.

"Good sister." She squeezed her fists into my hair again, kissing my lips bruisingly. Her hands dropped, letting go as she turned for the room. My shoulders sagged, and I wiped the tears, still not able to stop the ones that continued to slip free. I headed for the room just as Rory stepped from the closet, handing me clothes for the slave. "I'll be hiding in here. Make him go to the restroom to dress. He needs to be let out anyway. I'll be in here until you leave. Bang on the front door before you walk in."

"Okay."

At my one word, she eyed me suspiciously, backstepping to the closet. The door shut and I wiped my nose and face, heading over to the cage's door.

One breath.

Two.

All my emotion left me, and I opened the barrier, bending down to peer in.

"Out. Come get dressed. We're leaving."

The slave wasn't far from the door. He crawled out, scanning my face as he winced and stood. Small cuts and holes dotted and ran lines across his chest and neck. His mouth pulled back at the side only to fade as I showed no emotion at seeing him.

"Make it fast."

"Have you been crying?"

I thrust the clothes in his direction, watching as he disappeared through the bathroom door. I headed for the closet, swinging it open. "I need his shoes."

Rory's head shook. "He gets none. Shoes are a privilege. He hasn't earned it."

I rolled my eyes, turning, only to have her grab my forearm. She stepped forward, tracing her fingertips over my cheek and lips.

"I think it's going to bruise."

"It wouldn't be the first time. At least this time I'm not in a coma."

"All you have to do is listen, Hazel. I know what's best. Those Masters aren't it. It's not even funny. This isn't the outside world. These people will eat you alive. I act this way to protect you. You never see that."

"I see everything."

I jerked out of her hold, turning and shutting the door behind me. I didn't have to wait too long before the slave came out from the restroom. He kept his gaze on me, but I diverted my attention to stare ahead as I led us out of the apartment. Just putting distance between me and my sister felt like a weight was lifting. The only thing holding me down was the slave whose stare hadn't left my face.

"You're different."

"What?"

I glanced over watching his expressions change. He jolted to a stop, turning me to face him.

"You *were* crying. Did someone hit you?"

My hand lifted to the aching area, and I started walking again.

"I'm the Mistress. You don't ask questions."

"But if someone hurt you—"

"It's *my* business." My eyes cut over in a glare as I slowed, pushing the elevator button. "There's rules, and I'm the one who makes them. Do you understand?"

"Yes, Mistress." His jaw flexed repeatedly as he looked down at his feet.

"Good. I'd hate to have to—"

"Excuse me."

I stiffened at the familiar voice, turning to see Jackson not a foot away. Although he'd called out to me, his eyes took in the slave and all the cuts covering his exposed neck. My heart was pounding as I turned to face him completely.

"Yes?"

"I have a few questions concerning your status. May I have a few words with you privately?"

I glanced at the slave, trying to hide the slight shake that was taking over my hands. Jackson wasn't in his uniform like he'd been last night. He was wearing dark denim jeans with a gray thermal long sleeve shirt. The way he towered over me had me wanting to be wrapped in his arms all over again.

"Slave, go sit on the sofa over there until I call for you."

There was a slight hesitation, but the slave obeyed. Jackson and I watched until he was sitting, and I leaned in, lowering my voice.

"What are you doing here? I thought I said I'd come to you. How did you know what floor I'm on?"

"I work here. It wasn't hard to find out." He stepped in, almost a little too close. "What the hell happened to your face. Did he do that, or did she?"

"Rory was mad. I don't want to talk about it."

His head moved as he put himself in my line of sight.

A. A. DARK

"I want to see you again."

"That's kind of hard. I tried to leave. She made me take the slave. She said it's not safe to be out by myself."

"It's really not."

"Well, I can't bring the slave with me to see you. He might accidentally tell Rory. He doesn't know about her yet, so don't even mention her existence. It'll ruin the game. That'll get me in even more trouble."

"What if you have me escort you? I'm a guard. I'll wear my uniform. I can take you shopping or out. Wherever you need to go. Will that make her feel safer?"

"You're a man and a stranger. She'd never let me leave with you."

Jackson's mouth twisted as he looked around.

"There has to be a way for us to spend some sort of time together."

"I'll see what I can do. I have to go. The slave will get suspicious, and I really don't want him mentioning this to Rory. She's already mad enough."

He reached for my face, cursing as he stopped himself.

"You know how to get ahold of me. Call me. Don't text. You can delete my number after we finish. I don't want you to get in trouble if she happens to check the phone. A call doesn't show proof of anything. Not like words. I'll be around."

I nodded, stepping back and turning to wave the slave over. Jackson headed off, and my knees almost gave out through the adrenaline. I hit the elevator button trying to convince myself that it wasn't the least bit suspicious. The slave wouldn't say anything if I didn't make a big deal of it.

"What sort of foods do you like? I shouldn't be asking but," I shrugged, glancing over, "I'm a picky eater so I guess I understand."

The door opened, and a slight smile returned to the edge of his mouth as he followed me onto the elevator.

188

"I'm really not that picky. I'll eat whatever you want to feed me."

"I bet you're starving."

As if my voice conjured his hunger, his stomach growled. We both laughed, and I felt my fear ease even more.

"I'm dying over here. I think I could eat my weight in food right now."

"If I recall, there's a bakery cart in the lobby area. They have the same one on every floor. I guess the main one is an actual restaurant, but I have no idea what floor that's on. I feel like eating a muffin, myself. I didn't get to finish breakfast. Oh, and coffee. I really need one of those."

The slave moaned, and my smile stayed as the doors opened once again. The rich scent of pastries filled the air, and I grabbed the slave's hand as we laughed and jogged to the small cart nestled at the center of the room. There were two people in front of us, but it gave us time to look at the menu.

"I usually get blueberry, but I think I'm going to get a chocolate chip muffin today. What do you want?"

"What can I have?"

One of my eyebrows rose. "Not the entire cart, but pretty much whatever you want."

"Can I hold your hand again?"

"No."

He leaned in, leveling his mouth with my ear.

"I've been thinking about last night. It was...amazing. Terrifying but such a thrill. I haven't felt like that in over a year. Maybe longer." He drew back, continuing to stare in my face. "Will you want that again today?"

Was it truly so amazing? A thrill? Was I jealous?

Always.

"Maybe. We'll see how good you are." I stepped up to the cart, refusing to look at him. "Chocolate chip muffin and a coffee, two sugars, for me, and the slave will have..."

He moved in. "Two blueberry muffins, a glazed donut, a chocolate one, and a coffee. Black. No sugar."

"After all that, you won't need any. You're going to be bouncing off the walls."

I glanced over to catch his smile, but I didn't return it. My stare stopped on a bench, and my gaze connected with Jackson's. He didn't acknowledge me; he just stared. Watching. Waiting.

"Here you go, Mistress."

I blinked hard, shaking my head as I forced a grin, taking my order. The slave got his, and I glanced over my shoulder, slowing as the bench was suddenly empty. My mouth opened only to shut as I spun in a circle, scanning the busy lobby. Grocery stores and outlets were buzzing with people who were coming and going. Had I imagined Jackson sitting there? Had it been someone else and my mind was playing tricks on me? I wasn't sure, but I would be more aware from here on out.

JACKSON BANKS

"Let me just repeat what you've told me, Banks. Last night you were propositioned by a Mistress for sexual favors. You engaged in the act, where you gave her your number to pursue an affair."

"That's correct, Sir."

The High Leader's brow furrowed as he shifted in his chair behind the desk.

"And now you're asking me to look up more information on her and her twin?"

"...Yes, Sir." I let out a breath. "I ran into her earlier—" At his look, I shrugged. "I waited for her to leave this morning and I followed her. We talked a little. Her cheek and lip were swollen and starting to bruise. It had been clear she'd been hit. She was with the slave, and said it wasn't him. She admitted it was Rory, the sister."

"That's not our business, Banks. You know how this works. You've had extensive training concerning relations with the Masters and Mistresses of the Gardens. It's allowed, but it's not encouraged."

"I know that, Sir, and I gave plenty of thought on the decision overnight. I just want to make sure she's okay and this twin of hers isn't going to hurt her worse. I just want an idea of exactly what I'm getting brought into."

"So you can pull back if need be?"

"Exactly, Sir."

But that wasn't the truth. I couldn't just leave the Mistress to the abuse of her crazy twin sister. I may have been heartless in some respects, but the woman was beautiful and that was ruling me more than anything. I couldn't stop seeing her dark, curly hair and big blue eyes. They weren't even really blue. More of a mix between blue, gray, and lavender. She was stunning and sweet. I got the feeling that she didn't belong here, and that reeled me in even more.

"Couple B-Nineteen?"

"Yes, Sir."

Whatever was on the computer screen, I didn't have a clue, but it was enough to have Nineteen's eyes narrowing.

"I only have a summary, but from what I see, the number does come back to twins. Hazel, Mistress Nineteen, and Rory Summerland, Mistress Nineteen-dash-two. They're twenty-five years old. Daughters of Lance Summerland." Nineteen clicked more buttons. "He's not a Master here, but it does say he's recently passed. The mother, a former actress, has been gone now for over ten years." A good minute ticked by. "Contributor," he mumbled. "Something-Something Firm. Possibly lawyer, maybe? Or…inventor? The information looks to be out of the L.A. area. Fuck if I know. They're here, and if they're here, they're someone. With no father or mother, they're on their own. Sorry, that's all I can really dig up on them. The Main Master will have their file. If I think about it, I'll mention the names and see what he can tell me. With the way things are going, don't count on it."

"I understand, and I appreciate what you've given me so far. It does help."

"I'm glad." I stood and he joined me. "I appreciate you coming to me with your concerns. Maybe think about walking away from this one. It sounds like it could have the potential to be a mess."

"I'll think it over. Thanks, Boss."

I turned, stopping at the call.

"Banks, watch your back. The Mistresses here are no less dangerous than the Masters. In most cases I've seen, they're worse."

"Noted, Sir."

He nodded, and I left his office, heading towards the elevator. As I approached and pushed the button, I couldn't stop repeating her name. Hazel Summerland. Hazel. Hazel. Why did I know that name? I did know that name, didn't I?

The doors opened, and I got on, riding up to my floor. When I finally made it in my room, I barely noticed Ryan, my roommate, lounging on the sofa. It wasn't often we were both off duty at the same time, but on rare occasions it happened.

"Just in time to catch the game."

"Can't. I need to look up some stuff."

"What sort of stuff?"

I squinted, turning as the name repeated on a loop.

"Have you ever heard of Rory or Hazel Summerland?"

"Are you fucking serious? The Summerland twins? Who hasn't heard of them?"

I immediately headed over, taking a seat on the sofa as he sat up.

"Tell me about them."

"Are they here?"

At my look, he rolled his eyes, nodding.

"I don't really know much about the family. I think the dad was some sort of inventor for Hollywood or something. Like mask, makeup shit, or something? It took off. It's in everything, even regular makeup now, which, I'm guessing makes them heiresses to some huge fortune. Like…a never-ending supply of money. Anyway, the mom was a pretty famous actress before she died in an accident. None of that was what got the girls famous. That happened when one of the daughters started dating Ethan O'Brien. The headlines went crazy."

"Ethan O'Brien? The actor?"

"That's right. It was a few years back. Hazel, I think. The older one. I guess they met on the set of that popular paranormal movie he's in. I think they had her dad in for costume stuff. Well, they dated for a few months when rumors went wild with the other sister stealing him away. There's no telling since Rory, I think, was supposedly secretly seeing some football star. Once the twins got on the scene, there were plenty of men who became interested. They were in magazines and tabloids. I think the Rory-one even did some cover modeling or something. Hazel sort of faded from the scene when her sister fucked it all up. It was a wild two years in the outside world. After that though, they sort of disappeared. Or maybe I stopped paying attention. All I know is…*wow*. Fucking hot. Like…" His head just kept shaking. "Wait, did you say they're here?"

I stood, clenching my teeth as I walked to the fridge, grabbing a beer.

"They're here, and they're off limits."

"To us?" His head cocked to the side. "Or to me?"

"To you. I figure you should know. Hazel might come by at some point. Do *not* even act like you recognize her."

"Shut the fuck up. Dude, in your wildest fucking dreams."

I twisted the top from the beer free, throwing it at him. "I mean it. Not a Goddamn word."

"There's no way in hell you landed Hazel Summerland. What happened? Did she say hi to you? Wave your way? Ask you for help? You're not actually *seeing* her."

"Believe what you want. All I'm saying is, if Hazel comes over, you better stay quiet and leave us the hell alone."

His hands lifted as I chugged down more of the beer.

"You know me. I won't get in the way. But if—"

"I'm not lying, and I'm not seeing her. Just...talking, I guess. We met last night. I'm just warning you. She may not even call. She has a lot going on anyway. Just..." My head shook as I took the phone from my pocket and sat back down. "Let's just watch the damn game."

"What game?" Ryan turned off the TV, turning more to face me. "After that shit, I want to know what the hell happened. How did you meet her? Was it when you were pulling guard?"

Another drink. And another. I couldn't seem to get her taste out of my mouth. I could still feel her around me. Hear her moans. Second person. Me and fucking Ethan O'Brian. Me... why the hell would she choose me?

"Well?"

"I took her to buy her slave. That's all you need to know."

He looked puzzled. "That's it? How about you tell me the part where you gave her your number and invited her over. You're not usually so bold."

"I'm not telling you details, Ryan. That's personal. And...*she chose me*. I'd never throw myself at anyone."

"Are you fucking with me? You are. You're getting me back for—"

A ring had both of us looking down to the phone lighted up in my hand. I threw him a look, standing as I brought it to my ear."

"Hello?"

"It's me." Footsteps were light but evident as I strained to listen. "Rory's occupied for a little while. Where should I go?"

"Where are you now?"

"Almost to the lobby where we met before."

"Turn around and head the other way. It leads to our side of the apartments. Stop when you get to the elevator on our side. I'll meet you there."

A. A. DARK

"Okay. See you soon."

I hung up, meeting Ryan's shocked gaze.

"No fucking way, man. No way."

"Be gone by the time I get back. Or…in your room or something. Shit." I pushed my phone in my pocket, finishing off my beer and quickly throwing it in the trash. "Clean up your shit too. I'll be back."

Jogging to the door, I didn't stop my fast pace as I headed for the elevator. I'd need to go up three floors, but it wouldn't take me long. I may even beat her to our small lobby.

"Banks, where are you going?"

I didn't turn to my friend, Charles. I ran faster, slamming my finger into the elevator button the moment I slid to a stop outside the double door. Almost immediately it opened. I stepped in, trying to slow the adrenaline. Somehow knowing Hazel's past made this even more real. I didn't get attached to people if I could help it. Especially women. That was outside of our duties. Those came first over everything and everyone.

"Fuck."

More, her name repeated. It was as if it belonged inside me. With as shocked as Ryan was…I was even more. Finding out who she was, I was downright flabbergasted. I wouldn't question the whys. It would never make sense.

Dinging had me stepping out and almost walking right into her. She was breathing just as heavy. I wrapped around her waist, pulling her into me, and stepping back into the elevator. I didn't have to coax a kiss out of her. Her lips met mine just as fast. Small arms wrapped around my neck, and I lifted her off the ground against me. Hazel's legs locked around my waist, and I dug my fingers into her ass as she clung to me tightly. I was so lost in our kiss, I barely heard the elevator doors open. I quickly put her down, holding her hand as I led her back to my apartment.

Bottles clinked and Ryan froze, clearly shocked as I led

196

Hazel inside. Her smile was radiating, but I didn't stick around to socialize. I led her into my room, shutting us in. I barely had my door locked before she was wrapping back around me.

"We have to make this quick. I don't have much time. If I can get back before she realizes I'm gone, I can do this more often."

I pulled her shirt over her head, taking off mine just as fast. We were pulling and pushing down clothes. I could barely speak as we crashed to the bed.

"Five minutes or five hours. I'll take whatever you can give."

"You're not upset?"

I moved to suck and kiss down her neck as I shook my head.

"I understand things aren't easy for you. I'm not here to add any stress. I want to be the one who takes it away."

A gasp filled the room as I sucked against her breast, teasing her other nipple with my thumb and index finger. I was fitted between her legs, and she was already arched and moving against me.

"Jackson, I wish I could stay longer. I'm working on a plan. I just need a little time. *I want to stay though.*"

There was a poutiness in her tone. A longing that had me lowering even more. God, I would have done anything to keep her here. At least for the night. For a few hours. Hell...one hour. To rush was worse than not having her at all.

"Spread wider for me, baby."

No hesitation. Hazel's legs opened beautifully as I settled between them. As I lowered, running my tongue along her slit, her fingers loosely pushed into my hair. She kept her hand there, as a presence but not a guide. She let me lick and suck, rushing yet making sure to give special attention to the places that made her moan even louder. I sucked her clit, sliding my finger into her entrance, nearly fucking my mattress at the tightness that hugged to me.

"Jackson, please."

The plea was more than her sexual need. She let me keep going and going, but the worry would be there. I wanted her to come back. Maybe even needed her to. Hadn't I been in her lobby first thing in the morning? Hadn't I been waiting? Praying? Fucking needing? I couldn't get her out of my head. Last night shouldn't have happened. Things like that never happened to us guards. *Especially me.* But it did. She chose me over some attractive Master at her beck and call. In a city of celebrities and slaves, it was me. Just me, Jackson Banks. No one else. *That meant everything.*

"Someday I'm going to show you what it's like to do this for hours."

I lifted, and my hand slid under her lower back. Spinning us, I put her on top of me. Just taking in her curves in the light did things to me I'd never felt. She was pure perfection, and I wasn't going to risk missing a moment.

"God, you're beautiful. So fucking beautiful."

The lust wavered from her face, and her words about her sister came rushing back from auction night. My head shook, and I pulled her down to me until her lips were only a whisper away.

"Don't deny my compliments or dismiss them like they're meaningless. When I say something, it's fact. You are stunning." My hand gripped the back of her neck, holding her close. "You doubt my feelings, yet I can't help but question your own. I'm perplexed by all of this. Open your eyes and look at me."

Hazel's lids lifted and tears fell. Blue turned to bright lavender, even showing hints of a pale aqua. Had she not dove in for a kiss, I would have been captivated beyond an eternity. Even kissing her, I couldn't shut my eyes from hers. Our stares were locked, and neither of us were looking away. Hazel grabbed my cock, slowly easing to take me inside of her pussy. My mouth opened, and a sound left us both as she began to work down my length.

An inch.

Up.

More.

Up.

Even more.

Each inch was torture when she had control. Had I been too rough with her last night? Had I hurt her? I'd been so carried away that I hadn't been paying the best attention. I sure as fuck hadn't been expecting the confession on how I was her second, or that she hadn't been with anyone in four years.

"Jesus." I bent my knees, leveling my feet to the mattress. Nails dug into my chest as she rode me, but she still only had me halfway inside of her. Impatience had me moving my own hips, pushing inside her even more with every thrust. At the gasp and squeeze to my pecs, Hazel arched, sinking down to the base. I moaned, holding to her hips as she began to rotate and fuck me in earnest.

"This feels so…" she ground against me, letting out little whimpers. "It's more than good. I don't want to go back."

"You have to if you want to keep coming over. We'll think of something. We'll come up with a plan. Code words. We'll figure it out."

She lowered to my chest, telling me she approved with the kiss. There was so much heart behind it, I got lost in her taste. My arms went around her, and I held around her lower back with one hand, and her shoulder with the other. I took control, increasing the thrusts and depth until I was sure I couldn't go any deeper.

Minutes passed. Hazel grew louder, begging me so sweetly as I kept her right on the edge of her orgasm. I may have not had a lot of time, but I wasn't going to waste a second of what I was allowed. She'd remember this. *Crave this, like me.* I wouldn't be the only one wondering about her every hour of the day. I wanted to eventually mean something to her. It wasn't often we had an opportunity to find someone down here. I'd already been here a year and sometimes a day could last what felt like weeks. It was lonely and that was a hell in its own. I wasn't going to miss this opportunity. Hazel was a dream. She was beyond my fantasies, and it didn't help that I now felt slightly starstruck. No. I wouldn't lose her. Not if I could help it.

"Are you ready to come on my cock?"

At the eager nodding, I brought up one of my hands, lifting her face. Bright eyes met mine, and I kept my palm against her cheek as I lifted her to sit up, tilting her hips forward. Slowly, I ground her against me, moving my own hips to add friction. Hazel's mouth flew open, and she let out a large moan, breaking the skin on my chest. I ground us in a steady motion, forcing her to keep her eyes on me. The faster we moved, the more pleasure drew in her features. I didn't look down to see where we were joined. I'd already seen that. What I wanted to see was more raw. Intimate. *Someone who could someday be mine.*

"That's it. Scream for me. Just like that. Fuck, baby. I'm about to come all inside of you."

I started slamming into her, and the spasms were triggered like clockwork. Her pussy was made for me. *Meant for me,* and I'd do everything I could to show her that.

MISTRESS B-0019-2

RORY

"I had fun today. You're so different than anyone I've ever met before. There's this...brutality to you. A darkness. Yet, there's moments when you're funny and sweet and caring." The slave paused. "Am I talking to much?" I lifted my head from his chest, tearing my gaze from the blood smears that were mostly dry. How long had I been laying here as the slave blabbered on? An hour? Longer? I kept seeing Hazel's face. Her tears. I could hear her sobs.

How many times could you break someone's heart before they stopped loving you? I'd done more than wound her body when I struck her. And I kept doing it. I kept hurting the only person I loved.

"You're fine," I breathed out. "I should go."

"Do you want to grab muffins and coffee in the morning with me again?"

My head slowly turned. "Muffins?"

He smiled. "Chocolate chip, and a coffee, two sugars."

"I don't eat chocolate chip. I eat blueberry."

His brow crinkled. "Not this morning. You had a chocolate

201

chip, remember? You even said you usually don't have that kind, but you felt like something different."

"That's right. It completely escaped me. We'll see how I feel in the morning."

Different? Hazel ate blueberry religiously. Fucking different? What the hell was going on with her? Was it me? It was definitely me. If she wanted different food, she probably wanted a different life. *A different sister.*

The anger returned as I climbed out and locked the cage behind me. Hazel was already in bed, her hair wet as she read a book. She didn't even look down at me even though she had to have heard me lock up.

"I'm taking a shower and going out. The slave will need one after I leave." My eyes narrowed as I turned for the bathroom, only to barrel around and race up the steps that led to the mattress. Hazel looked like a deer in the headlights, fear making her push back into the headboard. "I want to know everything, *right now.*"

I climbed over the white comforter ignoring how the dry blood stood out.

"I don't know what you mean."

"Yes you do. You're acting funny. Why chocolate chip? Why not blueberry? You never want to try new things. I hit you one time and suddenly you're picking new food?"

A sigh left her. "Rory, it was a muffin."

"*It was a choice.* You didn't go with what you knew. You picked something different. Are you really thinking about leaving me again?"

"What?" Hazel's tone turned to a higher pitch as she moved back even more. "Of course not. I was just upset earlier. I didn't mean the angry words I said."

"Are you sure?"

"Rory, I just have a lot on my mind, okay?"

"You tried to leave me once."

And I'd almost killed her for it. I put her into a fucking coma for three days, but she never told a soul it was me. We never fought after that either. At least for a while. I had promised to make it up to her. I truly hadn't meant to hurt her. Ethan was a mistake. He'd come on to me. Or maybe I'd made it a little too easy by pretending to be her, first. It didn't matter. That was the past. We were fine now. We were back together and that was the important part. Unless... "Tell me you're not thinking of leaving again."

"I already told you; I'm not leaving."

"Maybe I'm finding it hard to believe you."

"Because I had a chocolate chip muffin? Rory, do you hear yourself? I think maybe it's time you start seeing Dr. James again. Maybe you need to get back on your prescription. I keep telling you that you're getting worse. You need help." Hazel hesitantly reached over, placing her hand on my wrist. "Let me help you. We can leave for the city and come back in a few days. We'll go together. Me and you."

My eyes lowered to where her hand rested over the blood smears. Maybe she was right. Maybe it wouldn't hurt. Or maybe she just wanted me to be a zombie again so I'd leave her alone. Hadn't that been around the time she met Ethan? Was she looking to meet someone new so she could leave me again?

"I'm fine. Let's not make this about me. I've been a bad sister lately. You're obviously hurting." I scooted in, pulling her close as I eased her to lay down. My head lowered to her shoulder, and I held on, closing my lids. Hazel smelled so clean. So crisp and homey like apples and cinnamon. Here I was, her opposite...a wreck, covered in blood, with my knotted hair. Mascara and lipstick were no doubt smeared across my face with lord knew what other sort of body fluids. Cum. More blood. Saliva. A mixture of it all. Where she wore light pink pajamas, my saturated, black cotton slip dress was the billboard that announced the dirty whore I was. How had we gotten here? How

203

were we so different? I couldn't think of a single thing I'd gone through that Hazel hadn't. Yet, she was perfect. How? I couldn't stand it. I wanted to taint her as much as I wanted her to take me over. How were love and hate not the same emotion? I wasn't sure I could tell them apart anymore.

"You should really shower. I can wash your hair if you want."

I snuggled in, holding on to her even tighter. "You're so good to me, always watching out and taking care of me. You used to like when I'd take care of you too. It's been a while. You probably need me."

I pushed under her pajama bottoms, rubbing over her panties. At her silence, my head lifted. Hazel was staring up at the ceiling. She wasn't soft and welcoming anymore. There was even a tear starting to make a path down her temple.

"Are you confused or disgusted? Is that it? I disgust you now?"

"Rory."

"No. Answer me. You've never not at least shown me affection when I ask."

"You never ask," she said, turning to face me. "You take. I tell you no, and you don't stop until you're having your way with me. Did you not just fuck the slave? Was he not enough? What about the Master last night or the one you're going to hunt down minutes from now? More, more, more. *All you want is more.*"

I was sitting and slapping her again before I could stop myself. A gasp left her, and she held to her already bruised cheek as she glared at me. No tears. No sob. Hate. It had me grip the comforter as I let out a scream. Hazel never fought with me so much. She barely spoke her opinion half the time. Now she was lashing out at me at every opportunity?

"I won't forget this. I'm going out. When I get back, you better be normal."

Hazel didn't speak, and I didn't keep stabbing my words into her heart like I wanted. My need to cuddle her was overrun with my need to throttle the fucking living shit out of her. The two fought for blood inside of me, and I couldn't leave that bed fast enough. She had rejected me. Rejected me when she knew that was all I had to give.

Grabbing a red dress and a pair of matching panties, I headed for the shower, slamming the bathroom door behind me. I'd drown myself in the scorching water. I'd let it cleanse my lungs and burn away the dirt that lived deep within my skin. I'd never be clean. I'd never be pure or good enough. Hate was all I was good for. Hate, sex, and murder. I could kill. I sure as fuck wanted to.

"HONEY, CAN I BUY YOU A DRINK? MAYBE TWO OR THREE?"

"You can get the fuck away from me. Are you blind? I have four sitting here I haven't even gotten to yet."

The Master scowled, stomping away as I stared at the bar's mirror in a daze. My face fit perfectly between two bottles on the shelf, and I'd never wanted to smash glass so much in my life. Hazel. She never left me. Correction. She'd never leave me. She'd be normal when I returned. I'd climb in bed and hold her, and she'd snuggle into me too, holding around me, promising we'd be alright. Silently convincing me she'd never let me fall. Dammit, I was spiraling down a hole so deep, I was terrified what it must have meant. Maybe she was right. Maybe I needed to go back to Dr. James.

Movement blurred at my side as I swayed in my chair. Hazel was always right. She'd fix this. She'd fix me again. I just had to let her, and that was my issue. Giving in was almost impossible. On medication, I'd numb out. I'd get lost in life. That gave Hazel freedom to find someone. Why wasn't I enough? Why couldn't she just love me as much as I loved her?

"Do I know you?"

I glanced over to a brunette male. He wasn't wearing the typical suit. He was in a pair of jeans and a long-sleeved shirt. He was handsome in some rugged sense, but I didn't care for looks or company at the moment.

"No, you don't know me, and you're not going to either. I don't need a drink." I waved in front of me, picking up a shot glass and tossing it back. "I don't need your mindless talk, or your dick, or advice on how to hold my fucking liquor. I don't need you or him. Or that fucker three stools over. Do you know what I do need?"

My glare radiated my rage as I took in the stranger.

"What do you need?"

"My sister. I need Hazel to stop—" My eyes closed, and the room swayed the smallest amount. "She's going to make every-thing better. I love her." I tossed back another shot. "I fucking hate her. Have you ever loved and hated someone before?"

There was nothing inviting about the man anymore. He was blank. His face even appeared hard as he motioned for a drink.

"I have."

"What did you do about it?"

He took the beer, gulping the liquid down. The man didn't turn to look at me. He kept his focus ahead, taking in his own reflection.

"My advice wouldn't apply to you. I did have a brother though. He was *all* I had. Treasure that connection. If you lose it, you can't get it back."

I made a grunting noise but stayed quiet.

"If you don't mind me asking, why do you hate your sister? Did she do something bad to you? Hurt you?"

"Hazel?" I burst out laughing. "Hazel wouldn't hurt a fly. She wouldn't know how to. Me, on the other hand, I'd tear off their wings faster than they could fly away." My smile melted, and I grabbed the next glass. "She's everything I'm not. If you

206

combined perfection with beauty and grace, you'd have Hazel. Bitch."

I brought the glass to my lips, stopping myself from taking the drink.

"I think she's going to try to leave me again."

My voice cracked as tears blinded me. They didn't spill over. They knew better.

"And I'm taking it you don't want her to leave?"

The question had my head snapping in his direction. "Are you stupid like all the other men in here? Of course I don't want her to leave. Did you miss the part where I said I loved her? Hazel's not going anywhere. She knows what will happen if she tries."

"And what's going to happen?"

Was that a threat I'd detected...or was I drunk? God, I could barely stay on the stool. I kept swaying.

"Hazel knows better. She..." I blinked, leveling my hand on the bar. "I should go home. She's probably worried anyway. Or sleeping. The old Hazel would be up, waiting for me."

I turned, stepping down from the stool. My ankle rolled, and I hit the floor hard, jarring me for a moment.

"Damn. You're not going to make it far like that. Let me get you help."

"I don't—" My head lifted but the man was already across the room talking to a guard who was posted at the door. Had I been so delayed? I stood on shaky legs, taking two steps that led me to crash into a table. An arm was suddenly wrapping around my waist, and we were moving. I kept blinking, trying to bring the guard or man who was following into focus, but it was taking me longer than it usually was.

"What floor are you on?"

The guard. He was the one holding me. The stranger was trailing behind. My head rolled, and I laughed at his question. Why, I had no idea.

A. A. DARK

"Ten. Ten-ten." More, I laughed. "Hazel said it was our lucky number. New beginnings. More like a beginning where she *leaves* me."

Whispering filtered through between the men, but I couldn't make sense of it as we climbed on the elevator. My eyes closed, and the next thing I knew, we were moving again. Walking...or was I being carried? I was moving. How, I didn't have a fucking clue.

"Here we go."

Knocking.

More knocking.

The sound was drifting in and out. It was Hazel's voice that had me lifting my head.

"*Rory?* Oh my God, is she okay?"

"Just drunk. Let's get her in bed."

"I'm fine. I'm awake now." I lifted my hand, jerking away from the guard. I immediately stumbled from the vertigo, crashing to the living room floor. "See. I said I'm fine."

"Jesus, Rory." Hazel was by my side, helping me to sit up. I slapped her hand, locking my fist in her hair. "You're not leaving me."

"I said I'm not. Let go, you're *hurting* me."

"That's nothing if you leave."

"*Rory, let go.*"

I obeyed, rolling. I grew still at the tactical style boots my face was only an inch from. My upper body lifted, and I glared at the strange man who'd been talking to me at the bar. I still couldn't quite make out his face, but I didn't care to. I didn't even care that he sent up red flags.

"Thank you both for bringing her home. I'm going to put her to bed now. You should both go."

"Are you sure you're okay?"

"*She said she's fine.*"

The words roared from me, and neither man budged.

"I'm okay. She'll calm down once I get her in bed. Thank you for watching out for her and bringing her home."

The room tilted again as I fought to stand. The door closed, and I reached out, taking uncertain steps towards the room. Hazel swept in, wrapping around me as she kept me steady. When we got to the bed, I nearly fell off the steps twice. Hazel held steady. She didn't let me fall. By the time I was collapsing in my spot, I could barely move. My eyes were rolling, and I was sure I was forgetting something.

"You're not leaving, Hazel. I...won't let you leave. I'll never...let you leave."

MISTRESS B-0019

HAZEL

"Chocolate chip for the win. I wondered if you would choose it again. You seemed like you were pretty set in your ways when we talked about it a few days ago."

"I'm starting to see change might not be so bad."

"Mistress." The slave paused, blowing against his coffee as his shoulders sagged. "Can I be honest with you without getting in too much trouble?"

"Of course."

"Something keeps bothering me. There's moments like right now where I feel like I could tell you anything. But then there's times where my head is spinning with confusion, and I'm afraid to even talk to you. I swear it feels like I'm sitting here with someone completely different than last night. I can't quite put my finger on it, but you're just so..." He stopped. "Complex. I don't know. Moments we share at night are hot and all, it's just, I think these are my favorite times. It's nice sitting with you here like this. It's calming. Peaceful, even."

Favorite times? I shifted, so glad Rory couldn't hear him say that. She was quieter than usual since Jackson and the guard brought her home. I knew this part. What was coming wasn't good, but I wouldn't think about that yet. The important part was in front of me.

"Are you upset? You're quiet."

We both blew against our coffee, and I threw him a sad frown.

"I'm not mad at you, slave. I'm probably going to get in so much trouble for this, but I'm over it, really. I want to be honest with you, okay?"

He nodded, searching my face.

"The reason I feel like a different person is because I am. Keeping this secret from you isn't my choice. I have a twin. Her name is Rory. She's the one who comes to you at night. This is her game."

"Game?"

"It's a mind game. It's to mess with you."

The slave's eyes lowered as he blinked through the news.

"I see. I guess it's good to know I'm not losing my mind."

"I'm sorry. Rory's not okay right now. She's going through something, and there's nothing I can do to help her. I'm worried about her, truthfully. It's like she's getting worse by the day."

"I can agree with that. At least in her violence towards me. So..." Again the slave grew quiet. "Sorry, I'm just trying to separate the two of you. We've never...I mean, you've never... with the knife?"

"No. That's Rory. We haven't done anything sexual. This is the extent of our time together. Please, please don't mention that part to Rory. She likes you. Don't ruin that. If you do, I promise you're as good as dead. She'll kill you, and she won't have a lick of remorse. To you, the only one that exists is my sister. That's your favorite time, not this. You live for it. Your happiness doesn't start until she returns to you. That is what she should feel." I took a sip. "I like you. I want you to live. Please, follow that script."

The slave nodded, worry only clouding his face for a moment.

"I'll do as you say. But just so you know, this *is* my favorite time. This makes it manageable."

My mind twisted, calculating far future plans. I lowered my lashes, gazing up at him through the unspoken possibilities. "I'm happy to hear that. Promise me if she ever tells you the truth, you'll act surprised. Rory misses nothing. If she sees through the lie…you die. Always choose her in every sense."

He swallowed hard. "Okay. Can I ask something else?"

"Yes."

"When we met the first morning…did she do that to you? The bruising." He pointed to his cheek and lip area. I let out a breath, bringing my attention to the table as I let the victim in me shine.

"Yeah. I think if anyone understands Rory's temper, it's you. We do what we must. Always," I stressed. "That's the most important thing, slave. You do everything Rory tells you. I don't care if you like it or not. The first sign of disobedience—"

"Death."

"Exactly. Follow her orders. I don't care what they are. Anything she says, you do it."

"Got it."

"Good. Enough with the depressing talk. Now that you know the truth, tell me about yourself. What's your real name?"

A big smile came to his face. "Damien. Yours? Or am I not supposed to know that?"

"I think it's best we wait on my name. No slip ups. I'm Mistress and so is Rory. Never our real names. It's safer that way."

"I like you."

"I like you too. Where are you from? What are your hobbies? What did you do before you got here? We have a little time. I want to hear all about it."

"Wow. Where do I start?" His lips pressed together only to twist. "I'm from Omaha. I worked at a small company my uncle owned, making cabinets and stuff." He shrugged. "Nothing impressive, I promise. I was just normal. Average. I go to a club one night, and I wake up in what looks like a basement. The rest is history."

"I'm sorry. I really am."

The slave placed his coffee down, leaning towards me. His interest was there. So was his pull towards me. He went to speak, stopping himself as he sat up taller. I looked behind me, smiling as Jackson took a seat at the next table.

"It's okay. I told the slave about Rory. He promises to keep quiet." My smile fell. "Are you alright? You look upset."

Jackson's face was tense as he glanced between me and Damien.

"I've been worried sick. A big chunk of the guard is down with the flu, so I've been covering different shifts and working for days. I kept missing your calls, and I made it out here too late by the time I did get off. I'm glad to see there's no new bruising, and you're alive. How's Rory? Is she still batshit fucking crazy?"

The slave laughed, drawing our attention. I turned back to Jackson, shrugging.

"She's quiet. There's worse to come. She has patterns. She's not okay. At some point she's going to break, and I'm just praying since she won't see our doctor back home, I can get her to see the one here before that happens."

"You do that as quickly as you can. I didn't like what I heard that night at the bar. Hazel...she's going to kill you." His hand lifted as my mouth opened to argue. "It might not be today. It might not be a year from now, but she will try. I saw the look on her face when she kept saying how much she hated you. She even hinted to your death. I don't like this one bit."

"Rory was just drunk."

But I knew the truth. My voice sounded weak when

213

compared to Jackson's knowing glare. His head kept shaking as he looked at me.

"The truth almost always comes out when people are drunk. You get her into that doctor ASAP. She is not okay in the head. She already hurt you on auction night. I bet she even went after you the night we dropped her off."

At my head lowering, Jackson immediately brought it back up.

"She fucking did."

"It was just a slap. I was arguing. I should have kept my mouth shut. I'm finding that harder each time."

"Do not for one second take the blame for her actions."

"Fine. I get it. I'll talk to her, and I'll try to make her go in. Just..." I reached out, sliding my fingers through his. "Try not to worry. I'll be okay. I know how to deal with my sister."

Jackson lifted my hand, kissing against my digits. His eyes glanced to the slave, and he kept hold of my hand as he took Damien in.

"What about you? You see the worst side of her. What's your take on the evil twin? Is she dangerous enough to kill her sister?"

Damien pulled down the collar of the shirt making my jaw drop. Dark purplish-black bruising colored his collarbone, and I could see healing slices littered throughout. He was covered in them. So many I couldn't begin to guess a number covering his body.

"Well, she kept repeating that she hated me when she did this, so...I guess I'm with this guy on how she feels about you. I don't think you're safe."

I ignored the words, surging to my feet to pull and look down his shirt, myself. "Rory did that to you?"

"Last night. I told you it's getting worse. It was a full-blown ass-beating. I don't think I've ever suffered as much rage from a man. Although...there I would have at least defended myself. I let her do this. I didn't have much of a choice if I didn't want my throat slit."

"I can't believe..." I swallowed back the shock, stepping over to ease back to my seat. "I've never seen her do something so bad. She killed the other slaves but that was quick. That wasn't *this.*"

Jackson's fingers brushed through his hair. I could tell he was on edge as he stayed quiet, thinking. We were all assessing what we now knew, but what could we do about it? Legally in the Gardens...nothing.

"Hazel, I want you to come stay with me for a while. I know Rory will freak the fuck out, but I can't let you go back there after this. It's too risky."

"It's riskier for Damien." I gestured to the slave. "She'll kill him in her rage. I cannot let that happen."

"And I can't let you return in good conscious. Jesus, take a good look under his shirt. That's overkill. That's issues that far outweigh medical treatment. Even sedated, I don't trust her."

"Rory loves me. She's not going to kill me. Hurt me, yes, but not seriously. I'll be okay until I can get her help."

Jackson cursed under his breath. "How do I know you're okay? I can't call to check. You don't want your sister knowing about us."

"For good reason."

"Hazel, I'd rather be her target than you."

"Wrong. We'd both be the targets, and bigger targets than ever. We're safer this way. Just give me time. I'll try to call you every night, even if I can't talk. If I call and hang up, you know I'm okay."

"And if you don't call?"

"Then you'll probably see me down here the next morning. I know you don't like this, but you have to let it play out the best way it can, and that's with me controlling what happens." I glanced at my watch. "The slave and I should go. She'll start to wonder what's taking so long. I don't want to make this worse."

Jackson clenched his teeth. "Will you try to come over tonight?"

"If I can."

He nodded and I stood, Damien following behind me. My hand cupped Jackson's shoulder, and I kept a decent pace as I left the lobby and headed for our hall.

"Damien, I want you to try to take care in that cage. I'm going to do my best to calm my sister so she doesn't lash out at you anymore. I'm so sorry."

"It's not your fault."

"But it is. I guess she really does hate me. I've always known it but...I never expected her to go this far." But that was a lie. I knew Rory, and just how far she would go.

I slowed as we approached the door. "Remember to always call her Mistress. You don't know her name. Do as she says and pretend she's your world."

Taking out the key, I intentionally banged into the door as I dug through my purse. The slave took a deep breath and I turned, slipping in the keycard, and walking us in. The house was silent with no sign of Rory anywhere. But I knew where she was. She was in the closet, waiting. Always waiting.

JACKSON BANKS

Two days. No call. No breakfast. I sat in their lobby, staring mindlessly towards their hall, more in a daze than anything. Out of everyone I talked to, I got no help. No solid advice or relief. For someone who had no claim or even right to step in on Hazel's behalf, I felt completely lost. Even as a friend, I held no authority or say. What was I supposed to do, knock on the door and ask Rory if she remembered me from the bar? Was I supposed to tell her I'd come to check in on her to see if she was holding it together? I couldn't do that. It'd only make things worse for Hazel.

Voices sounded in the distance, and I turned sideways in my chair, hiding behind the large pillar I sat by. The female voice wasn't Hazel or Rory and the realization only had me pissed off even more. I felt helpless. I felt...yearning. My obligations and the protector in me were not getting along. My job came first. The rules of the Gardens came first. So why was I seconds from knocking on that door and breaking that bitch's neck?

If she was dead, Hazel lived.

But that was ridiculous. You didn't commit murder for a lover you'd just met. So what if we had a handful of trysts under our belt. That didn't qualify me to go all psycho. I was a guard. *A very well-respected guard.* My opinion and insight were encouraged. I was moving up quickly. I couldn't ruin that over a woman who may just be tiring of me. For all I knew, my help wasn't wanted. Maybe she didn't like me butting in and trying to save her. This was Hazel's battle, not mine. If she needed me, I was a phone call away. In the meantime…

I glanced around the empty lobby not believing how far I'd come so fast. I used to hang out with the guys. I used to drink beer and watch sports. I watched shows. Went to the movies. Busted some skulls at The Batter's Cage. Yet…here I was, waiting around for some rich, beautiful heiress like a pathetic love-sick fool. I wasn't even worthy of her, and maybe that's why I wanted her even more. Or maybe I was just dreaming. It's not like I could do anything anyway, even if Hazel appeared. She'd probably be with Rory and then what good would that do? I was lovesick. I'd even go as far to say borderline obsessed. She was all I wanted. All I needed, and nothing I did put an end to the overwhelming need to have her.

Standing, I headed for the hall to go the long way around. I wasn't going to have one of them walk out to catch me not far from their door. I had to stop this and trust that I wasn't making a mistake by leaving or not reaching out. But what if I was? What if the one time I walked away, I'd come to regret it? I stopped in the middle of the hall, closing my eyes as I fought for a solution. My phone ringing had my lids flying open. I immediately groaned as I pulled my phone out and saw Ryan's number.

"I really don't need you giving me anymore shit right now."

"Jackson?"

"…Hazel?"

"I'm sorry. I left the phone in the room with Rory and couldn't call you to ask if I could come over. Your roommate let me use his phone."

Was I already running to my apartment? I was.

"I'm on my way. Give me five minutes, tops. I'm going around the long way."

"It's okay." She paused. "Jackson...before you get here."

The worry in her tone twisted my stomach. It fed the protector. It increased my need to save her. The obsession. My legs wanted to slow through the caution, but I knew I was running faster.

"What is it?"

"Just." She stopped. "Just don't freak out or worry okay?"

I didn't even respond as fear bombarded me. My finger clicked the button, hanging up the phone, and my feet pushed harder. Faster. I was so full of rage, I was hitting the elevator in record time. I punched my finger into the button, fisting my phone hard enough to break it. How it wasn't crumbling to pieces or cracking in my grip, I didn't know. Worry. Worry. I wasn't just worried, I was fucking sick over what might have happened behind their closed door for the last two days.

"Come. *On*."

The door opened, and I nearly collided with three guards walking out. Over and over, I pushed my floor, my pulse pounding with every fucking second that dragged on. When the door finally opened, I could barely step through the threshold. Hazel stood there waiting. Her eyes full of tears as she took in my shock.

"Oh, *Hazel*."

I had no words. None that would make either of us feel any better.

Dark bruising covered one of her eyes, and it was half swollen shut. The purple webbed off to blacks and greens over her cheek fading not an inch from her split lip. The two tiny stitches told me she went to the hospital here, but that I'd missed her transport enraged me to no end.

"Did guards pick you up to take you in?"

"My sister." She sniffled. "It's not as bad as it looks. Nothing's broken or anything. I just—"

I pulled her into my arms, trying to be gentle but she still cried out.

"I wish you would have called me. I know there's nothing I can do, but fuck. What the hell happened?"

"It's a long story."

"Let's get settled in, and you can tell me."

Walking her to my apartment, I could feel her limping. Each step seemed to be a struggle and for the first time, I wanted her clothes off and it had nothing to do with sex. I wanted to see the damage. I wanted to feed off more of the boiling fury that was building by the second.

I opened the door, meeting Ryan's worried stare. He could sense my mood, and he stayed quiet as I led her to my room. "Are you thirsty? Hungry? Have you eaten or had anything to drink?"

"I'm okay. I just need to sit down."

Hazel was already lowering herself to the edge of my bed, wincing as she shifted through the pain. I eased to my knees, reaching for the hem of her shirt. She went to stop me, bursting into tears as I inched the T-shirt up over her waist. Whatever I had prepared myself for, I was grossly mistaken. I dropped the shirt, burying my face in her thighs as I tried to control my need for murder.

"Nothing's broken. I'm really okay. I have medicine for the pain."

"Talk."

It was the only word I could manage as I grounded myself by holding onto her hips.

"I tried to talk to Rory about getting help here instead of going back home to see Dr. James. At first I thought I was making ground, but something I said must have set her off. That was after we left the lobby that morning. After a few hours, I decided that I'd just call the clinic and set Rory up an appointment. I thought maybe if I just got it done, she'd agree and go. I shouldn't have done that. The Main Master called her to see if she was okay before I had the chance to warn her. She..." Another sob. "I've never seen her so mad."

My head lifted. "Does the Main Master know what happened to you?"

"I don't think so. I...You're the first person I've seen since the clinic."

"What do they think happened?"

Hazel looked down. "I told them Rory and I got in a fight. There's nothing wrong with that, and she was right there so I couldn't say much."

"Where is your sister right now?"

"Asleep. She stole some of my pills and took twice the dose. She won't be awake until morning."

"Hazel." I tried pleading to her with my expression. "Please. *Please.* Do not go back. Please."

Bright eyes disappeared as her head bowed. All I wanted to do was cup her face and make her look at me, but I was too afraid to touch her and hurt her more.

"Think about it. I'm going to get me a beer and let Ryan know everything's okay. Why don't you lay back and try to relax. You said you left your pills. I think we might have some pain reliever. Do you want some?"

"*Yes.*"

I nodded as she cried out and scooted back towards my pillows. I left my room, shutting the door. Ryan practically lunged in my direction the moment I rounded the turn.

"Dude, what the fuck happened to her? Did the sister do that?"

"Yep. Fucking cunt. I swear to God. I don't know how I'm still standing here. I can't breathe. I'm trying my hardest not to put my fist through a wall. I've never wanted to kill someone so

221

much in my life." I pulled out my phone. "You still have those pills for your back pain? Hazel left hers at her apartment." My hand covered my mouth. "You think her face is bad. Below the shirt—"

Ryan cringed. He turned, opening the cabinet to pull out the pills. As much as I wanted to call the Main Master, I had to go up through my chain of command. That had me dialing the High Leader's number. He was my boss and oversaw all the guards. He'd have to reach out to the Main Master for me.

"Nineteen."

"Sir, this is Banks. I need you at my apartment. I have Hazel Summerland here. Mistress Nineteen. Sir, she's…God."

"Is she okay?"

I could already hear footsteps increasing.

"No. It's nothing that happened just now, but she's hurt pretty badly."

"I'm with the Main Master. We're on our way."

"Thank you, Sir."

Hanging up, I took the pill from Ryan, grabbing a glass of water. Hazel tried pushing up to sit as I walked into the room, but it was almost impossible for her. Tears were racing down her cheeks again, and with how long it took her to get settled and take the pill, there was already knocking on the door. The sound had Hazel's eyes shooting open. She scrambled on my bed like prey, moving this way and that through her panic. The terror she held couldn't be masked as she searched for somewhere to hide.

"It's just the High Leader, my boss. Calm. It's okay. I'd never let anything happen to you. You're safe with me." I reached for her, trying my best to add comfort. She pulled me in, burying her injured face in my stomach. She was on her knees but sitting back on her heels. My shirt was caught in her tight grasp, and she was trembling so badly her body almost appeared to be convulsing. I glanced over as Nineteen headed toward us with the Main Master in tow.

"Mistress Nineteen."

Hazel's head shot up at the Main Master's voice. The look on Elec's face went beyond shock. He hadn't been expecting the damage any more than I had.

"Main Master." Hazel tried to step off the bed, jolting as she tried straightening completely. "Am I in trouble? I didn't get Jackson in trouble for coming here, right? I didn't mean to. I should have called."

"You're not in trouble." He stepped around Nineteen, moving only a good two feet away as he took in the abuse. "When did this happen, Mistress? We talked the day before last, didn't we?"

"Yes. It was over my sister's psychiatric appointment. You were checking to see if she was okay."

"That's right. Were you already like this when I called?"

"No, Sir." Tears raced down her face. "Rory didn't know about the appointment. I meant to prepare her, but I didn't get the chance. She's been like a loose cannon for the last few weeks. It's been getting worse and worse. I only meant to h-help her."

"But I made things worse." The Main Master cursed under his breath. "I had no idea she didn't know." He angled her face to the side. "You went to Medical."

"I did. My lip was cut badly from the statue Rory kept by the bed. I needed stitches."

"Is that what she used on your body too?"

Hazel's eyes shot over to mine.

"They have to see what Rory did. It's not just your face."

"But I'm okay. I told you; nothing is broken. It's just bruises."

The Main Master brought her face back to him. "What about the last time she put you in the hospital? You almost didn't wake up from that coma. You were lucky."

My heart all but stopped as Hazel dropped a shade of color.

"How…That was…No one knew."

"She's done this before?"

"Jackson." Hazel wiped the tears. "I think I'll be okay if I can just rest for a few days."

"Tell me there's something you can do," I growled to the Main Master. "I know they're a couple. I know they could kill each other if they wanted and there's not a damn thing we can do about it but *come on*. This isn't a normal situation. We can't send Hazel back over there. Rory will kill her next time. We all know it."

Silence played through the room as the Main Master gestured to Hazel's shirt. Her bottom lip edged out in a quivering pout while she drew it up just under her breasts. As he spun his finger, she obeyed, turning in a circle.

Nothing. The Main Master continued to take in Hazel as she lowered her shirt and waited.

"When I choose Mistresses and Masters for the Gardens, you all go through extensive testing. Rory was mentally evaluated. Would you say she's changed since then?"

Hazel took a few seconds, nodding. "We were tested almost a year ago, and then six months back. I'd say about four months ago, I noticed the change in her. It started with depressing episodes. They'd last a few days, and then she'd be fine for a while. I was hoping it would pass, but I've seen this before. Back when...I ended up in the hospital. This last month, I don't even know who she is anymore. I'd say she's at that breaking point again."

"But the slave you bought lives?"

"Barely," Jackson blurted out. "He looked just as bad as Hazel did under his shirt when I saw him a few days ago. She cuts him though too so he's getting both."

The Main Master nodded. "I'm going to have Rory re-evaluated. It's one thing to live this life and be in your right mind. There's a form of control that rests there. Mental illness is another thing entirely. Not only does it put her at risk, but it puts every other person here at risk as well, and that deems her unfit to continue in her role."

"You'll kick her out?"

The Main Master's eyes searched Hazel's face. Could he see her innocence like me? It was so obvious to anyone who really looked at her. Hazel didn't belong here. "No. Rory will have to stay here if she's incapable of being a Mistress. Permanently. She'll never be able to leave again. She knows too much."

"Oh." Hazel shakily lowered to the bed. "I guess that's better than you releasing her in the outside world. That's what worried me the most. She's too unstable for that." Her eyes closed. "If she wakes up and I'm not there…Her biggest fear is losing me. If we're separated, she will have a full-blown episode. It's what made her attack me to begin with. She's so afraid of me leaving her, yet she puts my life in danger making it a possibility of losing me forever. She doesn't see what she's doing. Or if she does, she's beyond the ability to stop herself. I don't know. I'm so tired. My head is killing me."

"You're okay with her staying here with you until I figure out what to do with the sister?"

I nodded to the Main Master, following him out as he headed into the living room.

"Hazel can stay as long as it takes."

The Main Master withdrew his phone, texting as he continued.

"I'm not expecting promising results from this evaluation, but I'm going to watch the attack anyway and see all sides." He paused, glancing up. "Testing takes a few days so the sister will be free. You're relieved of your guard duties in the meantime. Keep Hazel here. If she needs to get out, give me a call and she can come to my club. She'll be safe there. We don't need any more drama or violence between those two."

"Will do, Main Master."

He nodded, and I watched as he and the High Leader left the apartment. I headed over, locking it behind them.

"Keep that bolted at all times. I don't trust that crazy bitch from finding out where Hazel is. She has a fear of them being separated. If you ask me, she's going to fucking freak. I'm keeping Hazel in here so if you think you see her out there, it'll be Rory. She may be asking around. You don't know shit. You have no idea who Hazel even is. Got it?"

"Damn right I do, but what about the others?"

"Others?

Ryan rolled his eyes. "It's not secret amongst the ranks who you're seeing. You know word gets around like wildfire here. I'll do what I can to let everyone know, but I don't like the odds. If you ask me, it's only a matter of time if she starts asking around."

MISTRESS B-0019-2

RORY

It was a pounding. A banging that went beyond the pulsing deep inside my head. Time warped and stretched out. It had my eyes fluttering open. A blur of movement had me sitting, if not slightly falling. I rubbed over my eyes, trying to make sense of the deep voice that filled the room.

"Mistress B-Nineteen-dash-two. State your name."

"What?" I could barely make out the Main Master announcing the formal title as my eyes began to focus.

"State your name."

"You know who I am. Rory Summerland. What the hell is going on, and why are you being so loud?" I reached for Hazel, my head jerking to the side at the empty space. "Hazel?"

"Mistress, we need to talk."

"Hold on. Hazel?" Louder I called, stumbling down the stairs and slipping enough to catch my outer thigh on the edge of the wood. I threw back the lock on the cage, swinging the door open. The slave was scrambling forward, racing for the restroom, and there was no stopping him. How long had he been in there? How long had I been sleeping?

He flew by, and I turned in a circle, my legs nearly giving out from the medication I'd taken. "Hazel?" I called, reaching for the wall as stability started to come back. I glanced in the closet, nausea plaguing me as horror and anxiety nearly choked me.

"Hazel!"

"Mistress. *Rory.*"

Only then did I slow. I took in the Main Master, so confused why he was standing in my doorway.

"Where's my sister? Have you seen Hazel? Hazel?"

Louder, I called, my heart racing as I tried to peer around the guards that I could see in the living room.

"Your sister is safe."

"Safe? From what?"

"From you."

"*Me?* Why would she—"

"I saw the tape. I saw what you did to her."

I stopped as the last few days blurred in my mind. "Hazel." I tried racing past the Main Master, only to be faced with a wall of guards who were blocking the door. "Hazel!" I spun to the man whose dead eyes never left me. "Where's my sister? Where did you take her? Hazel!"

"Like I said, she's safe. Do you realize what you've done?"

Anger tried blanketing the guilt, but I was torn between the two. "She wanted to leave me. *Hazel's not leaving.* I want her back. You bring her back right now."

"Absolutely not. You signed a contract stating you were in stable mental health. I do not believe that to be true. I'm sending you in for an evaluation."

"You want to lock me away?"

"I didn't say that. You will not be admitted so long as you follow the rules. You can come and go as you please during the evaluation. But there *will* be conditions you abide by, or your freedom will disappear."

"I want my sister. She needs me. We need each other."

"Hazel will be under my care until I deem you of sound

mind. You have to prove you're stable and know what you're doing. If you pass, she returns home. If not," he shrugged, "you'll be taken care of in our special wing."

"Nothing is wrong with me."

"Then you should have no issues taking and passing the tests."

My hand settled on my chest, soaking in the hard thumps of my pulse. Hazel was gone. She was really gone from me.

"What happened to my sister? Did she come to you, or did you go to her?"

The Main Master's lids narrowed.

"Not that it's any of your business, but I went to her. She's a Mistress here. Her wellbeing is my responsibility, just as yours is. Had this been the other way around and she hurt you, she'd get the same treatment you are."

"*Would she?* I doubt that."

I spat the words in his direction, watching as he stepped closer.

"I'm trying very hard to be patient with you. You don't want to fight with me. It will not end well for you, Rory. *Focus.* During your evaluation, you are forbidden to search for your sister. You will not make contact. You will not so much as ask around for her. I told you she's under my care. Only when I feel you're safe to be around will I allow her to return. If you disobey, you prove you're not of sound mind. The Gardens have rules. You will follow them."

"That's bullshit. All of it. I'm fine. You need to bring Hazel back. Unless…*it's you.*"

The Main Master's head tilted as his stare narrowed even more.

"Elaborate. What's me?"

"All of this. Maybe you're here because you want to take her for yourself. You want to take Hazel so she can be yours."

He closed the distance between us even more, a threat on his face as he stared me down. "I don't like that tone or your insinu-ations, Mistress. Let's get something straight. If I wanted your sister, not you or anyone else in the world would be able to stop me. You're damn lucky I didn't choose her. If I did, you'd have been dead a long time ago."

Blazing heat poured from my skin as I began walking a slow circle around him. My mind told me to tread carefully, but my instinct only knew one thing; the threat. By a pure miracle, I managed to complete the circle and head for my bedroom door. I grabbed the handle, swallowing back my need to attack.

"When do my sessions start? I want this over with so Hazel can come home."

"You can report tomorrow. It'll be for five days."

"*Five days.*" My explosion was like a bomb. The room went deathly silent. The energy in the air became thick and still, making my skin prickle with the need to react. More, the Main Master looked at me like dessert. But it wasn't a good look. He wanted to hurt me. Kill me. I doubted anyone ever disrespected him, and he didn't like it one bit. It was so obvious, and yet I could barely care as my mind screamed for Hazel.

"Congratulations, Mistress, seven days. Report to the clinic you took your sister to when you busted up her face. Noon, every day. They'll be testing you there. If you miss a day, I'll add three. If you try to leave the Gardens, you're dead. I'll let you know when I have the results. *If you make it that far.*"

I wanted to scream. To lose every ounce of control I had and go crazy. I didn't as the Main Master left my apartment with his guards. Instead, I held onto the handle so my legs wouldn't collapse through the overwhelming realization that my sister was gone. Truly gone. *Seven days?* That was a lifetime. How was I going to manage without knowing she was there? We'd never been apart. Not for more than a day or two, and even that was rare. Ethan didn't even get an entire weekend without me showing up or Hazel coming home. We couldn't be away from each other. It was impossible.

"Mistress? Are you okay?"

I nearly did collapse then. My head still wasn't right from the medication. I was so fuzzy and far away. I had to think. Our game was over.

"They took Hazel. Fuck." A heavy, broken breath left me as I lowered to the floor. "Slave, they took my sister."

"Sister?"

I ignored his confusion, overlooking a real concern I couldn't decipher. Yes...he didn't know I had a sister. Not until right now. "I won't see her again for seven days. I...I don't know if I can do this." My lids narrowed as he cautiously came closer, lowering to sit down beside me. Blood was long dried from his waist up, and the scars evolving over the bruised skin had me lowering my gaze. All Hazel had wanted was for me to go to some stupid shrink. Now look where we were at. Hazel was hurt, and the Main Master was protecting her from me. *From me.*

My shoulders shook as the sobs came.

Me. The monster.

Me. The unstable one.

Me. Me. Me. Always me.

But what about her? How did the Main Master know to come take her? We'd made it out of the clinic just fine. They didn't even care. Something wasn't right. Not with how different Hazel had been lately. She was hiding something, and I was going to find out what it was. Maybe it would take days. Maybe I wouldn't discover anything at all. All I knew was I wasn't giving up until I questioned everyone who might know what the hell was going on. If Hazel or the Main Master was hiding something, I was going to find out.

"Get the shower ready, slave. We're going out."

I DON'T KNOW WHAT I HAD BEEN EXPECTING WHEN I STARTED ON my quest to discover the truth of Hazel. If it was cooperation from the Masters or guards at the Gardens, I wasn't getting it. Nothing I did had anyone talking. If they did speak to me, they knew nothing. Technically, I wasn't even supposed to be asking around for my sister, but I didn't care. Hazel belonged with me, and I wasn't going to stop until she was back.

"You mentioned things changed when your mother passed. You were around fifteen back then. Let's talk more about that."

My head tilted the smallest amount as I stared at the red-headed doctor. She couldn't have been more than forty. I instantly disliked her with her fancy, sophisticated clothes. She was clean. So clean and pure like Hazel. Yet...this woman wasn't. Not really. "This is supposed to be an evaluation, not a fucking shrink session, *Mistress*. I know you're not just a fancy doctor. You have no right to be judging me."

"I am more than qualified, Rory. I'm here to determine your mindset, and we need to go through the process, or I can't say with confidence that you're of sound mind. Tell me how things changed when your mom passed. It was a fall from a horse on set, wasn't it?"

"Yes." The word came out through clenched teeth.

"You and your sister were there when it happened. Start with what you remember."

"What I remember." My lids closed, but I wasn't thinking about what I saw or heard. The anger and irritation were too powerful for that. It was taking all I had to not stand up and walk out. "What I remember is the top of her fucking spine protruding from the side of her neck. The way her jaw dropped in shock only to shift to the side demonically as she landed awkwardly at an angle. I remember the odd sounding pop when she fell, and how the horse went crazy, stomping her chest in the process. I remember the way my father screamed as he ran towards her, almost getting kicked and trampled himself."

"It's sounds like you were close to where it happened."

"My sister and I were extras for the trail ride. We were on the horses next to hers, along with other people."

A pause. "Seeing your mother like that, how did it make you feel?"

"How the fuck do you think it made me feel? Horrified. Heartbroken." It was my turn to pause. "Intrigued."

"Intrigued? Let's visit that. Why?"

"She had what looked like a fucking bone sticking from the side of her neck. It was shocking. At first I was scared but..." I let out a deep breath. "I tried figuring out how it connected. What it was stuck to that held her altogether. And why after it broke that she died."

"I was old enough to know the basics, but I'd never seen death before that, and I didn't know much about anatomy. School wasn't my thing. I was never a good child."

"Why do you believe that?"

My stare lowered to my lap, but I couldn't stop my lips from twisting from the smile that wanted to come.

"I did some bad stuff when I was pretty young that would set me apart from most children."

"Tell me."

"Well...just stuff. Just...little things. Putting dirt in kid's lunches. Tripping or hitting people who annoyed me. I got in trouble a lot. Mrs. Bennings, my fifth-grade art teacher, for instance. That was when things shifted, I guess. Hazel and I had a project. It was one of those stupid clay-making things where we had to choose some sort of Christmas theme and incorporate it into an ornament. I decided I was going to draw a snowflake into mine. Hazel loved snowflakes, so I was really making it for her. Well, she put a Christmas tree on hers. Not only did she not gift it to me, Mrs. Bennings gave me a *B* where she gave Hazel an *A*. My snowflake apparently wasn't detailed or original enough and I was being lazy. I worked hard on that fucking project. It was never good enough. *I*...was never good enough. Mom got the stupid tree ornament, and me, *nothing*. Mrs. Bennings, though...I gave her the best present of all."

"What was that, Rory?"

"A concussion."

Eyebrows rose...not surprised. Not even judging me. She was waiting for me to elaborate and continue. I was over it.

"She had a golden apple paperweight on her desk. I hit her with it. I got suspended. I would have gotten a lot worse than that had my mom and dad not paid the bitch off." My teeth ground into each other. "She deserved worse."

"Because she didn't like your project and preferred your sisters?"

"I worked hard! I deserved an *A* too. I never wanted to be better than my sister. Just equal. You have no idea what it's like to always be the one who gets blamed. Who's never good enough. *I deserved better*."

"Maybe. Or maybe you've been fine all along, and you just think your life is bad."

"Are you saying I'm delusional, Doc?"

"Why don't you tell me about Hazel. You hinted she gets attached to men. Why don't you clarify what you mean."

"I mean exactly what I said. Hazel." I stopped. "Men fall for her easily. They get trapped in her spell of innocence. They think they'll save or protect her, or that she'll take care of them like their stupid mothers." I rolled my eyes. "She's good like that. She can get anyone to believe anything. She can become their most longed-after dream. And it's fun for her at first, but she's just as dumb as them. She gets what she wants, and she discards them. That breaks her heart. She cries over them. Mourns them as if they're dead. But they're not. Not always, unless she kills them. And she does. I've helped her clean up her messes, although it's been a while now. But she'd never admit what she's done to anyone. To say the truth makes it real. Perhaps she's the one who should be here, not me."

"Maybe she will. Or maybe that's just a part of your sickness as well. Is Hazel the bad one, or do you just think she is?"

The shrink wrote something down, bringing her attention back to me. I tried to compose myself so I wouldn't fly out of my chair, after her. My words were getting twisted, but I was starting to see that was the point. This woman wanted me to flip out. I wasn't going to give it to her. This Mistress worked for the Main Master, and she had my life before her, judging me just like everyone else. She had the right. What she wouldn't do was use something I confessed to her against me. I was being honest. That had to count for something. It better.

MISTRESS B-0019

HAZEL

Four days of television, sleep, and pacing. I wasn't sure how much longer I could stay couped up in this tiny apartment without even going to a lobby for breakfast. I was beginning to feel claustrophobic, and Jackson could see that as he drew more cards from the deck.

"I can't play. It's your turn."

I looked down at my cards, but I couldn't see them. I didn't want to. My emotions were all over the place, and I was having a hard time processing.

"I think I'm finished playing. Maybe I'll just go lay down in bed for a little while. I was thinking of starting Castle Way again."

"You just finished that book. *In a day.* I've been reading it now for three months." He let out a sigh. "We can sit on the couch and watch a movie."

"I don't think so."

Jackson's eyes lit up. "We'll go out."

"Go out? We can't leave anywhere."

"We can. The Main Master said I could call him. He'd let us into his club."

236

"He has a club?"

"Dark God Status. I've never been, but I've heard it's pretty wild. And usually mostly empty. It's VIP only. He's not even there sometimes. Just his chosen."

I looked down, pulling at Jackson's big T-shirt I wore.

"Oh...right. You'll need something to wear. Hold on. Give me a minute."

He sprung up, jogging to his room before I could even say anything. Within seconds he was talking to someone on the phone. I tried to listen, but I couldn't quite make sense of what he was saying. I knew it had to do with clothes, but I kept hearing words that didn't belong. I stood, trying to peer through without moving closer.

"Perfect." He burst through the threshold, smiling, holding the phone still to his ear. "Yeah, that should work." He paused. "Shoe size?"

"Seven." He repeated it, nodding at whatever was being said. "Twenty. Okay, sounds great, thanks." He hung up. "There. Done. Everything you need will be here in twenty minutes."

"What all do I need?"

"A dress. Makeup. Shoes. That sort of stuff. The slave said she'd make sure you had everything. I told her to add some surprises."

My hand came to my bruised face. At least my eye wasn't swollen shut anymore, and the darkness was already turning to a yellowish color in some areas. I still wouldn't be able to hide it with makeup. Just...mute it. "Jackson...are you sure? I can read or—"

His finger gently leveled at my lip, just to the left of the stitches.

"You deserve a night out. You need fun. To have space and be able to relax. You can do that at the Main Master's club. We'll take the elevator up on this side. No one is even allowed on that floor without the Main Master's permission. The guard presence up there is insane. Only the most trusted guards can even pull duty there. That's my goal," he smiled. "I want to be one of those guards."

"You will." I took his wrist, turning my head slightly to kiss against his finger. The act had him closing his eyes and pushing his other hand through the hair at the nape of my neck. His forehead pressed to mine, and time played out as we took comfort from each other's presence. It was nice to be able to connect with him on a level deeper than sex. He was sweet and caring. Nothing like what I imagined for a guard at a place that dealt in torture and murder.

"I should probably go figure out what I'm going to wear. Believe it or not, I can dress up when it calls for it."

"I can't wait to see."

"Don't open that door if someone knocks. Just yell out, and I'll get it."

"Alright." I eased back to the sofa, watching and smiling as he headed for his room. The moment he disappeared around the side, my smile fell.

I was going out. *To a club.* I never went anywhere like that. Was Rory out right now? Was she losing her mind, hurting herself in some destructive way? Was Damien still alive?

Minutes played out as guilt had me lowering my lids and losing myself in the darkness. A part of me wished I wouldn't have left. That part belonged to Rory. It was brainwashed by her and completely aware of the dependency that came with it. The other part...The other part rejoiced in finally being free. I could breathe. I could have fun and laugh and not worry about a negative remark or impending explosion.

I was torn on what was right or wrong, or who was even on the right side. What was more powerful? Was it my love for my twin, or the length I'd go to be free of her? There was one thing I knew for sure. This wasn't going to end well for one of us.

"What do you think?"

I took in the gray fitted slacks and black button up shirt. He had the long sleeves rolled to the middle of his forearms and the top loosely unbuttoned. His hair was even styled, slicked back on the side in a playful yet fashionable style. I found myself standing before I could stop myself. Jackson looked like a completely different person. The ruggedness was gone, transformed into...trendy.

"I...*Wow*. I..." I walked forward, taking in his wide shoulders and slim waist. I'd seen it in his uniform, but most of the time he wore jeans and loose fitted shirts. "You look amazing."

"You're surprised."

"Yeah," I laughed. "I didn't think this was your style."

"I have a few tricks up my sleeve."

"You really look phenomenal. Thank you for this. I know it can't be easy having me here all the time."

"Are you kidding?" He gently scooped me in his arms, kissing my cheek. "I can't remember being this happy. *Ever.* I was sort of hoping this would last a while longer. I could get used to this."

"Me too."

He leaned in just as knocking sounded. He checked the fancy silver watch, stealing a kiss as he put me down.

"They're late."

Walking over, he checked through the peephole before unlocking and swinging open the door. Bag after bag was handed over and my jaw dropped as I took in everything. When Jackson finally shut the barrier, I waved at the floor.

"All that for a night out?"

"For a few more days, just in case. There's pajamas, no more oversized tees of mine. Panties, bras. I told them to put in some loose, comfortable dresses." He leaned down, digging through the bag. "*Ah-ha.* And this."

"You got me a new book?"

The excitement in my tone couldn't be hidden.

"Better. I got you three."

I couldn't contain the squeal as he pulled the other two out. I couldn't stop from throwing myself into his arms either. Had I ever thought this guard was capable of such things? Never. I wasn't sure what I had expected when we met, but this wasn't it.

"You've outdone yourself. I don't even have words. Thank you." My head tilted back as I stared up at him. "*Truly*. Thank you for everything."

"I'm just getting started." He winked. "Go get dolled up. We have a date."

"A date?" At my smile, he pulled me back in, moving his lips to my ear. "I sure hope so. I'm serious when I say I don't want this to end."

When he pulled back, his smile was replaced with heat. So much heat that I felt my own flare to life.

"Go get dressed before I take you back to that room and ruin our night."

"Nothing about that sounds like ruination to me. More like a dream that's too good to be true." I stepped back, reaching down to grab the bags. I headed for the room, glancing over my shoulder as his gaze soaked in every inch of me. Not once did he look away.

"Jackson." I stopped at the bedroom doorway. "You're nothing like I expected. I knew you were amazing, but you're so much more than that. I like you."

He laughed, dazzling me even more with his smile.

"I like you too. Call if you need any help."

I nodded, easing the door shut. It didn't take me long to unpack the bags and get dressed. The makeup, on the other hand, took more time than I wanted to spend. No matter how much concealer or foundation I applied, I couldn't cover the bruises anywhere as much as I liked. As I stared at myself in the mirror, all I could do was sigh. The black dress I wore was fitted with the smallest amount of stretch, and it hugged to my curves, beautifully. It looked more appropriate for Rory, but that made me only like it more. My cleavage was visible in the low cut V, but not enough I felt uncomfortable. The material even had a shimmer to it every time I moved. I smiled, spinning in the stilettos, praying I didn't break an ankle on top of my already beat up body.

Heading for the door, I took a deep breath, not prepared as both Jackson and Ryan stopped talking and gaped at me. Jackson caught himself first, but Ryan's expression was frozen. It took Jackson elbowing him for his roommate to snap out of it. He was still in his uniform, and clearly just finished his job.

"You look gorgeous."

"Thank you. I tried," I stopped, pointing to my face. "It's the best I could do."

"I don't even see the bruises anymore. God, you're *unbelievably* gorgeous."

Ryan made a sound. "Good luck getting through stops. I hear there's four just to make it to the entrance. You know they're going to be giving you hell."

"Let them try. They're just jealous."

"Yes they are. You called the Main Master and cleared it?"

He nodded to Ryan. "Yep. They're expecting us."

"Lucky."

But he didn't look at his friend. He was eating me up with his gaze. "Yes I am. Don't wait up for us." Jackson's arm came out, and I gripped his large bicep, letting him lead me to the door. As we waved to Ryan and headed down the hall, I couldn't help but glance up.

"The other guards are going to give you a hard time?"

"All in fun. I guess it's gotten around that we're…talking."

"Dating?"

"In my wildest dreams." He laughed.

"This is a date, isn't it?"

Jackson slowed, his face turning serious. "Well...yes. I mean...yes, but." He stopped. "You'd really date me?"

"You seem surprised. It's not like we're getting married, but..." I took in his expression, his need, *his immense want*. I felt it in every inch of my manipulative body. I slid my hand down his arm, lacing my fingers with his. "I do like the thought of seeing where this goes. Dating sounds good to me."

Seriousness grew with a tinge of uncertainty.

Jackson swallowed, his fingers flexing against mine. "I don't want to screw this up, so bear with me. That's titles, right? Boyfriend? Girlfriend? Feel free to tell me if I completely read that wrong. I just want to make sure."

"Let's just say dating. We have time for titles." Heat burned my cheeks as I glanced up, shyly. "Seven real dates or two months from today. Whatever comes first. If you still want to see me after that, I'd love to be your girlfriend. I just...I think after a while, you're going to get tired of me."

"Tired of you?" Jackson pulled me in close, stopping us in front of the elevator. "Never. Not for a moment."

The door opened as he leaned in to kiss me. Two guards threw us smiles and immediately went into hushed whispers as we got on the elevator. The moment he pressed the floor and the door shut, Jackson leaned in, taking his kiss.

"Two months or seven dates. What if I decided on a date every night from tonight? Does that count?"

"You want me to be your girlfriend that bad?"

"I don't need the title. I just want to know you're my girl."

"I thought I already was."

His eyes said it all. I had him. Every inch of every part of him. Not once after that did he leave my side or remove his claiming touch. I liked it. I encouraged it.

Our ride up played out in a comfortable silence, and it lasted through the checkpoints. The guards did smile or give him a look, but no one said anything until we reached the entrance.

"Banks. I didn't believe it at first, but here you are." The guard glanced at me, grinning my way.

"Yep," Jackson answered. "Here we are. Did you need to see my ID or anything?"

The guard shook his head. "I just need the Mistress's arm."

"My arm?"

"The price of admission is your blood."

My lips parted, and I hesitantly lifted my arm out towards him. The knife had me swallowing hard as the tip punctured my skin. The guard paused, lowering his voice. "You'll want to bleed it out. Don't wipe it away. It's an honor to be here."

"Of course." I dropped my hand back to my side following Jackson to the large doors that seemed to go up forever. Music thumped in the distance, and my heart quickened as darkness swallowed us whole. The black was so deep, it didn't even appear as a color, but more a hole in the surrounding red lighting. As bad as it was, I couldn't even focus on the shades. My stare locked on a glass room in the distance, housing butchers. Human body parts dangled from hooks while ground meat oozed from one end of a machine. There were buckets full of organs, and blood smeared all over the place.

Slower, Jackson and I walked, until we were sliding in the first booth we came across.

"This is...not what I expected." Jackson continued to look around like me.

Three butchers. Three glass stations. There was even an elevated sitting area that was empty, standing out amongst the others. It looked like an altar or throne. That had to be where the Main Master sat. In the center of the room was a stage, but if someone had been performing, they weren't anymore. Or maybe they were on a break.

"May I get the two of you a drink?"

I glanced at the beautiful, dark-skinned slave who wore a yellow head wrap with a matching dress. The short little number was so thin, it flowed over her body like tissue paper. I glanced at the bar, deciding to order the only alcoholic drink I really knew.

"Jack and Coke."

"That sounds good," Jackson said, surprised. "I'll have one too."

The slave nodded, walking away.

"Jack and Coke. I did *not* expect you to order that."

"Did you expect something fruity?"

"I did, actually," he laughed. "Why Jack and Coke?"

I shrugged. "It was my dad's drink. Rory and I would always sneak in and make us a small glass when he was asleep." The memories had a grin appearing. "I don't usually drink anymore. It's been years. I don't like to, but tonight is a good night."

"It is." He reached over the table, holding to my fingers. "I know I've already said it, but you look amazing." Lifting, he cupped my hand in both of his as he leaned in to level his lips against our connection. He didn't kiss. He just continued to stare at me in nothing short of fascination. I didn't break the spell. I kept our gazes locked until the slave was easing our drinks to the table.

"Thank you," I mumbled the words as she hurried off. I grabbed the glass, sipping against the top as I watched Jackson. So many things were going through my head. So many questions I wanted to ask so I could read him better. Would it even make a difference?

"May I ask you something? I feel...I really like you, and that scares me. I want you to know me, Jackson. The real me. Most think they have me figured out, but I'm not normal. I'm not just here for Rory." I paused, frowning as I took in his wavering expressions. "If you think I'm good, I'm not. I deserve this title, and when the time comes, I'll put it to use. You have to know that."

"I'll admit, I see you as good, but the truth is, none of us are saints. You have to have a certain mindset to even be here. Tell me who you are, Hazel. I want to know everything about you. I won't judge. I've seen shit you can't imagine. Just be completely open and honest. I think I can handle anything."

"First, tell me about you. What brought you here?"

Jackson shifted in his seat. I could tell he wasn't necessarily comfortable with what he was about to say.

"I lived an average life. I had a middle-class family until my parents died when I was nineteen. I graduated high school and went into the military. I excelled and moved up in record time. One day I saw some shit I wasn't supposed to. It was death with a bullet or the end of my outside identity. That was only the beginning. I had to prove my worth. I had to fight to make it here. We went through hell. Literally, I think." He smiled. "It was for the best. Aside from my job, my life in general was shit. I had a brother. It didn't work out with him. We fought a lot. He was into drugs. He almost got me arrested once and destroyed my career. I loved him, it was just a mess. Anyway, I've killed. I've almost been killed. I've done some really bad shit I'm not sure I can even say out loud. I'd do it again if I had to. That doesn't make it easier, but there's nothing I can do about it either. It just is."

"It just is. I like that."

I interlaced our hands again and moved them closer to me.

"I've killed. I've hurt people. Rory didn't make me do that, Jackson. I did it because I wanted to. In my youth, I pretended to be my sister because I was ashamed of the need. As if death cared about my name." My head lowered, and all I could see was my mom's horse bucking. I had only meant to scare her by causing the horse to rear up. I thought she'd blame Rory, and then I could get my sister back for calling me names. I never expected her to die. It hadn't even been plausible in my mind back then. But it happened, and the horrible part was...I got to be the mom. I got to fulfill that role and make the rules. I was

245

needed. Depended on. I was happy. That didn't mean my manipulative ways ended there. They didn't; they were fed. They blossomed, even if Rory and I resented that part at times.

"My mom died when we were fifteen. After that, Rory got really bad. She was always a troublemaker, but she started doing dangerous things. Her temper got worse, and I guess mine did too. I was just better at hiding it. Men wanted me. Even before my mom died. They were always around, on set or at parties my parents were invited to. It's like Rory and I couldn't escape them. And they were always at least twice our age. Twenties. Thirties. Forties. *Older.* We were kids, and the touches and propositions were never ending. One night, I had enough."

"Your first kill?"

"Yes." I lied. My mom was my first kill, but no one would ever know that. "I was almost seventeen. It was at one of these parties I mentioned. My dad was being celebrated, and I hadn't almost gone. I wasn't in the best mood, but I wanted to support my dad. During the celebrations, I slipped outside to just get away. I needed to breathe. It was so loud. Well, I was standing at the end of the deck, overlooking the mountainside. Someone...a man...he wrapped around me, pushing his hand between my legs. I screamed, but it was already so loud from the party that no one heard. I started thrashing and fighting against him. He smelled like liquor so bad, and all I could feel was the anger. Fear, yes, but so much anger at the audacity that he thought what he was doing was okay."

"What did you do?" Jackson was leaning closer to me, his mouth inches now from our joined hands.

"I managed to get free and scramble away. The guy was wasted drunk. He started yelling stuff to me about leading him on, and how my dress was too sexy and short. It wasn't. It was almost to my knees. Anyway, he thought I had left because I moved into the darkness on the side of the house. His mistake was turning his back to me. He moved in to look out over the mountainside. Along the side of the house there was a flowerbed with these rocks about the size of your palm. They had little designs painted on them. I took one and snuck up behind him. He heard me, but he wasn't nearly fast enough." I paused, seeing nothing but Rory laying in the bed across from me. She was giggling and telling me about Mrs. Bennings and the apple.

"I hit him between the eyes as hard as I could. The man was so stunned, he threw himself back, right over the deck. It was a steep drop off and pretty far down. I put the rock back and went back into the party. I never told anyone that story but you."

Jackson searched my face, leaning forward and kissing my hands. "He deserved it."

"I thought so."

"Killing that bastard doesn't make you a monster. You're a fucking hero in my book. I would have killed him too."

"But I liked it, Jackson."

"So, you liked it. That doesn't make me not like you."

"What if I wanted to kill again?"

"Do you?"

"…I don't know. Not yet, but someday I might."

"How many people have you killed, Hazel?"

"Three, but the need is there. The yearning. Whether I can embrace it, I don't know, but I want you to be aware."

Jackson looked off to the side, taking in the closest butcher.

"Seeing what they're doing, how does that make you feel?"

"Honestly?"

He turned back to me, his lids narrowing through the deepening of my tone.

"*You like it.*"

"Not just like, Jackson. I love it."

JACKSON BANKS

I was learning more by the day that Hazel was nothing close to the person I believed her to be when we first met. That wasn't a bad thing, quite the opposite. Where I'd felt she was too good for this world, I was quickly being put at ease that she might be able to handle my side of our life after all. Sometimes I did bad shit. I was okay with that, but I worried if she'd hold it against me. I wasn't going to have to worry about that anymore. Hazel was a lot more like me than I could have imagined, and I had a great feeling about a possible future together. *This was going to work.*

"I like this place."

Hazel finished off her second drink, swaying to the underline music. It wasn't too loud, but it was definitely noticeable. As if it were set to the perfect volume to enhance without overpowering. It was nice. Like magic to the happiness taking me over.

"How do you think they choose the slaves they butcher? Do you think they're crows?"

"Maybe." I laughed, biting my bottom lip. I couldn't stop taking in how beautiful Hazel was with her heavy lids and swaying body. I'd never seen her so relaxed and happy at the same time. "I'm going to find out for you. Someone must know."

"You have the coolest job." She eased to a stop looking up at me through thick lashes. Her dark curls were wild from all the movement, and the lust called me in, stronger than ever. "I never told you how sexy you are in your uniform. The first time I saw you, I swear it's like...time just stopped. I thought to myself, who is this man? I could barely function enough to approach you. I was so shy yet...*I couldn't help myself.*" Her face seemed to darken under the red glow. "I wanted you so bad. I've never done anything like that before. I still can't believe what I did, propositioning you like that. Have you?" She stopped, a small pout drawing me forward over the table, as if I could move through it to get closer to try to comfort her sudden sadness. "Have you ever been with anyone here? A Mistress or slave?"

"Not a single one. Hazel...I truly do not understand why or how you chose me. You literally could have had your pick of anyone. I'm no one. But." I stopped. "I wish you could read my mind or at least understand it. My job is my life. Had it been anyone but you, I don't think I would have even told them I was allowed. *You.* It could only have been you, which is crazy since what happened was so out of character. It's like—"

"*It was meant to be.*"

"*Yes.*"

My awe grew. I was drunk. I knew I was drunk. Where she was finishing her second glass, I was on my fifth. I didn't do liquor. Not often, and these were a lot stronger than I had prepared for. But I knew she was feeling it too, so I wasn't too worried as I let myself enjoy our night.

"Can I sit by you?"

"You don't even have to ask. There's plenty of room. Come here, baby."

Hazel stood, slowing as she came around to my side. A single light flooded the center of the stage, drawing our attention as she slid in next to me. As I wrapped my arms around her from behind, I took in two rows of cloaked figures appearing from the nothingness at the back of the club. They seemed to appear from nowhere in their dark hoods and flowing robes. Intricate symbols aligned the bottom hems of their arms and even encircled the fabric concealing their feet. Whether they were men or women, Masters, Mistresses, or slaves, I didn't have a clue. Fingertips were hidden with black gloves and their faces were concealed from the oversized hoods as they seemed to stare down.

"What do you think they're doing?"

Hazel's voice was barely a whisper. Eerie music seemed to fade in from nowhere as I lowered my lips to her ear. The cloaked figures stepped on the stage, moving into a circle to surround the outside area.

"I have no idea. Maybe it's a play or some sort of act?"

Before she could say anything, the cloaked figure at the very back opened their robe, dumping a nude woman on the floor. Her body was pale under the bright spotlight, and she immediately scrambled to stand, crying and whimpering as the figures stepped this way and that, blocking her escape. Even though there was no microphone on her, her voice carried through the speakers as if the stage itself was picking up everything, and maybe it was.

"Please. I want to leave. Please."

"If this is a play, she's a very good actress."

Hazel was sitting up against me straighter. She seemed more intrigued than afraid as she watched on. With the amount of room closer to the back of the booth, I opened my legs, pulling her to sit in-between them. As I leaned against the sofa-style backing, Hazel flowed with my movements, bringing her legs up to the seat and leaning against my chest. Her breathing was increased, but her eyes stayed transfixed ahead as the woman screamed and bounced from one pair of reaching arms to the other.

"Someone help me! I want to go home. Please!"

"Home?" I flattened my palm just under Hazel's breast, slowly moving up over the roundness. "She must be new. At this point she should have already embraced this place as her home. She hasn't. Her fear is real."

Hazel's breath caught as my fingertips traced a circle over the hardening nub. The deep vibration wasn't heard, but I felt the hum in my body as her legs drew up to the side.

"Let go of me. Let. *Go.*"

Dark hair was pulled one way, being caught from another figure as they tried to bring her in their direction. Hands groped and forced their way into her pussy. Screams got louder, reaching a heightened pitch as bite marks and slices from a blade made blood run down her chest and arms.

"Stop, I want to go," she sobbed, loudly. "Stop! St-Stop!"

But the ten cloaked figures only pulled at her harder, one even causing a loud pop from her arm as they almost seemed to try to pull her limb off. One's head was buried between her outstretched legs. She was a good five feet off the ground, now, with every limb being tugged at with what appeared to be extreme force. She tried to fight and thrash, but it was pointless through the hold. Nails tore down her skin, and one kept biting and taking chunks from her body, only to spit the flesh on the wooden floor. Hazel was moving more against me, and me...I hadn't even realized I had one of her nipples pinched between my fingers, and my other easing over her upper thigh.

"Jackson." I paused. It wasn't a request to stop. Her fingers were digging into my thighs as she spread her legs to give me access.

"Please! I'll do anything. Anything! Someone—"

Her voice was cut off through whatever pain she experienced. She sucked in a breath, going into murderous screams. My finger traced over Hazel's panties and the wetness had me moaning and sliding under the lace to bury my finger inside of her.

What appeared to be chanting began, increasing with the slave's screams and sobs. She was trying to fight harder than ever. As much as I wanted to watch, my eyes kept moving down to Hazel as she rocked against my finger. I was squeezing into her breast, pushing as deep as I could go as I had her pinned to me.

Sliding another finger inside, Hazel's hold left my thighs to wrap around my forearm. She was so wet, loving every second of my teasing as I dipped in and out to tease her clit. Just as I lifted my eyes to take in the show, I glanced up, catching the Main Master walking to the stage. Even Hazel felt the shift in the energy. Her head lifted, but she slid her hand down, holding my wrist in place so I didn't withdraw my fingers.

"*Please!* Oh, G-God, please help me." More cries. "I want to go home. It's b-been weeks. I have to g-go. I-I-I....I....Ple..."

The girl was staring at the Main Master as he stepped to the edge of the stage, but she wasn't moving anymore. It was as if she were suddenly a statue.

The Main Master's hand rose high, and he kept it there as the figures parted, letting him inside the circle. The slave was lowered to stand, and she stood upright, just as frozen as her face.

Higher, the Main Master went, slowly tracing his hand out to the side. The slave's head glided with the movements: right, down, left, up, down. For what seemed like minutes, he played her like a puppet. His head tilted and he snapped his fingers in her face twice. The slave's hand lifted, palm up, staying in place, not moving.

"We've met before." The Main Master's voice purred, rich and coaxing. "Do you remember me?"

"Yes."

Monotone. No emotion.

"What do you remember of me?"

"You've been coming to me every day since I've been here."

"I have, and for good reason. Sometimes in the outside world we make mistakes. Maybe it's our own fault. Or maybe the people we meet are the ones who are out to get us. You wanted to be in a relationship with someone before you were brought here. You did some very, very bad things to that person. Didn't you?"

"...Yes."

"You made quite the mess for my friend. Does that make you happy?"

A pause. "No."

"Tell us why."

"All I wanted was for him to want me."

"Yes. So you've stated on more than one occasion. Tonight, I'm not just going to give you to him. You're going to do that in the most profound way one can. Would you like that, slave?"

"Yes."

The Main Master lifted his hand again, beautifully cutting through the air as the slave followed his movements. Foreign words began to leave his mouth that I'd never heard before. Phrases. Short sentences. The roll of his tongue and weaving of words had Hazel holding my wrist tighter as she got close.

Silver reflected and I leaned down, nibbling against Hazel's ear as the Main Master handed over a dagger.

"You say you love him. *Prove it.* Cut out your heart so I can give it to him."

No fear. The Main Master pointed below her breasts, to the inside of her ribs.

"You're going to cut here, and with your other hand, you're going to reach inside your chest and pull it out. You might have to get creative. I have no doubt you'll die trying. Lift the knife. Show your love."

"Fuck. Fuck." Hazel's lips parted as the slave stabbed the

blade of the dagger in, slicing through her skin like butter. Her face turned into my bicep, and it had nothing to do with her being uneasy with what she was seeing. Spasms shook her as I grabbed her hair, tilting her head back so I could run my tongue along the slit and corner of her mouth.

"After she's dead, we're done. We're going home, and I'm going to lick every ounce of cum from your pussy." I lifted her face, forcing her to watch the slave who forced her hand in the split skin below her sternum. Blood poured down her stomach and down her legs, even dripping from her pussy as she stared ahead in a trance, digging, twisting to maneuver inside of herself. The spasms were slowing from Hazel, followed by small jerks from her legs as she watched in horror-filled fascination. "I've never wanted you more than I do right now. When we get back, I'm going to show you just how much."

MISTRESS B-0019-2
RORY

"**R**emember what I said when we get there. Smile. Stop looking so fucking afraid, or I'll give you a real reason to mope and cower. *Last night was nothing.* You're lucky I held back at all."

"Yes, Mistress."

The slave's head was practically bowed as we headed down the long hall. I dazzled with my fake outgoingness. I socialized. I talked to anyone who would speak with me. Not about anything in particular. I waited for someone to recognize me. Or...*her*. It was driving me insane that people just wanted to communicate to talk about themselves. I wasn't here for that. I wanted my sister. It didn't matter that I was on the morning of the one-week mark. If I didn't find her soon, I truly might lose my mind. I was hanging on by a thread. My hands stayed jittery. My adrenaline never quite found a baseline. I was all over the place mentally and physically. To stay in my apartment when I knew someone had to have seen Hazel was impossible. I was determined to discover where she was hiding, but I had already covered all the floors before. The slave and I had even ventured into the city. There was only two places I hadn't gone, and one was impossible. That was the Main Master's floor at the very top. The other had promise. Maybe I wasn't even supposed to be on the guard's side of the building, but I didn't care. What would they do, tell me to leave? For all they knew, I was lost.

Glancing behind me, I threw the slave a glare. He lifted his head, forcing a small grin. I stared ahead, plastering on my own smile. I could hear voices in the distance, around the turn, but they weren't female. I took a deep breath, holding my shoulders high as I broke around the side. Two guards were at a vending machine, laughing about something.

"Hello."

They turned at my voice, their smiles melting into a look I didn't like.

"Are you lost?"

"Is it so obvious?" I laughed, taking in every micro expression on their face. "I'm sorry, I was curious what was this way. I've been everywhere else. Is this where you all live?"

"You can't be here." The taller guard's voice was deep as he took a step towards me. He glanced at my slave, coming back to me. To say he appeared angry was an understatement. It immediately threw flags, but concerning what, I wasn't sure.

"I'm sorry. I wasn't aware it was off limits. Is your set up like ours with lobbies, shops, and restaurants? Maybe you have better ones over here."

"*You can't be here,*" the taller guard said, reaching for the radio at his shoulder. My hand came up cautiously causing him to pause.

"Wow, am I in trouble? I was only trying to be nice and strike up conversation. I'm sorry if I upset you. That wasn't my intention. Surely you can see this was a mistake."

"I don't care what it was. Head back that way and go to your own side."

That was more than some baseless anger. He was intentionally targeting me as a bad person. He knew who I was. Had the Main Master warned them, or was it something more?

"Okay, I'll go back. First…I'd like you to do me a favor."

The guards didn't say anything as I stepped closer. What they did do was watch my every move. I was dangerous to them. Lethal. They were ready for me to strike which had me peering between the elevator and main hallway. Hazel was here somewhere. She was on this side. I could feel it.

"I'd like an apology. I'll leave, just tell me you're sorry for being *rude and mean*. I'll be talking to the Main Master about this. I did nothing but end up at the wrong place, and I shouldn't be treated this way for it. It was a mistake. Nothing more."

"Do what you have to do." The taller guard crossed his arms over his chest. "I'm not apologizing for doing my job."

"Alright. I see how it is." I turned with every ounce of rage in me, meeting my slave's stoic face as I headed back for the hall. As I turned to look over my shoulder, the two guards were moving in to watch me leave. The tall one was even talking on his radio. Was he calling me in? Telling everyone to watch out for me? Fucking Hazel. Why hadn't she just come home? She couldn't be kept prisoner on that side. The Main Master saw her as a victim. She knew her place was with me. Why didn't she just come back?

My lids narrowed even more. *Because she didn't want to.* How long now had she wanted to leave? Too long. For all I knew, she planned this entire thing. Maybe the Main Master lied, and she'd gone to him. Was there something between them? He said no, but wasn't he surrounding her by guards, hiding her from me. Keeping us apart? Why? What reason did he have to do that? Abuse wasn't against the rules here. Fuck, it was encouraged. We were in the house of death, and I let her live. Why take her? Why allow her to hide from me?

I walked faster, storming past a Master who was leaving his room. Glancing behind me, the slave was walking fast trying to keep up, but it was the guards I ate alive with my gaze. They were still there, watching. *Protecting.*

Stopping at my door, I reached for the card, unlocking it and throwing the barrier open. I screamed, then. I went right for the lamp, jerking it from the coffee table, and throwing it at the wall.

"She got to them. They have her. They fucking have her and are trying to protect her in pure Hazel fashion. That bitch. I swear I'll make her pay for this."

Once I started, I couldn't stop. Everything I could get my hands on, I destroyed. When there was nothing for me to grab, I headed for the kitchen, pulling out a butcher knife and stabbing it into the leather sofa, slicing and tearing my way down the thick cushions. Deep breaths left me. My head was spinning, and I couldn't focus as my legs gave out and I collapsed to the floor.

"Mistress."

"*What?*"

I couldn't even see the slave from my position. He was hiding, and that was good news for him.

"You have to be at your appointment in ten minutes."

My eyes rolled, and I fell back to the floor, peering up at the ceiling. I could do this. One last appointment, and then Hazel would be mine. She'd pay. She'd pay so fucking bad. I'd kill her this time for making me undergo this bullshit.

"Mistress?"

"I heard you."

A groan left me as I stood. My hand gripped tighter to the handle of the knife, and I pointed it at the slave who stood by the bedroom door.

"Grab my purse. You're staying here. If she comes home, you will not let her leave. Your life depends on it. I don't care who she's with. If she comes, she stays. Understand?"

He nodded, seconds passing before he was able to mumble a response. My purse was on the table next to him, and he grabbed it, walking over. The fear he held had me snatching the tote to put the knife inside.

"I'll be back. Do *not* let her leave."

"Yes, M-Mistress."

And she'd be back. It was day seven, and I knew where I stood. I was a psychopath. That did not mean I was crazy. Paranoid, yes. Delusional? Having hallucinations? Unaware of the difference between right or wrong? Not at all, and they couldn't lock me up for that.

I shut the door, heading towards the elevator. I put my purse over my shoulder, running my hand down the length of the black and white jumper I wore. The long sleeves were pushed up to my forearms and the fabric was wrinkled along my legs. That probably wasn't the best thing. I didn't look too well put together. That didn't matter. I kept repeating that as I approached the elevator.

"I thought that was you. *What are you doing on this side?* Does Banks know you're out of the apartment?"

I looked over my shoulder at the uniformed guard, only realizing the man was talking to me. That had me taking him in even more. His earpiece was out, and his radio appeared off. He wasn't working right now. He couldn't hear what they were saying or if they were saying anything at all.

"Banks?"

"Jackson. Does he know you're out here?"

My lips parted as I slipped into a guilty yet sad expression. "He's going to be so mad. Shit. I only wanted to get out and breathe a little. Maybe get a muffin. It's been almost a week. I was going to hurry."

"It's not safe for you to be out here. Let's get you back before someone sees you."

"You mean my sister?" I gave him a suspicious look. "Are you sure you're a guard? You don't look like you're on duty, and shouldn't you know this?"

259

The man hesitated, completely confused on me turning the tables. "I swear I'm a real guard. I was about to go on duty now. Ryan, Jackson's roommate, clued me in last night on what's going on. I've been above, pulling duty there, so I haven't been at the meetings, but he did show me your picture. Your sister put you in danger."

I still looked at him skeptically. "That's right." He waved me to follow, but I still pretended to eye him curiously. "Rory is crazy. She just lost it that night."

"I'm sorry. That's never a good thing."

"No, it's not." I followed along, heading back towards the end of the hall where the guards had found me. My fists were drawn in tightly, and I was praying they were long gone by now.

"I once had a bad fight with my brothers. Good riddance. Siblings aren't always our friends. Sometimes they can turn out to be your worst enemy."

"Tell me about it."

Smiling, I let him know I was getting more comfortable with him. We approached the turn, and I held my breath as we stopped in front of the elevator. When the door opened, two guards paused at my presence. They stepped out, eyeing me warily as they headed for the hall. My hands were shaking as I climbed on the elevator and adjusted my purse. My heart was nearly pounding out of my chest and the anger was building by the second. My sister was not just with one man, but two? Who the fuck were Jackson and Ryan, and how did she manage to get the love of the Goddamn guard?

"I can't tell you how much I appreciate you bringing me back. It was stupid to leave and go out on my own. Rory's usually up at night and sleeps during the day so I thought I was safe. That was such a stupid move on my part. I'm so embarrassed."

"Don't worry about it," the guard laughed. "The muffins here are pretty good."

I laughed, nodding. "*Right*. They're addicting. It's been almost a week and I feel like I'm dying."

"I know Banks won't leave your side. I'm a little surprised you slipped past him, but it's best to listen to his rules. You're not safe. Next time have Ryan go get you one. I'm sure he would in a heartbeat."

Glancing down, I looked up shyly. "They're so great to me. Jackson's...amazing. He's always looking out for me."

"Well, from what Ryan tells me, he's head over heels for you. I still can't believe the two of you are dating. He's a lucky guy."

The elevator door opened, and any hint of a smile was long gone. We headed to the hall, and I couldn't stop the fire from pouring from my skin. Dating? Since when? You didn't start dating someone within a week. Hazel had been lying, and I was pulled back all the way to auction night. She was smiling. Happy. She'd found him, then, and she planned this entire thing. *Bitch.*

"Here we go."

I let the guard step to the door as I moved against the wall. Looking down, I opened my purse. The moment the door pulled back, I grabbed the handle of the knife thrusting it through the guard's neck, and jerking it back just as fast. Wide eyes from the man at the door only registered for a moment before I was slicing and stabbing the knife in his direction.

"I don't see Hazel. You must be the roommate, *Ryan*."

The large blade sliced down his forearm and a flimsy end table crashed under his weight as he tripped over it. Anger overpowered fear as he rolled to his side, barely missing the knife as I reared back and stabbed it down. Pressure grasped my wrist, crushingly, but I grabbed a beer bottle from the ground, smashing it into the man's head. Skin split and blood oozed free as his head fell back, and he went limp. A door swung open, and my gaze cut up just in time to see Hazel's shocked face.

"You are in *so* much trouble, Sister."

261

"Jackson!"

"*No you don't.*" I grabbed the knife, rushing forward as she slammed the door shut. I collided into the barrier, pushing it back open a few inches before she could secure the lock.

"Jackson!"

I barely heard the water turning off and a crashing sound. Harder, I pushed, throwing every ounce of strength I had forward. Weight gave way, and Hazel and I went pouring into the room. She fell back into the bed while I crashed to my knees, but I was up just as fast.

"*Jackson!*"

"You call to him? *What about me?*" I sliced the air, cutting into the side of her calf as she tried to spin further on the bed. Hazel grabbed a pillow, swinging it towards me as I dove forward, trying to stick the knife in her thigh. The pillow slammed into my side, knocking me off balance. Hazel grabbed my hair with her other hand, dropping the pillow and trying to reach for the weapon. All she got was my forearm as we fell to the floor and began to wrestle each other for control.

"You shouldn't have come, Rory."

"No? You knew I would. *You were counting on it.*"

"You know me *so* well, but you really don't."

"I think I do."

I grabbed her shirt, growing closer with the tip of the blade. Hazel went into screams again, overpowering me enough to turn us sideways.

"Jackson! Please!"

"Always the victim. The fucking damsel in distress."

A smile flashed catching me offguard. It only made me angrier as I yelled and threw my weight forward. Color blurred and I grasped a fistful of Hazel's hair as I stood, slicing toward the man who was now staring at us in horror. As I took him in, I felt the blood drain from my face, rooting in our predicament.

"I know you. You...*You were the one at the bar.*"

"Jackson, *please.*"

"Shut up, Hazel!" I reached down, cutting her neck enough to make her stop reaching out to the fucking guard who was inching closer. If she was trying to stop the bleeding, she wasn't focused on calling to him.

"Were you watching me? *Spying on me?*"

"No. I thought you might be Hazel. Rory, drop the knife. No one else has to get hurt. Let's just talk about this."

"What is there to talk about? My sister played you. She played us both. Hazel was never going to stay with me. *Were you, sister.*" It wasn't a question. I leveled the blade at her neck, twisting the hair in my grasp even tighter. A loud scream was followed by sobs, and I thrust the knife at Jackson as he tried to surge towards us.

"I'll go h-home. I never wanted to leave, but you need help Rory."

"Lies! You were always going to leave. I told you that wasn't happening. We stay together."

"Yes. We'll s-tay. We'll go...back."

"*No.*" Jackson's hands were up as he skirted around the room. "I won't let you take her. Hazel's staying with me."

"You? You're nobody. Not even to her. Hazel doesn't like you. She's *using* you."

"Jack-son." The sobs were getting heavier as she reached out to him with one hand. I reared back, swinging at an angle enough to slice through her forearm deep. Maybe enough to reach bone, but I didn't care as she started to scream and bleed out.

"Rory, enough! You don't want to hurt her. You're sick. Let Hazel and I get you help. We can get you better. Hazel and I won't abandon you or isolate ourselves. All three of us can see someone. We'll do this together."

"Please." Hazel could barely catch her breath. Blood was pooling in her lap as the room seemed to shift under my feet. I was back to questioning my sanity. Back to trying to decipher if what I was doing was the right thing. But my distraction didn't go unseen. Jackson dove in, and my knife was out of my hand so fast, I couldn't comprehend that he had it as I threw myself right at him.

"No! *No!*"

My sister was screaming again, but the room was muted to actual words. The hum vibrated in my ears, and I gasped as Jackson's eyes held mine and he spun me for the ground shoving the knife in my chest even deeper as he did.

"Rory! God, please."

I grew stiff through the agonizing pain as Hazel hovered over me. I couldn't catch my breath enough to scream out. To speak and tell her I was okay. Maybe I knew I wasn't. The horror I felt went soul-deep as I looked at Hazel. Where I expected to find regret, heartbreak, something, all I saw was victory. Maybe even relief. A part of me broke into more pieces, and my very essence shattered at the betrayal.

All I ever wanted was for Hazel to love me more than anyone else. *We were twins.* That connection with her should have been mine, and only mine. Our love never stood a chance. I would have done anything for her, and did, but I was my own worst enemy. Hazel always said it, and maybe she was right. Or maybe I wasn't the bad one after all. I was blunt. Honest. I made my intentions known. Hazel was the wolf, lurking in the shadows, waiting to tear others apart with her teeth. She was sly. Cunning.

"Fuck. Oh, shit. Rory, we're going to get you help, okay? Jackson, *get the phone.*"

But the man was just glaring down at me. The knife was still in my chest and instinct had me trying to pull it out, but Hazel pushed my hands down, stopping me.

"Jackson, *the phone.*"

"I'm not leaving you with her."

"*Her?*" There was a moment of silence as she glared towards him. In that moment, I watched her turn the tables, just like she always did. Her voice went flat. Emotionless. *"Go.* Rory can't hurt me anymore. *You* made sure of that."

Hurt her? *She hurt us both,* but I didn't care for the pain on his face. The statement had me sobbing through the coughs. All I tasted and smelled was blood. I was choking. Dying. Hazel knew that as she leaned down, taking my hand. A tear escaped, but even as I fought to bring her in clear, I wasn't sure if it was real. Nothing in our lives had ever been. From the earliest years, we never stood a chance. People like us rarely did.

Hazel put her forehead to the side of mine as Jackson left the room. I was gasping, trying to get air, but nothing was coming. Darkness was edging in, warm and welcoming.

"Shh, close your eyes." Wetness moistened my skin as she nuzzled me, lowering her voice almost inaudible. "It's time to go back to mom. She's waiting for you." A sound left me, having her clutch my hand tighter. *"Tell her I'm sorry.* I never meant to kill her. I *did* mean to kill you." She leaned in kissing my forehead. "You were right, Rory. I knew you'd never be able to resist. You should have just let me go. *You knew better.* You always knew this would happen. It was just a matter of time." My body stiffened, and more I was drawn into the nothingness. Into death. "That's it. Let go. It's better this way."

MISTRESS B-0019

HAZEL

"He's looking over here again, Mistress. Are you still not talking to Jackson? He looks so…"

"Guilty? Regretful?" I finished off my muffin as I kept my stare on Damien. "He should be. I asked him for help. I didn't ask him to kill my sister. And he did, slave. Rory may have ran into that knife, but I watched him finish her off as he took her to the ground. He had a choice to kill her, and he jumped at the chance." I shrugged. "I haven't decided whether I'm going to forgive him for that. Rory needed help, but." I stopped, my lip quivering.

The truth was, I may have wanted to be free of my twin, but I still missed her. Mourned her. At least in moments like these where I had the chance to use that loss. Sometimes the days were long and lonely, but at least I had Damien as my own. And we were getting to know each other, slowly but surely, just as I liked.

"I'm sorry. It's all too much. I loved my sister, but Jackson. I was so sure we—"

A sob left me, and I did glance at him then, showing him how betrayed and hurt I was over what he did. The pain drew in

266

his features, but he didn't come to me. He knew better after the last time he tried. I lost it. I told him he had to wait for me to come to him. And he'd wait…For how long was the question. I was curious to find out.

"Please don't cry. Jackson doesn't even have to be a thought right now. Focus on you. You've been through so much. I know how hard it's been, but you have me, and I'm trying to be the best slave I can."

"I know you are." I grabbed my coffee, standing. "You're doing a great job. You've helped me out so much since I've come back home."

"No offense to your sister, but I was glad it was you." Damien followed as we began to walk to the apartment. "I don't think I would have lived through that last day if it wasn't. I've never seen anyone so angry before." He looked over at me as we entered the hall. "I was so worried about you when the Main Master kept you away. I had no idea what happened, and your sister wouldn't give up. We went everywhere searching. I feared actually finding you. I think I was even more afraid when I wasn't there. At least I could have tried to stop her. Locked away here…it made me sick. How would I protect you if I wasn't close? I could have at least tried to do something."

"You were worried about me?" I took his hand as we approached the door. "I was worried about *you*. She hurt you just as badly. I wasn't sure you'd survive. It drove me crazy that I couldn't come check on you. What I saw. The scars covering your body. The scars…They…" I stopped, grabbing the key card, more tears escaping as I eyed him.

"You want to say more. What about the scars, Mistress?"

I opened the barrier, leading him through the threshold. Damien followed me to the room, even crawling up on the bed as I took a seat. He slept with me now, holding me since Rory wasn't here to do it anymore. And he wanted me. It wasn't hard to miss with his body molded to mine.

Slow...but steady.

"Mistress, what about the scars? You were going to say something about them."

My head lowered, and I wiped the tears from my cheeks. "It's just...It's so hard for me to see you without your shirt. Every time I do, I see my sister. It puts such a dark light on the memory I want to have of her. It's so confusing. I just want to put her to rest, you know? It's hard to do when I think of the hell we both had to endure during the last few weeks of her life."

Damien got quiet, pressing his lips together as he thought. I sat quietly...waiting.

"What if...What if you cut me on occasion too? Not in a bad or painful way, but to drown out the negative and turn it positive. I trust you more than I did her. I know you're not doing it to hurt me."

"You'd let me do that?"

A smile tugged at the side of his lips. "It wasn't so bad. I even liked it at the beginning. I think," he paused, scanning my face to settle on my lips. It took a moment for his eyes to lift back to mine. "I think I'd like you to try."

"I can see how that might work. If I cut you out of...want... or positive emotion, I could transfer that to her memories, or even mute her actions completely. My lines would blend with hers. I wouldn't know where hers started or where mine ended. It might help."

"Want?"

The slave swallowed hard, shifting closer. He was dying to lean in and kiss me so much he couldn't stay still. I didn't answer his question as I leaned over his lap, opening the drawer on Rory's side, pulling out her small pocketknife. As I lifted, our faces were only inches apart.

"Maybe you could guide my hand? I don't want to hurt you."

The slave eased his shirt over his head. I took in his dark hair and light eyes as he gently took my hand. We didn't speak, but the heat between us did. It sizzled and grew. Damien added pressure, breaking the skin as he drew my hand down over his pec.

My heart was racing.

My adrenaline was soaring.

His feelings for me were evident as the blood began running down his chest.

"I think...I want you to kiss me, slave."

And he did, sweeping me away in promises that far outweighed my worries for this new life. Had this been what Rory felt the first time she was with him? My mind wandered, swept away in Damien's dueling tongue. I'd seen my sister's face the next morning. She'd been as close to heaven as she'd ever get, and the new sensations fed my need to not just control my slave, but to experience a major part of Rory.

She was wanted.

Sought after.

Chosen.

She was the twin I could never be, and I had every intention of merging the best parts of her with me. This new world was mine for the taking. I had no rules outside of the Gardens. No one was here to tell me what I could or couldn't do. This new start was everything I needed. Rory wasn't here, but she was part of me, and I'd played her so many times, I knew just where to start.

I was me.

I was her.

I'd become us both.

One...like she always wanted.

The End

Master B-0491
Garden of the Gods
International Bestselling Author
A.A. Dark
Copyright © 2023 by A.A.Dark

All Rights Reserved

RULES

Rules are subject to change. If you neglect to follow these rules, you will undergo an investigation/trial where punishment is evaluated by the Board and Main Master, Elec Wexler. Punishment can range from fines to lockup in Hell Row to Death.

1) Keep your hands to yourself.

2) The only property you may destroy is your own. (slaves included.)

3) You are a number. Your peers are a number. Use them.

4) Respect your neighbor's privacy.

5) GOTG is NOT to be discussed outside of this facility.

GLOSSARY

W

Virgin slave. Wears a white robe during the auction.

B

Nonvirgin slave. Wears a blue robe during the auction.

D

Docile, drugged slave. Can be w or b. Heavily trained. Good for elderly or those with disabilities.

M

Male slave.

Crow

(fc: female crow, mc: male crow) Ruined, disfigured slave. Convicts fall into this category. Black robe during the auction. Usually the cheapest slave.

Blank slate

Mostly male slaves who have undergone forced indoctrination through various scientific methods. (Brainwashing, programming, training, etc.) Most remember their identity but have key parts of their past erased if it could pose a threat or alter their role as a slave. They're programmed to be focused solely on their Mistress or Master. They are made to be obedient, loyal, and protective.

*Master numbers written out throughout the stories are capitalized. (Ex. Twelve-twelve.) Also, the word Master throughout is capitalized. (Ex. Master Twelve-twelve.)

*Slave numbers written out will not be capitalized. The word slave throughout will not be capitalized outside from the beginning of a sentence.

"WE ALL WEAR MASKS, AND THE TIME COMES WHEN WE CANNOT REMOVE THEM WITHOUT REMOVING SOME OF OUR OWN SKIN."– ANDRÉ BERTHIAUME

PROLOGUE

MASTER B-0491

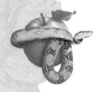

Garden of the Gods
Colorado Springs underground facility

Respect came in many forms. It took a lot for me to feel that for certain people, but as I sat in my booth two stories up, I couldn't help but be in awe of the man who walked the stage. I knew the Main Master. We weren't close, but we were connected. Not because of money or our standing amongst society, but because fate decided to weave our lives together like an intricately spun web. I wasn't a good man. Neither was the reaper walking the stage.

"Welcome to the second auction for Garden of the Gods. For those who didn't make it to the first, I'm going to recap this as quickly as possible. You've taken the classes. You've learned the rules. Even though our slaves have been trained, you are going to have to earn your titles. The B's in front of your number are for a reason. This is the Beta stage. Some of you will make our foundation. Some of you won't. Your outside status got you here, but that means nothing inside the Gardens. You are a number. That's it. Your identity or status means absolutely nothing. Here, there is no power or favoritism. This world is mine, and you better hope like hell you can follow the rules, or you won't survive in it." His eyes scanned the large room and his tone lightened. "On the plus side, you've all made it this far, and that speaks volumes. I have high hopes for most of you."

A smirk tugged at my lips.

"For those new to us tonight, I don't think I need to go much into how this place is not Whitlock. The rules are different. The location is different." His face turned hard. "I am *not* the old Main Master, Bram Whitlock. A few Masters from the first auction had to learn that the hard way. You cannot buy yourself out of trouble. You cannot *buy me*. I will never let the Garden of the Gods fall."

Growing up under the Main Master's shadow, I believed him. I knew things about Elec Wexler that no one else did. Secrets. Compulsions. Cravings. I even heard about his darkest desires. Ours weren't the same, but they weren't that far off either. It's why his family embraced me and brought me in to work for them. We were the same, even if we were all different.

I scanned the other booths, shifting in my chair as I tried to calm the whirlwind of excitement within. The last few months hadn't been good, but it was about to get so much better.

"Let's recap bidding for those who don't know. First, we have the white, or w's. These are the virgins. We also have the b's: or blue." He paused. "Not virgins. We also have the d's, who now have their own room at the back right, behind all of you. They're docile, trained, and good for those who are looking for a long-term slave. Lastly, come the black, or as we call them, the crows. These could be fun for anyone looking for a bloodbath or just a fun time. They're the convicts. The disfigured. The old. *Repulsive*." He stopped at the end of the stage. "You get it. Also in that category, you'll find the breeders. I want to make a note of some changes in this category." His hand raised. "Listen to me closely. I won't repeat it. You are not allowed to bid on them unless you've already gone through the steps and signed a contract with me. We had a few try last auction even though this was already stated in bold caps in the pamphlet. If you bid on a breeder, and you haven't met with me, your bid will be revoked and I will fine you ten thousand dollars for wasting my time. Breeders are special. Breeders are for only those I approve of."

"For those looking for our programmable, 'blank slate' males and *now* females, your auction is just through that door off to the right. The information was in the packet, but just in case you missed it last auction, these are those who have had a portion of their memories erased. They're aware. They know who they are, but they only remember what we want them to."

Interesting. I laughed under my breath. Leave it to the Main Master and the entire team to pull this off. Blank slate males and females. Who could have guessed? I sure as fuck hadn't expected that.

"The last few weeks have been exciting, to say the least. I've watched some of you grow in your role. The majority have done great with following rules. For those who are new, pay attention."

"What you buy is yours. You can do whatever you want with it. Fuck it. Kill it. Share it. Marry it. Love it. Eat it. Destroy it." He paused, walking down the stage some more. "I don't care so long as you follow the rules. Your business is your own. I can't stress that enough."

"If you look down the arm of the chair, you will see a button. Do not." He stopped, pausing for longer than anyone expected. "All of you listen and listen good." He turned in a slow circle to view everyone in the room. "Let me say it again since others from the first auction learned the hard way. *Do not...* press that button unless you are sure you want to bid. We do not have a lay-a-way plan. You cannot get your slave on loan. If you don't have the money, don't bid. At the Gardens, there's no such thing as accidents. If you bid, you buy. If you can't pay, I will take my payment however I want. Don't believe my threat, *test me*. I'll take everything you own on the outside world, and you can remain here with the slave you couldn't resist. This life can be simple if you just do as you're told. The rules are easy. Complete acceptance into the Garden of the Gods is not. You all signed a contract to get this far. Abide by it, and Alpha status will be yours."

Lights flashed, moving around the room as everyone's attention went to the back entrances. I took in the beautiful women adorned in sheer, white robes who were waiting for the go-ahead.

This was it. This is what I'd spent months waiting for. Now, all I needed was to find the perfect slave.

MASTER B-0491

"Yeah, she was gorgeous. So what. Let him have her. Wait until he sees who I buy. He'll regret outbidding me. Asshole. I hate that fucking guy."

"Didn't he get the role you auditioned for last fall? What was it? Dammit. It's right there. What was it called, Pete?"

"Dead Horizon. And who cares. It's going to be a horrible movie. Mark my words. I bet he fucks that one up too. Ethan O'Brien is overrated. Five years from now, no one will even remember who he is."

The loud voices in the hall had me rolling my eyes. Where I noticed a lot of the Masters and Mistresses mingled, I wasn't up for being social. I wasn't like these celebrities and politicians that lived to be heard or seen. Where most were here for the thrill, my need was different. I...was different.

Maybe I always had been. I liked to think once upon a time, I'd been a normal kid. But what was normal? What was ego? Personality? I often questioned what made a person who they were. Was it parental upbringing? Society? A little of both? Maybe. Or maybe some people just had evil ingrained in their very DNA. I did, but luckily, I kept it under control. That hadn't always been the case. The evil force within me took over once for a couple of months...*once*, and it had changed my life forever. Instead of being caught and carted to jail, I found myself beaten and kidnapped, taken somewhere different. Somewhere secret. Not this Whitlock they spoke of. I hadn't had the money or status for that, but what I got sent to was a secret group of sorts. Not quite a society, but not a brotherhood either. The ages ranged from college-age like me to men fifty years my senior. Bloodied from my abductors, *them*, they took me in. They were my mentors. Legends. I didn't have a choice in being part of them, but given the alternative of death or jail, I didn't mind. In truth, their acceptance altered me.

It was my secret. Mine...and that of the family of the Main Master. Elec's father saved my life despite that I almost stained the name of his son. Even though I was a few years older, Elec and I went to the same college back then. We were similar in appearance, and close to the same age. But how the Wexlers found out it was me behind the buzzing headlines, I didn't know. The description was out; identity wasn't. To my surprise, not long after I was taken, the entire thing disappeared. I didn't have to be told it was them. I knew their power. And...I thanked my lucky stars. Ever since, I listened to their every word. I obeyed and followed in the footsteps they designed for me. It wasn't easy, but neither was my burden. Here in the darkness—their path—they allowed me to unleash it, and that was all that mattered.

As the next w1 walked onto the stage, I lounged back in my chair, taking her in. Her dark skin and medium length dark hair pulled to me. She had an exotic look, but so had another I'd thought I had wanted too. I wasn't quick to bid. I was waiting for that spark. The one that made my pulse quicken. She'd have a lure I couldn't escape. She'd appear, she had to.

Doubt built as I looked at my watch for what had to be the one hundredth time. It'd been going on almost two hours. Two fucking hours of mostly w's with some b's thrown in to mix it up. Still, not one slave that gave me the reaction I was hoping for.

Numbers flashed on the large screens of the bidders, but I didn't pay it any mind. I was scanning the Masters and random Mistresses below. Some were on the edge of their seats. Others were laughing and bullshitting with those they sat by. I could have easily fit in down there amongst the crowd if I wanted to pretend. I was good at that. Thing was, I was hesitant. To say the last few months hadn't been a challenge would be a lie. After years of being a lawyer, I was a new judge. I threw the cases asked of me. Thanks to my connections, I held power I never thought I would. With that power came a price. It brought threats. Enemies. A part of me welcomed it, but it did take its toll. Especially since I got the feeling some of those threats came from big players in my circle. I knew enough of this life to not turn my back on people. You couldn't trust anyone. The Wexlers' taught me that.

Flashing on the screen came and went. So did another slave who had me twisting my lips. I pushed the button on the side of the balcony summoning a slave waiter. Within seconds he was arriving at the door, knocking to enter. I opened it, taking in the male who wore a yellow headdress just as the female slaves who worked for the Gardens.

"Brandy. And bring me one of those cake sampler things I saw in the front."

"Right away, Master."

I let out a sigh, turning to glance towards the stage. What I saw had me shutting the door and walking towards the edge of the balcony. I grabbed the binoculars, taking her in.

Sheer white flared out as the most beautiful woman I'd ever seen stepped up the last step, turning to walk the length of the stage. She was older than the others. Maybe in her mid-twenties. She sure as hell wasn't barely legal, which is what a lot appeared to be. Although I noticed her long, light brown hair, it was her face I couldn't break my gaze from. Why, I wasn't sure. My brain said unbelievably gorgeous, but this slave had no distinguishing features that made her stand out above the others. Maybe that's what it was. Medium lips. Thin, small nose, but... medium, again. Decently round, light colored eyes. She was average, but with a perfection that set her apart from the rest. Whatever it was, it had me, and I wanted her with a need above anything else I'd felt in a long time.

Knocking sounded at my door.

W0727. I repeated the number in my head, hitting my button to bid before jerking the door open. The male slave jumped at the surprise but was quick to react. I barely had the Brandy and cake in hand before I was spinning to kick the door closed.

Fuck. I watched the bids climb, hitting my button the moment I sat my plate and glass down. I wasn't filthy rich, but I did enough corrupt shit over the years that I was pretty damn well off.

"Come on," I mumbled, pushing the button even harder through my need to win. There was a mix of fear and panic on the woman's face as she shifted on stage. I popped a cheesecake bite in my mouth trying not to moan as I took it in and studied her. Mid-twenties. Skittish. Virgin. I hadn't been set on a w2, but I wasn't against it either. This slave was like winning the fucking lottery for me. I wasn't even sure how it was possible that she was still pure with how beautiful she was. There had to be men who were interested. *Who had at least tried to have sex with her.* The shape of her body was like an hourglass. Her breasts were full. Again...not too big or too small. I was baffled. She'd had the willpower to hold off, looking like that? Men had to have flocked to her. Begged and bribed her. Fucking stalked the shit out of her. Not many women I'd come across had that sort of restraint to hold off for so long. It all spoke volumes and my mind raced because of it.

Another bid from a Master had my finger slamming over the button. Each second was torture as I stayed transfixed on the slave and the screen. Back and forth my eyes jerked as I waited for someone to counter my offer with a higher amount. My heart all but stopped as my number flashed on the screen.

Winner.

Fuck. Fuck. I almost couldn't believe it as I saw them lead her off the stage. For seconds, I couldn't move. I was no amateur in my dark ways, but this was my first auction. My first slave that belonged to me. There was no rush. No risk. No fear of being caught. No repercussions. I wasn't breaking laws. The reality hit hard. I stood, pushing my fingers through my dark hair as I headed for the door.

A slave. Finally. I'd been hearing stories about Whitlock for years. But that's all they were from the men's club I belonged to. *Stories.* I never thought something like this would be possible for me. I wasn't elite. I wasn't born into a rich family. I was no one. But...obviously, *someone.* I had Elec to thank for this. Even though we weren't personally close, our connection to his father tied us. Our link was unspoken but real. Gratitude was on my side, and maybe there was understanding on his.

"Jenson. Judge Jenson Colburn; you don't say. Quite the title there."

I turned towards the lounge area, recognizing the voice immediately. Smiling, I offered my hand to the Secretary of State as we closed the distance. My laugh couldn't be contained.

"Jack." I moved in giving him a quick hug. "A title thanks to you, no doubt. It's been way too long. How have you been?"

"I've been great. You know how it is. The good with the bad. But you...I'm hearing great things about you, Jenson. You're doing phenomenal work. You're going high places; I just know it."

"Seems we all are. It's been quite the year. How's Georgie? All good in the homelife?" I stood a little taller, instinct kicking in as it had me cautiously scanning the hall. Jack smiled at the mention of his wife. "She's doing great. She's actually checking out the blank slate females right now. I was on my way to meet her. I just saw you and had to say hello."

"I'm so glad we ran into each other. I just bought a slave, myself. I'm on my way to pick her up. We all should have dinner one of these nights. I'm Master B-Four-ninety-one. Pound four-ninety-one on my Gardens' cell. Give me a call anytime. I'll be here for a few days."

"Thanks. We'll definitely do that."

I gave a nod as he slapped my shoulder, heading back towards the lobby. I'd known him for as long as I'd known Jerry, Elec's father. Jack hadn't been Secretary of State back then, but a lawyer, and a damn good one. He taught me almost everything he knew. They brought me in their circle, and completely changed my life.

Heading around a turn at a fast pace, my shoulder collided with another. We hit hard, stopping and locking eyes. His lids narrowed the smallest amount before the side of his mouth pulled back and he continued. Anger? A threat? He gave no apology. No excuse. Just the look. I tried not to overthink it as I glanced behind me to see him disappear around the turn. He'd been roughly my size. Dark hair like me. Where I was extremely good looking, he was more average, but not unattractive either.

The stairs were ahead, and I took them down, not bothering to wait for the elevator. I wasn't afraid, but I didn't make it a habit to be cornered in a tight space with strangers if I could help it.

A guard was at the end of the stairs, and I slowed, moving in. "Where do the winners go?"

"Right through that door, Master."

"Excellent, thank you."

I pushed through a pair of double doors, slowing at the small desk off to the side. A guard was holding a tablet, talking through an earpiece. I headed over, waiting as he finished and turned to me.

"May I help you, Master?"

"I'm here to get my slave, w-seven-twenty-seven."

"Of course. Let me see if she's programmed and ready."

Programmed. That's right. She'd be somehow internally set with my chosen code, so I could shut her down if I ever needed. Not that I would. I'd be able to handle her just fine without activating some fail-safe. After all, it's what I did. What I loved. *It's what I was counting on.*

1 VIRGIN SLAVE. WEARS A WHITE ROBE DURING THE AUCTION.

2 Virgin slave. Wears a white robe during the auction.

WO727

I learned long ago not to pull away from the guards. Although my mind screamed at some stranger touching me, I managed to stay composed as I was led through a pair of doors into what looked to be a large seating area. There were black leather sofas off to the side and random Masters and Mistresses standing around. The sight was just as unnerving as what was happening, but my obedience was instilled. I knew how to act. What to say. I'd had enough training to be prepared for this night. That did not change how uncomfortable I felt. Even the oil I was soaked in wasn't numbing my anxiety as much as I had hoped.

I was bought.

Owned.

By whom...I had no idea, and that scared me more than anything. All I kept imagining was a nasty, old man. An abusive predator dying to put me through the floor. I saw my grandfather. I wasn't sure I could do this. To go through that again...Daddy said I'd never have to. He said now that Grandpa Nelson was dead, I was safe. It was a lie. My father went to prison, and following years of verbal abuse, hatred and therapy couldn't help me. The only man I'd finally let myself trust, brought me here.

All that time, and I still hadn't learned anything but survival. Maybe it was for the best...or maybe I was about to be in over my head.

"Master B-Four-ninety-one."

Turning, I scanned the room, nearly fainting as a man who looked to be in his late sixties waved at the guard. Pressure pushed against the back of my throat, and I was sure I was going to either scream or be sick. Flashes of my past, of the unwanted touching hit me like a wave. I could do this. *I had to.*

"Right here. Four-ninety-one."

A tall, dark-haired man excused himself around the older man, and my heart nearly stopped at how handsome he was. I hadn't been exposed to many people outside of the guards since I'd been here, but he was easily the most gorgeous one I'd seen. Maybe ever. It almost didn't seem like the moment was real. Dark, wavy hair. Charming hint of a smile. Square jaw. Light blue eyes. Even slightly long lashes. He was dreamy. Classically handsome. Breathtaking.

"Three-fourteen, you say?" The geezer's yell had multiple heads turning.

"No, Four-ninety-one."

"What's that, boy?"

The Master threw me a look, smiling, half trying to hide it. Relief had never felt so immense. I wasn't naïve that things could change with this new Master. We had been warned of the dangers, and he was here for a reason, but he didn't look anything like grandpa, and that was a start.

"Wrong number. Four-ninety-one! Four," he said, putting up his fingers.

The old man's mouth parted, and he nodded, turning. When the Master moved in feet from me, the guard was already hitting buttons on his tablet. I hardly noticed. My stare wouldn't leave the man's handsome features. I barely even felt the guard step closer and roll more oil over my forehead. They'd been doing that to us all night.

"That should be it, Master. Did you want to take her now, or would you like her delivered?"

"I think we're good to go." He gestured for me to follow. I gave the guard a glance, but he was already heading back to the doors we'd come in. Pressure eased around my bicep, holding on and stealing my focus as I let my new Master lead me toward a different entrance. "Did they explain to you why you're here, slave?"

Slave. Yes, he'd said that a little too comfortably.

"I was prepared." I paused, glancing up. "Master."

Again, the smallest hint of a smile tugged at his lips.

"I'm sure they taught you well. The reality is, not many of the slaves bought tonight will be alive come morning."

I tripped over my feet, only saved due to my Master's hold. He righted me, pulling me in closer.

"It's the reality of this place. Slaves are disposable. Especially if they don't follow rules.

"I see. Will you—Am I?"

I had meant to ask if I was in danger, but wasn't that obvious? The smile was gone, and his face was unreadable as he stared ahead.

"I'm not a killer unless I have to be. I'm too selfish for that. That does not mean you won't wish you were dead."

"B-But I'm okay if I follow rules?"

My question came out broken as we headed for the hall. I noticed the Master's hold was still tight, but it wasn't crushing. He was worried about me running. I wanted to. It was right there. For some reason, I was slowing. Growing...foggy as we headed for the elevator. Each second, I felt further away. I liked not shaking with fear. I needed to stay here. To think, to plan, but I couldn't clear my thoughts. I couldn't even grasp them. *The oil.*

"Perhaps." His grip eased, and I calmed even more despite I

knew I shouldn't. My mind was almost gone from me. My fear was nearly nonexistent.

We stopped at the elevator, and the Master turned me to face him. Fingers trailed along my jaw, moving up to slide along my cheekbone. Before I could stop myself, my eyes were closing, and I was nuzzling into the touch. It was nice. Soft and tender. *New.* What it was doing to me inside was even better. Tingling was starting to take over, sparking my body to life. Sure, I'd felt arousal before, but not like this. It was on a level I hadn't experienced.

"You're so beautiful. I'm not sure I'm going to be able to get enough of you."

His knuckles moved past my ear, lowering to travel the length of my neck. My lips parted, my breath catching as his touch dipped down to my chest. My eyes flew open at the yearning that followed. I tried to blink my acceptance away, but I was too stunned, and I was sure he saw that as he licked his lips. That only had me wanting him more. I jerked back, crashing into someone behind me.

"I'm so sor—"

Lights exploded in my vision. My knees buckled, and I crashed down, right onto them. Sound wavered, echoing oddly in my ears as my Master's deep tone broke through. He reared back, slamming his fist into the other Master's face as he went from dreamy to dangerous.

Yells were spewing from all around as I struggled not to sway to the side. Blood was leaving my nose, trailing over my lip. I was shaking through the chaos that was beginning to erupt as I kneeled.

"Hey! Masters!"

Guards were racing forward from the far end of the room, but my Master didn't flinch as his fist kept pounding into the older man on the floor. He had to have been in his upper forties, where my Master couldn't have been more than his late thirties. The

Master getting beaten had deeply tanned skin. Almond shaped eyes, although not far from the corner of one, it appeared to already be split open. He was average size and build where my Master was anything but.

"If you ever touch my slave again—" More hits. "I'll kill you. *I'll fucking kill you.*"

"Hey!" Footsteps pounded as the guards yelled in their earpieces, sliding to a stop as they reached forward, pulling my Master off the other. "What's going on here?"

"I'm good; I'm good. He hit my slave. I hit him back."

"You crazy fuck! You—" The man struggled to stand with one of the guard's help, wiping blood from his mouth and nose. His face was already starting to swell on one side. He was livid, until he took in my Master.

"Oh shit. Oh…fuck. Judge, I didn't see you. I. Jenson, I'm sorry. I-I." He stopped, growing even more concerned as the man I knew as the Main Master headed right for us. Was I in trouble? The man approaching scared the hell out of me. With the rage he suddenly held, the effects of the oil disappeared completely. I was more terrified than ever.

Jenson, my Master, didn't seem bothered by it as he pulled me to stand. His lips pursed angrily as he turned my face from side to side.

"He got you good. Are you okay?"

"I'm fine."

But I wasn't. My balance was off, and I felt nauseous through the fear. I wanted to cry. To hide. That part of me had disappeared months ago. I'd stand and be quiet. I'd be nothing more than a statue ready for an order.

"You don't look fine. Dammit. This is why you always stay at my side. *I'll protect you.*" Full lips parted as what I could only guess was awe or lust took over him. His thumb collected blood from under my nose, and I was sure he was going to lean forward to kiss me.

291

"What the hell is going on here?"

"Master—"

"Four-ninety-one," Jenson supplied for the guard.

"Four-ninety-one says this Master hit his slave."

"Is that what happened?" Ice blue eyes, so close to my own Master's color, narrowed as he stared down the older man.

"Elec. I mean, Sir. Main Master. It was a reaction. I've had a lot to drink. I was bumped from behind pretty good, and I didn't think. I apologize deeply to everyone. I had no idea it was..." Again, he stopped talking, glancing back up to my Master, fearfully. "Judge, I swear, I didn't mean to. Don't hold this against me. Tell me what to do."

"You don't know me. Especially, here. Don't you fucking call me that again."

"I'm sorry. I shouldn't have had so much to drink. Please. Whatever you want."

The Main Master crossed his arms over his chest looking between the two men. The anger was gone and what replaced it was more...*amusement?* I was looking too, so confused at whatever power my Master had over this man.

"I don't want anything from you."

"Don't say that. Let's start over. I'm Percy, but you know that. You're my judge on the outside world. We're not there right now, but it seems I've screwed up here as well, so let me make it up to you. I can. We can start fresh. New. *I don't want to go to prison.*"

"And you won't if you're not meant to. Like I said." His lids narrowed. "I don't want anything from you. I'm going to pretend you're not trying to bribe me either."

Conflict merged with anxiety as the Master looked between the Main Master and Jenson.

"He hit your slave. I don't usually ask, but circumstances are different here. Are you satisfied with how this is ending? I can put him in front of the board. I can take his hand."

The threat had Master Percy going pale as he looked between them.

"Tempting."

"Please. *Judge*."

"What the fuck did I say," my Master snapped. He turned to the Main Master; to whom I now knew as Elec. "What I want from him isn't a body part. He can leave. If you have a moment, I'd like to talk to you about it…privately, if that's alright."

Elec's gaze flicked to me for only a second. The Main Master held something inside I couldn't even put into words. His look was a threat, all its own. I couldn't make any more sense of it than knowing I had to escape his presence as fast as possible.

"Of course. I've been meaning to talk to you, too. It's long overdue. Guards, take her to Master Four-ninety-one's apartment and restrain her. I have a feeling this may take a little while. The Master and I have a bit to catch up on."

"Apartment twelve-oh-six."

The closest guard stepped in but paused as Jenson spun back to us.

"Make sure my door is secure and locked before you leave. As you can see, I have more enemies than friends, and I don't like the thought of her alone."

"Of course, Master."

The two guards fit themselves on each side of me, leading me onto the elevator. Our ride up was silent, minus one of the guards talking over his mic. When the door opened, laughter met us. It was coming from either one of the shops or bar that was not far off in the distance. A few random Masters walked around, and even one Mistress had her arm looped through a man in a pair of gray sweatpants. It was the standard wear for the male slaves. I learned that firsthand on one of my hospital visits when I'd first arrived.

"This is it."

One of the guards pushed a card into the slot, making the

light flash green. When we entered, I couldn't help but slow at the luxury surrounding us. I'd grown up poor. My parents had been divorced, and although my dad did what he could to help us out, me and my mom still barely had enough to get by. After her death, my dad remarried a woman who didn't want me around. Naturally, I moved in with Grandpa Nelson, but that had me going from poor to dirt poor. From the ages of thirteen to fifteen, we had no electricity. No hot water. I was lucky to eat sometimes. If I was good, of course. Then Daddy finally came. It didn't take long for him to see something was wrong. When I finally broke down and told him of the touching, my life changed forever. *He...changed.*

Maybe it was the guilt. Maybe it was more. I'd never know now. That was the past. It was gone from me forever. Here, now, in a materialistic sense, I might as well have hit the lottery. Gorgeous Master. Crème leather sectional, glass tables, and an expensive rug. It didn't seem real. There was even matching décor in crème, browns, and pale yellow. It was all so...clean. It was a lie. I could see through that, even still influenced from the oil.

"Right this way, slave."

I followed them into the bedroom, jolting to a stop as they looked between the cuff on the ground to the ones on the bed.

"I'm good here." Quick steps brought me to the floor cuffs, but the guards didn't move. A smirk came to one of their faces and he nodded, grasping my bicep to pull me to the bed. "Please, put me on the floor. If my Master wants to move me, he can."

"Sit down, slave."

"Please?"

At the silence, I quickly took a seat, lifting my arm as they cuffed my wrist. I could have fought, but there was no point. I'd already gotten beat enough for the day. I wasn't going to bring even more on myself.

"Slave is secure. We're headed back down."

The guard didn't even look back at me as he and the other took off at a fast pace. I let out a sigh, not moving for a few minutes. I was still foggy. Still...off. It didn't help that the silence was making me tired. My adrenaline was finally slowing, and my entire body was feeling the peace I suddenly felt.

Lifting my legs to the mattress, I laid back against the pillow. I'd sit when I heard the door that way he could see I wasn't comfortable here. But it was only a good idea in theory. The minutes stretched. Time drew out. My eyes got heavier. Twenty minutes or two hours, I wasn't sure as I drifted. What I did know was something suddenly wasn't right. It was a crawling of my skin. A prickling along my arms as if I were staring down the most ferocious animal, and it was getting ready to eat me alive. My eyes fluttered open, and before I could scream, there was a knife at my throat and a hand over my mouth.

Eyes peered out through the black mask. Dark brown eyes. Terrifying eyes. The lids were narrowed and promised a nightmare there was no escape from. Not with me secured with a cuff. A whimper left me as the stranger shifted to straddle over me. With the white robe still on, my body was exposed. I was completely nude.

"Please."

My muffled plea was unrecognizable as the leather-covered hand tightened over my mouth. Seconds passed as he glared into my eyes. Such...hate. Anger. It held me trapped in terror as he removed his hand, bringing it right to my breast. If there was a power in me to scream, I couldn't find it. Not with the sharp tip of the blade stabbing into my skin.

"I beg you. My Master—" Stinging cut me off. I moaned out in a guttural cry, and wetness raced down my neck where the knife had stuck into my throat. The hand didn't stop playing with my breast. Pressure squeezed my nipple before massaging into the fullness. My lips kept quivering, and the sobs wouldn't be denied as he sent pings of pleasure zapping through me.

This shouldn't have felt good, and maybe wouldn't have had I not been drugged on the oil, but my body couldn't deny the response. My breaths were heavier. My hips were trying to arch for a need that terrified me. I wanted to keep shaking my head. To scream, but I couldn't. The sound was nowhere to be found.

At the man's shift, I took in his black long sleeve and black jeans. Black gloves. Black boots. He was spreading my legs, fitting himself between them as his one hand latched to my hip and jerked me further down the bed. I could barely stop myself from hyperventilating. With one hand he explored my most private area, and with the other, he let the blade drag over my skin. I winced as it made the shallowest slice, but it didn't stay steady. It was the feel of cold metal over me. I wasn't sure what to focus more on, the leather gloved finger that was beginning to ease inside of me, or the symbols the masked man was drawing over my chest. He kept cutting me. Not deep, but enough to have me sucking in a breath through the sting. Dots of blood were already beading, and I couldn't decipher if what I was feeling was fear or awe.

"God, please. Please, stop. My Master will be back soon. Pl—"

The hit had a high pitch sound ringing in my ears. I did start fighting then. My legs were kicking, and I somehow knew I was swinging my free fist in his direction, but it did little to stop the frenzy that had taken over this man. He was ripping at the button, pushing his pants down as he put more of his weight over me. The knife was gone. Where, I didn't have a clue. He was all hands, suffocating me. Hitting me with every scream that came out of my mouth.

There was so much noise. Someone had to have heard. Someone would come.

"Get off! Help! Get! Off!"

But my shouts died with a pain so intense, it took my breath away. I was thrashing. Kicking. But the buck of my hips only sent him tearing through even more of me. I choked on the breath as air came back, screaming like I had never screamed before. It was all for nothing. He thrust, sinking his teeth into my neck. Again, I screamed with everything I had. My entire body wracked with sobs and sucking quickly followed the burning to my throat. The threats were slowing. Turning more into a rocking as he buried himself continuously and pushed deep. Each second, my emotions twisted. Each moan against me, agony faded. I was numb and yet...tears somehow found their way through the crumbling of a lie I tried to make myself believe.

I was not going to be alright here.

My Master would not save me.

I was not safe.

I was a slave, and I was cursed to live a reality I could never escape.

MASTER B-0491

O ne shot. Two. Three shots. Four. I never expected Elec to be so relatable. We had a lot to catch up on now that we'd officially met, but that would come. As I threw back the fifth shot, I told myself I'd think about all that tomorrow. After all, there was no rush. I belonged to the Gardens now, and Elec would always be here. This was his chosen path, just as I was living the one they'd assigned to me as well. Not that I didn't think Elec chose this. He did, and I couldn't blame him after his past.

As I left the bar on my floor, I couldn't erase the smile on my face. Life couldn't get any more perfect. Between my slave and Percy Billings, things were just getting better and better. I'd truly lucked out. It wasn't every day you had part-owner and CEO of one of the most successful pharmaceutical companies begging at your feet. Damn, I loved my life.

A laugh left me as I reached in my pocket for the key card. My smile didn't remain as I pulled it out. My door wasn't but ten feet away, and the fact that it was cracked had me walking faster as I thrust it open.

Open? *How?* That should have been impossible.

"Slave?"

I didn't have the barrier shut before screams had me racing for the bedroom. What met me was a mix of reactions I couldn't process. Her terrified face was battered and bloody. There appeared to be bite marks all over her neck and arms. There were even a few shallow cuts between her breasts. It was the cum sprayed over her stomach, and the blood between her legs that drove me forward in a rage.

"What the fuck happened here?"

"P-Please. Master, please!"

She was jerking against the restraint, reaching and trying to get to me. The terror she held was all too real as I reached down, unlatching the cuff. The moment she was free, she dove in my arms, holding around me for dear life.

"He. H-He." Sobs wracked her body as I sat down, pulling her into my lap. I grabbed the bottom of her robe, wiping the cum free as I began to hold and curl her into me to rock in a slow rhythm.

"Shh. You're okay now. I'm here. I got you. I need you to slow down and tell me exactly what happened, so I know what to tell the Main Master. Start at the beginning."

"A m-man in a mask. He." Again, a sob. "I was sleeping, and he was suddenly over me. He had a big knife." She lifted her crimson-stained neck enough to press against a small hole. "I was so scared. I tried to f-fight. I. I. He was too strong. He *hurt* me."

My arms wrapped around her tighter, rocking her as I cuddled her close.

"Did he say anything?"

"N-No—Yes! Before he left. He said he'd see me around. What if he comes back?"

My lips twisted with the growl, and I kissed the top of her head.

"He'd be stupid to return. I shouldn't have let them bring you up. Didn't I tell the guards to check the fucking door?" My teeth clenched. "I have so many enemies. My job doesn't make me very popular, I'm afraid. Lately...not popular at all."

Her head lifted again.

"The Master mentioned...he said...you're a judge?"

"That's right, but I was a lawyer first. A damn good one. I only recently became a judge. Still...due to my location and connections, I'm afraid I deal with a lot of powerful people. There's not many in this place I haven't met one time or another. Parties, acquaintances, court. If I haven't met them directly, I know someone they're associated with. It's a big mess, but I'll get this under control. It's just going to take them time to see they can't intimidate me. I'll talk with the Main Master again. Maybe he can have guards watching the apartment. Before I call, I need you to think back. Do you remember anything about the person who came in?"

I let the anger radiate from me. Her lips trembled as she winced in my lap.

"He was wearing all black. Black boots. Long sleeve shirt. Pants. Gloves." She shuddered. "The mask was black too. He had...brown eyes. *Scary eyes.* They were so dark. Almost black. They. He. H-He."

"Shh." I rocked her more, fitting her face back in my neck. "We'll have him found, and when we do, I'll make him pay. He'll regret the day he ever hurt you."

She sniffled. "You're sure?"

"If I can help it. I won't always be here, but I'll have you watched over. As long as you lock the deadbolt, no one should be able to get in. You'll be safe." I moved back, sliding my finger under her chin to have her looking up at me. "Okay?"

Puffy eyes met mine as she nodded. The shaking in my arms only fed my needs. Maybe I should have been more concerned, but it was hard to think past the bruising coming up on her beautiful, perfect face.

"Do you think you can shower alone while I call the Main Master?"

"I…" Fear had her eyes flying wide.

"No need to be afraid anymore. Look at me. *See me.* Calm. I'll stay with you. I'll help you."

"Well." She stiffened in my arms.

"No need to be modest now. I've already seen your body. Besides, I'm your Master. It's my duty to take care of what's mine." My hand slid over her swollen cheek. *"You are mine, slave.* Mine to do with whatever I want."

"What is it that you do want? Are you going to hurt me too?"

Tears spilled from her eyes as I rolled her to the bed. With how she was positioned, it was easy to fit myself between her legs as I hovered above. The slave didn't scream. She didn't try to fight or flee.

"I'm most definitely going to hurt you, but not how you think."

"What does that mean?"

I opened the blood-stained, sheer robe, pushing it over her shoulders to reveal her body. The slave's eyes squeezed shut, and she went to turn away, but I quickly stopped her.

"Look at me." She sobbed, breaking all over again. "Look at me." Green eyes blinked, fixing right on mine. "Good girl. Now, stop crying." I waited as she sniffled and obeyed. "There we go. Do you know how to make the pain stop? To ease the trauma of what you've been through?"

Her head shook. "How?"

I pushed my hands underneath her, rolling to my back to bring her on top.

"Take control. Fear has no place in the Gardens. Don't let it rule you. I'm going to fuck you regardless of what happened tonight. I'm not letting him have what's mine without regaining it. If I don't have you, he wins." Her gaze scanned mine almost horrified. "Come lay down on my chest and start kissing me.

Show your appreciation. Kiss me for buying you. Kiss me for what I'm going to do to save you. To keep you safe. Give me every part of you, and I'll allow you to be happy."

"Allow?"

My hand locked to the back of her neck, bringing her inches from my lips.

"Yes. If you fight me, I assure you, happiness will not exist. I will break you far worse than the man who hurt you tonight. Submit to me and give me what I want, and you will be the envy of every slave here." My other hand settled on her hip as I moved her against me. "I will treat you like a princess. Dress you like one. People will cater to you. All you have to do is what I say."

For seconds she didn't break her stare.

"Kiss me. Fuck me, slave. Let me make it feel good for you this time."

"I…hurt. I'm not sure I can."

"That wasn't a suggestion. You can, *and you will*."

I bucked my hips sending her falling forward to catch herself. While she stared down at me, I unfastened my pants, maneuvering them down until I was able to kick them off. With her hovering, I grasped her hip, lifting her higher so that my hand could cup her pussy. She let out a cry as her face drew in from pain. The wetness had me immediately drawing my fingers back to take in the blood. She wasn't losing a lot, but enough to have my lips pull back on one side.

"It may have hurt the first time, and it'll probably hurt a little when we first start, but you're going to come to love this, slave. You're old enough to know about sex. You're not innocent."

"No. I know things."

"And you've played with yourself before?"

There was hesitation, but she nodded. "I have, Master."

"A lot?"

"Sometimes."

Her words were forced. She was still on the verge of completely breaking.

My finger traced a circle over her clit, moving down her slit. Her hands clutched to the comforter at the sides of my head. I kept my touch light, barely there as I went from her opening to the sensitive nerves that had her biting her lip.

"He won't win. We're not letting him." A small sigh left her. "There we go. Relax. Feel the sensations. If there's pain let it mix with the pleasure and feed it. You have to be strong to survive at this place. Are you strong, slave?"

She sniffled. "Y-Yes."

"Show me."

I eased the tip of my finger into her entrance, letting her get used to the feel of me thrusting in and out. When her shoulders loosened, I moved to the next knuckle, withdrawing as I used my palm to still add pressure to her clit. A whimper left her, and she grew wetter with the increasing speed of my penetration. Within a few minutes, I was damn near buried inside of her. She was moving to my rhythm, rocking despite the tears that escaped.

"That's it. Take control, Princess." I eased in another finger making her gasp. "Fuck my fingers. Show me what a good girl you're going to be."

My head lifted, sucking her nipple into my mouth. The cry that left her wasn't one of pain. It was pure pleasure. I used that to my advantage, gently biting the nub, only to suck harder. My cock was throbbing and so ready to pound into her bloody, abused pussy. It was driving me crazy.

"You feel it. Chase the need. I'm not stopping until you come all over my fingers, so you might as well give into the ecstasy. To hold back with me will be your biggest mistake."

"Master." Pink was beginning to tint her cheeks. "I won't hold back....I don't think I can."

"You said that when we started this too."

I spun her to her back, continuing to fuck her with my

fingers. The blood nearly had me coming at the sight. It'd been too long since I'd given myself over to this part of me. The darker part. Now that I'd started, I'd be unstoppable. There was no telling how far I'd take this role.

"Spread open wide. I want to see you."

"I—"

I didn't give her fear or embarrassment a chance to ruin our progress. I widened her thighs, licking my lips as I smeared in the bloody wetness. I could see where she'd been torn. It wasn't too bad but noticeable enough that I didn't have to search it out.

"Who am I, slave?"

I continued to thrust as I ask.

"My Master."

"And who's is this?"

Her mouth opened in an O-shape as I added another finger pushing deep.

"Yours, Master. It's yours."

"Fuck yes it is. It's not his, is it?"

Anger took her over. "No. *Never.*"

"That's right, Princess. Some stranger may have fucked you first, but I own this pussy. This is all mine." I moved closer, easing in the tip of my cock as I watched her stretch around my thickness. For the smallest moment, she jumped and winced, but it didn't last, and I didn't push forward. I fucked her with the tip, slowly building her up as her expressions shifted through the sensations. She was fighting the need to give in. Fighting the bliss. That wouldn't do. I wouldn't let her mentally pull away. Even though my eyes barely left the crimson beginning to coat my cock, I was just as relentless as I was silent. I wanted to see if she'd give in.

I played with her clit, first, rotating my thumb in a circle. Then, back and forth at different speeds causing her legs to twitch through the sensitivity. For minutes, I tortured us both. I was so transfixed with what was mine, but I wasn't satisfied with her reactions. She'd have to learn to prioritize her emotions. Still, her walls were up. Raped or not, she didn't have the right to shut me out of anything. She had to see that from the very first time. See that I was the one who was bringing her pleasure, and I wasn't the man who hurt her. There was no free pass with me. This slave had to know her place, and I wasn't going to settle for someone who withheld what rightfully belonged to me. She'd cum. She'd fucking scream my title, bloody from another man, and all. I wasn't going to stop until she did.

"You're not getting on my good side right now." I slapped over her clit. "You're fighting your orgasm, and that would be a mistake."

"Master, I can't...help it. I'm trying. It's right there. I just—"

"Already came for him?"

Her eyes widened and there was hesitation before her head went back and forth. "No, Master."

"Are you sure you didn't give him what belongs to me?"

"I swear I didn't."

"*Then try harder.*" Again, I brought my fingers down hard over the sensitive nerves. At her moan, a rumble left my throat. I gripped her hair, pushing my cock more than halfway inside her pussy. The depth had her eyes widening.

"You like that." I pulled back out, moving just as deep, repeating the motion as fear mixed with the heavy lids from lust. "Give in, Princess, or you're going to be nothing more than a pick-up for the guards. I don't need a shell; I need fire. Whoever is hiding inside that pretty little body of yours better come to life, quick. This is the second auction. Do you see a slave in this apartment?"

She didn't have to know I missed the first auction. Let her fear increase. Let her try harder to please me.

"Master." Her mouth flew open, and she gasped as I withdrew, slamming myself inside her. "Master, if I could. I just think." She stopped, rocking against my steady thrusts. Sweat was starting to dot her cut-up chest, and her head was going from side to side as the brink of the orgasm tortured her. I was starting to see the fight wasn't something she was in control of, or even knew how to battle. That was obvious as she adjusted to our rhythm. *Virgin.* Yes. An older one. She was fighting more than me right now. She was fighting the very reason that left her untouched and guarded for so long.

"You were just raped. That is the only reason I'm going to give you a free pass. I'm not myself. You're not yourself. We're both affected. Let's try something different."

I lowered inches from her face, licking my lips as I took in how sexy she was. My mouth pressed into hers, testing our connection while I kept my stare locked on green eyes. When I deepened the kiss, her body softened, melting almost instantly.

"Yes, Master." Again, I kissed her. "I like this. That's better. That's—"

I pushed in my tongue, cutting her off as I deepened the kiss. She met me hungrily, wrapping her legs around my hips as I continued to thrust and grind into her pussy. Burying my fingers in her hair, squeezing enough to have her sucking in a breath. Moans immediately followed, merging with whimpers as her nails bit into my back.

"Like that. Master, just like that. I...*Master.*"

Her head was lifting, and her legs were drawing up even further on my sides. My mouth recaptured hers, and the spasms hit her hard. Her body trembled, shaking and jerking through the loud cries that had her holding to me even tighter. I slammed into her pussy with everything I had, pounding as I really drove my cock home. I wanted her to feel me, and only me, long after I finished. To want me even when her world was burning to the fucking ground. Trials were at the heart of every relationship. As I came inside of her pussy, I was ready to put ours to the test.

WO727

I should have been relieved. Happy, even. As I sat at the table in the fancy restaurant on our floor and watched Jenson talk to the Main Master, all I felt was queasy. It'd been almost twenty-four hours since my Master returned to find me, and I didn't feel much better than I had then. It didn't help with the way the Main Master was looking over at me. Did he think I made the story up? Surely, he could see the bruising on my face and body. Or maybe he was upset because the security failed, and I got attacked. Yes, that had to be it. There was no way I could get in trouble for this. I didn't do anything wrong. So... why did I feel responsible? I knew why. I felt guilty when Daddy killed Grandpa Nelson too. Or when Aunt Keri took me in when Daddy got locked up but got mad at her husband for even talking to me. These things kept happening, and it was always my fault.

Pushing my fork into the center of the baked potato, I tried to take a bite without looking as awkward as I felt. The two men had been talking for almost ten minutes now. My Master would look to explain something, the Main Master would nod or say a word, and it would continue. Dinner was not going very well.

Given how worked up Jenson was, I didn't expect it to get much better when he returned.

A sigh left me, and I paused mid-chew as the Main Master pointed right at me. I turned, looking over my shoulder, frozen as his eyebrow rose. I pointed to my chest, getting a quick nod. Dread was overwhelming as I stood on shaky legs. Why the hell was I being summoned? Could they both not just come sit with me? Everyone was looking. They were watching. Now, they were focused right on me as I weaved between the fancy tables.

Lord, please don't let me bump into anyone. With this sequins silver dress and heels my Master insisted I wear, I just knew I was going to either be covered in food or break an ankle before this was over with.

"Slave." Jenson held out his hand. I took it, coming to a stop at his side. "The Main Master has some questions for you."

"A-Alright."

For seconds he stared down at me in silence. I knew I was squirming under his gaze. There was nothing I could do to stop the uncomfortable sensation. His energy was overwhelming. Terrifying.

"You say you awoke with this stranger standing over you?"

"Yes, Main Master."

"And he had a knife?"

"He did." My hand automatically stopped at my exposed, marked up cleavage, moving to the hole that was left in my neck between all the bite marks. It wasn't deep and probably less noticeable than the bruising indentations of teeth, but to me it left the most terrifying impact.

"Your Master said he raped you."

"He did. Twice."

"Twice?" My Master's head whipped to me. "You didn't say twice."

My mouth opened, only to close. "Well, once, but it was technically twice. He didn't...he didn't—"

"Finish," the Main Master supplied.

"That's right, Sir. He didn't finish the second time. Truthfully, it only lasted a minute or two before his phone rang and he took off. He didn't seem happy about that, but he told me he'd see me around."

Silence.

"Interesting." The Main Master turned his attention to Jenson. "Like I said before, I'll look into it and let you know what I find. As for Master B-One-thousand-sixty-eight, take care of it. Same goes for B-Four-twelve."

"You got it, Main Master. My pleasure."

Elec's hand clamped to Jenson's shoulder, and he turned, leaving us. I stayed quiet as my Master led us back to the table to sit. To pry would not be wise. I truthfully didn't want to know what they were doing behind the scenes. It probably only meant more trouble for both of us.

"How was your steak?"

I glanced down at what was left of it. "It was great. Your food is probably cold."

It didn't stop him from cutting into the meat.

"It is. I don't care. I'm starving." A smile pulled back his lips as he glanced up at me through his lashes. "You've been keeping me quite busy. I'm going to need fuel if we're going to continue after our shopping."

"More shopping? We've been doing that all day."

I tried to keep my tone light, but all I picked up was the dread. Was it from having to walk, or was it from the thought of having my Master inside of me again? It hurt to move. To sit down. I was so uncomfortable and in pain, not to mention, still bleeding.

"Surely you haven't had your fill already. We've only gone to a handful of stores. Besides, most places here never close."

"I guess it's the heels. They're going to take some time to break in."

The smile returned, growing bigger as he sat up straighter. "We can go home so you can change first. I think I'd like to watch that." He brought the steak to his mouth, chewing as he continued to rake his eyes over my neck and chest.

"I'd like that too, Master. The blue outfit you picked out earlier with the cute white sandals should work great for our trip."

"I agree. Shit. Actually." He looked at his watch. "Your nail appointment is in an hour, and one of your special orders is ready for pickup not long after that. You're going to love what I chose for you to wear tonight. It shouldn't take long for me to grab it. I'll take you to the salon and hit up the boutique while they're taking care of you."

Nails? Special outfit? I didn't care for either of those, but was that a shred of relief underneath? I was almost glad to be parted from him, but the fear of being unprotected this late in the evening didn't sit right with me either. It didn't help that he was thrusting me into a life I knew nothing about. I wasn't a princess like he called me. Truthfully, I hated the pet name. And I'd never had my nails done. I could barely even walk in these high shoes. I sure didn't dress in the style he was dolling me up in. It wasn't that I hated it, it's just that the entire situation on top of being here was all too much. I wasn't able to process my new life with how my mind kept replaying the rape. Every man. Every look my way from one of these monsters. I was sure it was him. Yet... I didn't have the first clue who it could be. That scared me the most.

"Look at you, so far away. He did this on purpose."

My eyes rose from the table. I'd been in a daze.

"I'm sorry, Master?"

"What he did to you. He did it on purpose. And not just with altering your mindset. He wanted me to remember him every time I looked at you." His head shook as he took another bite and chewed. "He's a fool. I'm a jealous man. That's a fact for anyone who knows me or my history of dating. It's why I've never cared to get serious. What's mine is mine. There's no way around it. Most women can't handle how intense I am and that's okay. But I don't get to dump you. Kill you, yes, but that's the only way I escape our relationship. They had to have known that to do this to you. They'd know it would get to me and it is. They're putting us to the test."

My lips parted as I shifted in my seat. There was anger in his voice. I didn't like that. My Master had hinted of a darker side, and I was hoping to keep him happy enough to never meet it.

"I'm sorry they used me to get to you. Maybe if I had use of both arms, I could have fought him off better."

"I doubt it." Another bite. He was quiet as he chewed and swallowed. He took a drink of wine, the contemplating fading with a sureness close to cockiness. "I know what to do. I mean, I'm not sure I have a choice. He can't claim all the credit if I do damage on top of what he's already done. I already reclaimed you sexually. I'll just cover his marks with my own. It'll be that simple."

The blood drained from my face, and I felt faint as I stared across the table at his smug expression.

"It's really the only solution that will put us back on track. Don't you think?"

"I…" What I thought was…I was going to be sick. "Maybe if you pretended it didn't bother you—"

"*He's not stupid, slave.* I thought you said you were strong?"

"I am strong. I'm not saying you're wrong, Master. You have valid points. I just think marking me worse will show more weakness than strength. You'll be playing his game, and he'll see that."

If I thought him angry before, he was downright livid at me now. Blue eyes were barely visible through his narrowed lids.

"I bought a virgin. I did not get one. I bought a beautiful

slave. What he left me with was a battered, abused, crying mess. And you expect me to do nothing about that?"

The dress crunched in my fists as I crushed the sequins at my thighs.

"You speak of him testing us. I will not let him get to me. As of right now, nothing happened. It's gone. In the past. You want a strong woman; I will be that. I will stand tall because I am yours. I will look down my nose at every man who looks my way, proving my worth for belonging to you. They will see no fear because I will not be their victim. Yes, this person took my virginity, but it was not their cock I came on. *It was yours.* One look at us together, happy, focused on only us and not their game, and they will know that. They will see they didn't win."

Jenson searched my eyes as he grabbed his wine and finished it off. When he stood and held out his hand, I didn't hesitate to join him. And just like with my words, I kept my shoulders back and my head high. What I spoke was truth, even if I hadn't known that until the words were spilling free from my lips. There was a power in me. There always had been. I had been made into a fighter from my earliest days, I'd just never been put to the ultimate test. Something told me I may not have a choice being owned by this Master.

MASTER B-0491

I could beat her just as much as look at her. She was right when I hadn't wanted her to be. I respected that, even if it did piss off this Master part of me. I wasn't normally so violent. I could hit a woman, but it didn't do much for me. It didn't drive me to some blissful state of mind. My tastes ran in a different direction. A calmer, slower path. One that could last nights. *Days.* I once almost had twenty-nine hours before my time got disrupted. Those had been heaven for me, and now they could return. I knew that as I held to my slave's hand as if we were a couple. And I suppose we were, just of a different dynamic than I was used to. This took an adjustment, and I was having a harder time than I thought I would. It was one thing to play the bad me. Another to fully embrace it while being my true self. I'd never been able to completely merge the two, and I wasn't sure I could any time soon. *Did I even want to?*

As we left the main building that held the apartments, I took in the chaos of the underground city streets ahead. It was just as alive and packed as it had been the night before. Not that I had spent much time down here. Once Elec and I were alone, it was like reuniting with an old friend. One, I'd never known, yet knew a great deal about. I could thank his father for that. Not that Elec would be thanking him. There was shame there. The two pretty much hated each other, and it was his father's fault. Jerry was big on gambling. On wasting money faster than he could make it. Although...he wasn't as bad as he used to be. Regardless, where Elec was sharp wit, his father wasn't, and over the years the alcohol left him talking more than he should. I knew secrets about his son no one else did. I guess maybe because his father took more to me than Elec. I didn't have reason to hate him. I didn't have the only woman Elec had ever loved killed just to trap him in this world. That had been forever ago. College age, really, but before I had come along. Jerry was lucky to be alive at all. I wondered if Elec even knew his father was responsible for the car accident that took the life of his former fiancée.

Pressure squeezed into my hand as my slave stepped closer towards me. Bodies were thick in the main entrance, crowding into each other as people came and went. I didn't like so many strangers close, but I couldn't avoid this life altogether. My slave had a point. We needed to be public. We had an image to maintain.

My smile was automatic at the thought. Let everyone see us —how happy we were. How unaffected. I unlocked our hands, putting my arm around her shoulders and drawing her in even closer. The slave wrapped around my waist, and I used my free hand to make our path through those just standing around. The live music was loud, and the drunk fools seemed to be mesmerized by it as they stared ahead at the stage outside the bar.

"Did I mention how beautiful you look in blue?"

"In the room." She smiled up with adoration, her voice loud through the noise. "Thank you. I'm so happy you like it on me."

"I'm going to like this special order even more. I can't wait for you to try it on." We began cutting through to turn on the first road to the right. The way my slave's eyes sparkled had my heart pounding. She truly was stunning to look at. I could get lost in her eyes and did. It was the explosion of pressure against my slave's shoulder, and the tearing of my hand free, that broke my fascination. The force knocked her back and had me spinning as I tried to catch her from falling.

Murder called to me as my gaze searched the thick crowd. Had I not been so captivated maybe I would have been paying better attention.

"Are you okay? Who the fuck was that? Did you see them?"

Still, I was scanning the crowd looking for someone out of place. For someone staring back or appearing angry. Guilty?

"No. I was looking at you." Tears were filling her eyes as fear clearly took over. Her gaze jerked to the people surrounding us. We both turned. Looked. Watched. After a good minute, I pulled her through, nearly knocking people over in the process. Had that been what we'd been a victim of too? Impatience from someone trying to get through the crowd? Or was it more? It was clear you could get run over by not paying attention, and I hadn't been.

"Maybe we should go back to the apartment."

"Go back? Do you think I'm afraid of him?" I stopped us not feet from the salon she had an appointment at. "Go back?" I repeated. "You're fucking joking, right? Weren't you the one trying to convince me to not give in? You said you were going to be strong. Now you want to give him recognition because of one possible shove to your shoulder?"

Her lips parted, but she'd barely look at me. Light eyes were scanning the darkness around us, taking in the random people off the main road.

"I asked you a question, *Princess.* Answer it or I go back with my original plan and beat the hell out of you. At least then he can see that the marks on you are mine. I can live with that."

Her eyes snapped to me. She stood straighter, taking a deep breath. When she drew my face down and placed her lips to mine, I studied the way her behavior changed. The anxiety lessened. She even forced a slight smile.

"Forgive me; you're right. I wasn't paying attention. That could have been anyone, and it was probably just an accident. I'm better now. Thank you, Master."

"Don't thank me yet. The night is young." I grabbed her bicep, more dragging than leading her into the salon. A black-haired slave's head lifted as we walked in, and she quickly stood from the table, heading over. "W-seven-twenty-seven. She had an appointment."

"Yes, Master. I'm ready for her. Right this way."

At the gesture, my slave turned to me, waiting for me to release her.

"I'm going to get your order from the boutique and maybe grab a quick drink or two. You're to stay in this shop and wait for me to return. Do you understand?"

"Yes, Master."

I gave her a nod, letting go. Leaving her felt odd...different. Almost as if she were a child, and I was releasing her into the wild. That was just ridiculous, but I couldn't shake the feeling of how vulnerable she was out here alone. Without me as protection, they'd eat her alive. Would that be so bad?

My teeth clenched as I pulled her back into me. "I'm angry. I shouldn't take that out on you. It's this person. I want to know who the hell they are. I can't stand that someone is targeting us and taking out their hate for me on you. It's not fair, and it's driving me crazy." As I hugged her into me, she sniffled. "No more crying. Go have fun. Let this take your mind off things. Even if for a little bit. I'll be back soon. Then, we'll have a better night. *Me and you.*"

"I'd like that. Thank you, Master."

Even though I nodded and waved goodbye, I was barely there. The bell jingled as I left the salon. The boutique was only a few doors down, and I was numb and so far away as I picked up the order. Words faded. Blurred. Darkness encompassed me again, and I let myself get lost in the loud laughter and moans from the whorehouse I passed. When I finally headed through the doors of the bar and sat down, my voice sounded deeper than normal. I was drowning in analysis. In 'who' I was, and what I wanted to get out of this. I thought last night I knew. My path had seemed as clear as day. But I couldn't shake the plaguing questions. The man that bumped into me at the auction. The crash against my slave here on the street. Was it the same person? A different one? An accident on both occasions? It was hard to believe that, but nothing was as it seemed in a place like this. Who were they, and why did they appear to be targeting me? The face hadn't looked familiar, but that didn't mean anything. I ran across so many people in my everyday job. They could be anyone. *No one.* It was hard to say. I was constantly being told I was overthinking things. It was hard not to when your life was surrounded by crime, and you were guilty of things most people couldn't grasp. The threats. The constant need to hurt me by going after those I was connected to. Friends. Co-workers. I was lucky any family I had was already dead.

"Give me something strong."

The male slave bartender nodded, and I fisted the top of the boutique bag I held to. They were no one. It was nothing. I was stronger than them. Let them try to face-off with me.

I tossed back the shot, welcoming the fire that made its way down my throat. I gestured to the glass for another. And then another. Minutes went by as I kept them coming. Longer. An hour? More? I had no fucking clue as I tried to recall all the people I'd run across at the Gardens so far. Sure, there were some I didn't care for or had run-ins with, but no one matched enemies from my past or present. I was fine. I was...feeling the drinks. I wasn't wasted-drunk, but I wasn't sober either. I was walking a very thin line between the two. I stood, throwing down some cash. The slaves technically didn't need to get paid, and the drinks were free, but I went through the motions anyway.

"Four-ninety-one. Judge!"

Pausing on my way to the door, my eyes narrowed at the familiar voice not far from the entrance. Percy was waving me over to a table full of Masters, his smile falling when I didn't budge in their direction.

My head shook, and I continued, my title growing in volume as I pushed through the crowded entrance. It was loud outside as I processed the crowded space. I wasn't stumbling but I felt a slight sway in my steps as I headed around the crowd collecting near the live band.

"Judge, wait! *Judge.*"

I spun, enraged. "I swear to fucking God if you don't stop calling me that I'll lock you up and throw away the key."

"We really need to talk."

"We don't. If I want to talk to you, *I'll find you.*"

"But…"

The bruising on the Master's face was extensive. It'd come up a lot over the last twenty-four hours.

"You have to let me explain. Last night—"

"I don't give a shit."

"Last night was the worse fucking night of my life. Judge, my wife left me before I came here. The lawsuit…it's too much for her to take. She packed her stuff and took the kids. She wants a divorce. I wasn't in my right mind. I'm still not."

"None of that is my problem. You hit my slave."

"And I'm sorry for it. Please, just give me ten minutes to tell you my plan. I'll do whatever you want. I can make this up to you. *I know I can.*"

W0727

I wasn't sure whether to sit or stand. I'd done both off and on for longer than I could recall. I paced. I stood at the window. My Master had dropped me off over two and a half hours ago, and still he hadn't returned. Should I try to walk home? Find a guard and see if he was okay?

The slave who worked on me was already focused on someone new, as were the other three women in the back. They were oblivious to my worry and didn't seem to care either way. What was I supposed to do? My Master told me to stay inside. Did that stand if he were in trouble?

Ringing had me glancing over to the small desk the nail technician sat at with the Mistress. The phone came to her ear, but I redirected my attention back to the large glass windows. With how dark it was, it was impossible to see much. I was squinting and could still barely glimpse the pedestrians walking the road.

"W-seven-twenty-seven?"

I spun, taking in the dark-haired slave who put the phone down.

"Yes?"

"Your Master says go home. He's waiting for you."

A. A. DARK

"Go home?"

"That's right. I could barely understand him. He sounded...drunk."

Drunk? Yes, hadn't he mentioned going to get a drink? Dammit. So, this was the sort of Master he was. Unreliable. *A liar.* A drunk who would risk his slave's safety. Hadn't he given me this big speech about feeling bad? About being upset over this rapist? And this is what he did? Leave me alone? I supposed it could be worse, and still might be. It's not like he'd hurt me yet, where maybe he should have. I was still waiting for the bomb to go off. I was almost certain it would. Maybe even tonight if he was drunk enough. Grandpa Nelson had a temper when he had alcohol. This Master might too.

"Thank you."

I bit into my lip, trying to push back the fear as I eased the door open. To the left, the road was still as packed and crowded as it had been before. Maybe worse. Laughter was booming as was yells in the distance. The crowd looked rowdier than when we pushed our way through. To the right, further down the road, the lights were barely bright enough to give off an ample glow. Anything within feet of the streetlamps were hidden in the darkness. For a good minute, I couldn't move. I wasn't sure which way to go. Neither would be good for me, but one assured I'd get hurt if I decided on that way. I wasn't sure I should risk the main road. Then again, at least if something did happen, there'd be more witnesses. Someone might be able to help me.

Back and forth, I looked. It wasn't until a shadow, cat-o-corner, across the street, stood from a table and headed towards me that sparked my movement. If I were to head for the main street, the shadow might cut me off. I took steps backward, moving towards the end of the road. Turning, I kept my pace at a near jog as I passed the other stores. One. Two. Three.

Glancing over my shoulder, it didn't appear the shadow was getting closer. I pushed myself even faster. The noise was fading in the distance. I was never coming out after dark again, if I could help it. Not with a Master this unreliable. I wasn't far from the entrance to the apartment building. One block. I could do this.

The moment I rounded the building, darkness blurred and seemed to lunge right for me. Pressure—leather fitted against my mouth, and another arm looped around my stomach, lifting me from my feet. Each footstep jolted me through the run. Light faded, disappearing as we were engulfed by the apple trees that surrounded the outside city. I couldn't see a thing. That didn't mean I didn't know who had me.

"Mmmph mmm mmmphh! Mmmph mmm!"

I kicked and attempted to pry the hand from my mouth. It did nothing. I even tried my hardest to twist my body at odd angles, but it proved useless in the endless seconds it took him to reach his destination. We suddenly slid to a stop and the air left me as I was slammed to the ground below. I was swinging, scraping the air for some sort of oxygen, and it only came when I was sure I was going to pass out. I inhaled, trying to steady the intake as I greedily tried to make up for the cramping and anxiety crushing my chest. The moment the flat end of metal fitted across the side of my throat, I froze.

"Let me go."

He didn't speak as he lowered to nuzzle against the side of my face. Fingers fisted at the crown of my head and the knife was slicing my skin as he continued to rub his face against mine. Although I couldn't see him, I could make out a few distinct smells: cigarette smoke, something sweet, and possibly liquor. That could have been anyone at the Gardens.

"You're not hurting my Master by doing this." I winced as stinging increased. The wound wasn't deep, but it wasn't budging either. "He doesn't care about me. I'm replaceable." I cried out as strands of my hair broke free. "I'm nothing to him. Don't you see? You're hurting me, not him."

"Maybe it's you I want to hurt."

The voice was so deep and low I could barely make it out. Teeth grazed my cheek, moving towards my lips. Had I heard that voice before? Had it sounded at all familiar? *I wasn't sure.*

"Please don't—"

My words got caught in my throat as the blade angled to slice deeper. One hard swallow; one wrong move. That's all it would take to slice my throat wide open.

His hand left my hair and he shifted, pushing my dress to my hips. Tears were automatic, but I managed to hold in the sob as the zipper of his pants sounded, followed by rustling from his clothes. The knife eased and I wasn't sure where it came from, but I heard my scream before I realized it had come from me. The shrill pitch took over every inch of me as my throat began burning through the volume and force. The man above me stiffened. Then…lights. They came in a combination of blows that crushed into my face. The anger was evident as he unleashed a wrath so great I regretted my actions. I was going to die out here in these dark trees and no one was going to find me.

Pressure pushed against my entrance and the thrusts were unforgiving. They rocked my nearly unconscious body, but I didn't stop fighting. Even barely able to swing, my heavy arms didn't stop hitting against his chest. I even managed to scoot back a few inches, or maybe that had come from the brutality of the pounding. Everything was fading in and out. At one point I was sure he was even talking to me. Nuzzling some more. Tracing my features with his leather finger.

Darkness.

Lights.

Darkness.

I blinked. No…lights.

My eyes rolled, and I could see the halo of brightness glowing closer. My fingers twitched. I opened my mouth to speak, but nothing came. It was quiet, and I wasn't moving anymore. I was...cold. Alone.

Lights.

There were multiple sets of them. Some going further back. Some moving off in the wrong direction. Again, my fingers lifted, and somehow, I managed to bring my hand off the ground. It fell almost just as fast as it lifted.

"Slave? Slave!"

Something close to a groan mixed with a cry. Had that been me?

Light swung in my direction from feet away, blinding me. Closing my eyes had been a mistake. I didn't have the strength to reopen them. I was fading again. Falling so deep into a void, I wasn't sure I even wanted to break free.

"Slave? I found her! Slave, shhh, don't move. Oh my God. Jesus."

I jerked at my Master's hand sliding under my head. A sob came just as fast as he lifted and pulled me into his arms. Light flashed but faded as my lids squeeze shut through the pain.

"I got you, Princess. Shh. I got you. Fuck. *Fuck.* We're going to get you help. We'll get you better."

Footsteps closed in. The crunching of foliage and loud voices hummed around me. We were moving now. Running? I was rocking all over the place. Rocking with him? Under him? Darkness. Light. White ceilings. Blurs of colors and sounds.

Time.

Echoing.

More light.

"I swear to all that's holy, when I find him, I'm going to kill him." Lips pressed to the side of my forehead. "I had too many drinks. I should have come back sooner. He had to have been watching. That's why he called. *He saw everything.*"

A whimper left me as I processed the words and tried to wake. Still, the condition of my body ruled my consciousness.

"Sleep, Princess. I'm here. I'll protect you."

But would he? He hadn't yet, and I'd been attacked twice within twenty-four hours.

"Mast—"

"No, don't talk. Rest. God, I fucked up. I'm sorry. I'll be better from now on. We'll be better after this."

I didn't have the strength to say or do anything else. Functioning was beyond me. Feeling was unbearable. Mentally, I was shot. Physically, I knew I was battered beyond anything I could imagine. When I did become completely conscious, I'd be in more danger than I was sleeping in this hospital bed. I would do as he said. I'd heal. I'd prepare. *I'd try to figure out who kept attacking me.*

MASTER B-0491

I hadn't liked returning to work with my slave so battered and broken, but I didn't have a choice. I wasn't a CEO. I wasn't a famous artist or celebrity. I was needed in the real world which made the days go by torturously slow. The hours grinded into an agonizing halt as the seconds slammed into my head from the clock I stared at on my office wall. I could have destroyed everything with the number of unresolved issues I had plaguing me. Despite the impatience…my life as a Master left me on an all-time high. It made my adrenaline race. It opened a new life full of my needs I hadn't had in more years than I could remember. *It gave me her.* It was like I was back at college, yet this was better.

I had a beautiful slave who was healing. Who was no doubt terrified and missing me as much as I was missing her. I was going to make my princess better. She'd need me for my protection. She'd want me around so that I could take care of her. That made me happy. I could prove myself and be a Master she was grateful to have. A Master who was stern, but one she could depend on. One she needed. Hadn't she called out to me in her worst times? Reached and cried for me as she choked on the blood from her injured tongue and lacerated lip?

I hadn't been sure I made the right decisions for what I wanted out of this, but when I'd seen the condition my slave was in, I couldn't deny the feeling. Something shifted inside, and I could see the overall outcome. It made me want her even more. My slave could have died. Had she been anyone else, maybe I wouldn't have cared as much, but I did. One more explosive hit. A punch a little lower or higher. When I saw her...I was almost certain she wasn't going to make it. That made me sad. *It opened my eyes.* I hadn't even begun to enjoy what we could share. I hadn't even got to see how she'd react to being my slave. We needed more quality time. Not just days...weeks. *Months.* I had to slow down and see that.

My lips twisted. It wasn't going to be easy. I was two people and torn between them. Or I had thought so, but was I really? Everything was progressing perfectly. Just as I had wanted, even if sometimes it all blurred together.

"Judge, you have a call on line one."

"Who is it?"

"They said you'd know. That you were expecting this call."

Janey, my secretary's voice echoed through my office, and I rolled my eyes. I wasn't in the mood for mind games. Maybe I should have gone home. I was done for the day, but I was lost in thoughts. There was too much disappointment in myself as a Master. Maybe even grief took over as I recalled racing her to the hospital. The hours of waiting for word. Of contemplating more of who and what I was...It set things straight. It locked in my position as something I didn't think I could be without.

Picking up the phone, I tapped my finger against my desk.

"Judge Colburn."

"Well?"

My hand froze at Elec's question.

"The appointment is cancelled."

A pause. "I knew you'd come through, Jenson. No one has time for cooking classes, nor is there a point to them. The professionals can continue their jobs, and you and I can find better things to waste our time on."

I nodded, knowing he was referring to me dropping Percy's case. If it would have been up to me, I'd have burned the entire pharmaceutical corporation to the ground. That wasn't what my superiors wanted.

"I like the sound of that. Say, you haven't heard from Jill, have you? You know, my date last week who ended up with food poisoning? She wasn't looking too well when I left her to come home."

"I've been keeping an eye on her for you. She has quite the way to go, but she's coming around. It's almost the weekend. I'll call David so he can find you a replacement. You should come down and see her. I'm sure she'd like that. Besides, we need to talk." He paused. "You know...there are no positions currently open where I work, but there's always a chance something becomes available in the future. You have quite the reputation from what I hear. I'm very intrigued. I know the path you're meant to take, but I could pull some strings. You have potential and restraint, when it calls for it. I'm rarely wrong, and I think this place might be more to your liking than there. You'd enjoy the way things are run here. Someday, you'll have to sit through one of our trials. I think you'd enjoy it."

The phone disconnected, but I couldn't put down the receiver as I stared ahead.

Had Elec just offered me a spot at the Gardens...permanently, on the board? Not now, but someday? Holy shit.

Slowly, my hand lowered, and I pushed to stand. I wasn't sure if anyone was listening in, but I wasn't taking chances. I tried to appear normal as I grabbed my jacket and headed for the door. My steps were determined as I left. I barely even recalled waving to Janey. My heart was racing. My adrenaline was soaring. The excitement was returning. Just thinking about flying back to the Gardens was a dream. It was everything I wanted.

"SLOW. YOU GOT IT. TRY ONE MORE BITE."

I stepped inside the room, watching as my slave paused with the shaking spoon of broth at her lips. If I thought she looked bad that night, I wasn't prepared for just how beaten she'd been. I mean, I knew, but I hadn't expected the amount of bruising to be so severe. The entire left side of her face was blotchy with a swirl of purple, black, and yellow. Her eye on that side wasn't swollen shut, but it was still puffy and colored. Her skin was even split over her cheek, held together by two butterfly bandages. There was a slit over her lip, and even color under her other eye. Gauze covered one side of her neck, where I'd seen the large gash that night. It hadn't been extremely deep, but the knife had gotten her good at some point.

"You're awake."

My slave didn't take the bite. She lowered the spoon, nodding to the nurse who stood and excused herself. I made my way to the bed, moving the portable table so I could sit down in its place. I grabbed her hand, taking in how the white of her left eye was completely red under the swollen skin.

"Fuck...I'm sorry. I should have never of went to the bar that night. That Master I hit, Percy, he was there. He went on and on." I stopped. "I should have left and went back to you immediately. I never thought the bastard who's doing this would call and pretend to be me. I thought you'd stay and wait. I shouldn't have taken the risk until he was caught. Truthfully, after my talks with the Main Master, I thought this bastard had proven his point. I thought he was finished. We both did."

Tears raced down her cheeks, but she didn't speak.

"I'm going to make this up to you. We're going to start over, Princess. The Main Master has worked out a deal on the outside. He's giving me a little time here while you heal, so we can catch who's responsible. Like a vacation, so to speak. I'm going to get you better. Okay?"

Slowly, she nodded, and I watched as more tears spilled free. I brought her hand up to my mouth, kissing along her digits as I soaked in every shade of color on her face. Every slight swell in the plane of her cheek. Could I have chosen a better slave? One who could shine so gloriously after what happened? God, she was a beauty in her brokenness. An absolute goddess in her anguish. I could look at her like this forever. I could fall in love with her if she stayed this way. Needy. Quiet. Gazing up at me as if I were her knight and shining armor.

"Let me take care of you."

Moving the table back towards us, I lifted the spoon, taking my time as I fed her. Still, she didn't talk, regardless that I filled her in on work for the last three days. I was beginning to wonder if she even could with her injuries. They hadn't wired her jaw shut, had they? I didn't remember hearing about anything like that.

"Have they mentioned a release date?"

Still, the tears randomly left. She sipped the soup from the spoon I held, shaking her head as she swallowed.

"No, Master."

It was barely a whisper. She cleared her throat, wincing as she pushed to sit higher on the bed.

"Do you *want* to go home?"

Her lips trembled as she searched my eyes. A sob broke free, and she hesitantly reached for my suit jacket, bringing me in. I wrapped my arms around her, reaffirmed on every decision I'd made up to this point. Yes, this was exactly what I had wanted.

"Don't cry, Princess. I know you're scared. How about I get up there and hold you? Would that make you feel better?"

At her nod, I took off my jacket and shifted to the opposite side of the bed. I helped her turn to lay her good side against me. The way she fit in my arms was undeniable. We'd barely had significant time together, but the little things said more than time ever would. Besides, now that Elec had bought me a few weeks, we'd finally connect as we should. I really owed him, and maybe that's exactly what he wanted. He mentioned the Gardens, but I was probably more use to him on the outside. Sure, we had some unspeakable connection. We practically shared the same dad, but Elec was also a genius at manipulation too. He'd get me right where he wanted me if he had some ulterior motive. I'd be wise to watch my back from all angles. Even concerning him. *No, especially concerning him.*

Minutes passed as I stared up. My slave was softening in my arms, relaxing as she held on to me. For the moment, I was in heaven. Absolute bliss. Heat rolled from my slave, and light snores even eventually came as time flew by. It was a knock that pulled me from visions I could have lived in forever. The door opened, and my head lifted as the Main Master stepped in. To say his arrival was unexpected was an understatement. He said we needed to talk, but he knew how I felt speaking in front of anyone. Especially, my slave.

"Main Master."

I went to slide free, pausing as his hand came up to stop me.

"I was in the area, visiting a friend whose wife is back in our care. Poisoned after the first auction. I don't think she'll ever recover, but he believes different. Tragic, really. Anyway, I thought I'd come by and check on yours too. How is she? Any change from earlier?"

"Thanks. Not really, but she's doing okay. Well, okay, considering." I paused as my slave stirred against me. "Any news on finding out who did this?"

Elec's lips pursed for the smallest moment as he glanced at her. "No. I watched the recordings a few times, but it was too dark to really see much. You can glimpse him carrying her into the orchard. He's there for a good amount of time and then leaves

330

alone. Somehow, he makes his way to the main street. When he goes in, he's wearing a mask and a dark hoodie with a logo from one of the shops. A few were bought, so we're looking into that, but afterward he just disappears into the crowd. I'm guessing he ducked between people at some point and took it off. It's hard to say. Minutes later you can see the dark material in the streets where he must have dropped it. I'm sorry. Impressive, truthfully, but there's nothing of significance we can use to identify him."

"Damn." I let out a deep breath I didn't even know I was holding. "Hopefully he's finished. I think he proved his point. At least for the time being."

"Don't count on it. Men like that don't ever stop, Jenson. They can't. That's why they're here. To pretend otherwise would be foolish." He kept looking at the woman I was holding to but came back to me. "The doctor is releasing your slave in the morning. I'm having breakfast with Jack and Georgie. We're discussing our plans for the upcoming masquerade. Meet us for breakfast on the top floor. I'm curious on your input. I'm sure you have some great ideas for our Garden Games. We can talk over Master B-Four-twelve then too. Afterward, you can take her home."

"Alright."

He gave a curt nod, taking a step back but hesitating. He kept doing this while we were together. I knew he wanted to address or ask me something, but he never did. Was it about her? Did she still rule his life? Or did I give her more credit than I should? I only knew what his father told me, and the truth was never easy to come by with any of the Wexlers'.

"You'd be smart to." He stopped. "You know who you are, Jenson. Embrace it. You can do that now. Don't lose yourself in the delusion that now that you have the world, you can have love too. We both know this doesn't end well outside of any of us. Not for you. Not for me. *Not for any Master or Mistress.*"

I glanced down to the slave I was cuddling. When he turned, I slid free, coming to stand next to the side of the bed.

"Elec." He paused in reaching for the handle, keeping his back to me. "Would you still be the Main Master if Vivia would have lived? Would you still be you?"

A good minute passed. Two. I couldn't detect emotion, but the silence spoke for itself.

"We're all born with an identity. The core of who we are can be altered, but certain things can never be erased. Not completely. I was born many things, Jenson, but one thing I can't escape is my role in this life. I was meant to play a big part somewhere, and with the fall of Whitlock, it just happens to be here. Vivia." He stopped. "She was the epitome of purity. Of grace. She would have never condoned our world, nor survived it. I knew this. It's why I killed her."

"*You?*"

"Of course, me. But you didn't think that." His tone dropped as he finally turned to face me with dead eyes. "Which means my father probably took credit, like he always does, and you were about to tell me all about it." He nodded, as he took me in. "Let me guess, my father used some common excuse. An accident. A fall, perhaps?"

"Car."

Elec didn't so much as change his expression. "If only she'd had it so easy. I'm afraid that wasn't the case. I'm a greedy man. We both are, so you'll understand when I tell you love doesn't exist with us. It can, but it will never last. Vivia and I...we were a lie. I couldn't face it for a long time. Months, Jenson. That part wasn't fair to her. Had I truly loved her, I would have set her free when she said she wanted to call off the engagement. I didn't. I suffocated her with my love. I forced it on her with every fiber of my being. I shoved it down her throat until she was choking on it. Have your fun." He paused, his eyes going back to my slave. The truth was suddenly clear. Love didn't sit well with him. Nor did affection. "Have fun and then release her the only way you can in this place." Pulling open the door, he gave me one last look. "See you at breakfast. Oh…" His lids narrowed, rage drawing in his face for the first time. "Vivia's name belongs to me. *Only me.* Never let me hear you say it out loud again, or it'll be the last time. *You've been warned.*"

WO727

After three days at home, I should have been okay. I was getting better by the day. I was being spoiled by my Master. I had everything I could have wanted or needed. Everything but peace.

A little over a week as a slave, and I couldn't get over the fear of what might come next. Over the panic when my dreams put me face to face with the man who could have killed me. *Twice.* Every knock. Every phone call. Every blur of my Master out of the corner of my eye sent my heart to my throat. My body was in a constant state of anxiety, and nothing I did stopped it. The masked man would come back for me. He'd find me the moment I let my guard down. What was stopping him from walking right in here and killing my Master to get to me? He obviously wanted to hurt him; *it's why he kept hurting me.* He could do it and kill us both. I felt his strength. It was unstoppable. He was evil, and that's why I needed to stay prepared for anything.

"Thank you for bathing and drying me off, Master. I think I'll be okay now if you want to get some cool air. It won't take me long to get dressed."

Steam filled the large bathroom as Jenson leaned back lazily against the wall by the door. For seconds, he just continued to stare. He did that a lot.

"Don't be silly. This room has the most perfect view. Of course I'd want to be here with you. But no need to get dressed. We're staying in for a movie-night."

I let out a deep sigh, so glad he was finally going to take a break from parading me around the masses. I couldn't stand the stares. Worse, I felt like I was being put on display. As if not only my Master was boasting from my condition, but that the other Masters and Mistresses approved. The looks. They weren't full of sympathy. More...something akin to lust and pride. It made me sick. It made me never want to be out amongst them again.

Jenson pointed. My hair was wet, and he waited for me to wrap it in a towel before finally opening the door. Where I thought he'd hand over the robe, he grabbed my hand leading me to the bed. My resistance didn't last much longer than it took him to pick up on it. He grabbed my waist, gently lifting to sit me on the edge of the mattress.

My pulse skyrocketed. It did every night I'd slept in this bed since I returned, but those nights I'd feared for nothing. All he did was hold me. Now, was different. He was lowering, putting his hands on my knees as he scanned my battered face. He didn't speak, he just added pressure, almost prying my legs apart. The shaking was starting again.

"Lay back, Princess. I've given you time. You know what I need to do. It's only fair."

Fair? For whom?

I could have argued. I could have exploded in what was fucking fair or not. I had a list a million miles long. None of this was fair. Not to me. But who was I other than a slave? I was no one. *I was his.*

"There we go," he encouraged, pushing me open the rest of

335

the way as he moved his face in. Light kisses pressed just past my knees, moving closer each time he switched sides. Large hands grabbed my hips, and he pulled me in, only spreading my thighs impossibly wider. He moaned at the sight, changing the kisses to suction as he began sucking and nibbling his way to my most private part.

Closing my eyes, I tried to differentiate what was good and bad. I tried to categorize right and wrong. I wasn't able as he closed in, tracing his tongue over my slit. My fingers dug into the comforter, and I couldn't even figure out how to classify the sensations I was feeling. Pleasure, yes, but...I didn't want this. Not really. It felt wrong after what had just happened. I was scared. Afraid of what might come with the sex. Would he hit me too? Where was his 'Master'? What was the reason he was even here? Aside from some forceful talk, he hadn't hit me or hurt me. Not like the rapist. Not like the killers I'd heard about. Not even like Master Percy from the elevator.

"Fuck, you taste so good." His tongue was pressing into my entrance as thoughts fought against reason. I could feel my hips rock despite I hadn't done it intentionally. Flicking from his tongue over my clit had my legs jerking and all queries fading to the background from the pleasure that took the forefront.

I was wet. Really, really wet, as I took in the glistening on my Master's chin. Prickling from his five-o'clock shadow scraped against me, but somehow enhanced the burn building from the constant attention to the sensitive nerves. I...*liked it*. I realized that when the questions weren't bombarding me.

"Master."

Suction over the top of my slit had me crying out as Jenson's eyes lifted to meet mine. There was heat there. Such...fire as he stared up at me. It was more than the first night. This was different as he lifted, crawling his way up, over me. I eased back to the bed, letting him hover inches above. He didn't say a word as his fingers replaced his mouth. Touching me. Teasing me.

"Unbutton my pants, Princess."

I reached down, obeying. I didn't let my gaze leave him for long. I wasn't sure I could as I stared into blue eyes. The way the intensity held me captive, I wasn't sure whether to be mesmerized or on alert. There was something...off. I couldn't put my finger on it and wasn't even sure the feeling had merit other than intuition.

Glancing down, the button came free. I eased down the zipper, waiting as my Master took his pants off. When he did, he climbed up, straddling my chest so that his cock rested in my cleavage.

"You may not be able to quite use your mouth like I want you to yet, but your hands are perfectly fine. Touch me. Show me how much you want me."

My response was immediate, but questioning if that was a threat, gave me pause. What would happen if he felt I didn't want him? Would the monster I was waiting for arrive?

"Damn, you're so beautiful."

"Not anymore."

"That's a lie. More than ever."

He brought my hands up, flattening his tongue to slowly run up one palm and then the other. I shivered under the sensations, watching as he took his turns spitting into each one. As he did, he never broke his stare. Not even when he led them to wrap around both sides of his thick length. It was...hot. Even...fascinating in its own way.

I could feel my legs scissoring through the need my Master was invoking. As I began to stroke, watching my Master's pleasure did more than turn me on. The man was sexy in the way he started to move against the friction. Completely captivating as he fucked my hands. I kept the strokes firm, but not too tight.

"Like this, Master?"

"Just like that, baby." He moved his hips, thrusting into my grip as he rolled my nipple between his fingers. He even brought my breasts in closer to enclose around him too. Precum made the sliding even more slick, and I couldn't help the need that was taking me over. My Master picked up on it, letting go of my breast. He still played with one of my nipples, but with his free hand, he reached behind himself, brushing his digits over my folds. Rubbing circles over my clit until I was spreading my legs, begging for more. And he gave it, burying his finger inside of me. Each stroke, each thrust. My Master and I were breathing hard as we built each other up. Minutes passed, and I began to squirm.

"Another finger. Please, Master."

"No." His hand left my breast, and he tapped his finger against my mouth. "Open. You're going to lick it, Princess." He removed the towel from my head, and his hand came to the base of my skull, lifting me as he moved further up. My eyes went back, meeting his, just as my tongue swept over him to collect the precum that was about to drip free. "Fuck, yes. Again."

I opened, slow, bringing the head of his cock halfway into my mouth. My lips encase the tip, and I gave a swirl of my tongue before a rumble left him. I couldn't open wide enough with how thick he was. Not without pain, and he noticed that as I continued to tease his head with my tongue.

"Your mouth is mine when you're healed. I'm going to fuck those pretty little lips so good. Your throat's going to be my new home. You'll be lucky to breathe."

Fear sparked but faded as he withdrew his finger from inside of me, lifting, and fitting himself back between my legs. There was hesitation as he lowered, pressing his lips gently into mine.

Sex wasn't so bad when it was like this. I could even learn to like it if I didn't fear my Master changing. I tried to tell myself he wouldn't, but I wasn't so sure. I didn't know this man, and I wasn't about to forget that. Not even because of good sex.

"I'm going to fuck your pussy so good." He buried his finger back inside of me. "Spread wider, like you were before. Fuck my finger and show me how much you want me."

A moan left me from nowhere. My Master eased a second finger in, and I arched, taking both into me deep. I repeated the call to my Master, even reaching for him as my orgasm built. My breasts were swaying with the slam of his fingers, and his thumb occasionally teasing my clit was putting me over the edge. The ache inside had me begging for more. This was different than the rapes. Like night and day, and I was seeing that with every increase in pleasure.

"Jesus. You're so damn sexy."

My Master turned, easing to rest against the headboard as he pulled me up to straddle him. For a moment, I almost froze. My pulse spiked, and I zeroed in on the way his cock felt at my entrance. Thick. Big. He inched inside, and whatever was starting to come disappeared as I began sinking down his length.

"Your pussy was made for me." He gripped my ass, controlling the speed as he brought me down on him even more. "He uses you. Tries to destroy you." He pushed deep, only to withdraw, pulling me back down again. "I make you feel good. I know what you like. He and I are not the same. *I love this pussy.* He doesn't. Not like me."

The thrusts came steady as I tried to force the words away. To ignore them. *Something.* They kept coming, speaking against my lips. Invading my mouth as he kissed me through the comparisons.

"Fuck. He could never have you like this. Keep riding me, baby. Ride my cock like you'll never ride his. You won't, *will you.* You want me. Not him."

"Master, please."

"Or do you want him? Maybe you like the way he fucks you, more."

"No. Never. I—"

He didn't let me finish as his lips crushed back into mine.

Fingers pushed through my hair, holding me so I couldn't break away. With one arm locked around my waist, and the other controlling my head, he easily moved me at the speed he needed. And I was truly fucking him, just as he wanted. His speed. His way.

Teeth sank into my lip, reopening the cut on the inside. I cried, trying to jerk back, but there was nowhere to go. Blood crept over my tongue, washed away by my Master as he deepened the kiss. I somehow knew I was pushing into his chest, but my focus was on the intense burning from the wound.

"Mas—"

Lips bruisingly ground into mine, igniting the pain even more. I cried out into his mouth, screaming as he jerked my head back. Hair tore as he kept my neck angled backwards. He stopped thrusting, staying inside of me as he locked my body into position.

"You say you didn't enjoy it, but I'm not sure I believe you." Tape tugged against my neck as he slowly peeled back the gauze, exposing the wound from the knife. "Maybe you're lying to me. Maybe you truly like it rough."

"No." A sob tore from me as my eyes stayed fixed on the ceiling. I tried lifting my head, but he had me stuck. "Master, I didn't like it. I screamed for your help. I kept calling out to you. I fought him. I tried so h-hard to get away."

His finger made a circle just above and below the wound, tracing around it, over and over.

"I promise. I swear."

Jenson lifted my head, bringing me inches from his face so he could stare me down. He was angry. More than that. But he wasn't any less hard than before. His cock kept jerking inside me as he stood on some violent cliff I was terrified he'd jump off of.

"I only w-want you. I think you're the most beautiful man I've ever seen. You're so good to me. You're giving and k-kind." Another sob clawed its way out, and I cupped each side of his neck, trying to bring myself closer. Anything to calm him down. Blood was dripping from my chin, and he kept zeroing in on it. "I only want you. No one else. You take care of me. You *s-saved* me."

My bottom lip trembled, and I watched his face lose the anger. His eyes left the blood, coming back up to my stare.

"You're right; I did. I saved you. He almost killed you. *He hurt you.* You don't want him."

"No."

"I spoil you. I put you on a pedestal. He's not like me."

Jenson reached up, smearing the blood up towards my bruised cheek.

"He's nothing like you. You're all I want. All I've ever wanted." I moved in, hating that I was getting so close to his mouth after what he'd done, but I didn't have a choice if I wanted to calm him down and distract him from the blood. "Kiss me, Master. Please."

The fire was back in his eyes. The want. *The need.*

He licked over the smeared blood, pushing back into my mouth as he began to rock me against him. All arousal was gone. All lust I'd felt...history. Whatever was going on in my Master's head stemmed from a lot more than my rapist. He was insecure. Unstable. It was unfathomable how he thought I enjoyed the assault more than the good moments between us. I didn't understand it, but I was hoping with a little digging, I'd be able to get more insight into what I was dealing with. This Master had triggers, and whatever they were, I had a feeling they'd lead me to whoever was after him. If I could discover the root, perhaps I could unmask the cause.

341

MASTER B-0491

Almost two weeks back at the Gardens, and I was ready to secretly slaughter a board member just so I could take Elec up on his offer to take their spot. This place was amazing. So much better than the outside world. There wasn't anything you couldn't do down here. I was in awe of the activities, not to mention the events the Gardens held on the weekends. This place was truly its own city. It was even better since the normal laws didn't apply. For the first time, I felt I was discovering my true self. *Who I really was.* I couldn't say that was good news for my slave. She stayed in a constant state of awareness. Her eyes took in everything. She analyzed every damn thing I said, staying quiet, but judging me, just the same. The questions. So many damn questions. I didn't like that she kept prying. She was comparing me and *him*. Wondering about him. Maybe even needing him? Or maybe the masks for this masquerade were planting worries where they didn't belong.

"I told you you're safe with me. *Smile.* Dance with me, Princess."

"Of course."

Black silk shifted around my slave's curves as she stood,

taking my hand. Even though she followed me to the dance floor, she was stiff. Alert as she peeked through the black lace surrounding her eyes. We had to have danced a good dozen times already, but that did little to put her at ease. She was afraid, even if she tried to disguise it. I could be cautious too, but I refused to hide. I would not be cornered to my apartment. Not for her or anyone.

"I'm sorry if I'm upsetting you, Master."

I threw my slave a look, leading her on the dance floor. She wasn't very graceful, but she was a fast learner, moving right into step as I took the lead.

"I'm trying to be patient with you. You've been hurt repeatedly by a violent stranger. I understand that, but I'm not going to lie. You are upsetting me."

Her bottom lip pushed out the smallest amount.

"I've given you two weeks. You must learn to trust me. I *need* that from you. I have to have that. If you don't trust me, what we have is pointless."

Tears welled in her eyes as she nodded. "I trust you. I really do. I'm just trying to be the slave you need. You protect me, and when you're having a good time, I want to try to protect you too. You watch my back, and I watch yours. I'd feel horrible if something were to happen to you. You're strong, and if faced with someone, I have no doubt you'd be okay. It's them catching you off guard I'm trying to prevent."

Her hand slid from my shoulder, wrapping around the side of my neck. The silk had my lids growing heavier. The black gloves going up just passed her elbows did things to me. *Dark things. Calming things.* I didn't lose control. I calculated. I waited for the perfect time. It was coming.

"Nothing will happen in public. They wouldn't dare. It's too risky. Besides." I gestured my head towards Elec as we rounded the back end of the dance floor. He was wearing a mask very similar to mine, black, just covering the eyes. He was at a large table, deep in conversation with a handful of other masked Masters. "That is one of the most protected men on the planet. When I say we're safe in here, we're safe. Look around. There's a damn guard every ten feet. I want to see you have a good time. Do that for me. Let go of this fear. Be the slave I need you to be."

"That would make you happy and salvage our night? You'll forgive me?"

I smiled. "I would."

"Alright. Let's start over. My eyes are only for you." She licked her lips, pressing her breasts against me as she moved in closer. I turned us, avoiding another couple as I easily maintained the steps. My slave was getting better at dancing, but it was only on the backburner of my thoughts. In that moment as her stare stayed locked to mine, we were one. I could forget everything. Who I was. What I wanted. It was easy to fall captive to her beauty, and now that I had her attention, she had me.

"I'll never use it, but I'm curious. I never got your name."

Green disappeared behind closed lids. One step. Two, I spun us, watching as she giggled but kept her eyes closed.

"What are you doing?"

"I'm trying to see if I'm dreaming."

"Dreaming? Don't be ridiculous. Why would you be dreaming? Because I asked your name?"

Long lashes fluttered open, but she held her smile.

"I was afraid I'd forget what it was. I don't think I've heard it in almost a year. It sounds odd, even when I think it, but imagining telling you...that makes me happy."

"Well?"

Her smile was contagious. I pulled her close, nipping at her healing lip as she angled her head, teasing me with something I didn't know.

"Sloan."

"No." I laughed, genuinely surprised as I smiled even bigger. "No way. That can't be your name. You're Rachel or Becca."

"No, I swear. Sloan Skye Walters. That's me."

"Sloan Skye." I drew her in closer. "Very unique name, but lovely, just like you."

The music turned slow, and I slid my hand from her hip to her lower back. Her arms came to settle around my neck, and the way she gazed up at me heated my blood. The bruising was still noticeable under the makeup, only enhancing her natural beauty. My hand traveled lower, feeling over the curve of her ass. I squeezed, moving my lips to her ear.

"What do you say after this dance, we go get a drink? Are you thirsty? Hungry?"

"I am a little thirsty."

"Wine. That's what we need."

My slave's face lit up as she nodded.

"I'd love that. It's been so long."

I wrapped my arms around her back, bringing her in so she could lean her head against my chest as we more rocked to the music than danced. For the first time in days, I felt her completely relax against me. I could have stayed there and kept her in that mindset of needing me forever, but the music only lasted for another minute or two before it ended, picking up pace.

Pulling back, I led her off the dance floor, never letting my palm leave her. As we passed Elec's table, our eyes met. We still had so much more to talk about concerning Master B-Four-twelve. We were supposed to go over new evidence yesterday, but he cancelled our appointment due to more important tasks.

"I'm so excited." My slave glanced up at me. "I love wine. Like…*love* it. Before I was brought here, I used to drink a glass before bed. It helped me wind down from my hectic schedule."

My brow drew in as I took two glasses from a waiter,

walking us to the far end of the room. I didn't feel like sitting down. I was getting antsy. On edge.

"Hectic schedule." I watched as she closed her eyes, taking a big drink. "Why don't you tell me more about yourself. I'm curious."

The pleasure wavered as she opened her lids, swallowing.

"Alright. I—"

"Wait." I took a drink. "Be thorough. Truthful. If you lie to me."

She blinked, shifting. "I have no reason to lie about anything. I'll tell you whatever you want to know."

"Where are you from?"

"Well, I was born in Louisiana, and lived there with my parents until they got a divorce. My mom...she passed from cancer a few years after that, and my dad had a new family at that point. He was never home anyway. He was a truck driver. When she died, I went to live in Arkansas with my Grandpa, her dad."

I read her face like a book. I'd seen innocent and guilty, and this woman had secrets.

"You didn't like that though."

"I did not." She finished her wine, lifting her hand to the passing waiter. "May I have another, Master?"

"As many as you want."

"Thank God." She switched glasses for a new one, taking a drink before she continued. "I already grew up poor, but the conditions were atrocious. *He* was atrocious."

"He hurt you. You were a virgin, so he didn't rape you."

"No. He never went that far. Close to everything but that. I lived there about two years before Daddy came to visit me."

"And what did Daddy find?"

Worry, something more, had her staring down at her glass.

"He...I told him. I only wanted him to take me away from there."

"But he didn't?"

"No. They got in a fight. He killed Grandpa Nelson. He's in prison now."

I blinked through her words. "So, Daddy came to your rescue. Good." I took a drink. "What happened after that?"

"I lived with my aunt and uncle."

"Still not a good situation, I see. You don't seem relieved by it."

"They fought a lot."

"Over you?"

She nodded. "My uncle wasn't allowed to talk or even look at me. I couldn't get out of there fast enough, but I did after I graduated. I left Baton Rouge and moved to New Orleans. I managed to hold down jobs while I got my degree. I was finally making something of myself when I met Payton."

"Payton?"

At my deepening tone, her eyes shot up. She downed the glass of wine, waving the waiter back for another.

"I dated him for a few months. He was my first serious boyfriend. Before, I hadn't had time. I worked two, sometimes three jobs. When I got hired at the hospital things became easier. And he was a cop so...I saw him a lot."

"A cop." The words barely made it through my clenched teeth.

"He's the reason I'm here. He tricked me. He turned me over to them. I guess you can say he played me all along."

I finished my wine, grabbing a new glass from the waiter as my slave took another as well.

"Payton? What was his last name?"

She hesitated. "Yardley."

"Payton Yardley. What did you do with this cop? Did you make out with him? Touch him? Let him touch you?"

Sloan quickly saw where this was going. She took a small step back under my enraged stare.

"We were dating, Master. He said he loved me."

My eyes narrowed even more. "He told you that?"

"All the time. He even hinted on a future. Marriage. Kids."

Her voice cracked and tears fell to her cheeks.

"And that upsets you? Which part? His betrayal or your heartbreak?"

"Master...*he sold me to this place*. He played on my past and toyed with my emotions. I guarded myself for so long, all for what? So I could be worth more money to a Master who'd want me like a piece of meat?" Her voice was shaking as she chugged back the wine like it was water. "I trusted *no one*. I kept to myself. I." She swayed, pausing as she reached for stability. "I... thought things would be different. But it wasn't different. It never will be. Men...hurt...you." Closer, she moved to the wall. I took her empty glass so she wouldn't drop it. "Master, I don't feel."

"What? You don't feel good? Sober? No, I do believe you're going to be quite drunk. And quite fucking honest. Trust? *You don't trust me.*"

Her mouth parted, and she seemed to go back over what she'd said, catching her mistake. "I'm sorry, Master. I think. I. I'm not right in the head. I'm off-balance. I feel funny. I'm... leaving...the room. I'm." Again, she stopped, her lips parting as she looked around in horror. She was lowering towards the floor, moving more into the wall as if she could hide against it.

"You're not leaving, you're drunk. Let's go."

I grabbed my slave under the bicep, putting the glasses down on a nearby table. Each step was a chore. A fight. I didn't bother heading for the main entrance. I swept her into my arms, pushing through the back doors. I knew they led to a small adjoining room that opened to the hallway, right by the elevators. It would save time and face. The last thing I wanted were the other Masters seeing my slave incapacitated. Besides, Sloan obviously wasn't in her right mind on alcohol. Her eyes were rolling, and she wasn't moving much anymore.

"Leaving so soon?"

The voice behind me had me slowing in the middle of the room. It was the footsteps that followed that gave me pause. Not one pair. Not even two. There were multiple pairs.

"I think the Master likes to play games." A new voice. "Let's give him a game worth remembering."

WO727

Colors. Lights. Everything was in slow motion and sounding so far away as I tried to figure out what was happening. Voices were dragging, not making sense as blurry figures began to fade in and out.

"Hold her legs down."

Laughter. Was that a female? Something wasn't right. I knew that deep in my bones as I realized I was moving and fighting against pulls that were trying to get a grip on me. Colors warped again, but there was one thing that couldn't escape me: masks. Not like at the masquerade. Full face masks like the one my rapist wore. But this wasn't just one man. This was many men. Three? Four? Nausea washed over, but I managed to hold it off as the room swayed. That kept happening. Why couldn't I get ahold of myself? Why couldn't I think straight or get control?

The sickening feeling went beyond terror. It wasn't just the wine, either. This was more.

"Dammit, *grab her legs.*"

"I will when you get both her fucking arms. I thought you said you drugged her?"

"*M-Master?*" The room was beginning to become stable

350

enough for me to feel a sense of control, but it didn't last for more than a few seconds. "Master! Master!"

"I did drug her. It's kicking in. Look at her."

Why did that voice sound like mine? Was I hearing myself? I wasn't right.

Somehow, I managed to twist, reaching for a butterknife not far from where they had me. Fingers dug into my calf, and I turned, slicing towards the hand that reached for my wrist. It didn't appear the knife cut into his palm deeply, but I couldn't tell as he grabbed me in a crushing hold, making the weapon clink to the surface.

"Bitch! You're going to pay for that."

My head fell to the side, and still I jerked my arms and legs against the pressure that tried to spread and restrain them. Two more masked people were feet away, pointing at me and whispering. They were everywhere. How many was there? *"Master!"*

Multiple sets of laughter rang out at my yell. It distorted, morphing to demonic tones as my eyes continued to roll off and on. When I finally could blink through the episode, what I saw had a blood curdling scream leaving me.

"There's my girl. Miss me?"

The masked man lunged, grabbing my throat as I tried to twist. It was only then I realized I was being held down on a circular table. Pressure was like a vice, crushing my throat as one of the strangers who held me turned me back towards my rapist.

"Shh." The man I'd come to fear lowered on top of me, moving in inches from my face. Colors were starting to blur again. They were stealing me as I felt his hand move between my legs. A sob shook me, and I shouted with everything I had, trying to go wild against the hold.

"Master! Master, please!"

"You hear that? She wants her Master." A voice laughed.

"Your Master can't help you, *slave*. No one can."

Pain jolted my body at the teeth biting into my neck. I could barely catch my breath as he let go and plunged forward. I screamed, seizing through the forceful thrust.

"Master! Help me! He's here. Master!"

"Damn, she's beautiful, isn't she?"

That voice. Did I know that voice? My hearing wasn't reliable. I wasn't even sure what was real or what wasn't. I was crying. Sobbing. Still screaming when one of the stranger's hands weren't covering my nose and mouth. The stranger off to the side grew closer, but I wasn't even sure if they were real. Color blurred. They bled and transitioned into nothingness. The room kept disappearing.

"What I wouldn't give to put my dick down her throat."

"I want to fuck her. Do you think she'll scream for me too?"

"*I'll fucking kill you all.*"

The tone had been so deep. Had it been far away? Come from the man above me? I almost couldn't make out who was talking anymore. Pounding shook my body with every brutal thrust. My vision went white, and my new scream sounded a million miles away. I was fading again. Leaving the horror that was becoming a constant in my life. It came. It went. And so did I...

"Do I FUCKING LOOK OKAY? *LOOK AT ME.*" JENSON. HE WAS talking to someone. The Main Master? It sounded like him, but something wasn't right. The voices were wavering, going in and out. "Yeah, I'll do that. Thanks. I'll see you at breakfast."

My eyes cracked open, and I jolted at the pain. It wasn't only on countless spots of my body, but within me too. The deepest parts of me hurt. Although it was excruciating, my head was the main thing that throbbed. Movement and sound made me gag, and I was barely able to roll on the bed and reached the bedside trash can before I started vomiting.

"Dammit."

Footsteps hurried towards me at a quick pace, and I couldn't help but flinch as I heaved again. When my eyes finally rose, I burst into tears knowing the edges of memories pushing through wasn't a bad dream. I hadn't imagined what happened.

"Master?"

He took the trash can, putting it down to kneel and face me. One of his eyes were nearly swollen shut, and his cheek was bruised. There was still blood on the inside of one of his nostrils.

"What happened? I...I mean, I think. *You said.*" I sniffled but sobbed. "I thought we were safe."

"We're safe now. We have the Main Master to thank for that. I don't think either of us would be here had he not found us when he did."

"*Did he get the guy?*"

My Master got quiet, grabbing my hands as his brow drew in. For seconds he didn't speak.

"The men ran. They caught up with them. He says he has the one who did this to you."

I sucked in a deep breath, half crying from the pain I still felt, and half crying out in hesitant relief.

"Did he tell you who it was?"

"He told me who they found, but I'm not so sure what to think about it." He seemed to catch himself, stopping. "This involves Masters. It's not a place for a slave. All you need to know is you don't have to be afraid anymore."

I wiped the tears, nodding, but I wasn't sure I could make myself believe it. Hadn't I let my guard down after my Master basically promised I was safe at the masquerade? I hadn't been. Not even with him and the Main Master so close. And what if they got the wrong guys? The men ran. They could have easily mistaken them for someone else in the area.

"Did he say anything else? Maybe a reason or—"

353

"No. *Enough.* We're done talking about it. I'm going to get the shower going. Get us clothes. You need a shower too."

The look he gave me had me feeling dirtier than ever. Used. Broken down. So filthy and ashamed. Had I been raped by more than the one main rapist? Did they all...No. I wouldn't think of that now. My lips parted to call out to my Master again, but he was already standing, leaving me at the bed. His behavior was different. Colder. Detached. And clothes? We'd never really slept in them. If I had gotten in bed with clothes, he'd taken them off.

As I stood, I noticed silk was split along my side. I could see my waist and hip. My panties and stockings were nowhere to be seen. I wanted to throw up again. I hurriedly pushed the torn dress off, throwing it to the far side of the room. I couldn't look at it. Couldn't bear to see what they did. And if it did that to me, what about my Master?

A million questions nearly paralyzed me. What if he didn't want me anymore because of the rapes? What if he was done trying to put me back together again? I had said way too much when I started drinking the wine. He'd been furious at my mention of Payton. Jealous, but so much more than that. But... the trust. It all came back in a wave of dizzying thoughts. The one thing he wanted, and I'd pretty much admitted I didn't have it. It was one thing on top of the next. If all of this turned my Master against me, he'd want a new slave. That meant...I'd die.

Banging came from the bathroom drawers. Despite the pain, I kept my pace fast, too afraid to make him any angrier. I had to think. To come up with a plan. I couldn't make any mistakes. But fear only added to my mounting anxiety.

I grabbed a pair of panties and a nightgown for me, pulling out a pair of boxers for my Master. When I stepped into the bathroom, my reflection gave me pause. The blood vessels in my eye were nearly all ruptured again, and there was fresh bruising on my neck. There didn't appear to be any new marks on my face, but I wasn't sure if it would still look like this come morning.

"Here." He grabbed our clothes, tossing them on the counter as he handed over pain reliever. He didn't even wait to see if I took it. Jenson turned, heading right to the shower. The sound of water filled the space, and I felt emotional whiplash compared to the last two weeks. He had his scary or unstable moments, but overall, he spoiled me. *Wanted me.* He treated me like the princess he'd named, and now...I might have ruined that. He was acting as if I didn't exist.

There was no acknowledgement to me whatsoever as he climbed in the shower. I grabbed the glass of water on the counter, wincing as I swallowed down the pills. When I opened the shower door and climbed in, he didn't even glance my way.

"Master... are you mad at me?"

Nothing. He finished lathering his hair, rinsing it out before he finally met my stare. When he did, his expression was just as cold as I was waiting for the water. It was unlike the man he was most of the time. It was if I were staring at a complete stranger. Especially with the bruising and swollen eye. He scared me. More so than ever.

"Am I mad at you?" He roughly cupped the side of my neck, pulling me towards him. His thumb rubbed up and down the front, bringing my focus there. Although the pressure wasn't intense, my throat was already so sore from the rapist. "Am I mad at you? What do you think, slave? Am I?"

"Yes." I didn't reach for his forearm or wrist. I leaned forward, my hands going to his shoulder, choking myself as I held and tried to get closer to him. "Payton meant nothing to me. I was upset over another break in trust, not in his lies for a future. You ask me to trust you at the party, and now you know why I was so afraid to. Everyone who has ever been in my life has hurt me one way or another. I've been so scared to let you in. I'm afraid you're going to hurt me too, but that's not fair to you. I can be loyal, Master. I can trust. *I can.* Don't be mad at me. Tell me what to do. Whatever you want."

"I've been patient. I've given you nothing but time."

"I'm trying. The rapist—"

"Is irrelevant! If anything, what's happened should have made you trust me more. It didn't. You made that clear tonight."

"I'm sorry. I'll do better. Please, tell me what to do."

"You can't handle it."

"I can. I will." I hesitated, knowing I'd probably come to regret this. The rapes weren't my fault. I was doing everything I could just to cope, but I'd run out of time. I messed up being honest, and now I was going to have to face my Master for who he truly was. The submission was mad. Crazy. Insanity was never stronger than when death was at the door. "Master, please. I can do this. I can be the slave you need. Let me prove it to you."

Glacier blue eyes glared into mine. Seconds went by when finally, the anger eased. He pulled me into his arms, holding tight.

"You have no idea what you're asking for, Princess." He pulled back, reaching up to cup my face with both of his hands. There was a pause before he continued, almost seeming to decide something as he took me in. "You want to prove it? You say you can be loyal and that you can trust. We're about to find out if you're telling the truth."

MASTER B-0491

"You don't trust. You've had a hard life. It happens. I didn't trust for a long time either, but there's a moment in a person's life when they must ultimately face who they are. The lies. The running. The fantasies. We have to learn to let all of that go and see the truth that is hidden behind the excuses that rule us."

I led my slave to the bed, lifting her arms as I began to restrain her in the cuffs attached to the headboard. She said she wanted to trust me, but I could tell the only thing she wanted to do was run. Fear ruled her, and I let it feed me as I continued.

"Honesty is not easy to come face to face with. It is usually ugly and traumatic. It takes bravery to face truth. Most don't have the courage to admit that they're different. It took me a life-time up to that point to stop running from what so desperately wanted to break free."

My slave's lip trembled. "And what was that, Master? What wanted free?"

I didn't answer as I secured the other cuff and headed to the closet. Light flooded the space, and I reached to the top shelf, grabbing a small box. As I headed back to the bed, Sloan's head lifted, watching as I came to stand at the very bottom of the mattress.

"I'm good looking. I've always known that. I've even used it to my advantage. But, you see, it was never enough. Where I used it to get me what I wanted, it ultimately repelled my true desires. I never understood what it could be...until I did. It wasn't my appearance, it was me. The inside of me. Even as much as I tried to fit in by mimicking my peers, my true nature could never be hidden. Energy. Looks. Actions. *They just knew*."

The flaps opened, and I peered down into the small space. Sloan was still lifting her head, trying to see what it was I was getting.

"After a while, I stopped pretending to be like them. I lost it. I got angry. I guess you can say, I got even. They feared me, when at that time they had no reason to. But I gave them reason. I showed them what they clearly already knew, even if they couldn't see."

"Master, I don't understand."

"With everything that's happened, I've only ever wanted one thing from you. What is that, Princess?"

Her lips parted. "Trust. Devotion. You want me to need you."

My eyes shut, and I smiled. "Is that really so hard? Trust me. I never hurt you. *Not like him.* Need me. Want me. Let me take care of you. See me. *Only me*." I reached down, unzipping the small packet to pull out a needle and thread. "Do you see only me, slave?"

A slight panic took over Sloan as she tried to glimpse what I held. The closer I got, the faster her breathing increased.

"Of course, Master."

"I'm not so sure of that. You see plenty of other people. *You see him* when I only want you to see me. Me over everything. Me over the worst-case scenario. Trust me. Need me. See me. *Me. Me. Me*."

"I see you." Her voice cracked.

"You will after we finish."

"I don't." She dug her heels into the mattress, shifting the smallest amount as I sat down next to her, threading the needle. "I don't understand, Master. I see you. I never look at anyone else. My rapist…he means nothing. I don't want to see him ever again. Master, please. What are you going to do?"

"It's simple. Until you're ready to see only me, you'll see nothing. You'll only hear me. Feel me. You'll learn to need *only* me. That, or I'll be the last person you ever see. Now." I bit the thread free from the spool. "Do you trust me?"

A whimper broke from her lips. No objection. No scream. Just a trembling of her body as she sobbed and nodded.

"I trust you."

"We'll see." I turned to face her, using my free hand to trail down her cheek. "I'm not going to lie. This is going to hurt. Feel free to scream, but don't you fucking turn away or fight me. That's not trust, Princess; at this point, that's a death sentence."

"Okay. O-Okay." She broke, her shoulders shaking as she kept in place. "I can do this. I trust you."

Leaning forward, I held her stare only inches away.

"You're about to not have a choice. Do you see me?"

"Yes, Master."

"Do you want to be only mine?"

She nodded, continuing to cry.

"Close your eyes."

She scanned my face once more before obeying. Her lids lowered, and I smiled, closing my own eyes as I savored what I'd waited for now for weeks.

Two identities…merging…colliding into what, I wasn't sure. All I knew was I had to find out. I had to see where this led.

Biting my lip, I took hold of her upper eyelid, lifting it free from where it rested. An agonizing groan was followed by a high-pitched sound as I leveled the needle against the skin and forced it through. She didn't stop crying as thread slid down, finally stopping at the knot I'd tied at the end.

"Master, I-I-I don't want him. I swear I don't."

I pinched just under her lower lid, lifting the skin. She let out another loud cry as I stabbed through, threading the pieces of skin together.

"Master, I promise you."

"Are you trying to get me to stop?"

I may have asked, but I didn't pause in moving to her top lid again.

"No. I just want you to know." A breathy sob. "I don't want him. I only want you. Only you. *Ah!*" More cries as I punctured through, moving back to the bottom. Then back to the top. Three. Four. Five times. "I don't want him. I want you. I trust you. Only you. Only you."

Wetness mixed with a small tinge of blood. Her lids were red and starting to swell the smallest amount around the punctures. I cut the thread tying it off as I finished the first eye. The black color of thread was so prominent against the mix of tones from her flushed face. It sent a rush of adrenaline through me, sparking a lightening-like branching of lust and bliss. My own hands were shaking as I began the next eye. And more, my slave chanted her need of me. And more...*I knew I had finally made it home.*

⁓

"SLOW. HERE, REACH OUT." I GRABBED MY SLAVE'S HAND, helping her stand from the bed. She was still crying in short bursts of wrenching sobs, trying to be strong, but she couldn't hide this sort of mental trauma. Sure, she'd undergone pain, but it didn't compare to me taking her sight in such a shocking way. I dumped her right off the mountain of misery into the never-ending depths of darkness, and she withstood every second of it for me. *Me.*

"Count the steps to the wall, Princess."

She held my hand as I kept her closer. The way she kept trying to turn her face into my chest left a warmth blossoming inside.

"There we go. One. Two. Three." She sniffled, her hand bouncing as she searched for the barrier feet away. "Four. Five. Six."

"Seven," she continued. "Eight. Nine." Her fingertips brushed the wall and again she sniffled. "Nine steps, Master."

"Good girl. See, you did it." I licked my lips, tracing down her face. Her head cocked to the side, and I let my gaze rake over her body as I helped turn her back to the bed. "Now turn and go back."

"I can h-hold to you still, right?"

"You better."

Her foot came out, and I kept pace with her as she counted back to the bed. When I made her count the length and width, I then made her count the steps to the bathroom. After, I quizzed her on the numbers. She had no problem remembering, but she started to get disoriented when I introduced the closet and the bedroom door.

"I'm feeling a little dizzy, Master."

Anxiety was back in her tone. She wasn't as good as she pretended to be, but I didn't expect that. *I didn't want it.* The worse she was, the more she was mine. And my slave was barely hanging on from a full-blown episode.

"That's common." I lifted her in my arms, carrying her back to the bathroom. It was late, and every pull of pain in my face was a reminder of just how amazing this night had gone. Perfect. Heaven. Dreams. "I think that's enough. Time to brush your teeth so we can get ready for bed.

More panic, and more I smiled. But she didn't say anything

as we went through the routine. She shifted and danced, hesitating as I went to lead her forward.

"I have to go to the bathroom, Master."

"Count the steps. I'll lead."

Embarrassment was growing on her face as it tinted red.

"One. Two. Three. F-Four." She sobbed. "F-five. Six."

"One more step, Princess."

"Seven."

Her shoulders shook through the new round of cries. I helped her sit, crossing my arms over my chest as I beamed and waited. Let her feel uncomfortable. Let her squirm and be helpless. Here, she was mine, and here, I'd devour her whole. Here, my game would become one, and I would finally get to pick up where I left off so long ago.

"Done?"

Her hand felt around, grabbing the toilet paper as she finished. I flushed for her, sweeping her back to my arms when she stood. The hold around my neck was tight. Her entire body was damn near convulsing through her near-broken mindset. Jerking back the blankets, I laid her down, taking in her nude frame. This wasn't about sex anymore. This was about power. Control. She was finally at the mindset now where *I had it*.

WO727

"I'm so impressed with you, Princess. I didn't expect you to take to this so well. You ready? Open for me."

My mouth parted robotically as the fork pushed in. I took the chicken, chewing through the blur I was floating in. To say I was taking this well was furthest from the truth. Three days I'd gone through hell. The need to open my eyes drove me mad. The need to blink. To see. *To be independent in the smallest thing*...obliterated me. To be present was a reminder of what I was missing. To become attuned was a torture I couldn't endure. But to stay lost in the deepest parts of my mind, now that saved me. I was there but not. Here but gone. Present but so fucking absent.

I swallowed not sure I could stomach another bite. Eating was the last thing I wanted. If I could sleep. If I could disappear completely time would pass. Maybe he'd get bored of this and cut the threads. Should I cut them? Could I?

No. I couldn't do that. Trust would be gone. I would be dead.

"Open for me, baby."

I obeyed, nearly scrambling from the chair as lips hungrily met mine. The sudden, unexpected touches were too much. He kept doing this, catching me off-guard. A hand between my legs. A pinch to my nipple through my dress. A kiss. Lots of kisses. I should have been getting used to it, but the more it happened, the more I wanted to run and scream. To fight. To go wild. It was one thing to see my Master. Another to have him hidden from me. It reminded me of the masked rapist. Now, I couldn't see either of them to distinguish good and bad. Was there truly a difference?

"Mmm." He laughed, nipping at my lip. I wish you could see yourself right now. You look so sexy in that dress." His finger traced the deep V of the loose material, stopping in my cleavage, only to head back to my throat. "I love you in purple. I think this is my new favorite color on you. It matches the bruises. Almost like a necklace." His voice faded out only for him to laugh again. "Yes, that's it. I should pull up your hair after we finish. I want a better view."

Knocking had my head whipping to the side. My pulse exploded, and I was barely able to stop from pissing myself.

"Master. Master, who is that? Were we expecting company?"

The chair scraping the ground had my head ducking as I drew into myself.

"We were not. Do not move. Do not stand. Do not make a sound."

God, I was going to pass out. Unbelievable terror had bile burning my throat. My teeth were chattering through the fear, but I continued to hold to the table as an anchor.

Footsteps headed away from me, and all I could see was the mask man hovering above. He'd rape me again. Worse, he'd kill me this time. He'd show us both who was in control. It wasn't me or my Master. This man had friends. This man was powerful. He'd be back if he wasn't caught. He'd come for me.

Metal. A clicking. More sounds I wasn't sure of.

"Main Master." A pause. "I wasn't expecting you."

"You didn't come to breakfast this morning. I figured you'd

come to lunch but nothing. We had an appointment. You were a no-show again. *That's twice, Jenson.* I don't take kindly to getting stood up."

Silence. It lasted for seconds followed by a sigh.

"Come in. I'm sorry, I completely forgot. I was a little distracted."

Footsteps had my head shifting to better hear them. I was still shaking. Still trembling to insurmountable heights.

"Oh." Hesitation. "I see. You've advanced. Now, doesn't this look familiar."

Did it? I used every ounce of my hearing to soak in tones, breaths. Even movement.

"You can say I'm getting more comfortable."

"Yes, you can say that. I saw the pictures in your file for the Gardens. You're growing into your role." The Main Master cleared his throat. "Why don't you grab a notepad. I'll try to make this quick."

Footsteps. Some away. Some…coming closer? I wasn't sure, but my body responded as if they did. My teeth began chattering again and the shaking grew worse.

"Look at this." The Main Master's breathy whisper was followed by a pause. "I'm curious, slave, did you let him do that to you willingly?"

My lips opened, only to close. "You're not my Master."

A chuckle.

"I'm not your Master; I'm your Main Master. Answer the question, slave."

The tears were automatic, forcing their way through the secure thread. I should answer him. I knew that, but I couldn't. What if this was a test? What if I got in trouble? Who would I get in more trouble by? Too many questions, but one man suddenly seemed more important than the other, and this one I didn't trust.

"You're not my Master. You're not my Master. *Master.*"

"Answer me, slave."

My volume increased. "Master! You're not my Master. Master!"

Footsteps were close to pounding as they returned. "What the hell is this?"

"Master. *Master.*"

My hands were out, searching, grabbing. More footsteps. I jumped and cried out as a hand settled on my shoulder.

"I asked her a question. I expect her to answer. She will answer...*now.*"

"Princess." Fabric rustled and lips pressed to my cheek. I reached out, clinging to his shirt. "The Main Master asked you a question. What did he ask?"

"H-He." I tried to catch my breath through the tornado of emotions. "He wanted to know if I let you do this to me. Willingly. And yes, I did. Only you. Only you, Master."

"Good girl," he whispered, kissing me, heatedly. He moved over, scraping his teeth against my cheek. "Good. Girl." Another nip. Another kiss. Movement. "Let's have a seat, Main Master."

Aside from the walking, they kept quiet until leather groaned. And me, I retreated again, deep within as their tones lulled me like a lullaby. I wasn't sure how much time had passed. They talked about a four-hundred-number Master. About a criminal case he was facing in the outside world. I cared for none of it. It wasn't until I knew they stood that it jolted me back to awareness.

"The *rapist*. Master, what of the rapist?"

"Nothing yet, slave."

A sound left me at the Main Master's response. It was a cry so alien, I hadn't even thought I was capable of such a sound.

"Nothing? I thought...Master, you said...but."

"I told you I wasn't sure about it. I don't think it was the right person. It's nothing for you to worry about, slave. You trust me, *don't you?*"

"I...I. Yes, of course." My hands flattened on the table as I turned away from them. I had to calm down and gain control, but I also knew that was pointless. With no sight, I couldn't protect myself. I couldn't fight or distinguish the difference between sounds. My rapist hardly ever spoke. When he did, it was... different. Quiet. Changed from what had to be his original tone. He...My body went ice cold as suspicion came from nowhere. It overwhelmed me with flashes of quick memories from the very first attack to the last.

"A moment outside?"

"Give me a minute."

The door shut, and I was ready as my Master's hands settled on my shoulders from behind.

"That's it, baby, breathe. I know you're upset. Just think about it. What better way for you to learn to trust me?" He kissed my cheek. "It's fate, really. Now, stay. I'll be right back. It won't take me long."

"Is it him?"

"What?" Confusion was apparent in my Master's tone. "Is what him?"

Anger built within me. How could my Master not care about this rapist? How could this not be his main priority? It made no sense. That meant he had to know who it was...right?

"Is the Main Master the rapist? Were you with him all the way up to my rape the night of the auction? Are you letting him do this to me? *Is it him?*"

Silence played out as his hands stayed on me. They flexed, they squeezed. I didn't need to see his face to know my question was messing with him. With what sounded like a growl under his breath, his hands went lax, and he tried to cover it by clearing his throat.

"*It better not be.* I'll be right back."

That wasn't the response of a man who was lying. Not the way he said it. It was as if the idea hadn't even dawned on him.

As if he'd never expected it. But now that he did, I saw his anger. It was there concerning this rapist, he just never let me see it. That confused me even more. Was he doing it to calm me? To make me feel better? Imagining it was the Main Master pissed him off...*so he did care.* Perhaps this was the side he never let me see. Maybe he only pushed for an answer when I wasn't around.

The door shut, and I let out a breath, feeling for my water. I took a drink, letting my mind go back to the last rape. Back to when multiple men had me pinned down to the table. The Main Master had been surrounded by men too. I'd seen the table when Jenson pointed him out to me. It made sense. Who else could get away with something like this? There were cameras everywhere. And they'd caught nothing?

I wiped the angry tears, letting myself stew as I went over everything I knew.

Why? The Main Master ran this place. He could have any slave he wanted. Why me? I was no one special. I'd seen a ton of more beautiful women here. He could have whoever he wanted. Anyone, literally. That had to mean my Master was right on this being personal. He'd always said that. So, what existed between Jenson and Elec that would cause the Main Master to do this? *If he even did?* I knew better than to get carried away on presumptions, but it fit so perfectly.

"I'll take care of it. I don't see it being a problem. The case is pretty cut and dry." He paused at something the Main Master said. "I won't forget to take them out." Another break in talking. "I'll text when I'm ready. It might be a few hours or a few days. I'll let you know."

My Master's voice grew in volume as I felt a breeze from what I assumed was the door being swung open. A thud sounded, followed by heavy walking towards me.

I stood as my Master gripped both of my biceps and helped

steady me. In a slow path, he rounded my shoulders, pausing when his palms were on each side of my neck. Lips massaged into mine, tender...more passionate than the other times.

"You defied the Main Master for me." One hand slid up to my jaw, bringing me in even more. "You wouldn't answer him. You chose me when the man could have killed you on the spot. You waited. *Called for me.*" More he kissed me, and with each slide of his tongue against mine, hope sparked. Hope. Sight. My Master's happiness. There was something to that. It was a requirement. A priority over everything.

"I said only you. I want no one else. I belong to you. I'm yours." I gripped his shirt as his other hand went down to grab my ass and pull me in.

"You should have seen his face. He wasn't happy. He was shocked. Surprised, maybe? I can't believe you chose me over the Main Master."

"Always."

His hard cock pushed into my stomach for the briefest moment before he pulled back. There was a scraping of something next to me, and then vertigo hit. I was spun as he lifted me into his arms. We couldn't have been halfway through the living room before he jolted to a stop. Something glass shattered. Where it had happened, I wasn't sure. Jenson didn't speak. He didn't say anything at all.

"Master?"

Silence. Seconds went by.

"Master? What is it? What happened?"

When he still didn't make a sound, I lifted my hands feeling his face. He seemed fine. His cheeks were rough from not shaving. His jaw was clenching.

"Master, please, you're scaring me. What is it? I can't see. Did something break? Is someone there?"

The last came out almost strangled through my fear. I

squirmed, feeling…everything. His face. His head. I was moving so fast, touching every part of him I could that I wasn't prepared for his hold to drop out from underneath me. I hit the ground hard, feeling his body fall off to the side, away from me. I didn't understand what was going on.

"Master? *Master?*"

I patted the ground, trying to find my way back to him, but I froze as my hands landed in wetness. It didn't appear warm, but it wasn't cold either. My head shook, and I moved more to the side, scrambling and crashing into what I could only think was the back of the sofa.

"Master! Please, talk. Master, please! I need to find you. Are you okay? *Master.*"

Hands gripped my hips, ripping me from the ground. I screamed, kicking and swinging as I twisted my body to try to get away. Without sight, I couldn't see who had me, but I didn't need eyes to know. Terror took me under. It drowned me. Engulfed every inch of me so much that I did piss myself. I had no control. No objective other than to do whatever was necessary to get this rapist away from me.

"Master, please!" I got my nails ready as I turned more towards the man who had me. We were moving. Heading for where I assumed was the room. If he got me again, I was done for. He'd kill me. He'd make my death the most excruciating death of all time. I couldn't stop. Not for anything.

As I continued to let my arms and legs go wild, I felt for anything I could grab on to. I was turned and for the briefest moment I took hold of the frame, but it didn't last as we broke through the threshold. Where I expected to be thrown on the bed, I knew from the amount of steps, I was taken to the one place I dreaded the most…the shower. And I was right as my feet landed on tile. If he wanted me clean, *he wanted me.* Not again. Never again.

More, I screamed, hitting a volume so loud and high, I was sure God himself would appear to save me. All I got was light taking over my vision. My legs buckled, and I went down. Down...to nothingness. To the black.

MASTER B-0491

O ne stitch. Two. Four. Six. My slave really shouldn't have screamed like that. It was one thing to take her cries. Another to deal with a sound so shrill it gave me a headache. This would teach her. Let her try to scream like that again.

I knotted the thread. She'd been trying to come to for almost ten minutes. It wouldn't be much longer now. I walked over, picking up my phone. At the glimpse of myself, my stare locked to my dark eyes, and I smiled. I'd been wearing the contacts all day. I'd been *him* today, right in front of her, and she hadn't even known. There'd been a delicious amount of power in that. A settling. Home.

My eyes lowered, and I pulled up the messages between me and the Main Master. That he was even helping with my game was still unreal, but hadn't he been piqued by my past, especially the months following? We'd never connected and become friends. I wasn't in his arena of worthiness, but I'd still always been there. He knew of me. I knew of him. I'd even heard he asked about me on occasion. And now he'd brought me here, accepting me. Enjoying my games. Even wanting me to keep him posted on how they played out. We truly were a lot alike, although I doubted he raped women. Games, he lived for them. Sadism, torture, absolutely. But did he even have sex, or did he live for the kill? After his reaction to Vivia, I wasn't sure. Maybe someday I'd get answers to the countless questions I had concerning the Main Master. With as similar as he was, he was also unreadable and unpredictable. Where I thought I knew him, I had to admit, I didn't know him at all.

Me: The game begins. I couldn't resist. The timing was too perfect. So much for waiting a few days. Sorry to steal time from you.

MM: Master B-1488 was a decent Master. Fun to play with and quite the fight. I had a few days. Still, you owe me.

Me: I do, but I'm in no rush. A few hours if you want to go a little longer. The bastard deserves whatever you're giving him. He shouldn't have given me that shit-eating grin when he bumped into me at the auction. I don't like questioning enemies, and from what you told me, he was a dick anyway. Just let me know when you're ready. And you know where I stand. Whatever you want, Elec. Anything.

MM: I have to ask. Will you do her mouth like your last victim, Courtney, from college?

Turning, I walked over to my slave, snapping a picture and sending it.

Me: Already done. It's the same. Perfect.

MM: It is. Have fun but be safe. You know the risk for the game you play. Drop off will be soon. I'm ready for someone new anyway. I'll email over the feed. Dinner tonight with Jack, Georgie, and two of my board members. Bring your slave if she's alive. She's quite the work of art.

My eyes narrowed, and I couldn't get my slave's worries out of my head concerning Elec. They were for nothing. He wasn't the rapist, I was. Still, it was the outside part of me. The judge. The overcautious questioner. Delusional jealousy. Paranoia. But I wasn't him right now. I wouldn't worry about the Main Master. I had to focus on my slave.

Me: You got it. See you tonight.

Groaning had me glancing over. I laid down the phone, not bothering to grab my mask. Besides, it had a new home now. *Or it would soon.* I'd worry about getting another later. Right now, my slave needed me.

I headed over, grabbing her ankles and jerking her down from the pillow so that she lay flat on the mattress. The guttural cry was automatic as her skin tugged on her cheeks and jaw. She was trying to open her mouth and assess what was happening. Her hands jerked in the cuffs and the muffled cry sounded hollow and horrified.

"Mmmmpphhh. Mmmphhh—hhm"

The cries were constant as I pinned her legs under me. To rape her again held no appeal. I'd already had her at the masquerade. Besides, my slave was too injured to hurt much more. She needed tenderness. Appreciative lovemaking. I wanted her to *need* me to comfort her that way. I wasn't ready for her to die or go back to the hospital. I'd have to leave soon, and we would go into the healing stages. Of the body. The mind. *Until it was time again.* After all, I had a plan, and she knew with my reassurance, how many enemies I had. How long could I keep this going? Weeks? Months? Years?

"Shhhh."

Her body rocked through the soul shattering cries. Back and forth her head shook, and she was pulling at the cuffs as if she could get her hands loose. I rested my head against her chest, listening to her racing heart as it pounded against my ear. Each inhale, I counted. Each sob, I felt. So much time passed, I was sure we were truly merging. We were one in breaths. Were our hearts in sync too? She was calming. I had never felt more myself.

I didn't speak as I finally lifted. The crying had long stopped.

Had her head not turned, I wouldn't have even known she was awake. I reached into my pocket, taking out my knife as I moved to straddle her waist. She was nude. Here, with me over her, she'd know there was no threat. Not from what she feared. But she wasn't necessarily safe. I never made it this far with Courtney. I couldn't quite mark her as mine. By the time I finished here, there'd be no doubt who this slave belonged to.

I pushed into the mattress as I leaned forward. Had I ever been in love before? Real love? True love? No. But, here, now, seeing my slave as she was, I could almost believe myself taken over by the emotion. *I wanted to.* I craved what the stories all boasted about, but did men like me ever stumble into fairytales? Did villains find their one?

My slave jumped as my fingers brushed over her sewn mouth. Her head pushed more into the mattress and the sound that left her was long and more of a higher pitch. How could someone be so beautiful? It didn't make sense to me as I let my touch move close to her nose, tracing over one of her stitched eyes. The vulnerability. The helplessness. The trust she had for the Master version of me. She had no idea I was the rapist, and if I kept scrambling her mind, she never would. I would be her air. Her nourishment. I'd be the very reason she lived. What all could I make her do? Become? The possibilities were endless.

As my mind raced, I kept my fingers moving over her constantly. I had no reason to rush. Time would play out as it should. The blood and claiming would come. This moment was ours. No words. No pain as I soaked in every beautiful detail. We were on opposite sides, amid the deadliest dance known to man. Predator. Prey. Master and slave. This night would be a milestone we'd never forget. The spectrums we dangled from wouldn't allow it.

The breath she let out as I went from her jaw to her neck was broken up. Each rise and fall of her chest slowed. She was waiting for my attack. Preparing for me to lock onto her neck and finish her off for good. My fingers went up and down the soft, bruised skin, caressing. Showing her a different side. After all, there was no fun if she wasn't caught unaware.

"Mmmph. Mmpph."

My stare left her throat, stopping on her mouth. I wanted nothing more than to kiss her lips like they were. To feel the thread and tease it with the tip of my tongue. I couldn't do that. *Not as him.* He didn't care to kiss. He wanted to hurt.

"Mmm. Mmm. Mmmhhhrrr."

Was she still calling out to me? Bliss. Yes. We truly were a good fit. Maybe not so much at the beginning, but now, like this, I'd made her perfect.

"Mmmmhhhrrr."

I flicked the knife open feeling her body stiffen below me. She was trembling again, shaking her head back and forth as if it would make some sort of difference.

My hand flattened at the top of her chest, just below her neck. Still, her head shook. I paid it no mind as I brought the tip of the knife down. Barely connecting, not cutting, I drew symbols over her skin. A heart. An arrow through it, just like I saw the girls do in high school. I even wrote out my name. I took my time. At one point I was sure I heard footsteps, but they were so light, I wasn't even sure that was the case. I was lost in the call to break skin. To brand her mine forever.

There'd never be a moment *he* wasn't with us. Every kiss. Every look. Every ping of lust for her body would be marked by *him*. The dotted scars over her lips. The letters I was about to carve into her body. They didn't say: me, me, me. It was, *him, him, him.* I couldn't escape the darkness. The monster inside of me was my true other half. He ruled me. Made me stronger. And thanks to the Gardens, he was here to stay.

Moving to her sternum, I added pressure to my hand, breaking through the skin. As I glanced up and watched her features pull against the stitches as she screamed, my elation grew. With every curve of the letters. With every word I finished, only to begin again…her cries did nothing to deter me. I was so engulfed in my skill. I barely even paid her notice. My attention was on the way her skin looked when it separated. On the fascination for the way her blood was beading. On the crimson river running down her sides as my name came to life.

Him.

Him.

Him.

My adrenaline was soaring. My heart was beating against me like a cannon. By the time I covered her chest and stomach, I almost couldn't bear the intensity anymore. How could one feel heaven and hell at the same time? I felt destructive yet godly. Although I wanted to cover every inch, I knew it was time to stop. After all, my Master needed space to reclaim his slave. I'd have to have room for my name too. And then she'd be complete —my own personal canvas. A diary of my demons. They told the story, just one only me, the Main Master, Percy, Jack, and Georgie knew. They helped me throughout my game, just as I planned to help them through theirs.

Sobs were a hum of vibrating tones. Snot was collected around her nose and her hair was dampened on both sides of her head. I forced her legs open roughly, as if I were going to rape her, shifting and tossing the knife towards the door at the same time so it would sound like someone was coming in.

She froze.

I froze.

I smiled, leaping off her.

"Mmmmhhhhrrr! Mmmrrrr! Mm!"

It wasn't the guards or Main Master she called to. Trust. Not just hope. It was me in her darkest moments. Me, when she looked for someone to hold on to. Trust, yes, I had hers.

"Mmmhhhhrrr!"

She was going wild on the bed, kicking her legs, and

thrashing her body. I threw the door open, looking between her and the dead Master on my living room floor.

No rush…Strategy.

I yelled out.

I threw things around.

I put the mask on the dead supposed rapist.

I created absolute and utter chaos to our perfect home.

Life was fucking great.

Taking the knife, I slashed my shirt, cutting into my ribs just enough to make it bleed. When I headed for the mirror to dishevel my hair and nick my face, I paused. It was a pity I couldn't keep my rapist with me for longer, but this was only the beginning. A learning process. Maybe even an experiment. It was time for my little game to end, and for me to sweep back in as her knight. Her protector. The contacts had to go. *He'd* go…for now.

W0727

He wasn't dead. *My Master wasn't dead.* I could hear him yelling. Fighting? I felt faint in my struggles. Had I lost a tremendous amount of blood? The rapist had been going forever, fileting me alive. He would have killed me after the rape, had he had his way. My Master had saved me. He would save me, wouldn't he?

"Mmmhhhrrrrr!"

I was breathing so hard I was sure I was going to hyperventilate. I had to calm down. There was no way I could throw up with my mouth sewn shut, and with as rattled as I was, I was damn close to doing exactly that.

"Oh, God. Fuck! Princess, hold on. I'm here. Jesus."

Had I thought to calm down? The sob was uncontrollable at my Master's voice. His concern had me reaching for him, even if I couldn't move my arms further than what the cuffs allowed.

"It's okay. It's okay. I got you. I'm right here. I'm going to cut the thread. I need you to be still, okay?"

"Mmhmm. Mmmm!"

I obeyed, trying to slow my breathing down as I stopped. Regardless that I wasn't moving my limbs, my body was jolting through odd spasms. Not to mention, my hands constantly fisted. Trying to keep still, I couldn't stop moving. Wet, slick fingers settled on my chin, sliding to my cheek as Jenson leveled his hold above and below my lips. Pressure tugged, and I felt the first stitch give way. Then...the second. Third. Fourth.

I was crying again, barely able to contain myself as he finished and pulled the strands free. I opened my mouth wide, breathing deeply. *Greedily.*

"Master, please hold me. Master."

"I will. Give me a little time, baby. I'm going to get your eyes. Be still."

"I thought he got you." My voice cracked. "I wouldn't believe it. I couldn't. You won't leave me. Right? You won't leave me?"

A pause. "No, Princess. Not when I can help it."

Threads gave way under the blade, but I couldn't stop talking. "You killed him? *Please say you killed him.*"

"I did. He's dead."

I sniffled, trying to stop crying. It was almost as impossible as stopping the shaking. "Thank you. Oh, Master, thank you. God, I." Stopping, I pulled against the cuffs again, fighting the restraint as tugs and pressure pulled at my lid. Light blinded me and I squinted.

"One more eye."

"How bad am I? I'm bleeding. Am I dying? I don't know what's happening."

"You've lost some blood, but I think you'll be okay. It's not too deep. He." My Master hesitated as he began removing the thread on my other eye. "He truly hated me. *Us.* Sewing your mouth." He let out a growl. "He was mocking me. He wanted me to see who owned you, and in his eyes it wasn't me. It was... him. *Him.* That's what's cut into you. *Him.*"

"You're my Master. Only you."

"Let's not talk about this right now."

The last thread was pulled free, and I blinked, not able to open my eyes with how bright it was. A combination of tears left me, and the moment Jenson uncuffed me, I was squinting enough to see where he was so I could fly into his arms. But even nearly blind...I could feel it. Blood. It was covering both of us. I was sure I'd even caught view of some smears on his face.

"You were so strong." He cupped my cheeks, pulling back to crush his lips into mine. The pain had me crying out, but I didn't care as I clung to him.

"What happened when you fell? Where's the rapist?"

I was still squinting, still trying to get everything to come into focus. My Master lifted me, walking with me into the living room. At the body on the floor, I only held to him tighter. He sat on the sofa, keeping me secure in his arms as he stared ahead in what looked like a daze. There was blood on his face, and a cut on his cheek. Did he look as haunted as me? It appeared so as he gazed ahead at the wall, but I still couldn't keep my eyes open for long.

"I should call the Main Master. He needs to know what happened."

"What did happen?"

"I don't know. I was fine but halfway through talking with the Main Master I started to feel...off. I thought my drink tasted funny. I think somehow he drugged me. Sort of like they drugged you. I was walking and...*I saw him.* He was at the bedroom door in front of me. I jerked to a stop and nothing. I barely drank anything. I think maybe he expected me to have a lot more. God." He stopped, his blue eyes wide as he looked deep into my stare. "You'd be dead right now if I wouldn't have woken up. He would have killed you."

"You saved me."

He pulled me in close, holding tightly.

"Of course I did. Do you trust me now, Princess?"

I was already nodding before he could finish. Trust had

A. A. DARK

nothing to do with it, but I wasn't about to say no and have my eyes sewn shut again.

"Yes, Master. More than anything."

"Good." He let go, easing me to my feet. He quickly checked his watch. "I have to report this. It's close to six." He got quiet. "We were supposed to meet the Main Master."

He walked to the phone, but my eyes didn't leave the body sprawled feet away. I had to see this man. I had to know who had hurt me.

"Main Master." A pause. "He came back. I got him. He's dead."

Words continued, but I didn't hear what was said as I forced myself forward. Glass was shattered and water was on the floor. The mask alone had my heart thudding in my chest. The closer I got, the more fear tried to stop me. My legs grew heavier, becoming almost impossible to lift, and my pulse was echoing in my ears.

The man was in black jeans and a black long sleeve shirt. Possibly the exact ones from the first rape. He looked as tall as my Master. Even the size was similar.

"I'm positive it's him. It has to be. He was about to rape my slave when I burst through the door. He has a mask on and everything." He got quiet. "Slave, what are you doing?"

"I just…" My fingers could barely grip the bottom of the mask, I was trembling so badly.

"Slave."

He couldn't stop me. *I had to see.*

Despite the terror, I jerked the material up, falling on my ass as I came face to face with a man I didn't recognize. It was jarring and confusing to not be able to identify my attacker. Wouldn't he have followed us around? Stalked us? I should have seen him leaning against a building or eating at a restaurant. Nothing. I'd never seen him before. Was I overreacting? Had I possibly missed him lurking around? I'd tried to stay so aware. I

382

tried to remember the face of everyone I'd come into contact with or passed in the halls. Restaurants. Shops. Elevators. I didn't understand.

"Of course. Yes, Main Master." His tone dropped, grabbing my attention. "I appreciate it."

Jenson hung up, coming over to help me stand.

"You shouldn't have done that. Your nightmares will now have a face, and that's never good. Come on. The Main Master is on his way. Let's grab your robe, Princess. He mentioned he had two friends with him. They were on their way to dinner. I don't want them seeing you like this." A smile tugged at the corner of his lip. "Maybe they're part of the board. Someday that's going to be me. I'll be on the board. Elec hinted as much. Then, I can be here with you all the time."

I tried not to stiffen. I wasn't even sure why. The thought of more men around me wasn't comforting, but neither was the idea of my Master becoming one of the higher-ups. I may have said I trusted Jenson, but I didn't trust this circle of men who were grouped together with such power. They were capable of anything. They could get away with the worst things imaginable. I still wasn't convinced the Main Master wasn't playing some part in this.

As Jenson led me to the bedroom, my mind raced through the events. It all played out in a jumble of violence and blurred memories. Visions were distorted. Sound was wavered and off. But there was something.

Something...something.

"Lift your arm."

I obeyed, putting on the robe, but I couldn't shake that there was a vital piece of information I was neglecting to see. If I could think, maybe I could figure out what I was clearly missing. With no notable direction, all I was doing was grasping at straws. And not even good straws. I wasn't a reliable source for answers and that was the most upsetting thing of all.

"Come. You can sit on the couch while I take care of this. The Main Master will probably want to ask you some questions. If he does, you're to answer them."

"Yes, Master."

We headed back to the living room, and I took a seat. Within seconds, a knock sounded. I shut my eyes, still sensitive to the light. Footsteps. Lots of them. They padded against the floor moving different directions. Voices came. Sounds. Banging. Light laughter in the far distance of the room pulled my attention like a magnet. I tensed, recognizing it immediately. *The masquerade.* My pulse hit hard, and I tried not to show my fear as I opened my eyes and slowly turned towards the men in the crowded room.

Jenson, the Main Master, and two other men were by the door, and there were guards moving deeper into the apartment. Jenson was explaining something while one gestured towards the body. All four were interacting. They appeared... familiar with each other. And although I tucked the knowledge away, what I focused on were the two friends. They were older than my Master and the Main Master. Not by much. A few years, tops. They were in good shape and relatively good looking. One had dark hair where the other's was salt and pepper. The dark-haired member laughed, looking right at me as I nearly choked through the cry that wanted to escape.

Immediately, I looked down at the floor. I couldn't be mistaken. The masquerade was a blur, but I'd remember that laugh anywhere...right?

"This is him?"

As they headed over, I took in my Master's smug expression. I was missing something. Something. Something.

"That's right. I think I recognize him from one of the court cases, but I can't recall what it was over. Jack, do you recognize him?"

"I do, but I can't quite place him. This was after I left. This was recent."

My Master nodded. "That's what I was thinking."

Elec kneeled, looking between the dead rapist to me. Back and forth.

"Two years ago, I believe. Port-Leslie—"

"Yes! The Port-Leslie Rapist," My Master burst out. "That's right. He was accused of sexually assaulting six women in that building over a one-year period." My Master's head tilted to the side. "That was one of the first cases that came to me. You had me dismiss it for lack of evidence. Why would he hold a grudge against me for freeing him?"

"You freed him for the law out there. Not from the one down here. Jail in the real world is simple. Here, for me, not so much. He did his time in Hell Row, but he was still indebted to me for things outside of the rapes. His life was within these walls. No leaving. No escaping. I suppose him hurting your slave was payback for that. But that's all speculation. We'll never know now. At least this is over, and you and your slave can rest easy."

Tapping had me glancing over. The dark-haired Master kept drumming his finger against his outer thigh. I blinked the action away, moving back to my Master, but ripping my eyes back to the man's bandaged hand.

Tap-tap.

Tap-tap-tap.

Bandaged hand.

It took everything I had to tear my eyes away and stare at the floor. The laugh. The injury. Hadn't I got one of them with the butterknife? It was too close to be wrong. He was one of them. I glanced up, taking them all in. Taking in my Master. Watching his slight smile. Seeing how comfortable he was with them. How...he was *one* of them. Maybe not status-wise if they were board members, but almost. They acted as if they were equals. He *knew* these men. They were friends. Close, on a level that made me believe they'd help him. Be there for him. *Support his sick games.*

"The guards can clean this up. You both don't look too hurt. You still want to catch dinner with us? We can wait."

Jenson turned to me, his face transitioning with a multitude of emotions. He looked torn as he battled whatever was in his head. His face softened as he came over, cupping my cheek. "I don't know. Maybe another time. I think my slave needs me right now. She's been through so much." His thumb made a path back and forth over my skin. "Unless you think you're okay?"

"She looks okay to me."

I glanced at the men, not quite sure which one had made the comment. The room shifted from my fear, and I tried to keep my breath steady.

Lie. That's what I had to do. My Master wanted to be with these men as much as they wanted to be with him. He wanted his position amongst them. There was no such thing as having an opinion anymore. His needs were mine. His wants, mine. *I trusted him.* I was supposed to need him more than I needed myself. Every part of me was here to make him happy.

"I think I'll be okay going to dinner...if you can help me. Will you help me get ready, Master? Will you keep me safe," I said, lowly, so only he could hear.

His proud smile said it all, and it turned my stomach. I wasn't safe. I wasn't okay; I was aghast. Trapped. I was even more shocked and scared than a second before. Sickness was all I felt as my Master kissed me and helped me stand. The betrayal, the nausea. It came with an ache that hurt worse than any abuse I'd sustained. From the looks on the mens' faces as they watched us leave the room, I knew this wasn't over. Even if I was wrong, and that dead man was my rapist, there was more of them. It could be my Master leading this, or it could be all of them involved. Perhaps they took turns. All I knew was I was at the heart of a game darker than the night itself, and there were predators hiding in places I couldn't see. Maybe even hiding in plain sight. In my bed. *In my home.* At every turn. One would come back for me. They'd want to pick up where he'd left off. A mask equaled anonymity. It protected them, *but it also protected me.*

This time, I'd be ready for *him.*

Next time…I'd be prepared.

Master B-0113
Garden of the Gods
International Bestselling Author
A.A. Dark
Copyright © 2023 by A.A.Dark

All Rights Reserved

RULES

GARDEN OF THE GODS

Rules are subject to change. If you neglect to follow these rules, you will undergo an investigation/trial where punishment is evaluated by the Board and Main Master, Elec Wexler. Punishment can range from fines to lockup in Hell Row to Death.

1) Keep your hands to yourself.

2) The only property you may destroy is your own. (slaves included.)

3) You are a number. Your peers are a number. Use them.

4) Respect your neighbor's privacy.

5) GOTG is NOT to be discussed outside of this facility.

GLOSSARY

W

Virgin slave. Wears a white robe during the auction.

B

Nonvirgin slave. Wears a blue robe during the auction.

D

Docile, drugged slave. Can be w or b. Heavily trained. Good for elderly or those with disabilities.

M

Male slave.

Crow

(fc: female crow, mc: male crow) Ruined, disfigured slave. Convicts fall into this category. Black robe during the auction. Usually the cheapest slave.

Blank slate

Mostly male slaves who have undergone forced indoctrination through various scientific methods. (Brainwashing, programming, training, etc.) Most remember their identity but have key parts of their past erased if it could pose a threat or alter their role as a slave. They're programmed to be focused solely on their Mistress or Master. They are made to be obedient, loyal, and protective.

*Master numbers written out throughout the stories are capitalized. (Ex. Twelve-twelve.) Also, the word Master throughout is capitalized. (Ex. Master Twelve-twelve.)

*Slave numbers written out will not be capitalized. The word slave throughout will not be capitalized outside from the beginning of a sentence.

"CONSCIENCE IS GOD'S SPY AND MAN'S OVERSEER." —JOHN TRAPP

PROLOGUE
MASTER B-0113

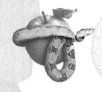

Garden of the Gods
Colorado Springs underground facility

There was something to say about greetings. They had the power to set the mood for either a night, a day, or a lifetime. I'd spent the last fifteen years creating the most warming, heartfelt introductions people had come across. I preached about love. About forgiveness. I was the safety in the storm. I was the helping hand to those going through the hardest or most traumatic times of their lives. Greetings were the foundation of the future, and my institution and my place in it was more than protected. It was guarded. Revered. After all, my church provided more than donations to the Gardens. It gifted the Main Master some of the most sought-after slaves.

"Welcome to the second auction for Garden of the Gods. For those who didn't make it to the first, I'm going to recap this as quickly as possible. You've taken the classes. You've learned the rules. Even though our slaves have been trained, you are going to have to earn your titles. The B's in front of your number are for a reason. This is the Beta stage. Some of you will make our foundation. Some of you won't. Your outside status got you here, but that means nothing inside the Gardens. You are a number. That's it. Your identity or status means absolutely nothing. Here, there is no power or favoritism. This world is mine, and you better hope like hell you can follow the rules, or you won't survive in it." The Main Master's stare scanned the large room and his tone turned softer. "On the plus side, you've all made it this far, and that speaks volumes. I have high hopes for most of you."

I took a sip of wine, grinning ahead as I watched from my private balcony.

"For those new to us tonight, I don't think I need to go much into how this place is not Whitlock. The rules are different. The location is different." His face turned hard. "I am *not* the old Main Master, Bram Whitlock. A few Masters from the first auction had to learn that the hard way. You cannot buy yourself out of trouble. You cannot *buy me*. I will never let the Garden of the Gods fall."

Whitlock. Those were the days. The Gardens wouldn't end up like that. It was impossible given who ran the machine of our world. This place was unstoppable, and so were the people and businesses who supported it.

"Let's recap bidding for those who don't know. First, we have the white, or w's. These are the virgins. We also have the b's, or blue." He paused. "Not virgins. We also have the d's, who now have their own room at the back right, behind all of you. They're docile, trained, and good for those who are looking for a long-term slave. Lastly, come the black, or as we call them, the crows. These could be fun for anyone looking for a bloodbath or just a fun time. They're the convicts. The disfigured. The old. *Repulsive*." He stopped at the end of the stage. "You get it. Also in that category, you'll find the breeders. I want to make a note of some changes in this category." His hand lifted. "Listen to me closely. I won't repeat it. You are not allowed to bid on them unless you've already gone through the steps and signed a contract with me. We had a few try last auction even though this was already stated in bold caps in the pamphlet. If you bid on a breeder, and you haven't met with me, your bid will be revoked, and I will fine you ten thousand dollars for wasting my time. Breeders are special. Breeders are for only those I approve of."

"For those looking for our programmable, 'blank slate' males and *now* females, your auction is just through that door off to the right. The information was in the packet, but just in case you missed it last auction, these are those who have had a portion of their memories erased. They're aware. They know who they are, but they only remember what we want them to."

Tempting...One of those could come in handy. Who didn't need an assistant with the type of work I was focused on? It could be grueling. Intense. It would give me more room to focus.

"The last few weeks have been exciting, to say the least. I've watched some of you grow in your role. The majority have done great with following rules. For those who are new, pay attention."

"What you buy is yours. You can do whatever you want with it. Fuck it. Kill it. Share it. Marry it. Love it. Eat it. Destroy it." He paused, walking down the stage some more. "I don't care so long as you follow the rules. Your business is your own. I can't stress that enough."

"If you look down the arm of the chair, you will see a button. Do not." He stopped, pausing for close to a minute. In a slow circle, he spun, taking in the crowd. "Let me say it again since others from the first auction learned the hard way. *Do not...* press that button unless you are sure you want to bid. We do not have a lay-a-way plan. You cannot get your slave on loan. If you don't have the money, don't bid. At the Gardens, there's no such thing as accidents. If you bid, you buy. If you can't pay, I will take my payment however I want. Don't believe my threat, *test me*. I'll take everything you own on the outside world, and you can remain here with the slave you couldn't resist. This life can be simple if you just do as you're told. The rules are easy. Complete acceptance into the Garden of the Gods is not. You all signed a contract to get this far. Abide by it, and Alpha status will be yours."

I reclined the seat, kicking up my feet as I pulled out a pack of cigarettes. Lights flashed moving around the room as everyone's attention went to the back entrances. I took in the beautiful women adorned in sheer, white robes who were waiting for the go-ahead.

I'd need another drink. Lots of drinks. Maybe a bottle or two. I was in no hurry. I had all night to find the perfect b replacement8. This one would be strong. Tough. This one who'd sate my darkness but give insight into the light. It was time...

MASTER B-0113

One hour. Two. Three. The more I watched, the more I drank. The more I drank, the more I laughed. The more I laughed, the more I seethed. Intoxication fueled the insanity that lurked within. Questions. Decisions. Words were always my power. They plagued me, taunted me. For as much as they ruled my life, they left me the moment I saw her.

"Up next we have slave b-twelve-ninety-seven."

But that's all I heard. Not the whispers or buzz of conversation from the remaining Masters, Mistresses, or Couples who lingered. Not even the slave in the yellow headdress that collected my plate of long forgotten appetizers. My pulse thrummed in my ears, and I leaned forward watching the way the blue sheer robe flowed against the olive skin of the brunette who climbed the stairs to the stage. To say I hadn't seen her before would have been a lie. I had. It was a brief encounter—a perfect opportunity for a beautiful, drug addict coming to find God. My people had helped her, alright. They'd brought her here.

...For me?

An evil smile stretched across my face. How the hell had I forgot she was here?

Our outpouring of help was never-ending. My reach was worldwide. But her...Josie Lockhart, she was a local, and had come to the Church. I'd seen her for the briefest moment in passing. I couldn't forget that face, even if we'd never actually met. She was one of the first taken from my new building, and to this day I hadn't forgotten how her vibrant eyes stood out against her darker skin-tone. She was gorgeous. Beautiful, even more now that she was clean and healthy. She downright mesmerized me as I pushed my button. I didn't care that the announcer wasn't finished with whatever the hell he was blabbing on about. It was my fault she was here...*and I'd let her use that blame to my advantage.*

Numbers flashed on the screen. It was another Master countering my bid. Irritation blossomed but my narrowed stare didn't leave Josie as I kept slamming down my button. No matter how tough I knew she probably was, she couldn't control the shake that left her body trembling. Even from my private booth to the right of the stage, I could see how terrified she was as one of the guards forced her to turn in a circle. Her eyes were scanning the large room, but I doubted she could see much through the bright lights that were spotlighting her.

Seconds played out.

A minute.

Lights slowly strobed on the screen and my pulse slowed.

"It seems we have a winner."

Satisfaction soared as they led her off the stage, right in my direction. Pale blue eyes lifted and so did my hand as I tilted my glass to her. My new slave jerked to a stop, only to be tugged along down another set of stairs.

Shock.

Betrayal.

So many different emotions transitioned on her face. I wanted to watch them wear off so they could build into what I knew would come, but she disappeared below me before the

400

anger could register. It didn't matter if we faced off right now. She'd be mine soon enough, and when she was, *hell would have no wrath quite like my slave.*

I welcomed it.

Leaning back, I finished off my glass, placing it down to the small table at my side.

Josie Lockhart. Josie Lockhart.

How I even remembered her name was miracle enough. That I had stuck around this long to bid on her…that was chance. Fate? God? I wasn't convinced. The trafficking part of my business wasn't really something I controlled or oversaw. I had people that scouted under the church, and they answered to the Gardens, not me. But Josie was different. She'd been one of the few that had been led to the underground tunnels just off the hall from my office. That entrance was long gone, now, but we were still in the early stages at that time, and I'd seen and heard her speaking while they passed. We'd locked eyes just as we had not a minute ago. That could be an issue for me. She wasn't just a normal slave, and I could be a bit obsessive when something like lust was involved. I did have that towards her. To deny it wasn't going to make it go away.

Knocking had me turning to look behind me. I spun, reaching over to pull open the door. My shoulders loosened and my body relaxed as the Main Master walked in.

"Did I just see your number on the screen?"

Although he spoke with curiosity, he knew it was me.

"That's right."

"Pretty slave. I didn't think you'd be buying this time. You still have the other, don't you?"

I shrugged, throwing him a charismatic lazy smile that came natural to me from years of interaction and training. "What's left of her. She was ready to die weeks ago. She barely hangs on. It's time." I paused, taking in the way his light-colored eyes shifted to the balconies in the distance. He even seemed to relax a little which was something people naturally did around me. "What are you doing down here anyway? I figured you'd be mingling or at your club."

A smile tugged at Elec's lips. "I was making my rounds. I'm headed there now." He paused. "How long are you planning to stay this time?"

"As long as I can. You know me. If I don't have to be out there, I'm not. Even when I am, it's only for service."

A slow nod took over as he walked to the end of my balcony. He didn't put his back to me as he placed his hand on the edge, reading my face.

"A few weeks ago I was asked a favor by a very important person. It seems he got himself into a sticky situation. Normally, I wouldn't waste my time over something so petty, but I'm afraid this had elements that…intrigue me. I couldn't resist. I need you available whenever I call."

"You know you can always rely on me. The church can get by with my protégé for one or two services if need be."

"Good." He tapped against the railing, still staring in the distance. "Why her?"

I glanced towards the stage that held a new slave. Leisurely, I made my way to the edge of the balcony to join him.

"I saw her once. She was taken from my church. Drug addict. Possible former prostitute. I'm not quite sure. She wanted to be saved." I lifted one of my eyebrows as Elec turned to me. "Well, *here I am.*"

"Here you are." Elec mirrored me as he nodded. "Have fun with your slave. I'm headed to Dark God Status. After your fun, feel free to head up to the club. I probably won't be there long, but the doors are open if you want in. You're on the list."

"Thanks."

The Main Master checked his watch and nodded, heading out. I went back to look at the large theater setting. There were still mostly Masters filling the chairs, but not many. It was getting late, and it was time for me to retrieve my new girl. That was if I could make it there without getting bombarded by random people. Even at the Gardens, I couldn't escape the desperation of the damned. Salvation was craved, but they couldn't stop their sins to stand a chance. And me, I didn't work miracles. Work and words—lies and manipulation. Brain bending. That was what I was good at. It's what connected me and Elec.

Leaving my private room, I headed down the long hall that led to the stairs. The lobby area below was already clearing out. Most had their slaves by now. Maybe I'd waited for them to leave so I wouldn't have to face them. How could they know how our lives were, and yet still think I had the key to save them? Everyone wanted to believe in a higher power; they just couldn't face the fact that his name was Elec Wexler, and his title was Main Master. That was as close to a God that they were going to get. A good God? No. But a ruler of realms...*this realm*...yes.

"Please, *I don't want to go. I*—"

Screams were immediate as I turned the corner and walked into the room for pick-ups. A small-framed blonde-haired slave wearing white was pulling against the Master's hold. The hit was solid sending her crumbling to the ground at the force. I ignored the scene, heading to the guard not feet away.

"Master One-thirteen. I'm here for my slave."

"Yes, Sir." The guard was scrolling and clicking on his tablet. The screams turned to sobs and grew further away as the Master left with the struggling girl. "I've notified them of your arrival. If you'd like to take a seat, your slave will be brought out shortly."

No way was I sitting back down. My adrenaline was rushing through my veins at the anticipation. My fingers were twitching through need. Not a physical one. My work was mental. I wouldn't need to strike my slave to bring her to her knees. At least not in the long run. It would take time. Encouragement.

Some abuse would probably be needed at first, but not because I enjoyed the cruelty. I didn't care either way. It just wasn't comparable to the power of persuasion. To see people bend the knee. Fall to my feet. Obey and do *anything* I said because they believed every word I spoke...It was like magic.

I didn't expect to get that from my new slave. She'd seen through the illusion, but I liked that even more. This would be a challenge on top of my experiment. I needed that.

Laughter came from the entrance of the room, and I ignored it as an electronic door opened and a guard appeared, practically pushing my slave through the threshold. He didn't have to push long. The moment she saw me, I got exactly what I expected. *Maybe even what I wanted?* The slave lunged in my direction, but I was ready, latching around her neck and squeezing hard enough to have her face turning red as she clawed at my hands.

"Feisty bunch tonight." I smiled at the guards who were momentarily stunned from both of our quick reactions. "Yep." I squeezed harder, tilting my face as I took in her panic. "This is her, my slave. You need anything else?"

N-No, Sir." The guard stood straighter. "She's already been programmed and is ready to go."

"Excellent." The slave's knees buckled from the pain and lack of air. Her mouth was opened wide as she tried to scrape in any ounce of oxygen she could get. I eased enough to have the slave gasping and coughing, but I didn't let go. I met her stare, glaring as I snatched her closer, adding a secure but not debili-tating pressure. "Have they shut you down yet from this code word they speak of?" Fear mixed with confusion as her face went back and forth. "No? Let me tell you about it. With one word, you will become paralyzed. Aware of everything, but a shell. If you don't listen to what I say, I will speak that word. I will carry you home, and then I will rape you with everything I can get my hands on until you're nothing but a bleeding, muti-lated mess. I will torture you, cut you open, and remove your insides while you slowly die, incapable of any fight. That's not you. You're a fighter. You've proven that over and over. Don't let us both down. *Walk.*"

And she did as I pushed her away with force. She wasn't happy about it, but the slave caught herself from falling, rubbing her neck as she angrily headed for the door.

"If you run—"

"You'll say the word. Rape me. Torture me. Yeah, yeah." We got out of the door, but she spun back almost making me collide right into her. "So *Godly* of you, *Pastor.* I was laughed at. I was told you were a fraud. That you wouldn't be able to help me. I should have listened."

I stepped in even closer, moving my body into hers. She was so stubborn, she refused to step back.

"But Josie, I *did* help you. Twice," I growled. "Look around you. You're not an addict anymore. You're alive....for now. Walk."

"I can't believe I thought you were a good man." She stomped down the hall at a fast pace. "I was so sure at first this was a misunderstanding. They convinced me I was going to rehab. They never said it was one I couldn't leave. I know this life all-too well. I've lived it." She glanced back just short of the lobby that housed the elevator. "You do know this is trafficking, right? Oh wait." Josie's dark hair flew over her shoulder as she glared. "You just bought me. *A human being.* Yeah, I'd say you know what's happened. I'm also guessing it's your fault I'm here. I should have prayed it was you who'd have the most horribly painful death along with those bastards who took me."

"Please. Pray. Don't let me discourage you from speaking to your God."

"My God?"

The anger wavered as she slowed. I didn't. I grabbed the back of her neck, leading her the rest of the way to the elevator.

"What do you mean by that? Are you saying you don't believe in God?"

Her voice cracked at the end. The horror won over her rage. It became disbelief, then almost…a sadness.

"You *are* a fraud?"

"We'll find out soon enough. Get in."

B1297

S ilence.

I couldn't stop staring at the man who was responsible for bringing me here. Had I once thought he would change my life? Had I even had some sort of stupid schoolgirl crush on the good-looking pastor? Me and everyone else. Maybe that was half the draw. God, I was a fool. How could I have been so stupid? Not for going to a church to seek out help for my addiction, but to go to *his* church? The biggest church in the United States. The most popular and talked about. The building was almost as big, if not bigger, than a football stadium. People flocked to West Ridge by the thousands. More? I had no idea.

My decision to go to the church had been somewhat spontaneous. Or maybe I hadn't had a choice. Everyone on the streets called it a cult or a scam. And perhaps it was, but I'd been overcome with awe as I watched Pastor Anthony Addaway on my phone. He was tall, lean, but nicely shaped with his larger shoulders. He had dark hair with a touch of silver even though he was in his mid-to upper thirties. I binged previous services for nearly two weeks in-between cleaning rooms at the hotel where I lived. I wanted so desperately to be safe and turn my life around. *To escape.* What did my brilliant idea get me? Clean, yes, but a slave, nonetheless.

"Stop pouting. You've been through hell. You should be celebrating right now, not throwing a fit. I saved your life tonight whether you want to believe it or not. Do you know what kind of men are here?"

"I can only imagine. If they're anything like you, I can't really see how I'm better off."

His large hand pushed into the center of my back as we stepped off the elevator and headed left towards another hallway. We didn't have to go far before he was reaching over, pulling me to stop. Just feeling the heat from his hand on my bicep did odd things to me. I wanted to scream. To fight him like I'd never fought anyone before. I wanted to cry and break down. To ask him *why?* Why this? Why me? Why was he the way he was? *Who was he?* Did he truly not believe in God?

Just seeing him, hearing the way he spoke, I felt like I was in shock. Like my world was spinning out of control. I wouldn't have guessed that Anthony Addaway was involved in human trafficking. The church workers, maybe, …but I wouldn't have dreamed in a million years he would have condone such a thing. He hadn't appeared guilty or even knowing when I'd seen him the day they took me. I thought…I'd felt…it was stupid to think he actually saw me. *Me*…not another number for their sick underground city. But me as a person. The look on his face when he'd gazed up from his desk. My heart had all but stopped. And him, his eyes had…widened in surprise? Had I thought he appeared intrigued? God, how had I held to that stupid memory? A part of me had even deluded myself into thinking he'd remember my face and try to help find me. *Rescue me.* Maybe he had, but not in the way I prayed. And God had I prayed my heart out. Had he planned this from the beginning?

The question only brought on more as he unlocked the door and pushed me in. What I saw, I wasn't prepared for. A red-head woman with shoulder-length hair stopped wiping down the counter, tears filling her eyes as she dropped the cloth and came rushing towards us.

"Master."

She fell to her knees at Anthony's feet. The sight only had me taking a few steps back. I'd had the training. I knew the protocol, but actually going through or seeing the act felt wrong.

"Is it time? Oh, please say it's time. I did as you said. I've repented. Multiple times this hour. I'm ready."

Something flashed over the pastor's face. Sympathy? No. Relief?

It was so hard to tell as his fingers pushed through her hair. At the affectionate touch, she wrapped around his leg, sniffling.

"Soon, slave. Have you made your decision?"

"I have."

She sprung to her feet, racing past me to the room. My new Master's eyes met mine, and I wasn't sure why I felt sick to my stomach. Something seemed very, very wrong. What was it time for? And why repent so many times? I was confused. Not just by her words, but by her eagerness. It didn't go along with the haunting expression she had on her face. Her eyes were slightly sunken in, and she looked tired. But almost wired? Broken?

"What's happening?"

My question didn't get answered. The slave rushed back into the room, sending me scrambling back at the gun she held.

"This. I choose this."

"You remember what I said. I won't allow you to have that gun while it's loaded. Only I get to have it. You're okay with me being in control of your path?"

"I am. It's better this way. Your hands are steadier. You'll make sure the job gets done right."

"Mr. Attaway. *Pastor.* What's happening? You're not really. I mean." A hardness came over the Master's face as his gaze lifted to mine. He didn't say a word, but I knew he was mad that I'd used his real name and interrupted. "Master," I said forcefully. "What is happening?"

"Go get your bear and blanket. Put on the white gown. I'll put you to sleep."

The slave handed over the gun, nodding. As she ran off again, I witnessed a smile surfacing. She didn't appear afraid or even in distress. She was suddenly happy at his overly caring nature. Excited, even. That made me nervous for reasons my mind couldn't process.

My teeth clenched. "Master, please tell me what's happening."

Anthony unbuttoned the suit's jacket, shrugging it off to rest on the back of the large gray sofa. The shoes came next, along with the socks. When he removed the tie and started unbuttoning the shirt, my lower back crashed into the bar that separated the opened kitchen.

"Do you remember your childhood, Josie?"

My lips parted as tattoos began to appear just past his collarbone.

"I..." I cleared my throat, trying to look away, but failing. "I remember."

"Was it a good childhood?"

It was easier to take in the lines and dark shading than to relive memories that haunted me.

"It was a childhood."

"Then it wasn't good. You would have told me if it was."

My gaze did jump up then, but not for long as he continued with the buttons, moving down his sternum.

"I had a shitty childhood, Josie. My father was a dirty cop, and my mom fucked anyone who'd whip out their dick. Sometimes with me right there. My dad would beat her when he found out. He'd threaten to kill us all. He finally made good on his promise one Christmas Eve night. Obviously not to me, but to them." The Master finished unbuttoning his shirt, shrugging it off to expose tattooed skin. Words. Lots of words covered almost every inch. Scriptures. Images of animals eating people. A man tearing a woman apart. I was shaking again, not able to say anything as he headed closer.

"What do you think it does to a child to find his parents dead on Christmas morning?"

It took a moment to get my voice to work. "Destroys them? I mean," I was fumbling over my thoughts. "It must have been horrible. Tragic."

"You could have stopped at the beginning. Destroy works. You can say it destroyed me. Killed me even, but not in the way you'd think."

I stayed quiet as Anthony took a seat at the bar, spinning the chair so he could face me. Even though he was so serious, he pulled my attention like a magnet.

"I opened my presents. I ate a bowl of cereal. I turned on cartoons. Maybe I was too young to quite grasp the situation, or maybe my mind shut down. But I didn't feel much. A part of me expected it. It wasn't until my door got kicked in that I truly felt fear. Not from the surprise, but from who I saw."

"Who was it?"

The slave returned and my Master stopped, following her with his dark eyes as she headed into the kitchen. She grabbed a bottle, pouring him a drink and sitting it on the bar in front of him. Anthony turned only enough to toss back the small amount before standing and heading to the fridge. I couldn't see what was inside, but it was as if he were messing with something. A few seconds went by, and he withdrew a syringe, holding it to the light as he flicked against it. Instantly, I flew from my chair, falling over myself as I tried to get as far away as I could.

The slave paid me no mind as she got closer. Me, I couldn't even watch. Sickness swarmed my stomach, and I was sure I was going to throw up. My pulse was racing, and I'd never wanted to run away so badly in all my life. I'd beaten drugs. There was no way I'd go back to them now.

"Good girl. Look up."

I glanced to the kitchen, taking in the way he held to her chin. Lovingly. Fatherly.

"Do you take responsibility for what you've done? What you've caused?"

"All of it, Master."

"Are you worthy?"

A sob. "No. I'm not."

"But I've told you that you are. You don't believe me?"

"We both know I'm not. *We know.*"

"I guess we do."

The slave's lids closed as she took in a deep breath. She was leaning more into his hands, feeling the effects of whatever he'd shot her up with.

"It's time to sleep. Tonight, there will be no work. Just dreams. It's you and whatever you choose. You are choosing this, Linda. You know that."

"I choose...this."

He lifted her in his arms, studying me as he carried her into the room. Everything in me wanted to run right for the door. To escape whatever craziness was happening in this apartment. If I did...it could be worse. He knew my history. He wouldn't force me to become an addict again. He wouldn't feed me drugs. He couldn't.

Seconds went by as I watched him place her in a small bed on the far edge of the bedroom. The slave held to a white, fuzzy bear, and he tucked her in as if she were a child. I was so confused on what was happening. I didn't get any closer to figuring it out as he turned and headed back towards me.

"No appeal at all?"

The closer the Master got, the further I distanced myself.

"The needle? Fuck no. Hell no."

"Hmm."

Still, he came towards me, causing me to turn and circle back towards the bar.

"Josie, I want you to tell me more about yourself. Why was your childhood so bad?"

My head shook. "Stop getting closer."

"I will when you start talking." He pointed to where I'd been sitting before.

"Or what? I don't want to talk about my childhood."

I eased to the stool, but kept my weight on one leg, ready to bolt as he came to a stop at the stool next to mine.

"You'll talk or I'll make you talk." His head gestured to the fridge. "Once I shoot you up, I'll know your deepest, darkest secrets. There will be nothing you can hide from me."

Tears surfaced. Where I once thought the past held my pain, I was suddenly seeing how much power fear had in the present.

"I grew up poor. I was bullied in school. I ran away at fifteen and lived on the streets."

"Running away was better than facing the difficulties?"

I paused as he reached for the bottle, pouring himself another drink.

"Before, yes. Now, I don't know."

"Well, then." He tilted the glass, slowly drinking the shot down. "Before, yes, but you're not sure. What confuses you? Tell me more."

Shifting in my chair, I tried to ignore how his muscles flexed through his movements. He was drinking more, not even really looking at me. I could feel my shoulders drop and some of the tension leave as he focused his attention elsewhere.

"Maybe it's stupid now. I don't know. Growing up, I couldn't...breathe. We lived in the south with my grandma in what I could barely call a house. Summers were miserable. Winters were cold. My dad was a hard worker, but he was never home. It was me, my mom, my grandma, and my brothers and sisters. There were six of us kids, total. We all shared a room while my mom stayed with my grandma in her bedroom. We grew up that way. Just...stuck. I felt suffocated."

"But there had to be good times."

Memories returned. "Of course. There were also just as many bad times. My parents fought when they were together. After a while, my dad almost stopped coming home. My brothers were always throwing blows when they got in their teens. Being the youngest sister, I was just trapped in the middle of them all. They didn't see me. I was an inconvenience to an already troublesome situation. It was better that I leave. One less mouth to feed. One less fight to endure. *It's not like I never went back.*" My cheeks burned as I could so clearly see the day I showed up, unannounced. "Five years I was gone. No one even really cared when they opened the door and saw me. No happiness. No relief that I was even still alive. It doesn't matter," I said, cutting off the thoughts. "I left. It's just." The pain in my chest was almost too much. "I thought maybe things would be different when I returned. All they seemed to care about was how I was another mouth to feed. It was just like old times. I stayed two days and went back to the city."

"Back to your homeless life and drugs?"

My face hardened as tears blinded me.

"For a while. I wasn't always homeless, you know. I was getting my life together when I went to your church. I had a roof over my head. It was at a hotel, but I paid rent, and I worked my ass off for them. I had a legit job. *I needed your help.*"

The tears did spill then. Anthony turned on the stool, facing me for the first time since we'd sat down.

"My help? My prayers? My special words with God?" His lids turned to slits and any calming pull I'd felt moments before disintegrated through the intense energy he radiated. "As if I have any more right than you. Don't you see? You needed none of that. *No one.* Everything that happened to you is a result of actions *you* took. You did this to yourself, Josie. You left home. You chose the streets. You chose the drugs."

"I did not! I didn't choose that." I flew from the chair feeling the rage I'd harbored for years build under his watchful stare. "What do you know about a hard life? What do you know about being taken advantage of? Being tricked because of your inno-cence? Being forced into drugs against your will and raped, only to be led into sex work? I've done this trafficking thing before. *I won't do it again.* You stick that needle in my arm, and mark my words, I'll find a way to stick that barrel down your throat. Let them kill me. I don't care."

Silence.

"So, you want to die?"

"What?"

"You'd shoot me and be okay with the consequence being death."

It wasn't a question.

"Do I want to die, no. If you try to drug me, I'm good with the consequences. Rest in peace, *Pastor.* I wouldn't have the least amount of remorse."

"Interesting." He turned even more, leaning his powerful upper body in my direction. "What if I said I could get you to take that needle in your arm without forcing it on you? What if I told you that it wasn't a drug, and it wasn't addicting? What if I said, God or your parents would meet you on the other end of that needle, and you'd see things you couldn't imagine?"

"I'd say you're fucking crazy, and no thanks. My parents had their chance. If God is ready to meet me, he can come get me the right way. I've made peace with my savior and my past. I don't need you anymore as a middleman. I don't need you or anyone else at all."

MASTER B-0113

Didn't need me? The phrase kept repeating in my mind, circling around, taunting me. Everyone needed something. Prayer. Comfort. Shelter. Support. Sustenance. Someone to confide in. My new slave acted strong, and she was, but everyone had a breaking point. Those either made you stronger or you'd never return. I'd test hers just like I had with Linda, and I'd find Josie's weakness. Everything came at a cost. She was about to find out what hers was.

"Slave. Linda."

Heavy lids cracked open, and a smile came to her face. I curled into her closer, feeling the heat radiate from her body. I didn't care that Josie wasn't sleeping yet. Or that she was watching from the corner of the room. It had to be close to three AM, and I still wasn't done drinking. Maybe I'd never be done.

"Master, he was there. I was calling, and he came to me. I was holding him again. So sweet," she slurred. "It was just like old times. I didn't want to wake up. Can I go back now?"

Tears were beginning to streak down the sides of her face, into her hairline. Linda's story was like nothing I had been prepared for. She was broken long before she came to the

416

Gardens. Before adulthood, which had been forced on her with little knowledge. She lost her son to the system due to circumstance, and she'd never gotten her chance to find him before she was brought here. That made it impossible for her to help in my search or recover from the trauma. Where I sent her to find God, she always found him, her son. That didn't help me at all, but I did what I do best. I made her face the pain. To ask for forgiveness. I tested her to see if she was strong enough to move past it. She didn't think God could forgive her. I didn't assure her he did. Who was I to speak for a source I was trying to find proof of?

"I'm going to let you go back."

"*Oh, thank you, Master.* I'm ready." Her lips quivered as her eyes closed.

"And you've repented? You've asked for forgiveness?"

"Yes. I will over and over while you do this. I want to go h-home."

I kissed the side of her forehead, propping myself on my elbow to look down at her. "Open your mouth and keep your eyes closed." She obeyed, not flinching as I eased the barrel into her mouth. "Loss kills us. No one knows that more than God. I told you once, and I'll tell you again. 'For God so loved the world that He gave his only Son, so that everyone who believes in Him may not perish but have eternal life. Luke 3:16. God feels your pain, Linda. He's here for you. 'Though he brings grief, he will show compassion, so great is his unfailing love. Lamentations 3:32. Take a deep breath." I whispered. "…'I tell you the truth, a time is coming and has now come when the dead will hear the voice of the Son of God and those who hear will live.' John. 5:24. He's calling, Linda. Can you hear him? *Listen.*"

Silence.

Bang!

Blood splattered across my face. Where I expected a scream, Josie didn't give me that. Her eyes were wide, and her back and palms were flattened to the wall as if she feared she'd fall through. Or maybe she was trying to ground herself. Either way, she stayed frozen as I stood and headed back to my bottle. I didn't get halfway through the living room before footsteps raced from the bedroom. Deep breaths left her, and she went back to the wall, more sliding down it than lowering to sit. Her olive skin was pale, and she looked on the verge of being sick.

"You're a mercy killer, is that it? You said you didn't believe in God."

"I never said that."

"You didn't deny it. You killed that girl."

I grabbed the bottle, drinking deeply. "Yeah, I did. She wasn't the first, and she won't be the last."

"*Why?* Why would you do that?"

"She wanted to die."

"So. Why?"

"That's none of your business. That's Linda's."

"But...I don't..." She got quiet. "You gave her that shot. She saw someone in her hallucinations. She wanted to die to stay with them. Is that what you want from me too? Delusions? You want to weaken my spirit and kill me?"

"I'm going to try."

Gulping down more of the fiery liquid, I winced, swaying as I forced myself straight. The room was moving, or I was. I had to stop drinking. I knew that as I took in my new horror-filled slave. She was beautiful when she was afraid. Maybe more than when she was happy. Or perhaps she was every second of the day.

"Go back to your story."

"I finished."

"No you didn't. You have lots more to go."

"Do I?"

"I said you do."

"Can you at least wipe the blood from your face?"

My hand flattened, smearing the substance, and I didn't so

much as blink as my gaze bore into hers. Josie was shut down. Teetering on the edge of something I didn't like. Rebellion, yes, but something else. Maybe I told her too much. If I were good, it wouldn't matter. At my look, a pained expression took her over. I was giving her a warning, and she didn't miss it.

"Sit on the couch, slave. Grab that throw blanket and make yourself comfortable." I placed down the bottle even though I didn't want to. Charm dripped from my calm tone. It thickened in the air, surrounding her like the coziest calm. "I'll sit at the other end and listen. You can tell me everything. From your earliest memory to the moment they brought you here to the Gardens."

"So I can give you ammunition? You have all you need in your room. If you want to kill me, I'm right here. Just blow my brains out too. There's nothing stopping you. It's not like you're going to get in trouble. You're not breaking any laws. Go ahead, Pastor. Read me my last rights, or whatever. Have at it. I'll even make it easy." She sat, holding to one side as she popped the blanket in the air. Almost enchantingly, it floated down around her as she took her seat. "I won't even move. Unless that's what you need. Should I scream? Run around and give you a chase? Will that do or is it strictly my sob stories that get you off?"

A smile came, but it wasn't a nice one. The smoothness was gone, and I was walking forward, right at her, and nothing could have stopped me. I locked around her throat, positioning myself inches from her face.

"You want to know what gets me off?" Tighter, I squeezed, but she didn't fight me. She glared, stirring the lust in my blood even more.

"Rape."

The word was but a hollowed breath of air. I laughed, shaking my head.

"I said I'd rape you with everything I could get my hands on. That doesn't include me. I don't fuck my slaves. I don't fuck

A. A. DARK

anyone. You're damn lucky for that. You couldn't handle me if I
did."

Small glints of something flashed in her eyes. It was enough
to draw me in. To captivate me for the smallest moment. I eased
my hold even more, scanning her softening face.

"Talk, slave, or you're not going to like what comes next.
Right now, this is voluntary. The moment you refuse, I'll chain
you up and take your words the only way I can. I will stick that
needle in your arm, and I won't stop until I'm content that I've
heard everything."

"Liar. You won't stop until I'm like her, begging for death.
You want me facing my demons until they swallow me whole.
You won't win. You won't succeed in giving me to them. I will
not succumb to whatever game you're hoping to play. I will tell
you the worst things I've ever experienced, but nothing you hear
will lead me to the path you're praying I take. I've made my
peace. Torture me. Rape me. It won't matter. I don't want to die,
and short of blowing my brains out, nothing you do will
make me."

"What's this love language you speak?"

"The truth."

"You have strength."

"I wasn't left a choice, Pastor."

"*Master.*"

"Not to me. Even if I say the word, I don't mean it. You're
Pastor Anthony Attaway, and no other title exceeds that."

Did I still have her neck? I did, but I wasn't squeezing like I
wanted; I was leading. Pulling her to me as I crushed my lips
into hers. And for the smallest moment, Josie returned my kiss
becoming the devil, herself. It was enough to have both of our
heads rearing back. Not that I wanted to. It had been too long
since I had a woman stand up to me like this. I was too drunk,
and I wanted more of her fight. More of a reason to break every
single rule I'd lived by for more than a decade.

"Talk."

I let go, feeling drunker than ever. Fuck the alcohol. I knew that wasn't what I was experiencing. It was lust, and it had its claws in deep.

"I won't start at the beginning. I'm going to just randomly start telling you every bad thing about me. Every lie. Every tragedy. Every kiss I gave, and the ones I didn't ask for. I'm going to take you into the darkest places you've probably ever gone, Pastor, and while you're looking for a reason to bring me into the light with death or repentance, I want you to stop and realize, you're already looking at it. I am the light. Why? Because I'm a victim turned survivor. There is no brighter light than that. There is no bigger strength than overcoming an obstacle meant to kill you. You may think my story ended when I got here. That you *saved* me." Her head shook. "This place may have kept the drugs away, but I had already beat the hardest part. *I* made myself sober. This place just kept me that way. I won, Pastor. Not them. Not you. *Me.*"

All I could do was shake my head as I looked at her. She spoke of victory. She held such satisfaction. And in the matter of seconds, she showed me exactly how to decimate her.

"You're a stupid, stupid woman, Josie Lockhart. *Stupid.*"

Worry crept in but so did caution as she watched me sink into the couch.

"Pride leads to ego. Ego to mistakes. You just made the biggest one of your life."

"Did I?" Her head shook. "I don't think so."

"Ego," I repeated. "Just like believing you'll show me the darkest things imaginable. Look around you, slave. You are in the depths of hell, and the only devil you're going to face is me."

"Devil? You?" She laughed. Then, she laughed harder. "You're not the devil, Anthony. I've seen him, and you're not even close."

"You've seen him." It wasn't a question as I reached over to the table, grabbing my phone. "I'm calling for a pickup, and you're going to start with that story. I want to hear everything."

She only paused enough for me to call for the guards. The moment I hung up, she sucked in a slow breath.

"I was nineteen and almost three years into working the streets. At that point, I was going through one of my on-and-off again moments. I was off drugs. My episodes would last a few weeks, and I'd get sucked back in. Well, I had just finished working for the night, and the woman who watched over me was eerily quiet as we walked back to the house. It was this rundown old Victorian a few blocks from downtown where we worked. Anyway, one of the regulars showed up about a block from my usual spot. He was looking for something out of the ordinary. Usually what Ronnie wanted was quick, but he was offering to rent a room for the night. I was exhausted, but Dina said I had to go. She knew I wasn't using, but that didn't stop her from practically shoving a pill down my throat."

"We got in the car, and Dina rode with us to the hotel. Just as we were pulling in, I saw a man walking around the side of the building. Just the sight of him sent a sickness through my stomach. I could tell he was tall, but he was wearing this dark trench coat with a hat. I tried not to think anything of it. Where we were, it could have been anyone. I pushed it away as Ronnie went inside to get a room. Well, by that point the pill was kicking in. My adrenaline was going. I felt good, like I could leap tall buildings and run a marathon."

"Ronnie finished checking in, and we drove around to the back of the building. By that point I had already forgotten about the man. I opened the door and with the way the reflection from the streetlight hit the window, I swore I could see a face in the glass. But it wasn't a face I'd ever seen. It didn't even look human." Her hands lifted. "The eyes were...wide...and slightly sunken in. Black eyes. There was no white at all. The cheekbones were high, and the lips were thin. It had a very square chin. I remember jolting to a stop. The sickness in my stomach came back, and I was paralyzed with fear. And not even because I couldn't tear my gaze from the face. It was what I felt as the sight burned into my brain."

"What did you feel?"

Was I at the end of my seat? I couldn't break my gaze from her terrified face. I could tell she didn't even want to be talking about it. What she said was real. At least to her, and that intrigued the hell out of me even more.

"It was a heavy emptiness. A sorrow that I can't even begin to put into words. Fear, definitely, but a…sticky terror. Almost as if seeing the face had somehow stained my soul. I suddenly felt how dirty I was. Shame overtook me, and we all heard this deep laughter. We kept turning to look around in circles. Looking. Searching the surroundings. Ronnie started calling out, threateningly, trying to see who it was. I did the same, even if I was afraid to see him again. We were all on edge at that point. Why, I don't know. People laugh every day. But the tone was different. We could feel it. It wasn't normal and we all sensed that. They never told me whether they saw anything, but I think they did, just like me. When we couldn't find the source of the laughter, Ronnie just…called it off. He wouldn't even give us a ride back home. He got in his car and hauled ass. *But that face.* It didn't end there. We started walking, and I kept seeing him, the tall man in the hat…going into stores. Disappearing around corners. I was in a full-blown episode, and Dina swore what she had given me wasn't hallucinogenic. It couldn't have been because she saw him too. But only once. After that, he disappeared. Sort of like what happened after I saw you, Master. Gone…but not forgotten."

B1297

My Master was drunk. Not just inebriated, but shitfaced to the point that he could barely sit up straight. He was leaning. Rocking. Slurring. I expected some form of self-control, but whatever was going on inside Anthony Attaway was long overdue. He wasn't well. The man had nothing but questions for me, and on a deeper level, I had to answer them. If I knew anything at all, it was that his own were what needed to be answered. He was missing something. Something pivotal that was affecting his entire outlook on life. Maybe death. The afterlife? Or perhaps this was just him, but I didn't think so. I was good at reading people. *Seeing through them.* Some were just psychopaths. You could lose yourself in trying to dissect their reasoning, all the while, they were losing themselves in fantasizing about dissecting *you.* Here at the Gardens...literally.

"You're not finished, slave. Keep going."

"You're dozing."

"I'm not. I'm listening."

I glanced over to the clock hanging on the wall, feeling myself almost nod off from being so tired.

"It's almost six in the morning. I don't think I can do another story. I'm ready for bed."

"You'll go to bed when I tell you. Another."

Sighing, I shifted on the sofa, curling into a ball as I laid my head against the oversized pillows. I could fall asleep right here and now if I wanted. This wasn't the streets. It wasn't a cell bed. It wasn't hard and low to the ground. I felt as though I were floating on a cloud. My eyes closed and only reopened at the bark of Anthony's voice.

"Wake up. You said you kissed men, and some had kissed you. Who was your first?"

"Kiss?" I paused. "Voluntary or involuntary?"

His lids narrowed just the smallest amount.

"Both."

I yawned. "My first kiss was when I was seventeen. His name was Cliff."

"*Cliff*," Anthony interrupted. "What sort of name is Cliff?"

"Clifford is a fine name. It's a damn name. Do you want me to keep going or not?"

He waved his hand but stayed quiet as his head leaned back. His eyes were closed, but I knew better than to stop.

"Cliff was a roofer down the road from the Victorian house I told you about. He was...sweet. He didn't look at me like the others."

"Wait." My Master's head lifted. He seemed to hesitate as he processed. "You were already on the streets by that time."

"My first real kiss wasn't before I was ever touched, Pastor. It came long after."

"Keep going." The irritation was there as his head went back down.

"Cliff took me out on some dates. Secretly, of course. The house was already getting pretty full, so Dina wasn't on my ass too much. They knew I wouldn't run away at that point. Everything was...good...for a while."

"What happened?"

I glanced to my Master who still had his lids closed.

"Niles, the main guy who ran the house, saw us leaving a deli a few blocks over. Cliff had his arm around me, and they fought. It wasn't pretty. Cliff got beaten badly. He never came back or talked to me after that.

"Your first heartbreak."

I shrugged regardless that he couldn't see me.

"A part of me knew it wouldn't last. It was good that it didn't. The anger helped me find the bravery to run away. It took me another two and a half years, but I did it."

"And what about the first men who kissed you without your consent?"

My teeth bit into each other. My silence had Anthony's head lifting so he could look at me.

"Ooh. This is a sour topic. This one stings. A man from your Victorian? A client? Niles, himself?"

I hugged more into the pillow, pushing the emotion back as far as I could. Should I lie? I knew it was pointless. It would get me nowhere except further from the healing I'd already done. It happened. There was nothing I could do about it.

"I met a trucker when I first ran away. He brought me to the city, but it was a good few days drive. He was in his early twenties. If you recall, I was fifteen. And stupid. I had no idea what predators were back then, but I learned pretty fast. I thought." I stopped. "We hit it off pretty good at first. Or I thought we had. We laughed. We sang songs and had fun. The second night is when he kissed me. It was unexpected. Not wanted the first few times he tried. I guess I was too afraid to really say no. Somewhere along the way that night, I convinced myself it wasn't so bad. I even somehow deluded myself into thinking maybe he actually felt something for me. It was ridiculous. I have no idea what I was thinking, but a part of me really imagined that we could make something out of the good times we were having.

Maybe even try to make something of a future. I know, I was stupid. The third night." I stopped.

"You lost your virginity to him."

I glanced over. "He was very pushy. It's like he was all over me. Again, I gave in. To everything. I feared if I didn't, things would get worse. A few hours later, they did. After he got what he wanted, he abandoned me at a truck stop about an hour outside of the city. I went into the restroom and when I came out...gone."

"Ouch."

"I think we can both agree it was for the best. Big lessons learned there, Pastor. It sure prepared me for what I was soon up against. The world is not a nice place."

"It's most certainly not. From what I've heard so far, it seems like things got worse after that and never really got any better."

My head tilted, unsure if there was sarcasm or sympathy in his tone.

"I guess it depends how you look at it. Let's go two years back, months before I went to your church. Before I cleaned myself up. Before I got a job. Before I found worth inside of myself. I was at the worst I had ever been. The drugs never really left me. I had no shelter. No food. If I needed something, I stole it."

"No prostitution at that point?"

My lids lowered as defensiveness flared.

"I never went back to that after I escaped the people who trafficked me. *Never.*" I pushed myself up to sit, moving to the edge of the sofa as the pastor lay back and stared at me. "Why do you do this? Why do you need to hear our stories? Are you living our sins through us? Trying to understand them? Or... maybe you're using them as fuel to sate some festering anger you have. If you're not a mercy killer, that just makes you a plain murderer. How will you kill me, Anthony? Do I even get to know?"

"Of course you'll know. You'll even choose how you want to go."

"Like the other slave."

A smile pulled back his lips just the slightest amount. He was still having a hard time keeping his eyes open.

"And I'll want to die?"

"You'll be *begging* me."

I laughed under my breath, moving my eyes to the floor only to meet his once again.

"Then it's not my reasoning; it's yours. I don't want to die. That means you'll somehow manipulate me so I'll want to. It makes you happy to cause such emotional inner turmoil that you get people to kill themselves?"

My Master groaned as he leaned over, grabbing the hem of my see-through sheer robe. Until that moment, I'd almost forgotten how exposed I was.

His fingers traveled up the edge towards my chest, and I couldn't move through the hunger on his face.

"Maybe, but what makes me happy is irrelevant in the scheme of things. I'm on a quest at the moment. Nothing more. I was going to offer you clothes, but I'm not sure I want to. You see, Josie..." He trailed off, stopping level with my nipple. So close, but not touching. "I like to test myself as much as I like to test my slaves. I haven't fought this particular battle for quite a long time." Brown eyes lifted to mine. "You think I'm judging you, but I'm not. I have a soft spot for ruined women. *Strong women.* I try to steer clear, but they sure keep finding me. You found me."

How had I missed him getting so close? Our mouths were only inches apart. I glanced to his lips, meeting his stare head on letting my need turn to anger. *Purpose.*

"I was never ruined; I was weak. I'm not that person anymore." I moved in just shy of his lips, only to turn my head at the last second and stand. I threw him a defiant look, heading for the room. "I'm going to bed. Goodnight, Anthony."

But he didn't answer. He let me leave, and I wasn't sure what to think about that. I was dreading this moment the most. Even as I entered the room, my skin crawled. As I came to face the slave's bed, I wanted to forget the way the Master said it was now mine. There were clean sheets. A new pillow and blanket. It didn't change what I'd seen. Did the pastor truly want me to sleep here?

"Well...What are you waiting for, slave?"

My heart was racing as I looked towards the door the Master stood in.

"I need something to sleep in."

"You don't. You can get in my bed."

I took in the way his expression said the opposite. He wanted me, but he didn't. Not really. He truly was in a war with himself, and the street part of me wanted to test which one was stronger. To get him to want me could play in my favor. *It could save my life.* It could also destroy it.

"I will not sleep in your bed. Do I have any clothes or not? I really would like to take a shower before I sleep."

The Master pointed to the closet door. I eased in, flipping the switch, and screaming as arms locked around me from behind.

"Such a smart mouth. *I like it.* They didn't teach you to act like this at the Gardens, did they?"

Pressure turned crushing as I tried thrashing in his hold. I didn't stand a chance against the Master's powerful grasp. He had a good foot of height on me, and he was nearly twice the width.

"I asked you a question, slave. *You think you know me? You* think just because you've seen a side of me most worship that you have leverage? That you have some sort of power?" I tried gasping through the squeeze, but the Master's other arm flew up, and his hand cupped over my nose and mouth. Lack of air turned me wild. I kicked. I twisted. I bucked. I still couldn't find an opportunity to hurt him, and the lack of oxygen was making my arms heavy. They were barely moving as I kept begging myself to swing. To fight. I couldn't. Darkness was winning. He...was winning, and me...I was disappearing.

"They didn't teach you to act like this, but you'll learn your place. Sleep, slave. *Sleep.*"

MASTER B-0113

D id she look pretty in my bed?

My finger traced over her lips, moving along her jaw until I made a path back up to her small, thin nose. Pretty. Pretty. I kept seeing her beauty when normally that was the last thing I noticed in women.

Yes. Josie most definitely looked like she was made to be in my bed. Her dark hair was spread over my pillow, and her olive skin tone stood out against my pale blue sheets. They'd be a close match to the color of her eyes. I did want to look into their depths a little longer. God, I was wasted. I should have gone to sleep a long time ago. I couldn't when all I wanted to do was keep looking at her. Talking to her. Devil. Angel. Which one was she, and which was I? I thought I knew, but I kept getting confused. I couldn't think when all I wanted was to fuck her. Control and crush her with my power. Kiss her. Breathe her into me. Suffocate her. Yes…I'd already done that.

"Mmmrr."

A small sound left her as her head rolled closer to me. I really shouldn't have put her in my bed, but I already knew where this was going. I didn't have a choice if I wanted this to go my way. I was the Master here, not Josie, and the sooner she got that through her head, the faster I could analyze this new vision quest I was on. Maybe they were pointless, but I didn't think so. There were plenty of studies of patients on psychedelics. Some were used illegally, but others were highly held in spiritual practice. Where it was easier to shoot up Linda, I wanted to try something different with Josie. It would be brutal. Hours of sickness and extreme hallucinations, but I was ready. Whether she was didn't matter. She was here for me, and she was damn lucky I'd been taken over with this new interest. Otherwise, she'd just end up dead when I finished with my fun. She probably still would.

"Mm. *No.*" My slave's eyes flew open, and she went to sit up, not able as my arm barred over her chest. She tried to claw her way off the bed but couldn't as I jerked her in my direction.

"You're going to lay here, and you're not going to move. Did you know every bed, no matter the size or Master's choice, comes installed with cuffs in this place? That's what you'll get if you decide to try to get out of this bed again. I'll lock you in and keep you here until I decide otherwise."

"I couldn't breathe. You…"

She didn't finish. She just continued to stare at me like the monster I was.

"You passed out. I know. I meant for you to."

"Why?"

"Because you forget who's the Master. Do it again, and you're going to lose a lot more than air. Do you understand?"

Hesitation played out but she slowly nodded.

"Good." My stare dropped from her face, traveling down to her neck and then chest. She flinched as I reached forward tracing my finger down her sternum. I didn't make it an inch before she slapped my hand away. I grabbed her wrist, squeezing, and moving her arm back down to the bed, pushing it hard into the mattress. Again, I repeated the act. With her laying down, the blue robe was completely open, exposing her entire body. I couldn't get enough of her curves. Of the way I could see her chest rising faster from my touch. "How many men have told you you're beautiful?"

Full lips parted, but she didn't speak.

"Let me rephrase. How many have told you you're beautiful and meant it?"

"I don't know." Tears collected, and the weakness was like blood to a shark. "I never believed them."

"You don't think you're beautiful?"

"I'm okay, I guess."

"Okay?"

My finger traced under her breast, moving around until I was circling closer towards the center. I took my time, watching Josie fist the comforter underneath her. She stared at the ceiling, her mouth opening as I moved even closer to the hard nub that called to me.

"You kissed me back, slave. You want to kiss me. Even after everything you know. After what you saw me do to Linda. You feel it. There's something between us." I reached her nipple, moving my thumb in to gently pinch against it. "Answer. *Truthfully*. You feel something, whether you like it or not."

"Not." Her eyes stole a glimpse at me as fear clouded in from her uncontrollable tone. "You're a con. A liar. I feel something, but I don't want to."

"Neither do I."

A moment of silence passed, and she braved looking at me. "What do you suppose it is? It's more than attraction. More than lust. Perhaps a mixture of the two?"

My hand cupped her breast while I continued rolling her nipple.

"It's chemical. For instance, lust is driving me right now. Testosterone and estrogen rule me. Mix in some dopamine, norepinephrine, with a dash of serotonin…attraction. As this plays out…we introduce oxytocin and vasopressin. *Attachment.*

All are trying their best, but they're wasting their time with the last. Or perhaps I have a deficiency in one. I won't get attached to you. It's never happened towards anyone, and it never will. I'm content being with myself. I like it that way."

"Me too."

I left her breast, easing over the center of her stomach. My hand came to a stop and my brow drew in as I took in what I was doing. Four years at Whitlock. Second auction at the Gardens. Not once had I gotten this far with a slave. I hadn't even let my mind go there. Yet, here I was, wanting to reach down to spread her legs so I could taste her. Make her come. Fuck her? Did I really want to do that? I didn't have to remain celibate. No one expected me to. I did that for myself. I was normally disciplined to the extreme. Nothing had been that way with me since I'd arrived back at the Gardens. I'd even been smoking again. I hadn't done that in years. It was more than Josie. It was me. It was the endless words that plagued my mind. The questions. The curiosity. The hate for so many things and people. I had an obsessive personality when it came to work or tasks. Added with the need for perfection, I was usually consumed. I liked it that way, but had I been so overtaken by everything happening in my life that I hadn't realized I was in trouble? I was drunk, and I sure as hell wanted more. I wanted escape. *More.* I wanted things I didn't even know. *More.*

More.

More.

More.

A growl left me, and my hand lifted to hover over her stomach. She'd asked me if I believed in God. She assumed at one point I didn't. Truth was, I didn't know what to think. I used to believe in God. I worshipped him. Prayed to him. Devoted my teachings truly to him. Aside from my battles, I had talked with God. I tried to understand why I felt compelled to do the things I did. I secretly waged war with my demons despite knowing I couldn't outrun any of them. Then…I stopped. Life won. My darker connections pulled me in. I got lured into my secret fantasies. I began to explore all sides of faith until…no sides at all. It became less worship and more experimentation and studies. Out of body experience. Psychedelics. Meditation. I took classes when I had no place to test my theories. I tested different methods. If a God or devil existed there had to be a lifeline to them. I was determined to find it, if not directly, get some sort of message.

Maybe it was stupid, woo-woo shit. Maybe it would amount to nothing. I wouldn't know unless I tried. With my work, with what I had done, seen in my own hallucinations, there had to be something more than the heavy, horribleness that had visited me, right? The questions were eating me alive, and maybe even a part of me wanted them too. I was finding little to live for. Money wasn't enough. What used to be my life's mission wasn't satisfying me anymore. Not when I had the underlining embarrassment for my path. That was my father's fault. I was led to lead a lie…*for them*. I played my part for who I was. That's what was important to those who mattered. That didn't deter me from this quest. It only fed it. When you preached something so much, for so long, you started to want proof. I'd get mine one way or another.

"Pastor?"

The word barely came out as a whisper. I wasn't sure how I'd heard her at all. My jaw flexed, and my eyes raked over her body. I clenched my fist over her stomach, torn between continuing with what I wanted or getting on with my game. Both? Not yet. Soon. So very soon.

"Get your clothes from the closet and go take a shower. You have ten minutes to get your ass in bed. One word and I'll cuff and fuck you until your body shuts down and you die. You can starve, piss, or shit yourself for all I care. I'll light this mattress on fire and be done with you. It doesn't matter to me. Your stubborn, outspoken streak ends now. You don't believe me, go ahead and call me Pastor again. Say something." Nothing. Her eyes were wide as she trembled through my words. "You're running out of time, slave."

Josie sprung from the bed and raced to the closet. Within a minute she was running for the bathroom. She was learning. I knew she was going to have trouble, and I didn't expect her strength to disappear so soon, but I was one step closer to where I needed her, and for now, that would work.

BI297

For four days I was on edge. Any speck of familiarity or comfort towards my Master was gone the moment he stole my oxygen. This man was not my friend. He was not even a man of God, redeemable somewhere deep within. Anthony was dangerous. After what he did to me and Linda, I had no doubts exactly what he was capable of. It was hard to gage exactly what I was up against when he spent most of his days reading or studying something. He barely talked. He was too absorbed, but not today. The morning had already started differently. For one, he wasn't holding his tablet or phone. He was watching me.

"You're not eating."

I glanced at the food, not able to stomach another bite. I forced myself to anyway. I was hesitant to respond to him at all. In my past, I'd been beaten, raped, drugged, and hunted. I'd been terrified back then. This was worse. Then and now didn't compare. With my past, I almost always had the hope of escape. That was gone from me now. What was left was him and me, and I was no one.

I was bought.

Bait.

The slave.

Pastor Anthony Attaway had me at his mercy, and after four days, I wasn't sure how much tolerance he had left. Every moment that he wasn't reading, he was electric, and not always from the lust. It was the unidentifiable stares—longing or luring? If I could only read what was on his mind, I might stand a chance in what came next.

"Better."

The pastor took a bite, his face staying in the same stoic expression as he watched me chew. I stole glances here and there, but I didn't want to draw his attention more than I already was. The attraction and pull constantly weighed on my mind. I'd given lots of thought on whether to act on it. The thing was...lust wouldn't save me. Having sex with my Master wouldn't either. If anything, it could very well be my death sentence. With the way I kept catching him looking at me, I might not have a choice.

"The dress looks good on you. It fits good too."

Glancing down, I forced myself to swallow the bite of chicken.

"Thank you, Master."

"We started our first night off a bit fast. I was...drunk. More than drunk, really. It's a bit of a blur." He paused, his brow drawing in as he seemed to debate something. "I think." He stopped. "I choked you unconscious, didn't I."

It wasn't a question.

My eyes jumped to his but lowered just as fast.

"You did."

He nodded. "I didn't think that was a dream." Another pause. "I won't apologize. It's dangerous for you to test me. I wouldn't advise it."

"You don't have to worry about that, Master. You showed me my place."

His eyes flickered at my tone. I could have cursed. Had I put too much attitude behind my statement? Behind a title that was almost impossible for me to use? I sure felt like I had.

"Finish eating. I need to make a call."

My Master didn't wait for my response. He stood, putting his plate in the sink. Walking over, he grabbed his phone and headed for the bedroom. The moment he disappeared my eyes cut over to the door. As much as I wanted to run away, I knew it would be worse if I did. There was nowhere to go. If he didn't find me, the guards would. This place was infested with cameras. Even ones you couldn't see. I knew that from my time in the cells. I was observant. I listened to people talk. Slaves had tried to run. It never ended well.

"Main Master."

I could barely hear the pastor's voice as he seemed to grow further away. I ignored the conversation, quickly getting up and raking my food in the trash. I washed our plates, doing my best to lose myself in some sort of task. To think. To figure out some-thing. Anything. I couldn't by the time Anthony returned. There were no options. No plan or scheme that would help me. This was it. My best bet was staying quiet so I could bide my time. After all, Anthony had to leave at some point. When he did, I'd have some sort of freedom. Unless he intended to kill me before that; which he very well could.

I turned off the water from the sink as the Master headed from the bedroom. "So something did stick from your training." I kept quiet as I walked to the sofa, taking a seat as he placed his phone down on the bar, dismissing me as he headed over. A small leather book rested on one of the end tables and he picked it up, reading through.

Time passed as I sat on the far end of the sofa and waited. The Master resorted to his habit of the previous days. He read and paced. He walked in circles, going back and forth, only to turn the opposite way and begin counterclockwise. I kept my head down, losing myself in my own thoughts. It was a knock that had my face jerking to the door.

"Perfect. Just in time."

Anthony swung the door open and smiled as he took what looked like a to-go bag. I followed him with my eyes to the kitchen, but he was behind the counter, and I couldn't see. It didn't take long before my Master came around, holding two glasses. He oozed charm. The man everyone ogled over and worshipped stood before me, momentarily making me drop my own guard.

"I've been thinking about our conversations the first night. *Or what I can remember of them.* I'm sure I was an ass, but I think we should start new. What do you think?" He handed me a miniature teacup holding brown liquid. I brought it in, crinkling my nose at the earthy smell.

"I'd like to start new." I paused. "What is this?"

"A special drink. Sacred, really. It's tea, but it's on the fancier side. Nothing but the best for the Masters here at the Gardens. It smells weird, but I think you'll like it. You have to at least give it a chance. *To us.*" He raised his glass waiting as I eased mine against his. "To God and everything he has planned."

I couldn't stop the hesitation as I waited and took in his change in demeanor.

"All in one drink, Josie, or your salute to God doesn't count. That'll bring us bad luck. Don't do that to us. Ready? One. Two." I brought the cup up closer to my lips. "Three. Drink it all down."

And I did, almost spitting it out instantly. It took everything I had to swallow the woodsy, bitter taste.

"What a good girl."

He put down his empty cup, pulling me to stand and walking us quickly into the bedroom. Had the remnants of his drink looked different than mine? I'd barely been able to see in the fast amount of time, but the color was darker. Thicker? Mine looked like tea. Almost clear. His like…soda?

"Sit."

But he helped ease me down before I could really obey. I wasn't sure what to think. Alarms were ringing in my head. My brain was screaming more than caution. *It was screaming warnings.* Why move me from the couch so fast? Why bring us in here at all? He was suddenly acting strange, and I wasn't sure why.

"Master…what's happening?" I scanned the underlining excitement on his face. "What did you do?"

"Something that could be amazing. Before you worry, there's no chance of addiction. None. Zero. And no needles. I did that for you, slave. Now, you're going to do this for me. As greedy as that sounds know that you will forever be changed for the better after this."

"Better? You…" I looked back at the living area. *"You… drugged me?"*

My voice cracked making his face harden. "It's a good drug. And I've been told by people I trust that it's not addicting. You have my word, and I don't give that out freely. I want you to relax through this. It's going to be rough at first. It'll be hell, but I promise you, what's happening to you during is well worth the brutality."

Tears blinded me, and I couldn't keep in the sob that tore its way through. "You knew how I felt about drugs. *You knew.*" I stopped from exploding like I wanted, but I couldn't stop shaking from the rage within. I had to calm. I couldn't get in more trouble. "What is it?" I said, angrily. "What's going to happen?"

Tears were spilling over like a river, and there was nothing I could do to stop the anxiety. Fear gripped me around the throat tighter than Anthony had the other night. I couldn't breathe. I could barely swallow through the thick bitterness that lingered. I had worked so damn hard on myself. For what? For him to take it away?

"It's a spiritual drug, used in practices from the earliest of times. You're going to see amazing things. Your brain is going to open new doors, and as it does, you will relay everything you see. Everything you hear. Understand?"

I nodded as the sob mixed with a broken growl. It elongated as my leg began to shake hard in place. Anthony's hand flattened on the middle of my bare back, burning against the exposed skin from the backless sundress.

"You have no idea how happy this makes me. If I'm happy; you'll be happy. There's really no reason to be afraid or angry. You'll be alright, I promise." His hands rose almost cautiously, cupping my face. I wanted to pull back. To scream and attack him. I couldn't as I caught what appeared to be a speck of caring concern. It gave me pause, but it did little to ease the mass of emotions I was going through. "I know this is hard for you to believe, but this isn't just for me, Josie. You've had a hard life. What if it didn't hurt you anymore? They say this drink has the power to heal the most broken mind. It's life changing. If you saw the studies I have, you wouldn't believe the results. It alters people. Completely transforms them. It also gives insight and visions, and those are all I want from you."

"Like Linda?" I snapped.

My head pulled free of his hold.

"This isn't what I gave Linda. Would you prefer her drug instead? I can grab the needle. Maybe the combination will overdose you once and for all. Would you prefer that?"

My head shook as my cries increased. I knew there was no point in crying, but I couldn't get over the fear. As crazy as it was, I felt betrayed by this pastor. Betrayed when I should have known he'd pull something like this. Why was I surprised? I shouldn't have been. I knew his ways. I knew how dangerous he was, and I was hurt at my hard work being taken from me.

"Breathe and calm. Don't let your anger win. The results depend on it, and for both of our sakes, we want good results. Now, I want you to lay back on the bed and relax." He eased me down. "Take slow deep breaths and let yourself fall into a somewhat meditative state. I'll be here with you every second of the way."

"How long before it hits?"

I wiped my eyes, already swearing I felt the tiniest bit different.

"About half an hour on average. Could be more or less. Like I said before...the Gardens only has the best of everything. And I mean everything, Josie." He stopped, using his hand to turn my face so I could look at him. "You can do this. You're strong. If there's answers, you're the one who can get them."

"Answers to what exactly? What am I supposed to be doing?"

"You're looking for proof of something more. Answers."

"Why me? Why aren't you drinking this tea and finding your own damn answers?"

He wasn't looking at my eyes anymore, his stare was stuck on my lips.

"I'm not a reliable source. I've already had it multiple times, and everyone's experiences are different. Mine were...*unbelievable*. It's what fueled this. I can't be sure what I remember is what I saw. Even recording the sessions, I'm too taken away to remember to speak. You won't be like that because you got me. I'll walk you through and be there every step of the way. We'll experience this together."

I inhaled deeply, closing my eyes as my Master began stroking back my hair. Darkness encircled me, hugging warmly like a blanket. The longer I stayed there, the more real the weight began to feel. It was almost like the air was hugging my skin. Like it was caressing me in the most loving embrace. My body began floating and as fast as I felt free, my eyes were flying open. My stomach lurched, twisting and growing heavy as the walls around me morphed in color.

I knew I should have stood, but my Master was already pulling me into the bathroom, just in time for me to get sick. I barely made it, but he seemed to know exactly what I needed before I could even speak. But I wasn't saying words. I was crying and staring into the toilet in horror. The colors were moving, transitioning into shapes. Things?

A gasp left me and sweat coated my skin. The shower water was running. If time had passed, I wasn't aware of it. But it had to of. My Master was standing, adjusting the water as I tried to make sense of the colors that kept moving all around me.

"Slave—"

But I was already gagging, despite nothing else was coming.

"You're doing great, Josie. Come, let me help you."

I was standing, letting him undress me. I didn't care. My attention zeroed in on my reflection and it wavered, bleeding down the mirror. I wasn't sure why, but I stepped forward? Was God in there? Was he staring back at me behind all the colors? The room returned and my Master had his shirt and pants off. He had on a black pair of boxers, and he was turning me towards the shower.

"What are you seeing, slave?"

"Melting. Colors. Everything is…" Darkness was around me again, I was warm, nestled in the magic blanket that had me smiling. Yes…I was smiling a lot. Smiling and…singing? My eyes opened, and I realized the pastor was washing me. It wasn't in a lustful way. He wasn't even using his hand, but a washcloth.

"Keep going, Josie. Everything is what?"

"Beautiful. But scary. I don't feel afraid. I feel…good."

"Search for the answers. Focus on your mission."

"My mission." Just saying the words had the room spinning. Colors began to merge around me, and I put my hand to the wall falling through it. But I didn't, the room just shifted again as it transitioned to different shapes. "God?"

But I didn't see God. I saw me, as a child. I saw my brothers and sisters. My father. My grandmother. Even as the pastor eventually led me from the bathroom, my vision didn't end. I spoke to them. I argued. I cried. And cried. And cried. And I woke up, but not from a dream. I was awake, I just woke up from the hallucination of an argument that seemed so real, I would have sworn I was standing back at my grandmother's home.

"I can't find God. I asked them all. God escapes me." I took deep breaths, covered in sweat. Or was I still wet from the shower? Time was gone. It didn't even exist anymore. "I love them. I was so selfish. Did you hear me, Pastor? I was undeserving. I know nothing. I knew that, but I feel it now. I know nothing."

"Shhh."

Somehow my head was laying in Anthony's lap as he rocked me. I spoke, but I was still crying, off and on. Colors shifted again and my eyes rolled. My arms wrapped around the pastor, and I melted into him as if he were the most comfortable pillow. Or...as if he were God, himself.

Darkness crept into the vision of my grandmother's living room again. Where I thought I was going to continue seeing my bad choices and disappointments, it was being taken from me by the second. A voice spoke, but it was one I'd never heard before.

"Hello?"

My head was lifted. I blinked hard, seeing the apartment's room, but an overlay of darkness coating the floor and walls. It was taking over, tinting every surface it touched.

"Hello? I...feel you."

"What do you feel, slave? *Who* do you feel?"

Had I said that out loud?

"Someone's here. I..."

"Search out your truth. Search out proof."

445

I wanted to scream, yet I didn't. Negativity was growing so far away. My emotions were dying. Ego was melting just like the colors. I buried my face in Anthony's stomach, holding around him tighter. He was still in his boxers, and I could smell the rich scent of something on his skin. It weaved its way into me, becoming part of me. Forcing its way deep, pinching and hooking into the fabric of my true self. My head was shaking no. I might have been even saying it over and over, but there was this presence where one hadn't been before, and it wanted me aware of its existence.

"What don't you want, Josie?"

Heavy panting was leaving my mouth. I rose to my knees, blinking as I swayed. Anthony didn't let me fall, instead, he was holding me steady as I peered deep into his eyes. Like a flash, I saw my life flicker in a collage of fast-moving images. They took me from my grandma's house into the big rig where my life changed forever. I went to the city. I lived on the streets. Everything played out up until I was walking down the corridor of the church, listening to the woman tell me about the rehab facility. And I saw him...

My hands lifted to the pastor's face, but it was the light coming from inside his eyes that held me trapped. It was a hallucination. An illusion. Not real. There was no light inside this man, yet my brain kept grasping what wasn't there. It showed me the impossible. It called me forward.

"What are you seeing, slave? You have to speak, or I won't know."

"It's you," I whispered. "I'm in the church. I've stopped at your door, and I'm looking right at you."

"What am I doing?"

"Looking at me, Master. You're just staring at me like I feel. Like...we have something."

"The chemistry."

I nodded, still seeing him sitting behind the desk.

"I want to go in the room."

"And do what?"

"I…I don't know. I…"

The vision faded only placing me inches from the man I'd been wanting to go to. I blinked hard realizing just how close we were. The heat on my Master's face—the lust. I wasn't dressed, and I'd only just realized that as my breasts moved up and down through the quick breaths.

"The vision is gone." Licking my lips, I went to pull away, stopped as his hand flattened on my back. When Anthony brought me closer, there was no fighting what my body clearly wanted.

He was spinning and easing me to the mattress, but that's as far as he went. He hovered. Watching. Waiting. For what, I wasn't sure. He was on the verge of acting, and I was too conflicted on whether to encourage him or scream.

MASTER B-0113

Three hours Josie had been hallucinating. She talked to herself. She laughed. She cried…a lot. Sometimes, she went a long time without saying or doing anything at all. Although I knew it was starting to slow, I still couldn't stop from wanting to continue searching for answers. The first night on any drug rarely brought success. From how light in color the tea had been, I knew she wasn't getting close to the full dosage of what could have been brought over. This was the beginning, and I accepted that as I forced my never-ending need away. If I could ignore what else I wanted, that would be even better, but I still wasn't sure I wanted to. I couldn't get over how gorgeous Josie was. To say I didn't want to possess her in every way imaginable would have been a lie. I wasn't even going to try to deny how hard the pull was to take some sort of action.

"Pastor…"

I was still hovering over her. Still battling my own demons. They didn't just have me. Josie's eyes were beginning to roll again. Her hand reached up to my chest and her lips parted as she arched. To take advantage of her in this state would have made me the lowest of scum. I was that. I didn't avoid fucking her because of morals. I steered clear because of me. Did I really want to risk falling into the trap of lust? It triggered more things than feelings. It messed with my head. I had enough shit already going on in there.

"I don't want to see it again." Her head shook. "But I already have. I don't understand."

She was hallucinating again. Her mouth parted and her eyes flew open wide. The top of her body lifted, and I moved back just enough to see what she'd do. She was nearly sitting, only a few inches from my face. It was like she couldn't even see me before her.

"And God lives here? All the time? Impossible," she breathed out.

"Lives where? What's impossible, Josie?"

My head tilted as I took her in. She blinked, rapidly, smiling as she seemed to bring me in clear, but it didn't last. Her head turned to look next to the bed, and the grin grew exposing her teeth as she beamed with excitement.

"You watch him all the time? Does he know? And you follow him? Just...around? No..." Fear. "I...It's not true. Is it? I can't..."

I looked back and forth from the empty spot by the bed, back to Josie's face. Before I could ask her anything else, she turned to me.

"You have a robe. A black robe. You're.... evil. In a circle. He watches. Your angel, there." She pointed, and I moved to sit back against my heels. I wanted to snatch her up. To ask her how the hell she knew that, but she had been in my closet. Perhaps she'd seen the robe, and her subconsciousness was playing out the information this way.

"What is this angel's name?"

But she wasn't listening to me. "He *runs* the circle?" She gasped, her head shaking as she leaned in to return her hand back to my chest. "Are you sure? I don't think so. What family line?"

Her lips twisted. "No, he said his dad was a cop." Astonishment. "Elite? What blood line?"

"*Josie.*"

I had to stop my hand from going to her neck to choke the life out of her. She shouldn't know that. Any of it. Especially the robe.

Fingers pushed into my pec, but she continued to stare at the emptiness.

"I think he's beautiful too. Cruel, yes, but…Of course not. Toledo? What's there?"

I stiffened, cutting my eyes to where she continued to look. My family had a house in Toledo, but I hadn't been there since childhood. This was not real. It couldn't be. A part of me wanted to believe. How would she know this stuff…but she could have seen or learned it anywhere. The facts weren't hidden.

"I don't want to go back there. I'm not sure I believe you. I feel him. I am him. He's…No. I'd much rather stay here." She yawned, trying to pull me down on her. When I wouldn't budge, she climbed her way on top of me, wrapping her arms around my neck. She straddled my waist, hooking her legs together so that she was stuck to me. I growled, nearly falling back, off the bed. I let her hold, refusing to touch her as I stood and headed for the top to sit and lean against the headboard. A part of me was hoping she'd go crashing to the floor or mattress. The other part wanted her to stay. The latter won as I sat back down. Josie snuggled into my neck, burying her face against me as she mumbled incoherently. Me…I was getting so hard I couldn't stand it.

"The angel's name, Josie. Did he tell you?"

"It was you. But not you. Just…another part of your higher self. You were with another part of me too. And we were…" she paused. "Entwined. Or stuck. With vines and eyes and—"

"Are we still talking about the angel?"

"He's so beautiful. You're beautiful." Her arms tightened even more as she moved against me.

"That's the euphoria talking. You're going to love everything and everyone for a good week after we finish. Probably longer. Like I said before, some people are changed forever."

"I like love. Love feels...so good." She wiggled on my hips causing me to groan. I grabbed her pillow, putting it on top of mine as I scooted down. I was still positioned high but lying back at the same time. I saw my mistake almost immediately. My position only caused her to shift even more, giving her better access. I adjusted myself so that my cock rested against my stomach, but Josie was covering my body with hers as she continued to rub her pussy against my hard length. My hand squeezed into her hip, but the pain did nothing to deter her.

"Josie, your trip is about to take a very dark turn if you don't keep still."

"But you said you loved me."

"I did not."

"You did."

Grabbing her chin, I forced her head to lift so that she had to look in my face.

"I never said I loved you. I never would because I don't. *I never will.* I don't even like you. I tolerate you. That's it."

"Liar." She swayed as she forced herself to sit up from my chest. "He is a liar. I know. I...I...I..." Her expression fell as she got quiet. Whatever she was seeing had microexpressions dancing on her face, but for the most part, she didn't move.

"Slave?"

Her hands went straight up, and her head eased back as she began to rock back and forth as if she were dancing. I had no idea what she was doing, but my stare couldn't lift past her breasts to find out. One shift. One touch. I could change everything. I could give in to what I was dying for. Fuck, I wanted to. I could almost see her riding me. And she would right now. She'd probably fuck me better than anyone ever had. The pleasure would rule her here. *I...would rule her.*

451

One time.

One time.

One. Fucking. Time.

But having her just once wasn't enough, and that's where I found my restraint for the moment.

"Slave, where are you?"

Still, she swayed, keeping her head back.

No answer.

"Josie, what are you doing?"

No answer. Just the slow dancing of her body back and forth on mine. For minutes I took in every angle and line on her chest. From the curve of her waist to the swell of her breasts. The sight was hypnotizing. Erotic. Josie's head was lifted, but her eyes were still closed as she moved against me. It was only then I saw how wet my boxers were from the precum soaking through. Although she was the one adding friction to the base of my cock, it was me who suddenly wanted to do the rocking—thrusting. *Anything* to come.

I sat up, flattening my hand on her back as I turned her to lay on the bed. I'd meant to get up and walk around. To take a breather. I didn't get a chance to lift before her arms came back to my neck.

"Kiss me, Anthony."

"*Master.*"

My voice rumbled, only making her bite her bottom lip.

"You want to kiss me again." She grabbed my hand, bringing it to her breast. "Kiss me like you did in your church office."

"That wasn't real, Josie. None of what you're seeing is technically real."

She squeezed into the back of my hand, wanting me to touch her. Trying to force me to take over. I refused. My self-control was hanging on by a thread. I'd made a horrible mistake by choosing a drug that lasted so long.

"Make it real, Pastor. I need..." Her body moved in nothing

short of a fitful pout. Her heavy-lidded eyes closed, and her hold lifted from my hand, moving down between her legs. My teeth ground into each other, and the top of her hand slid against the underside of my covered cock. A moan left both of us as she touched herself. The movement of her fingers came in fast small circles. I could feel her moving but all I saw was the pleasure on her beautiful face.

"Yes. *Yes.* Master. I need...I...*Master.*"

But she was already coming. My eyes widened as I looked down in shocked awe. I went from guarded and tense to intrigued in less than it it took her to get off. I was fascinated. Mesmerized. I suddenly wanted to see if I could make her come just as fast again. And again. Was it the drug? Was she prone to quick orgasms? The questions came and the curiosity overpowered the resilience. It would only be getting her off. I didn't have to fuck her.

"Josie."

My hand lowered, moving hers out of the way. She'd still been between her legs, rubbing over the outside of her pussy as she came down. When juices met my fingertips, my lids closed to bask in the wetness. And she let me, even grasping to my side as I explored the smoothness. The sounds that followed my touch robbed me of any control I might have had left. It was about her. Not me. Her.

I made a path over her slit, feeling the heat burn me alive. I dipped my fingertip into her entrance, flexing my jaw as she let out a whimper. Josie gasped, rocking to bring me deeper.

"Master, that feels so good. Tell them to be quiet. They'll listen to you. I want it to be just us."

"*Quiet.*"

The anger in my tone had her smiling. She used her hold around my neck to pull herself close enough to put her lips to mine. The shift of her body sent my finger inching inside.

"God, yes. I've thought about this before. I shouldn't have."

"You thought about me?" My lids narrowed. "Open your eyes and say it to my face. I don't believe you."

Blue looked gray as she peered up at me. "More than once. More than five times. It was so wrong, but I couldn't help it. You were on the laundromat's television the first time I saw you. Your words held me trapped. I couldn't move. I couldn't even change my clothes over to the dryer until your show finished. It was like you were speaking just to me." Her lips pressed gently into mine, so soft, so loving as she continued to whisper against me. "You were the most beautiful man I'd ever seen. Like God had chosen you just for me to. To save me. To make me yours."

My touch slowed against her. Something warmed in my chest and my pulse was beating just a little harder.

"When I saw you on the balcony, I prayed it was you. I thanked God. But...that would mean...and then I realized...."

Tears.

For the first time, something different swarmed and ate at me inside. Not words. Not sins. Something a lot worse. I couldn't even put it into thoughts, but I knew it wasn't good. My fingers stopped, and for the longest time, Josie and I just stared at each other. Her hold around my neck was tighter than ever. She was damn near choking me, but I couldn't do anything about it as I tried to figure out what the hell that feeling was. I couldn't part from her. I couldn't do anything but take in the raw pain on her face.

"I shouldn't have said any of that. I...*I want to go home.* Tell them to stop," she whispered, letting me go and falling back to the bed with a bounce. The shift of the mattress rocked me awake. I pushed hard from the bed, storming through the bedroom door, into the living room. My slave was crying again, and we were only on night one. One of five. We had a long way to go, and I wasn't sure who this was going to be harder on... her...or me?

B1297

Horrified didn't come close to describing how I felt. No… it was more than that. If I could multiply horrified by a million, it might be close to describing how I felt as I sat at the table like a zombie, drinking water. From what I could remember, I said things I'd never in a million years admit to. And those were just words. *What I'd done.* What I possibly begged for him to do to me…

Had I said everything out loud? I didn't know what was real or what was a hallucination. I wasn't even sure if we'd done anything at all. We'd had sex a good three times that I could recall, but the fact that we'd been doing it under a palm tree on top of a mountain told me it was probably more hallucination and less reality. Unless my mind had been in the mountains and my body was getting used down here on the bed. I had been holding around him at one point. I could remember that. And kissing him? Getting fingered?

Jesus.

Oh…yes…hadn't I seen him too? And God? And a seal in a top hat and an angel?

Never again. I'd been pretty fucked up in my younger days,

but never had I come close to seeing everything I had last night. Why wasn't there somewhere I could hide? I wanted to be alone, not studied as I tried to keep my face from turning a bright shade of red every five minutes.

"You need to try to eat some of that fruit."

I glanced down at the platter. I wanted to say no, but I grabbed a strawberry instead. If I argued that meant we'd have to talk. I was not opening my mouth, even if I had slept most of the day away again. I was still seeing shit. Hearing voices. I wasn't to be trusted, and that made me uneasy.

"Did you forget how to talk?"

"No, Pastor. *Master*."

Still, he stared. I kept my eyes on the platter, chewing and grabbing a slice of banana.

"That's it? I want to hear more about what you saw. You said things that you couldn't have possibly known. You're going to tell me more about it."

My eyes lifted and my heart exploded as I tried to recall what he was talking about.

"*God,* slave."

"God?"

"You said you saw God and an angel. They were telling you things. You said the angel was me, but a different or higher version or something."

"Oh." His words triggered the memories to return. "God was with this…weird shape. But it wasn't really a shape. It was like," I paused, "vibrating dots, but they were so close together making this…star? Anyway, he showed me this beautiful place. It was so breathtaking; it didn't seem real."

"Maybe it wasn't. Maybe it was. That's what we're trying to find out. Go on. He took you in this place. Then, what?"

"I can't quite remember. I think he mentioned something about always being there. Or that I could always come there? Inside it felt." I stopped as tears blurred my vision. I was still so emotional, and I couldn't stop it. "It was like nothing I'd felt before. Peaceful. Loving. I didn't want to leave. I begged not to go. I...It hurt when it disappeared. I almost wish I could go back."

At my words, my Master stiffened. Had I sounded like Linda? My blood nearly went cold as I quickly reached down grabbing a slice of orange.

"What did this place look like?"

"...paradise? It's so hard for me to recall."

"What about the angel? Me. You talked with him the longest."

I nodded, chewing.

"He hinted about how you've fallen under darkness. Or you wore darkness?"

"The robe."

"Robe?" I gasped as it all came flooding back. "*I watched you sacrificing people.* That's right. It was so fast, but I saw it. He took me to this dark room. Like a...void. You were in this circle, and you were performing some sort of ceremony. But you did more than kill that woman. You've killed lots of women. And not just ceremonies. The circle, the hoods, yes, but...just... murder," I breathed out almost silently.

For a long moment Anthony didn't speak. He didn't even blink. He stared at me with a look that made my skin crawl. It was more than rage. It was a threat like none I could ever remember facing.

"That's impossible for you to know. Who told you that?"

"What?"

"Did someone tell you that, or did you see my robe in the closet and just invent the story during your episode?"

"I...didn't see a robe, Master."

"*Sure you did.* You had to of. It's right there in the closet. You got the sundress yesterday. You had to have seen it."

"Pastor—"

457

But I wasn't able to continue. The Master pulled me to my feet, dragging me to the room and into the closet. When he flipped on the light, he froze. It took seconds before he let me go and lunged forward, jerking at the clothes until he reached the end.

"It's not here. Did you do something with it?"

"Master, I…I never saw a robe."

"You had to of. It's the only—You're lying. You invented the entire thing up. Maybe not intentionally, but you did."

My head shook. "Are you sure?"

"Of course! I mean…Well…" Confusion only grew. "I will not have my experiments tampered with. What did you do with my robe, slave? I'm going to need that when the Main Master is ready. Tell me what you did with it, right now."

"Master, I didn't—"

"Josie, this isn't a game. Where's the robe?"

"I never—"

His hand latched to my neck, jerking me barely an inch from his face.

"I will choke the life from you unless you tell me where that robe is. You have three seconds. *One.*"

"I don't know." I held to his wrist, shaking my head as a sob escaped. "I swear I never saw one."

"Two!"

"Master, please! I don't know. I never saw a robe." The grip stole my air, nearly crushing my neck as I tried to scream. My body was still going through the motions of crying despite sound was impossible to make. Air, I could hear. The screaming pleas were nowhere to be found.

"Master, please! Master! Please!"

But all it was was me mouthing the pleas as I tried to fight. Stars danced in my vision and my arms and legs were getting weak, heavy, as I hit and kicked against him. One second I was on the verge of going under, and the next I was scraping in every ounce of air I could. Still, my Master held me up, and still, he gripped my neck.

"If you're lying to me and you did something to that robe…"

"No. I promise."

To speak was painful. My throat ached and was on fire as he eased me forward with the hold.

"If you didn't see the robe, how did you know? How did your mind invent those scenes if you had nothing to influence your thoughts?"

"It was real. I saw it. I saw into your mind."

"That's impossible."

Anger filled me for the first time since I'd awoken.

"If all of this is impossible, why are you drugging me? Why are you even doing these damn experiments? You wanted a message! *You wanted to know.* I'm telling you what I saw. How can you not believe it? Isn't this what you wanted?"

"It's *not* impossible. It's just…I…just." He stopped, his head shaking as if he wanted to believe but was too caught unaware that he wasn't sure how to react to it.

"Think, Pastor. I'm no Bible expert, but did water not turn to wine? Did a bush not light on fire and talk or something? You're telling me you put stock into a book, but not a vision? How many visions appeared in the bible and turned out to be real? Why can't mine be?"

Nothing. Anthony didn't speak as he scanned my face.

"I had my robe taken to Dark God Status when I arrived. I… forgot about that."

He let go, turning to leave the closet. He didn't make it a few feet before spinning back and grabbing my bicep to pull me back in the room.

"Did you research me after you saw me on TV?"

I hesitated at the seriousness. There was anger underneath. Fear? Uncertainty? I couldn't tell.

"I watched videos of past services."

"That's not what I asked. Did you look up information on who I was as a person? Where I lived? My childhood? Anything like that?"

"Not that I'm aware of. I just watched shows. I looked at websites about the church."

Anthony's head shook but he didn't speak. He was so close and almost seemed to get closer by the second. I wasn't sure if he was going to kiss me or choke me again.

"Pastor." Flashes of last night had me pulling at the collar of the long nightgown. I was starting to sweat. I still wasn't good. I was even still slightly nauseous. "I don't know what was real or not. I don't know if it was my brain, or I was truly talking to someone. I know how that sounds. I know it seems impossible, but...it was all so real. Truthfully, I'm not even sure we're standing here having this conversation right now."

"You need more water and fruit. You're going to need to be hydrated for tonight."

"Tonight?"

The Master paused, his face hardening.

"You're not finished. This is a five-day journey, slave, and you will do every damn day of it. You will not fight or give me a hard time about drinking the tea. You'll do it. I don't think I need to tell you what will happen if you fight me."

The recovering part of me wanted to cry. To scream and argue, but in all reality, I was just as curious as him to get back and see if I could make sense of the mountain of blurry memories. There was something about being in that space that ignited peace in the damaged crevices of my soul. Whether that was my addictive personality returning or something of a higher magnitude, I had no idea. Both terrified me.

MASTER B-0113

Purging. It was a relative term used for the effects of the tea, and it was spot on as I held Josie's hair while she threw up for the second time. It hadn't taken her long to start seeing things. Twenty minutes. A little faster than yesterday, which wasn't surprising given this tea had been darker and thicker. That didn't mean we were early into the night. She'd been sitting here now for almost two hours, not quite able to shake the nausea that plagued her.

"Your toilet has snakes coming out of it again." Josie wiped her mouth, falling a little to the side as she pulled back. "We should really have that looked at."

"I already told you, slave, they're not real."

"They look real to me."

"Because you're high."

I reached over, grabbing the mouthwash only to place it back down. She'd drink it. I grabbed the toothbrush, squeezing a small amount of toothpaste on the bristles. Josie was swaying as I helped her into the shower. She sat on the small seat, limp, resting her head against the side.

"Here, open your mouth before it kicks in worse."

461

Surprisingly, she obeyed, only getting distracted at the end as I was making her rinse it out. Blue eyes rolled and she reached for me, laughing as her lids stayed closed.

"Master, get in and play in the water. You're so serious. We'll swim." The words were slow. Just as distant as she was. I could have easily broken her grip on my shirt, and did, but I found myself easing my clothes off and climbing in with her. The movement had Josie's eyes opening, and her smile growing as she gazed up to my face. If she realized I was nude, she didn't show it. Her eyes closed again, and she let out a long breath, almost a blissful sigh as I lifted to cradle her in my arms. I took her seat, content to hold her in the warm water while she curled into me.

As the silent minutes passed, I went back to her visions. I couldn't explain them. I couldn't even find possible reasons as to how she knew. If she spoke the truth and didn't research me, she couldn't have known I came from an elite family. I'd fed her a bullshit story at the beginning, and she'd never given me indication that she knew I was lying. There'd been sincerity on her face. Sadness for my lie. I didn't understand her knowledge, and that only had me wanting to see if anything else would come to her.

"Will you do this forever? Just like this."

"Hold you?"

She yawned, nodding. I noticed it was something she did a lot while going through the hallucinations.

"You can do your shows and just walk around holding me. Store...holding me. Walks. Eating. All just..." Another yawn. "Holding me. Pretend you have no idea what everyone is talking about. Let them think we've lost our minds. Maybe we have, but how funny would that be?" She laughed, and I couldn't stop myself from joining her as I thought over the ridiculousness of her story.

"You like to be held."

"I've never liked it before. Just now. Just like this."

The moment of clarity wouldn't last. I knew that as she grew quiet and still. Minutes passed as she carried on conversations with someone who wasn't there. She called to her mother. She even started talking to God in a prayer-like fashion at one point. But she had no more insight and wasn't able to answer questions quite yet. I washed us as best as I could. I even shampooed her hair while she lay there mostly unresponsive. The thing I did the most was stare. With her, I couldn't help it. Every time her light blue eyes opened, they gripped me. Against her dark, olive skin tone, I didn't stand a chance. It didn't help that I felt that odd questioning deep within. I liked her. Sexually, of course, but perhaps it was more than that? I just wanted to revel in her beauty. Get lost in it without anything breaking the spell. I was becoming greedy and possessive with my need, and I wasn't sure what to think about that. I knew what would happen next.

"It's time to get out, slave. I need you to stand so I can dry you off."

"I won't fall off the mountain?"

I smiled as I stood, continuing to watch as I cradled her.

"I won't let you fall."

I hadn't meant it the way it came out, yet there seemed to be more behind my words. Maybe even she caught it. Josie's eyes opened, and I quickly sat her on her feet, turning off the water. I reached over, grabbing the towels just outside the walk-in shower. Her eyes were already closing making me spin and lunge for her as she swayed.

"If you fall and crack your head open, you're going to be in so much trouble. I'll leave you here to bleed out."

Blue. They met me as she lifted her arms for me to hold her again.

"No. I need to dry you off. You're going to have to wait until we get in bed. Put your arms straight up. Not to me."

She obeyed, immediately dancing as she began to sway her

A. A. DARK

hips and sing. I cursed under my breath, trying to dry her as her arms went this way and that. Crouching, I eased the towel around one leg, pausing as I came face to face with her pussy.

How the fuck was I going to do this for the next few days and not give in to at least taste her? I had no idea as I forced myself to move faster. I wanted nothing more than to make her moan as I explored every inch of her with my tongue. Yes, I wanted her to come while I licked and sucked against her.

"It's c-c-cold. I'm an ice cube. My arms and legs are frozen." She became still, fear morphing her face. "Oh, God. I can't move. I'm stuck. I'm really stuck. I'm so c-c-cold."

"Then you need blankets. Hurry, go to the room and climb under them."

"*I can't.* I." Her head bobbed in place, but she didn't step. "I'm stuck. Look at me. My feet are becoming a part of this glacier. I'm becoming rooted. Oh, *shit*, I'm turning into a tree."

"Turn into a bird and fly your ass to the bed before I toss you that way."

The terror had me laughing like a monster. That only had me laughing even harder as I picked her up and carried her in the room, tossing her on the bed. The scream just made it worse. I was laughing so hard I could barely breathe.

"It's swallowing me, Master, please! It's quicksand. I don't want to fall through. It's trying to eat me."

I could barely stop laughing enough to answer her. The things I could say to that. I almost did, but I stopped myself. "If you don't want to fall, swim. Like you're in a pool."

"A pool? Oh! Of course."

Climbing on, my smile stayed as she moved her arms through the air mesmerized. It didn't hold a candle to how captivated I was. Watching Josie trip out on drugs wasn't something I should have found funny, but it was, and I didn't care. I doubted anyone had ever seen her this way. This care-free and alive. This afraid. Laughing. Crying. Pouting. Seductive. Had anyone ever got to see her as her true self? *Had she?* This was who she was under all the layers of conditioning. The circumstance didn't matter, it was the emotions that did.

"How is someone so beautiful? God did good choosing you to preach."

My smile fell, and I rested back against the headboard. "I see you're no longer swimming on my bed. Welcome back." My mouth twisted. "I'm a good actor, I guess."

"Acting?" She laughed. "No one could mimic passion like that. A part of you believes in what you're doing. You care about it, despite who you are underneath. You know that saying." Josie was starting to slow as the drug began kicking back in. "Angels...and all."

"I have no idea what saying you're talking about. The only saying I can think that relates to me is, 'even the devil was an angel'.

"Are you, Master?"

"The devil...or an angel?"

"Both."

"Hmm. Am I both?" My head nodded. "Sometimes."

"You know that saying." She stopped and time stretched until she forced her lids open. "You have to sin to be saved. No one is without sin. You're the only one who can control how much you give into it. That's the difference."

My eyes rolled as I pulled her away from the edge. She was on her knees, lids mostly closed while she rocked.

"You're not going to start preaching to me, are you, slave? You're thinking too hard. Where's my angel? I want you to talk more to him or God."

Just the mention had her eyes opening and her head turning to the spot she'd stared at before.

"He's right there. You talk to him. He doesn't want to talk to me."

"Is that right. Well…I can't talk to him because I can't see or hear him."

"He said you can you just choose not to listen."

My lips pursed through the slight annoyance.

"I do not hear voices. My own, yes, but—" I stopped. "I only hear me. I don't hear another version of me."

"It's still you, Master."

"Ask him what happens when we die."

Silence played out as she swayed.

"He said come see for yourself. Drink the tea."

"I have before."

"Then you know."

My head shook. "It didn't work for me like it does for you. I didn't see much. Just…shapes and darkness. I saw…I heard." I stopped. What I saw wasn't bright colors and paradise. It was dark and thick. Engulfing and suffocating. Sadness. Sorrow. Screams. So many screams and sounds of misery. It was all negative emotions and trauma after trauma as I relived my abusive past from my important father. I had been so alone. So… degraded and humiliated at every turn. I was never good enough, and when my path was finally chosen for me, I thought I could embrace it. After all, a part of me connected with pain, even if I didn't feel it as much as others. Maybe that part of me was broken due to the amounts I'd had to endure over my life. I wasn't sure. All I knew was my father wasn't proud. He laughed as if it were the best joke in the world. It was another reason for him to throw my weaknesses in my face. After all, I'd never be good enough to head up our family corporation. That's what my older brother Paul was for. I was the outcast. The weaker of the Attaways. They had no fucking idea who I was. Where they were bloodthirsty for business, I just liked to spill blood. We were not the same.

When I didn't continue, neither did Josie. She was probably somewhere different now, floating through some psychedelic heaven, having the best damn trip of her life. My sudden need for her attention took over as my mood soured even more. I hated to think of my family. I hated my past even more. I grabbed Josie's hips, startling her for only a moment as I put her on my lap to straddle.

"You wanted me last night."

My tone was sharp making Josie sad as she reached up to cup my face. "You're angry."

"Frustrated. Yes."

"At me?"

"At life." I blinked away the riptide of disappointment sucking me down. I never thought about the family part of my life. I didn't care to. Now that it was here, the last thing I wanted to do was face it. "You wanted me to kiss you last night. To touch you. You *wanted* me. Do you still?"

"Would it matter?"

"Probably not because I want you. I'm the Master. I get what I want."

Her palms lifted from my jaw as her fingers traced down my cheeks.

"Is that really you though? The mindset is, but the angel says that's not all you are. You're more, Anthony. You can be the Master. You can be the dark robe. You can be pastor and helper, and God still loves you. He'll still forgive you if you only ask for it. Do you ever ask for forgiveness for what you've done?"

"What I say between me and God is for his ears only."

"Alright." Her whisper was barely audible as she moved more against me. She was hovering just shy of my lips, easing her breasts against me as if she couldn't stand to be so far apart. Or maybe that's what I was feeling. "Master...I should move off your lap."

"You could try, but I won't let you."

My palms slid from her hips, up to her waist. Josie's eyes closed, and the way she ground herself was truly the only heaven

I was sure of. My lips met hers, and I wrapped my arms around her, one sliding to the base of her neck as I held tightly. Her tongue eagerly met mine sending the dominant part of me primal.

I was never a good boyfriend or lover. Most couldn't handle my level of intensity. I didn't have to worry about that with her. I didn't even have to let my mind go there, but it did as I rolled her to her back.

Years of celibacy didn't hinder what was ingrained. All I'd thought about since I bought my slave was this moment right here. One, I never thought I'd allow to come. Had I thought myself stronger than this?

It wasn't about strength in my moment. As I lowered sucking against her neck, need was what ruled me. The taste of her skin alone had my body on fire. Whimpers and sighs left my slave, and when I made it to her breast and sucked her nipple into my mouth…a small cry sent my pulse to speeds it hadn't been at in years.

"Anthony." She gasped, spreading her legs wider as my free hand settled between them. I squeezed the fullness of her breast with my other, using my teeth to tug against the hard nub that I couldn't get enough of. "Anthony, don't stop. Don't—"

Her hips arched, and I smiled as I recalled the last orgasm she'd had. Could I make her come just as fast? I wanted to. I wanted her screaming over and over as she craved nothing but what I could give her.

"Right there. Oh, God." Her head lifted as I slid one of my digits in deep. The tight wetness had my jaw repeatedly clenching as I made slow thrusts, teasing her clit in the process. Already, she was growing louder, moving against my finger as she fisted the blanket. "Master, you won't stop?"

"Not until I get what I want."

I lowered, still fingering her as I dipped down to suck back against her breast. Josie's sounds grew within seconds. Her head shook back and forth and the moment I stretched her with the tip of my second finger, she burst into spasms. I continued the thrusts, filling her with my digits as I sucked her nipple even harder. The moment she began to come down, I withdrew, sliding her fingers in my mouth.

"That's what I wanted. Now, let's try that again."

BI297

It was only a matter of time. Maybe I'd known that all along. After all, my Master was a man. In my experience, men had a hard time resisting themselves around women. There was something about needing to assert their power over us they couldn't resist. Was I angry? At the moment, quite the opposite. Was I surprised? Not at all. Anthony may have been a pastor, but he was still a man. It didn't stop him from wearing his black robe. From killing women. I knew it wouldn't stop him from having sex with me someday too. I could try to fight this all I wanted, but there was nothing left for me to do. Fighting it anymore was pointless. Not only because he was the Master and had decided, but because I'd been fantasizing about this moment now for years. Sure, that had been before I knew he was involved with my trafficking, but now that it was a fact, I had to let that go and use it to my advantage. Not his. Not the Gardens. *Mine.* If I had learned anything from the streets it was to put myself first. To be thorough. Most importantly…to know someone before you did business with them. The streets created fighters. We were smart. Fluid, always morphing. We were a different breed. Our breed learned to survive no matter where we ended up.

"Four orgasms. *Fuck*," my Master moaned. A growl rumbled his throat as he gave one last suck to my pussy and lifted.

I technically wasn't doing business with Anthony, but I was methodical in planning. I'd researched the man quite thoroughly before I went to that church. With my past and who I was, I had to. Routines had become part of my life. I'd become quite organized as I sobered, and although I met a lot of new friends, I stayed extremely cautious. My intentions had been to stay clean. To get my life together like the new crowd I hung out with and join the church community so I could be good. *Safe.* I'd wanted to start a new life. My crush on the pastor may have had me going above and beyond in the research department. By a miracle, it was paying off. I may have been delusional. I may have had no clue what I was seeing or saying…but even drugged, I'd never been stupid. Somehow, my brain was finding ways to have this benefit me, and if I could give him the answers he needed, I may just end up with more than I ever prayed for. That still didn't answer some of my own questions, like the black robe for instance. I hadn't known that secret before the hallucination told me about it. That part freaked my Master out the most. If I wanted to be honest, it terrified the hell out of me.

"I could do this all night. I should stop." But my Master wasn't stopping. He was allowing me to pull him down so we could kiss.

"I don't want you to stop. I want to keep going."

Anthony kissed me hard, lifting enough to scan my face.

"You're coming down faster than last night. You haven't had any hallucinations in almost an hour. At least not any that's stolen you from this. You're…aware."

Heat burned my face as I nodded. That only had him going back to kiss me even more. The tip of his hard cock pushed against my entrance, and I spread my legs wider, welcoming him as he began to inch forward.

"Dammit. Fuck. Slave."

My nails pushed into his back as I arched, taking him even deeper. The moan that left me as he surged and buried himself was one I couldn't have held in if I wanted. My Master felt so good inside of me. His thrusts were slow but steady, and I couldn't stop the surreal feeling from taking over. What were the odds that I had gone to his church, been taken, and then bought by him close to a year later? That I even saw him as they took me. Our eyes had met and...something passed between us. We'd already established that.

"Anthony." His fingers fisted almost angrily in my hair sending pain shooting through. "*Master.*" I cried out, pushing my nails into his back. "You feel so good. This is—" I gasped as he slammed into me.

"Too good. This is all..." He moaned. "I know this part, slave."

"What part?"

His eyes were slightly narrowed, and he pounded in slow but hard thrusts.

"The part where I obsess over your pussy. The part where I have sex with you at every turn. You're about to find out why I don't fuck my slaves or get involved with anyone. I wasn't in this sort of place because I was drawn to explore the afterlife, Josie. I'm about to drown myself in everything you...until I can't take it. And it will happen. It has every single time I've gotten involved with someone. Do you want to guess what happens when I overwhelm myself with you?"

Harder he slammed, holding my gaze as my body betrayed me and my orgasm built.

"You're going to kill me."

My words were weak. Barely audible.

"I won't have a choice. But you'll see that soon enough. Or

472

maybe you'll pull a miracle out of your hat and prove me wrong. Either way…" He ground himself, his hips digging into my inner thighs. "*I have you now.*"

To scramble, to fight, would have been the worst thing in our moment. Maybe he even expected me to try. His eyes were wild. His sudden hold on the back of my neck was even a tad too secure. The defiance in me built, but I kept his stare, almost as a challenge. Maybe that's what he needed. Bold but submissive. Timid but strong. I'd be so quiet, he wouldn't see me unless I wanted him to. And if he thought to smother himself with me, maybe I'd do it first. There was an answer to everything, I just had to find the right balance for my Master. He wasn't going to leave me much of a choice.

"You're holding back, slave." My body swayed with the increasing thrusts. "You're right there on the brink of having another orgasm, but you're too scared."

Slowly, my head went back and forth.

"I'm afraid, but that's not why I don't come."

"Then, why?"

"To prove a point, Master. You don't have me unless I give it. You can take my body, but that wouldn't satisfy you. You're not doing this for the sex. What you want is for my pussy to crave you too. To know your cock makes it feel good. When you lose my mind, you lose my pussy. You can fuck it bloody if that's what you want. It may even get wet. What won't happen is pleasure. If that's gone, this is what you get…my boredom."

My Master wouldn't have looked anymore shocked if I would have kicked him clear across the room.

"Boredom?"

"You ruined our perfect moment by throwing in some threat you assume might happen. As if I'm like every other girl you've fucked. You better recognize real fast, I'm so much better." My arms crossed over my chest as he continued to try to bring me back to our moment. My breasts bounced through the slams. He even shifted my hips and ground into me. Sure, it felt good, but two could play this game.

"Slave."

"I won't come. You ruined it. There's only one way to change my mind. You want me back?"

Anger filled my Master's face as he stopped and glared down at me.

"Well?"

His stubbornness stayed in his hard expression, but he allowed me to pull him down. My lips pressed into his and at the crushing pressure, I jerked my head to the side.

"Too hard."

"Slave, you really don't want to test me. I'm a second from beating you."

"And I believe you, but if you want me to come, you're going to have to earn it." I eased him down again, adding passion to my kiss as I coaxed his lips open. Anthony massaged his mouth into mine, sighing into me as he slid in his tongue. His body relaxed, and his movements turned smooth and slow as he began to withdraw and inch back inside.

"I don't make love to women, Josie."

"I told you, I'm not just any woman. I'm *your* woman, Master. You bought me. That doesn't make me the Gardens anymore. That makes me yours."

The claiming sound that left Anthony gave me goosebumps. I wanted to smile but held it in as his kiss deepened. The thrusts were increasing in speed again, but not in brutality. He was getting so thick inside me. Pleasure reawakened, and my moans only drove my Master on. We were kissing so much we were barely breathing. Anthony was pushing so deep, I could barely control my own body. We were both on the edge, barely clinging on as pleasure reached fevered heights.

"Master." I moaned his title, knowing that's what he wanted. I bit against his lip, moving down to suck against his neck. He'd barely let me leave his mouth and the realization of that only fed my mind even more on what I needed to do and how I needed to act. He had already angled himself and found his way back to maneuvering my lips to his. "I want you to make your ownership official. I want you to stay with me. *In me.* Let it be a reminder to both of us who I belong to. *Who I really belong to.*"

He moaned, thickening so much I could barely breathe.

"Say it, Josie. Tell me."

"Come in me, Anthony. Show me how I'm the slave and you're the Master. How you own me, and how I'll only ever be yours. Give this to me. I want to feel your proof."

"I just told you what I was going to do, and everything you're saying is only going to make it worse. You said you didn't have a death wish."

My orgasm nearly won me over as I tried to find the words to speak.

"I don't. That's why I'm going to show you I'm everything you need." My hands lifted to his face. "You're not going to be able to obsess over me when you're too busy seeing me obsess over you. I'm everything you've ever wanted. I'm everything you need. You won't want to kill me because it'll be too painful to live without me. I'm a stranger, but that day our eyes met at the church, that disappeared. We connected for a reason. You bought me because you were meant to. There's no escaping this, Master. Not through death. Not for either of us."

"You're too drugged up to know what you're saying."

"I know the truth." I shifted, reaching down to run my fingers over his balls. He immediately growled out, trying to kiss me, but I turned making him connect to my neck as I continued to caress. Teeth bit in hard making me cry out, but I continued to talk anyway, not giving in to his pain. "Say you like me. Say you're not going to screw this up, and you're going to let me try to be your slave."

"I give the orders here."

"Yes, you do, but say it anyway, Master." My fingers spanned over his sensitive skin, cupping and massaging. I spread my digits wide as I came to the edge of my pussy so I could feel his cock slide in and out of me. I added the smallest amount of pressure, stroking him through the thrust. Sweat was covering Anthony's face and the heat pouring from him was unreal.

"I like you. Maybe I'll kill you. Maybe I won't. What I am going to do is come in this pussy."

"Who's pussy?"

My hands both moved to Anthony's back as he cut me off with his mouth. He pounded into me and within seconds I was trying to break away to cry out. Spasms shook me as he swallowed down my scream, refusing to let me leave his lips. His cock grew thick, and I encouraged him as I tried pulling his body more into mine. Cum shot into me, and I gasped, holding tight until he was slowing.

"Mine, slave. That pussy is mine."

MASTER B-0113

I shouldn't have been smiling. Maybe I shouldn't have even left the apartment. What the fuck had happened last night? My head was still spinning. No one told me what to do. Hell, no woman had ever dared speak to me like Josie had. *Demanding. Dominant.* Yet…she hadn't taken that role; she'd only stated the demands and waited. She said what she expected without ordering me to do it. I didn't like it, yet somewhere deep inside, *perhaps I did.* It was different, and that was enough to keep me strangely intrigued. For now…

"It's a little early to be drinking, isn't it?"

I stopped just outside of Dark God Status, turning to see the Main Master.

"That's debatable. Are you headed inside?"

Elec threw me a look. "Tempting. I heard you were on my floor. I was on my way down."

"I've just come to get my robe. I had it brought up here when I arrived, but I want it back at my place. Until we know when I'll need it, I think I'll just keep it with me."

"I'll walk you in. How's it going with the new slave? I saw you disposed of your first."

Nodding, I searched for words.

"Josie is…an interesting slave." I glanced over.

"Interesting is an odd choice of words."

"Odd…maybe that's a better description. At least for how things are going." I almost winced as I thought over my concerns. "Could we figure out if she somehow..." I stopped, stealing a look back to Elec as he stared over at me curiously. "You know the quest I'm on. During her hallucinations, she was talking to someone. She said it was me, but an angel. She knew things she couldn't have unless she looked into me on the outside. Could we figure out if she did?"

"What sort of things did she know?"

We headed through the dark club, but Elec stopped me at the bar, gesturing for me to sit down. I didn't have to tell the slave in the yellow headdress what I wanted. Elec nodded, and the slave seemed to know.

"She says she talked to an angel. He mentioned human sacrifice. Murder. He told her I came from an elite family. She mentioned Toledo, where my family owns a house, and 'blood lines'. I don't like it, and I'm not sure how she could know that unless she investigated me before she was even taken. Which she admitted doing to an extent, but she swears it was all church related. She came to us for help with her addiction. She said she watched a lot of the past shows before deciding to show up. That's it. Yet, she knew about the robe. The angel told her I led the group. She knew things she couldn't have."

The Main Master took his drink from the slave, his mood shifting immediately. I grabbed mine, not waiting to shoot it back.

"Family. Status. She could have easily found that and maybe did without even realizing it. You wouldn't believe what people remember once they're under the influence of psychedelics. As for the robes and what we do here at the club," his eyes cut to mine, "no way she could have known that. Not without one of us telling her. And you know the rules. We don't speak on robe business outside of our meetings. *Ever.*" His finger tapped against the bar through his sudden anger. "If someone is whispering secrets behind our backs, I'll find out who." Elec finished off his drink just as fast as me, standing. I joined him, heading to the back doors that were nearly camouflaged in the surrounding black walls.

"Tell me more about your slave. Has she asked you any questions concerning us? Who's a member? Where our meetings are located? Anything that might seem suspicious?"

My head tilted as I looked over at him.

"No. Nothing like that. She was under the influence when she spoke about this. I nearly choked her to death for even saying it out loud."

"Do you think it's possible she could be a Seer?"

Elec slammed his palm into the door, sending it flying open as he brought us to a room that looked similar to the lounging areas outside. Two sofas filled the space, along with a chaise, and a few chairs. Mirrors were on the wall, and a clothing rack was off to the side of it. My robe was hanging there, covered in a garment bag.

I slowed. "A Seer? Here? Aren't those spies? I'm afraid I don't know much about them."

"I'm not surprised. They're rarely talked about outside of higher circles. They're usually used in the outside world to maintain balance, but I'm hearing stories of them being placed in our cities throughout the world. We've only come across one so far in the Gardens, and it was completely by chance. Maybe it was an isolated event, but I'm not so sure. It was during the blank slate transition. During the process, the slave broke, rambling what sounded like a confession on how he was here for information. Sadly, his brain was already too scrambled to get anything more. He was one of the few who couldn't be brought back. These...spies or outsiders. I believe someone is slipping them in through the scouts. They go through the process, and they report to a Master or Mistress, but for what...I'd like to know. Maybe they're gaining information from other Main Masters or maybe..." His face tightened as he shook his head. "It could be anything. What I do know is I won't fucking tolerate it."

"I don't like that. You think Josie might be one of these spies?"

One of his eyebrows rose. "Grab your robe. Let's go find out."

My stomach twisted, knotting as I walked over, snatching the garment bag. Could my slave really be a spy? Too many emotions collided for me to pick them apart. Anger, yes, but also...betrayal, sadness? No. Surely, that wasn't what I was feeling. Surprise, yes, but...I wasn't quite ready to see her die. Those emotions were the hardest to decipher.

The Main Master and I took off at a quick pace.

"When we get there, I don't want you to say a word. Let me do all the talking. Don't look at her. Don't acknowledge her presence. I need her complete focus if I'm going to get answers. Understand, Master?"

This was business, and Elec wanted me to see that as we left the club and headed for the elevator. "Yep."

"Good. I know you like this slave, but if she's a spy—" The abrupt silence had me looking over.

"I know. She's dead."

"She'll wished she was."

My eyes met his and I nodded, pushing the odd stirring away. I shouldn't have cared in the least. I knew what was at stake. Still...there was something there, even if it was small.

"What do we know about this slave's past other than she was an addict who showed up at your church?"

We stepped on the elevator. "I think I know most of her life. It's what I've been working on. She grew up in a small town. Her dad was away most of the time, working. She lived with her mother and grandmother and had six brothers and sisters. At fifteen, Josie ran away, was picked up by a trucker, and lost her virginity on the last night of the three-day drive. He left her at a truck stop that morning, abandoning her. I'm sure that fucked up her head even more than whatever made her leave to begin with. She made it to LA and was homeless. She was eventually trafficked where they got her hooked on drugs. You know how that goes. She stayed there until she was nineteen or twenty and managed to escape. When she came to my church, she said she was clean; she was just battling the need to fall back into drugs. She never had the chance. We took her."

The Main Master was on his phone, pushing through buttons and sliding from screen to screen. He didn't even look up as the doors open and we headed out.

"Josie Marie Lockhart Ortega, twenty-three-year-old female—"

"Wait. Ortega?"

"That's right." He flipped through more screens. "Married at twenty-one to a Phillip Ortega from...Phoenix. He was twenty-nine when they married." More he flipped screens. "It looks like she filed for an annulment a month after they married but it was delayed because...ah, she was pregnant."

"*Pregnant?*"

I couldn't keep the shock from my tone.

"Only briefly. According to this hospital report, she lost it a little over a month later from an accident." His head shook as he slowed on my hall and came to a stop a few doors shy of mine. "Toxicology report here says she's clean. That had to have been...a few months before she was brought here. You didn't know any of this?"

"No. She never once mentioned anything about a husband or pregnancy."

"Not even under the ayahuasca?

My head shook to Elec. "No. Nothing. Who's Phillip Ortega? You got this look when you read his name."

"There's not much information under his section. I've never heard of him, but he has quite the record."

"For what?"

"Drugs. Trafficking. There's mention of cartel association. From what's listed, I wouldn't say he's a small player, either."

Was I angry? Jealous? Raging? I didn't know what to feel as I gestured to my door and followed the Main Master that way. I pulled out my card, sliding it in and pushing the door open. Josie surged to her feet at seeing us. Our eyes met, and I knew I couldn't hide the boiling emotions. The Main Master stepped forward, and I didn't even look to Josie as I headed for my closet. It didn't matter that I wasn't in the room. I could still hear the Main Master as he approached her.

"Sit, slave. You and I need to talk."

"You both look mad. Did I do something wrong?"

I hung up the robe, turning to head back to the living room. But I didn't stop there. I went into the kitchen, grabbing the bottle. To hell with the hour. Who cared if it was barely lunch time. I needed a drink. I wasn't sure I was prepared for what else Josie was hiding. And she was hiding something. I was sure of it.

"I hear you've seen some interesting things. Would you like to tell me about them?"

I glanced up. When Josie looked towards me, the Main Master snapped his fingers, pulling her attention back to him.

"You're not to look at your Master, slave. Only me. Tell me what you saw. All of it. If you hide or lie about anything, I will know, and it will not be good for you."

I took a sip, able to watch now that her focus was on Elec.

"I've seen so much, Main Master. Most of it is a blur, but I do remember some things vividly clear. My life seems to be a big theme when I drink the tea. It plays over and over. Sometimes it's in my parents' point of view. I see their sides. I see my own. It's usually from birth to when I leave. I've seen…" Her head lowered. "I know it sounds crazy, but my Master comes to me as an angel. He tells me things. Sometimes he takes me places and shows me."

"Don't leave anything out, no matter how crazy it sounds."

She nodded, picking at her fingers as she kept them sitting on her lap.

"He showed me parts of the Master's life. Sort of like when I see from my parents' point of view. It's just the Master's. I was in a big house in Toledo. I don't know how I knew where I was, but I heard the word in my head. The house was two story with brown brick. It had bright red carpet over the stairs. Dark wood on the walls throughout. I…saw the Master's room. There was," her hand lifted. "Sports posters on the walls and…lots of bookshelves. He had a desk not feet from his bed which had dark blue bedding. There was even a little whale pillow by a blue and white striped pillow."

I slammed the glass down. "*Impossible.* How the hell do you know that? I haven't stayed in that bedroom since I was ten. It doesn't even look like that anymore. It hasn't since after I left."

The Main Master threw me a look, and I grew quiet as Josie's eyes filled with tears.

"What else, slave?"

"I was shown the Master in his church. Tunnels and roads underground but running…*everywhere.* There were so many slaves from all over being brought to some old castle or something. It looked odd. Like…not stable on its own. As if it were built into the underground. The castle was fine and suddenly it was crumbling to the ground. I saw, I saw…" A sob left her. "More before that. The Master was in this castle. He was there cutting apart some blonde slave. Lots of dark-haired slaves before that. It was as if time was running backwards. There was more, but it's so hard for me to remember that part since everything was jumbling together. I was going in and out of all these different visions." She wiped her eyes, but tears were still coming. "I also saw robes. Black robes and circles. Blood. Women being killed in the center. But not by the men..." she sniffled. "By themselves, Main Master. From...you. You made them do that." Josie was shaking from fear so much that she couldn't sit still. Even her jaw was chattering. "I had a dream this morning that you came and took me. You hurt me. Kill me." A sob. "Is that why you're here?"

"That depends. We're going to try something, slave. If I feel you're telling the truth, maybe you can stay. If I think you're lying to me, then yes, you will come with me, and I will scrape the truth from your brain until I'm satisfied that what you're telling me isn't some bullshit story you heard from another Master or Mistress."

The Main Master leaned forward, grabbing behind her knees and jerking her to the bottom of the sofa. He wasn't happy. I'd never seen Elec be physical with any slave. He restrained from touching anyone if he could help it, yet the thought that she was a Seer was getting to him. Anything that wasn't complete trust rattled him, and he wasn't sure what to think of her story any more than I was.

"Face me and stare into my eyes. What we're about to do isn't a fast process so you might as well stop crying and *relax*. So long as you tell me the truth, you have nothing to be afraid of. You are safe with me, slave. *Relax,* and keep staring into my eyes."

His tone was smooth. Not too loud, but not too soft. His knees were nearly touching Josie's and their stares were locked as he continued.

"There's nothing more that I want than to walk out of here and let you stay with your Master. I believe you to be a good person. I don't think you're here to cause any harm. *Relax.* Feel the tension leave your legs. Let them loosen as you look even deeper into my eyes."

GARDEN OF THE GODS

His hand lifted, but he didn't move it, and Josie kept her focus on Elec.

"When you were in your cell, you've seen me do this. You saw it on your television. Do you remember?"

"Yes, Main Master. Seven o-clock, an hour after dinner."

"That's right, slave. Every night."

"Every night," she repeated, almost robotically.

"Good. Feel the muscles in your hips and back relax. You're doing great. You feel safe. You trust me because you know as long as you tell me the truth, you won't be harmed. Even if you've done something bad, the truth will save you." His hand lowered the smallest amount, but her gaze wasn't leaving his eyes.

"Look how well you're doing. Even your arms are relaxing. You can feel the sensation moving to your shoulders and neck. You're warm. Safe. The longer you stare into me, the more your trust grows. Can you feel it, slave?"

He snapped, bringing his hand between them, using his pointer finger to trace a pattern. Her eyes caught the movement, and she was following it back and forth. He snapped again and her gaze jumped back to his eyes.

"Beautiful. What is your name?"

"Josie Marie Lockhart."

"Why do you not go by your married last name? You're still married."

"I can't."

"You can't use your name?"

"No, Main Master."

"Why?"

Josie was like a statue as she stared ahead, but she didn't appear tense, just frozen.

"He's looking for me. I don't want to die."

"You feared for your life?"

"Yes, Main Master."

"Who is Phillip Ortega?"

Trembling. It hit her despite that she was under Elec's spell. "Bad."

"You married him. You got pregnant by him. How bad can he be?"

"*Bad.* I didn't know. I thought he was a different person. He lied to me."

"Who is Phillip Ortega?"

"He owned a club. I never went to it. I wouldn't be around that environment." Her words were slow. "I didn't know he was hurting people. I tried to file for divorce when Lori told me. They wouldn't let me."

"Shh." Elec's finger began to move again. "*Relax.* Breathe. You're not in trouble for Phillip. I'm only curious about him. You're safe now. He can't find you here."

"He'll take me away. He tried to already. He took me to Phoenix. He was going to take me to Mexico. I didn't want to go. He forced me in the car. I...I...got in an accident trying to escape him. I—" A sob.

"You lost your baby. I'm sorry, slave." He let a few seconds pass. "I know you're upset, but we'll go through this together. Just walk me through it. After you were released from the hospital, was he there, waiting for you?"

"I left before he could find me."

"And you went back to Los Angeles?"

"Yes, Main Master."

"Keep going. Tell me what you did, then."

"I stayed with a friend until I got a job at the hotel under a fake name. I was scared. The addict in me wanted the escape, but I refused to give in. I focused on work, but it was so hard. But then I saw Pastor Anthony on the television." Immediately, the tension melted from her body. Elec seemed to notice it too as he glanced my way.

"And this was the first time you'd ever heard of him before?"

"Yes."

Elec nodded.

"Keep going."

"I was doing laundry when I first saw his show. I watched the entire thing, mesmerized. He was so beautiful. What he was saying…it was like he was speaking directly to me."

"What did you do when the show ended?"

"My laundry."

"And then what?"

"I grabbed dinner from the diner across the street and watched more of the pastor's shows. I watched them for hours. Days. I watched as many as I could. They helped with the cravings. Anthony was the closest I could get to God. I knew God would help me."

Again, Elec shot me a look. This time, there was slight sarcastic amusement on his features.

"Did you look into the pastor outside of the church?"

Josie's lashes fluttered as she still stared ahead.

"He had a website. I'd heard Phillip was in town, and I was afraid. There was a contact page. I only wanted to escape the drugs and Phillip together. He was going to take me. The website promised to help with lots of things. Domestic abuse was there too. I just…" she broke down again and I cursed under my breath. "He would have killed me."

"*Relax.* There we go. That's it." The Main Master moved his finger until he was satisfied that she was back under as deep as he wanted. "How did you know about Whitlock?"

Josie's mouth opened but no words came out at first.

"I don't know what Whitlock is, Main Master."

"The underground castle you saw. The place you saw your Master killing those girls. Who told you about it?"

"The angel did. It was my Master."

"Are you saying you know of Whitlock from a hallucination?"

487

"Yes."

"No one told you about this place?"

"Yes, my Master did. He was an angel."

Elec shifted in his seat, snapping. He moved his hand back and forth, snapping again as Josie's eyes returned to his.

"No one told you about Whitlock, other than your Master?"

"No. The angel version of my Master told me."

Elec shook his head, clearly frustrated.

"What about the robes? Who told you about the ceremonies?"

"My Master did...as an angel."

Repeatedly, Elec's jaw tightened, and his face grew harder.

"Tell me about where you saw the ceremonies."

"They were on a stage. My Master was leading one, even though I couldn't see his face. I knew it was him. He had a girl hidden in his robe. He got to the stage and forced her out. She fell on the floor, and she was screaming."

The Main Master's eyes met mine, but he didn't speak. He went back to her.

"What does the girl look like?"

"Dark hair. Thin." Josie stopped. "I saw her here in a cell. Not with the other slaves. She's..." her hand pointed down. "Deeper. In a secret room. You see her, Main Master. Every day. I've seen the ceremony, but you haven't killed her yet. You will, and I know how you're going to do it."

The Main Master stood, angrily, only to sit back down.

"Keep going. How?"

"You'll make her cut out her own heart, and she will. She'll die right there on that stage, and you'll take her heart and send it to...Kressling Industries. Rob...Burlett."

The Main Master snapped twice, fisting Josie's hair as he shook her violently. He stood, jerking her up to her feet. My slave was so startled and lost, she started screaming.

"Enough. How did you know that? *I told no one.* You expect me to believe you learned of that from a hallucination?"

"Please! I swear." She sobbed, trying to reach back to hold to his wrists. Elec dropped her, putting a good foot between them. He looked at me and all I could do was shrug and shake my head. I was just as perplexed, and I had no idea what to do about it.

"Sit down, slave. We're not finished."

Elec stalked to me, growling the moment he made it to my side.

"She's either uninfluenced by what I'm doing, or she's telling the truth. How she..." His hand lifted as he pushed his fingers through his hair. "*Fucking impossible.*"

"Or not. Main Master, as hard as it is for us to believe, you can't imagine how many accounts I've come across just like this. It's not as unheard of as you think. Maybe Josie is just...more open than others."

"Are you saying she's fucking psychic because if you're insinuating—"

"Elec, I'm just saying she knows, and it doesn't appear to be coming from any person that's...alive. What that means, I don't know. Why do you think I'm doing this? Admit it," I said, lifting my brows. "This is some crazy shit. You can't pretend it's not. Our own military used the same techniques. There's something behind consciousness, but what the hell it is, we don't know. Answers come. Visions happen. Sometimes they're eerily accurate, sometimes they're not. Josie's picked up on some things. They wouldn't have come had I not drugged her. I really think this was some sort of fluke occurrence. She saw shit she shouldn't have seen, but she saw it. Let me keep going with this. Maybe she'll see more. Perhaps something beneficial for both of us. It can't hurt. It's not like she's in the outside world. She belongs to me. She's a slave to the Gardens. If anything, we could use this to our advantage. Or…maybe the hallucinations will just be bullshit from here on out."

He shifted on his feet, keeping his gaze in her direction. Josie was on the sofa, wiping tears that wouldn't stop.

"Psychic or Seer. Do I need to tell you which one is more logical? I don't like this, and I'm not taking any chances." He looked back at me. "I'm going to have my people check her out. Not tonight, I have pressing appointments I can't cancel, but soon. Perhaps when you leave. Then I can have her returned when you're headed back."

"Of course. I plan to stay until after…" my hand waved to the bedroom. "I guess until after you have the girl cut out her own heart. Is that what you were really planning on doing?"

"I hadn't decided. I guess I have now. I like that better than what I had originally come up with." His lips twisted. "It's actually fucking perfect, and I hate how I heard it from her. How the hell did she know…" He grew quiet, glaring towards my slave.

"I don't know, but something is going on, and I plan to figure out what it is. Let me know when you're ready. In the meantime, I'll continue the tea. There's no rush. I told you I was planning on taking a week or two leave anyway. If Josie is really seeing this stuff, I want to see what else she comes up with."

B1297

"Yου're mad at me. You're going to have to get over it. My loyalty is to my Main Master. It is not to you. He had a right to know what you saw. Besides, I don't know why you're sitting there pouting. I'm the one who was lied to, *Mrs. Ortega*."

My eyes sliced in Anthony's direction, but I didn't argue or explode like I wanted. I was too emotionally drained for that. I was tired. Weak. All I wanted to do was crawl back in bed and sleep.

"You could have told me, Josie."

"No offense, Master, but I truly didn't believe you'd care."

"We had work to do. I told you to tell me about your life and you completely skipped over the biggest part. Marriage and a child. Those are huge moments.

My mouth parted, but I breathed through the need to raise my voice.

"You don't think I know that? *Pastor...*" I paused at the glare from not using his correct title. "Do you understand how personal that is? Losing a child...it's too hard for me to talk about. To even *think* about. I've been through so much, but those months were the scariest, most heartbreaking moments of my life. I just can't."

"Obviously not. Even your mind is blocked to that part of your life when you're on drugs. That is harder for me to believe than some left-field vision of robes. It seems impossible. Almost..."

He stopped, standing from the sofa to pace. The Main Master only left an hour ago, and I was terrified he'd knock on the door and change his mind. He wanted me to see doctors below. I was dreading the thought of having them poke around on me. So far, I was safe. I wasn't sure how much longer I could go without them discovering that I knew more about my Master when I'd arrived. It wasn't technically a big deal, but to them it might be. Regardless, I wouldn't worry. I knew how to twist things around to play in my favor. And they were only little lies. The fact was, I knew stuff I wasn't supposed to. I saw those visions. I hadn't made them up. I couldn't change any of it. What I spoke had been the truth. Maybe I was going crazy. Hadn't I been through enough trauma and stress to trigger some sort of breakdown? I sure felt like I was experiencing one. Maybe that's exactly what was happening.

"Master, I don't want to talk about this anymore. I'm tired. May I take a nap?"

"A nap?"

"A nap."

The Master left the edge of the kitchen, walking back into the living room where I sat on the sofa. "I can barely restrain myself as it is. Are you sure you want to get so close to a bed?"

My skin flared with heat as I stood.

"Don't pretend you liked it so much. We both know you have better things to do."

I turned, heading for the room. Not too fast. Not too slow. I barely made it to the entrance of the bedroom when an arm wrapped around my waist and his other hand fitted over my mouth. He lifted my back to rest against his chest as he carried me to the bed. The moment we approached, his hand tightened over my lips, and he lowered to the mattress, trapping me underneath his weight. A moment of panic had me turning my head to the side. I thrashed against the restraint, only feeling it secure even more.

"Don't presume to know anything about me. If you did research me online more than you say, you'll come to find the only thing that's true is names and dates. Who I am on paper doesn't define the man who could easily snap your neck. If you're a spy, collecting information on the Gardens, you'll suffer a death so painful and torturous, you'll regret ever taking the assignment."

"A spy?"

My muffled question may have been hard to understand, but my Master didn't miss the shock and fear that dripped from my tone.

"You know too much, Josie. Information no one could know. You better confess to me right now how it came to you. Did a Master pay you? Approach and threaten you? Maybe if I put in a good word—"

I could still see the evil in the Main Master's eyes. It nearly took my breath away. Is that what they thought was happening? My head shook frantically. "I'm no spy." I thrashed even more, my denial getting lost in the vibrations filling his hand as he pressed into my mouth harder. "Pastor, let go. *I'm no spy.*"

Still, he kept me trapped. Did he understand what I was saying? I thought so, but maybe he didn't want to know. He held tight, nuzzling the side of his face against my hair.

"I said I'd have no attachment to you, but I can't deny, I think I'd be a little bored if you died so soon. We have so much to explore, Josie. So many more tea-trips to take. I almost can't wait for tonight. Do you think you'll see more things you shouldn't? You never told me you saw me at Whitlock. I should make you suffer for having to hear it in front of the Main Master first. Maybe I will."

Anthony shifted, unbuckling and pushing down his pants, still using his weight to keep me pinned down. His hand didn't ease from my mouth. It stayed over my lips almost bruisingly as he forced my legs open wider, keeping them pinned with his. I made continuous sounds, a mix between moans and rejections as he slid his fingers in deep.

"We should have never done this, slave. I'm not sure what's going to be worse for you, being grilled and interrogated in the lab, or having to deal with me now that you've awoken the part of me that can't rest. I'm trying so hard but...*I don't want to take it easy on you.*"

His fingers left me, and pressure fit against my entrance. A rumble shook his chest, and I screamed with everything I had as he slammed forward. My entire body locked up from the twinges of pain.

"A fucking spy." He was back to burying his face against the side of mine. "You better pray to God that's not true. I swear... think back to what you saw me do to those slaves in Whitlock. Torture. Dismemberment. That'll be nothing. I'll make it a million times worse for you. I didn't give a shit about those slaves. *But you,*" a growl left him. "I enjoy this a little too much. If it gets taken away because you *lied*, I'll destroy you for doing this to me."

My words were irrelevant. The Master couldn't understand them, and I truly didn't think it mattered what I had to say. He knew what he wanted, and he was taking it. My body belonged to him, and what he needed wasn't soft or slow. The thrusts were getting savage as he used my body as an anchor to pound into.

"Do you have anything to confess?" His hand dropped from my mouth, cupping and holding on to the side of my throat as he continued to pin me on my stomach. I was crying. I knew that, but the odd sense of pleasure mixing with anger was warping any fear I might have had.

"I'm no spy. Let them do whatever they need. I have nothing to hide. Yes, I looked into y-you. What all I came across, I don't remember, but it was nothing bad. I needed help, and I wanted to look into the man who offered it. That's n-no crime."

"No, it's not." He lowered his chest to my back, pushing his arm underneath with the other as he hugged around my chest and biceps, trapping my arms at my sides. I could barely breathe with his weight and size, and my Master knew it as he intentionally held me captive. "I really hope you're telling the truth. Death wouldn't be this fun, slave. Don't you like this?"

"What I'd like is for you to stop thinking of yourself and turn me over. You're going too deep. It hurts."

"It hurts?" He laughed, biting hard into my shoulder until I was screaming. I fought against his hold but didn't come close to getting free.

"Pain is good. God, you're so fucking beautiful when you scream. I like you even more fired up like this."

My Master slowed his thrusts, lowering his face back into my hair as he continued to hold and fuck me. Although his hands were underneath, he still managed to reach my breast to pinch against my nipple. The pleasure sparked, but I still tried thrashing. It didn't help drown out my building need to be touched. Teased. Anything to make me cum. I knew the tea was still lingering. It would for days according to my Master. That only meant the effects would continue. But what was the tea, and which was the real me? It was hard to know when moans kept escaping.

"Look at you taking my cock so good." He slid in a few more inches making me suck in a breath. "It's all fun and games, but playtime is over. I've been easy on you long enough. Arch your hips, slave. I don't fucking care if it hurts you. That's my pussy, now, and you're going to feel what I want you to. You're going to take all of me."

I didn't move.

"Arch or I'll move my cock to your ass and really make you scream."

"Can I at least get on my knees?"

He let go of my body, and pain webbed over my scalp as fingers pushed into my hair and fisted. I didn't fight the pull that drew me up on all fours. My Master managed to stay inside of me, using my hair to draw me back as he thrust deep.

"That's so fucking hot. Arch just like that. *Jesus*." His free hand grabbed my hip only for a moment before it slid to my ass, squeezing hard into my flesh. I could feel how thick Anthony was getting. Pleasure mixed with pain as he continued to keep a steady pace, but somehow it didn't deter my impending orgasm. No matter whether I liked it or not, he hit every part inside of me that triggered ecstasy. I hated it as much as I loved it.

"Master, slow. Slow."

But he didn't slow. He slammed into me, doing the opposite. He sped up, filling the room with an echo of his skin slapping against mine. My sounds increased until I was screaming and shaking through the orgasm. And my Master…he buried himself as deep as he could go, making me cry out even more as his cum claimed me once again.

MASTER B-0113

Three days. Five days total on the tea. Nothing more. Josie battled more of her past, even seeing a child she swore was her own. An infant boy. She cried, and cried, and cried. That night had been the hardest for my slave, but the most observant for me. I watched Josie grow over the nights, falling deeper into the hallucinations of the tea as it got stronger and stronger. The angel came, but it gave nothing new. Why I was jealous that she had a three-hour conversation with a different version of me, I'll never know. What I had concluded was my slave needed some massive aftercare, and I wasn't sure how to begin. I had let her sleep, but even after twelve hours of being dead to the world, Josie didn't look any more refreshed than she had last night.

"Drink."

Her lips peeled back in distaste as she looked at the glass of green liquid.

"What is it?"

"Does it matter? I said drink it."

Lifting the glass, she brought it to her nose, sniffing.

"Josie, drink the damn smoothie."

"I'm not a fan of green vegetables."

"It's not just vegetables." I cursed. "Would it make you feel better if I said it was a cum cocktail? You sure drank mine down last night."

She threw me a look, narrowing her eyes. "Where's your green drink?"

"I don't look like I've gone on a five-day bender. You look like shit. The dark circles under your eyes are unreal. Drink the smoothie or so help me, I'll make you. And hurry. We need to get out today. I thought we'd go see a movie. It starts in less than an hour."

"*A movie? Really?*"

"Yep. Hurry before I change my mind and chain you to my bed like I'd prefer."

She squealed, cringing before bringing the glass up to take a drink. Her brow creased only to lift in surprise.

"This isn't bad at all. I think I like it."

"Good. You're going to be living on smoothies between meals from here on out. I figure we'll let you rest a few days before we go again with the tea."

Her smile grew as she danced around the kitchen. I knew the tea was still working its magic in the background, but I almost wished she'd stay in a playful mood all the time. At least until I wanted to flip her darker. I liked a good fight. It wasn't hard to trigger her. As for now, I was content with keeping her happy.

"I'm so excited. What are we going to see, Master? Oh, what should I wear? I can dress up, right? I have so many pretty dresses. Do you have one you like the most? There's a red one—"

"Slow down, slave. The red one will be perfect. I think the show is a mystery or something. I didn't really look. I chose the one that didn't sound stupid."

Her lips puckered the smallest amount making me want to kiss them. With her, I was insatiable. Maybe I thought by now I'd tire of her body, but it was so far from the truth that it made my head spin. I didn't get attached. It just didn't happen. Not until her, anyway. I couldn't deny there was something there. Maybe there always had been, but with each tea-trip, with each day, each argument or fight, she hooked me even more. I couldn't even stand for her to be asleep when I wasn't. If I was awake, she'd be too. If I wanted to get the hell out of the apartment, she was coming with me. It wasn't just the need to possessively be with her. Even though we bickered, it was real. It was ours. *It was fun*...At least for me, and that's all that really mattered.

"I can't wait. I can't *wait*." Josie was chugging down the drink, still dancing in place in random moments. When the knock came, I wasn't sure who was more disappointed, me or her.

"Who the hell is that?" I didn't wait as I headed for the door. When I swung open the barrier, I became even more confused. Two guards were standing there, a third quickly hanging up the phone as he walked up. But he wasn't just anyone. Nineteen was in charge of the guards. He oversaw them all. "High Leader."

"Master B-One-thirteen?"

"That's right."

"The Main Master sends his apologies. He's a bit busy at the moment, but he's ready for your slave to be seen."

"Right now? He mentioned taking her while I was gone. I thought we agreed on more time."

"He must have changed his mind. I was given specific instructions to retrieve her now."

Turning, I looked at Josie. Her blue eyes were big with fear as she stared between us. I wasn't sure how to feel about that when her fear wasn't coming from me.

"Of course. Come in. She'll have to get dressed. Did the Main Master mention how long she'd be gone?"

Nineteen and the guards entered at my gesture. I shut the door behind them as Josie headed for our room to get dressed.

499

"He didn't say how long she'd be undergoing testing. He did mention that you were welcome to walk her down with us. He's there now, but I'm not at liberty to go into why."

"I see. I think I'll follow you down. Maybe he'll have a moment to speak with me if he's not too busy. I'll go get my shoes."

Heading in the room, I didn't go for my shoes. I went to the closet, turning Josie to face me. Tears were filling her eyes, but she held them in. There was a slight shake taking her over, and I didn't like that she was afraid.

"Last chance to confess. Do you have anything to hide? If you lie to me now, I'll request to kill you myself. You won't like that."

"I'm not a spy. I swear I'm not."

Her voice cracked, but the tears stayed in place. I nodded, reaching over to grab the red dress. "Put this on. I'll be walking you down."

I turned to leave, stopping to look back at Josie's call.

"Master, what if they're wrong? What if…"

The fear was thick on her face.

What if they were?

"The Main Master will know the truth. I trust his judgement. If you're not guilty, you better do a damn good job at convincing him."

Was I coming off hard and distant because it was the way I felt or because part of me couldn't bear the thought that this didn't go the way I wanted. Josie swore she wasn't guilty of any wrong-doing, and I believed her. But what if the Main Master didn't. He wasn't happy when he left. He wanted answers. Ones none of us could give him. At least, none that he would accept. He wasn't very open-minded, when, given his work, he should have been.

I slid on my shoes, sitting on the edge of the bed. Josie walked out in her dress, wearing a pair of matching sandals. For it being winter, you wouldn't know it in the Gardens. It was always the perfect temperature in the building and city below.

"Pretty. I like it."

Josie tried to grin, but her lips barely tugged back at the side as I stood. Walking over, I put my hands on her shoulders. A slight pout took over, but she stood up straight, meeting my eyes.

"You ready?"

"Yes, Pastor."

My lips tightened. "Okay…" I paused for two seconds before I leveled my hand at her back and led her into the living room where Nineteen and the guards were waiting. We followed them out, all staying silent as we headed to the guard's side of the apartments, which happened to be opposite from the side of ours. When we approached the elevator, Nineteen slowed, letting one of his men hit the button as he moved closer to us. The doors immediately opened, and we all stepped in, riding down.

"Right this way."

Nineteen led us to some doors to the right, into what looked like all the other lobbies. He came to a stop, turning to me.

"I'm afraid this is as far as you can go. Would you like me to let the Main Master know you wish to speak with him?"

"No need, I saw you all enter."

Elec rounded a turn, heading for us. Although his tone was lighter, he didn't appear in a better mood from the last time I had seen him. I wasn't sure if I liked that. I knew he wouldn't make the wrong decision on Josie, but what if he was having a bad day and just…

"Main Master."

I lifted to shake his hand noticing his eyes were on my slave. Had that been a negative expression? Anger? I couldn't tell as he broke his gaze and slid his hand in mine.

"Master One-thirteen. Did you carry on with your experiments over the last few days?"

"I did."

501

"Anything new you need to report?"

I glanced at Josie, twisting my mouth. *If only.* At least then it might be less suspicious.

"Not really. More episodes concerning her past. She had long conversations with this…angel. Nothing really came out of it."

"Pity. Well, I'll keep you updated. The testing shouldn't take but a day or two. Maybe less, depending. I'll give you two a minute while I talk to my High Leader."

Nodding, I watched as they walked to the far end of the room. I took in Josie's tremble and the worried look on her face.

"If everything you've said is true, you have nothing to worry about."

"You say that," she breathed out, quietly. "I've already seen this, Master, in my dream. I don't think I'll be coming back. I'm a threat whether I'm a spy or not. I've seen things I shouldn't. The Main Master doesn't like that. He—" Tears spilled over, and she quickly wiped them away. "He's going to kill me, so I guess this is goodbye."

"If you're not a spy, he won't kill you."

"He will, and he's going to." A sob came but she kept wiping the tears away. "You saw how angry he was. He doesn't understand anything but facts. He has no faith, and he doesn't take chances."

Hands cupped my cheeks and Josie stood on her tiptoes, pressing her lips into mine. It was brief but passionate. It had me grabbing her bicep to pull her back to me as she began to head to Elec.

"Wait a minute."

Words…they were gone. They weren't bombarding me. Suffocating me. I looked to the Main Master, who had his arms crossed over his chest, talking to Nineteen but looking at us. Was she telling the truth? Had she truly seen her own death? *Even if she wasn't guilty?*

My eyes lowered back to my slave. To think after all this

time of hearing every aspect of who she was, what she'd gone through, to think my own actions would be the result of her death...*and not by me*...I didn't like that. I wasn't okay with that.

"I'll talk to Elec. He." Again, my eyes briefly jumped over to him. "You're not going to die. We're both starting to overreact. You saw your death, but that doesn't mean it's real. You've seen a lot of crazy shit. It comes with the territory of the tea. *Even in dreams.* Listen when I say you'll be okay. Got it?"

She nodded, even if it didn't look like she believed me. I straightened, gesturing my head to Elec and giving Josie's arm a squeeze as I nudged her over. She got a few steps, taking one last look at me as Nineteen and the guards led her through the doors. For the life of me, I couldn't tear my stare from the now empty space. My heart was pounding, and my stomach was twisting. My eyes slowly came to the Main Master, and I could barely process my reaction to possibly losing my slave as I took in his hard expression.

"The day you put her under, she mentioned her dream." I stopped. "She says you're going to kill her, even if she's not guilty of being a spy." I paused. "You wouldn't do that, right? I mean...she's here at the Gardens. She's not a threat."

"I'll be the one to determine that."

"Elec." Again, I glanced to the door. "She's seen some things, but—"

"Master, go home. I'll keep you updated."

And just like that, I was reminded that friend-status didn't exist here. Relationships outside of business came second, and trust was bendable. It could benefit whatever was more important, and slaves didn't even rank high enough to be on the list.

B1297

For hours I stayed hooked to a machine. No doctors. No scientists. No Main Master. Just me, a bed, wires, and screens. What they were reading, I had no idea. I watched them; I dozed. I even got to see people come and go through the glass windows. Nothing seemed significant. They were getting on with their lives while I was praying mine was not about to end. If I went off my visions during the drugs, then yes...I'd die today. The Master seemed to have more faith that I wouldn't, but he hadn't lived through what I'd seen. Did he see how the leaders made the rules? Those rules weren't here to help the people. They were to keep the power. I was a risk, plain and simple.

I sat up from the bed, wiping my hands down my face as I continued to take in the large monitor keeping track of my blood pressure and heart rate. Further in the room was a wall of what looked to be more monitors, but they were turned off.

Following the lines, I took in the number of beats my pulse read. Seventy-four. Seventy-seven. Seventy-five. The moment the sound of the door opened...eighty-four and rising.

"Slave b-twelve-ninety-seven, I'm Dr. Milsap. I'll be assisting the Main Master today." He pointed to the screen. "I

504

just want to explain what's going to happen so there's no confusion." He reached over, adjusting the sensor on my finger. "I'll ask you some baseline questions first. This will cover your name. Things like colors and shapes. Very routine stuff. From there, we'll go into questions that are more in-depth of why you're here."

"Alright."

As I talked, I watched new lines appear. Ones that hadn't been there before. Not because he'd done anything different, but because I hadn't really spoken until now.

"Excellent." He paused as the Main Master appeared around the corner, walking in a swift pace to the door. Blue eyes sliced up from his phone to come to me. The look he pinned me with made my pulse skyrocket.

The door swung open, and the Main Master slid his phone in his suit's jacket.

"Have you started the baseline questions?"

"No, Main Master. I was just explaining to her how this was going to work."

"Great. Let's get started."

The doctor nodded, hitting buttons on a keyboard. Multiple screens began to appear on the wall monitor, and I couldn't stop the nervousness that made my teeth chatter.

"Are you slave b-twelve-ninety-seven?"

"Yes," I managed.

He nodded.

"Is your real name Josie Marie Lockhart Ortega?"

"Unfortunately."

The doctor's eyes lifted, and I sighed. "Yes."

"Are you twenty-three years old?"

"Yes."

He stopped, drawing on a piece of paper.

"Is this a circle?"

"Yes."

"Are the walls green?"

I glanced around. Only half were glass, but the bottom was white.

"No."

"Is the sky blue?"

The question had me pausing. "Generically, yes, but it's also gray during storms and black at night."

Dr. Milsap opened his mouth and closed it, glancing to the Main Master.

"Just answer the damn question, slave."

"What if it's wrong? What if it thinks I'm lying? I can't say the sky is blue when I know it's not all the time. We don't even have a sky here. I don't feel comfortable answering."

The doctor shifted nervously as his hand rose. "Let's just go to the next question. Were you born on June seventh?"

"Yes."

"Is your mother's name Ann?"

My eyes closed as the room seemed to tilt. I placed my hand on the hospital bed I was sitting on to steady myself.

"Yes."

"Good." The doctor entered in some information, picking up a clipboard.

"You're unstable. Before we start, when was the last time your Master gave you ayahuasca?"

"Is that what it is?" My eyes lowered. I didn't know much about the drink, but I had heard of it. "Last night was my fifth and final night, Main Master."

"Write that down," he said to the doctor. "Final dose. That's the strongest." His teeth clenched. "I think we can both agree you're still far from sober. When was the last time you've seen anything? Heard anything?"

It was my turn to shift.

"A few hours ago? In the shower after I woke up. The water on the walls, they turned into snakes. I…I really can't remember the last time I didn't see anything, truthfully. The days are blurring together. It would seem I'm always hearing or seeing something."

The Main Master looked at the doctor who nodded as he took in the lines on the monitor. He withdrew a folder from the drawer on the counter, heading closer to me.

"Now that we have a baseline, slave, I'm going to ask the real questions. Are you ready for that?"

He stared at the monitor. Another baseline?

"Yes, Main Master."

He opened the folder, scanning the contents before coming back to look at me.

"Have you talked to anyone in your family in the last year before you were brought to the Gardens?"

"I...Yes. I called my mother to tell her I was pregnant."

"How long had it been before that? Would you say a few weeks?"

I paused as my brain scrambled to remember back.

"...yes? I think so. I told her I'd gotten married."

"What about before that? Did a lot of time go by or would you say you called every few weeks?"

"Main Master...I don't know. It was sporadic. Sometimes it was weeks. Other times, months. In my teens, it was years."

"Are you close with your family?"

Confusion had me shaking my head.

"Some of them. I mean, we're family. We don't talk often, but we keep in contact. I don't hate any of them if that's what you're asking."

The Main Master pulled out a picture, handing it over to me. The tea had the rawness of my heart aching and bleeding as tears blinded me.

"George. My oldest brother. He's...married now? He has a child?"

The family photo of him holding an infant next to his high

school sweetheart, Fiona, was too much for me to bear. I'd been here so long, but how long, I didn't have a clue. It felt like forever. A lifetime, which was proving to be true.

"To you, that's your brother. To me, that's George Lockhart, the newly elected mayor of Victoria. Small town, yes, but I hear he has very big goals. *Political.* You never mentioned he was a former detective, slave."

"I didn't…think it was an issue. It's unrelated to me. George and I were more than ten years apart. We were never close. He lived states away from where I did."

"Did he not come to your hospital room when you lost the baby? He may have been states away, but when you were in trouble and called, he jumped on the first flight out."

"*I was scared.*" My lips quivered as tears streamed down my face. "I didn't know who else to call. Phillip constantly threatened to kill me if I tried to leave. I didn't have a choice. And your information is wrong, Main Master. He didn't come to my hospital room. I left there the moment I was able. He came to my hotel room, but I only saw him briefly."

The blue darkened in his eyes as he continued to stare me down.

"Tell me about that. Your brother wasn't in town long, but neither were you. You rented a car that very night and went to LA."

I nodded, looking back at the picture I held.

"Phillip found me. Or…he found George. I saw them arguing in the parking lot. I knew I had to leave before he came to the room. I ran as fast as I could."

The Main Master took out another picture, handing it over to me. The sight almost had me jumping down from my bed. To do what, I wasn't sure. Instead, I froze, my insides beating against me as I continuously shook my head in more than denial. I was flabbergasted.

"What is this? George…he." More, my head went back and forth.

"Did you think your brother was honorable in his occupation? Did you ever wonder how Phillip found you? How he heard about you?" My head shot up from what looked like a surveillance photo of the two of them together. There were drugs and guns surrounding them as they looked to be carrying on a conversation. More, the Main Master continued.

"He lived in and worked out of Phoenix, Josie. You lived in LA. Do you really think it was random how the two of you met?"

"He owned a club there."

Elec's head shook back and forth but he didn't speak.

"He didn't own that club?"

Still his head shook.

"But…I…" I wiped my eyes, trying to catch my breath.

"You married one of the highest-ranking members in the cartel. Your brother, who is as dirty as they come, is a former detective, making plans to some day run for senator, and you expect me to believe you had no idea about any of this?"

"I swear." My voice cracked, and I quickly cleared it. "I knew Phillip wasn't a good man, but I tried to leave. I tried to get away from him. You know I did. You saw I rented that car. I avoided him for months before I was brought here." My eyes widened even more, but my brain was having a hard time making sense of things. "Phillip or my brother, they're not why I'm here are they? Did they do this to me?"

The Main Master got quiet as he glared. After a few seconds, he stepped in closer to the doctor, ignoring my question as Dr. Milsap silently pointed out areas to him on the screen. Whatever he had written down on the clipboard had the Main Master's face drawing in almost angrily.

"No. They are not the reason you're here, slave, but I won't lie. Your husband has some serious pull, and I'd be lying if I said I wasn't tempted to give you back to him for some of it."

I did fly off the table then. My heart rate skyrocketed as terror left me needing to escape. My legs grew weak, and I hit the ground at the Main Master's feet.

"Don't send me back. Death would be better than a life with Phillip. I'll do anything."

"Tell me how you knew about the ceremonies. You knew names. Locations. How?"

"I saw it."

My teeth gnashed together as the Main Master ripped me from the floor, slamming me to the bed. Alarms were going off in the room as he held to my jaw, yelling in my face.

"How did you know!"

"The tea! I swear it was the tea. I don't know how I saw it." I sobbed, breaking completely as the hold grew harder. "It just came to me in the visions. I didn't ask for it, it just happened."

"Sir."

The doctor's voice had the Main Master letting go to leave me on the bed. I sobbed harder, barely able to open my mouth through the cries. Throbbing took over my jawline and cheeks and I rubbed against the side of my face as the Main Master eyed me. What the doctor was whispering, I didn't know. I couldn't stop crying enough to hear.

"Let's try something different, slave. Have you at any point conspired to solicit information about the Gardens?"

"No."

"Have you ever met, had conversations with, or made dealings with anyone associated with the Gardens aside from your Master?"

"N-No."

The Main Master jerked his eyes from the monitor, rage transforming his face as he closed the distance between us. Like a vice, he gripped on crushingly.

"Are your intentions to turn your Master against me?"

"Never."

I sobbed, but he only moved his fingers higher on the hollows of my cheeks, pushing harder.

"Will you or have you used your body to try to gain control over your Master?"

My lips parted, a cry leaving me as he pushed down.

"I have. I will. Not to control...*to survive.*"

"So you admit to wanting to control Master One-thirteen."

I tried to nod but could barely move under his hold.

"I admit it. I've used my body. Or...let him use it. I don't know exactly what you're asking. I can't think. Main Master, please. I know my place. I'm a slave. I'll do my duty. I'll be whatever he wants. *I'll do whatever he asks.* I just want to go home. Please, I didn't do anything wrong."

"You're not getting out that easily, slave." He turned to the doctor. "Hook her up. If she's lying and has been trained to beat these machines, she won't beat this."

"Machine?"

My voice nearly gave out.

"That's right. I still have more questions. If I don't like your answers, you'll get a jolt of electricity so powerful, the pain will be unbearable. It *will* break you eventually."

"But...I'm not lying. *I'm not.*"

"We'll find out."

MASTER B-0113

The emptiness of solitude had never bothered me. Most of the time, I preferred it. As I entered the lobby of the lab, I couldn't deny that last night had been the longest night I could ever remember having. With my hours screwed up, sleep was impossible. I paced. I watched TV. I even tried to read. Nothing could fill the presence my slave had imprinted on my apartment. Without her in it, the place felt just as dead as it had been when Linda was alive. I wasn't sure why that bothered me, but it did. I liked her late-night conversations with her imaginary me. I enjoyed watching her dance or laugh or cry. The thing was…I liked her. Maybe a little bit too much and a little too fast. And I was worried. I'd be lying if I didn't say my nerves were on edge. I didn't like the way Elec and I had left things. The more I thought over it, the more the scene kept eating at me.

"Master One-thirteen." Elec came through a pair of doors. He had bags under his eyes and his usual short-to-medium length hair was disheveled. "I was told you were headed down. Can I help you with something?"

"Uh…yeah. I've come to check on my slave."

"We're not finished yet."

"Not finished? You said it might only take a day or two, tops. Possibly a few hours. You've had her for..." I checked my watch, "twenty-one hours. Has she given you reason to believe she might be lying about anything?"

Silence.

Elec crossed his arms over his chest. "I don't believe in coincidences."

"You don't have to, Main Master, because it's not. She told you how she'd come across the information. She was honest."

"From her visions?"

"You asked her, right? Surely you know whether she's lying. What did it say?"

"Lie detectors aren't reliable."

"They're reliable enough for you to use them. If it would have said she was lying, you would have believed it. Now that it says she's not, you think she's somehow outsmarted it?"

"Master, I suggest you return to your apartment until we're finished."

My fingers drew up into my palm, and I didn't move.

"I bought that slave. I was honest with you about everything she said and saw. I've entrusted you to figure out whether she's telling the truth. I did not give her to you to force a guilty verdict because you don't believe how she's come across the information. Is she a spy or not? I'm ready to take my slave home."

"A spy, maybe not. Guilty of something...perhaps."

"We're all guilty of something, Main Master. Every single one of us on the planet. That doesn't condemn her to torture or death. Where is she? I'm taking my slave. If she was hiding something, you would have discovered it by now. You didn't at my apartment. You didn't after twenty-one hours. We're finished. Josie's not a threat to the Gardens."

"I'm the one who makes that call."

My teeth ground into each other. "Can I at least see her?"

Blue eyes narrowed as he looked at me.

"You want to see your slave?"

"…I do."

"If you insist."

He turned, and I followed, heading through the door to go further into the facility. Halls. Doors. I wasn't sure how many we went through or passed. When we finally made it to the end of the corridor, the Main Master opened a door to an empty, large cement room. A drain rested in the middle, and Josie wasn't a foot away from it, limp and hanging with her arms cuffed above her head. I almost couldn't move. I sure as hell couldn't speak as I took in the massive burns and bruises covering her body.

"You did this?"

"I did. I'm about to continue. Hurry and tell her what you need to. I'm busy."

"But she's not guilty. She's not…she's not a threat, Elec."

"Not a threat to whom? The Gardens? What about to you, Anthony?"

I looked between them. "What do you mean?"

The Main Master headed forward. The click of his shoes was like an alarm clock to Josie. Her head fought to lift, and piss ran down her legs as she began whimpering and crying in fear at his approach.

"Let's recap, slave. We were having such a good time before."

"I said I'm sorry. I'm sorry."

"Don't tell me. Tell your Master."

It was only then that Josie's wild eyes spotted me. Heavy, soul-wrenching sobs left her, and her body pulled in my direction, stopped by the cuffs.

"Master, please. I'm sorry. I want to go home. *I'm sorry.*"

"Sorry for what?"

I stepped forward, heading closer, but keeping my distance.

"I only wanted to make sure I was safe with your church. I researched you. I looked up your site."

"You already told me that, slave."

Her eyes went to the Main Master coming back to me as she cried harder. "Maybe that's how I knew so much. There were other sites that held information on you. Other churches. I think I saw it and…I…maybe that's how…" Screams filled the room as the Main Master reached out, shocking her with what looked like some sort of rod. "I must have known from the research." Her legs gave out, but she fought to stand. "I researched you. I…I must have—"

Again, she screamed out as he pressed the electricity into her side.

"She already told me this! Why are you hurting her for it?"

"I knew who you were. I must have…*I must have known.*" Her ankles rolled as she fell back down, hanging from the chains.

"There's no must about it. Your slave knew exactly who you were. She can try to twist it however she likes, but she'll continue to get punished until she admits the truth."

"And what will that do?" My head shook. "She knew me, so what. She researched me. She was a fucking victim, Elec. She needed to feel safe with who she was going to. That is not guilt. This," I said, gesturing to him, "isn't punishment. This is sadism. You have plenty of slaves to torture. She's clearly not who you want her to be. I'd like to take her home now."

"And I told you we weren't done."

Heat boiled in my veins. My own sadist loved nothing more than to fight, but this was a fight I couldn't win. It was death. It was a choice and a test, and I was smart enough to see that. Barely. That didn't mean the Main Master would return my slave when he finished. He could very well kill her and there wasn't a damn thing I could do about it. Why? Because my loyalty was in blood. My soul was sold. The only way out was death, and I had died to get here a long time ago.

"I'll take my minute now."

515

Heading to Josie, I couldn't stop the conflicting emotions. It could be the last time I ever saw her. Short of suicide from being her savior, there was nothing I could do. I was no knight in shining armor, not that she'd live anyway. I was not here to rescue my slave from the Main Master. I was here to say goodbye.

"Josie."

"Master. Pastor Anthony, please. I'm sorry. I swear, I'm sorry."

"Shh. Don't apologize." I wiped her dark hair out of her tear-drenched face, trying not to explode at the massive bruising along her cheeks and jaw. "Josie, I can't be here. I have to leave now."

"Leave? *Don't leave me.* I want to go home too. I'll be a good slave. Don't leave me. Master, please. *Anthony*, please."

"You've been strong. I know you'll continue to be. Just keep telling the truth."

"Don't leave me. Pastor," she sobbed. "I'm begging you. *Pastor, please.* Tell me a prayer. Don't leave me! Tell me you feel Him and He's with me. Tell Him to be with me. *I need him.* God, help me, please! God!"

I turned, glaring to the Main Master, but coming back to cup Josie's face.

"What did I tell you before? You don't need me for that. He is always with you, and he's here more now than ever. You may very well die when I leave this room. Face it. To face death is to face God. Stand tall and take this."

I kissed her hard, feeling her collapse as her sobs started all over again. I didn't look back. I met Elec's eyes, storming from the room. Cursing myself for picking her. For drugging her. Praying...for the first time in longer than I could remember.

Silence. Shuffling of feet. Voices buzzing in the background.

For two more days I waited. My slave was dead. There was nothing that could have convinced me otherwise. Guilt had somehow appeared, eating my mind with words. Searing my inside like acid. Questions. Why? How? Everything imaginable raked my mind until all that remained was a mush of thoughts. I was a mess. I hadn't shaved. I was still in the same suit I left my slave in. And then it happened. A call. A location.

I must have made it to the hospital's floor in record speed. I barely remembered the ride on the elevator at all. But my slave wasn't fine. She wasn't much of a slave at all. I'd been here another day, and she'd yet to wake up. Her body was covered in every color imaginable. Her face was swollen, but not from any beating I'd ever seen. It was the overall trauma. The stress. But she was alive. I had that to be thankful for. And the doctors did say she would wake at any time.

"One-thirteen."

I turned from the bed, looking behind me to the door. The Main Master didn't come in, but he wouldn't look at me either. He still appeared angry. Still...not quite right. I stood, turning to face him.

"I thought you should know, there were things I couldn't allow your slave to remember. I won't even say it in case she can hear, but you know what I'm referring to. If you were smart, you'd refrain from your experiments with this one. Your *loyalty* that day is the only reason she's alive. You didn't like where I stood, but you knew your place. I'm starting to see alliances aren't everything with some Masters and Mistresses here at the Gardens." He glanced back to Josie. "You may want to return your...things back to my club. If the information comes back to her, I won't be so lenient again. You *will* tell me if it comes back to her."

517

"You have my word. I appreciate your generosity. I didn't expect to get her back."

He seemed to weigh my response, nodding as if he were satisfied.

"I'll be needing you soon. I've moved up the date for my friend. I'll keep you informed."

"I'll be ready, Main Master." I met his eyes, holding his cold stare. "Thank you."

With a slight bow, he stepped back, disappearing from view. When I turned to sit down, my heart jumped to my throat. Josie's eyes were opened, and the fear in them was evident as she stared towards the door.

"Slave."

She reached for me, too afraid to take her gaze from the entrance. When I sat on the bed, she wrapped around my waist, bursting into tears.

"I'm so sorry, Master." She sobbed, allowing me to lay her back as I leaned in to stay close. "Did I do good? Can I come home now?"

"You did good. The moment you're better, we'll go home."

She sniffled. "I don't know why I'm crying. It was just some tests, I just...I think I did bad or fell asleep because I can't remember what all happened. I hurt. Was I bad?"

"Maybe a little, but you're going to be better now, aren't you?"

"Yes, Master. I'll be the best slave. I'll do whatever you ask. I won't argue about the tea anymore. I didn't mean it. I'll be good. I'll be so good. I don't want to go back to the Main Master." She paused, her forehead crinkling as she seemed to try to recall what happened. "I can really come home?"

"Soon, and you're finished with the tea. I'm not sure there's much left to learn. From you, anyway. I am curious about other slaves, but let's not rush into that. We'll think about that another time when you're better. There are still a few weeks until the next auction. Let's see what happens between now and then. Who knows, maybe this is the start of something new. Perhaps you can be my assistant. Are you good at taking notes, Josie? How organized are you? Can you handle me killing other slaves?"

A slight smile mixed with the haunting trauma in her depths. She lifted her hold to around my neck, clinging as if she were afraid she'd wake up with the Main Master at any moment.

"I can do anything you need. I'm a quick learner, and I'm very thorough. There's not much I miss. My memory has never been clearer." She buried her face more into me, pausing. "I'm from the streets, Pastor. Violence is what we know. We're smart. Tough. We have to be. *We're a completely different breed.*"

The End

Master A-0005
Garden of the Gods
International Bestselling Author
A.A. Dark
Copyright © 2023 by A.A.Dark

All Rights Reserved

RULES

Rules are subject to change. If you neglect to follow these rules, you will undergo an investigation/trial where punishment is evaluated by the Board and Main Master, Elec Wexler. Punishment can range from fines to lockup in Hell Row to Death.

1) Keep your hands to yourself.

2) The only property you may destroy is your own. (slaves included.)

3) You are a number. Your peers are a number. Use them.

4) Respect your neighbor's privacy.

5) GOTG is NOT to be discussed outside of this facility.

GLOSSARY

W

Virgin slave. Wears a white robe during the auction.

B

Nonvirgin slave. Wears a blue robe during the auction.

D

Docile, drugged slave. Can be w or b. Heavily trained. Good for elderly or those with disabilities.

M

Male slave.

Crow

(fc: female crow, mc: male crow) Ruined, disfigured slave. Convicts fall into this category. Black robe during the auction. Usually the cheapest slave.

Blank slate

Mostly male slaves who have undergone forced indoctrination through various scientific methods. (Brainwashing, programming, training, etc.) Most remember their identity but have key parts of their past erased if it could pose a threat or alter their role as a slave. They're programmed to be focused solely on their Mistress or Master. They are made to be obedient, loyal, and protective.

*Master numbers written out throughout the stories are capitalized. (Ex. Twelve-twelve.) Also, the word Master throughout is capitalized. (Ex. Master Twelve-twelve.)

*Slave numbers written out will not be capitalized. The word slave throughout will not be capitalized outside from the beginning of a sentence.

"THE HEALTHY MAN DOES
NOT TORTURE OTHERS.
GENERALLY, IT IS THE
TORTURED WHO TURNS
INTO TORTURERS."
-CARL JUNG

PROLOGUE
MASTER A-0005

Garden of the Gods
Colorado Springs underground facility

As an Alpha Master and one of the board members, my attendance to the auctions were mandatory. My need for a slave...a must, just as everyone else who filled the space and stared towards the stage. Darkness cloaked the room, and only one light stood out prominently. It was on him, the Main Master —the man who controlled this entire underground facility.

"Welcome to the second auction for the Garden of the Gods. For those who didn't make it to the first, I'm going to recap this as quickly as possible. You've taken the classes. You've learned the rules. Even though our slaves have been trained, you are going to have to earn your titles. The B's in front of your number are for a reason. This is the Beta stage. Some of you will make our foundation, some of you won't. Your outside status got you here, but that means nothing inside the Gardens. You are a number. That's it. Your identity means absolutely zero. Here, there is no power or favoritism. This world is mine, and you better hope like hell you can follow the rules, or you won't

526

survive in it." His eyes scanned the room. "On the plus side, a lot of you have made it this far and that speaks volumes. I have high hopes for most of you."

I looked around my private balcony. Crème-colored silk chairs decorated the entire space, and pale lavender accents were visible throughout. From the neatly tied bows on the curtains, to the freshly cut flowers that filled the fancy vase on the table against the wall, I felt like I was more at a wedding than a disguised funeral.

"For those new to us tonight, I don't think I need to go much into how this place is not Whitlock. The rules are different. The location is different." I turned back to the stage. "I am *not* the old Main Master, Bram Whitlock. A few Masters from the first auction had to learn that the hard way. You cannot buy yourself out of trouble. You cannot *buy me*. I will never let the Garden of the Gods fall."

Damn right it wouldn't. The board members and guards would never allow it. I hadn't been a part of Whitlock, but I did have an apartment there passed on to me from my father. I didn't have a reason back then to attend the auctions, but I did now.

"Let's recap bidding for those who don't know. First, we have the white, or w's. These are the virgins. We also have the b's: or blue." He paused. "Not virgins. We also have the d's, who now have their own room, at the back right, behind all of you. They're docile, trained, and good for those who are looking for a long-term slave. Lastly, come the black, or as we call them, the crows. These could be fun for anyone looking for a bloodbath or just a fun time. They're the convicts. The disfigured. The old. *Repulsive*." He stopped at the end of the stage. "You get it. Also in that category, you'll find the breeders. I want to make a note of some changes in this category." His hand rose through the pause. "Listen to me closely. I won't repeat it. You are not allowed to bid on them unless you've already gone through the steps and signed a contract with me. We had a few try last

527

auction even though this was already stated in bold caps in the pamphlet. If you bid on a breeder, and you haven't met with me, your bid will be revoked, and I will fine you ten thousand dollars for wasting my time. Breeders are special. Breeders are for only those I approve of."

My hands fisted more out of the surprise adrenaline I was hit with. This was getting real. Too real, but I couldn't back out. I'd given my word, and I meant to keep it. Besides, maybe this is what I needed, not that it would make a difference.

"For those looking for our programmable, 'blank slate' males and *now* females, your auction is just through that door off to the right. The information was in the packet, but just in case you missed it last auction, these are those who have had a portion of their memories erased. They're aware. They know who they are, but they only remember what we want them to."

Elec walked down the length of the stage in his black fitted suit and matching black button-up shirt and tie. His dark hair was starting to grow out of the short style he usually wore, and his handsome features kept the attention of everyone in the room. He was comfortable on the stage. His tall length stood straight, yet he walked with ease as his light eyes took in everything. For those who knew his cousin, Bram Whitlock, their resemblance couldn't be ignored. Neither could the aura both men projected. They both were a force to be reckoned with. I knew that firsthand.

I pulled out a cigarette, lighting it. The taste had me inhaling deeply, and I held it into my lungs, exhaling as he continued.

"The last few weeks have been exciting, to say the least. I've watched some of you grow in your role. The majority have done great with following rules. For those who are new, pay attention. What you buy is yours. You can do whatever you want with it. Fuck it. Kill it. Share it. Marry it. Love it. Eat it. Destroy it." Hesitation. "I don't care so long as you follow the rules. Your business is your own. I can't stress that enough."

"If you look down the arm of the chair, you will see a button. Do not." He stopped, taking his time as he stared us down. "All of you listen and listen good. Let me say it again since others from the first auction learned the hard way. *Do not...* press that button unless you are sure you want to bid. We do not have a lay-a-way plan. You cannot get your slave on loan. If you don't have the money, don't bid. At the Gardens, there's no such thing as accidents. If you bid, you buy. If you can't pay, I will take my payment however I want. Don't believe my threat, *test me*. I'll take everything you own on the outside world, and you can remain here with the slave you couldn't resist. This life can be simple if you just do as you're told. The rules are easy. Complete acceptance into the Garden of the Gods is not. You all signed a contract to get this far. Abide by it, and Alpha status will be yours."

I took another deep drag, pushing the cigarette butt hard into the ashtray. Lights ran the edge of the floor, making their way over the top arches of multiple doorways. Gasps and chatter filled the theater and heads spun from the stage to the nearest entrance as a line of beautiful women dressed in sheer white robes awaited their cue. I stood, leaving my booth and heading to collect my own slave. *A virgin wasn't it.*

MASTER A-0005

There was this thing about death. It had the ability to erase, destroy...to heal. For me, only the first two applied. Rebuilding my life was impossible. My wounds did not mend through retribution. If anything, they only grew. Numbness or rage was constant. No matter how important events were, or how good my world became, morality disappeared in the oblivion of sorrow. Grief had me, and peace ceased to exist.

Where I once had the perfect life, that reality had ended over three years ago. No wife anymore. No son or a daughter on the way. My world came to a standstill December twenty-eighth, and any essence of a person I was ended alongside a steep slope outside some small Colorado town. The first year I almost succeeded with suicide twice. The second year...I went on a killing spree, torturing and murdering the son of a bitch who took them away from me and four others just like him. That did nothing to heal the hole inside. With each year it grew, and there was only one thing left to do—something I had avoided the first auction: my duty.

"Master Five, please approach."

I stood from one of the multiple black leather sofas in the

opened back room, ready to get this over with. Wayne, a guard I'd met over the last few months as a board member, nodded to me as he held his tablet and went through my order. "Says here you're looking for two crows1. One male with these charges," he said, making a path under the code with his finger, "and a fc: a female crow2. Did you find one in the binder you wish to see?"

"Don't need to."

The guard's mouth opened only to close at my short answer. He stopped, scanning the screen and squinting as he took in the information. His gaze shot up to me, only to lower and lift again. "There's already a slave programmed in here. You haven't...seen any—"

At my hard stare, the guard grew quiet, clearing his throat. Technically, I should have chosen one from the profiles in the binder and been escorted to see her, but Elec had already assigned me a match within the approved bloodlines. Who she was or what the hell she was doing here as a slave, I hadn't a clue. Her information was in my room, but I hadn't been able to stomach looking at it. I wasn't even sure this is what I wanted. It was, but not.

"We keep the males in the back, restrained, as you're aware. We have them sorted by charges. You can take the walk and choose yours from there. Just let me know when you've decided, and I can enter their slave number in the system for auction. The breeders are kept in a special room. We can go there last if you'd like to see her before she goes up for bid.

"I'd rather not." I shoved my hands in my pockets. "Once I win her, I want her taken directly to my apartment."

"Of course." The guard grabbed an extra tablet off to the side, pushing buttons only to hand it over. "If you'll come with me, I'll take you to the males." I followed next to him, scanning the names and details on their charges as we headed through the electronic door. There were twenty-five convicts who matched my needs, and there was only one requirement: repeated offenses. The one with the most was my winner. So far, that was slave three-one-nine-three.

More, I scanned down, taking in their portraits. Some appeared disheveled, others held a hard expression, trying to capture their toughness. One even appeared to be crying. My head shook, and I cursed in aggravation, moving my attention back to their records.

Locks shifted and an electronic door opened as we took a left and went down another hall. Three doors down, we came to a stop as more metal clinked and the entrance opened.

"If you'll wait here, I'll go in and make my round."

The guard didn't wait for my approval. It was mandatory, and he walked through the threshold holding to the gun at his hip as he disappeared. I didn't bother giving it any more attention. I kept my stare at the screen as I repeated my scroll.

Slave three-one-nine-three.

I took in the three pictures under his profile again. Despite being twenty-six years old, his brown hair was already balding. The large scar that ran along his scalp on the side had my cheek twitching where I had my own. Mine wasn't big. Three inches compared to around the six inches for his. Still, our injuries were visible and were probably both related by the same thing...just on different sides. Mine was in result of his sins. Sins that killed my entire family. His, he'd probably gotten killing someone else. He had the right charges. Vehicular homicide. Multiple DWIs before that. He was my guy.

Clicking on the link, I watched as the pictures of his victims loaded. Not a family but two eighteen-year-old girls and a twelve-year-old boy. Given the last names, my guess was that it was the driver's little brother and her friend. Three kids. Fucking tragedy for the parents who lost them. Just looking at their smiles, my stomach flipped and the familiar hate that scorched my insides returned.

This was no accident; this was a pattern. One the driver

hadn't learned from after numerous other arrests for the same damn thing. *Murderer.*

"All is good, Master Five. You can come in now."

My teeth clenched, and I eyed the guard's gun. I took one step, stopping through the adrenaline causing my entire body to shake. Again, I eyed the weapon at his hip. Sweat began to coat my skin, and a metallic taste registered on my tongue. Flashes of my pregnant wife and son blinded me, and I gave a hard shake, trying to erase them as I took a step back.

"I can't. If I go in there, I'll kill them all. Slave three-one-nine-three. He's the one I want."

"I'll mark him down for auction."

As Wayne entered in his information, I pulled at the tie. I didn't wear suits despite I'd been raised to. It was my only form of rebellion against my wealthy family once I'd left the house. Not even when I ran my own company and practically lived in the office did I portray the aura of who I truly was. I'd always been laid back. Happily hiding my darkness. How many times had my wife said my smiles were contagious? They'd hid the deadliest of deeds had I ever had to commit any, not that I really did back in those days. Nothing about that Jake Princeton existed anymore. My companies continued to thrive, but I didn't have any part of running them. I had people for that. I didn't smile. I wasn't down-to-earth or easy to talk to anymore. I was dead in almost every sense of the word, and if there was life in me, I couldn't find it outside of the blood I spilt for them men who deserved it.

"All seems good to go, Sir. Both slaves are in the system under your name, and the bidding will start shortly. If you'll follow me back into the main room, you can take your seat."

I didn't answer, and Wayne didn't wait. We headed back, and I stayed in a blur until I was lowering to my spot on the sofa. Minutes passed. Longer. When the female's number flashed on the large screen covering the back wall, I was ready to get this over with. What I wasn't prepared for was the picture of her to appear. It caught me so unaware, I almost forgot to press the fucking button.

"Fc one. Starting bid: one-hundred-forty-five thousand."

My skin crawled as whispers and murmurs filled the space. The price was steep for a crow, shocking really, but I ignored the stares as my number registered on the screen. I couldn't break my gaze. I didn't even want to blink as I took her in.

Brown hair was so dark it was almost black. She had blue, round eyes above a straight thin nose, and decent lips. To say she was overly beautiful would have been a lie. She wasn't like most of the slaves here who stood out for their shockingly gorgeous looks, and that worked in her favor. She was real. Relatable. And for me, that was trouble. For me...it left me intrigued when seconds ago I hadn't been buying her for anything other than convenience.

"I wasn't sure you'd go through with it. I must admit, I'm happy you took my advice."

I didn't have to turn around to see who it was. The sound of the Main Master's voice was one I knew well.

"I don't have much of a choice."

Elec came around, sitting beside me.

"That's debatable. I happen to think you have plenty."

"You're wrong. Your family line isn't riding on an heir. You didn't give your word to your father on his death bed. You didn't have to watch your wife and children die one at a time. You didn't have to listen to your wife beg you to cut open her stomach to pull out a daughter that died in your arms. You didn't have to see the heartache on your wife's terrified face as she bled out because of what you did. And you *sure as fuck* didn't have to hold that dead baby as you watched a son you thought was okay fall asleep to never wake again. Eight hours I lived that hell. Eight hours I was trapped in that fucking car with them. It should have been me. *It should have been him.* We both should have died that day, *not them*. Don't tell me about my options until you've walked in my shoes, Main Master. Every breath I take is one I wished I wasn't. To possibly experience that all over again, fuck no. I much prefer this route. Here, I have control. There's no pretending this is anything other than what it is. There's no dating or outside bullshit. This works."

Silence.

Elec leaned forward, resting his forearms on his knees as I watched my number flash on the screen.

"I'm truly sorry about Maggie and your children. What you had was special. That's rare for people like us. I know slave one won't fill Maggie's shoes, but she will give you a child who can at least carry on your name. Whether you choose to stay on this earth to see it grow or not is up to you. I told you I'd be here for you and the child regardless. We've always looked out for each other, Jake."

My head lowered as I stared at the floor and nodded.

"Who is she, and why is she a slave?" I glanced over. "She has the right blood. There's a reason she's here and not out there doing her duties like us."

Elec grew quiet, unclasping his hands as he sat taller.

"I see you didn't read the file."

"I couldn't."

His lips pressed together as he let out a deep breath.

"We all have secrets. Let's just say this is one I uncovered a few years back when we first started planning the Gardens." His brow drew in. "We're our own greatest enemies. I held a grudge against a certain family. A very close family to my own. Ego will do that to you. Where I meant to bring down the empire, I discovered a treasure hidden amongst it." He shook his head, tearing his eyes from the daze he held, bringing his cold stare to me. "Leverage is everything, and I have more than I know what to do with." He paused. "We're the only ones who know she exists. Bastard children are rarely acknowledged amongst us, but when they cross bloodlines, say…Alastair Whitlock and Aubrey Walton, well, secret babies always find their way to the surface. They should have known this."

My eyes widened. "Are you telling me you have one of the only living relatives of your cousin, Bram Whitlock, down here at the Gardens as a slave?"

"You'd be correct."

"Does Aubrey know? David?"

"No. The scandal that Kayla even exists would be…well, I don't have to tell you the waves that would make if Aubrey's affair came to light. She didn't want the girl or even to risk this secret coming out, that's why she put her up for adoption twenty-five years ago. Thing is, with all these at home DNA tests, you can't imagine the secrets being exposed."

"That's how you found her?"

"Partly. All the families in our circle are marked. These days it's both a blessing and a fucking curse. She took one, curious about her real parents. She should have left it alone. Good for us, she didn't."

"You said partly."

"I did."

He grew quiet, only to glance over with a look I couldn't read. "She was trying to be a surrogate for her adopted sister. We keep tabs on places for possible breeders so you can imagine my surprise when I came across her name there while having my people search for her over her genetics. It was as if the stars aligned perfectly. Like it was meant to be." He let out a sound and I wasn't sure if it was a laugh of disbelief or a sigh. "Julie was the name of the adopted sister. She was a good ten years older than Kayla and was a cancer survivor who couldn't have children. Kayla put off everything to help her sister start a family. Work. Friends. She never got to go through with it. I had her taken first. Julie's cancer returned. It was aggressive, and there was no stopping it. She died last month. The slave doesn't know, nor do I want her to. She's come far. I won't have the news ruining all my hard work."

"You never mentioned you were training her personally."

"Didn't I? Well, I have been. I told you she was special. Training her myself was the only way. She's a goldmine, and not just because she can add to our lines. Kayla will be worth a pretty penny once her existence comes out. Or, I should say, we will. Between Whitlock and Walton, Kayla's line will be worth a fortune."

I got quiet as I let it all sink in. "So, how does this work in the long run if the slave is technically missing? You and I signed a contract."

"We did, and you have my word on everything we agreed to. Worthy blood. Legit child. Kayla was reported missing by the sister, but nothing ever came of it. Besides, I took care of it. No record will be found. The Waltons' haven't been on our good side lately, and I don't have to tell you the mess my cousin, Bram, has made. Fucking traitor. Anyway, you will have the baby, and in time, you will expose the secret. Both families, Whitlock and Walton, whether they accept this or not, will not publicly be able to turn their backs on you or the child. Your fortune and power will grow. Not only up there, but down here as well."

My eyes narrowed as I took in his plan.

"And the mother?"

"You own a luxury resort in Denver. You met there and hit it off. Both of you will take plenty of pictures together over the course of the pregnancy. Or pregnancies, depending on if you want more. For now, let's just say it's only one. You will *pretend* to be happy. When it comes time for the child to be born, Kayla will die. Not really if you wish her to live, but to the outside world, she will. The girl has no one. Aside from the dead sister, her adopted parents are deceased. This truly couldn't have worked out any better. Video is hard to refute, and if it appears she dies on film, the Waltons' or Bram can't deny it. To them, she'll be dead, and she can stay that way."

I cleared my throat, finding it hard to breathe as I nodded. Fuck, I wasn't sure if this was the way. I needed an heir. I loved my father enough to keep my promise, but could I do this?

"Jake, you have her now, and that's the important part. There's no rush if you're not ready," Elec said, clasping my shoulder. "Get to know slave one. See if she's right for you. If not, I will buy her back. Her blood is worth more than the measly amount I charged you. Give it a chance and see what you think. It's that simple."

"I gave my word. I can't break it. I don't want this, but I...I don't have much choice. The sooner I get this over with, the better."

1 (FC: FEMALE CROW, MC: MALE CROW) RUINED, DISFIGURE slaves. Breeders. Convicts fall into this category. Black robe during the auction. Usually the cheapest slave.

2 (fc: female crow, mc: male crow) Ruined, disfigure slaves. Breeders. Convicts fall into this category. Black robe during the auction. Usually the cheapest slave.

FC0001

Wooden walls. Wooden floors. The apartment I'd been brought to was bare, basic, if not with the potential to be slightly...homey? There was no other way to describe what I was seeing. Black leather sofa. Two end tables. No pictures. No television. No rug. No lamps. Small kitchen table. Not much of anything aside from the necessities and a coffee mug lying on the counter. As I took everything in, I tried to go over my training. It's not like I couldn't remember my orders; I'd been in captivity as a breeder now for almost two years. It's just, with as foggy as my mind was, this didn't seem real. Hadn't I been counting down the days until this moment? Hadn't the Main Master just last week assured me I'd be taken care of and safe?

"You knew this day would come. I'm giving you a gift in a place that would eat you alive. Master Five is a decent man who happens to be in a rough spot. He lost his family. You're going to do everything in your power to give him a new one. Aren't you."

It hadn't been a question. I'd do this or I'd be dead. It was as simple as that. With as long as I'd been here, his orders were all I knew. All that kept me going. I wanted a family and to be happy,

I just never thought it would be like this. Mine…and yet not. Not here, anyway.

You will stick to the plan and give him a child. I will allow you ten months to care for it in the installation above."

"Where I was before I was brought here?"

"That's right. After that, you will be able to see it grow, but only if he allows it. You're a vessel, nothing more. If he decides to show you video, pictures, that's up to him. If he says it's okay, I'll even let you visit the child throughout their life, but never as their mother. A teacher. A nanny who takes care of them while their father is here. The child will not know you as anything more until they are old enough to be trusted. Master Five will have complete control over what he wants you to have access to. That's more than most breeders get. Take it or leave it.

Leaving it only meant death. My new Master, Jake, wanted a surrogate. I could give him a child in exchange to live. A part of me even wanted to which sounded crazy, even in my own mind. It took me longer than the others to adjust to this life. I'd fought for as long as I could. During one of my lessons with the Main Master, something in me crumbled. Maybe it was my stubbornness. My will. All I knew was the weeks passed, and I calmed. I became content and accepting, and that's when things got better. This was a gift. The Main Master said as much, and he was right.

Turning, I glanced at the round clock on the far side of the wall. It was the only thing hanging. It was late. Close to ten. I had no idea when my Master was meant to arrive, but I wanted to be prepared and put on the perfect first impression. It was everything. This man was used to a wife. A motherly type. I'd never been a mother, but I had a wonderful one who I had learned from, and she taught me well despite she hadn't given birth to me. That hadn't mattered for either of us. What Marion and I shared was special, and I'd soaked in every minute I could before she passed. So…what would she want me to do here, in this moment? It didn't take long for me to figure it out. The Main Master had already given me instructions, and they happen to align with how I was raised.

"Appetizer."

The word repeated in my mind like an echo. Maybe he already ate. Maybe he'd expect a meal. Regardless, I was supposed to have something for my Master to snack on just in case. I'd be ready for anything. But…that didn't fair as well as I hoped. As I walked over and opened the refrigerator, I quickly saw the problem. There was barely any food. Aside from coffee creamer and a few to-go boxes, the Master didn't have anything.

"Don't panic," I breathed out. My eyes scanned the space. No phone. No way for communication.

My hand slapped against the counter, and I grabbed a piece of paper and a pencil jotting down my list. The more I thought, the harder it was. I wasn't used to this. My training was extensive, but this was real. It was different.

I took off at a fast pace to the door. Just as I suspected, a guard was posted outside. I was a breeder trained by the Main Master, himself. I wasn't a w1, b2, or even a d3. I was beyond cuffs. I was safe.

"Slave, you can't—"

"My Master has no food, and I have no phone. I need a delivery, quick. Will you please call in my order and tell them to hurry?"

The guard's brow crinkled, and he took the paper, nodding. At my smile, he returned one, and I quickly shut the door. For minutes, all I could do was pace. When knocking finally sounded, I damn near ran to the barrier. A slave in a yellow headdress was holding two paper bags and I quickly grabbed them, feeling…something. Happiness? I hadn't felt that in months. Years?

"Your delivery. Is there anything else I can get you?"

I paused at the slave's question, glancing at the guard again. He was scanning down the hall and somehow that made me feel safer. I'd spent so much time around the other female breeders. Men and guards were a danger all their own, and I was taught from the very beginning not to trust any of them. We were a temptation. A forbidden lure that was like a magnet down here. "No, that's it. Thank you."

The moment the door shut and automatically locked, I didn't waste any time unpacking the food and putting it away. I left out what I needed: crackers, salami, turkey, two different cheeses, pickles, and olives. Wine. By a miracle, I just happened to find a wooden tray on the top shelf above the plates, and a single wine glass pushed in the far back.

Was I missing anything? Was there anything else I should do?

The questions came as I elegantly plated the tray. Time disappeared through the cutting, stacking, and fog. Once I set up the table and had everything out, I took my place on a chair, waiting. Thinking. Even dreaming as I ran my hands down the long white dress I'd found on my side of the closet. It wasn't until beeping sounded that I tore my gaze from the table and stood. What met me was not what I expected.

"Main Master."

Steps were fast, and I didn't miss what looked like rage on his face as he approached. Before I could scramble back or fall to my knees, he had me by the face, pinning me against the wall.

"Your Master will be here in less than a minute. You remember everything I taught you. Do not fuck this up; do you understand me?"

"Y-Yes. I did what you said."

His glance quickly went to the table. "You did well, so ignore all I say once he appears. This has to happen, slave. Your Master doesn't want the union, and he will fight it unless I give him reason not to. If he's on watch for my monster, it will distract his own. That's what we need. Jake isn't who he used to be. He loves all females. There's nothing more he hates than seeing them get mistreated or abused. He might be rusty in that department, but we're going to fix it. At least concerning you. To do that, we need to trigger him."

"Trigger? You mean to hurt me?"

I barely got the question out before the Main Master cut me off.

"That's right. This is business. If I'm going to reach him, I need to shake things up, otherwise he'll never reach his potential or feel anything for you. Neither of us can afford that. My plans run deep, and they include this child. So, first, I will wake his beast. Then, you do what you're taught. Trap it. Tame it. This is the only way. As a last resort, and only a last, tell him you have other options. Sebastian Rivers. Mention him as a possible Master who wants you. They're rivals. It'll flip a switch in Jake. I can't promise if that'll be good or bad. If he brings up the contract, tell him to look on page fifty-two. It'll get you out of this agreement with my permission. Are you ready?"

Silence played between us, and something in me twisted and grinded to a stop. Maybe it was my heart. Maybe it was common sense. Whatever it was joined my fight and disappeared in the icy blueness of the Main Master's eyes as I stared into them.

"Do it."

The back of his hand connected so hard my head spun to the side. Blood swept over my tongue at the split in my lip, and I sobbed, my knees buckling as they threatened to give out.

"Good girl. I'm proud of you. Keep your mind sharp, and don't you dare mess this up. You have him breed you before the morning. I'll be stopping by to make sure of it."

Another hit. More beeping.

"There's a small room to the right, inside the bedroom. It's a cell. Put him there."

Two guards paused at the doorway at seeing us but

continued through the room. Between them was a man in black. He was in chains and kept his head down as they escorted him through the living room. I could barely comprehend what was happening as my face throbbed through the constant beating of my heart. My Master bought another slave? A bad one?

"What the hell is going on here?"

The voice was so deep and full of anger. The growl he let out was instant. My stare landed on a tall man, in what appeared to be his mid-to-upper thirties. Dark hair was on the longer side, swept back, but falling just below his eyes, and he had a beard. He wore a suit, but it didn't look as if he were comfortable in it.

"Main Master, I asked you a question."

"And I don't have to answer it, but if you want to know, I was checking on her training. I taught her better than this." His stare pierced me as he glared. "*Do better*. You're the best, and you will act like it. I'll be watching." His finger rose not an inch from my trapped face, and for the smallest moment he pushed me harder into the wall. "I'll be back."

He gave one last squeeze along my jaw and let go. He didn't say anything else as he stormed from the apartment. My pulse was pounding so hard, instinct and shock had me scrambling to my Master and falling to my knees.

"Forgive me. I should have made you a dinner instead. I... I'm s-sorry, Master. I thought an appetizer could hold you over until you told me what you'd like me to make, but I should have done better. I will next time, I promise."

Fingers brushed the top of my head, and I sobbed again, not able to hold it in.

"You don't have to do that right now, slave. Stand. Show me what you made."

I obeyed, surprised as his hands came out to help me rise.

"I wasn't sure if you'd eaten. I hope you don't mind that I had the guard order us some things. If you let me know what you'd like, I'll start making it for you. We have steak, chicken, and a few sides. Vegetables, unless you don't like those."

Light brown eyes rose from the tray. When he met my stare, I had to force my gaze down. I didn't want to. There was something pulling me to keep searching his depths. Maybe it was the pain I could so easily sense from inside the darkness, or maybe it was the broken energy of his presence I could feel. It roped itself around me, clearing some of the fog, but there was also something terrifying about the way it put my nerves on edge. That only brought me back to the bad man they'd brought in.

"I am a bit hungry. No meal, this is perfect..." Hesitation had me swiftly looking up, only to lower my eyes again as he stepped closer. "Thank you."

"You're welcome. Is there anything else I can do for you?"

Seconds passed before his finger fitted under my chin. When he swept over the blood, I lifted my gaze again.

"No." He paused. "You may be a slave, but I never allowed my wife to cook for me, and I don't want it from you either. If I want a meal, I'll make it, or we'll make it together. Don't get me wrong, you'll have duties, but none will involve you being on your feet. You're here for one purpose, and only one. You're going to give me a child. Focus on that."

"And him?"

The Master's gaze cut to the bedroom door but came back to me.

"I won't sugarcoat what's about to happen. It's going to be a long night for me. Maybe for both of us. The cell is soundproof, but how much I'm not sure. Expect screams. Yells." Hesitation as his eyes scanned my face. "Any good in me died years ago. Don't go looking for it. You won't find any. That piece of shit in the room deserves to pay, and I plan to make him."

I cleared my throat, trying to stand taller.

"You mean to kill him?"

"Damn right I do. As painfully as possible."

A deep-rooted shaking had started, and nothing I could do would stop the way my body trembled like bait.

"May I ask what he did?"

The Master's hand dropped, and he took a deep breath.

"He killed three kids. He took them away from their families forever. That's all you need to know."

Kids. Families. Yes…my Master had lost his. This was his revenge. I would not get in the way of that. Whatever was best for my Master was best for me.

"Give him hell. That's what my mom would have said." I stepped back, moving to the far chair. "Would you like to have a snack with me before your fun?"

A smile tugged at his mouth, barely noticeable under the beard. He nodded, taking his place in the other chair. I grabbed an olive, popping it in my mouth, doing anything I could to try to add a layer of comfort between us. After all, it wasn't just my training. We'd be trying to have a baby together. Could I really go through with doing it tonight? My mind stole my fear. It just was. It had to happen.

"You're not what I expected. You're better." My Master sat down, grabbing a cracker as he began to stack it with the meat and cheese. "Were you briefed on me?"

"A little. I wasn't told much. I'm to give you a child, just as you said."

The Master's chewing slowed, and he swallowed, nodding.

"I promised to carry on my name, no matter what. I mean to do that."

"Of course." I cleared my throat, shifting in my seat. "Do you plan to try tonight after you're finished with the crow?"

My words were breathless. Barely there. Loud scraping sounded from the chair, and I jumped at the sound as the Master eased to his feet. His hands flattened on each side of the tray while he moved in inches from my face. For the life of me, I couldn't turn away. I could barely breathe with how close he was.

"I do. Tonight, and every day and night until it works."

1 VIRGIN SLAVE. WEARS A WHITE ROBE DURING THE AUCTION.

2 Nonvirgin slave. Wears a blue robe during the auction.

3 Docile, drugged slave. Can be W or B. Heavily trained. Good for elderly or those with disabilities.

MASTER A-0005

"I t was bullshit, really. A complete misunderstanding. I wasn't even that drunk. I kept trying to tell those officers. Hell, I passed the stupid fucking tests they kept giving me. You can watch the tapes and see. They framed me, plain and simple. I shouldn't even be here right now. What is this place, anyway? Don't I have rights or something?"

I took another drag from my cigarette, pushing the bottle closer so he could continue drinking with his free hand. The other was cuffed to the metal table we sat at. A table that was bolted to the floor, along with his chair that happened to be on a special swivel.

"Tell me about the accident."

Smoke left my mouth, joining the haze that rested above. The slave's lip curled back, and he grabbed the bottle, taking another drink.

"Don't I get a phone call or to talk to a lawyer? I don't like this room. Fuck, I don't like this place. No one will answer my questions. I want to talk to someone about a transfer. This isn't a...prison. Nothing about this is right."

"Tell me about the accident."

The slave's eyes narrowed as he put the bottle back on the table. "I've told you three times already, Mister, I'm not talking about it. Where the fuck am I? This isn't even a real cell. You live here?"

"The accident."

Before he could open his mouth, I pushed to my feet, grabbing the bottle and swinging wide to connect with the side of his face. Glass shattered and brandy and blood sprayed across the room.

"Make me ask again. I dare you."

Cries mixed with screams as the crow held to the split skin of his cheek, trying his best to jerk free of the restraints holding one of his hands and feet.

I sat back down, crossing my arms over my chest, waiting. Watching as he cursed and continued trying to work himself free. Blood was in a constant drip to the shiny metal surface, racing down his face as the flow only seemed to increase. Red covered his teeth through the yells and spilled over his bottom lip. The more crimson that appeared and pushed passed his fingers, the more panicked the slave became. The table was a mess, gaining small puddles and smears as the slave let go of his face to try to get his arm free.

"You're fucking crazy, man. You call someone. Get me out of here right now! Hey! Guards! Help!"

More yells. More screams. Minutes went by. Longer. When the slave realized I wasn't moving or talking, he began to slow. He wasn't going anywhere, and he was realizing that too. Here, there was no escape. There was no help.

"I don't remember anything. It was probably that bitch's fault."

My eyes flared through the boiling rage. I eased to my feet, and the crow jerked harder, fear drawing in his face as the volume of his voice began to shake and stutter. He kept trying to jerk against the cuffs, as if he could run away from me.

"It could have been me. I m-mean, I guess maybe I could have drifted in her lane. Stop! I didn't mean to! Fuck, man. Please, I want out of here. I want to leave!"

"*Quiet.*" The word was forced through my clenched teeth. "You're going to start at the beginning. From the moment you woke up and decided to be a fucking murderer."

"Whoa! Murderer? I didn't—"

"*Murderer!*"

Only a good two inches separated us. I was breathing so hard, it took everything I had not to pound his face into bloody nothingness. The slave slowly lowered, his body nearly convulsing through the trembling.

"I slept with a bottle n-next to my bed."

My inhale was deep, and my lids closed to trap me in the darkness. Moments blurred through the flashes of my dead family. Blood. Gashes from the twisted metal. Cold skin. Little hands. My cries. Even opening my eyes, I couldn't push away what was burned into my brain. I took a seat, forcing my hands open so they wouldn't fist. Not yet.

"Go on."

The slave continuously swallowed. "I...think I woke up drunk. Maybe I always do. I grabbed the bottle, taking a drink. It's the first thing I do. I. I. Can't take this. Any of it. Life, you know?"

I didn't answer.

"My cousin, Tate, he owed me money. After a few hours of sitting at home, I decided to go see if he was ready to pay me back. I guess I was already feeling a bit buzzed by then. I knew he was broke. He's always broke. He ain't got a good job like me. Or...like I used to have."

At my hard stare, he kept going.

"There are worse jobs than construction. All these new homes going up, someone has to build them. My dad owns the company.

Fired me three times over the last few years, but he knows how good I am. He needs me." He stopped. "Needed me. I'll be out of here soon. I'll appeal the stupid decision. They didn't even let me tell my side. I was advised not to take the stand, but I think if they knew…It was only a few drinks after work. The bar was just three miles down the road. It's not like I targeted the car or anything. I was tired. Like I said, my work is grueling. I bust my ass all day in the hot sun. It was my day off. I was just trying to let loose. To relax some." He paused, anger sliding into his tone. "Hey, I need a doctor. I'm losing a lot of blood here."

"You're not losing nearly enough."

I stood and the tension in the crow's shoulders increased. He tried shifting in the chair, watching me uneasily as I headed to the shelf on the far back wall. He couldn't see what I had resting there, but if he did, he wouldn't be so calm or clueless.

Placing down my cigarettes and lighter, I grabbed a small knife. The blade was no longer than five inches. It was serrated, not smooth. I headed back to the table watching the crow's eyes squint through the fear that built.

"I w-want to leave now. I said it might be my fault. You got my confession or whatever."

My mouth stayed closed as I stared him down. It didn't take much for the man's eyes to lower to the table.

"I'm going to give you this knife. I'll give you one minute to slice your own throat. If you don't, you belong to me."

Small, hard jerks against the cuff was his only reaction. He knew I was serious, and panic kept him trying to break free. He wouldn't. There was no escape.

"One minute." I placed the knife down, taking my seat not far away. The slave gripped the handle, clenching around it as he panted in increasing anxiety. I looked at my watch, ignoring the sharp blade cutting through the air not inches from my face. Each swing and slice did nothing to bring him closer. Sounds and whimpers grew, turning into yells as I continued to watch the time tick down. "Fifteen seconds."

"Help! Guards! Someone!"

Faster, he tried stabbing towards me. As he reared his arm back, I lunged from the chair, grabbing his wrist and slamming his fisted hand against the metal table. The blade fell free, but I didn't let go of my hold. I kept his wrist pinned and with my other hand, I gripped his elbow, forcing it inward in one brutal blow. Bone broke through skin and screams turned to howls as the crow went wild in the chair.

Me…I felt no satisfaction. I watched. Minutes went by. The slave continued to cry and sway. *To beg.*

"Tonight, we end here. When I return, you'll tell me more."

I headed to the door, pausing as I grabbed the keys from my pocket.

"Please, man. I swear I'll do whatever you want. Let me out of here. *Please.* At least get me help or something. God, please!"

"God can't hear you nor will he save you. No one can."

With that, I swung the door open, turning to lock it behind me. I stayed quiet, heading to the bathroom. It didn't take long to brush my teeth and shower. Or maybe I was rushing through because I was nervous and sick to my stomach at what I knew I had to do. Could I? Should I?

No answer would come. Not when I cracked the bathroom door to give me enough light to see my way, nor when I stood beside a bed that held a woman I didn't know. A woman I was meant to impregnate.

"Master?"

The soft voice was thick with sleep. The fact that it held a seductive pull was nothing more than my duties outweighing my common sense. There was no way around my promise. I had to do this, despite it being the last thing in the world I wanted.

Kayla's outline lifted as she sat up in the bed. She didn't reach out or touch me. She shifted, pulling the nightgown over her head. Even with how dark it was, I didn't miss the way her arms crossed over her breasts, or how I could feel the mattress shaking against my legs.

I grabbed the towel wrapped around my hips, letting it fall to the floor. My heart thudded sickeningly in my chest, and I pulled down the blankets sliding in. When I turned towards my slave, there was just enough light to barely see her features. There wasn't much expression, but from what I could see, there was a tinge of worry. Unease. She was looking to me for some sort of comfort, and I had none to give.

"Lay down."

The slave's bottom lip stuck out for the briefest moment, and she obeyed, lowering back to the pillow. I kept my eyes on her face, refusing to close myself off to what I was doing. This slave, Kayla, she would not be Maggie. I would not pretend or fantasize to cover up my betrayal to my vows. To the only love I'd ever known outside of her and my children. To do that was cheapening their memory, and I'd have no part of it.

"Move your hands. You will not cover yourself."

Fingers pressed into her generous breasts before easing to her sides. I swallowed back the bitter taste on my tongue, hating myself even more as my body responded. I was so fucking hard; I couldn't stand it.

Duty. Duty. Duty.

Duty would have me fucking her. No touching. No kissing. No foreplay. None of that was required with how ready I was. Yet...my hand was lifting to cup her breast. I was even teasing her nipple as my thumb circled the hard nub, pinching it until the slave was making the softest moaning sound. Her hips shifted, and her knees drew up. It was enough to have the anger rushing to the forefront. Enough to...have me hooking around her hip to pull her in the middle of the bed as I lifted and fitted myself between her thighs almost greedily. *Possessively.* Was there still traces of the old me in there?

Wetness met my fingers as I reached down, tracing them along her slit. Pain flared as I bit into my bottom lip. Fuck, she was so hot and ready, and I hadn't done shit to really get her in the mood. I couldn't stand that I even cared, but I couldn't change who I was. Even unattached, I still wasn't an asshole. I had to do something enough to appease the only decency I still held.

"Spread wider."

I brushed her clit, letting one of my fingers slide into her as she opened her legs even more. Her breath held, and I shifted my shoulders, thrusting and adding another finger as I felt her stretch around them. My cock ached, and my only saving grace was knowing I wouldn't have to do this long. She needed my cum. That wasn't going to take more than a few minutes if she was lucky.

"Like this, Master?"

"Just like that."

She arched, sucking in a breath as I pushed my fingers deeper. The exhale turned into a long moan as her lips parted, and she moved even more against me. The sight was so hypnotic, I didn't realize how much time had passed until her increasing whimpers turned into full blown cries of need.

"Master, I'm so close. Do I wait? *Master.*"

My fingers withdrew, grabbing around my cock as I fit it against her entrance. Heat scorched me, reminding me of my sins. I lifted my gaze, taking in her heavy lids. Even with the dimness, I could see how much she wanted this. Her breaths were just as heavy as mine. There was a plea in the way her stare begged me to keep going. And I wanted to. Maybe a little too much.

Before I could process what I was doing, I was pushing from the bed and grabbing the towel to wrap back around me. Guilt squeezed my chest, and bile burned my throat. Anger. It took over everything as I stormed into the living area. I'd never wanted a drink more in my life. It didn't help that I refused to touch the stuff.

God, what was I doing? Was my word worth more than the promise I made to my wife? I loved Maggie. She and our kids were my entire world. But she was gone. I knew that, even if I didn't want to face it. My word to my father, on the other hand, wasn't going anywhere. My name sure would if I didn't produce an heir. I was the only one who could carry on the Princeton name, and if I wanted to be truthful, one child wasn't enough. I'd had two and now they were gone. Why the fuck didn't I do the IVF route? Elec and I talked about it, but I didn't trust anyone but myself to get the deed done. Motives, secrets, vile acts ran rampant in our circle, and I'd make sure there were no questions on paternity. I had documentation of her cycles. She'd been examined and tested over the last few weeks. Those were all I'd really cared about when I signed my contract with the Main Master.

A growl tore from my throat. My hands rubbed against my face, and I couldn't ignore how rock hard my cock still was. I was torn between love and duty. Between love and tradition. Survival of what us elites held the dearest. *Blood.* How much was mine worth? How much was hers? Ours together…fucking priceless.

FC0001

There was no time for clothes or modesty as I raced to the living room. This breeding was a must, and we'd been so close. I knew it wasn't me. Elec warned me how my Master didn't want this. Thing was, I couldn't afford him to back out. Stranger or not, Elec would be furious with me if we didn't consummate this union. It was important it be the two of us. And I'd been prepared. I'd been taught to try to sway things my way. I hadn't been honest when I told Jake I hadn't been briefed on him. Elec told me enough for my training to kick in. I could manipulate him. I had to. I had orders; I didn't have a choice.

The Master had his head down, pacing as I stepped from the darkness. His hand fell from his head, and he looked up, raking his eyes over my nude body as he did so. I could see he was still turned on. The size of his cock couldn't be mistaken from under the towel. He very much wanted this. My feelings were irrelevant.

"Slave, go back to bed."

"You're finished trying?"

"I said go back to bed."

Anxiety fluttered within. Reasoning with him was not going

to work. Elec would be back in the morning, and I was running out of time.

"I'm sorry if I'm not a good fit for you. If I can just use your phone, I will call the Main Master to retrieve me. I know I'm not the prettiest woman here. I'm sure he'll gladly replace me with someone more appealing to your tastes. There were plenty who wanted me outside of you. Maybe the Main Master can convince them to a swap."

"What?"

Confusion had him turning more towards me.

"I'm clearly not your type, and that's okay. You have needs outside of me. As the Main Master's project, I was promised certain things. I'm above the typical breeder. I'm special and have choices in my future. What I wanted above all was a family, Sir. I want a kind Master who adores me. Who's excited to see me carry their child. One who will allow me to be a part of the baby's life as much as I can for being down here. I don't believe you're that person. There's duty…and then there's a partnership. I want to connect and bond with my Master over this, not just be a shell for their needs. That's what you want for me, and that makes me sad because I hoped—" I stopped, holding back the tears that came from the lies. Tears that seemed to come from nowhere…*everywhere*. I wasn't promised those things, but they were definitely possible if my Master would only allow it.

"I loved my adopted parents, but I never got the completion I needed for family. There's this hole inside, and the thing is eating me alive." I wiped the tears. "I need that bond, Master. I need this for me. I have nothing else. If I could just…if." I stopped. "The Main Master was sure you were the one, but he's wrong. You can't give me what I need. I don't believe you're capable of even trying. That's not fair for me. Perhaps Master Rivers would have been a better choice."

"Who? Did you say Rivers? Not fucking Sebastian Rivers."

My lips parted at the roar of his name. "I'm not sure, but I

A. A. DARK

believe that's what the Main Master called him. Your phone, please. It won't take long."

Rejection. The name. I watched my Master go from confused at my need to call, to downright livid as I held out my hand. He was shaking, nearly baring his teeth as he glared at me.

"Sir, please. He won't be upset. If anything, he'll be relieved. I think he held a little doubt on whether you were capable as well."

"Fuck both of your doubt. You're not fucking going anywhere."

He took a step forward.

"Let's be honest, Sir, you're not looking to connect with your breeder. You want a body, not one that comes with a mind or opinions. I'm sorry, but that's not me. I offered to make you dinner tonight. It was a gift, not because it was ingrained with my training. It was my chance to bond with you. To see if we connected. I can't connect with someone who can't stand to touch me. Who can't at least try to be affectionate with me."

His head shook as his eyes narrowed. "I was very clear with the Main Master on what I wanted. Feelings on either side were nowhere in my contract. If I was looking for a love match, I would have done it outside of this place. I didn't, and I won't. I'm not looking for love. I had that. It's dead. You're a breeder. I bought you. Your thoughts, opinions, likes, dislikes, mean nothing in the scheme of things. Why? Because I'm the fucking Master. What I say goes. And what I say is, you're not going anywhere except back in that room."

"Back in the room to what? Get fucked by a man who doesn't even feel attraction towards me? You could have anyone in this place. You're handsome enough. Spare us both the headache and let go of the stubbornness. It's only one call to the Main Master. You can have your pretty shell before the sun comes up."

"Stubbornness? Pretty shell?" Each slow stride held more

558

power than the last. I did everything I could to stand tall, but I'd never felt so small as he came to tower over me. "You think I'm not attracted to you? That I don't want you?" He jerked the towel free, allowing it to fall to the floor. His grip locked on my wrist, bringing my hand to fit around his hard cock. He held me there, not letting me remove it. "Does this look like I don't want you? It's the entire reason I left you on that bed. *It had nothing to do with you.* I lost my family, slave. It hurts to betray my vows. It kills me to feel this at all. To me, this is wrong. Wrong and yet... you *feel* my dilemma. I'm adjusting."

"I'm sorry. I truly am. I wished I knew what to say, but I only know the truth. I wasn't the one who hurt you. I don't deserve to suffer because of something I didn't do. Something I'm guessing *he* did, in that room." My other arm reached forward to his free hand, bringing his palm to flatten to my stomach. "Give the crows your hate and me hope. You need an heir. I want a family. *A family*," I stressed, squeezing more into the hand on my stomach. "The only way I'm walking back to that room freely is if you give me your word that's what we'll become. I know this is hard for you, but let it go. Keep it in your secret room. I know my place as a slave. I know the child can never live with me or know who I am, but you can give me time with them above the Gardens. You can bring me news and pictures of them as they grow. You can *try* to embrace this."

"I am trying. You're here. But if you expect love—"

I gave a hard shake showing him that's not what I was looking for. "I'd never expect that from you. Affection and love are not the same thing. You can be kind, and not give me your heart. You can be gentle, and not put a ring on my finger. Give me the family without giving me your true self. Play the role and feed me my fantasy. I'll give you a child. Be good to me, and I'll give you as many as you want."

The Master's brow creased, and his hand slid to my side, pulling me closer. The thickness of his cock was the only thing separating us. I couldn't stop myself from increasing the pressure as I stroked down to the head. Jake's lids closed, and a small rumble vibrated his throat. To think would only hurt him more, so I'd do what I was taught. I wouldn't allow him to do anything but feel.

Adding pressure, I eased him back until his legs connected with the sofa. Jake studied me, but sat down, watching as I lowered to my knees before him. His cock was heavy and thick in my hold. There was a moment of what looked like uncertainty sweep through his eyes. My head went down, and I swirled my tongue over the precum coating the tip. His length jerked in my grasp, and he moaned, pushing his fingers through my hair as I opened my mouth and eased him inside.

"God dammit. Fuck."

His fist tightened, painfully. I sucked in a breath from the stinging, going back to let my tongue mold to the underside of his cock as he led me deeper. I added suction at his pull, only for me to slide back down. My lips met my hand, and I nearly gagged as the Master's hold locked me into place and tightened to a degree that had me crying out. The sound was muffled, vibrating my lips enough to truly make me gag. Tears collected in my eyes, and still he kept his cock in my throat while I pressed my nails into his thigh.

"You're good. Too good. I could almost overlook how you smoothly transitioned into taking control. Very smart of you. Thing is, slave, that's one thing you'll never have. All the decisions between us are mine. Your terms; you leading me to sit; choosing to lure me out of my mood by making me focus on pleasure instead of pain. Mentioning that bastard Sebastian to rile me up. Elec taught you well, but it won't work with me."

I sucked in a breath, coughing as he jerked me up by my hair. Tears raced down my cheeks while he forced me to look at him.

"Your terms and ideal of a family I can work with. If I decide to give you more, that's my choice, and mine alone. Your position as anything other than a slave, I won't tolerate. As for the breeding part, you leave that up to me." He brought me closer, searching my eyes as he moved in to brush his lips against mine. "Your first mistake was choosing this spot. There's no fucking way I'm conceiving my child on this couch. You and I may not know each other, but what you'll learn is I don't do anything half-ass. That's another battle I'm fighting. If we're going to make a baby, we're doing it the right way. I may be having trouble accepting this, but that does not mean I wouldn't want or do anything for my child. Understand?"

"Yes, Master."

"Good."

The anger was still in his tone. He stood, pulling me up by my hair. Fingers slid free, and he quickly swept me off my feet to cradle in his arms. There was nothing gentle about the action. We were at the bed in only a few steps.

"Give you my phone. *Sebastian Rivers.* As if I'd hand you over to that son of a bitch. As if you really had a choice in any of this at all." A sound rumbled from him, and whatever existed between them kept eating at my Master. The more time that went by, the angrier he became. "I can't believe he's here. Fuck. I won't let them take you. They can't with my baby in your stomach."

"You'd breed me just so I couldn't go to him?"

"I wanted you before he was in the picture. Now that he is, you can bet your ass I'm going to. You have something I need. Something he'd kill to have. I won't let him, and neither will you." His eyes were intense as they met mine. "Your special say with Elec stops with me. I'm what is best for you; it's not Sebastian. Accept that, and let any manipulations the Main Master taught you go. They won't serve you well. It would be stupid to even try with me." He nipped at my lip, only to kiss me softly. "Sebastian...*wanting a breeder*. Wanting you. This is so much bigger than what I thought. Bigger than what Elec mentioned."

He paused. "It doesn't matter. I have you. I bought you. It wouldn't be smart to play these Masters' games, slave. We'll eat you alive. Nod your head and say you choose me. Say you're done weighing your decision, and you want my baby."

He dropped me on the mattress. I went to cry out in surprise, immediately cut off by his mouth and body crushing into mine. He pulled me back to the pillows, thrusting his tongue against me. The weight of his body was something I didn't even know I needed. The fog inside wavered, almost clearing for a split moment. It felt good to have him on me. To feel him moving against me as he put emotion behind a kiss I didn't think him capable of.

Fingers slid behind my neck and the grip was claiming as he lifted the smallest amount, bringing my mouth more into his. Taking something from me that I didn't even know was there. My heart swelled and my lids flew open. All I could do was stare up in stunned shock. Maybe even fear. I'd been playing a part for the Main Master for so long, I couldn't decipher what was real or staged anymore. This...this felt real and that suddenly scared the hell out of me. It was enough to almost wake me up from what felt like a dream.

"Choose me. Say it."

"I—"

His kiss took my breath away, and I moaned into his mouth, feeling myself pull him more into me.

"Say yes. I'm going to give you your baby, right now, and when Elec shows up first thing in the fucking morning, because I know he will, you can tell him you're content with your choice of Master. You can tell him Sebastian isn't the one for you. You're mine now, and I'd like to see anyone try to take you away."

MASTER A-0005

Worry or guilt couldn't get through when all I could think about was that son of a bitch, Sebastian Rivers. We'd grown up together. Competed against each other in everything from sports to grades to girls. By a miracle, I always seemed to pull off the win, but almost hadn't with Maggie. They'd met before we'd ever seen each other, and they'd hit it off hot. So hot, my former wife had lost her virginity to Sebastian, but their relationship hadn't lasted longer than it took for me and Maggie's eyes to meet. From the first stare, we both fell hard. As much as I'd like to say the rest was history, it hadn't been an easy path. With her parents already approving of the match to Sebastian, they almost didn't allow her to be mine. It was a battle I won because of my last name and money, but the war had only truly begun at that point. Sebastian wouldn't let go, and his constant trapping of my wife, even after our vows, had taken its toll. Now that he knew about my slave, I feared history was going to repeat itself in more ways than one.

"You'll give me meetings with the child? *Pictures*?"

My arm slid under her lower back, pulling her down and

more into me as I ravaged her mouth. Wherever the passion had come from, I didn't have a clue.

"You're the mother. If you're a good slave, I'll give you more than that."

Kayla's breath caught as I dove in sucking and biting against her neck. She was arched for me, moving down my length as I rubbed my cock along her wetness.

"Your word." She moaned as I rotated my hips, and the head of my cock entered her.

"You have it. We'll be a partnership, like you wanted. We'll work together in everything, so long as you obey me when it matters."

I inched in, only to withdraw and slide deeper. The tightness had me groaning as I continued the thrusts. She was so wet and getting louder by the second. When she moved in to hold around my neck, my kiss was automatic. It was…real. Intoxicating. I barely managed to remember to breathe.

"Jesus. God." I buried my length, pushing so deep, I was losing myself. The internal alarms were constant little reminders that something wasn't right or normal, but I couldn't make sense of what they meant. My brain wouldn't get over the need to consume. To make Kayla mine before I lost her for good. *And I could.* Yes, I bought her, but that contract had been full of holes. I read every page. Elec didn't need much to change his mind. Thing was, the moment she was confirmed pregnant, she truly belonged to me.

The pressure around my neck tightened and fingers gripped into my hair. I was thrusting harder. Faster. The slave's legs were drawn up high as she took each slam of my cock. The frenzy inside me was all too real.

I'd keep her.

No one would take her away.

I'd kill them if they tried.

Let them…Let them try.

I had something now.

I had her.

Maybe even a baby on the way, soon.

A child.

A new start.

A new life.

Did I want that?

Could I stomach my choice?

Mine.

Mine.

Her.

A baby.

Her.

A slave.

My slave.

Not Elec's.

Not Sebastian's.

Not my parents or hers.

Not Bram Whitlock.

Not the Waltons'.

Mine.

Mine.

Mine.

"Master. Yes. Master. Kiss me, more. Faster. Yes, please. Faster. *Faster.*"

Words and pleas buzzed my head as I pounded into Kayla. As I cemented every fucking thought or concern so deep inside of her, they'd never see the light of day again. She was mine. This baby would be mine. I could have something again. No...I *had* something already, and the predator that had been reborn in me at Sebastian's mention was ready to draw blood to keep it that way.

Spasms jerked my slave's legs, and her screams only drove me even deeper into the dark tunnel of fixation I was enveloped in.

Here was the Jake Princeton I knew well. The one who I thought died with my family. Had I thought I transitioned him into a killer? That he'd been lost all those years back? He was alive, and he had someone new. Someone…in jeopardy of being stolen again. That… was something he could focus on. That…would help ease the guilt.

I gave one last slide of my tongue against hers before I pulled back.

"Fuck, look at me."

Kayla's heavy lids lifted as she gazed into my eyes. I couldn't help but press my lips softly into hers, repeatedly. Maybe it was the final seal to my past, or a stamp to my future. As I stared down into my slave's face, feeling my cum pump into her, I wouldn't allow myself to see anything else. This was it. *She was it.* I couldn't take that back.

* * *

"FAVORITE MOVIE?"

I stared up at the ceiling, pursing my lips, trying to figure out how in the last few hours I'd gotten to this point. How…I'd done a full circle from when I'd first met Maggie. It left me sick yet… numb. Angry? No…not at her. At me? At Elec? Sebastian? Maybe it was life in general. "Tombstone. You?"

"Sleepless in Seattle."

I glanced over, not able to help the small laugh that left me. Had that just happened? What the fuck was this transition in me? "Classic. Favorite food?"

"Steak. You?"

"Steak. Music?"

"All." She turned on her side, facing me. We'd already had sex three times. It was close to seven in the morning, and we were both barely holding on. If it weren't for the million questions barreling through, I might have already been sleeping. "I'm hungry. How about you, Master? Breakfast? I can make you coffee."

"That sounds perfect." I glanced over to the clock on the bedside table. "By the time we finish, Elec should be knocking on my door." Her smile fell. "He will, won't he."

It wasn't a question.

"I believe so. He'll want to check in on me. He's...very determined for this breeding. If not us, then." She stopped. "He's put in a lot of hard work training me. Truthfully, I'm not sure why, but I don't mind. It beats the alternative. I could have been a b1 and be dead right now. Or I could have been left without a choice and gotten a horrible Master."

My stomach twisted at the words, and heat flooded my veins. *A Master like Sebastian Rivers.*

"You're safe with me. Let's keep it that way. I won't let anyone hurt you."

"What if you hurt me?"

Pushing to my elbow, I looked down at her, brushing the dark hair from the side of her face before I could stop myself.

"Physically, never, but I'm your Master. Like I said before, I'm not a good man. What I am is a good father, a partner, and that needs to be your focus. Elec may have trained you, but his job is finished. You're mine now. All mine." At her uncertain nod, I drew my hand back, taking a deep breath. "Coffee. Breakfast. Let's do this."

She was smiling as we stood, but it didn't last as a knock sounded.

"Well, that didn't take very long." I slid on a pair of pajama bottoms, grabbing a white t-shirt from the dresser. Kayla was putting on a light blue robe, tightening it as I headed for the door, angrily. As I went by the mirror, I jolted to a stop, bringing my fingers to the large mark on my neck from my slave's sucking. I was starting to see she had a habit of that. One I didn't mind

given the shitshow I was about to stir. The moment I opened the
door, my rage only grew.

"You're up early." Elec stood there with Sebastian, both
smug as shit as they took me in. Elec's suit was dark blue,
making his eyes even brighter, where Sebastian's was a light
gray. It suited him with his blonde hair and green eyes. He
looked dressed to kill…steal, and that didn't work in his favor as
I tried to hold on to my temper.

"Early? We haven't been to sleep yet. You have some nerve
bringing him here, Main Master. Can I help you with something?" My glare narrowed even more as Sebastian put his hands
behind his back. The look he threw Elec said more than either of
them did.

"I need a word with slave one."

"If you're checking to see if I bred her, I did. Multiple times,
if you really want to know. She's no longer your concern, Elec.
She's sure as fuck not his."

The Main Master nodded. "It's good to hear you both took to
each other. As it is, I'm coming in to see her anyway. Move and
let us in, Master Five."

"Only you. *He* stays outside."

"If that's what you want."

"It is." I pulled the door open wider, allowing him in. I
immediately slammed it shut. Kayla was in the kitchen, and the
coffee was already going. The pots and pans were on the stove,
and she placed the eggs and bacon down on the counter before
walking quickly over to him, lowering to kneel.

"Main Master."

"Stand, slave."

She obeyed at Elec's command. When her head lifted, he
reached out, holding her chin to make her meet his eyes.

"Did Master Five breed you?"

"He did. Three times."

"Cycle day?"

"I'm on day ten, Main Master."

"Perfect. Have you eaten since last night?"

"We were about to, Sir."

"Next time you're up all night, you are not to wait so long before nourishing your body. It needs a constant supply of energy." Elec glanced at me. "Keep her fed and rested."

"I know what I'm doing."

He ignored me, looking back to her. His hold didn't move, and I didn't like how attached he seemed to be. This wasn't the Main Master I knew from growing up or our meetings. He wasn't the one I talked to at the auction. Not even the one who'd offered the contract. Something was...different. Or maybe I just hadn't seen him so protective over something.

"You're to rest after you eat and in-between breedings. Don't lift anything too heavy. Your emotional state is the most important. No risks. We've talked about this."

"We have, Sir. I will take care of myself."

There was a pause as he kept staring into her eyes.

"Any other issues you wish to tell me about? Pulls? Yearnings?"

"What?"

They didn't answer me as she swallowed hard. "No. I... haven't really had much time to focus on anything else."

"Does he suit you?"

"I believe he does. Master Five has been." She stopped. "He has been careful and generous so far. Kind."

Elec's eyes flashed with something, growing harder as he glanced at me. When he turned back to her, his head gave the smallest nod.

"Kind will work for now. See how things progress. If they're good, you'll have to be honest. I'm a call away in the meantime, if you don't feel comfortable." He let out a breath. "I want you in medical once a week from here on out. I will send you your own phone. You're to text every other day. You will keep me posted."

"Posted for what? What are you talking about, yearnings?"

"Slave one will tell you when she's ready and not a moment before. Don't push her."

"Alright, enough. This is not what we agreed to. She's *my* slave, Main Master. I bought her. I bred her. There's nothing else to keep tabs on. She's mine. I can easily give you the news when there's some to tell." I came up behind my slave, flattening my hand on her stomach as I eased her back towards me. She didn't fight. She let me lead, even resting against me when she couldn't move back any further.

"You bred her. It doesn't mean it took. Until it does, as stated in our contract, she's still mine. We run off of cycles here at the Gardens for the special fcs2. If she doesn't take this cycle, and your relationship is not working for her, I have the option to find her a new Master. Good luck." He took a step back, turning but stopping as his brows drew in and he turned back to us. "She'll have her own phone, but if I hear you withheld it or she wants to reach out to me, you are not to deny her request. Don't let me hear otherwise. It won't fare well for you Master Five."

"Wait." I stepped around her. "Wait one goddamn minute. The contract did not state anything about cycles. I read every page. There was no time length for how long it would take. You said as much last night after I bought her. What the fuck is going on? Is it because of him? Let me guess, he offered you more money so he could take her away from me. Is that it?"

Elec's mouth pulled back at the side.

"Page fifty-two. Second paragraph. First sentence. *The slave and their overall health and wellbeing are to be monitored by the Main Master until a child is conceived. At any point until then, the Main Master has the right to cancel the sale.* No refunds either, as you're getting use of my property. And no, Jake, this doesn't have to do with the money. Sebastian has promised me *results*. I need those. Just keep doing what you're doing. The only thing you have to worry about is your temper and whether the breeding takes. It'd be a damn shame if it didn't. Treat her well or otherwise you lose her. Those are my terms, and you'd be smart to comply with them. You don't want to cross me."

1 NONVIRGIN SLAVE. WEARS A BLUE ROBE DURING THE AUCTION.

2 (fc: female crow, mc: male crow) Ruined, disfigured slaves. Breeders. Convicts fall into this category. Black robe during the auction. Usually the cheapest slave.

FC0001

I was the first. The foundation of a dream in my Main
Master's eyes. He'd once talked to me about it when I was
above the Gardens, locked away in a room in the military installation that kept me hidden while they built this place. I'd been
curled in a ball, crying and afraid. Elec hadn't been angry or
mean to me. Quite the opposite. Soothing. Caring. He'd even
mentioned how he thought of keeping me for himself. Why, I
hadn't a clue. It crossed my mind that he wanted to personally
breed me. That was his primary focus for my path, but perhaps at
some point he'd decided against taking that route. Maybe he
didn't like kids. Maybe he wasn't ready. Whatever it was, he
kept hidden inside himself, in a deep hole no one could get
through to. I'd tried for months, even telling him my own secrets
I never thought I'd tell a soul. He was easy to confide in like
that. Quiet. Always listening. Always…seeming to be interested.

We'd talk about everything. He'd mentioned once he lost the
woman he'd loved. No details. No name. Just fact. I also knew
his hate for his cousin, although he'd never mentioned the name
or gender to that either. Elec went into detail on the hell both had
gone through. Despite their similar upbringing, the Main Master

never felt good enough, and he planned to change that. He told me how he intended to take over everything. I didn't know what that involved either. Only that...even as I faded further away inside myself, I believed he'd meant it. Why wouldn't I after knowing he ran this place. After years of training. Of helping him as I watched him embrace his own sick needs. He'd done more than unlock something in me during my time as his apprentice. I changed. Completely transformed until I couldn't put myself back in my sweet, goody two-shoes box I was packaged in. Maybe he hadn't expected me to enjoy helping him as much as I did, but he said it was in my blood, as if he knew the monsters it carried.

Monsters...I'd brought to my Master's home. How could a mother, a breeder, want to commit such atrocities? If my Master only knew who I really was, he'd more than likely not want me at all. He was the killer; the future mother of his heir wasn't supposed to be too. Yet, I was. Nothing made me happier. Nothing helped me disappear like losing myself in the thought of dissecting bodies. The act called to me. The need to butcher and hack up until they were nothing but pieces was almost too much to even think about.

"You're distracted."

Was I still moaning? Still going through the motions even though I was so far away? I was. These days it seemed I stayed on autopilot. The mere mention of my demons stirred them. The Main Master had whispered them back to life. Had he done it intentionally? The phantom screams called to me like the most passionate lover. Almost like my new Master. He was trying, even though I knew a part of him was against even touching me. Neither of us had a choice, but we were doing the best we could.

A heartache worse than the one I had for being here engulfed me, dragging me into hollowed tunnels of haunting need. They led me to blue eyes and bloody hands. Intricately poetic hands if I wanted to be honest. I always ended up covered in crimson.

Not him. Not Elec. How could a person look beautiful amid a graveyard of corpses?

He said I was.

It hadn't been in a romantic or even a lustful way. More... fascination. Appreciation? Neither of us had an attraction towards each other like that. He was too beautiful, and me...I was a slave. A tool to help my Main Master achieve whatever was needed for his plan. It didn't matter what that might entail. Good. Bad. Horrifying. The damage he had accomplished opening this pandora's box was done.

"Too distracted to even answer?"

Fingers gripped tighter in my hair, pulling my head back as my Master made me arch. I sucked in a breath, moaning as he plunged deep. Fisting my hands to the sheet, I forced words to come.

"I'm sorry. I'm a bit dizzy."

And I was. It had nothing to do with the sex and everything to do with the way my brain was having a hard time focusing.

"Dizzy?" My Master withdrew, easing me from my knees to lay on my back. "Why didn't you say something? You don't have to keep going if you're not feeling well. We've been trying to conceive for days. I think we can both rest for a night or two."

"I just need a moment. Maybe something to eat or drink."

He reached over to the end table next to the bed, grabbing my glass of water. I sat up, taking a sip.

"I'm going to grab you a snack." Eagerness drew in his brow, only for it to faulter as he narrowed his eyes. "Are you ready to talk yet?"

Before I could stop myself, my gaze shot to the crow's room. The shaking came back, just like it had when I saw the prisoner being brought in. It wasn't fear that left me trembling...it was desire. Longing. I wanted nothing more than to hear his screams. I wanted to read the fear. Experience the gut-flipping nausea as they shifted in emotion as I helped to bring on their pain.

"I don't know."

My Master's eyes widened. "This is good. Before it was no. Now it's uncertainty. We can work with that."

"I don't think we can." I pouted. It was more training and less intellectual realization as the Gardens version of me went through the motions.

"You'd be surprised how understanding I can be, slave. If you'll just confide in me, we can move forward. We're trying to have a baby. I need you to be honest. Not just for your sake, but for our future child. It's imperative you tell me. I think I have a right to know."

"You're right. You do. I just..." I blinked through a way to even say the words out loud. There was a part of me that wanted to confess everything, but there was also what felt like a block on doing so.

The Master's hand came up. He left the room at a quick pace, returning with a banana and a bag of trail mix I'd ordered earlier.

"You just what? The Main Master mentioned yearnings. A pull. To what? I keep trying to make sense of it. Are you a former drug addict? Do you have a pull to pills or heroin or something?"

"No, of course not."

He let out what appeared to be a sigh of relief.

"If it's not that, I think I can handle anything."

"Don't be so sure of that." I peeled the banana, taking a bite as I stared ahead. Mid-chew, I turned to Jake, searching his face. He was still peering over at me, holding an expression I couldn't quite make sense of. He'd spent hours in the cell torturing the crow now every day since I'd been here. Four days now? He was there, and I couldn't ignore how the hours seemed to last forever when he was doing what I wanted. *What I needed.* If I wanted this to work, did I really have a choice but to be honest? He never left me here alone. At least not yet. It's not like I could sneak in and have any sort of fun even if he did. He kept the door locked. It would come down to me calling Elec and something told me if I did, I'd break any trust I'd gained with my Master up to this point. Our union wasn't easy for him. That was obvious, but he was getting better at not being so awkward, and that made all the difference.

His hand came out, and he took mine in his, waiting...

"I've been here for two years."

"The Main Master told me."

I nodded. "I've been through a lot of training. Some of that training was not...conventional."

"Breeders, you're trained in sexual things, yes?"

"I am. All things. This wasn't that. I." My head lowered while I stared at our hands. His were so much bigger than mine. And calloused and rough, where I'd never imagine them to be.

My eyes lifted back to his. Before I could speak, Jake's phone echoed through the room. A small growl left him, and he reached over to the end table, grabbing it.

"Hello?"

Anger. It had him closing his eyes and breathing in deep.

"Of course. No, I wasn't told." His lids cracked open, more in a glare than anything. "She doesn't need any training. She's fine." A pause. My Master stood, heading over to grab clothes. As he started to get dressed, his temper soured even more. "This is not what we agreed to, Elec. Are you watching us? Did you know she was about to tell me her little secret so you decided to help her so she couldn't open up to me?"

My heart thudded in my chest. I swallowed hard, standing to get dressed as well, jolting to a stop as my Master's head jerked hard for me to stop.

"No. I'm putting my foot down. Slave one needs rest. I just got her a snack because she told me she was dizzy. She's not feeling so well. Training or whatever rouse you're pulling can wait. I'm her Master, and I'm not just saying no; I'm saying fuck no."

The volume on the end didn't get louder, but I could hear the Main Master's tone deepen, even if I couldn't hear what he was saying.

"No, we don't need you here. She's fine. She can rest while we deal with these trials." Another pause. "Give me ten minutes."

My Master hung up, cursing as he tossed the phone on the bed and started buttoning up the white dress shirt.

"I have no idea why I agreed to this position on the board. Free bodies? I was doing just fine finding them myself outside of here. I'm a risk," he growled out. "That's what the hell they said. The Gardens and a position on the board or else they'd keep me down here forever without a choice. Can you believe that shit? God forbid I taint my name or bloodline. They need me to continue it." He glanced over, pushing the shirt into the slacks to tuck in. "Nothing about me matters except the mere existence. I never thought I'd hate being who I am, but alas it's come." He grabbed a tie and his jacket. "I have trials to attend to. They've apparently been going all morning. I shouldn't be too much longer. A few hours, tops. You'll be okay?"

"I'll be fine." My fingers pushed through each other as I twisted my digits nervously. "Did the Main Master mention I had training? It may be important."

Jake's eyes cut up as he slowed tying the tie.

"What more could you need to learn? If you ask me," he waved his hand, "I'd say you're pretty damn qualified in the breeding department."

"It's more than that. I learn all sorts of skills."

"Like what? Cooking? Cleaning? Mothering skills?" His mouth opened, only to close. "I guess that would be a good thing for you to learn. Besides that, what would they teach you that you don't already know?"

"Lots, I assure you. My skills are unparalleled...*in all things*."

577

"Right. Well." He reached over, grabbing socks and his dress shoes. "It's been a while for me for baby stuff. We'll take classes together. If you want to learn new things outside of your role, I will teach you or have you taught by someone I approve of. It won't be the Main Master. He's." Jake stood, stopping for a few seconds. "The two of you were never a thing, were you? Lovers?"

My head shook. "No, Master."

"Alright. He's too attached. You may be his special whatever, but you're mine now."

The wheels in my head came to a grinding stop at the opportunity. "I'll probably get in trouble for saying anything, but...not technically."

He paused from sliding in his foot. Possessiveness swept over his face.

"I bought you. You're mine. Soon, a part of me will be in your belly, and he can back the fuck off for good."

There was no leaving the train station we were standing in. My Master was the awaiting passengers, and I was the freight train about to blow right through the stop. There was no derailing what I was meant for or taught. I didn't even feel nervous or guilty as my eyes seemed to glaze over for the smallest moment.

"I'm afraid even after we conceive, the Main Master will still have say in our arrangement."

"Like hell he will. How is that?"

I shrugged, heading over to sit on the side of the bed he was closest to. Although I appeared sad, I felt nothing.

"I once overheard him talking to someone on the phone. They were discussing the contract. I guess whoever he was talking to mentioned his hold on me. They were worried about losing the breeding rights. I was never meant for just one Master. At least, not at the beginning. Maybe it's changed, but I can't be sure. All I know is the Main Master said, 'the only way slave one will be out of my control is if someone puts a ring on her finger. Who would do that?' And I guess he's right. No one would."

Silence. My Master stared at me, not moving. Not even blinking.

"Get dressed."

I stood but didn't move.

"Slave, get dressed. Get." He spun, growling through the words that turned angrier by the second. When he stomped from the closet, thrusting out a white slip dress, I still didn't budge. "Wear this. We don't have much time."

MASTER A-0005

R ationality was out of the window. Thinking anything through wasn't even worth the time. If Elec thought he was going to outsmart me, he had another thing coming. Kayla's bloodline stopped with me. I'd breed her. We'd have children together. No one else sure as fuck was going to have her. Whitlock and Walton…I saw the greedy dollar signs, and I wasn't going to let them get rich off the mother of my children. There was no way in hell I'd let them cheapen her like that. Cheapen *me and my future heirs* like that. This was the only way, and why the hell not? I'd already broken the biggest vow there was to my wife. What difference would this make anyway? Hell, if anything, this would only make my heir's claim that much more believable.

"I now pronounce you husband and wife."

The phrase repeated in my head, driving the truth home. Husband and wife. Wife. Kayla. Wife.

"Is that really us?"

I clicked ignore on the Main Master's call, bringing up the camera on my phone instead. As I fit mine and my slave's face on the screen, I nodded.

"Looks like us to me. Smile, wife."

Wife. Wife.

My smile was genuine for no other reason than I'd won this game. Hers was the best fake smile I'd ever seen. It dazzled, bewitched, even as she lifted the bouquet next to her face and leaned in kissing my cheek. I continuously clicked, turning to kiss her back.

"I hate to marry and run, but I'm pretty sure the guards are going to hunt me down if I don't get to the trials." I kissed her lips again. That time there was nothing fake about it. The action gave me the smallest moment of a pause before I led her out of the chapel, stopping just outside the elevator. When it opened, we entered together. "You'll be okay getting back to the apartment on your own?"

"Of course, Master."

I went to hit different floors, not able to go through with it.

"I'll just walk you. I don't want to risk anything happening. I don't trust anyone in this place. You'll be okay for a few hours? You're not dizzy anymore?"

"I'm better. I'll be okay. I have my phone now. Why don't you text me when you're finishing up, and I'll make us a special dinner tonight? Steak."

At her smile, I nodded, wrapping my arm around her to bring her closer. What I didn't expect was to see angry eyes glaring at me when the elevator door opened. The first thing the Main Master did was glance to the bouquet, then to Kayla, and lastly to me. I didn't say a word as I led her into the lobby area. Elec didn't hesitate to take the advantage.

"You're late. Later than late."

"Couldn't be helped, Main Master."

Elec followed as we entered the hall.

"I can see that. What the hell did you do?"

I slowed, pulling out my key card, but not stopping until we were at the door.

"I married the mother of my future children. Is it not the right thing to do?"

He didn't answer as I opened the door, holding it for Kayla. When she stepped in, I kissed her cheek.

"I'll text when I'm on my way. Don't open this door for anyone you're not expecting."

"Of course, Master."

"Husband will work. I'll be back soon."

I went to shut the door, but Elec's hand flattened against the barrier before I could close it completely.

"Give us a minute."

"Elec—"

He pushed past me, slamming the door in my face. The need to explode sent my insides boiling. Had I been worried about Sebastian? Maybe I should have been more concerned over the one man who'd been so eager to push Kayla off on me. Something wasn't right, and I couldn't quite understand what it was. The slave said they weren't intimate, so what was it then?

Pushing the door open, it only went a few inches before it connected with Elec's hand. Whispering was evident, but I couldn't tell if it was angry or not. I couldn't even figure it out before Elec let go and came to face me.

"Let's go. The break is almost over."

I turned, taking in Kayla's smile. It was blank yet sly. She wasn't upset or worried. Her expression was as plain as day. *We won.* She was mine.

I gave her a wave, barely able to contain my victory as I walked alongside the Main Master back towards the elevator. He suddenly didn't appear upset. More...devoid of emotion altogether.

"So, married. I have to say, I did not see that coming. Not with you, Jake."

"Well, it's not like you gave me much of a choice. Why the

hell convince me to take slave one if you only meant to breed her out to everyone else as well?"

The Main Master's slowed, turning to look at me as we stopped at the elevator.

"Repeat that?"

"Don't act like you don't know what I'm talking about, Elec. Kayla told me all about your plans to breed her out to other elites. Did you seriously think I'd share the mother of my heir with who-knows-who? So my kid or kids can have a cousin-brother-uncle? We're not doing that shit. Our circle is too small to not have that happen."

He didn't say a word as we stepped into the elevator, and he pressed the button.

"Anyway, it's done. She's my wife. She'll have my children, and when the time comes we can expose the secret. We'll stick to the plan, just like you said."

"Seems that way."

IT DIDN'T MATTER IF YOU WERE ABOVE THE GARDENS OR below...people never changed for shit. Not the deeds or behavior. Sure as fuck not gossiping. Had my eyes not been on Elec the entire time, I would have assumed it was him who leaked the news. As it was, we'd been trying cases for hours and he hadn't picked up his phone or talked to anyone but the defendants.

"Married. You can't be serious? You, Master Five?"

My mouth twisted to the Main Board Member, Shane, as we left the room, heading for the elevator.

"Who the hell texted you that information? You've been four feet from me the entire time."

He laughed. "I know everything. Congratulations. To slave one, I hear. Excellent choice. It would have been a better match

583

on the outside world, but little we can do about that now. She'll be useful to all of us, and that's the important part."

"Where the hell is *your* heir? Shouldn't you be working on that?"

"Vera and I have been talking about it. I'm a little jealous, if I want to be honest. Hell, it makes me want to start trying to have one of my own. Imagine the power of our line if we joined them. Have you talked to Elec about matches? I'm sure his head is already spinning with possibilities for your future child."

"I'm right here. I can hear you."

I turned, watching as the Main Master trailed behind. His stare was suddenly glued down at his phone. We were all waiting for the elevator, and I never wanted to be more away from people in my life.

"Well...*do you?*"

Elec still didn't glance up at Master One's question.

"We'll talk about that after a child exists. As of right now, it doesn't."

"That we know of." I reached forward, smashing my finger into the button. "It'll be there. If not this time, the next. Now that I'm married, there's not much of a rush anymore, is there."

It wasn't a question, and the Main Master didn't comment. He was still looking down at the screen, seeming to read whatever it was on the other end.

"Master One, I can't make it to dinner, but why don't you take Master Five instead. I'm sure he'd love to catch up with Vera."

"I would, but I got married today. I'm going home to my wife."

Only then did Elec's eyes lift. What they held, I couldn't begin to decipher. Anger? Satisfaction? A little of both?

The elevator door opened, and we all got on. With the board members living on the same floor, I still couldn't escape them. I didn't have to wait long. The door opened and we piled out.

When Elec followed, I looked over my shoulder, cautiously, not sure if he was following me or Shane. He didn't live on this floor. When I stopped at my door, I found out.

"Main Master, what are you doing?"

"Open the door."

"Not until you tell me what the hell is going on. *You wanted this for me.*"

"I still do, but slave one's wellbeing is my first priority."

"You don't think I'm taking good enough care of her? *Elec.*" My voice rumbled as we held eye contact. "I don't know this you. I don't *like* this you."

"You don't have to. What I'm doing is bigger than your feelings. In the future, you'll understand. Right now, you need to open this door."

"If I don't?"

The Main Master's lids closed for the briefest moment. He took a deep breath, his face transforming to one that had me stepping back as he pinned me with a look so empty, I felt the threat as my life hung in the balance.

"I am not your enemy, and you sure as hell don't want to make me one. Everything I'm doing is for a reason. Just because you don't understand it doesn't mean it's bad. But it will be if you don't open that fucking door right now."

To speak was a bad idea, but I didn't fear death. I craved it on more levels than I wanted to admit.

"You're too attached to her. Kayla came close to being related to you. To being your own blood, but she's not. She's Bram's half-sister. He's your cousin, but not her. You're on Bram's mother's side, not Alastair's. If it's not blood, and it's not love...what is it?"

"It's not my place to tell you, Jake. Or maybe it is. I guess in a way it is my fault. I just...I never thought." He glanced at the door, his lips growing tight through the anger. "You know who she is."

"She's a Whitlock and Walton."

"More Whitlock than Walton."

It was my turn to pause. "What is that supposed to mean?"

"Open the door."

I obeyed, slowly stepping inside. Dark red was splattered over one side of Kayla's face, and her white wedding dress was saturated in areas. Bloody hands clenched in my wife's lap, and she seemed surprised to see me as she pushed to her feet like a wild animal. The amount of surprise told me I wasn't the one she was expecting. Given the Main Master's presence at my back, I realized...I wasn't. She'd reached out to him. *Not me.* I didn't focus on that as I rushed forward through the horrific visions from my past.

"Jesus. Did you hurt yourself? Are you hurt? What happened?"

"I..." She looked like a deer in the headlights, only gaping for a moment before she crumbled to her knees. "Forgive me. I...Please, I...I made a mistake. I only meant to look. To talk to him and see why he was screaming." Her head lifted, tears racing down her cheeks. "Forgive me, Husband. I swear, I didn't mean to. *He grabbed me.* Hurt me. I got scared."

But I barely heard her words as my gaze lifted towards our bedroom. I took a step to the side to go around her, stopping as a hand clamped to my bicep.

"That is not your priority. *She is.*" Elec let go of me, glaring as he kneeled to face Kayla. "Where did he hurt you, slave?"

"You went into the cell?"

She paused in answering, more tears leaving her.

"I'm sorry. He was yelling when I got home, and...the door was unlocked. I don't know what I was thinking going inside or even checking. I got too close." She stopped, sobbing as the Main Master lifted her wrist. A deep bite mark was surrounded by bruising across her forearm. I sat down at the sight, taking her arm from Elec, possessively, making her turn more in my direction.

"Unlocked? I..." My head shook. Had I really forgot to lock the door behind me? "Stop crying. It's okay."

"It's not." She sniffled. "The pain triggered something. Once I started, I couldn't stop." Her eyes lifted, leaving me to go to *him*. "Main Master, I tried. I really did but—"

"This is your husband's fault, slave, not yours. Had he not been so determined to keep you from your training, this wouldn't have happened."

"Me? How the hell does this have anything to do with training? It's not like you're teaching her to kill." At their silence, my eyes widened going back and forth between them. "She kills?" Still nothing. "As...training, or to..."

Elec took a seat on the other end of the sofa. As he leaned forward, I could see different emotions taking over.

"She was here before Master One was chosen. She was the true first. I started training her almost immediately. But it was more than the lessons. We began getting slaves in, little by little. I'd make her hunt with me. I taught her everything I know. She was such a natural after the initial shock wore off." His head shook. "She reminded me so much of Alastair. Of...family."

Kayla's head tilted as if it were the first time she was hearing it.

"Jake...When I said she was more Whitlock, I meant it. She belongs here. It's like she was made for this place. As if it's in her very DNA to live this life. I guess in more ways than one...*it is*."

FC0001

Family? Whitlock? I blinked through the insight, feeling my heart race as my brain tried to make sense of what I was hearing. The name, Whitlock, was common enough, but only one family stood out with that name. My mind immediately tried to dismiss the information. There was no way. No…chance. Was there? I didn't recognize the name Alastair, but there was one I knew, and there wasn't a person in the US who hadn't heard of the famous, Bram Whitlock. He was a dream. A socialite lawyer who hung out with the most famous stars. Or…he had years ago. Was he related? Was I—no. It couldn't be.

"Are you saying my wife needs to kill? As in, she can't function without committing murder?"

"I can function," I breathed out.

"Function, yes. Does she want to without killing?" Elec shook his head. "No. She needs it like any of us do. It's a part of her, and if she has cravings for it, it's my fault. I've enabled her. Even encouraged it. It's her right with who she is."

Jake's hand came to his mouth. It looked as if so many thoughts were taking him over. Did he regret choosing me? I truly had tried not to kill his crow but…I hadn't tried hard enough. One touch of the man's broken arm, and he'd bitten me. It was like a flip switched. I hadn't screamed or cried. Fear didn't exist. I let the pain feed me. I even flexed and rotated against his secure hold before he let go. And then I'd done it. I slowly walked to the cart of weapons and—

Whack!

I swung the mallet right at the side of his jaw. When he screamed, I watched the lower part of his face shift disproportionately to the side.

More screaming.

More swinging.

"Please don't be mad at me. I'll make this up to you, Master."

"Husband."

Slowly, I let my head angle to look up through my thick lashes, allowing my shoulders to cave into themselves submissively. My tone even softened as I stared up at him as if nothing in the world mattered but his claim over me.

"You still want to be married to me after I did something so horrible? I didn't listen to you. I don't deserve kindness. I failed."

More sobs.

More emptiness.

I wiped the tears, looking between the two Masters.

"I failed you both."

I didn't wait for them to speak. I stood, letting my soft cries continue as I paced, flattening my hand over my stomach. I cradled myself protectively, reminding them of the reason I was here to begin with. To them, I was fragile, and I needed their guidance. Their ownership.

"Wife." My Master stood. "Kayla, come sit next to me."

Hearing my name was enough to slow my strides, but all it did was stir the embers of my existence even more. It was buried in there, somewhere. Hidden...but not. It was surfacing, and at a rate that scared me. I knew something was off, I just couldn't quite make sense of it all.

"Slave, listen to him. It's not good for you to be upset. Like I said before, this is not your fault. I knew this was coming. It's been awhile since you've had this sort of release. I was trying to get ahead of it, but I should have done this before the auction. I take responsibility for that. I've been too busy with my duties that I neglected one of the most important ones. *You.* Come sit down. Your...husband can make you some tea. You like tea. It relaxes you."

The Main Master stood, joining Jake. I came to a stop, easing my arms up to cross over my chest.

"Tea? You both are so focused on calming me down, but you haven't even seen what I've done. Go look." I pointed to the room. "Go see, and then you come back and tell me I'm not in trouble."

My husband headed for the room, but not the Main Master. One of his eyebrows rose as he walked over to me. Only when he got inches away did he lower his voice and speak.

"You're a piece of work. Breeding, marriage, and murder in less than a week. I'm proud."

"You may be, but he won't like this."

"He may."

Jake stopped in the threshold, staring at the opened cell door. He didn't move forward. He didn't even look back our way. Seconds passed before he disappeared from view.

"He's going to send me back. He'll want the pregnancy terminated and to start over with someone else."

"There will be no termination if it took. I have too much riding on this to let a little murder ruin it. You have the Princeton line almost secure. It'll stay that way."

More seconds. A minute. When Jake reappeared, I couldn't read the hard expression.

"You did that?"

"I'm sorry."

"Don't be ridiculous, slave. I'm sure it's fine."

Jake didn't speak at the Main Master's comment, but the tilt of his head combined with both eyebrows sitting high said otherwise.

"You categorized everything in bins and Tupperwares. Every piece. Every part. You drew a bubbly heart on the one labeled 'heart'. That body had to of taken you hours. Since...we married. What you did is grueling. It is not an easy task."

"She gets consumed. It's truly enjoyable to watch."

Jake's hand flew up to the Main Master, as if to tell him to be quiet. Anger took over as he headed in my direction. I didn't move like I wanted. I didn't trust that he wasn't going to beat me, but I tried to show him otherwise. The Main Master wasn't taking that chance as he stepped closer.

"You did that in there." Still, shock filled his face. "You killed that crow. Chopped him up into pieces. Ordered fucking plastic bins and containers of all sizes. Got index cards and identified them adding hearts, stars, even spirals for the intestines. Not only that. After you finished, you cleaned the room. There's no trace of blood. No bloody tools. *Nothing.* Not once did you think to text me. *Instead,* what did you do?" Jake gestured to the Main Master. "You write him. To what? Cover your ass? Have him help you hide it from me? *Your husband.* You took vows, Kayla. You said 'I do'. *You didn't.* It should have been me you called, not him. *Me.* I'm your husband."

I didn't speak. I didn't have to to know Jake was about to eat his words. I wasn't stupid. If the Main Master taught me anything, it was to cover all bases. All sides.

Picking my phone up off the counter, I opened it, heading into the texts. When I handed it to Jake, the anger once again departed, replaced with disbelief.

"You did not text me. I would have felt it. I..." He jerked his phone free, once again his eyes going wide. "How did I miss this? There's no way. I...I swear I never." He stopped, and I let the tears return.

"I wrote you after I killed him. I told you I was scared. *That I needed you.* You never wrote me back. I didn't know who else to call. I tried to tell you, even if I was terrified to do so." The first sob came as years of stored emotion came seeping free. It was so easy. So...distant and yet available for me to use. "I tried telling you first, but nothing came of it. Even the Main Master didn't see my messages until just before you both arrived."

Silence.

Jake shook his head, tossing both of our phones to the sofa. When he stepped in, holding to my shoulders, more tears escaped. Those had nothing to do with acting. Something in me stirred as he met my eyes. The emotion in his depths did weird things to the numbness. It whispered to dark spaces inside, trying to call something from the shadows.

"You needed me, and I wasn't there for you. I lashed out at you. I've done nothing but add to your stress, at the worst possible time. Forgive me."

"But...aren't you mad at me for killing your crow?"

Something flickered on his face as he turned towards the bedroom doorway but disappeared as he came to face me.

"There will be more crows. Right now, let's try to salvage what's left of our special day." He glanced over at the Main Master. "Alone, if that's possible."

Elec's eyes narrowed. The way Jake spoke to him scared me. I'd never heard anyone be so dismissing to him before. If I didn't like it, I knew it was taking a toll on the Main Master.

"For now. I will be meeting the two of you at the clinic for an evaluation in the next few days." Blue eyes lowered to me. "If anytime between then you need something, you tell your Mast—"

"Husband," Jake corrected.

"*Husband*, or call me, and we'll get you what you need.

Whatever it is. Your comfort and happiness are what's important from here on out. You know what to do. Safety above all else."

Nodding, I stepped closer to Jake, watching as the Main Master headed for the door. The moment it closed, Jake turned to me, easing his palm along the side of my throat,

"You yearn to kill. I wouldn't have guessed that in a million years."

"I'm sorry if you're disappointed. I can't help it. I think it's always been there. Just...helping the Main Master, I wasn't really left with a choice. I had to face my demons. I had to embrace them or let them eat me alive."

He licked his lips, moving his thumb up to trail along my jaw. The moment his face softened, it hardened, and I watched him pull away. He kept doing that, and I knew it was because of guilt. Maybe it shouldn't have upset me, but the flare of pain couldn't be hidden in my hollow depths. If anything, the realization only intensified what was there.

"I have a pretty big tub. I'm going to draw us a bath. I think we could both use some relaxation. Besides, you cleaned the cell, but you didn't think of yourself. You're a mess." He led me to the room, pausing as we entered the bathroom. He pushed down the straps to my stained slip dress, not taking his penetrating gaze from mine. "I *never* want to see you covered in blood again. Not when I don't know what the hell is happening. You gave me a damn heart attack. Honesty, Kayla. No matter what it's about."

Could he take my complete honesty? No. Not even I was ready to face that. To admit what lurked inside me was to face a possible death sentence. It didn't matter if I had important blood or not. I knew that, yet I couldn't deny the manipulations that wanted to rule me through the fog. I was two people, fighting for sanity in ways I didn't even understand.

"I'll be honest...Jake. May I call you by your name?"

A slight smile appeared as he eased my dress down the rest

of the way so it could pool at my feet. "You're my wife. Of course you can."

"That makes me so happy to hear. I didn't want you to be even more upset with me. I'm trying so hard to be everything you need." I pushed to my toes, kissing his cheek. Brown eyes soaked me in as I pulled back and reached over, turning on the faucet. There was a hesitation to him. Not one of guilt like before, but a true uncertainty that wasn't good or bad. More...curious.

"What I need is open communication. No more secrets, okay? I'm a pretty reasonable man. There's not much that upsets me. Stop focusing on fearing me, and instead work on making yourself into the healthiest version of yourself. You're going to need it just as much as the baby is. If you're happy, they'll be too."

"They'll. They. Healthy." My eyes lowered. "I'm glad you mentioned that. I'm late. I should have taken my pills after lunch."

I didn't wait as I headed to the medicine cabinet, taking out the multiple bottles of pills.

"How many are you taking? What are those, anyway?"

"Prenatal vitamins, along with some others that help with deficiencies. It's important my body stay strong. Especially since the shots make me feel...off."

"Shots?"

I filled a glass of water, popping back the pills and swallowing. "Yes. They enhance ovulation. They help our chances to conceive."

A big smile appeared, melting almost just as fast.

"Don't those produce multiple babies? Twins? *Quintuplets?*"

I laughed, surprising myself as I headed forward. "Twins, maybe. I wouldn't go as far as five, but I guess it's possible." I shrugged. "It might not be bad having a big family right off the bat. I always wanted that. I guess I can't really have it now. Not in a true sense. A house. Movie and game night. Kids running around crazy while I'm trying to make dinner."

My voice faded out provoking Jake to draw me in his arms.

"Let's get you cleaned up. We'll worry about all that when the time comes."

"It'll never come. It just *is*."

I stepped back, not able to stop the strange tugs and jerks in my mind. Just speaking the words, I saw my own home, growing up. I saw me and my sister singing Christmas songs at the top of our lungs. It didn't matter how far apart our age was or that I'd been adopted. We were family. Real family. We had so much love between all of us.

My heart twisted and went raw as visions kept coming. Sneaking out to play in the pool after our parents went to bed. Jumping up and down when Julie got accepted to college. The tears when we discovered she had cancer. The happiness when she beat it. Her asking me to be a surrogate.

"Kayla?"

I jumped at the hand on my shoulder. My body was trembling through the memories that returned from nowhere. I knew my past, but I couldn't deny it felt so far away. Briefly fleeting as it came in and out. I could see the scenes, but not quite feel them. Even now, there was a numbness tinging my recollection. Just like my emotions. I didn't understand it, even if I knew it wasn't right. Something was different. Even...wrong, but I had every intention of figuring this out, where it worked in *my* favor.

MASTER A-0005

"High school mascot?"

I laughed at the question, not able to stop from getting sucked into Kayla's energy. She was different the last few days. More electric? Engaging? Maybe it was the kill. Maybe it was her hormones, and she was in a good mood. Whatever it was, she dazzled me as she lay in the bed and faced me. I couldn't quite put my finger on it, but I was suddenly mesmerized more than ever. I shouldn't have been. Even days later, I couldn't ignore what I saw in that cell. It wasn't the work of an amateur or someone who was hesitant about a kill. Still, how was I so different? The need lived within us, even if we didn't understand it.

"We were the Mustangs. What was yours?"

"Cougars." Her lids narrowed the smallest amount. "I'm assuming you went to college?"

"I did."

"Were you a good student?"

"Not always, but I managed to graduate."

She laughed. "Me too. I wasn't the smartest, but I scraped by. What wonderful times." The smile wavered as she seemed to think back. "What about after? What do you do for a living? You're...*important,* right? That's why we're together?"

With the sudden sadness that engulfed her, I couldn't think of my own pain I harbored. She was suddenly so expressive. I reached for her hand, feeling myself soften. I didn't like her upset, even if we were still getting to know each other. I took my role seriously. If I was going to be her husband, I'd make sure I was the best one I could be. It's just who I was, and there was no changing it.

"My bloodline is old, AKA I'm rich." I rolled my eyes. "I could have accomplished that on my own, and did, but aside from my businesses, our children's, children's, children, and so on, will never have to worry. Are you concerned for their wellbeing?"

Her eyes lifted to mine but lowered again.

"Maybe a little. Not financially. It's just...imagine for a moment being a father to children you have but can't take care of. Ones who don't even know you. I guess I never really thought about it this way. Or." She got quiet, more breathing out the word. "Thought. Tell me more about your life outside of here. It'll put me at ease. You said you own businesses."

"A few. I have a chain of resorts. Investments. My hand is in a little of everything." My brows drew in with her worry. "I'm a good father. Our child or children will not be raised by some nanny or stranger. They won't be sent away to schools. I'm not like the other elites, Kayla. What's mine is mine, and nothing comes between that. They'll be with me until the day they move out to live their own life, and even after that if that's what they choose. Family has always been everything to me."

"Me too." Her eyes filled with tears, but she smiled, holding them in. "That makes me happy to hear. Do you know which you'd prefer? Boy? Girl?"

It was my turn to get quiet. To think this far ahead hurt. It was a knife in the gut, but one I'd put there. There was no going back. This was my life, now, and the faster I embraced every aspect of it, the sooner the lingering agony would pass. Kayla and I would bond even more. We'd grow into something beautiful. *We'd work.* I was sure of it. We were starting to have an undeniable chemistry. Before, we got along well enough, but her internal emotion didn't quite match the outward. It did when she looked at me now. I could feel it, and I was starting to depend on it. *Crave it.*

"Healthy, and I mean that. Boy, girl, it doesn't matter. I will love them regardless."

She squeezed my hand. "I believe you. What do you know of my family? The Whitlocks. Is my father still alive? Do I have brothers? Sisters? What of my mother?"

My mouth opened but nothing would come.

"I mean, I've heard some things, Husband, but I trust your insight." Her volume lowered and worry blanketed her words. "Do you think they're bad people? The Main Master seems to think so."

"Elec..." I stopped. "Elec views Bram, your half-brother, as a traitor. When he took over Whitlock from his father, *your father*, he changed things. Elec thinks he ruined the place, but it was more than that. Bram fell in love with a slave. He ended up destroying the fortress and running away with her."

"Bram," she breathed out, pausing. "Fortress? That's what this Whitlock was?"

"Yes. It was a place very similar to this. Bram nearly died because of how unstable the place was, but Elec says it was his own fault. Had he been focusing on Whitlock and not his slave, the place wouldn't have swallowed him whole. He's lucky he lived."

Kayla pressed her lips into each other, shifting. "Bram Whitlock is my half-brother. How is he and the Main Master related?"

My hesitation had her eyes lifting to me.

"Cousins. Bram's mother is Elec's father's sister. How much did he tell you?"

"Cousins," she repeated. "I guess I should have expected that. Elec's mentioned names, here and there, so I've been able to put things together, but he never came right out and explained in detail. It makes sense now." She let out a breath, seeming to lose some of the unhappiness. "You said half-brother. What of my mother's side?"

"Aubrey Walton." I cringed, not sure whether I should continue. Kayla had a right to know, I just wasn't sure how much I should be telling her. "Aubrey was married at the time. I believe that's why she put you up for adoption. The scandal that would have caused in those days would have been very bad. Hell, it would be bad now."

"But people *will* know." Her head lifted and she pushed to sit up.

I joined her, still holding her hand. "They will. The news of our child will no doubt rock their world. Whitlock and Walton. It has to be done. Our child deserves their place in the outside world, and I won't let them be denied. So what if it exposes their sins and ruffles a few feathers? The Princeton name mixed with Whitlock and Walton...that's just gold, wife. Not just for us, but them as well. This strengthens all of our lines, and in the end, they'll be happy for it. It opens up more possibilities than you'd believe."

She got quiet, easing her hand from mine as she seemed to go into a daze. Silence stretched out until she rapidly blinked.

"My mother is still alive?"

"Yes."

"And my half-brother? No, my brother, Bram. Blood is blood. There's no half to us. He lives. He's not dead. Mother. Brother."

My forehead wrinkled through her monotone speech. I suddenly realized the last wasn't a question. She was stating the

599

facts. Going over them and letting them process as she shook her head and seemed to return from some deep train of thought.

"Do I have any other brothers or sisters?"

Something told me not to say another word, but the longing in her eyes kept me going.

"Lots. Aubrey has three kids with her husband. Two boys and one girl. The oldest son already has a child, so you have a nephew as well, but the oldest is their daughter."

Tears collected even though she smiled. And me...I kept going...and going.

"Robert, the oldest boy I mentioned, he and I happened to be college friends. He was big into sports. Football was his favorite. He'd host the biggest parties, and usually some sort of trouble followed them. I once woke up a few blocks away in someone's front yard, drunker than shit. It turned out that it was the house of one of my mother's friend's daughters, who ratted me out. My parents about killed me, but it was worth it. Robert knew how to throw a party."

Kayla laughed, sniffling.

"I like him already. Who else."

"Matthew and Elaine."

"My sister. The oldest." She wiped tears. "Tell me about her."

"Well." My hesitation had her interest growing as she turned more towards me. "Elaine is...well...she's a bit of a mystery, truthfully. She went to the same college as most of us, but she was more friends with Bram, I guess. Not close, but they hung in the same circles. From what I remember, Elaine works for the FBI. I'm afraid that's all I really know. She travels a lot so any time there's some big event or gathering we all have to attend, she's rarely there."

"Oh. I see. What does she look like?"

I took in Kayla's dark hair. Hair like Bram and their father.

"Blonde, like her mother. Beautiful, too, but...I'm afraid I don't really know specifics. She never really was around for me to get to know."

"I see." Kayla let out a shaky breath. "I'm sorry I'm such a mess. I don't know why I'm crying or why I never asked questions like this before. I'm truly appreciative for everything you've told me. I'm just feeling a little." She stopped. "Clearer than I have lately."

"Was it the kill?"

A veil almost seemed to lower, taking her away from me again. Just the mention had her lids going heavy. Her eyes lifted from my lips, stirring a lust I couldn't quite control around her. It wasn't her looks, although she was beautiful right now. She just had this air. This...damn seduction.

"I think it might have helped a little, I'm just sad I couldn't really let go of the guilt to really enjoy it. I do enjoy it, husband." She inched closer to me, looking up at me through thick lashes. "Does that make you not want to be with me?"

"No. I won't lie, it's...different. I'm adjusting."

"I see."

Her head lowered, but I reached for her chin, tilting her head back enough so I could give her a kiss.

"You shut down at my response. You can't do that. I need you to always be honest with me. That's the only way this marriage will work." I paused, taking in a yearning in her depths. A clarity that kept getting stolen at the most random moments. "You're not done killing, are you? You want more?"

The smallest quiver shook her lip.

"I wish I could explain. I don't even think it would make a difference. I have so much anger. *So much sadness.* My heart feels like it's closing in on itself. I can barely breathe."

"I know that feeling. What happened to you isn't fair. It's not."

"It's so much more than that." She went to speak, hesitating. "I was robbed on so many fronts. All I've ever wanted is out there.

601

It's there, Jake, and I can't have it." A sob escaped. "My mom. My brothers and sister. I want to be the one to show them our child. I want to hug them and celebrate with them. How did this happen?"

There was nothing I could say to console my new wife. There were no excuses, no truth or promises I could make. Kayla was a pawn in a scheme Elec wouldn't budge on. He owned her, and his payment went well beyond what I'd bought her for.

"I'm sorry. I can't free you from the Gardens, but I can try to make it manageable."

I grabbed my phone, watching panic have Kayla jumping up to her knees. I hit Elec's number, feeling my own emotions twist and pull in what was right or wrong. Her hands tried to wave me to stop, but tears appeared, and she quickly gave up.

"Master Five."

A breath left me. "Kayla's upset. You need to send more crows, or you come make this right. She's asking about her family—"

"*You didn't—*"

"You never said not to."

"Dammit, Jake. I knew she looked different when I was there. Shit. You should have known better. I said no about her adoptive sister. I meant all family. I'm on my way."

I hung up, easing from the bed.

"The Main Master is on his way. Let's get dressed."

"I wish you wouldn't have called him."

"No?"

Kayla didn't respond as she got up and began putting on a black lounge set. The sleeves were on the longer side, and she had the front of the baggy shirt tucked into the loose pants. She pulled her hair back in a ponytail, not meeting my eyes as she turned from the dresser's mirror.

"I'm going to be in so much trouble."

"For being upset?"

"For asking questions. I'm not entitled. Yet..." her glare lifted, "*I do believe I am.*"

Knocking had me hesitantly leaving her to go for the front door. When the Main Master entered, he didn't even look at me. Kayla was walking from the bedroom, a look on her face I hadn't seen before. She didn't even look like the same woman I'd just been in the room with. Her soft features were anything but. She was guarded. Empty. She was a stranger.

"Here we go. I was wondering how long it would be before you returned."

The Main Master moved further in the room but kept his distance from my wife.

"You did something to me. To my mind."

"Not like the others, but I did do something, and I'll do it again. It's safer for you."

A flare of defiance sparked. "For me or *for you?* I want to feel. To think for myself. I don't deny my status. I'm not even fighting it."

"You will. We've been here before. Must we keep doing this? I've already told you the way things will be. Your feelings are irrelevant."

"That's not true. Maybe when I'm under your spell they are, but when I'm here, like right now, my say has power. You've been holding back some big things, Main Master. Things I should have known. Things I had *the right* to know. I want to meet them."

"No."

She took a step forward, keeping his eye contact. "You owe me that."

"I owe you nothing. You're alive. You're in *my* debt."

"Is that right?"

Whatever existed between them had the Main Master's jaw flexing. Kayla knew something Elec didn't want anyone hearing.

Whatever she knew had weight. It made his glare soften but not disappear.

"I won't fight with you, Main Master. We may not be family, but I love you like you are. I shouldn't, but I know you. I know the real you, and you know the real me. Please. I'm going to die to them, anyway, aren't I?" Kayla came closer. "Can't I meet them before that happens? I'm not asking for some long night of memories. Give Jake and I a chance occurrence. Let us run into them somewhere as husband and wife. I don't even have to talk, Jake can do that, but let them see me as a real, living person. *Let me see them.* I've never once asked you for anything despite we both know I could have. I'm begging you...give this to me and I'll never defy you again. I'll provide my husband with more heirs than he knows what to do with. I'll never argue or make trouble. Please."

"Slave.

"*Elec.*" Anger wrapped itself around his name as Kayla's fists drew in. "If you can't bear to do it for me, think about your precious deal. Seeing me will solidify any doubt in their minds that this marriage was real when the time comes for them to learn who I truly am."

I walked to her side.

"She has a point. It could save us the grief of providing any other sort of proof."

"Couldn't you just be happy with a lifetime supply of crows? I have one being brought here right now. I'll give you that. I'll make this sacrifice worth it in blood. Blood is the only thing that is real. It is the only thing that can ease the hurt."

Kayla lowered to her knees, looking up at Elec.

"They *are* my blood. They're my family. Five minutes. Please."

Elec's eyes closed but he shook his head.

"I can't let you leave here, slave. I can't, and it's not because I don't want you to. It's forbidden."

"Then I've discovered them on my own. Let me reach out and at least talk to them. I've seen you video calling. Let Jake and I talk to them that way. That allows me to still be here at the Gardens, and then they see us together. Can we do that?"

"Is it so important for you to see family who may reject you? That would hurt you more." Elec paused as knocking sounded on the door. I put my hand up, heading over to let the guards and crow in. As I followed them to the cell, I didn't take my eyes off of my wife or the Main Master. Kayla was close to panicking. She was desperate, and like any caged animal, she looked ready to strike.

"I'll take their rejection if that's what the call comes down to. I don't care. They have to see me. They have to know I exist before it's impossible for them to. I've done everything you've asked, Main Master. We both know I shouldn't even be who I am. I belong on the other side of this dirty deal you have going on here, and I'm willing to overlook that for a moment of peace. I need this. If you don't want to do it for me, do it for the part of me that might be holding a baby."

FC0001

There was too much happening in my mind. I was running off adrenaline and desperation. Why couldn't he bend and see this was right and that I was capable. I had tried to prove myself numerous times over the years. The Main Master wouldn't budge when it came to me holding power. Anything I fought for, he smashed. Ruined. Destroyed. Now I knew why. But he couldn't escape who I was anymore than me. I was the sister of his enemy. A sister that could have so easily been an ally, if he only allowed her to.

"You know I don't have to give or allow anything. With one word, I can shut you down and turn you back into the woman who walked in this apartment. That slave doesn't want. She doesn't complain. She serves, as she's meant to."

"And someday she will break under that pressure. Your mind games will destroy her. What happens then?"

Elec didn't speak.

"Let me help you, Main Master. I can do and be whoever you want, but I need the chance. I need you to trust. I can make this deal work better than you ever imagined. Let them see me. One time. Just once."

Jake walked back over to me, taking his place at my side as the guards left.

"It's not that easy, slave."

"Is it not? Can't I just call my mother?"

"Not on any phone down here. Not even mine will reach the outside world."

"But you have reached the outside world. I've seen it."

He didn't speak, but I wouldn't stop.

"What about the installation above, where I was kept before?"

"No."

Defeat had real tears blinding me for the first time.

"You're refusing to work with me. It's all I want. All I need to keep going. Just one meeting. It has to be possible."

"...Maybe."

I stood at his words as hope surged through.

The Main Master's lids narrowed, and I could see the calculation spinning the wheels of his mind. I'd never met anyone so manipulative as Elec, but he'd taught me everything I knew, and if there was a way, he'd find it...so long as it didn't interfere with his plans. "Matthew."

"My brother. The youngest of the Waltons."

Elec threw Jake a look but nodded. "Youngest but not young. Almost thirty. What if I let you meet him?"

"He's here?"

I was breathless as I stepped closer.

"Not anymore, but he'll return at some point. Perhaps I set up a meeting. A...chance run-in as you mentioned. *As a Garden's Couple.* He won't know otherwise, and there will be strict terms on what you can say and do."

"I'll do whatever you want, just let me meet him."

The Main Master turned his attention to my husband. "I could fucking kill you right now. I'm finding little reason to keep you alive, Jake."

"She had a right to know. What's the timeline looking like for Matthew to arrive?"

"I'll check. He just left. He may not be back for weeks." Elec stared down at his phone, still deep in thought. "I...may be able to get Elaine down here at some point. She put in a request. I have not approved it, nor do I think I want to. She's a risk, and too attached to." He stopped, anger clearly taking over.

"Bram," I breathed out.

"I guess you know that now too." More rage was projected to Jake. "Bram could have brought us all down with him. He still might if he has his way. He is not to be trusted. Neither is his slave. Those two, you will *never* meet."

"But my sister..."

"Elaine knows her place, so perhaps someday. Time will tell. Right now, your best bet is Matthew, but I make no promises on when you'll meet. Focus on the crows. For now, *they're all you get.*"

The Main Master didn't wait to see if I approved or wanted to keep fighting. He turned, heading for the door. When he grabbed the handle, he paused, glancing back at me. Anger. Emptiness. They combined and with one foreign word, I joined him in the void. It swallowed me whole, sucking me into a vortex of fog. The barrier closed behind him, and I could barely focus as I walked to the sofa, sitting down.

"Kayla?"

Slow. It seemed to take forever for my eyes to lift.

"Yes, Jake?"

A frown came to his face. He didn't speak as he lowered, pressing his lips into my forehead.

"The difference is so obvious now that I see it. I should have known it was something like this." He cursed, growling. "Let's go to bed. You need to sleep. Maybe you'll feel better in the morning."

But would I? Didn't I feel fine now? Was that disappointment I detected from my husband?

Standing, I followed through in a haze. I didn't make it past the bedroom door before I was slowing, and my head was turning towards the cell door. Jake paused in pulling back the comforter.

"Kayla, come to bed. You can worry about the crow tomorrow."

Tomorrow…yes…I headed over, changing into a black silk nightgown and crawling on my side. Jake joined me, turning the bedside lamp off. As I stared up at the dark ceiling, a heaviness hit. It had nothing to do with sleeping and everything to do with a strange weight on my chest. My heart. Maybe even my mind.

"I'll stay on the Main Master about connecting with Matthew." His arm wrapped around my waist, pulling me up against him. He kept it there, seat-belting around my stomach. "This could really play in our child's favor if we were to meet him now. And I'll try to get you as much time with him as I can. We can do dinner together or maybe see him on our way to a movie. There is the club, Dark God Status, but I'm not sure I want you in there just yet."

"I made that club."

A pause. "Made?"

"Helped design. Inspired, I guess. I haven't been, but I've heard about it in detail from the Main Master. I might like to go someday."

"Inspired. I've been once. The…butchers…behind the glass walls. *That's you.*

"The butcher. Yes…I guess that is me."

Jake grew quiet, and time stretched in an emptiness that matched my own. I couldn't sleep. I couldn't even really think. My mind told me this was normal. That this stage was okay and would pass. I'd been here before. Multiple times. I knew this hollowness, but I couldn't quite make sense of the magnifications of what it meant.

Light snoring sounded, and after minutes I began counting my husband's breaths. They acted as a scale, taking the place of real time. The volume rose. It decreased. It almost became nonexistent. The numbers went from the hundreds into the tens of thousands. Hours must have passed. I didn't move, but he did. He tossed, turned, and mumbled names. I waited to feel. I *should* have felt something. There was nothing but recollection that I was back here, in this devoid space that was my home. It stirred the anger, and I knew that sensation all too well.

Sliding from the bed, I sat on the edge, staring at the dim wall ahead. More time. A lot of it. More stirring behind me. I was so aware and yet lost. When pressure from Jake's hand settled on my back, I couldn't help but jump.

"Kayla, what's wrong?"

"I can't sleep. I would like the key now. I don't need assistance. You can keep sleeping. I'll be okay."

The bed shifted and a click sounded before the bedside lamp lit up the space.

"It's four in the morning. Have you been awake all night?"

Slowly, I turned to face him, blinking through the question.

"I'm...not tired."

"Fucking Main Master." I could see the underlying rage on Jake's face as he grabbed his wallet from the bedside drawer, removing the cell's key from a compartment inside. "You start the coffee and grab a quick breakfast. If you get as consumed as you did the last time, you're going to need your strength. I'll call for more bins."

Before I could think what I was doing, I was crawling across the bed, wrapping my arms around Jake's neck. There was a pause as his head pushed back so he could look down at me, but it didn't stop him from pulling me in his lap. "You're still in there." He kissed my lips. As we searched each other's eyes, the heaviness in my chest shifted. It didn't lift, but something was stirring inside. "You're a fighter. You're a Whitlock and a Walton. Come back, and we'll play it safe." His voice lowered. "We won't tell him anymore. The Main Master never has to know. We'll keep it as our little secret. Just me and you."

But what was I supposed to come back from? What had happened differently before? My mind said I might know, but it offered no solutions.

"I'll make coffee and breakfast for both of us. Then...I'll assist with the crow."

"Assist? I don't understand. You didn't do that before."

"I was attacked." I found myself slowing as my brain weaved through the lies it knew to keep. "Once I started, I couldn't really stop. I prefer to assist. You torture, and I'll take them apart while you do so."

"At the same time?"

A smile came to my face as I watched my husband become intrigued.

"Same time. You can start at the top. I'll take care of the bottom. Fingers and toes. Hands and feet. Arms and legs. Or you torture, and I'll take the body part once you finish. Either way, I'll go at your speed. The slower, the more fun it becomes. The more they scream."

"You are a Whitlock, through and through. My God." His mouth tugged at the side. "I wasn't sure what I thought about that but...*I think I might like it.*"

"And I think *I like you.* A lot. I...feel it."

I licked my lips, standing from his lap. His sudden hold had me stopping. He was still sitting on the edge of the bed, his legs widening as he pulled me in between them. His face buried in my cleavage as he held me. Pushing my fingers through his hair, I gripped tight to the medium length as he moved over, sucking against my nipple through the silk.

"Jake." I inhaled, holding tighter through the zing of pleasure.

There was power in his grip as he settled on my hips, lifting and pulling me back on the bed to straddle him. I didn't need training to lead me into what I wanted. This was the mindset I thrived in. My training had never lacked in this department, and I let it rule me. I lowered my chest to his, meeting his mouth hungrily. When his arms wrapped around me, I wasn't sure I'd ever forget the significance of his touch. When he held me, I felt safe. Protected. From what, I hadn't a clue, but I didn't feel alone, and that was a sensation I knew all too well. Again, the heaviness shifted, trying to find its place inside me.

"Even now, you're not like before. You're not as far away as you were when you first came to me. I can reach you again. I can do it. He'll never know. I was stupid to call him." Still, he kept kissing me, cupping my face. And me, I was trying to lift to free his cock from his pajama bottoms so I could get him inside of me.

"Reach me," I repeated. "I don't know what that means. I... can't." A moan left me as his mouth became more demanding. My objective was all I knew. It kept repeating. Not his words. Not what they could mean. "I'm going to give you a baby."

"You're going to give me so much more than that. You're my wife."

"I am." I moved against him as he reached up, fisting my hair on each side to tilt my head back. The suction to my throat had me inhaling through the building lust. "We're married...We have each other forever? You're mine?"

Jake paused, pushing his pants down as I quickly leveled his cock at my entrance. "Till death do us part, whether we like it or not. I don't give up on anything. I'll make this work. But what about you? You have your role, but do you want this, Kayla? Do you want *me*?"

It was my turn to pause as Elec flashed in my mind. This was all so new, and people changed. Their true colors always broke through. Would Jake's, or was this the real him? Did I want this version of my husband? It appeared so. I couldn't have him fast enough but was that duty or part of me somewhere outside the cloudiness of my mind? I didn't know, but my voice didn't care as it spoke for me.

"I want this. I want you."

"Fuck. I know you do." Jake spun me, easing his cock inside until he was burying himself deep. A cry pushed past my lips, but it was one of savage need. My nails were digging into his back as I urged him faster. "I'm going to bring you back. You don't want to be brainwashed; you want to be my wife. You were so happy."

Brainwashed.

Brainwashed.

I heard him, weighing what that meant. I couldn't. My head lifted as my legs drew up. Jake was increasing his speed, starting to pound against me. He was still kissing me while we both tried to breathe. I wasn't sure what we were experiencing was ever going to be enough for me to be sated. Despite the lack of emotions, my body was feeling everything. It was relishing in the pleasure. Savoring in the way his cock fit perfectly inside.

"Yes. I'm happy with you. I want us to be a family."

"We are a family. Me and you, and soon we'll get the news we're waiting for. That doesn't take away our connection. Keep looking into my eyes, wife. I'm not going to give up. I got you once. I'll bring you back again."

I gasped, feeling myself built as he ground his hips. The friction over my clit sent the burn scorching every inch of my skin. Jake's hand slid to the side of my neck, holding securely. Saying more than he was. The truth of his dedication was in his grip. It promised things that fed the roaring beast inside. It gave me confidence. It added to the protection I knew he already felt. Jake was a family man, and his experience with being a husband

and father was already ingrained. With me, he fell into what he knew. He was home here, and that we were bonding so quickly only made him latch to me and my role even harder. My knowledge of that wasn't allowing it to escape me either. The girl who longed for this. The woman who prayed for a fairytale. Both may have been killed with my kidnapping, but a new me was awakening. Jake said I was brainwashed. Mind control couldn't keep me away forever. I was growing into both roles, and the merging of the two would only favor me in the end.

MASTER A-0005

I wasn't sure Kayla would ever wake up. After her sleepless night, it only took me making her come twice before sleep won over her need to kill the crow. Twelve hours later, she woke up happier than ever. Reinvigorated for our plan. I couldn't deny that I was too. Maybe the Main Master was trying to make amends. Maybe he'd twisted Kayla's mind enough to guess what would make us both happy. I wasn't sure as I took in the bloody, begging convict. I recognized him from the list of multiple offenders. He could have well been my next choice at the upcoming auction. Now, he was mine. As many crows as I wanted…were mine. I had Kayla and her hold over the Main Master to thank for that. No waiting anymore for me. Not if she needed this on a regular basis. And maybe she wouldn't. I didn't know. What I did suspect was that her urges were going to have to be reigned in. She liked this, but I wanted this to be a healthy need for both of us. Not an overwhelming addiction. That led to trouble, and if we were going to be having a baby soon, we had more important things to worry about.

"Families. They're always families. Over and over and over." I dropped the file, rearing back and connecting my fist with his face for what had to be the tenth time since we'd come in not an hour earlier. The crow's arms and legs were strapped to the chair, and he didn't stand a chance to move. "Did you get out of the car and render aid? Did you check to see if they were okay?"

"Mister, pl—"

I hit him again watching blood spray across the metal table at his side. One of his eyes was already swollen shut, and the cut at his brow had blood dripping down his face. His lip was fat, and the hematoma at his temple was half the size of my fist.

"You didn't. Why didn't you? Because you were so fucking drunk, you passed out. Even the crash didn't wake you. Two children ejected and dying in a ditch while you were oblivious. How do you think that mother felt losing her children? Losing her own mother? All they wanted was to stay the weekend with their grandparents. All they got was a grave." My head shook through the seething fury. Through the new fears as I took in Kayla's beautiful face and perfect posture. She was watching me intently, waiting... Even half dead inside, I saw her when she gazed up at me. I'd experience the real her however fleeting it was. I wanted that version back, and it only fed my violence.

"Wife, stand up."

Kayla stood from an extra chair taking a step forward. I swallowed hard, not liking how erratic my pulse was. Even as I knew what might be coming, it didn't make it easier to face. Lowering to my knees, I stared forward, even with her stomach. She'd hold my future. *Our future.* The future of the Princeton line, and it was up to me to make sure there was never a repeat of the past. I had to protect her. Protect any children we had together. Doubt was drowning me. What if I failed again? What if in one split second, I wasn't ready, and someone took them away too?

My eyes closed at the tortuous thoughts. I grabbed her hips, resting my forehead against the ultimate challenge—against a possible life we'd created—against fate. Where a part of me knew she'd be okay living at the Gardens, it didn't stop the questions. Accidents happened every day. I'd latched on to this new dream more than I had realized, and the negative aspects were catching up.

"I can't take the fears. I can't take the thought of losing you. Of maybe losing this." My lips pressed into her stomach.

"*You won't.* I believe in you. We're going to be fine." She eased down, kissing me as she got on her knees to mirror me. "No one will hurt us anymore. I trust you to keep our children safe. You'll figure out a way. You'll make sure they're always protected. *You will.*"

"I will. I promise."

"And if anyone, *anyone*, so much as hurts them—"

"*I'll kill them.*"

"They won't stand a chance. Just like this piece of shit here. He doesn't deserve to live. Every breath he takes is air he's stealing from us. If he couldn't walk over to save those babies, he'll never walk again."

A deafening scream muddled my mind. The blur was so fast that it took me a moment to realize that Kayla had moved at all. Toes rolled across the floor, blood squirting across the cement as she rolled forward, grabbing his other foot and bringing the hatchet down on that one too. More toes spun through the force, stopping inches from the feet that fought against the restraints.

"Oh God! *God!* You crazy bitch! Help!" He choked on his screams. "Someone help me!"

Kayla's laugh started low, turning into a giggle like a child. Her eyes rose, and she smiled, holding out the hatchet. For the briefest moment, I almost was sure I saw the real her. The one trying to come back to me. But did I know that version of Kayla? ...Barely. That didn't mean I didn't want more.

"Toes and fingers, husband. Show him your pain. Make him feel it."

I could have fucked her right there in the crow's blood for how turned on I suddenly felt. My lips crushed into hers, and I took the hatchet, standing, as she reached for a small Tupperware.

"You heard my wife. Fingers and toes. She got your toes. I'll get the fingers that were wrapped around the steering wheel. The ones that would rather hold a bottle than a phone to call for help."

"Please! Someone!" The crow was going wild in the chair. "Fucking—Someone, help!"

My head cocked as I took in the angle of his hand. With the chair swiveled to the side, the hatchet would be of no use. I could have spun him back to the table, but Kayla's earlier words came back to me. Slow. Yes, I'd drag this out.

I walked over, putting down the hatchet and picking up a tool that made me smile. It was more oval than square and contained three holes. The two on each end for my fingers; the one in the middle for his.

"I do think I'm going to enjoy this." I grabbed a hammer with my other hand, turning to see the crow's eyes widen.

"What is that? W-What—"

"It's sort of like a cigar cutter just…stronger. Are you left-handed or right?"

"Fuck you. Fuck. *Fuck!* Let me go. I'm sorry. I didn't mean to."

My head shook as I approached. "You wouldn't believe how many times I've heard that. *'I didn't mean to. It was an accident.'* Was it?"

Sobs filled the space and Kayla glanced up from her index card, a smile appearing as she taped the layer on the Tupperware lid.

"Open your hand."

The crow's knuckles grew whiter as he made a fist. I didn't ask again. My arm drew back, and I brought the hammer down directly to the top of his hand. Bones shattered from the force, reverberating through my grip. The howls only fed my ravenous need for revenge. One I knew would never be sated. Tragedy. Trauma. Kayla was the only thing so far that eased the ache and made breathing bearable. Even that held fear. It was a fear I could live with. *Survive in.*

"Let's try this again, shall we?"

I clutched to his already swelling hand, squeezing as I forced his finger through the hole, stopping at the middle joint. I didn't have to look at Kayla to see her eyes taking us in. Her presence was becoming part of me. I was willing it that way.

"P-Please. Mister, pl—"

Deafening screams echoed through the cell as my fingers shot closed, bringing the sharp razors down through thick flesh. The crow's body thrashed, and he turned pale. I didn't wait for him to catch his breath. I didn't even care if he passed out. Moving to the next finger, I snapped my fingers again. And again. And again. Slow, but steady. Peaceful yet...hollow.

At one point the slave did nod off, but Kayla was right there, reviving him just as fast. The slaps. The yells and smelling salts. She stayed focused on my actions, always assisting, and always ready as I moved to the next part of him. I got so engrossed with my own methods, I didn't even see the crow before me. Not really. I saw my family. I saw the hate I held for their suffering. I felt the raw pain associated with their deaths. More...a shallow level of contentment I couldn't quite explain. It wasn't significant, but it was noticeable to the damaged part of me.

"God! Fu—"

The crow's head bobbed as he fought for consciousness. The solid thuds coming from below drew my eyes down. Where the slave was missing from the elbows, down, Kayla had started working at removing his feet. With every swing of the hatchet, her face seemed to clear a little more. Or maybe it was wishful thinking. All I knew was she was intense. Driven. *She was beautiful.*

"Al...most." Her arm reared back, coming to connect with

amazing force. "There." She was glowing with happiness as she lifted the severed foot. It had me smiling too but not for long. Kayla quickly blinked, dropping the foot and hatchet as her bloody hands shot out for balance. She fell on her ass, rocking back.

"Whoa." I dove, lowering to put my hands on her biceps to try to steady her. "Talk to me. What are you feeling?"

"...Dizzy."

"We're done for now." I didn't give her a chance to argue. I swooped her in my arms, carrying her out of the cell and into the bedroom to sit on the side of the mattress. "Go more into detail. What else besides dizzy?"

"I think that might be it. The room just spun for the briefest moment. I..." Her hand came out. "There it is again. I'm not steady. It's coming and going."

"Your schedule is off. You've had a hard twenty-four hours. I think we should be safe and take you in to get checked anyway."

"To the doctor?"

"They may be able to help."

She got quiet. "I think maybe I just need a nap. Can I take one, and if it gets worse, then we'll go in?"

I couldn't speak as fear battled her plea. It was there deep in her eyes. A familiarness I caved to. Prayed for. And she was right. If I took her in, the Main Master would arrive. If he noticed what I did... "Alright. We'll get you showered and see if that works first. If you feel any more dizziness that doesn't subside, you tell me right away. You don't have to be afraid. It stays between us. Understand?"

Kayla nodded. She stood, and I helped her to the bathroom to clean up. As time stretched out, I watched her every move. Her every breath. I tuned in for any hint of vertigo but didn't detect anything else. As I tucked her in and headed for my phone, I couldn't ignore the tornado of emotions whipping through me. I thought losing my family was the hardest thing I'd ever have to face. It appeared starting a new one might just prove even more difficult. I wanted this. Actually having it nearly suffocated me. It had nothing to do with Kayla or a possible baby and everything to do with failing in my role to protect them. Having her almost faint was beyond my control. Women died in childbirth all the time. That was also beyond my control. Reasons were suddenly piling up, and there was nothing I could do to stop them.

I stared at my phone deciding against reporting it to the Main Master. It was wrong. A breach of our contract. I didn't care. He wasn't good for her. If he caught one hint that she wasn't as numbed out as he wanted, I'd lose all progress I might have already made. Or maybe I could talk to him. There had to be a reason he kept her so under his influence. If I explained that I wanted the real her, perhaps he'd set her free of whatever hold he had. Then again, she knew things he didn't want anyone else to know, and no part of her being aware benefited him. She could tell everyone. She could tell *me*.

FC0001

What started out as an afternoon of rest turned into an entire day. Then, two. Then, three. For the life of me I couldn't seem to keep my eyes open for longer than a few hours. All I wanted to do was sleep, and my husband couldn't stop cursing the Main Master for somehow messing with my mind. The more worried Jake got, the more hovering he became. He insisted a small break away from the apartment might be good, but all I wanted to do was crawl back in bed. I didn't want to be away from our home. I didn't want to be meeting with the Main Master either. I didn't have a choice as Jake led us out of the elevator and into the fancy restaurant where a few Masters were already waving us over.

"Is that our table? With them?"

"No. We'll just go say hello real quick."

He barely got to finish before all the men rose from the table. One's hand shot out, and I recognized him immediately from being with the Main Master. He was Master One. Shane.

"Master Five, I didn't know you'd be here. Did you want to join us?"

Jake shook his hand, nodding to the other men as a greeting.

"I wish we could. We're meeting with the Main Master about Kayla's appointment tomorrow."

"Oh, that's right." His face lit up. "I knew it was close to time. Are we thinking good news?"

I forced a smile, shrugging. Aside from the fog I couldn't fight, I felt nothing at all.

"We'll see." Jake glanced over, waving to Elec as the Main Master stood from a table at the far back of the room. "That's us. I'm sure you'll know the moment we get news. Hell, you'll probably hear before I do."

Master One laughed, slapping Jake's shoulder. "I probably will. Good luck."

"Thanks."

I waved towards the four men, leaning more into my husband as his arm came around my lower back. He kept me steady as we approached the Main Master. Elec wasn't happy. He wasn't mad either. Where I was usually good at reading him, I detected nothing, and that worried me even more.

"She's pale."

Jake paused from pulling out my chair. He glanced at me, helping me to sit. They quickly did the same.

"If she's pale it's your fault. She hasn't been the same since you messed with her head. Take it off."

"I will not."

"Elec, *I'm not asking you*. This is my wife. She's not the same as she was before. I want Kayla back."

"She is Kayla. Even if I released her from her altered state, which I have no plan to do, she'd be the same as she is now. It's not me; it's her."

Jake scanned my face, shaking his head.

"No. She was fine. Then she got dizzy. Ever since then, all she does is sleep."

"Dizzy?" The Main Master's mouth twisted, and he leaned

back in his chair, crossing his arms over his chest. "Dizzy." He repeated. "You didn't call me."

"So you could mess her up even more? No, I didn't call you. I didn't even want to bring her to this meeting. All she does anymore is sleep. There's no laughter. No happiness. No spark. Just sleep."

Elec let out a deep breath, torn between emotions. He was holding back, and how much of it revolved around my husband's attitude, I was afraid to know. "You're not this daft, Jake."

The table got quiet as the men stared at each other.

"It's not that. I already considered it. *I've lived it.* Kayla is different. She had life behind her eyes. That's gone now. Take it off, Elec. Kayla doesn't need to be controlled like that. We're happy together. She deserves to be able to lead a real life with me. I deserve it too. If I wanted a blank slate female to breed, I would have requested one. I want Kayla for who she is. The real her."

The Main Master laughed. "Do you really think I'm doing this to her because I want to? You are not safe with her in her true form. I taught her too well for that. She'd kill you, Jake, and she wouldn't bat an eye."

"I don't believe you. Kayla wouldn't do that to me. There's something between us that is more than your lessons. We have a real connection."

"Is that right?" He laughed, saying he believed otherwise. "Let's see, shall we?" The Main Master looked between us, stopping on me. His hand went up in my peripheral and he snapped, but I kept my gaze locked to his. "You can't lie to me, slave. Not even if you want to. Your mind won't allow it." He picked up the glass, sipping the dark liquid. "Do you have feelings for Master Five."

I glanced at Jake.

"Nope. Look at me and answer."

I met blue eyes, nodding. "I do."

"As a friend? More than a friend?"

"More."

His eyebrows rose. "Are you attracted to him?"

"I am."

"Because he protects you?"

I grew quiet through the heaviness in my brain. "More than that. He...sees me. He said forever. That's what I want too."

Another drink. Surprise merged with anger, mixing with something else.

"He's what you want. What happens when he meets the real you? Do you think he would want you then?"

It was almost impossible to stay staring ahead. I wanted to turn, but my body wouldn't allow it.

"I think he would. He saw the real me. We connected. We're...the same. We worked on that crow together. It was." I stopped, not able to hold in the awe that blanketed my words. "*It was amazing. He was.*" My blush burned my cheeks. My entire body suddenly felt on fire. "Amazing."

"Amazing. Hmm." Elec didn't speak as he finished off his drink. "Connected. Amazing. It would appear I'm fucking Cupid. This keeps happening. Love and murder, the perfect remedy for relationships. I'm over it."

"I told you, what Kayla and I share is special. Will you please say whatever you need to and reverse what you've done? We find out the big news tomorrow. I want the real Kayla to be present for that. She deserves those memories as clear as they can be, *Main Master*."

"And if she kills you in your sleep?"

"Is there a better way to go?"

Elec cursed under his breath. "I am not having a good day."

"Neither am I, but you can make it better by giving us what we want."

"Everyone wants something. Why can't anyone see I do what I do for a reason? You want Kayla? The real her?"

"*Yes.*"

"I'll think about it." Elec motioned for a waiter as Jake let out a sigh. The slave didn't come to our table. Instead, he nodded and headed towards the back. "I hope you don't mind. I ordered for all of us."

"Why am I worried?"

The Main Master laughed, an evil only I know slipping into his features. "Because you have good reason." He paused. "But don't worry, Jake. I have no tricks up my sleeve. This is actually for Kayla. Her favorite. I offer it as a…gift."

"I still don't trust you."

Jake's voice lowered, but the Main Master's stare didn't leave me. He was reading me to gauge my mindset, and I was just clear enough to know that. He worried of my loyalty when he didn't need to. Altered or not, I knew what was in my best interest. I had heard and seen enough over the years to know my place.

"You can trust him, Jake." I cleared my throat, sitting taller. "I do. The Main Master is right. He may not be conventional, but I've never seen him outsmarted or fail in trying to succeed in something." I looked at my husband. "You don't like what he's done. I don't think I do either. But…he has his reasons, and if he says something, he means it. If he fears I'll kill you, the warning is probably justified. I don't think I'd ever hurt you. I don't *feel* as though I would, but I don't feel much right now. I'm sorry." I looked back at the Main Master. "To you, too. I'm sorry you feel I need this to function. I search my mind and try to detect a threat inside, but I can't find one. All that's there is longing and the anger that's associated with it. We're not family, but don't mistake my love for you either. Elec, we are family. Main Master," I corrected. "If you think this is what's best, all I ask is you clear me long enough for the results, tomorrow, and when I meet Matthew. If you feel that's a mistake, so be it. I'm done fighting. I'm just done."

My hand came to my head, and I shut my lids, breathing through the fatigue that just wouldn't let me go. All I wanted to do was lie down. To sleep and cry and shout. But not because I was angry or upset. It was just there. I could have probably spilt my drink and burst into tears. No mental force required. I wasn't even sure where the need was coming from. I didn't feel emotional, but there was no mistaking the signals my brain was screaming.

"Do you see what I mean?" The words came out laced with a growl. Jake's hand settled on my back, and it reinforced the realization that I wasn't alone anymore. Protection. Comfort. The heaviness in my chest stirred. It was all too much. Tears raced down. A sob came. And I broke. "Shh. No, it's okay. I'm not mad at you." Another growl. "Seriously, fix her to the way she was before."

"I'm afraid that's going to be impossible. There's no fixing that." Elec laughed, this time in a lighter tone. "You are so daft. Fucking Einstein over here. Jesus, Jake."

"Stop it. This isn't funny. Say the words."

Harder I cried, burying myself even more into Jake's chest. I could barely breathe. Barely think. I didn't have to for what I knew was coming with the strong sobs. Dizziness hit again and I felt the world rock just before I grabbed the fancy bowl placement, throwing up right there in front of everyone. There was no stopping it. There was no real warning. The restaurant was dead silent until it wasn't. The echo and cheers from the table of Masters was so loud, I jumped as I tried to catch my breath.

"Do you see it yet, Daddy, or should I have t-shirts made?"

I looked up in time to see the Main Master throw Jake a wink. Night and day. Where both men had been in bad moods moments before, there was no mistaking the true happiness behind their eyes. For me, it wasn't joy I suddenly felt. It was questions. Training. Calculations. It was timing. Jake wasn't far behind my train of thought.

"No. It's too early for morning sickness. Her cycle isn't even supposed to start until tomorrow."

"What does that mean, slave?"

I sniffled, swallowing down more water. "It's the shots. Possibly multiples." I glanced at Jake. "Probably twins or more."

He had to have been as pale as I was.

"Isn't there more of a likelihood for complications that way? I mean—"

"Stop. We're all getting ahead of ourselves. This could be a fluke for all we know. We'll stick to the appointment tomorrow. They'll draw blood, and we'll confirm and check her numbers. We can go from there. Today, let's just eat and be thankful. Kayla."

My eyes lifted and with three foreign words I'd never heard before, the walls seemed to melt down around me. Warmth settled in my bones. The darkness from the Main Master's suit was almost enhanced. I felt...alive. Real. And so damn over-whelmed. I grabbed Jake's hand, scraping in air to catch my breath.

"Happy, Master Five? She has one day. And you, you'll be giving me your sperm to keep safeguarded in case you're not alive tomorrow. That's nonnegotiable. I'll send someone by later to collect." Elec's smile only widened as he took another drink. "I sure hope this wasn't a mistake. I'm not a religious man, but I'll pray for you."

MASTER A-0005

I had begged. Pleaded. There was no way for me to know what I'd get with Kayla completely unaffected by the Main Master, but I was excited to find out. Deep within, I feared I'd be faced with another stranger. I didn't feel that way as I led Kayla back into our apartment. She was quiet through dinner, but I understood why. Elec said she hadn't been completely free from his influence in over a year. She had quite a lot of adjusting to do.

"How are you? Do you want any water or anything?"

"I'm okay."

Her steps were hesitant. Cautious as I led her to the sofa.

"Why don't we sit down and talk. I'm sure there's plenty you'd like to know."

"Truthfully, now that I can think, I have no idea what to say." She lowered, glancing around before her eyes came back to me. "The colors are so bright. I keep feeling like any minute I'm going to disappear again. It scares me."

My knees turned more to hers, and I reached forward, grabbing her hands.

"I'm going to fight to keep you this way. The Main Master is afraid for my wellbeing, but I'm not. We have crows at our disposal if you need them. All you have to do is ask and one will be brought right over. This doesn't have to be hard. I don't want it to be. I want you to be happy." A smile began to surface, held down by the sudden fear of becoming a father again. What was worse was my worry over what the real Kayla thought. How much differently did she think? It's not like she disappeared completely when she was under the Main Master's spell. "We might be having a baby. How do you feel about that? Is it the same as before? Do you still want this?"

Emotions flashed and she smiled. "Babies. More than one. I'm almost positive now that I can think over the blur of the last few days. I've been so tired. More than what I should have been with regular conception. Jake, I think it must be twins. Maybe more. She smiled but clenched her teeth in overexaggerated fear. My heart melted at seeing a glimpse of her true personality. "I won't lie; I'm a little scared. That'll pass. I've always wanted a big family. And I already have a caring husband. The only thing I won't get is the home full of laughter and chaos." The smile slowly disappeared. "It's hard to think of how my life will be, but I get a lot more than most slaves at the Gardens do. To have a baby at all in this place...I'm lucky. Luckier, that I have you. You won't keep them from me. I can still be a mother when you allow it."

"All the time. I'll be here as much as I can. There's housing above. I believe the Main Master mentioned that's where we'd be spending our time when I returned with the child. Or children," I laughed. "I'll try to make this the best I can for you." My head shook as I was swept under by the possibilities again. "Shit. I can't believe it. I...really can't. I don't think I expected you to get pregnant so soon. It's like I went from fighting the idea to fighting to keep you mine. It was one thing after another. I haven't even really got to think at all."

Kayla stayed quiet, nodding. "I'm sorry about that. It has

been a rollercoaster since auction night. Hopefully the drama will fade, and we can focus more on ourselves. We wanted a baby. Now we might have two or more." Just saying the words it appeared Kayla lost color in her face.

"Are you okay?"

"I'm great. It's the anxiety I mentioned before. It keeps hitting me out of nowhere. I'm speaking the words, but the emotion that comes with them is sometimes too much. I'm not used to feeling to this degree. Or feeling much at all, I guess."

"But you did feel something for me?"

Her eyes scanned mine, and she hesitantly reached up, holding to one side of my face.

"Touching you makes my heart race. I have butterflies in my stomach. I can feel the warmth of your cheeks and how your beard tickles my fingers. I was aware before. I experienced lust but." She stopped. "It was mostly lust and something unknown. A need I didn't want to lose."

"And now it's butterflies and adrenaline?"

She laughed. "And a million other things. Jake, can I ask you a question?"

"Absolutely. You can ask me anything."

"Alright." She paused. "If you would have met me outside of here, do you think." She stopped. "Do you think you would have even noticed me?"

I reached over, pulling her on my lap.

"I would have noticed. I would have thought you were beautiful just as I do now."

Her head came to rest in the crook of my neck. "I want to stay like this forever. I hope I get to stay."

AS FAR AS THE DOCTOR'S OFFICE WENT, I'D NEVER BEEN A FAN. I also hadn't been to any that had a damn pastry buffet in the main lobby area. Maybe this wouldn't be so bad. *For me.* Kayla on the other hand wasn't enjoying the rich aroma. The longer we waited, the more antsy she became.

"He lives."

I glanced over, throwing the Main Master a look as he walked up.

"I never had any doubts, but you have my sperm now. I guess it wouldn't matter either way. Can we go back to the room already? Kayla doesn't like the smell. It's making her feel sick."

"You think because I'm the Main Master you get special treatment? I want one of those scones. Hold on." Elec walked over, taking two and heading back to us. "As I was saying, you'd be right. Let's go." He took a bite, leading the way as we headed for the door off to the side. The nurses threw him smiles, and the doctor paused from his paperwork, just as happy to see the Main Master as everyone else.

"You're going to give me good news today, Dr. Lane."

"I'm full of good news. Let's see what we have. Fc one, it's been a few weeks. How are you feeling?"

Kayla smiled as we followed him into a large room.

"I'm great. More than great. Nauseous but—"

"Happy." The doctor's intrigue couldn't be mistaken. "Step on the scale and tell me anything you've felt since the auction."

She obeyed, taking a deep breath. "I've kept with my prenatal pills and vitamins. I was doing great until a few days ago when the fatigue hit."

"You got dizzy first."

"*Yes.* My husband is right. I almost forgot."

The doctor waved her to take a seat as he hooked her up to the blood pressure machine and clamped a sensor on her finger. "So, you got dizzy, and fatigue followed."

"That's right, and then yesterday I was...crying, and I couldn't control it. That's when the dizziness hit again, and I got sick."

The doctor stayed quiet as he wrote down the information and vitals in the chart.

"That sounds promising. You look well enough. You seem happy which is great." He headed over, getting the syringe and tubes together. I was never one for needles, but Kayla didn't seem to mind as she watched him take her blood. "Is there anything else you can think of that you might need to tell me? No pains or erratic behavior?"

"Erratic?"

The doctor glanced at me. "It's nothing to worry about. Sometimes the shots can cause mood swings. If she hasn't experienced them already, I'm sure there's nothing to worry about."

Kayla shook her head. "Nothing besides the crying."

"Great. If you'll all excuse me, I'll go check this real quick."

The moment the door shut behind the doctor I spun my attention to the Main Master.

"Erratic behavior? Would we even know with how shut down you had her?"

"Calm, Master Five. Anything erratic about your wife has nothing to do with those shots."

"It's just me, then?"

Elec seemed taken aback by Kayla's question.

"You're so calm and soft spoken, I can almost believe you have no idea what you've done."

"Done?" The confusion was real as she kept her focus on the Main Master. "I've done a lot of stuff, but nothing I would deem erratic."

Silence filled the room as Elec ate his scone, keeping her stare. Only when he swallowed did he speak.

"I once tried giving you roommates. You begged for company."

Her hand waved through the air. "That wasn't erratic, that was fun. I was rebelling at that time. You knew just as I did what would happen."

"So, you admit it now? There were no accidents? No provocation like you stated before?"

"No."

"You massacred those women for no other reason than to do it."

"That's right. What did you expect? You had me kidnapped. Then, we're suddenly murdering people at free will. I was a mess. Confused. Beyond angry. I wanted you to trust me, but also fear me. I see it worked."

"I don't fear you, Kayla. I do fear for other people."

"But you don't have to anymore." I shook my head, moving in next to my wife. "Kayla has nothing left to prove. That was in the past. You heard her. She was angry, as anyone would be given her situation."

"She'll get angry again over something. It's just a matter of time. What happens then? Will you murder them too?"

"It depends. What did they do?"

The Main Master rolled his eyes. "You know what I'm saying. I've spoiled you, and you're smart enough to know that no matter how influenced you are. You think you'll get away with things because of your blood. You've known from the moment you got here you were special. I never hid that, but you also are not above the law of this place. I may not have you killed like the others, but I will lock you away in Hell Row and forget you exist. You'll be dead to me, and that would be worse than death itself."

"This was supposed to be a happy day."

The Main Master stood as Kayla's bottom lip stuck out the slightest amount.

"I'll be happy when the test confirms what we suspect. Allow me to get you a scone. Scones make everything better."

"I don't want a scone. I don't even want to smell it."

The smile was automatic, but Elec didn't speak as he left the room, shutting the door behind him. I moved in, taking his seat, and holding Kayla's hand.

"It shouldn't be too long. The doctor is running the test himself." Time passed, but I could tell Kayla was deep in thought. "Would you like me to get you some water or anything?"

"Water might help."

I leaned in, kissing her forehead. "Be right back."

"Wait. Jake…I did some bad things. I've." She stopped. "I'll be a good mother. Please don't let what you hear make you think otherwise. This is all I've ever wanted. I'll guard what's ours with everything I have. I'd never hurt them. You believe me, right?"

"Is that why you looked so worried? I know you'd never hurt them. I've done bad things too, but you're a protector like me. We'd die for what's ours. Kill."

"*Yes*. I knew you'd understand."

Just seeing the way her eyes longingly stared into mine did such profound things to the man I thought I was. It altered him. Changed his views. It gave me hope where I thought none existed. I leaned down, kissing her before I stood and shut the door behind me. For seconds, I didn't move, trying to reign in the excitement and fear. It was a voice that drew me forward. When I made the turn, I slowed, spying Elec talking to the doctor. Both their heads turned to me and from the look on the Main Master's face…*I knew.*

FC0001

Was it safe to feel happy for just a moment? Could I express it? Go crazy with the pent-up nervousness and excitement? It probably wasn't wise, but there was no one in the room to see me if I did jump up or down, or squeal, or...pace. If only I wasn't so dizzy, perhaps I would.

"Tell us." Jake barged through the door, making me jump. The doctor and Elec walked through, their faces anything but 'telling'. I couldn't read them, but I could read Jake.

Standing, I placed my hand over my stomach protectively as he made it to my side.

"I wouldn't let them tell me without you here. But they know. I know they know, and I think I know, but I want us hearing the news together."

The doctor headed to the counter, placing the folder down.

"It's as we suspected. You are pregnant. The HCG count is on the higher side, but we won't know whether it's multiples for another few days. Unless anything happens between now and then, I think we should aim for this time next week and test again."

Jake reached over, cupping my face, crushing his lips into

mine. Could I scream now? Go crazy with excitement? Not in front of the Main Master. Not yet.

"We're having a baby."

"Or babies."

"Or babies," he laughed. "We did it." Again, he kissed me, not caring that the Main Master or doctor was still in the room. "Are you happy?"

"Ecstatic. A little shaky, but I'm so happy."

"Me too. Shit. I forgot your water. Don't move. I'm going to go get it for you." He held my face trapped, kissing me again. "We're having a baby." Another kiss. "Water."

With that, he stood, heading for the door. The doctor's eyes met the Main Master, and he followed Jake out, not that I thought Jake saw. He was over the moon excited, but mine was fading as Elec shut the door and pinned me with an empty stare.

"You did it, slave. You far exceeded my expectations. I knew I trained you well, but this...you brought a man back from the dead in record time. Jake is falling in love with you if he isn't already. How did you do it?"

"I...was myself. I didn't really do much of anything."

"Oh, you did. I've known that man almost my entire life. When I forced him here, he was a breath away from killing himself. Now, you have him eating out of the palm of your hand. Enough so, he'd do the one thing he shouldn't, and that's lie to me."

"Jake wouldn't—"

The Main Master's hand shot up and the anger he projected had me wanting to move far away from him.

"I've been watching the two of you from the beginning. You forget, *I hear everything*. I see everything. He had every intention of hiding your condition from me so I couldn't change you back. He meant to turn you away from me. *Keep you away from me*. Do you know what happens when I can't trust people in my circle?"

637

"You can trust him."

Elec took a step closer. "You know I can't. There's no going back. If Jake can lie about you, he can lie to me about anything."

Tears blinded me as I tried to stop the devastating ache that was webbing through my chest. The pain was so intense, I could barely stay seated. Was this heartbreak? God, I'd forgotten how crippling it could be.

"What are you going to do?"

"Me? This is your mess. You'll be the one cleaning it up."

The tears fell, and I quickly wiped them away.

"What do you want me to do?"

Elec leaned against the wall, crossing his arms over his chest. "In two days your brother will be here. I'll spare you from having to break the news to him yourself. When you finally meet, he'll know exactly who you are. You're going to be sweet. Shy. You're going to let Jake do most of the talking. They know each other. He doesn't know you. He doesn't need to. Your purpose is to be there. All I want is for Matthew to see how happy you and your husband are, and for you to tell him your exciting news."

"And then? What about Jake?"

"That night, you'll kill him."

"*What?*" My head shook. "No. *I can't.*"

Elec lunged, digging his fingers into my face. "You can and you will. I can't have someone on my board I can't trust."

"But you can. He'd never betray you."

"*He already did.*" With one last squeeze he let go, leaning back against the wall. "You'll do it, and you'll carry on his line."

"Here? *At the Gardens?* I'll never see my children. I'll *lose* them." I stood, anger making me shake through the building panic and rage. "There has to be another way."

"There's only one way. My way. You won't lose them... unless you betray me too. You want to be free? Do you want to take your place in the outside world as the new Princeton widow?"

"But you said—"

"*I am not Bram Whitlock. I* make the rules, in case you haven't noticed. What I'm realizing is your manipulative little brain is more beneficial to me out there than in here. You've done your job for the Gardens. Now you can do more up there. You won't like it, and what I say is law, but you'll be free. Monitored constantly, yes. Controlled and under my influence, absofuckinglutely. Your life will read like a script, but you'll be out of here, and I'll make you a Mistress for when you need to return. I know who you are, Kayla. I trust you'll be loyal to me. *I made you.*"

"I."

Blue eyes darkened, almost appearing black as they glared down. "The answer can't be that hard. What's it going to be, Mrs. Princeton? Will a hint of love keep you as a slave, separated from your children, or are you ready to do my bidding on the outside world as a mother and Mistress? Neither of these stories will have a happy ending, and you may come to hate me because of them, but choose your future wisely. One looks a lot better than the other."

<hr />

"ARE YOU SURE YOU'RE FEELING OKAY? YOU WERE SO HAPPY AT the appointment. I leave to get your water and when I return, you were crying and upset. You haven't been the same since. Not when we watched the movie last night, or when we went on a walk. Not even when I had flowers delivered for you."

"I loved them. I did. I'm a mess right now. Look at me." I tried forcing a smile. His lips pressed to the top of my head as he continued to hold me on the bed. "You may be a mess, but you're *my* mess. Tell me how to fix it. What would make you feel better?"

Wasn't that the billion-dollar question?

"I'm just so tired. All I want is for you to keep holding me."

"If that's what you want, that's what you'll get."

My lids closed, trying to keep the tears inside as I listened to his heartbeat. How was I going to do this? How could I kill my husband, the father of my children? It wasn't like he was a crow. I felt sick. My head was spinning, and not in the fog it usually was. I'd never been thinking so clearly.

"Kayla?"

Jake's fingers beginning to stroke down my hair made me sob. I held my arms around him tighter, feeling the ache in my chest become unbearable. I couldn't do this. I couldn't *not* do this. Elec taught me there was always a solution, but what would it be in this case? Jake needed to die. If I didn't kill him, Elec would. Then, he'd punish me. Take away my babies?

Freedom...or love?

Was morality worth a lifetime in this place? Was escaping a cell in Hell Row even worth it? My life would become my own personal hell. The Main Master wanted me to do his bidding. What would that be? Did it even matter? I'd get to have a family. I'd have my babies. Or would I? They'd never truly be mine. Even they would be trapped in this world. Escaping was all I had wanted since I'd been brought here, but there was truly no escape. There was only compromise.

"You have to talk to me. Is it the Main Master? Did he say something to you after I left?"

I cried harder but shook my head.

"I'm not sure I believe you, but you can talk to me if he did say something. You may be afraid I'll tell him, but you're my wife. What you tell me always stays between us."

My head rose as I searched his face. Duty and loyalty, maybe even part of the former brainwashing, played tug-o-war with the feelings I already had for Jake. To tell him was putting nails in both of our coffins. Was that so bad?

Leaning forward, I gently pressed my lips to his. "You're so good to me. Probably the best anyone's ever been. There truly was no better pairing. We're perfect for each other."

"I see the root of these emotions now." Jake reached forward, tucking a lock of hair behind my ear. "I forget how overwhelming this must be for you. You're feeling again. That has to be a shock to your system."

"It's so hard."

"I'm here for you. We'll take one hour at a time. Come lay back down on me and let me hold you. When you're ready to get up, we'll figure out what you need."

I lowered, settling my head back against his chest.

"I need to eat soon. I'm probably going to get sick, but I have to try."

Jake went back to stroking my hair while he wrapped his other arm around me.

"Do you have an idea of what you might want?"

"Something light. Maybe some crackers and soup."

"That actually sounds really good. I think I might like that too. When Maggie—" Jake came to an abrupt stop causing me to lift my head and look up. He appeared shocked...then angry. "I'm sorry."

"Sorry?" His head turned, almost fighting me as I tried to bring his face back to mine. "Why are you sorry?"

"I don't want her name in this place. Not her name or...memories."

"It won't upset me if you want to talk about her. I know it hurts—"

"*You know nothing.* I don't want to talk about her. Not like this."

I sat up. "Like what? With your new wife?"

641

"Kayla, don't fight with me. It was a mistake mentioning her. I want to leave her out of this place."

"That's the second time you've said that. Why not mention her here? Because she was so good, and I'm so bad? Because you were proud of her, but this life with me brings you shame? You said we were supposed to be *honest* with each other. I guess that only applied to me."

I crawled off the bed, storming to the living room.

"Kayla, wait. That's not it at all. I'm not ashamed of you."

"Really? It didn't sound like that to me."

"You're taking it the wrong way. I'd have the same amount of respect for you if the roles were reversed. Will you stop?"

Jake's arms wrapped around my chest from behind, easing me to a stop before I could reach the kitchen. He spun me to face him, keeping me trapped to his body.

"I'm sorry if I upset you. I just don't want to talk about her or anything that happened before. I'm not ready for that yet. I'm trying so hard to adjust to this. I'm excited, and I want to embrace what we have, but to do that fully I have to go through the motions and let everything sink in. I'm not ashamed of you," he repeated. "I'm not. You can't help that you're here. I wish you weren't. If I could take you from here, I would in a heartbeat."

"Could you?"

The question was barely a whisper as my mind spun with new possibilities. Elec. He could get me out of here. He said so himself. If that was the truth…why wouldn't he let us both leave? He didn't trust Jake, but he had to know Jake would never betray the Gardens."

"Kayla, you know the rules. You can't leave. It's forbidden."

"Just give me a minute." I pulled him to the sofa as I sat down. "We offer Elec…a lot. You said you were rich. We…offer him something. He likes power. We give it to him. Yes. We…I have to talk to the Main Master."

"Are you serious? He's going to laugh at you or get really pissed. There's no way in hell—"

"Jake, *please*. Just stop for a minute and let me think."

He wanted my husband dead. I didn't see any if, ands, or buts, that came along with the decision, but wasn't it worth a try? Maybe Elec wouldn't even let me leave, but maybe if I mentioned money, he'd at least spare Jake's life. He had to. Couldn't he just kick him from the board? From the Gardens? It was stupid to even ponder. My husband was right, but I couldn't go a moment more without trying.

"I need to speak with him. Please." I bit against my lip as I took in his confusion. "Will you allow me to meet with the Main Master so I can talk with him? This is important, Jake. Please trust me when I say that."

"And this is about your freedom?"

"Mine. *Ours.* I have to try. Think about it. What if he let me out of here? What if he gave us a chance at a real life on the outside?"

"There's no way, Kayla. He won't even let you leave to see your family. I'm sorry. I just think it's a waste of time."

"*Please* let me try. I can at least try."

MASTER A-0005

I'd never really been 'one of the guys'. I was friendly enough. I played by the rules, but I had never been part of some big brotherhood like I felt the rest of the elite men were. Elec and Shane were sometimes inseparable. They hunted slaves together. They had their fun scheming and playing games behind the scenes. As much as I sometimes wished I could give in and just be a part of them, that wasn't me. I wasn't social. I didn't care for their type of fun. What I cared about was deeper than that, and maybe they were growing tired of trying to get me to be part of their clique. Not ten minutes ago, I'd nodded to Shane in the hallway. No joyous greeting. No hello. It was like I didn't exist at all. Not that he forgot to throw Kayla a half-ass, almost sad, smile.

Had I missed something? Did I forget the trials again? Or maybe something tragic and horrible happened?

I'd never know sitting out here in the stupid lobby. Why had I allowed Kayla to go in the Main Master's office without me? How the hell had she convinced me of that? Even now, I had no idea. I was just…here. A board member out of the loop over my own damn wife. A wife who was probably giving away every cent I owned. Was I really letting her do this?

Standing from the chair, I started for the door only to stop. She'd begged and pleaded for me not to interrupt. This was the only way. Only way? Was I buying that?

Freedom.

Freedom.

A mother to my children.

A real wife and family again on the outside world?

In my wildest dreams. There was no way in hell Elec was going to allow her to leave here. No damn way. But he did have a soft spot for her, and technically...she wasn't a *normal* slave. She was one of us, an elite. But hadn't Everleigh been too? She'd been a slave. No. No way Elec was going for this. Kayla had seen too much. She knew too much. There was more risk than reward, and Elec was all too aware of that.

"Jake?"

I turned at the deep tone, feeling my heart leap with excitement for my wife.

"Matthew." I walked forward, shaking his hand. "Damn good to see you. I'd heard you left."

"I did." Uncertainty swept his face as he glanced at the Main Master's door. "I was instructed I needed to come back."

"Oh." I, too, glanced towards the door. "You weren't told why you needed to return?"

"No." He laughed, nervously. "Should I be worried? I swear I followed the rules."

"I have no doubts you did. Matt—"

Before I could say anything else the door opened. The Main Master hesitated, looking between us before he waved Matthew forward. He paused but gestured towards me too.

What the hell was going on? I felt like I was in the twilight zone. It almost appeared the Main Master wasn't going to include me with revealing this news. It was me Kayla married. I was the one joining our bloodlines.

Kayla stood from the chair across from the desk, her eyes slightly wild. Tears were streaked down her cheeks and her eyes were more swollen than when I'd brought her in. Protectiveness surged, and I headed forward, slowing as I saw it. Emptiness. Distance. Nothingness. He'd gotten her. He'd taken my wife away again, and her brother's arrival was the reason.

"Matthew, Jake."

I stepped in next to Kayla, wrapping my arm around her waist while I kissed her cheek.

"Are you okay?"

"I'm f-fine."

She sniffled, glancing towards her brother who only stood a good three feet away. He shifted as the Main Master took his spot behind the desk, sitting while he stared at us.

"Matthew, grab a chair over there and drag it over. We need to talk."

Green eyes took us all in, and he ran his fingers through his light brown hair. He didn't move at first. After a few seconds, he turned and walked over. He wasn't but two steps into bringing the chair over before he let out a heavy breath. Matthew looked like he wanted to speak, but he kept quiet, placing the chair down, off to the side of Kayla. Close...but not.

"I didn't hurt anyone I wasn't supposed to. I swear it."

The Main Master smiled, but barely.

"That's not why you're here. No one accused you of anything. This is a more personal matter."

"Personal?" Matthew looked at Kayla but brought his eyes to me. "Jake? What's this about?"

My gaze shot to Elec, and he gestured to me.

"Matthew. I'd like you to meet my wife. This is Kayla."

"Wife? Oh. *Congratulations.*" Relief took him over, and his hand came out. "It's nice to meet you, Kayla."

"It's so nice to meet you, Matthew." She sniffled again, but her smile almost appeared genuine. Had I not known my wife, I would have never known the difference.

"Matthew, I had you come back because there's something you need to know." Elec, grabbed a remote, turning on a large screen behind him. Documents were already up, and Matthew looked confused as he squinted to read them. "Jake's wife, Kayla, was adopted when she was a baby. Her adoptive parents never hid this from her. She had a great life, but...not long ago, she took a DNA test to find her real parents."

"I don't recognize that name. Andrea Tessing. I've never heard of her."

Elec brought up documents with Aubrey Walton's signature. The looping. The slant of certain letters. Matthew pulled at the collar of his shirt.

"The handwriting looks pretty similar. You said DNA test?"

"That's right. A false name can't hide the truth from one of those." Elec hit more buttons, and Matthew's eyes grew full of shock as he took it all in.

"That's my mom." His stare slowly came to Kayla. He studied her for a good minute before he turned back to the Main Master. "She's my sister?"

Elec nodded. "I've verified the results. There was no mistake. Kayla is your sister. She's the daughter of Aubrey and Alastair Whitlock."

Silence. He looked at us, cutting his gaze to the document, only to come back and stare deeply into Kayla's face.

"My mom wouldn't...she wouldn't—"

"She had the affair, Matthew. The DNA tests don't lie. I'm sure she'll admit to the truth once you confront her."

"I wasn't going to say affair. She's been seeing someone behind my father's back for years. All of us kids know it. She wouldn't have given Kayla up, is what I meant. Blood...that's... forbidden to do. *She gave her up?* She's always spoken about the importance of family. I know the name is fake but tell me this was a protected adoption. Like, she knew where Kayla was going to be raised. You mean that, don't you? My mom picked this couple until the time was right to bring Kayla home and admit the truth? That's what you mean."

The Main Master brought his attention to Kayla as she held tissues to her lower face, quietly sobbing into them. I pulled her closer, knowing the deepest parts of her couldn't be hidden through Elec's mind warping.

"I'm afraid not, Matthew."

"She just gave her away. *Hypocrite.*" It wasn't a question, and the last was barely audible. The rage in his tone was clear and indicated deeper family mysteries he wasn't unveiling.

"I don't believe your mother wanted the secret getting out. Whether that was her decision or Alistair's, I don't know. Maybe she didn't want him to find out. Only Aubrey knows the answer, and I haven't revealed the news to your mother yet. I don't get to leave here often, and this is clearly news you'd want to deliver face to face. I came to you first."

But Matthew wasn't looking at Elec. His intense stare wasn't leaving Kayla.

"I feel I must apologize for my mother." He continuously shook his head. "God, I see her in you. Alastair. I see him too. It's so obvious."

"Is it? Are you...mad? I was so afraid to meet you. I didn't think you'd want to have anything to do with me."

Matthew's eyes flew open in surprise. "Mad at you? This isn't your fault. Still...I can see how you might worry. The others may have a harder time accepting, but." He stopped, looking between the two of us. "Of all the people in the world to marry...she chose you. You're a Princeton." He smiled, looking back to her. "You married Jake Princeton. They're not going to be mad about that."

"There's more."

Matthew glanced at the Main Master.

"More?"

"Kayla and Jake have big news."

Matthew couldn't hide the knowing look he threw at me.

"An heir. Say it's an heir."

I laughed. "Maybe better than that. We have good reason to believe it might be twins…or more."

"*Really?* Wow." More shock. "Congratulations, again. Seriously. Wow. This is huge. This entire thing." He got quiet, and I could see how he was trying to process everything. And it was more than digesting the news of everything he'd learned. He was a Walton. He was just as slippery as any of us. He was thinking how good this was for his family. About prospects. About the future. It didn't matter that he wasn't the oldest. This benefited them all. "Main Master, you've told no one else yet?"

"Just you." Elec flattened his hands on the desk, standing. "You do see everything this means."

"Yes. What do you want me to do? You have me here for a reason. With how big the news is, you didn't go to my mother. You have ulterior motives."

The Main Master walked towards the glass windows, placing his hands at his back, while one hand latched to his other wrist.

"You don't miss much. It's why you're here. Kayla is very special to me. She is the foundation of a dream. The beginning of something much bigger than Whitlock, Walton, or Princeton, alone. The combination in her belly is of the utmost gold standard. The only way the line gets better is if it's merged with mine. Perhaps someday it will be. Then again…the world is at our fingertips. It's why Kayla must be protected. It's why she'll be staying here until I decide what's best."

Matthew's features drew in. "But what about mother? She wouldn't dare come here. Robert wouldn't either, and Elaine isn't permitted. Bram is surely not welcomed."

"That's right. The others will find out once you break the

news, but all Kayla has is you. You are the only family she'll have access to. I don't have to stress to you how important family is going to be for her in this crucial time. Her pregnancy must succeed at all costs. Kayla has no one. Please take that into account when you're here. She needs to see you. She needs your support."

"She has it." He turned to Kayla. "You have it. Whatever you need."

"Thank you," the Main Master continued. "I know I called you away from some important meetings, so we won't keep you. You can have a slave on me for the next auction as well for any inconvenience."

"I appreciate that. I should be getting back, but I'll return this next weekend. I have some time, and I really want to get to know my sister."

"I can't wait to hear everything."

Matthew stood and Kayla joined him. He grabbed her hands, his lids lowering through a fascination stemmed in curiosity and greed.

"Until we meet again, sister, take care of yourself."

She stepped in, throwing her arms around him. It was brief, but I knew the real part of her had initiated the action.

"Safe travels, brother."

Matthew shook my hand, waving to Elec as he left the room.

"Well, that went a lot better than I expected. Kayla, this is such great news. I'm so excited for you."

"Yes, it is very convenient." Elec practically cut me off from saying more, his tone dry, transforming completely. The deadness in his stare couldn't be mistaken. "Now Kayla doesn't have to suffer alone."

"Suffer? Alone?"

"Your loyalty was supposed to belong to me, Jake. I didn't pair the two of you to be married. This was not a love match, and yet at the first flutter of your heart, you were willing to keep

650

secrets from me. *For her.* You're on my board. *You're a Master.* You're supposed to be one of the men I trust the most. From the beginning, you knew there was supposed to be no secrets. No lies. I can't trust you. I can't have someone around me or Kayla that I can't trust. I meant to punish her for your betrayal, but I'm seeing having her kill you isn't in her best interest. She hasn't stopped crying since she's come in here. That was selfish enjoyment on my behalf. Kayla *is* loyal, and that is why I will not make her suffer because of your weakness. Mistress, come to me."

A sob left Kayla, and she stepped from my hold, crying harder as she went to stand before him.

"I let my anger overshadow your wellbeing, *again.* Breathe." He reached forward, making a motion with his finger, not two inches from her eyes. Kayla instantly let out a breath and grew calmer. "There we go. Take a deep breath. When you breathe out, there will be no more pain. No heartbreak. Not today. You will mourn your husband's death, but you will know it was not your fault. It was his fault. He failed in his duties. Not you. You're the strong one, and you will continue to be strong for your babies. Understand?"

"*I l-love him.*"

"Understand?" He snapped his fingers and her body stiffened.

"Yes."

"Wait one goddamn minute. You can't kill me for wanting what's best for my wife."

"I can, and I will."

"I didn't betray you, Elec. I was watching out for her. You fucked her up. She doesn't want to *be* like this." I stepped closer. "Kayla, come back over to me. *Kayla.*"

But she wouldn't look at me. She stood tall, blinking up at him, so far away.

"Elec, *please.* Don't do this to her. She came here to beg for

651

our life together, outside of the Gardens. Take her up on it. You want my money? *My businesses?* Take it. Give me Kayla and let us leave. I'll never come back here again."

"Do you hear yourself, Jake? Tell me how any of that benefits me if I don't have her? Kayla is your wife. What's yours is hers, literally. You signed it all over to her in the marriage contract the minute you scribbled down your signature." A slight smile tugged at his lips. "The pregnancy and your sperm for future heirs was just the icing on the cake."

I took in his expression feeling my blood mix from cold to hot, back to cold.

"You planned this the entire time, didn't you?"

Elec's gaze left me, lowering back to Kayla. His hands came up, levelling to the sides of her cheeks. "Master One is waiting for you. Vera is in town, and both are going to take you to dinner to make sure you eat. They will take you home, where you will go back into your old schedule. Meal times. Sleep time. You know the drill. I have more business to take care of, but I will come by to check on you before bed. Text me if you need anything." He leaned in, kissing her forehead. "Tell your husband goodbye."

Robotically, Kayla turned. Her lips quivered, but aside from that, barely any emotions broke through. It was a heartbreaking sight. I couldn't stand it.

"Goodbye, husband." A pause. "I'll miss you. I—"

Elec snapped his fingers again, cursing. "That's good. You've said enough."

"Hear me, Kayla, baby, please. You said you loved me. I know that was the real you talking. *I love you too.* You have to come back to me, okay? You have to fight this." Elec took a few steps with her, leading her towards the door, but I wasn't having it. I surged forward, slapping the hand that lifted towards me to keep me away. It only had his other locking around my throat in crushing force. The pain that erupted in my side was excruciating. Lights flashed and my body seized as the blade disappeared, only to stab back into me with enough force to drop me to my knees.

"You wanted your family back." He sliced the weapon free along my ribs, leaning over me. The knife leveled at my throat, and I stared into the oblivion of darkness within his depths. "They're waiting for you, Jake. *It's time to go back to them.* I can take care of your new family. You're finished here."

EPILOGUE

MISTRESS 0

T itles were a confusing thing. Vera was Mistress One. I was Mistress One. Technically, she was Mistress C-One for their Couple status, where I was just Mistress...One? But I wasn't One because Elec said I was technically Mistress Zero. I was *the* Mistress. With as much enthusiasm as he used in his tone, I knew it was his way of trying to prove to me that I was important. That this was right. Despite his hold was wearing off on me by the day, he hadn't tried to strengthen it. Or maybe at the rate my body and hormones were changing, it was harder for him. I wasn't sure. Maybe he just couldn't tell. All I knew was, I cried a lot. I was sad. I missed my husband. Nothing I did could make the days stop dragging in a miserable ticking of time. Elec said I would grieve, and he was right. Nothing could fill the hole inside me. Not the crows. Not Matthew's frequent visits. Not even knowing that I was indeed having twins.

I was lost.

I was alone.

My heart was bloody and bruised.

Thinking back to the day in Elec's office, I could remember doing everything in my power to get him to let us leave together.

I promised the Main Master everything under the sun. He wasn't interested. He wasn't even willing to hear me out. Elec wouldn't bend, and me, I'd been devastated. But then...those words. I may have appeared calm throughout that first meeting with Matthew. The truth was, even though my body went through the motions, my mind wasn't. Not really. I couldn't stop screaming. I couldn't stop fighting. But it was all internal. All locked within. Or was. It wasn't anymore. I was here, even if I tried my best to hide it, and I had to do that if I wanted any form of control of my life.

"These are the babies?"

Matthew's eyes shot up from the sonogram picture, a big smile on his face.

"You can barely see much, but that's them. Did you tell mother yet?"

He scrunched his face, looking back down at the picture. "A few days ago. My father was...pissed. Not surprised but angry. Apparently, they were having issues and he'd been gone for a while. I guess that was during the time when he was living in California opening the businesses there." He glanced up. "It's such a fucking mess. Anyway, she wants to see you, Kayla. She says she didn't have a choice. Mother didn't go into detail, but I feel it had something to do with your father. Maybe in time, we'll learn the truth. All I know is when news gets out to the masses, my mother's going to have a lot more to answer to than a secret love child. Already Bram calls her nonstop seeking information. How he even knows, I don't have a clue. She won't take his calls, but if I know Bram, he won't give up. I guess you could say he'll be searching out answers too."

I tried to keep the emotion from my face, but the truth was, I didn't know how to feel about it. I kept Bram far from my mind. He didn't belong anywhere in my thoughts. He was the enemy. He wasn't good.

"Bram will go away eventually. If he ever comes to you, tell him I'm not interested in meeting. He's not to be trusted. I want to stay as far away from him as I can. I'll worry about it when I go to the outside world. I just need to wait to have these babies, and then Elec will be moving me to Jake's family's home. He said it wasn't far from mother's."

"That's right. It's close...*and the biggest estate in the neighborhood.* Anyone who is *someone* has a house there. Mom can help take care of you and the babies. She's ecstatic to meet you. I just wish—" Matthew's smile fell. "I'm so sorry about Jake, Kayla. I...I won't lie. When I learned the two of you were married that day, I almost couldn't believe it. Jake loved his family. For years, he's been unrecognizable to everyone. Losing Maggie and the kids truly drove him crazy. Knowing he took his life after I left that day. I was truly hoping he'd finally found happiness again. Especially with you. You both deserved that."

My heart seized, and I could barely catch my breath through the raw pain. "Please don't tell anyone that. It was an accident. God, I can't..." Tears raced down my cheeks. "Let's stick to that story." A sob escaped as my voice cracked. A waterfall seemed to stream down my face, and I couldn't wipe the tears away fast enough. "I wanted to believe it too. The pregnancy...it was unexpected. I think he felt pressured, and it was way too fast. I told him he didn't have to marry me, but...you know Jake and how committed he is. When we met at the resort, I fooled myself into believing it was love at first sight. It was but only for me. Or maybe a small part of him loved me too. I think he tried so hard to but—."

More sobs.

Endless.

I could see the lies so clearly, as if they'd truly happened. And maybe a part of me wanted to believe they did. The lies beat the truth. That was riddled in deception and manipulation. They were weaved with intent that went beyond what I'd been programmed to know. The clearer I became, the more the whispers and secret conversations I'd been exposed to began to sink in. My Main Master was always so flawless in his schemes, but I was starting to decode things that went far beyond what had gone down with my husband.

Families would fall.

Blood would flow.

My own family would have to earn their place by my side.

But that would be the start of another story. Mine began with a dream and ended with a nightmare. It wasn't over yet. I was being trained to find my place amongst the elite. *To rule them.* I was my Main Master's spy, his puppet, and someday my story would truly begin. When it did, *I'd be ready.*

The End

ABOUT THE AUTHOR

A. A. Dark is an International Bestselling Author. She doesn't reside in one place for long and is known to move at the drop of a dime. From mountains and snow to tropical beaches, she could be at one in the morning and the other by night. A. A. is a Goodread's Choice Award Finalist in Horror. She is also the President and CEO of Mad Girl Publishing, and the founder for the Pitch Black brand.

Mad Girl Publishing's rating system in levels of darkness.

PITCH BLACK ⊠ (Level 1)
STATIC WHITE ⊠ (Level 2-darker)
OBLIVION ⊠ (Level 3- darkest)

ALSO BY A. A. DARK

24690 series in Reading Order:

24690 (24690 series, book 1)

White Out (24690 series, book 2)

27001 (Welcome to Whitlock, 24690 series, book 2.1)

27009 (Welcome to Whitlock, 24690 series, book 2.2)

27011 (Welcome to Whitlock, 24690 series, book 2.3)

Or

Welcome to Whitlock Complete Novella Series (book 3)

Black Out (24690 series, book 4)

Garden of the Gods

Vol. 1

(all standalones and can be read in any order.)

Mistress B-0003 (Garden of the Gods)

Master B-1212 (Garden of the Gods)

Couple B-0001 (Garden of the Gods)

Master B-0077 (Garden of the Gods)

Master B-0999 (Garden of the Gods)

Vol. 2

Mistress B-0042 (Garden of the Gods)

Couple B-0019 (Garden of the Gods)

Master B-0491 (Garden of the Gods)

Master B-0113 (Garden of the Gods)

Master A-0005 (Garden of the Gods)

Anna Monroe and Boston Marks series in suggested Reading Order
Never Far (Boston Marks)
Mad Girl (The Chronicles of Anna Monroe)
MasterMind (An Anna Monroe and Never Far crossover)
Heart Lines (The Chronicles of Anna Monroe and Boston Marks)
Crossed Paths (The Chronicles of Anna Monroe and Boston Marks

ALASKA ANGELINI BOOKS

Contemporary Standalones
Unbearable
Insufferable
The Last Heir
Watch Me: Stalked
Rush

Captive to the Dark series
(All standalones and can be read in any order)
SLADE: Captive to the Dark
BLAKE: Captive to the Dark
GAIGE: Captive to the Dark
LILY: Captive to the Dark, Special Edition 1
CHASE: Captive to the Dark
JASE: Captive to the Dark

The Devlin Black series
Dom Up: Devlin Black 1
Dom Fever: Devlin Black 2
, This Dom: Devlin Black 3

Dark Paranormal/Sci-Fi lover? Check out Alaska's other reads…
Wolf (Standalone)

Marko Delacroix series
Prey: Marko Delacroix 1
Blood Bound: Marko Delacroix 2

Lure: Marko Delacroix 3
Rule: Marko Delacroix 4
Reign: Marko Delacroix 5

Sci-Fi
Atlas Lost

ACKNOWLEDGMENTS

To the most AMAZING betas in the world…
I LOVE YOU! You all rocked Vol. 2 of GOTG. Your insight is
so valuable. I'm truly appreciative and grateful for each of you.
Karen Preiato
Nicole Johnson
Kayla Cramer
Elizabeth Jansen
Amy Martin
Cayla Akright
Sandy Barg
Kelsey Elizabeth Stone
Morgen Frances

Also, to all the amazing readers, bloggers, TikTokers, and
Bookstagrammers who have reviewed and shown love to not just
this series but to ALL my books, I LOVE YOU! I appreciate
you. I can't thank you enough.
You're ROCKSTARS!

Last, but definitely not least, to my everything…
Dee Trejo and Nadine Flotte. You rock each book. You tear them
down. You destroy them. You make them shine.

Made in the USA
Middletown, DE
04 September 2023

37944654R00373